Quest

The author is fascinated by the early civilisations and how they were created, additionally, by the way that some civilisations have persecuted the beliefs of others, often causing unjust persecution and genocide. His story of mankind's domination of the world often depicts the inadequacies of this form of control, which so often causes hardship and cruelty. He realises that it is very difficult to suggest an amicable compromise, but sincerely believes that we may one day achieve a realistic goal that allows different beliefs to exist in harmony.

**Published Work:**

If Only They Knew (2008)
*Olympia Publishers*
**ISBN: 978 1905513 37 6**

Masada (2009)
*Olympia Publishers*
**ISBN: 978 1905513 94 9**

# Quest

# Peter Cordwell

## Quest

*Olympia Publishers*

www.olympiapublishers.com
OLYMPIA PAPERBACK EDITION

Copyright © Peter Cordwell 2010

The right of Peter Cordwell to be identified as author of this work has been asserted in accordance with sections 77 and 78 of the Copyright, Designs and Patents Act 1988.

**All Rights Reserved**

No reproduction, copy or transmission of this publication may be made without written permission.
No paragraph of this publication may be reproduced, copied or transmitted save with the written permission of the publisher, or in accordance with the provisions of the Copyright Act 1956 (as amended).

Any person who does any unauthorized act in relation to this publication may be liable to criminal prosecution and civil claims for damage.

A CIP catalogue record for this title is available from the British Library.

ISBN: 978-1-84897-039-7

This is a work of fiction.
Names, characters, places and incidents originate from the writer's imagination. Any resemblance to actual persons, living or dead, is purely coincidental.

First Published in 2010
Cover design by Bronowski © 2010

**Olympia Publishers part of Ashwell Publishing Ltd**
60 Cannon Street
London
EC4N 6NP

Printed in Great Britain

# Dedication

I would like to dedicate this book to the memory of Rev Dr Leonard Barnett for his constant guidance and encouragement, although he never saw the final result. He was an author himself and gave me a lot of inspiration and advice in producing this book.

## Author's Note

This story is set in the Fertile Crescent, in the Middle East, around 1100 BC. The story is fictional although it is based on fact. Some of the places did exist, the Empires and their struggles for supremacy did occur. Also some of the characters and scenes depicted in the book occur in the Bible. I hope the reader will forgive my playing around with chronological historical fact, which may not follow more recent findings.

# Contents

**PROLOGUE** ................................................................. 17
  **1** LEAVING HOME ................................................. 19
  **2** THE ROAD TOUR ............................................... 34
  **3** CAPTURE AND REVENGE ................................. 52
  **4** THE TRAINING CAMP ........................................ 70
  **5** A BRUSH WITH DEATH ...................................... 92
  **6** THE CROCS ...................................................... 111
  **7** ESCAPE FROM VICTORY ................................. 137
  **8** SIMEON ............................................................. 154
  **9** REPAIRS ON THE FINAL DRIFT TO KISH AND BABYLON ............................................................................. 172
  **10** THE HANGING GARDENS ............................... 194
  **11** THE ROUTES CROSS ...................................... 212
  **12** THE CAUSE OF WAR ...................................... 228
  **13** SAVING ASHKILON ........................................ 248
  **14** THE COST OF VICTORY ................................. 270
  **15** "SKREE" .......................................................... 289
  **16** KINDNESS RETURNED ................................... 306
  **17** THE EMPTY SECTOR ...................................... 324
  **18** OF HEALING LEAVES AND SANCTUARY ....... 344
  **19** NEW POSITION, NEW CHALLENGES ............. 361
  **20** TROUBLES IN TIMON ..................................... 378
  **21** ON THE ROAD AGAIN ..................................... 398
  **22** MEETING WITH SAMSON .............................. 421
  **23** TRAINING AND PREPARATION ..................... 441
  **24** SAMSON'S FATE ............................................ 459
  EPILOGUE ............................................................... 480

**GLOSSARY** ............................................................. 485

# PROLOGUE

Come with me across the vast areas of time and space as we travel far, far to the south and the east, beyond the shores of the Inland Sea and on to where another sea commences. This place is where a great river flows into the Inferior Sea (for that was what it was called at the time). This river is called Euphrates, by which name it is still known today. We are standing on the bank of the great river near a town called Lagash, at the mouth of the Euphrates. Today this place is called Basra and it is very important, but now for different reasons. It was important in those days, but as a trading place where ships entered the Euphrates, laden with goods from the far shores of distant India and the lands to the east. Here they travelled up the Euphrates to Ancient Babylon where merchants traded goods from far away Egypt, which were brought in large caravans to trade with the goods from the east.

This was a great time of change in the 'Cradle of Civilisation', as it is the period when the Bronze Age finished and the Iron Age began. But history is uncertain of the exact dates and much that is known is supposition. There was a great change in the political and imperial fortunes at that time. The Trojan Wars had vastly depleted the might of Ancient Greece, and the Second Hittite Dynasty was long dead. The Assyrians were stirring, as were the Babylonians. To their north the Persian Empire was rising. Egypt, possibly under Rameses II, was licking its wounds after the departure of the Hebrew slaves. Therefore, no major power was in command and everything was there for the taking. It was also a great time of changes in religious beliefs: the old-fashioned polytheistic religions were being questioned by certain parts of the civilised world, and the new monotheistic religions were beginning.

Mankind's search for a comprehensive understanding of the world's creation and of life itself was a whole area of question. Many new ideas were thrown into the melting pot and many new cultures were growing up, or at least seeds of those cultures were beginning to germinate. Mankind's eternal search for the truth affected a large percentage of civilisations. This brought about many cultural changes and many new ideas were taking shape. This is the setting to our story.

# 1
## LEAVING HOME

The boy threw back his head and laughed delightedly at the antics of the sand crabs that were fighting over the large dying fish that had been washed ashore. His teeth were very white, in the bright afternoon sunshine of the early summer. There was not a cloud in the sky and the heat bounced off the burnished gold surface of the river, which would normally be painful to those who were not used to the sunshine in that area. Indeed, his hair was bleached even lighter than his normal colour and his lighter than usual skin had darkened more to the natural colour of light golden brown, that was familiar amongst most of the people living in that region. But the boy was used to the riverbank and the sunshine reflecting from the water. This fish had been the very one that the fisherman who he had just left, had been talking about. It had broken the net, but in doing so had torn its scales and fins. These had bled and been nibbled by other fish, which had disabled its break for freedom. That, in turn, had made it more vulnerable to the gulls and other seabirds that were found along the tidal estuary. So now it was so badly injured that even the crabs tore chunks of pink flesh from its dying body.

Ruben was ten years old, or at least he thought he was ten. His father had left on a journey to seek his ancestors' homeland. Rumour suggested that his ancestors had travelled south-west and then disappeared. Another source then reported that they had reappeared in a distant land and were now fighting to establish a kingdom. His father left for his journey shortly after Ruben's mother had died. He was still a baby then and had been brought up as one of his uncle's children, but he had only recently been told that he was not of their family. This fact had not surprised Ruben, but confirmed in him a belief that he was different from the other children that he grew up with. After all, he was very large for a child of only ten and had different hair and eye colour, and even his features were quite different from those he had originally thought of as siblings. His hair was fine and the colour of dirty straw and generally unruly, unlike the other children whose hair was thick, dark and curly. His eyes were bright blue, unlike the usual brown of most of the children living in the area.

He was standing on the riverbank, where it became the shores of the Inferior Sea near Lagash, where his uncle had sent him on an errand. He had often performed the same errand and enjoyed the long walk to Lagash. Solitude did not worry him and the area in the summer was very peaceful, as was Akkad, the province of his hometown of Sumer. He enjoyed watching the great ships pass into the Euphrates and he often spent long periods listening to the tales of the sailors and the fishermen while they sat mending their nets.

His errand from his uncle was to another ship builder in Lagash, bringing down plans for new ships that the other merchant was building, together with a request for new materials to be sent up the river with the ships to Nippur, where Ruben's uncle would finish off the final work.

Ruben was a restless child and always wanted to see around the bend in the river or over the next hill. While he was journeying to Lagash from home he thought about following his father on the search to find their true homeland. His father was the descendant of a great man in the past called Abraham, who supposedly journeyed northwest from a place called Ur of the Chaldees. Ruben had been to Ur, which was to the southwest of Lagash, and could find nothing of particular significance that either confirmed or denied this rumour of his father's distant relation, Great-Uncle Abraham.

All these thoughts were going through his mind as he was standing watching the wildlife of the estuary and the ships that entered the Euphrates, or those that came down from Babylon. He did not notice the large, powerfully built but squat and ugly captain of the uniformed Babylonian Guard who came up behind him and grabbed him roughly by the shoulder. The captain's strong gnarled hand dragged Ruben round to stare up into his gruesome leering face, as he demanded in a harsh barking voice, his breath rank with stale beer, "Oi, you little brat, why aren't you at a training camp?"

All boys from the age of twelve were now conscripted into the Babylonian army and were sent to training camps to learn their trade of fighting for their new Empire. Ruben tried to explain to this rough captain that he was only ten years old, but the captain would have none of this, mainly because of Ruben's size. However, the other boatbuilder, who had fortunately hurried after Ruben and confirmed that he was indeed only ten and that the captain should leave him alone, prevented his arrest. The captain noticed by the man's finery that he was an important merchant and therefore let go of Ruben, but gave him a menacing look that suggested that he would catch up with him later. All this strengthened Ruben's wish to follow in his father's footsteps, as he had no desire to join the army and fight for the Babylonian king.

The important merchant, who wore the silver torque that denoted his standing in the Lagash Merchants of Privilege Chamber, had chased after Ruben, having dispatched him a few hours previously with details of the delivery, of which he now had minor changes to impart. His name was Mutek and he was of a kindly nature with a round jovial face, and he had always been friendly to Ruben and seemed to like the boy. He urged Ruben to put distance between himself and the Guard captain who was currently based in Lagash. Bearing in mind that it would take more than the remainder of that day for Ruben to reach his hometown of Nippur, he encouraged him to join a caravan of merchants who were making their way north-westwards up the Euphrates, with the particular instructions that Ruben should not be left unattended. Ruben was mindful to heed Mutek's advice and made sure that he slept well within the surrounding circle of campfires of the caravan that evening. As he lay listening to the frogs croaking in the night by the riverside, and the noise made by the crickets, his mind started wandering again to where his father had gone on his journey, and what, indeed, had happened to his father. He rolled onto his side and felt the bruising on his shoulder, which was a harsh reminder of his near-capture by the brutal captain of the Guard, and it was at this point that he finally decided that he must try to trace his father's footsteps and seek his ancestral home.

The following morning he rose early with the rest of the caravan and continued north-westwards, arriving shortly after midday at Nippur. He felt he ought to tell his uncle of his plan, but then decided at the last moment not to speak about it. Instead, he left a message with the girl that he had always thought of as his sister, Miriam. Although she was a few years older than he, she was a lot smaller than Ruben. She sighed deeply as he told her. She then came close to him put her arms around his neck, laid her head on his chest and said that she had always feared that he would follow his father one day. She told him that she would greatly miss him even though not everyone in her family would have that view.

"Yes, I know that," responded Ruben, "your mother always complains that I eat as much as everyone else put together." But before she released her grip on him she made him promise to let her know, somehow, of how he fared on his quest. As he quickly shoved his few belongings into a small knapsack he decided, on the spur of the moment, to risk his chances of being caught by the Guard captain, and seek the advice of Mutek, the merchant. So he slipped out of the house and wandered down the main street of Nippur, going deliberately towards the boatyards down by the river. The small squarish buildings of the town were mostly only one storey high, often with skin or woven cloth awnings or roofs that were brightly decorated and stood out starkly against the sun-bleached walls in the bright afternoon sunshine. As he walked along, he exchanged a couple of greetings with various townsfolk, which gave the impression that he was just wandering back to his uncle's boatyard, taking with him various items that may very well have been requested. But before he reached the river, he slipped down a side alleyway, checking that he had not been noticed and skirted east of the boatyard, deliberately avoiding being seen. When he reached the riverbank he slipped off his leather sandals and waded into the river until the water reached well above his knees. He then turned east, following the course of the river, and waded amongst the tall rushes that mainly concealed his presence. He continued for quite a while until he was well out of sight of the town before he waded ashore again and dried his feet. He then slipped on his sandals and continued his journey towards Lagash. There was no one else on the riverbank and certainly no party of travellers to which he could attach himself, but he did notice a couple of large boats that were going down river, full of soldiers from the Babylonian army. As the day wore on into evening, he began to look for somewhere to spend the night, all the time keeping a watchful eye for any passers-by. He finally saw what he was looking for, a small stunted tree near to a fairly dense patch of reeds and rushes that had recently been used as a resting place for one of the large river crocodiles. Concealing himself in this hideout, he curled up in the warm evening and soon fell into a deep sleep.

The sound of many voices and the tramping of feet and then harsh laughter that came from very nearby broke his sleep in the night. Keeping out of sight he made his way carefully through the rushes until he could see where all the noise was coming from. A party of Babylonian army, with a couple of Babylonian guards attached to its number, had marched westwards up river from Lagash and was camping just by the stunted tree on the riverbank. They had not bothered to post a guard as they were in friendly countryside and were all sitting round a fire, drinking millet beer, which was common in the army. Crawling closer, yet making sure he was not spotted, Ruben moved to a position where he could overhear the conversation.

"By the gods, that Captain Gershnarl was in a foul mood this evening," said one of the men, as he took a long draught of ale from the goatskin before passing it to his colleague.

"Yes," responded another soldier, "But I'm sure he'll be in a better mood tomorrow, because I heard him order another guardsman to be lashed, simply so that he could have the man's wife," he chuckled.

And so the conversation continued in typical bawdy revelry. This conversation was mainly meaningless to Ruben, although he quickly realised that the captain, Gershnarl was the same ugly but powerfully built Guard captain who had almost captured Ruben two days previously. As Ruben listened to more of the conversation he learned that the company of soldiers were on a routine patrol on their way back to Babylon, to the northwest. They had been instructed to keep an eye out for a large gangly-looking youth with sandy-coloured hair, who should be in one of the young soldier training camps. Realising that they were talking about him, he quickly retraced his footsteps to his original sleeping place and grabbed his possessions, and then went stealthily past the camp, keeping close to the river's edge. He knew there was no danger from the crocodiles that were often seen along the riverbank, which were only deadly in the heat of the day or early evening, particularly if they were aroused by the scent of blood in the water. He hurried along in the dark, keeping close to the bank so that the reeds and bulrushes occasionally hid him, and not worrying whether or not he was sloshing through water or mud, or on the dry ground. His only and immediate concern was to get to Lagash as soon as possible, preferably by dawn, and then to seek the help and advice of his uncle's friend – the merchant Mutek, who had been so kind to him before. Without realising it his movements became faster and less stealthy, until he was almost running without carefully watching ahead.

It was still dark when he could half-sense and begin to see the outlines of some of the houses on the outskirts of Lagash, and because of his exertions and fear, he was half running and half stumbling along, his breath coming in deep gasping sobs and his eyes damp with the beginning of tears. It must have been a sixth sense that caused him to slow his pace, because he almost stumbled into a soldier who was relieving himself by the river. He quickly darted behind a clump of reeds as he heard the gushing stream of urine splashing into the river. The soldier adjusted his dress and murmured drowsily in his semi-awake state and wandered off back to his bivouac that was not more than fifty paces away. Ruben desperately tried to calm himself and with a great effort of will managed to stop his racing heart that was beginning to pound in his ears, as he took stock of the immediate area around him. By now the dawn light was brightening to the east and he could make out some of the larger buildings in the distant town, and see that there were quite a few hastily erected bivouacs where groups of soldiers were sleeping in the close vicinity. He calmed himself as he tried to puzzle out the reason for so many soldiers, who had not been there a couple of days previously. He then remembered seeing the boats full of soldiers that had been going down the river, and realised that they must be new arrivals and would have had no contact with the previous group of soldiers whose conversation he had overheard. This realisation eased his fears and he knew that there must be another reason for their presence. He hastily ate the remaining dates that he had brought with him and a couple of wheat cakes that Miriam had stolen from her mother's kitchen before he had left Nippur.

He was a lot calmer now, but was very tired after his desperate flight along the riverbank, and this weariness made it difficult for him to think clearly. He knew something unusual was happening, but felt certain that he was not the reason for the large party of soldiers sleeping nearby. But he was also aware that there could be others like the ghastly Captain Gershnarl who had so very nearly enslaved him. In order not to alert any of the soldiers to his presence, he slipped off his sandals and stuffed them into the knapsack, checking that it was securely fastened to his shoulders. He waded out into the cool river, trying to avoid making any loud splashing noises that would awaken the soldiers. As he had always lived by the river he was quite a strong swimmer and could swim without making a lot of splashes. Using a strange style of swimming that he had taught himself, using his arms like the river frogs but wiggling his legs together in a motion like the large dolphins that came up the coast and occasionally into the river's mouth, swam for a considerable time. When he slowed and took stock of his position he was almost in the centre of the town and the sun had risen in the east, as it did so quickly in that region. He swam to the shore and found his way into a quiet street, where he slipped on his sandals.

He was fairly sure that if he were noticed no one would pay any attention, as it was common to see an errand-boy out that early in the morning and perhaps having a swim in the river. He quickly realised exactly where he was and made his way to Mutek's house, which was not very far away. Rather than awaken anyone in the house, he went up the outside steps to find that the roof was unoccupied, although people often slept on their roofs in the summer. This was not surprising as Mutek's house was fairly large and had marble walls and floors so that it was always cool, even in the heat of the day. Ruben lay down in the early morning sunshine and lined up his few damp possessions, which he knew would dry quickly in the bright summer sun. After a few minutes he fell into a deep dreamless sleep brought on by sheer exhaustion. His sleep was deep and he was not even woken by the normal noises of the awakening town. These sounds grew in intensity, with street traders calling out the wares that they had on offer, as did the smells that rose in the city as carts of freshly caught fish trundled by, mingling with the smells of cooking and freshly opened coconuts.

He awoke sometime later, refreshed after his much-needed rest, to look up into Mutek's jolly face, and hear the merchant say, "Hallo, Ruben, I didn't expect to see you back so soon. Put your things back in the bag, come downstairs and join us for breakfast. Then you can tell me what brought you here, obviously in great haste."

So Ruben followed him downstairs to where a large table was beautifully laid with lots of delicious things to eat and plenty of orange and pomegranate juices as well as wine to drink.

Over breakfast, Ruben told the story of his return to Nippur and then his decision to try to trace his father's footsteps, and possibly find out what happened to his father and whether or not he was still alive. He was quite honest as he told the story of how he left his uncle's house, pretending to go to the boatyard but slipping out of the town quietly, and then his trek along the riverbank and his sleep being interrupted by the camping soldiers. He spoke in detail of what he had overheard and his realisation that they had been ordered to capture him if they found him. He went on to explain to the astonished Mutek that he had then crept away, and he described his mad rush down the riverbank by night, and how afraid he had become, particularly when he almost bumped into the soldier who was pissing into the river. He continued by telling Mutek about his final swim down river to avoid all the soldiers who were camped just outside the town. He finished his detailed description of his return to Lagash, and asked Mutek about why his father had left, why he had run off in such short order and what had really happened to his mother, and finally, why there were so many soldiers around Lagash.

"Whoa!" cried out Mutek, "Just one question at a time, young Ruben. I will tell you what I know of your father's leaving and of why there are so many soldiers around here. But there are large gaps in the story that I have to tell you, there is much that I do not know. I can tell you this of your father, Uriah. He was not a coward, as some people might lead you to believe, but a brave man. He left your mother for her own safety, but her identity was betrayed. I do not know what has become of him, but I will help you in any way that I can. Before we start on that sad and long story let me tell you the reason for the presence of the many soldiers from Babylon."

He then took a drink that one of his servants had brought him and waved the man away so that they could continue undisturbed.

He explained that the new Babylonian king had signed a treaty with the powerful king of Assyria, which was far away to the north-west, and that that ruler, the tyrant Tiglath-Pileser, was a hard man. Having heard that there had been murmurs of dissent about the treaty from the council of the Merchants in Lagash, Tiglath-Pileser had requested the Babylonian king send a large force of his troops to quell any potential uprising. Therefore, even here Ruben was not safe because Mutek could very well be arrested, although he was safe for a day at least. He then went on to explain to Ruben that his father, Uriah, had got into an argument with the same Captain Gershnarl who had tried to arrest Ruben, but that even Gershnarl did not know where Ruben came from. The evil Gershnarl had his strange affinity with Ruben's family; it was he who had an argument with Uriah, when Uriah had accused him of cheating at the gaming tables.

Gershnarl always cheated, because he lacked the ability to remember pictures or numbers, unlike Uriah who was a skilled games player. However, Gershnarl had sought his revenge on Uriah by taking his wife, treating her brutally and forcing her into his bed. Mutek did not know the full story, but Ruben's mother was believed to have taken her own life. He showed a kindly reluctance to go into great detail as to what had happened, but intimated that it had been a nasty affair. However, he would certainly try to help Ruben escape from the area, which indeed was what he counselled. He then silenced Ruben's interruption by placing a hand on his shoulder and saying, "I think you're wise to follow your father and to try to find out what became of him."

After a long pause, allowing what he had said to really sink in, he explained that Uriah had started his journey from where the fabled Great-Uncle Abraham was supposed to have started his journey over one thousand years earlier. That place was called Ur of the Chaldees, and was to the southwest of Lagash, in the marshlands. He told Ruben that there was an old trade route that went to Ur from the south of the river, but it was overgrown and was hardly ever used these days. He went on to warn Ruben that he was setting off on a long and difficult road and he must be careful not to get caught by Captain Gershnarl, who was indeed an evil man.

Mutek then asked Ruben whether he had eaten enough and was sufficiently refreshed. He realised that the boy was still tired after his long journey through the night. He took him to a small chamber below ground level that was fairly cool, even in the middle of the day, where there was a bed made up. He told Ruben that he should rest, he could then start his journey in the evening after the heat of the day had passed, and one of Mutek's servants would row him across the broad Euphrates to where the old trade route to Ur started. While he rested, Mutek would prepare a few provisions for his journey. Mutek then left Ruben and the boy realised how tired he really was. After removing his sandals and slipping out of his light shift, he crawled onto the comfortable bed, pulled the cover over himself and was soon fast asleep.

He slept for a long time, but the evil and ugly face of Gershnarl, who seemed to torment his life as it had his father and mother's before him, troubled his sleep. When he awoke, it was to find Mutek moving around quietly in the room, and it was then he knew what a good friend he had found in him. He understood that Captain Gershnarl was a horrible reality that he would one day have to face. He hoped he would avenge his family of the injustice that this evil brute had brought upon them.

Seeing he was awake, Mutek said to Ruben, as the boy rubbed his eyes to remove the sleep from them, "Ah, I'm glad you're awake. It is now late in the afternoon and you must get away soon. I have laid out some clothes for you. Now go and wash, refresh yourself, and then join me for something to eat before you set off."

Ruben went into an antechamber where he found servants had poured a bath full of clean water, scented with coconut oil. As he bathed he felt that he was washing away the past, and came out fresh and newly invigorated. He put on a clean shift, and as he dressed he found a new belt with a scabbard and small bronze knife. He then came from the room, up the short steps to the main room of the house, to find that a light dinner of grilled fish was being served. He had not been aware of how hungry he was until he sat down and started to eat. After he had filled himself with two plates of food and plenty of mango juice, he was about to refill his plate yet again when Mutek stopped him. "Hold on young Ruben, we have to get you across the river, and I don't want you to be so heavy that you sink the boat," he said jovially, chuckling to himself. He showed Ruben a map drawn on a papyrus scroll that had been folded and placed into a waterproof bag that went into Ruben's knapsack. He noticed that the knapsack had been cleaned along with the rest of his meagre possessions. As well as the map, Mutek had supplied him with a tinderbox to light a small fire, and to add to the bronze knife he gave him a quarterstaff. He said that the guide, who would row Ruben across the river and start him on his journey, would also show him how to use this staff to flatten the reeds and prod the marshy ground ahead to ensure that he did not fall into a bog.

Mutek led him out of the house and into the courtyard, making sure that he carried all his new possessions with him. Here, a huge black figure was squatting under a fig tree. As they walked up behind him, one of the largest men that Ruben had ever seen rose from the ground and smiled his flashing white teeth at Mutek in a gesture of recognition.

"Ah, Ishmala," greeted Mutek, "This" – and he put his arm around Ruben's shoulders – "is the young man who I would like you to take over the river and start on the ancient road to Ur." He turned to Ruben, "and here you must seek out a man called Simeon."

Ishmala nodded and offered his hand to Ruben in a gesture of greeting and friendship.

"Ishmala has lost his tongue, Ruben," Mutek explained. "He is one of my closest and dearest servants, and he will not only row you across the river but will see you safely on your way and will not let you come to any harm."

Ruben's hand seemed so small inside one of Ishmala's. The Nubian's head was completely bald and projected from his huge shoulders like a giant watermelon. It was obviously oiled, as it shone in the late afternoon sunlight. All Ruben's fear of Captain Gershnarl seemed to evaporate as he stood only chest high beside this enormous man, who was obviously going to look after him and start him safely on his journey.

"As Ishmala cannot speak," said Mutek, "You will have to speak with him in a sign language that is easy to understand. I am sure you will have no trouble. Now he will take you to my boatyard down by the river and take you across to the southern shore, and guide you on your way."

Ruben turned his face to thank Mutek, but he was too slow as he was still gazing in wonder at Ishmala, and by the time he turned Mutek was already hurrying into the house. He did not know it then, but this would be the last time he would see Mutek. Ishmala took him by the hand again and led him stealthily along the side of the house, before entering the street and peering around the corner. He then hurriedly retraced his footsteps back into the courtyard, dragging Ruben behind him. He grabbed a rolled up carpet that was leaning against the wall. This he unrolled and motioned to Ruben that he should lay on the carpet with his few belongings. Ishmala gave Ruben the pole that the large carpet had been rolled around. This was so that when he rolled Ruben in the carpet the pole would protrude and make space for air so that Ruben could breathe. He quickly rolled Ruben in the carpet and without showing any sign of effort, raised the boy in the rolled carpet onto his shoulder. Only then did he walk around the house and away from the group of people watching the activity around the front door. Little did Ruben know, they were only just in time, as the gruesome Captain Gershnarl was pounding his gnarled fist on Mutek's front door at the same time as they left the courtyard.

Ishmala walked away from the crowd gathered around Mutek's front door and slipped down the alleyways until he came to Mutek's boatyard. Here he unrolled the carpet, allowing Ruben to stand up, but even then he motioned to the boy to keep quiet. He rolled up the carpet and stowed it in the large warehouse, outside of which a rowing boat was standing. Ishmala half-lifted and half-dragged the boat into the water and lifted Ruben completely off his feet and sat him in its bows. He sat in the centre of the boat and taking one oar in each of his huge hands, he began to row the boat away from the bank. Ruben knew that two men normally rowed this type of boat, one on each oar. But with this man, whose arms were like tree trunks, the boat soon left the shore, which rapidly fell into the distance and became shrouded in a mist that rose up from the river. Ishmala quickly settled into a slow, steady rhythm as the boat rose and fell in the swell of the estuary. The sky was a deep azure above them and brightened towards the west, where the sun was beginning to sink like a huge golden ball into the haze that was covering the town. As Ruben looked out towards the east from the front of the boat he could make out some of the stars as they began to glow in the night sky, and he could also see some of the fishing boats with oil lamps strapped to their main masts. Their own boat was painted dark blue, invisible to someone unless they were right on top of them.

"Ishmala, can I help?" Ruben asked, feeling completely useless. Ishmala paused in his stroke and turned to Ruben, smiled, and shook his head, but pointed to Ruben, then to his eyes and then to the distant shore, indicating to the boy. Ruben realised that he wanted him to keep an eye on the bank, and to look out for boats or anything that might break their passage in the water. Feeling that he now had a job to do and was beginning to earn his passage, Ruben took to this new job with great eagerness, scowling intently at the now-looming shoreline, where he could see small waves breaking. Without even turning to look, or seeming to check his bearings, Ishmala drove the boat directly into a small inlet that had appeared in the shoreline, as if by magic out of the mist. They were gliding along, up the inlet, and were soon shielded by the large bulrushes and reeds that grew thickly on the riverbank. The water became gradually more shallow and the hull of the boat juddered as the bow rose onto the sandy bank. Ishmala stowed the oars, and then with Ruben's help, or at least with his hands on the side of the boat as well, he dragged the boat above the high water mark, so that it would not get washed away by the incoming tide. Ishmala took out a huge wicked-looking curved sickle that was hidden in the recesses of the boat. With a few wide swipes he cut a large armful of reeds, which he used to cover the boat so that anyone passing would not recognise it for what it was, unless they stumbled right on top of it. Then, showing Ruben how to follow him close behind by grabbing his broad belt, he took the quarterstaff and parted the reeds in front of him, prodding occasionally to ensure that the ground was firm.

After a while they came to a small semi-overgrown track that headed southwest. It was now completely dark except for the bright stars that hung like lanterns in the sky, but the moon had not risen yet. However, it was far from quiet with the frogs loudly croaking by the water and the crickets that were in the undergrowth. Ishmala signed to Ruben that they must walk for a short distance, by moving two fingers and making a short gap between his hands, and indicating they should move off the main track before they slept for the night. This he showed by putting his palms together and resting his head on one side. So they moved for a short way off the track to where a few thorn trees were growing; here Ishmala used Ruben's staff to flatten the reeds in the shelter of the trees.

Although Ruben had done comparatively little that day, the

excitement of the last few hours had made him tired. As he sat down he noticed that Ishmala carried a large bag slung over one shoulder, which he now took off, and brought out some bread and goat's cheese. They hungrily shared this, washed down with a few mouthfuls of a pale golden wine that was surprisingly mild to the taste. Ruben felt very safe with this large powerful man watching over him, and he soon fell into a deep, untroubled sleep.

He woke early with the dawn light and was alarmed to realise that Ishmala was no longer sleeping next to him. He wondered what had happened to his huge companion and was amazed how the man could have stirred without waking him. He heard a movement in the trees and saw a large flight of ducks rising into the sky. He saw a few of the ducks knocked out of the sky by a well-aimed throwing stick. Moments later Ishmala appeared carrying the dead ducks, which he roasted over a small fire that he lit from branches he had already gathered. He smiled at Ruben as the boy rubbed his eyes and wandered across the clearing to squat by the fire. The roasted duck smelt good, but it was a shame that it had not been plucked: the burning feathers gave it a strange odour. However, Ruben ignored this and tucked in hungrily to the meal, which tasted good, and had some more of the golden wine that they had drunk the night before. Ishmala scattered the embers of the dying fire into a nearby patch of damp weeds, which sizzled and steamed as they quenched the fire. He pointed to Ruben and motioned with his fingers that he must start walking, and pointing to the sun that was just rising in the east, he indicated that the boy must walk on until at least midday. He led Ruben back onto the track and pulled the map out of Ruben's knapsack, and pointed to a place that he marked with a charred stick with a small cross to indicate their position. He gestured that Ruben should go southwest, but that he himself would go northeast, back to the boat, showing with a rowing motion that he must go back to Lagash. He held out his hand and took both of Ruben's hands in his, and placed them on his large chest – his heart would be with Ruben. He held the boy strongly by the shoulders; holding his head up and smiling that genial smile with the great flashing grin, and then turned on his heel. Ruben sighed deeply, and realising that he was now alone, simply hoped that if the evil Gershnarl was coming after him, somehow he would have to meet and pass Ishmala. This gave Ruben some comfort as he set out towards Ur.

\*\*\*\*

Mutek himself eventually answered the loud hammering on the front door. "Why, Captain Gershnarl," greeted Mutek with a smile. "I am so sorry that you have been kept waiting, but most of my servants are out and I have only just returned home from my boatyard." Mutek smiled in a polite greeting. Not put off by this politeness, Gershnarl shoved his large bulk through the door and past Mutek, allowing some of his soldiers to follow him. "I have been ordered to arrest you, on a charge of high treason," Gershnarl growled. As Mutek protested his innocence, his hands were firmly tied behind his back with a leather thong. He was roughly dragged out of the house and into the street, where a group of onlookers had gathered, realising that something was about to happen – as it often did when a party of Guards led by the much feared Captain Gershnarl appeared. They pushed the stumbling Mutek along as they marched him to the guardhouse. Mutek turned to protest, as the cell door was thrown open, but his objections were ignored, and Gershnarl's large booted foot slammed into his back, hurling him down the few rough steps to land sprawling on the floor. "Get in there, you dog," snarled Gershnarl. "We'll see you in the morning."

****

As Ishmala's boat ran ashore alongside Mutek's boatyard, the man was surprised to find that his arms were grasped by several pairs of hands, and even his great strength would have been futile against some of the twenty armed Babylonian Guards. Ishmala was well aware that these Guards were the elite fighting force of the Babylonian army. Each man had been carefully selected and chosen for his ability with the weapons that were the tools of his trade. Before he could react, he was assisted out of the boat, and heavy bronze manacles were forced around his wrists and ankles, joined by a heavy chain. The guard in charge of the party led him up to Captain Gershnarl and raised an enquiring eyebrow. "Where to with this one, Captain?" asked the Guard.

"Up to the bloody guardhouse, to meet his governor," said Gershnarl with a happy smile. "And remember this one can't talk." He deliberately stamped on Ishmala's sandaled foot. He smiled to himself as he followed the Guards who were trying to jostle and trip Ishmala as they took him up the alleyway and into the street. But their efforts were in vain as the large man went slowly with his head held high, seemingly oblivious of their manhandling. With this big black bastard out of the way, their job would be so much easier, thought Gershnarl to himself.

****

Mutek was led out blinking into the sunlight of the bright day after the dark dank cell in which he had been imprisoned overnight. He had been without food or water, still bound and without anyone to wash from his face, the ugly graze and bruises that he had sustained when he was thrown into the cell. The blood had dried on his swollen lips, but he ignored the pain and smiled when he saw Ishmala, who was standing tall and proud. But this smile froze on his lips and turned into a frown, as he saw the heavy chain binding his friend and servant.

The chain that joined Ishmala's wrists to his ankles was made from the new metal called iron that was quarried out of the mountains to the north. But as they had not learned how to temper it, the result was that the metal was either too soft or too brittle to be used to make weapons. So its full potential was still not realised, although there had been fierce fights with some pirates from the east, who had such weapons.

"Bind him to the lashing beam," shouted Gershnarl, pointing with his finger at Mutek, "and we will soon get a confession out of the bastard."

"But I demand a fair trial," shouted Mutek in protest.

"Oh dear, we have forgotten to give him a trial," mimicked Gershnarl, as he twisted his face into a more gruesome grimace – even though that was almost impossible. Mutek winced as his wrists were bound to the beam. But this was nothing in comparison to the sting of the lash. Six wicked strokes hissed out across his back, tearing his cotton shift, exposing his flabby back and leaving dark red angry wheals. Captain Gershnarl stepped up, leaning towards Mutek, "You were going to lead the revolt against the king's treaty with Assyria," bellowing so everyone could hear. Mutek sobbed with pain and shook his head in denial, but managed to keep his teeth clenched as he knew further protest would be useless. Seeing that he would say nothing, Gershnarl ambled over to the bare-chested executioner who was administering the punishment. "Try this," he said, handing the man a whip of scorpions. Ten more lashes with this ghastly weapon soon had the whimpering Mutek sobbing in agony, as the barbs in the lashes tore his back to shreds. The blood ran down his back and legs to soak into the ground and mingle with the scraps of flesh that splattered to the ground. He was only just alive as Gershnarl came over towards him, lifted his face and shouted, "Yes, what was that?" for the benefit of the surrounding crowd of soldiers, knowing that there would be no answer, as Mutek could barely breathe, let alone speak. So he ordered the flogging to continue.

Watching his friend and former master meeting his death in such a brutal and unjust fashion was more than Ishmala could bear, so he cast his eyes to the ground – but he kept this memory fresh in his mind.

"Shall we do the same with this one, Captain?" asked one of the Guards holding Ishmala's chains.

"Don't be a stupid arse," barked Gershnarl. "That bastard can't talk; just take him back to the cells."

It had been a good day, thought Gershnarl. He could always invent some story about Mutek's death for the commander, knowing that none of his men would speak out against him as they were all terrified of his reprisals. So now he could lead an expedition across the river to try and catch that little runt that he was sure the big black bastard had rowed there. Strange, he thought, how that large, gangly kid had looked like the "sod" Uriah with whom he had had an argument some eight years previously, when Uriah had accused him of cheating at the gaming tables. Uriah was correct, Gershnal always cheated, but Gershnal hated to be made a fool of, so he had got his revenge on Uriah by taking his woman and forcing her into his own bed.

## 2
## THE ROAD TOUR

As Ruben walked along in the early morning sunlight, the air was fresh and invigorating because he was still near the sea and the ozone from the salt water gave it a heady quality. He noticed many of the tiny flowers that grew in the damp soil around the vast clumps of reeds: the pale blue periwinkles, the small red blood-drops with bright yellow centres and the orange and yellow star-flowers, and others that he could not name. He wished he knew more of the plants and the masses of wildlife that he passed, not only the croaking frogs and chirping crickets, but all the many insects that were buzzing around, each performing their own task, completely oblivious to the human world. He paused to watch a long insect that he believed was called a dragonfly, but did not know why. Its bright blue body was about as long as his hand but thinner than his little finger, and it hovered on gossamer wings that kept it quite still above the ground, while its bulbous eyes seemed to be looking in every direction at once; then in a flash it was gone. Apart from these few distractions he walked along completely alone for what seemed half the morning, catching glimpses of the river to the north every time the path rose a few cubits and he could see above the reeds and bulrushes.

He paused for a moment to take a few mouthfuls of the drink that Ishmala had given to him, and as he unstoppered the flagon, it occurred to him for the first time that it wasn't a wine that he was drinking but a pale gold cordial; it was very refreshing, particularly as the day was now getting warm. As he walked along, the reeds and rushes seemed to get higher about him and then, quite suddenly, the track forked in front of him. He pulled out the map and studied it carefully, but could see no indication of a possible fork. As he stared closely at the papyrus, he saw that the old map, which must have been folded before it was stuck onto the new scroll, had then been refolded. This area was on one of the folds, which made it difficult to be one hundred percent certain that there was nothing on the map. Having to choose which path to follow, he chose the path on the right, knowing that he could always retrace his footsteps if this path led nowhere.

He set off along the path and after a while the ground became more and more marshy, and the reeds and bulrushes began to close in around him as the path grew narrower. He then noticed through a gap between the reeds that he was on a spur leading out into the river, as there was now clear water on both sides of the track. He stopped, wondering whether to go back or possibly try to strike off back towards the path to the left that was obviously on higher ground. He decided, as he could see no evidence of crocodiles in the area, to risk either wading or swimming across the short stretch of water.

Slipping off his sandals and putting them in his knapsack, he made a small latticework that he wove into a rough raft out of large reeds that he cut with the bronze knife, and placed his knapsack onto it. He then waded into the water, which came up to his waist. A few more steps and he had to start swimming as the water, although bright and clear, was surprisingly deep. As he headed for the other bank, pushing the raft in front of him, he noticed for the first time the unusually shaped prow of a boat that was half-wrecked, sticking out of the river. He swam closer to the wreck and secured the raft to the prow before inspecting it. He swam along the side of the half-submerged craft and as he ducked his head under, a bright flash caught his eye. He dived deeply to investigate the source of this flash and soon saw the bones of a hand, grasping the hilt of a sword with an ornate bright blue stone in it. He surfaced, trying not to feel frightened by the skeleton that had obviously been picked clean by the fish, for the boat was not that old and the flesh could not all have decayed away naturally in the time.

He had a vague memory about a story that some pirates from the east had fought with the Babylonian Guards a while back, something about a cargo they had been trying to capture. He took a deep lungful of air and dived back to where the hand was gripped around the hilt of the sword with the blue stone. The sword was embedded in a sack of what must have been dates, as there was an oozing black mass around the sword where it went into the sack. It was remarkably easy to remove as the bones fell away at Ruben's touch, and the sword slipped out of the black gooey mass.

The sword was heavy, even under water, and Ruben had to kick hard to regain surface. When he tried to lift the sword onto the raft with his knapsack he fully appreciated how heavy it was, as he had to use both hands to lift it clear of the water. He realised how sharp the sword was as it almost cut his fingers, even though there was still a lot of the black gooey mess on the blade. The raft containing the knapsack began to sink, as the sword was obviously far too heavy. He had to swim to the small sandy beach, which he had originally aimed for. This took a considerable effort, as the sword constantly tried to drag him below the surface. However, he eventually made it, leaving the sword temporarily above the waterline. He then returned to the prow of the boat, untied his raft from it and swam back to the beach.

Sitting cross-legged on the sand, he inspected his new trophy. It was a long sword that stretched from his feet to his waist, with a sharp point, broad and thick in the middle, and shaped like one of the leaves of the bulrushes. Both edges were still sharp as it had not been in the water for that long, and had been preserved from rust by the black oily dates. (Although Ruben knew nothing about iron and its rusting qualities at that time.) It was dull grey and did not shine like the bronze knife that he carried, but he was intrigued by its weight and sharpness. It must have belonged to a fairly strong man, who would have been able to wield it. The bright blue stone that formed the pommel of the sword was set amidst tiny white stones, which sparkled with all the colours of a rainbow in the strong sunlight. He recognised the blue stone as lapis lazuli, which the merchants from Egypt were keen to acquire, and for that alone it was a valuable prize. As it was now the hottest part of the day, with the sun burning directly overhead, he grabbed his belongings and made his way up the bank to the original track, where he could see a few small trees that would give him some shade from the midday sun.

Rather than take a short sleep, as was the custom during the hottest part of the day, Ruben was so excited with his new treasure that he sat in the shade with the sword on his lap and cleaned it with a wad of weeds, which he plucked for the purpose of polishing it, so that it shone a dull silver grey in the bright afternoon sunshine. He decided to weave a scabbard, using a latticework of reeds interwoven with strips of bulrushes, so that he could carry the sword on his back, which was how he had seen soldiers in the army carry their large swords. As he was also very keen to test the sharpness of the edge of the sword, he cut the appropriate grasses from the riverbank using it, as Ishmala had previously done with the sickle. He was amazed at how quickly and smoothly he could cut even the toughest reeds and rushes, and how the edge still seemed just as sharp afterwards, unlike his bronze knife that continually needed sharpening on the small stone that he carried for this very purpose. He used reeds just over the sword's length, crossed with the occasional stout reed, to make a lattice, which he then interwove with strips of thick bulrush. It took him a long time as the sword was long and he was meticulous to ensure that the scabbard did comparative justice to his fine new treasure. It was quite late when he rose from his labours and slung the sword in its new scabbard over his shoulders yet beneath his knapsack, and recommenced his journey.

He walked on for a long time, keeping to the track that was heading generally westwards into the setting sun and realised that he was very tired. Fortunately, in the dying rays of the sunlight he saw some reed buildings to his left where the smoke of a small cooking fire drifted lazily in the darkening sky. He walked towards the huts and as he came nearer an old man, sitting outside the nearest hut, called out to him in greeting, asking him where he had come from and where he was going.

"I have come from Lagash, from where I set out two days ago to the north of the Great River. And I am trying to make my way to Ur. Can you tell me if I am heading in the right direction?" asked Ruben politely.

"Why, yes," replied the old man. "Though it is still a good day's walk from here, and we seldom see travellers these days. So why don't you put down your burden and sleep here for the night, and tell us what is happening these days in Lagash?"

"You are most kind," said Ruben. "For I am tired and could do with a good night's sleep, as well as some food, which I will be happy to pay for."

"The news will be payment enough," said the old man. "We have food in plenty, providing of course that you like fish," he chuckled.

"My goodness," said Ruben. "Anything to fill my empty stomach, and by the smell of the food that is coming from your hut it will be very welcome."

So Ruben set aside his knapsack, which he ensured covered the handle of the sword that protruded from the scabbard, so that no one could really tell what it was that he carried. The man led him into one of the dome-shaped huts, where an old woman was serving some delicious smelling fish that was freshly grilled, to three small children squatting on the floor. The old man introduced Ruben to his wife, and explained that the three children were his grandchildren. His son was in the army and was being visited by his wife, so they were looking after the children in their parents' absence. As they sat down, Ruben noticed that the hut was woven from reeds that were in fact growing out of the ground and had been pulled over to make the dome shape of the hut, and that the thatching of rushes was extremely intricate and ornate.

The old man asked him about Lagash and it soon became apparent to Ruben that the man thought he was a deserting soldier, running away from one of the camps where the newly enlisted boys were sent to train. Ruben also realised that the old man was more than happy to keep this a secret, so he went along with it, knowing that it would be a good excuse for his presence.

He told the old man and his wife everything he could think of about various changes in the town, and then of the new treaty between Babylon and Assyria, at which the old man quickly nodded.

"Ah yes, we thought something like that was happening, and I believe that some of the army are being sent to the northern hills, where the Persians are mustering their forces."

And so the conversation drifted on during the meal, talking of this and that and nothing in particular. The old man then rose to his feet and said, "You look tired young fellow, so follow me with your possessions and I will take you to my son's hut where you can spend a quiet night's sleep."

Ruben followed him out of the hut and picked up his belongings, careful still to hide the decorative pommel of the sword, and followed the old man to another, even more ornately woven dome-shaped hut, where there was a latticework bed above the reed-strewn floor. Ruben gratefully put his belongings at one end of the latticework, on which he lay and quickly fell into a deep sleep.

He awoke fairly early in the morning to see the sun was already up and one of the children was looking intently at him from the doorway.

"Gran says you can come and have some breakfast," invited the child.

And so Ruben took breakfast with these kind people, who then set him back on his journey towards Ur, informing him that if he kept to the track, which shortly afterwards turned more to the south, he would come to the town before evening, providing that he kept to a good pace and did not stop for too long during the midday heat. Thanking them for their kind-hearted charity, Ruben shouldered his burden and went on his way.

Keeping up a fair pace was no great effort for Ruben, as being used to running long errands for his uncle he had ample stamina and he was growing used to the weight of the sword beneath his knapsack. He even tried trotting for short periods, as he had seen soldiers do on forced marches, particularly as it was still fairly fresh and the sun was not yet too hot. The track soon bore round to the left and headed more to the south, and it gradually started to rise out of the marshes. He rested for a short period beneath some bushes during the hottest part of the day, but was soon on his way again, following the old track that was more and more overgrown. He neither saw nor heard any other person but once again noticed the small flowers and the many insects, as well as some of the wild ducks that flew overhead. Before long he sighted the small town of Ur in the distance, which was on higher ground, overlooking the marshes to the west. As he drew nearer to the town, the bright afternoon sunlight reflected a pale gold from the top of the buildings that were very much like those in Lagash, mainly one-storey high and of bleached clay.

As he entered the main street of the town, he realised that the pale gold was reed thatching on the roofs of the buildings, which seemed to be the normality around here, unlike the woven, brightly patterned cloth awnings that decorated and roofed many of the buildings in Lagash. He had prepared his story so made for the town's main inn, noticing as he passed that there were a few of the reed-type buildings at which he had spent the previous night, with the family on the marshes. A great silence fell over the room as Ruben walked into the inn, as most of the inhabitants turned to look at the stranger who had entered. Taking his courage in both hands he walked boldly up to the innkeeper, who was sitting at one of the tables, and asked if he could hire a room for a few nights.

"How long is a few nights?" inquired the innkeeper.

"As long as my business takes me," replied Ruben extracting some of the money that Mutek had given him, to show the innkeeper that he could pay for his lodgings. The innkeeper agreed that he could stay as they had spare rooms, and then said, "We so seldom receive travellers these days. Would you like to come to dinner, or should I send one of my servants through with a meal for you?"

Ruben did not reply at first, but waited until he had looked around the room that he was shown. It was small, but quite pleasant as it had an open window overlooking the marshes, and a small table and chair as well as the bed.

"I am quite tired," he said. "I have journeyed from Lagash, so if you would be good enough to send in some supper, that would be excellent." He put his burden on the bed, being careful to keep the sword hilt covered by the knapsack, and sat down at the table, waiting for the food to be brought in to him. His meal mainly consisted, not surprisingly, of fish, with dates and olives, which was served by a young girl who carefully kept her eyes lowered all the time and said nothing as she placed the platter of food in front of him, together with a mug of beer.

Ruben ate hungrily as he looked out of the window into the darkening marshes. A pale mist rose up from the water, completely obliterating the view. It was rapidly becoming dark as the sun was setting quickly. Ruben was almost finished when there was a knock on the door. He rose and opened it, only to find the innkeeper with a small oil lamp that he kindly brought in and placed on the table. He told Ruben that when he had finished, all he had to do was put the empty plate and mug outside the door and it would be collected, but there was no rush for this, and then went out, apologising for the intrusion and wishing Ruben a comfortable night's rest. Ruben was rather surprised that he had not been questioned at all about what he was doing, but was nonetheless glad that he did not have to use the story he had invented. Before he finished the remainder of his meal he decided to inspect his sword once more under the light from the oil lamp. As he grasped the ornate handle and drew the blade into the light, he was shocked to see that there were little brown flowers of rust starting to form on the metal. Thinking hard about this strange phenomenon, he came to the conclusion that the layer of slimy grease that he had wiped off the metal had previously stopped it from going rusty. So he chopped the remaining olives and dates and mixed the oily mash into a paste that he then smeared onto the blade, after rubbing off the particles of rust. The blade was then greasy again, rather than place it back into the scabbard, which he knew would rub off the oily paste, he put it on the ground beneath the bed. He then finished up the meal and did as he was bid with the empty utensils. He blew out the lamp, lay down on the bed, and quickly fell asleep.

He awoke early as the dark window paled with the early morning light. As he lay on his bed, stretching and yawning, he heard a noise outside the door. He rose and opened it, and found a bowl of fresh water that had been left there for him to wash with. He brought the water into the bedroom and washed away the sleep from his eyes and completely rinsed himself down as he was quite grubby and sweaty from the warm night. As he dressed and took the bowl out of the room, he met the innkeeper who enquired.

"Would you like your breakfast brought to you, sir? Or will you join us in the main room?" he enquired.

Surprised at being called 'sir' for the first time, Ruben tried to conceal his astonishment, and said, "No, I am happy to join you in the main room, if you will give me a little while to finish getting dressed." He quickly went through in his mind what he was going to say about being on business from Lagash, and also his story of being of foreign origin, which he knew would be believed because of his sandy-coloured hair. After tidying his belongings and ensuring that the sword was safely hidden, he went through into the main room, careful to close his door, and said good morning to the people who were gathered in the main room.

He sat down to breakfast, which consisted of a maize mash and wheat cakes, served with dates and mangoes, which were washed down with surprisingly clear spring water. Then he casually asked whether anyone knew of the whereabouts of a man named Simeon, the one whom he had been instructed to ask for by Mutek. Another strange silence hung over the room as enquiring faces looked from one to the other. Finally the innkeeper said, "You must mean S'meon, the old man who lives out in the marshes. We haven't seen him for three or four months, but I am sure we will soon, when his floating house drifts this way as it normally does this time of year."

Greatly relieved that someone knew the whereabouts of the man he was looking for, Ruben enquired whether there was any way of getting a boat out to the man's floating home, but he soon realised by the blank stares and muttered conversations that no one knew exactly where this old man was. A new conversation started about some of the army being sent to the northern hills where there had been some trouble on the border with

Persia. Ruben was glad of this change of conversation and listened eagerly, but learned little as most of the subject was speculative. Breakfast was soon over and people began to drift out of the inn to go about their own business.

Ruben left the table and wandered out into the main street and was pleased to see the bright, early morning sunlight had burned off a lot of the mist from the marshes and that only a few wisps hung above the water, and even those were quickly vanishing. Looking down the street, Ruben ambled towards where a crowd of people had gathered around the well from which the clear water had obviously come. Already a few people were standing in a queue waiting to fill various water containers, which would then be taken back to their respective homes. He noticed the girl from the inn at the front of the queue, with two large pitchers that she was just filling from the bucket and was then presumably going to take to the inn. The girl was still rather shy with Ruben and did not look into his eyes, but readily agreed to his offer of assistance to carry the heavy burden back to the inn.

"Are you the innkeeper's daughter?" he enquired politely.

"Oh, no!" came the reply. "I have only recently started working at the inn so that I can assist my family, as my older brothers have been drafted into the army and we have little money to go round," she answered.

"My name is Ruben," he said as he easily picked up one pitcher in his left hand and helped her carry the other one between them.

"You are very kind, my name is Lialah," she answered conversationally. "I overheard you asking about S'meon this morning. He is known as the old man of the marshes and is a distant relative of mine. And I can confirm what the innkeeper was saying, about him turning up fairly shortly."

As she seemed quite willing to talk, Ruben asked her more about S'meon. He was interested to learn that his house was another ornate reed building that floated on a large mat of reeds. This drifted mysteriously around in the currents of the marshes, but it normally came close to Ur at this time of year. Lialah seemed to be pretty talkative once she had got over her initial shyness, and told him a lot of fascinating things about this old man who seemed to be something of an oracle. As they arrived back at the inn, she said that she had to go and clear up the breakfast dishes and then clean the bedrooms before she started the other washing tasks and jobs for the day. Ruben told her not to worry about his own room as he had only a few items and was not untidy. It had been clean when he arrived late yesterday and he would rather his items were not disturbed.

Having left his new friend to carry on with her chores, he wandered back down the main street and again began looking for any indication that there may be some truth behind the rumour that his great-uncle Abraham had come from Ur over two thousand years earlier. Finding nothing of particular interest about the small town, he ventured further along the old caravan route to find that it turned westwards again into marshes. The track began to descend until the ground underfoot became damp with large puddles of water. As the track wound on endlessly with no one in sight he halted, and after a pause for thought he decided to retrace his footsteps back to Ur and await the coming of S'meon.

****

Gershnarl was amazed at the rumpus that Mutek's death had caused, and the great difficulty that he had in convincing his commander that he was innocent of the brutal murder of a respected member of the Merchant's Council. Fortunately for Gershnarl, he had heard the rumour that the whole situation had been contrived by a rival boatbuilder in Nippur, and he had quickly altered his story to suggest to his commander his innocence of the murder of Mutek. Although he had been present at the arrest of Mutek, he had protested that he was absent when his men had attempted to gain a confession, but he had arrived too late at the flogging to save Mutek's innocent life. No one seemed concerned that Mutek's servant was still imprisoned and Gershnarl had not even informed his commander that Ishmala was still being held in the guardhouse.

All this ridiculous business had taken the best part of six days and so it was not going to be until first thing in the morning – that being almost a quarter moon after Ishmala's arrest – that Gershnarl could lead a patrol to follow the boy into the marshlands. As he left his commander's office, Gershnarl turned his mind to the woman who was coming to see him that night. She had appeared earlier that day and had begged him not to send her husband with the soldiers who were going north to the borderlands with Persia. He made it clear to her that he would have to bribe his commander and was delighted to hear that she could afford little to offer as a bribe. He therefore suggested, making quite clear what he expected, that she should come to his quarters that night to discuss the matter. Grinning with pleasure at the prospect of having this rather attractive young woman in his bed, he walked briskly back to his quarters after a long day spent making plans for an early departure in the morning.

The Babylonian Guards were the elite of the Babylonian army, and would often spearhead the attack on an opposing army, and were feared throughout the known civilised world. Captain Gershnarl was one of the common sort of soldier, who rose to captaincy by virtue of bullying and maltreatment of his men in order to have his commands obeyed. This made the guardsmen extremely tough and a powerful fighting force, as they were used to obeying orders without question, no matter how brutal or degrading the task might be. Therefore, Gershnarl knew that whatever went on in his quarters would not be questioned. Apart from which, witnesses had overheard the woman agreeing to come to his quarters that night.

Gershnarl entered his rooms and went into the bedroom where he slipped a coil of rope under the bed and tied a loop with slipknots at each end of the rope. After inspecting his handiwork he made sure that the loops were out of sight. Hearing a light knock on the door he went out into the main room and barked out, "Enter". The door opened and the young woman entered, turning and closing the door behind her. Standing with her back to the door, she said, "What exactly do you expect from me, Captain Gershnarl?" Gershnarl noted that she wore a simple but quite revealing gown that rose and fell to the rhythm of her hasty breathing, which outlined the contours of her ample breasts. He spread his hands in a mock gesture of surprise.

"Well, surely you must appreciate that I do not have full control over the men in my command, so I must offer my commander whatever price he requests for a man to be posted to do another duty," he said, moving closer.

She screwed up her nose at the rank smell of stale beer and his unwashed body as he moved yet closer.

"But I informed you earlier that I could pay very little," she murmured in a timorous whisper.

"I may be able to fix things with my commander, at my own expense," he said, as he moved still closer and placed one hand on her shoulder. "The only price I expect is having immense pleasure with you," he chuckled, as he cupped her left breast in his hand.

It was not rape as such, as she had come to his room. But it was nonetheless extremely brutal and her cries of protest soon became sobs of agony as he relentlessly continued. Finally he rolled off her with a groan of satisfaction and slipped off the retaining loops around her wrists. She rose shakily from the bed and grabbed her clothes to cover her nudity. She cried out to him, "I hope you are satisfied, you evil brute. And I trust you will ensure my husband is not sent north to the border to fight against the Persian forces."

"All that has already been arranged," murmured Gershnarl, now drowsy after his exertions.

"By the Gods, you evil bastard," she cried, as she hurried from his rooms, slamming the door behind her.

Gershnarl smiled to himself. It had been even better than he had expected. He had really enjoyed hurting the bitch and knew that he was completely free from any reprisal. After a short sleep he could get after that little sod had run off into the marshlands, he thought, and with that he slept.

\*\*\*\*

Ishmala was getting fed up with waiting. He was in the same guard house where Mutek had been imprisoned, although he had not been thrust in so roughly and had been fed daily, if you could call the small bowl of watery porridge food. As the days passed, the guards had stopped taunting him and were not even polite, but he could not talk to them and he missed human contact, quite apart from the freedom that he so dearly desired. He was still bound by the chains, although he had made no attempt to escape. However, he felt that he could break his bondage and escape, but with every passing day, living on these meagre rations, his strength was diminishing. He had heard the guards talking about a party, led by Captain Gershnarl, that would be departing early the next morning to go after someone who had run into the marshlands, and it was at this point that he had decided that he must escape and try to protect Ruben, as had been Mutek's wish.

After he was served his evening ration, which he greedily bolted down, bringing the empty dish back to the guard, he quietly awaited the guard changeover that night. Whilst he waited he tried with all his might to break the chains, but because he could get no article to use as leverage he was unsuccessful. The guard finally changed late that night and Ishmala pretended to be asleep until the early morning, when everything was quiet. He moved to the doorway and started a low moaning noise, which was the only sound that he could make, but also rattled his chains against the cell bars in order to wake the guard. In this he was successful. He then moved behind the door as the guard looked in. Believing he was lying in the corner, and as he was still fettered, the guard opened the door and came into the cell to see what all the noise was about. As the guard entered, leaving the door open, a chain was quickly thrown around his neck, the chain that was still fastened to Ishmala's arms. The chain was tightened and the guard's windpipe was crushed and his neck broken before he could even utter a warning cry. Trying all the guard's keys in the bronze restraints, Ishmala eventually found one that unlocked the manacles on his ankles and wrists. Heaving the guard's body into the dark recesses of the cell, Ishmala took all the keys with him and left the guardhouse, carefully closing and locking the door behind him. He then slipped quietly away down to Mutek's boatyard, where he knew a large pile of mangoes was waiting to be shipped up the river to Babylon. Having eaten his fill, which left a sizeable depletion in the number of mangoes, he went to where the soldiers had a wharf a short distance up the river from Mutek's yard, where he would await the coming of Gershnarl and his party of Babylonian Guards.

He did not have long to wait. As the sky was beginning to pale towards the east he heard marching footsteps and Gershnarl's barked order instructing that the boat be launched into the water.

"Where to, Captain?" asked one of the guardsmen, and he heard Gershnarl order, "To Ur, you arsehole, I'm sure that's where the little runt went to, as it's the only town of any size on that side of the river." So the boat was launched into the river and filled with a dozen guardsmen, five on each side with an oar, one on the stern with the steering rudder and one as lookout in the bows of the boat, with Gershnarl standing roughly in the middle of the boat. They rowed into the centre of the river, and headed southwest to Ur as the sun began to come up over the eastern shoreline. Because of the dark shadows they did not notice the black shape slip into the water and swim with a strong stroke after them.

\*\*\*\*

By the time Ruben had returned to Ur it was time for the midday meal and then a short rest during the heat of the day. On his way back he had noticed once again the tiny flowers amidst the reeds and bulrushes and the many insects that buzzed around totally oblivious to the world of humans. On reaching the town he went back to the inn, to find that he could get a drink of ale and a few dates and olives, plus a few rice cakes, for just another small amount of money that hardly made a dent in the pile of coins that Mutek had given him. Whilst he sat in the shade, slowly sipping his drink and enjoying the food, he looked up into the sky as a faint shadow crossed the sun. It was a large flight of rather strange-looking birds. They seemed to him to be a vivid pink colour, but he could not be sure of that, maybe it was because of the sunlight, but they were obviously tall birds, with long necks and large beaks. He wondered where they were going and where they had come from. He thought about the flowers, the insects and the birds of the marshlands, and wondered if S'meon knew all about them, as he seemed to be the authority on most things, according to Lialah.

All in all, he stayed for another three days in Ur, gradually getting to know some of the people and some of the history in the town. At one time, Ur had been considerably larger and originally the old caravan route had been busy, but over the last fifty years the main river that flowed into the Euphrates had silted up. Therefore, the large galleys could no longer reach Ur, so that its importance had diminished, as the importance of Lagash had risen in comparison. He also learned that many people had moved away in favour of living in Lagash, as there was little in the way of employment in Ur, with the exception of the few fishing boats that fished for the shrimps, lobsters and crabs that could be caught in the brackish waters of the river, in addition to a man who hunted crocodiles for their hides.

During his stay, his friendship with Lialah grew to the point of him assisting her with some of the chores around the inn, as he had little else to do to pass the time. The money that Mutek had given him was dwindling, and he realised that he only had enough for another couple of days, but decided that he would wait until he had nothing left, and then try to help some of the fishermen to earn his keep. Fortunately it was on the third evening, when he was sitting outside the inn awaiting the evening meal, that he saw in the marshes a large bank of reeds floating towards the shore. On this large bank of reeds he thought he saw an ornate domed house, looking like a small palace – but it was evening and the mist was beginning to rise from the marshes and darkness was falling, so he could not be positive. The bell sounded for dinner in the inn, so he went inside, and over the meal, when she came near him, he told Lialah about what he thought he had seen. After dinner, when he was helping her tidy up the empty plates, she told him that it sounded like S'meon's floating house. But when they looked out of the window they could see nothing because of the mist rising from the marshes. Ruben went to bed, hoping that what he had seen, or thought he had seen, was not an illusion, but that the old man of the marshes had finally arrived.

He spent a fitful night, and rose as soon as he heard the washing basin outside his room being filled. He washed, and as now was customary, joined the others for breakfast, where he sat with his back deliberately to the door. He hardly dared to look around when the sun came up. Finally breakfast was over and he turned around and wandered to the window, where he looked out and was greatly relieved to see that it was true, there was a large floating house down by the bank. Trying to look unexcited, he walked down towards the bank, but found that his pace soon became a run, and he almost bumped into an elderly man tying up his large raft of floating reeds to the stakes in the riverbank. The old man straightened to his full height and Ruben realised that he was tall, although slim and burned dark from hours in the sun. His beard was entirely white and his head topped by a beautiful bright green turban. A huge beaky nose dominated his wrinkled face, but deep-set, under white bushy eyebrows, were two piercing blue eyes that fixed Ruben with a steady gaze.

"You must be Uriah's son," he said. "I saw the boatbuilder, Mutek, last year, and I have been expecting you for some considerable time. My name is S'meon." He held out his hand in greeting.

Ruben was shocked at being recognised by a stranger, but he eventually found his tongue and greeted the old man, saying he had been told by Mutek to seek his help. Just to be sure that he was correct he said, "Is your name really Simeon, or should I call you S'meon?"

The old man smiled and said, "Yes, my real name is Simeon and that is what I like to be called, but the folk around here generally shorten my name because it is their custom and S'meon slides easier off their tongue."

Having recovered his wits, Ruben properly introduced himself, and then asked if he could possibly join Simeon on his raft. "Surely," said the old man, gesturing to the raft behind him. "You are very welcome, and I am sure that an extra pair of hands will help the running of this veritable museum."

Although Ruben did not know what a museum was, he excitedly ran back and took his belongings from the Inn and went to settle up with the innkeeper. Lialah, who had come to see her uncle, joined him on his return to Simeon's raft. They were greeted at the riverbank by Simeon, who said, "Welcome aboard," and with a wave ushered them into his palatial home. The main room was large and had a domed roof like the smaller reed houses, but much larger and far more ornate in the weaving. At each corner of the square central chamber there was a small domed room, which is why the place looked like a palace from the outside. Walking past these rooms there was a raised part at the back with three chambers leading off it. Simeon said, "I will show you everything in detail later, Ruben, but these three chambers in front of us, on the left is my bedroom. The room in the centre is the cooking area, and the room to the right is the guest bedchamber, where I would like you to put your belongings and where you can sleep."

Ruben was amazed at everything he saw, because although it was woven from reeds it was a remarkable structure, and awe-inspiring. He went into his bedroom and deposited the sword and the knapsack on the bed and was so excited by the prospect that he did not even worry about whether or not the sword hilt was covered.

He came out of the bedroom only to find that Simeon was deep in conversation with Lialah, giving her a list of various items that he required from the town. She finished the list and Simeon slipped his hand into his long flowing robes and extracted two large golden coins that he placed in her hand.

"This will be more than enough to cover the cost of the items that I require, but use the rest for your family, as I know that money is scarce these days."

Ruben had not been listening to the conversation as he was gazing around the large room and trying to peer into the small side rooms that led off the central chamber. Whilst he was doing this Lialah said to Simeon, "Thank you so much, Uncle S'meon, I will make sure that I get everything for you, and the extra money will certainly be of great assistance to my mother."

As she turned to go, Simeon said, "We may go off tonight, depending on the currents. I think that we may drift back into the marshes for a few days, but we will return, so if you could have the provisions ready for when we get back in a day or two. Oh yes, and I will then be happy to see anyone who requires my doctoring skills."

She turned to leave, but instead of walking straight through the doorway, turned and came over to Ruben, and before he realised what was happening she kissed him on the mouth and said, "I will look forward to seeing you in a few days." And with that she hastily left the house, and jumped down onto the bank and made her way back to the inn.

Simeon was at Ruben's side quickly and said, "Yes, she is a nice girl, my niece, I can rest assured that she will get all the provisions I need." He then turned to Ruben and said, "It was easy to see that you are Uriah's son as you have such similar looks, but you are far bigger than I would have thought for a boy of only ten or eleven years old."

This was the first confirmation that Ruben had heard about his real age and it certainly seemed to him to be about right. He turned to Simeon and said, "Can you show me what is in all the other rooms that lead off this room, as they look and smell interesting." With his arm still around Ruben's shoulder, Simeon ushered the boy towards the room on the left of the doorway and said, "All the four rooms off the main chamber are part of my museum of the marshes. This first room shows all the plants and flowers that you will see in the marshlands. They are placed around the wall and I know all their names and where they can be found."

Ruben was astonished at the vast amount of reeds and flowers that had been carefully dried and preserved and then placed with reverential care into reed bindings holding them to the wall. Before he came to the flowers, he noted that a lot of that he had originally thought of as being reeds were in fact one of forty or fifty varieties. This came as a surprise as he followed Simeon around the room. The old man pointed to various items, out strange flowers that he said were rare and could only be found in certain areas. Before he could fully take in the intricate splendours of this room, Simeon led him back into the main chamber and then into the next one on the far left of the house. In this chamber there were pinned, with small bronze wires, a host of dead insects that were held onto the wall, and Simeon said, "These are most of the flies and insects that you will see in the marshlands." Again he steered Ruben around the room and pointed out various insects that Ruben had simply thought of as flies or common bugs, but realised that they were all different, and many of them had vivid markings. He was excited to see one of the large bright blue dragonflies that he had seen earlier, but this was pinned in a separate section, amid lots of other dragonflies of various sizes and colours, some with intricate and highly decorative markings. As he gaped with wonder Simeon steered him out of the room and said, "Now I will show you some of the other creatures of the marshlands."

Simeon then led him to the right, to the corner chamber of the house. In here were many feathers, wings and even dead birds that had been preserved, and Ruben was delighted to see that one of the birds that he had seen flying high the other day had been preserved. Simeon said, "Yes, that is a flamingo. They do not often stop in the marshlands, but they do fly over this land early in the year and in the late summer, when they must be flying south for the warmer weather, and then returning in the spring to the north, where they spend the summer months." Leading the amazed Ruben out of this chamber he went back to the right-hand chamber off the front corner of the house. He said to Ruben, "Beneath the waters of the marshlands there is an entirely different world that few people have seen, and in this chamber there are just a few of the many wonderful creatures that exist in that under water world."

Ruben was dumfounded by the vast array of fish that had been dried out and placed onto rush plaques on the walls. There were even the bones and teeth of some of the crocodiles that infested the rivers. As Ruben gaped with awe at all these new things that he had never known existed, Simeon said, "But I can show you more of these things later. I can feel the raft beginning to be pulled out by the currents, so let us go and loosen the fastenings to the bank and drift away; it is always my wish to move as the Great Creator wishes me to move, following his lead."

They went to the side of the large mat of reeds and undid the twisted reed ropes that Ruben saw were formed from the raft itself and had been secured to the riverbank. They quickly boarded the raft as it drifted away from the bank. Ruben was surprised that Simeon had detected the movements through the floor of the raft, while he had noted nothing himself. Simeon turned to him and said, "Come now Ruben, let us go back to your bedchamber and you can tell me all about that fine sword that you have, and of what has been happening in Lagash, and of my old friend Mutek."

Realising that this old man missed nothing, and that those bright blue eyes could almost read his mind, Ruben went with Simeon back to his own bedchamber, sitting on the bed next to him. He explained all about the sword, how he had discovered it and how it had been preserved, how sharp it was and how it managed to keep its edge. But of how it was of a strange metal that was heavy and needed to be kept in greasy oil because otherwise it turned brown and began crumbling. Simeon told him that this came from the east, and he himself had a small knife made of this strange metal, which was called iron. He went on to say that this metal would soon replace all bronze weapons that had been used in humankind's battles, sadly shaking his head, showing his disapproval of warfare or indeed anything brutal.

Simeon laid aside the sword and said, "Enough of such things. Now I want to hear all the recent happenings in Lagash, and what finally brought you here."

So Ruben told him all about his recent errand to Mutek, his meeting with the odious Captain Gershnarl, and his decision, when he arrived back at Nippur, to retrace his father's footsteps, and how he had gone once again to Lagash to seek Mutek's advice. He told him of his flight down the river, of all the soldiers around Lagash, of his meeting with Mutek and his introduction to Ishmala, the dark giant of a man who had rowed him over the river and set him on the road to Ur. Having satisfied Simeon's requests for information, Ruben then asked the old man about the legends of his great-uncle Abraham who left Ur two thousand years earlier.

"My dear Ruben, as you can see it is now evening and the sun is beginning to set. So let us eat our meal and while we eat I will answer your questions to the best of my ability. I can also inform you about how your father left on his journey, and I can possibly give you some advice as to how you may retrace his footsteps if that is what you feel is your destiny." And with those words echoing in his mind, Ruben was led into the small cooking area where there were many things being boiled on wood that had been placed in a thick layer of clay above the reed floor. Simeon served food from all the different pots and said that they were all vegetables. He never ate flesh, as it had come from one of the Creator's animals, which were all his friends and wonders of the marshlands.

As they ate their meal, Ruben was delighted at the variety of food and how similar some of the things tasted to meat. Simeon said, between mouthfuls, "Let me tell you about something that I have only recently discovered, but which is apparent in all humankind." He paused as they finished their dinner and stooped to pick up the dirty plates, which he carried outside and placed just beyond the doorway. On his return he explained that they were his daily offering to the insects and animals of the marshlands. They would clean all the small bits of food that were left on the plates; this meant that nothing was wasted, and all he had to do in the morning was wash the dishes and everything would be fine to resume his daily living. He then said to Ruben, "Now let me tell you about my recent discoveries. It is all about the colour that surrounds a person. It can be seen if you look at people in a certain way, and try to think what they are thinking about, what their manner is and what their emotions are. This can be seen by the colour that surrounds them and gives an indication of their feelings; if they are normal and peaceful, the colour will be a pale blue leading towards dark blue and indigo." He went on to explain how the colour of people changed to yellow and green when they were agitated or restless, of how the surrounding colour would change to dark or even bright red if they were annoyed or angry, and how this colour seemed to dominate the blues and eat them up. Then Simeon paused, looked across at Ruben, sighed and smiled. The boy was fast asleep.

# 3
# CAPTURE AND REVENGE

The next morning Ruben awoke late. He could not remember going to bed, but when he looked around him he remembered that he was in the floating reed house. As he looked around the room he noticed that his new sword had been secured, like the exhibits in Simeon's museum, above his bed. He lay there for a few moments thinking about everything that had happened the day before: of the marvellous reed house, the four museums, then of the delicious meal and the sharing of Simeon's newly found discovery of the aura surrounding a person. He could not remember when he had dropped off to sleep, or even going into his room, which now felt like his home, particularly as the sword clearly identified it as such.

He knew that the floating house was still moving as he could hear the faint swish of water beneath them. He rose to his feet and went outside to look for Simeon. He found the old man outside the house, where he had just washed the plates from the previous evening's meal.

"Ah, there you are young man," said the lean green-turbaned figure. "Come inside and we will have a few reed barley cakes, with some ass's milk for breakfast." Turning, he led the way back into the main house.

Whilst they were eating their light breakfast, Ruben asked exactly when he had gone to sleep the previous evening.

Simeon chuckled. "Whilst I was talking about my discovery of the colour that surrounds a person, which depends on his feelings and intentions."

This greatly relieved Ruben, as he had not missed anything by falling asleep when he had. He could remember all the wonderful things that he had discovered the day before. He then asked Simeon how he could experience this discovery. "That is what I was hoping you were going to ask," said Simeon, "before you take a further look into my museum, which seems to fascinate you, as do many of the things put here by the Creator."

Ruben realised that his thoughts had been read by this wonderful man, and hearing once more a mention of 'the Creator', rather than a reference to one of the many gods already known to Ruben, each with their own particular responsibility, he was bemused. He was about to ask Simeon what exactly he meant by 'the Creator', only to find that Simeon was rising to his feet and saying, "Come on and follow me, young Ruben."

He followed Simeon out of the house and onto the platform of reeds.

He looked in the direction that Simeon was pointing and saw a small fishing boat in which some fishermen were seated.

"You see those two fishermen? Now, look at them through half-closed eyes and try to think of their intentions – what are they trying to do and why they are doing it?"

Ruben did exactly as he was told. He half closed his eyes, and looked at the men and tried to read their minds, expecting all the time images to break into vivid colour. Unfortunately, he met with absolutely no success and everything still appeared the greenish grey to light brown with the sunlight glinting off the water. "I am not sure what you mean, Simeon," said Ruben. "I can't see any changes at all."

"Well," said Simeon. "What are those men trying to do?"

"They must be trying to catch fish," said Ruben, still with his eyes half closed and concentrating harder than ever.

"And what kind of fish, and why are they trying to catch them?" asked Simeon.

Just as he was about to reply, Ruben's attention was diverted by a loud splash to his left, as one of the fish in the river leapt out to catch a hovering fly above the water. In that instant, as he spanned his eyes back towards the fishermen, he began to notice that in the shadows cast by the reed clumps he could make out the shapes of objects moving beneath the surface. He stared even harder and tried to visualise the shapes of the fish. His eyes then moved back to the fishermen and he began to notice a sort of halo around each man. He thought at first that their auras were a smoky grey colour, but then saw that they were blue-green coloured, each of which was differing, and one was more intense than the other. Suddenly, realising that he was seeing exactly what Simeon had told him about, the focus of these auras became brighter. "Wow, there they are," exclaimed Ruben. "I see what you mean. The colour around the man standing up in the middle of the boat is a lot brighter and is now growing stronger, as he is pointing at something in front of the other man. He is now telling the other man to throw the net in the direction that he was pointing." Ruben was utterly transfixed by what he saw. He was so intent that he did not notice Simeon staring at him in wonder.

"And he is now shouting at the other man and his colour is turning reddish and reaching out to the other man's colour, which is light blue, and his colour is being sucked in towards the red."

Simeon's gaze of wonder turned into a smile as he realised the boy had a natural gift. His smile broadened to a grin, and he reached out to calm down the excited Ruben, who was getting carried away describing the scene in front of him. Ruben stopped mid-sentence, as he realised that Simeon was smiling at him. As his eyes fully opened and he looked at

Simeon, the aura around the fishermen vanished instantly and everything returned to normal. "Oh," cried Ruben. "It's all gone."

He turned his disappointed face towards Simeon, who said, "Don't worry Ruben. Now that you have discovered the secret it can easily be regained. All you have to do is to repeat the same exercise and it will come back quickly, particularly if you are calm and concentrate your whole self." He still smiled at Ruben as the words sank in. Ruben felt that those piercing blue eyes were again reading his thoughts. Simeon placed both his hands on Ruben's shoulders in a friendly gesture and said in a serious tone, "You have a natural ability, you quickly grasped the idea. It is a real gift that is not open to many people; it certainly helps if you believe in what you are trying to do. But you must also empty your mind of any grievous thoughts." He went on to ask Ruben, "Did you notice anything else when you saw the colour around the men in the boats?"

"Yes," said Ruben. "Everything else seemed to be a lot brighter and I was able to see the fish under the water, and flowers and insects all much more alive and noticeable."

"Yes," said Simeon. "That is because your whole mind was concentrating on the work of the Creator."

Quite unexpectedly there was a bump and a jarring, grating noise as the platform stopped moving. Simeon turned around to look back towards the house and saw that the platform behind the house had run aground. Here the bulrushes were thick and tall, and he walked round the platform and stepped off onto a patch of dry ground. "Oh, yes," he said as he looked around. "This is the old caravan route. We will have to wait until the current changes again, which I am sure won't be long." Ruben jumped down beside him, and said, "I know where we are. I came almost this far when I was waiting for you in Ur. How long do you think it will be?"

"Oh, not very long," said Simeon. "When the current changes it will take us back to Ur. However, there is a minor repair job that I have to do. Unfortunately, it is high up in the cooking area and I am afraid that only I will be able to reach it, so I suggest that you walk back to Ur and try to see the auras. Remember, you must be in tune with the Creator and his wishes. Remember to ask Lialah to tell people that I will see them on my return to dispense my doctoring skills."

Ruben said, "Yes, I can easily find my way back and I am sure that the walk will help me get my thoughts in order. I will wait for you in Ur and pass your message on to Lialah. I did not know that you were a doctor." Simeon told Ruben that he would see him shortly, back in Ur. Before he set off, Simeon made sure that Ruben took his knapsack with a few things to eat on the way. Then he bade him farewell with the promise that they would meet again in Ur.

****

Gershnarl kept his men hard at work pulling strongly at the oars. He made sure that their pace did not slacken, but kept the boat heading west up the river. Realising that the current in the middle of the river was strong against them as the tide was out, he turned the boat more to the south until he had crossed most of the river and was out of the main current where the water was calmer. Instead of crossing the river completely, he turned the boat back into the west, keeping a short distance away from the bank to make sure that there was no danger of running aground on the low water sandbanks. His men were still fresh. They were all hand-picked Babylonian Guards, strong men who were used to hard work, either rowing a boat or on a forced march.

For the first short while of the journey Ishmala had kept up with the boat, but after a while he allowed the boat to press on ahead. He decided the best way to keep the boat in sight was to swim directly across the estuary and then trot along the riverbank. He crossed at the small inlet where the pirate boat lay half submerged and swam ashore. He walked up the same beach where Ruben had sat with his new sword on his lap. Here Ishmala paused briefly while he slipped on his sandals, which he had fastened to his belt. As he did this he noticed that the salt water had cleaned his wrists and ankles, and that they had been chafed by the bronze manacles and were now oozing blood from the sores. Knowing that they would soon heal, he ignored the slight discomfort and ran along the old caravan route and finally caught sight of the boat, just before it turned southwest into the old silted up river that came from the direction of Ur.

Gershnarl's men were starting to tire, as they had been rowing hard all morning. Much to their relief, he allowed them a short rest, and whilst they were resting, the inevitable goatskin of beer was produced and passed around, quenching thirsts. Gershnarl finally grabbed the goatskin and emptied it in a few gulps before tossing it aside. He ordered the men to get back to the oars, shouting at them.

"Pull, you accursed dogs, I want to get to Ur by midday."

Once more they strained at their task until their backs were aching and the pain in their shoulders made them groan, as the hot sun baked down upon their sweating bodies. Fortunately, Ur came into sight just before noon, so Gershnarl ordered the men to row the boat onto the shore, where they gratefully clambered out, pulling the boat up the bank and fastening it to a couple of small trees. They then had a rest under the trees, as was customary during the hottest part of the day, and once again a couple of goatskins of beer were produced and passed from man to man.

Even Gershnarl was tired, as he had not had a long sleep after his exertions of the previous night, and he was soon snoring in the afternoon sunshine. He slept until mid afternoon, far longer that he had originally intended. He awoke in a foul temper and shouted abuse at his men for not waking him earlier. He ordered the men into two ranks and marched them off at a fast pace towards the small town.

\*\*\*\*

It was only just over one whole day previously, but it seemed longer because he had seen and learnt so much in a short space of time. Ruben knew that he had met a wonderful and extraordinary man. In fact, the more he thought about Simeon, the more he thought that he was more than just a man, almost a deity. However, Ruben was honest with himself and admitted that Simeon's uncanny ability to apparently look into his mind with those piercing blue eyes of his, was unnerving and almost frightening. He was not aware of it, but his own eyes were similar and at times he had the same quizzical stare. He walked along the old caravan route feeling in tune with nature. He kept stopping to inspect things more closely. Everything seemed so much brighter and more alive to him, even his hearing seemed more acute. He found himself almost talking to a large beetle that was climbing up one of the rushes that he had stopped to inspect.

As he was rising up from inspecting the rush he heard a faint buzzing in his ear and turned slowly around to stare right into the eyes of an enormous dragonfly that was hovering only a hand span from his face. Once again those huge, bulbous, multifaceted eyes, which seemed to look in every direction at once, appeared to be inspecting him, but he had no fear or revulsion at the unusual creature, even though it was as thick as his little finger and as long as his outstretched palm. It had vivid brown and green zigzag markings along its body that would make it almost invisible when set against certain backgrounds. He stared back into those eyes and said, "And what do you think you are looking at, you strange little fellow? Yes, I too am one of the Creator's creatures. But I do not know yet what my role is or even where I belong."

After a few moments staring at each other, the dragonfly seemed to nod its head, wink at Ruben and in a flash it disappeared. Ruben smiled to himself and plodded on along the track that began to rise out of the marshes.

He was hungry, as he had not stopped to eat since he left Simeon, so he started munching the barley cakes, but he did not stop walking. He was soon on the higher ground overlooking the marshes, and pausing to look back into the late afternoon sunshine, where his keen eyesight made out the distant reed house that he had left behind.

He was still in the same euphoric and blessed mood, feeling at one with nature. Everything around him was brighter and more vividly enhanced. He then caught sight of three people who had been collecting the peat that was often used, when it had dried out, as a substitute for firewood, as there were very few trees in this area. All three people were deep in discussion whilst they staggered along carrying their burden. Ruben thought that this would be a good opportunity to visualise the colour of the air surrounding them, so through half-closed eyes he stared at them, trying to read their thoughts. Very soon he could make out a smoky blue aura around each person. They were obviously discussing who was carrying the heaviest load, and the person in the middle of the group was clearly insisting that his load was far heavier than that which the other two were carrying. He became more and more annoyed as he insisted that he was carrying an unfair burden. All the time that he was getting more excited, Ruben watched the colour of the surrounding air become a faint orange at first, becoming darker, until it was dark red – matching his mood. Additionally, the size of the aura expanded as it became redder. Eventually the person on the man's right gave in to him and took some of the load himself. Whilst this was happening, the colour surrounding this man seemed to be engulfed and swallowed up by the first man's dark red aura. But the other man on the left hand side remained stubbornly argumentative, the air surrounding him at first was green and then turned more orange and gradually turned red as he became more aggressive in his argument. At that point they all put down their loads, and the one who had at first given in to the angry man told them to stop arguing because it was a stupid squabble and they simply had to get all their stuff back and each man could carry a different load according to his strength. Whilst this happened, the air around him burst out bright orange, seeming to diminish the colour surrounding the other two men. Finally an agreement was made and the colour of all three men returned to the original smoky blue. Ruben watched all this, and could even overhear the arguments, and was greatly fascinated by what he saw.

By this time they were approaching the town and Ruben thought that it would be an interesting exercise to go and watch the crowd of people who were always around the well. He therefore hurried past the three men, calling out a cheerful greeting as he passed them, and headed towards the well. Many of the townsfolk recognised him as he passed, and he stopped to exchange a greeting with them, confirming that he had been with Simeon. He heard that his friend Lialah, had been buying up half of the town in order to supply Simeon's floating reed house with provisions.

Ruben settled himself a little way from the well, but just within hearing distance, and composed himself to watch the aura of the people around the well. He was soon able to see the colour of the air surrounding them and could easily tell what sort of mood they were in just by observing their colour. He watched in total absorption for a long time, watching the petty arguments and friendly banter that often went on amongst the people, many of whom he had come to know during his brief stay in Ur. By that time the sun was sitting in the west, over the marshes where the customary haze or fog came off the water as the light began to fade. Suddenly there was a lot of noise from the end of the town, and every gaze was turned towards the inn where Ruben had stayed, which was the focus of the commotion. Still watching with half-closed eyes, Ruben saw the air around the inn was glowing bright red and in places even a vivid purple, he noticed that a lot of people were shouting and that some of the people around the inn were dressed as Babylonian Guards. One word was then shouted out, and it had a remarkable effect on Ruben, as all the colours suddenly vanished.

One man, a fairly small person who often did odd jobs for the innkeeper, had been bodily thrown out of the window to end sprawling in the dust outside. "You cheeky little bastard, you don't answer back to Captain Gershnarl in that manner."

Ruben was truly astonished, all of a sudden the terror that this name evoked, his memory of his flight down the river and his fear of Captain Gershnarl returned, with the realisation that he was now in Ur. He quickly quelled his fear as he started worrying about Lialah. He stood up with the rest of the crowd and walked towards the inn to see what the fuss was about.

"Get this rabble outside," yelled Gershnarl. "We are simply looking for a sandy-haired boy who has run away from one of the camps, he is a gangling, tall bugger who is probably around 13 or so, and we know for certain that he came this way about a eight days ago," barked Captain Gershnarl, as he grabbed the closest onlooker and gave the man a fearful shaking.

"One of them must know, Captain," said a sergeant of the Guards, as he grabbed hold of another onlooker.

"I don't know nothing guv'nor," said the man jerking his finger at Lialah. "But the maid probably knows."

"We'll get the truth out of this little bitch," barked Gershnarl as he grabbed hold of Lialah by the hair and jerked her off her feet. He raised his hand to give her a stinging slap across the face. But his hand never landed, instead a ball of damp peat splattered itself against his neck, leaving a red mark where the missile struck him. It had been thrown by

Ruben, who had been standing next to one of the men who was still carrying the peat over his shoulder.

"Leave her alone, you brutal swine."

Gershnarl froze rigid to the spot. No one normally dared prevent him doing as he pleased. He slowly turned, wiping the peat from his neck, immediately spotted Ruben and barked out an order.

"There he is! Grab the little sod."

Ruben ran off in the direction of the marshes, shouting behind him, "You try and catch me then."

Some of the guards chased after the fleeing figure. Ruben was quick as he darted this way and that, but he was not as fast or as strong as one of the tall Babylonian Guards who quickly overtook him and held the struggling youth.

"I'll teach the little sod not to throw mud at me," snarled Captain Gershnarl as he strolled over to the riverbank, where the struggling Ruben was firmly held by two Guardsmen. "Pull down the little runt's pants and double him over," yelled Gershnarl taking a whip from his belt. "I will put a couple of stripes across the bastard's arse for that insult." He paced about six large steps away from Ruben and was standing knee deep in the river where he turned and drew out his whip. It cracked in the air as he drew it back. Ruben, who was blushing deeply at the indignity of being undressed in public, gritted his teeth and waited for the blow from the stinging whip. But, for the second time in just a short while, Gershnarl's blow never landed. A huge black hand seized his wrist from behind and Gershnarl's powerful figure was lifted bodily out of the water, by Ishmala, who had risen wraith-like out of the river.

Every face turned in amazement, the hands holding Ruben relaxed and he stood up, automatically redressing himself, whilst he gazed at the incredible scene. The sight of Captain Gershnarl being held by one arm like a puppet above the water by the huge black figure, sent a hushed silence over the whole gathering crowd. Even Captain Gershnarl turned his ugly face to stare into Ishmala's once benign and happy face, and saw his own death in those eyes. Whilst he was being held above the water, in one swift movement Ishmala twisted and kicked Gershnarl in the stomach, sending him hurtling into deeper water. Landing with a loud splash, he quickly regained his feet, although in great pain from a ruptured stomach. Gershnarl turned to face the oncoming Ishmala and tried to draw his short sword, but before his sword could be pulled free from its scabbard, his arms were pinned to his sides as Ishmala grabbed him with both arms and once more lifted him out of the water.

The Guardsmen on the bank could do nothing, for fear of shooting an arrow or throwing a spear that might hit their own captain. And everyone watched in horrified silence as Ishmala gradually squeezed the life out of the evil Gershnarl. Slowly the blood from Gershnarl's ruptured stomach began to ooze out from his mouth, and his cries of pain exploded into a gurgling shriek as his entire rib cage collapsed. The blood erupted from his mouth and the sound of his cracking ribs could be heard above his cries. The onlookers stared in horrified fascination as the water boiled and heaved, with both men disappearing beneath a welter of foam, blood and spray. The human combatants had been silently joined. A giant crocodile hit the two men, dragging them below the surface. It was by far the largest that had been seen for many years. The huge beast had been following the scent of Ishmala's blood as it oozed from damaged ankles. After a few more moments the crowd watched in stunned silence as the huge crocodile slowly swam away from the water darkened by blood, with what was obviously the remains of a body in its jaws. The dying rays of the sun shone weakly on the water as the ripples died away, and then someone in the crowd coughed. The silence was broken and the sergeant from the Babylonian Guards was the first person to recover his wits, averting his eyes from the grisly scene.

"Hold the boy," he ordered his men, and in almost subdued silence they grabbed hold of Ruben and bound his wrists with a leather thong.

"There is nothing we can do now, men," said the sergeant. "So we had better go back to the boat with the captive that we came to collect." They turned to march Ruben back towards where they had left their boat, but before they had gone more than a couple of paces a small figure dashed in between the guards and before they could stop her, Lialah threw her arms around Ruben's neck.

"Thank you," she said. "I will tell Uncle S'meon about your bravery and everything that has happened." She was about to say something else when one of the guards took her firmly and gently led her away from their prisoner.

Ruben was led away, still staring back towards the bloodstained river. Trying to remember the exact scene, Ruben wondered what had happened to Ishmala. Was his body that the crocodile had swum off with? He knew that Gershnarl was now dead.

****

It had been a bad fortnight for Commander Schudah; his last report to his commanding general had mentioned the feeling of unrest by the Council of Merchants in Lagash concerning the King's treaty with Assyria. Although this was only a minor matter, he had included it in his report more for the want of something new to report, hardly realising the alarm that it would create. Without warning he had been sent two boatloads of soldiers to quell any potential uprising. Although he knew that there was not going to be an uprising, as he had made up the story in the first place, he had to play along with it, and now he had the inconvenience of having to re-deploy all the additional soldiers. What was even worse was the fact that in order to appear to be acting, he had ordered the arrest of Mutek, one of the leading merchants, who was in fact a decent man who had often given a pleasant dinner followed by an enjoyable evening, to the commander. And to be completely honest the commander was rather fond of the merchant's daughter, and had hoped that the arrest, which he would subsequently revoke, would put him in a good position with her.

But everything had gone wrong, and as he paced up and down his quarters he was quite convinced that the whole reason behind this was that cunning swine Captain Gershnarl. By the gods, he thought, Gershnarl was a bloody nuisance, every soldier seemed to be frightened of him and in all honesty the commander himself was rather dubious about getting on the wrong side of the ugly brute.

When he had been offered the posting to Lagash as its garrison commander, a couple of years previously, he had been delighted to accept. Lagash was a pleasant, peaceful town, and quickly growing in importance as, being at the entrance to the river Euphrates, it dealt with a lot of the trade that came from the east. The only reason for the garrison and the small company of elite Babylonian Guards, was to deal occasionally with pirate forces that attacked the merchant shipping, or the robber bands that attacked the overland caravans. However, there had been very little trouble since he had arrived and he had to admit that most of the reason for there being no trouble was the presence of that same swine, Gershnarl. The very mention of his name and a party of men led by him would soon stop any problem that could arise. Even his spies in the robber bands had said that all the chiefs were in mortal fear of being caught by Gershnarl, as his reputation for torture was quite devastating, and sadly, undeniably true.

He had never intended that the order to arrest the merchant Mutek should have been given to Captain Gershnarl, but due to some blunder the order had been taken by Gershnarl, and the next thing the commander heard was that Mutek had been flogged to death. Obviously this had ruined his plans, apart from causing uproar in the Council of Merchants. Needless to say, Gershnarl had denied complicity in the flogging and had somehow wheedled his way out of being held responsible. Now, this very morning, he had been informed that when the guard on the small prison cell in the guardroom had been changed, the replacement had found the cell open and the guard had been found inside the cell with a broken neck. He had not even been told that there was anyone in the prison cell. Not that that itself was of any great importance, but whoever it was, there should have been a closer watch over them. The man in the cells had been the large servant of Mutek, a huge black Nubian whom the commander had seen at Mutek's house on various occasions. He had in fact been introduced to him – he was dumb, and had been so for a long time, but was a genial person and Mutek had told him that he was utterly reliable.

Now, to crown the whole strange business, when he had sent for Gershnarl to demand an explanation, he had been told that Captain Gershnarl had left town early this morning with a small force of Babylonian Guards to chase an apparent escapee from one of the young soldiers' training camps. Certainly, it was quite often that a young, newly conscripted soldier would run away from one of the camps, but this was hardly a job for a force of the elite Babylonian Guards. Frankly the whole situation was a bloody mess and Gershnarl would have a lot of explaining to do. And there hadn't even been a report from any of the training camps of a deserter. Commander Schudah was extremely annoyed and worried. It now looked as if his anticipated promotion was in jeopardy.

There was a knock on his door, and his lieutenant aide informed him that the boatload of men that had accompanied Captain Gershnarl on this ridiculous mission had rowed up river and had headed in the direction of Ur, and that they would certainly not be back this day. Realising that he could not change the situation, he decided that the best thing he could do was write a report to his commanding general and inform him that everything was in hand. Having made the decision, he sent for a scribe. As a commander he could read written instructions, unlike the average soldier, but most of the writing that was done was an art that was a profession in itself, and not something that was the prerogative of a fighting man.

The scribe appeared, carrying ink, brushes and rolls of papyrus. Commander Schudah could remember his grandfather telling him that when he first joined the army, a fine chisel marked a clay tablet, which was then baked. But this had all changed and a more fluent script that, once learnt, was far easier, had replaced the old cuneiform marking, and the writer could express his thoughts far more easily. The scribe sat on a stool and took out his brushes made of feathers and horsehair. He placed a fresh roll of parchment over his drawing board and dipped his brush in the ink. He turned an enquiring face to the commander.

"Is this the normal report, sir?"

"Yes, of course," came the irritated reply. "So just start with the normal greeting."

This was followed by a detailed account of how the new troops had been deployed and how he had interrogated the entire Merchants' Council. But when he came to the account of Mutek's death under interrogation and the rather bizarre story of another merchant in Nippur, and the clumsy account of the new boat building contract that had come from Gershnarl, he found that the right words would not come, even though he tried three or four times. He finally sent the scribe away in exasperation and said, "Come back and see me first thing tomorrow morning." He then resumed pacing up and down the chamber. "Damn that Gershnarl, it's all his bloody fault. Where is the accursed swine?" He knew he would have another night of restlessness. He had to know what had happened, he knew Gershnarl was behind the whole fiasco, but didn't know where he was or what was going on.

****

Ishmala had been dragged down, and sensibly had not tried to tear his punctured legs out of the crocodile's mouth. But when he knew that he could not hold his breath for much longer he reached down and grabbed the ends of the large gaping mouth. Even though the large teeth gouged lumps of flesh from his hands he managed to force open those huge jaws allowing his legs to come free. But by the gods, the brute was even stronger than him and he only had time to drag himself clear before the huge jaws slammed shut again. Fortunately there was a floating mat of reeds, which now covered him and the crocodile, and by grasping the reeds with his torn fingers he was able to pull himself away from the brute. The crocodile obviously went for the far easier prey and fastened his jaws around the remains of Gershnarl, and swam off to where it could store its catch of meat, until that meat decomposed. Crocodiles do not eat fresh meat, far preferring decaying flesh.

Ishmala had reached the far side of the floating mat of reeds and surfaced, gulping down huge lungfuls of air. He knew he had to get out of the water, because it would be infested with other crocodiles due to the blood in the water. But he knew he could not get to the shore as his strength was almost at an end. And anyway, Gershnarl's Guardsmen would soon finish him off. So he tried with his last remaining strength to pull himself onto the mat of reeds. Twice he failed, and he was just about spent when he was aided from above. He lay back on the bed of reeds. In the last remaining light he looked up into a wrinkled, frowning face, with bright blue piercing eyes beneath a green turban. Then he passed out.

****

Ruben was marched away with the Guards back to where they had left the boats. It was now completely dark and the sergeant decided that they would make a campfire and have a short rest, and wait until the moon rose in order to catch the tidal flow down river to Lagash. They made the campfire and sat around eating most of the remainder of their provisions, and the goatskin of millet beer was produced and passed from man to man. The guardsmen's treatment of Ruben was respectful. As he was right in the middle of the circle of soldiers, any attempt to escape would be completely futile. He was extremely quiet and only spoke in a polite manner when directly addressed; they untied him and allowed him to share the provisions – even extending a cupful of beer to him. Ruben was shattered by the events of the late afternoon. Strangely, Gershnarl's certain death had not even pleased him. He just felt empty and alone.

Some of the Guardsmen were comparatively lighthearted and even jovial. Gershnarl's death had simply been a release for them and nobody really mourned his demise. Being hardened troops they were not unused to blood, gore or death. Some of them amiably chatted to one another, whilst a few others laid back for a brief rest. But it was not long before the sergeant roused them and told them to get back into the boat, which was quickly launched into the river. They soon had the boat out in the small river that led to Ur. They rowed into the middle of the current flowing down river, and made surprisingly quick time on the final leg of their journey to Lagash. By this time it was early morning and the sergeant gave orders for the boat to be secured, dismissed most of the men, and then with just the remaining corporal, who had re-secured Ruben's wrists, marched him up to the commander's quarters. They were pleased to find that Commander Schudah was already dressed, and, leaving Ruben outside his quarters with the corporal, the sergeant went in to report what had happened.

Commander Schudah was feeling terrible and looked it as well, due to two nights of loss of sleep and worry about what he was going to put in his report. However, he was delighted that the sergeant had come directly to report to him and asked him firstly, where the hell Captain Gershnarl was.

"I'm afraid he's dead, sir," said the sergeant impassively.

"Dead?" repeated Schudah, astonished. "But when, I mean why... er... I mean how?"

"Well, he was killed by the black slave who must have escaped from the guardhouse," explained the sergeant, trying to find the precise words to make an accurate report, as he realised this situation could possibly lead to his promotion. And so the full story came out, albeit in a slightly incorrect order. Then the commander carefully cross-questioned the sergeant to find out exactly what had happened. The commander suddenly shed his tiredness and brightened up, he could hardly believe his luck. Things had turned out well, he could heap all the blame onto Gershnarl, particularly as the bastard was now at the bottom of the river being picked at by fish or inside some crocodile, he didn't really care which, he was just glad to have a scapegoat. Being rid of Gershnarl had other benefits as well. He knew that within a few hours he could get the full story about the death of Mutek. He hastily dismissed the sergeant by saying, "You have done very well, and must be tired. So go back to your quarters and wait until I send for you again." The sergeant was pleased at the praise, which he knew by experience was something that Schudah would not give lightly, but before he left he stubbornly continued,

"But what of the youth that we have outside, sir?"

"Oh yes, I had almost forgotten about him – is he dangerous at all or likely to run off again?"

"No sir, quiet as a lamb, sir, and in all honesty, he's quite a nice kid," said the sergeant sincerely.

"Well, let's see," said Schudah as he rang his bell for his lieutenant aide. He told the lieutenant to look after the boy, and said, "Get him something to eat and somewhere to rest and then I will interview him."

\*\*\*\*

The corporal of the Babylonian Guard waited with Ruben outside the commander's office. As he feared that they might be in for a long wait, he left Ruben for a few minutes before reappearing with a couple of stools. He sat Ruben down, and sat down himself, facing him. He untied the leather thong binding Ruben's wrists. As the lad was still withdrawn and quiet, he tried to engage him in conversation.

"That was an extremely brave thing you did, young fellow," he said. At first he thought that Ruben was not going to answer, but finally he looked up at the corporal and said, "I'm sorry, what was the question?" He had been lost in his own thoughts and had only just realised that he was being spoken to.

"But at least you did hear me," said the corporal. "I was complimenting you on what you did back in Ur, throwing mud at Captain Gershnarl."

"Oh yes, I see what you mean," said Ruben. "I suppose it was rather silly really, I only made him more angry than he already was. But I could not stand by and watch a friend of mine being bullied by that evil man."

"I am afraid there are quite a few captains like Gershnarl… was," said the corporal. "Remember not to stand up for what is right when you are in the army, when they send you back to the training camp. It is far better in the long run to steer clear of any arguments and simply do as you are instructed by your commanding officers," was his sound advice.

"But I never came from a training camp," protested Ruben, "I am only ten or possibly eleven and I was simply an errand boy, before Captain Gershnarl decided that I should be in the army."

This surprised the Corporal, and he felt sure that Ruben wasn't lying, but was simply a large boy for his age. So he said, "Well, surely someone can vouch for your age?"

"Yes," brightened Ruben. "The merchant, Mutek. He will confirm my story."

The Corporal stared at him. There was obviously a great deal behind this that he knew nothing about. Now that he had managed to break the ice and engage Ruben in conversation, he did not want to alarm the lad. He could not tell him that Mutek had died whilst being tortured, under the orders of Captain Gershnarl, who was supposedly trying to get a confession out of him. The corporal was only eighteen years old himself, and was also big and strong. The advice that he had given was something an old soldier had taught him, and by following his advice he had quickly risen to be a corporal. He was proud of being a corporal in the elite Babylonian Guard, and was hoping to be the first sergeant under the age of twenty. He stopped speculating about his own personal ambitions, to concentrate on the lad before him. He noticed Ruben looking at him questioningly, but did not want to reveal what he knew of the situation, which was obviously not very much of the complete story.

"I know little of what has gone on before we were ordered to arrest you, but I do know this: there is a great deal happening because of the treaty between Babylon and Assyria, and it would appear that unfortunately you have been caught up in momentous events. Therefore I cannot say with any certainty that you will be allowed to go free." He added, "Because you look as if you should be in the army at one of the young soldiers' training camps, you may well end up there. Now I'm not saying that this will happen, but it is a possibility that you should bear in mind."

"Even though I am not yet twelve years old?" asked Ruben. "And although someone can vouch for my age?"

"I am afraid that could be what will happen," replied the corporal, with a shrug. "I know it seems rather unjust, but you are an unimportant person as far as matters of state are concerned. But try not to be too discouraged. Life in the army isn't all that bad, particularly if you manage to do well in all the training. You could even become one of the elite Babylonian Guards, like myself. You see, although we often are used to spearhead attacks against enemy forces, there are many advantages. For example, we get all the best equipment and provisions and are well catered for," he continued proudly.

Ruben looked rather glum, but continued the conversation. "So you think I will probably have to go to a training camp?"

"As I say, I am not really sure, but I think you would be wise to prepare yourself for that happening," said the corporal, trying to sound as lighthearted as possible. And seeing that Ruben had not brightened up at all, he went on to try and comfort the lad. "You know, we could well meet again – remember my advice about staying out of trouble and simply obeying orders." Here, the opening of Commander Schudah's door interrupted him – so he added quickly, "My name is Corporal Belthezder, but all my friends call me Bel, and that is what I would like you to call me." He rose to his feet and snapped to attention.

Commander Schudah stood in front of him, and said to the corporal, "You and the sergeant have done very well. The sergeant informed me that it was your speed, agility and quick thinking that were responsible for capturing the young rascal, and I have told the sergeant that you can now go back and get some well deserved rest."

The corporal saluted and said, "thank you, sir." But before he left he put his hand on Ruben's shoulder, giving him a friendly squeeze and said, "Cheerio lad, remember we might meet again."

"Well, now young man," said Commander Schudah – noticing the friendliness that the corporal had shown the boy, and also remembering what the sergeant had said about the lad. "You seem to have got yourself embroiled in a complicated situation. It is going to take a while to get to the bottom of all this, particularly due to the death of Captain Gershnarl. So I will now send you off with my assistant," he continued, pointing to his lieutenant-aide. "He will get you something to eat and make sure you get a rest, and then I will need to interview you in detail."

So Ruben left the commander's office, following meekly behind the lieutenant, who was also a young man, but with a serious face that showed no emotions whatsoever. He led Ruben to what was obviously the main eating area, which he said was the mess. On the table, he first placed his officer's seal, which was a large embossed bronze coin that had a small spike extending from its reverse (the purpose of which was to be hammered onto parchment to denote the sender). He then led Ruben over to where they were serving food. He gave Ruben a plate and said, "Just ask for what you would like to eat. Fill a plate and come back and join me, I will go and get us something to drink. What would you like? Wine, water or possibly some millet beer? Frankly I would recommend the latter, it is a good brew here."

So Ruben first became acquainted with the soldiers' mess in this rather strange fashion, of being treated somewhere between a prisoner and a guest. He ate a large meal of maize mash with grilled fish, washed down with beer as recommended by the lieutenant, who also had a drink whilst he sat silently watching Ruben. Having finished his meal and when both clay mugs of beer were empty, the lieutenant led Ruben out of the mess and into the large barracks hall. He told Ruben that this was where most of the soldiers slept, but at the moment they were out on exercises. He led Ruben to a small side chamber and told him to try to get some sleep, but that it would be useless to try to escape, as he had to get past about six guarded doors. He left Ruben there and said he might see him later, and then walked away, shutting the door behind him.

Looking around rather despondently, Ruben lay down on an empty bed and tried to sleep. Even though he was tired, he was unable to sleep as his eyes kept filling with tears. But he didn't want anyone to notice that he was so upset, and tried to put on a brave face to appear unworried about his circumstances.

He continued to remember the strange events of the last couple of days and to reflect on what Corporal Bel had told him. He guessed that something had happened to Mutek, and not wishing to involve his uncle's family at all, and betray the fact that he had come from Nippur, he considered it far wiser to wait and see what would happen. Altogether he was miserable. The thought of going into the army was the last thing that he wanted, and the memory of his new found friendship that had suddenly been snatched away was a grief that seemed too hard to bear. Then the indomitable spirit that was inside Ruben suddenly kicked into life and said, 'No! You can train me as a soldier, simply because the training would come in useful. Indeed it would be sensible to be able to fight for what I believe in.'

But the Babylonian empire was not what Ruben believed in. He wanted to find his homeland. He wanted to know what had happened to his father. He wanted to see Simeon again and above all he wanted to follow in his father's footsteps. So let them take him into the army, he would work hard, he would follow Corporal Bel's advice, but at the first possible chance he would use the skill that they would teach him to go about furthering his own plans. Now he had a goal he felt more secure in himself. Already he felt the stirrings of manhood. In a few years he would be big and strong and what better training could he have than to be in the army. With that thought he fell asleep.

He was woken just as the light was fading, and the evening was beginning. The large barrack room was filling up with young conscripts who had been on training exercises. Someone was shaking his shoulder to wake him, and he turned and looked to see the lieutenant, Commander Schudah's aide.

"Wake up, young man, the commander wants to see you now."

So Ruben stirred himself, shook away his drowsiness and followed the lieutenant out of the barracks and along to Commander Schudah's office. The lieutenant briefly tapped on the door, but walked in before the commander even answered.

The commander had his back towards them and was gazing at something outside. He said, without turning, "Leave the boy with me and wait until I call you again." He turned around slowly and looked at Ruben for a long time before speaking. He seemed to realise that there was a new defiance in the lad, which had not been there before – or if it had it had been masked by his misery. The few hours' rest had obviously restored something in the lad. Meanwhile he had found quite a considerable background to the case. Mind you, the information that he had gleaned from the Guards had been more about Gershnarl's reckless lifestyle. There had also been a complaint from one Guardsman, that Gershnarl had raped his wife. Anyway, all this was not relevant to the boy standing in front of him – and when he really thought about it, this boy did look about thirteen and a large thirteen at that. But he was also aware that none of the training camps had reported a deserter.

"Now you know everyone says you are not yet twelve years old. Can anyone vouch for that?" he asked.

"Only the merchant, Mutek," answered Ruben clearly.

"Well, he is not around at the moment," the commander said. "But you didn't work for him anyway, did you? Surely there must be someone else whom we can ask."

"No, not really," Ruben responded, rather defiantly.

Commander Schudah shook his head in bewilderment. "Well, I'm sorry young man, but I haven't got the time to worry myself over your case. Therefore, I have no alternative but to send you to one of the training camps." He inspected Ruben while he waited for an answer. He was amazed that all this provoked was a small shrug, as if the boy was fully prepared for it. After a pause, he asked, "What is your name, boy?"

"Ruben Ben Uriah," came the clear reply.

Oh well, so be it, thought Commander Schudah, he had done his best for the boy. He could now wash his hands of the whole business and get back to more important matters.

# 4
# THE TRAINING CAMP

The next day Ruben was taken to a training camp for new soldiers, about half a morning's march northeast of Lagash, near the border of the province of Sumer, on the road to Sousa.

The training camp had been hastily erected within the last couple of years, so its buildings were mainly just wooden posts with branches woven in between. Some of the walls had been daubed and finished with clay, but many remained in their unfinished state. This gave the whole place an air of temporiness and hasty construction. Ruben was handed over to the commanding captain, whose name was Uglis. He was accompanied by two other twelve-year-old lads, both of who were considerably smaller and of a lighter build than he was. Captain Uglis came out of his office and dismissed the soldiers who had brought the new conscripts. He read the names that were written on the scroll of parchment he had been handed and after reading what had been noted beside Ruben's name he singled him out with the order, "Ruben Ben Uriah, one pace forward." He said, "It informs me here that you were picked up as a stray, and nobody knows your real age. Now as you are considerably larger than the other two boys here, and look to me far more like a thirteen-year-old, I am going to work you bloody hard, and hopefully transfer you to an older boys' unit once your basic training has been achieved. So you had better work very hard, you arsehole."

"I understand, sir," said Ruben automatically – he was already following Corporal Bel's advice.

"Are you anything to do with that young rascal my old friend Captain Gershnarl was pursuing?" he snarled.

"I don't know what you mean, sir," said Ruben noncommittally.

"Well, just behave yourself. And remember, I'll be watching you." He leered at Ruben while he looked him over. He was a big man with a large beer belly, and his name suited him very well as he looked rather like a toad, with large bulging eyes on a wart covered, speckled face that seemed to stand straight out from his shoulders, with no neck.

Ruben's initial thought was that Corporal Bel had been perfectly correct when he had said there were many other captains in the Babylonian army that were like Gershnarl, and he made a mental note to try to steer clear of this rather nasty character.

Captain Uglis bellowed a command and a sergeant came out of the officers' mess. "Here are three new recruits for your new platoon,

Sergeant Tryone," he said, and instructed the sergeant to show them their barrack room. The sergeant told all three boys to follow him, and he led them over to one of the new huts. This hut, like many of the others, was brand new and did not have any clay on the sides, which Ruben noted had only been daubed onto the officers' quarters.

Sergeant Tryone led the three lads into the hut and pointed to three of the empty shelves above three rough mattresses. He explained that this was where they should put their belongings, as eighteen of the other places had belongings on them. He told them that as soon as they had done this they should join his platoon in the main mess hall, behind their hut. He went on to explain that although the platoon was now twenty-one persons strong, his full platoon would be thirty – he had been promised the next nine recruits to make his platoon up to the required number. He said that the eighteen lads had only just stopped for midday break, so that if they hurried themselves they would not be too late to get something to eat. He left them and returned to his own meal in the officers' mess.

Ruben looked at the other two boys, who had already started to empty their small knapsacks of the few items they were allowed to bring. However, as he had nothing himself, not even a change of clothes – as his few possessions were still in Simeon's floating house – he looked around on the floor and found a couple of pebbles, which he put on his own shelf, denoting that it was now occupied. Without waiting for the other two boys, who were already friends and ignored his company, he went into the main mess hall. There was another tall but skinny lad who was sitting on his own. He smiled at Ruben, who took a plateful of maize mash and went over to join the other boy. He learnt that the other lad's name was Latich and he was sitting alone because he had come last in the latest training exercise. All their exercises to date were ways of building up strength and stamina. Latich said that they all had to pick up stones that were arranged according to their height, and his stone had of course been the largest, and as he was not particularly strong he had come last. Ruben smiled back and said, "Well, you are no longer the largest, as that dubious privilege seems to be mine."

Ruben thought that he had seen Latich before in Lagash, but did not say anything more for the present. However, Latich said that he had been an errand boy in Lagash, where he had worked for the shoemaker, and he felt sure that he had seen Ruben before. Ruben confirmed this by saying that he was also an errand boy who had worked for one of the boatbuilders, but had often been sent on long errands and was therefore not very well known to the town-folk. So gradually, over the first meal, Ruben made his first friend in the army.

Immediately after the meal, despite the fact that it was the hottest part of the day, Sergeant Tryone assembled the boys outside. He said their next exercise would be similar to the last, but this time they had to work in pairs. Now with the three new recruits they were twenty-one strong, so he singled out one boy and said, "You will have to work with me, lad."

Latich told Ruben that this sort of thing had happened before and that the boy singled out was Sergeant Tryone's nephew, so he had an easy job.

"The rest of you pair off and come over and pick up these logs." Naturally Latich stayed next to Ruben, as he could well imagine that Ruben was strong. As they anticipated, they were given the largest and heaviest log. Sergeant Tryone then informed the boys that they had to carry the log up to a post that they could only just see on the top of a small rise, and then return to the starting line, which he drew in the ground with his sword. All the boys were allowed a short while to practise the best way to carry the log, and nearly all of them opted to carry it cradled in their arms, both boys standing side by side. As Ruben had carried large things for some distance on his own, he knew that the best way was to carry it on his shoulder, and he took the front and heaviest end himself and told Latich to pick up the second part and stand behind him.

Sergeant Tryone, who had also adopted this position, said, "Go!" and all the lads dashed off towards the distant post. Sensibly, Ruben told Latich not to rush, but to keep up a good steady pace, and before long they were second, only just behind Sergeant Tryone and his nephew. They rounded the post about fifty paces behind Sergeant Tryone, but still well ahead of the rest of the platoon. When they were about half way back, Ruben could see that Sergeant Tryone's nephew was beginning to tire and that as the log was angled down towards him, he was becoming a drag on the sergeant's brisk pace. Realising that they could win if they hurried, he shouted to Latich to run as hard as he could.

Captain Uglis came out of his office to see how the new recruits were getting on, and was amazed to see that Ruben Ben Uriah, with that tall skinny boy who had finished last in the exercise before the midday meal, was overtaking Sergeant Tryone and his nephew, virtually dragging along his companion. Captain Uglis decided that he would wait quietly and watch the next exercise, to see whether or not that result was purely accidental.

Sergeant Tryone had also been shocked at being beaten at the finish, but was gracious with his praise for the winners. The rest of the platoon finished a long way back, the last pair trailing in some distance behind, with one of the lads severely limping. They had dropped their log on the boy's foot, which although it was not broken, was badly grazed, and was a blood-drenched, swollen mess. Sergeant Tryone called for an orderly to wash and bandage the boy's foot, knowing that this recruit could take no further part in the exercises that afternoon. After allowing all the boys a short break, which they certainly needed, he explained that (although he had not told them, as the best way to learn was by experience) it was far easier to carry heavy weights a long distance if they were carried on one's shoulder or even on one's head. As the boy who had dropped out was of a similar size to his nephew, he paired his nephew with the other boy and said to the others that they should keep the same partner.

The next exercise was a simple three-legged race over the same distance, where each pair of boys had one of their legs tied to the other boy's leg. He lined them up at the starting point, and once more shouted "Go!" Some of the boys rushed off, but were soon in difficulty because they did not work in co-ordination with their partner. Ruben and Latich began cautiously, but soon found that their steps were naturally even, as although Ruben was taller, he was no longer in the leg than Latich, and it was an easy job to ensure that they kept in step. As Latich had also been an errand boy he was used to running quickly and the only thing that had slowed him previously was that due to his skinny frame he was not very strong. Carrying weights was difficult, but this challenge suited him better and once again they were first across the finishing line. It was only then that Ruben recognised that he had a natural ambition to win.

Captain Uglis noticed this and came over to Sergeant Tryone and whispered something in his ear. Sergeant Tryone looked at the captain in surprise, but thought it best not to argue and he disappeared briefly into one of the huts and then came back, carrying a length of chain made from the new metal called iron. He went over to Ruben and said, "I'm sorry young man, but the captain wants you to be handicapped, and insists that you carry this chain." He clipped the chain around Ruben's waist and still had a lot left, which he passed over one shoulder and put another couple of loops around Rubens waist. He then passed it over the other shoulder and clipped it back on to the length around Ruben's waist. The chain was very heavy and Ruben understood that it would certainly slow him down.

By now it was late in the afternoon, so the sergeant said that there would be no more races that day, but they would spend the last part of the afternoon on a forced march. The boys lined up in twos and set off, with the sergeant calling out the rhythm. Ruben realised that he was being picked on quite deliberately, but was defiant and said jokingly, "Well, that will certainly stop me running away." The march took the remainder of the afternoon and comprised twenty lengths of the same route, around the post on the rise and back to the barrack room, altering their pace each time from a quick march to a trot. At the end of the afternoon Ruben was absolutely exhausted, but had managed to keep in step with the others, although he was bathed in perspiration and almost collapsed when he finished. The sergeant untied the chain, told Ruben that he had done very well, and sent the whole platoon off to the main mess hall for their evening meal.

It was whilst they were having dinner, Ruben having finished his first portion and gone back for a second plateful, that Captain Uglis emerged from his quarters and came over to the table where all the lads had been sitting, talking about the day's events. A silence fell over the area as Captain Uglis approached. The captain seemed to ignore the fact that everything had gone quiet, as he still bawled out, "Why have you removed those chains?" This was obviously directed at Ruben, who had already feared that this would happen. He turned round, looked Captain Uglis directly in the eyes and said, "I didn't remove them. The sergeant took them off, sir."

Captain Uglis was momentarily at a loss for words and then growled, "We will see about that." He marched over to the officers' mess and barked out, "Sergeant Tryone, out here if you please." There followed a short altercation, which Captain Uglis obviously won, as he walked away with a smiling face. However his smile soon turned to a frown as Sergeant Tryone shouted after him, "I will do as you order sir, but I do feel that you are unnecessarily persecuting one of my recruits." This brought Captain Uglis up short. He knew that Sergeant Tryone was a relative of Commander Schudah and it was Commander Schudah who had broken the friendship between Uglis and Gershnarl. He had had Uglis taken out of the Babylonian Guard and transferred to the training camp. So this was a veiled threat and Uglis did not want to get into trouble with Commander Schudah again, as he was hoping to do a good job with the new recruits and then regain his position in the Babylonian Guard.

After the meal, during which Ruben had two portions of everything washed down with two refreshing mugs of millet beer, Sergeant Tryone came over to Ruben and said, "I'm sorry lad, but Captain Uglis wants you to wear the chains all the time. Have you any idea why he is singling you out for this sort of punishment?"

Ruben answered, "No sir, I really have no idea – but it doesn't really matter. Don't worry about it. I will wear the chains as instructed."

The Sergeant was puzzled by Ruben's calm resignation at what seemed an unmitigated form of victimisation, but shrugged and put back the chain. He showed Ruben how to unclip it, as there was one link, which was cut, and he told Ruben that he did not have to sleep with it on, but should make sure that he came out of the barrack hut wearing it. He explained that this would keep the captain content, but sleeping with the chain on would be extremely uncomfortable and would only lead to bruising and leave a rash on the skin. Ruben considered that Sergeant

Tryone was fair and considerate, and thanked him, before rejoining his platoon, which was just returning to the barrack hut for the evening.

None of the recruit camps had any form of evening entertainment for their new conscripts, who were simply secured at night behind a bolted door. The lads went into the hut, where an oil lamp was lit. It had sufficient oil to allow it to burn for a short period before it went out, leaving the young trainees in darkness. The training camps were closely guarded, as it was common for the lads to run away. At this camp in particular, Captain Uglis prided himself in ensuring that there were no escapees, which he hoped would keep him in a good light and would aid his request to be transferred back to the Babylonian Guard.

There was not much conversation in the hut that evening as all the boys were tired. It had been an exhausting day, and they had been warned that there was an early start in the morning. Latich arranged to swap places with one of the other lads, so that he was sleeping next to his new friend. Nobody except Latich mentioned anything about the chain that Ruben had been forced to wear. As they both started taking off their clothes, he mentioned, "That Captain Uglis is a real sod, making you wear that bloody chain. But at least he has stopped picking on me because I'm so thin."

"Well, that's one bonus," said Ruben, as he unclipped the chain and dumped it at the foot of his mattress. "At least Sergeant Tryone told me that I don't have to wear the damn thing at night," he exclaimed with gratitude, as he pulled off his shift and crawled beneath the rough army blanket that had been issued. There was little talking as the lamp died out and everybody fell into an exhausted sleep.

It hardly seemed like a whole night, when they were woken up just as the sun was lighting the sky to the east. As the door was unbolted, an orderly brought in a couple of stone pitchers of cold water for the boys to wash in. Sergeant Tryone appeared at the doorway and said, "Now then lads, we are off to the seashore this morning, and we have not even got time to have breakfast. But not to worry," he said amongst the stifled groans that came from the half naked lads who were still washing. "I have a pony that is laden with goodies to eat and drink." He chuckled.

All the boys quickly came out of the hut, and he lined them up in twos, as he had done the day before, and marched them out of the camp, directly south towards the Inferior Sea, and not on the road that led southwest towards Lagash.

Ruben was in the third row and Sergeant Tryone was pleased to note that he was wearing the chain, which did not seem to impair him much at all. The chain did not worry Ruben, particularly first thing in the morning as it was cool, but after his body started to warm up with the marching, the chain began to become more and more uncomfortable and seem heavier and heavier. The sore places where the chain had rubbed the previous afternoon when he was perspiring freely, began to hurt again as the chain began to chafe. It was a vicious circle. The more the chain chafed, the more Ruben sweated and the more the chain seemed to dig in through his light cotton shift. At first he tried to ignore the discomfort, but as the sun rose into the sky and the heat began to increase, the worse the discomfort was felt, and the heavier the chain seemed to be.

Much to his relief, Sergeant Tryone called a halt at that point, and told the boys that they could break for a short period and eat some breakfast, as they were approximately halfway to the sea and well clear of the camp. The wheat cakes were handed round and the lads refreshed themselves with a goatskin full of clear water (this would soon be replaced with a goatskin of millet beer – once they had done the first year's training, as they were not normally allowed beer outside the camp). Sergeant Tryone noticed Ruben inspecting the sore places on his shoulders where the chain was cutting into him. He went over to Ruben and told him to unclip the chain, which he helped the boy remove. He then told him to strip off his shift, which was slightly bloodstained at the shoulders as well as totally soaked in perspiration. A few of the lads gasped when they saw the dark red grooves that were just starting to ooze with blood on Ruben's shoulders, where the chain had been chafing. Even Sergeant Tryone grimaced when he saw the injury that had been inflicted on the young boy. Sergeant Tryone said, "I am not happy about this, as it is my duty to ensure the well-being of the soldiers under my command."

Ruben answered him by saying, "It's not the weight so much, sir, its just the discomfort from the chafing."

Sergeant Tryone picked up the chain and said, "You're not wearing this anymore today, young man. I don't give a damn what Captain Uglis says." He wandered over to the pony where he placed the chain and fished out of the saddlebags a small stone jar, which was full of a dark greasy ointment. He came back and smeared some ointment on a couple of lengths of cloth which he also produced from the saddlebag, and laid these strips of cloth over the sore places on Ruben's shoulders. He picked up Ruben's shift and laid it on a stone beside the road. Much to everyone's surprise he then walked back to the pack pony and took off all the equipment and pulled off the saddle, revealing the blanket underneath, which he brought over. Making a ring of stones he placed the saddle blanket over the ring of stones and then poured some fresh water from the goatskin into the depression made by the blanket. He quickly swilled Ruben's shift around in the pool of water before the water all drained through the blanket. Picking up the shift, he wrung it out, and gave it to Ruben, saying, "Put this back on so that the sun does not burn and blister any other part of your body."

Ruben was greatly relieved to put on the damp shift, and despite the slight initial sting of the ointment on the sore grooves on his shoulders, they now felt a lot more comfortable. The sun was now quite hot. The onlookers quickly moved back and resumed eating their much-needed breakfast, whilst Sergeant Tryone replaced the damp blanket on the pack pony, which also seemed pleased at the cooling effect.

After their brief rest, whilst having their breakfast, Sergeant Tryone called them back into ranks and marched them onwards once again. Just before mid-morning they reached the final crest of the hill and saw the Inferior Sea in front of them. Sergeant Tryone halted the platoon and said, "You see that clump of trees over there?" He pointed down the slope. "That is where we will make our base for today." He had obviously been here before and knew the area well.

He split the boys into four groups, and appointed one boy in charge of each group, and called them patrol leaders. Ruben was pleased that he was chosen as one of the patrol leaders. Each patrol leader was told that he could appoint his own second in command, and Ruben obviously chose Latich. The sergeant then allocated various tasks to each party. One party, led by the sergeant's nephew, was instructed to build a low rock dam around a small spring that ran down into the sea in order to make a freshwater pool. He sent Ruben's party to gather firewood in order that a fire could be lit so that they could cook some fish. He then took another patrol leader, who was a fisherman's son, over to the saddlebags. From these he produced a small circular net and said to the boy, "See what you can do with this, and try to catch some fish for dinner." He went back to the last party and told them that they were going to be the afternoon's cooks and it was their job to prepare the meal when the fish were caught. He said to the remaining boys, "You can be the first party to bathe in the sea water, but be sure to take your clothes off and rinse them in freshwater once the dam has been made because otherwise the salt will dry hard on your clothes."

All the boys worked well at their allotted tasks, much to the sergeant's pleasure, and the patrol leaders encouraged their charges to even greater achievements. Plenty of fish were caught by the fishing patrol, who received great praise from everybody. Ruben's wood party collected a pile of dried up branches from the surrounding area and Sergeant Tryone, who used his tinderbox, soon started a good blaze. The dam of small stones produced a large knee-deep pool of clear water, which everyone used to wash their clothes in. The patrol of cooks managed to produce a pleasant meal of fish grilled on sticks suspended over the blazing fire.

Sergeant Tryone came over to Ruben as he took off his shift to wash it in the pool of clear water. He peeled off the strips of cloth which were soaked in the ointment and said to Ruben, "Go and wash your shoulders in the sea water, but after you have bathed come back to me and I will place new dressings on your shoulders."

Ruben quickly took off the rest of his clothes and dashed down into the sea, where he waded in and ducked his head underwater. The salt in the seawater stung the wounds at first, but soon the stinging was forgotten and Ruben started to swim around. He was surprised to find that only a few of the other boys could swim, as many of them had not come from towns near the river or the Inferior Sea. However, he was pleased to note that Latich could also swim, as he had come from Lagash. Sergeant Tryone also noted not only that Ruben could swim, but that he was a very good swimmer and moved effortlessly through the water.

The sergeant picked out five of the lads who could swim and measured off a length over which he got them to race. He was not surprised when Ruben won the race easily. He then got all the boys out of the sea and told them to rinse themselves in the freshwater pool. The boys put on their damp clothes, which soon dried on them as they rested in the warm afternoon sunshine. They then ate their meal of grilled fish, which was eaten with some wheat cakes left over from breakfast, together with some olives and dates that the sergeant had also packed. By then it was late afternoon, and the sergeant showed the boys how to strike their camp, by clearing up the ashes from the fire and burying them in the sand. He ordered them to scatter the rocks that had been used to build the dam in order to leave the place without any trace that they had been there. He told them that this was a sensible camping skill that they would have to use when they were on long-distance patrols. All the boys had enjoyed their day by the sea, even the lad who had hurt his foot the previous day. When he grew tired of marching and began to limp, the sergeant lifted him onto a spare pack pony that he had brought along for this very purpose.

As they marched away from the seashore, the sky to the east was darkening with the coming evening and the sun in the west setting. Sergeant Tryone kept them marching briskly, with only a short pause for refreshment. The sun had set and the stars were starting to show in the clear sky as they entered the camp. Sergeant Tryone marched all the lads in front of the officers' quarters before shouting, "Halt." He came round to where Ruben was standing, grabbed him by the arm and said, "Follow me, Ruben." He marched straight into Captain Uglis's office, brushing aside the guard who tried to stop him. Captain Uglis looked up from the scroll that he was studying, and allowed it to re-roll itself. He looked up at Tryone and said, "I didn't hear you knock, Sergeant." The sergeant didn't immediately reply, but in answer threw down the heavy chain on Captain Uglis's desk.

"Look at what your gross discrimination has caused," he stated as he turned Ruben around and lifted up his shift and peeled off the new dressing that he had laid over the ugly weals in Ruben's shoulders. "I really cannot understand this – sir," he almost shouted.

There was no expression on the captain's face, but when he looked at the sores on Ruben's shoulders he realised that he had gone too far. "Been complaining, have you?" he remarked.

Before Ruben could answer, Sergeant Tryone shouted, "No, the boy hasn't been complaining. It is me who is complaining, because I am responsible for the welfare of my charges – a fact of which you constantly remind us. Nothing justifies this form of treatment." Sergeant Tryone realised that he was getting emotional, but nonetheless felt comparatively safe, as Captain Uglis knew that he was a good training sergeant and also a relative of Commander Schudah, who was the last person that Captain Uglis wanted involved. There was a long, expectant silence, as each man weighed up his next move.

Ruben interrupted them, by saying, "I don't mind being handicapped, sir, but could I not wear some padding to prevent the chains causing the sores on my shoulders?"

Both men saw this as a satisfactory compromise, as neither of them really wanted to make it a big issue, but neither could be seen to step down. Captain Uglis said to Ruben, "Wait outside Ben Uriah, whilst I talk to the sergeant."

So Ruben waited outside the door, which the guard now closed behind him.

"I will tell you what I will do," said Captain Uglis, speaking directly to the sergeant. "I will get the leatherworker to fashion a supportive jerkin that will protect the boy's shoulders. Until then we had better let those sores heal."

"Thank you, sir," said Sergeant Tryone. "I will be far happier with that arrangement." He was about to leave, when a thought occurred to him, and he quickly turned round. "There is another thing I thought I'd better mention. The boy is a very good swimmer as well as his other obvious talents, and I sincerely think that he is a possibility for the Babylonian Guards."

"Yes, I see what you mean," brightened Captain Uglis. He knew that a recommendation from him would also be a merit in his favour. "Very well, that is what we will do. In the meantime make sure those sores get daily treatment. Apart from that we will have to work him hard to make sure that he graduates with a high rating. Thank you very much, Sergeant Tryone," he said, dismissing the sergeant.

So Sergeant Tryone left the office in a contented mood, told Ruben to follow him and went back outside to the waiting platoon, who had obviously overheard part of the exchange of words. He led the lads back to the main mess hall, and told them to get a light supper and then retire. Sergeant Tryone left the boys to see what there was still available in the mess, whilst he went to see the leatherworker. He didn't entirely trust Captain Uglis and wanted to ensure that the job was correctly carried out. He found the man, who had just finished his day's work, repairing leather breastplates. He turned round as Sergeant Tryone entered and greeted him as an old and trusted friend. Sergeant Tryone explained the problem and the leatherworker nodded his head in understanding of the situation. "What I could do," he said, looking round the door to make sure that they were not overheard, "is use some soft calf skin and then build it up to an outer layer of crocodile hide, the uncured sort, which is as hard as baked clay. It will be heavy, but it will do the job well. Do you think the weight might be too heavy for the boy?"

"No, I don't think so," answered Sergeant Tryone. "He is a strong lad, and I think he will soon get used to the weight. But can you get calf skin without arousing suspicion? I don't think Captain Uglis would approve."

"Yeah, no problem. We received a new batch in just the other day, and I'm sure I can put a few lengths aside without any questions being asked. So bring the boy over to me right away, and I can start taking measurements."

Sergeant Tryone thanked him, and went straight back to the mess hall where he found the boys just finishing their meal and having a drink of beer to wash it down. They all looked up at him expectantly as he entered. He said, "There's no rush, boys," but pointed to Ruben and said, "Follow me, lad."

They had been discussing what had happened, and had all overheard the arguments between the captain and the sergeant, but no one knew what the outcome was as yet, because the guard had then shut the door when Ruben was sent outside. There was much speculation, which was why they were all so interested to see what was going to happen.

As the sergeant led Ruben out of the mess hall he explained to him in a quiet voice, so that nobody could overhear them, what he had arranged with the leatherworker, who was an old friend of his. He said to Ruben, "Now you must not tell anyone that I have arranged this myself. You must not say anything about the soft leather that will be over the places where the chains have been digging in as you will get me into trouble if you do," he said, smiling wryly.

"Thanks very much, sir," said Ruben in a conspiratorial whisper. "I think you have been very considerate," he added.

"Fine, Ruben," the sergeant said. "Just be sure to keep your part of the bargain. Don't tell a soul." He paused and looked Ruben straight in the eyes, which he noticed were almost on a level with his own. "Another thing, I will be working you very hard, as the bargain I have made with the captain is for you to be trained as a possible recruit for the Babylonian Guard. You know this is the elite regiment of our army and it is only the best that make it, so be sure not to let me down."

They went in to the leatherworker's workshop, which smelt wonderful to Ruben and was very tidy, with a place for everything, and every thing in its place. The sergeant put his arm around Ruben's shoulders and said, "This is the boy, Master Tanner, and you can see the dressings cover the parts of his shoulders that need protection." The Master Tanner came over to Ruben. He was a short, slightly built man but had strong calloused hands, which Ruben noted were surprisingly gentle as he ran his hands over Ruben's shoulders.

"Uhmm, big lad isn't he. And he'll probably grow quickly, so we better make it with overlapping plates that can be moved out with the removal of a couple of stitches as he grows," said the little man. He went over to one of his racks and withdrew a freshly cut length of reed. "What's your name, son?" he asked Ruben, half mumbling to himself.

"Ruben Ben Uriah, sir," said Ruben politely.

The little man cut some small marks into the length of reed, and then came round Ruben holding the reed up against various parts of his body, and making notches in it. After a while, he dismissed them, and said that they would be hearing from him within the next few days.

The sergeant led Ruben back to the barrack hut, where the rest of the boys were getting ready for bed. All the boys looked up expectantly at Sergeant Tryone, hoping that he would volunteer more information about the result of his argument with the captain. However, the only thing he said, as Ruben went to his sleeping mattress was, "I do not want to hear a lot of chatter after the light has gone out. You have had a busy day, so you can have a short lie in tomorrow morning. We will be joined by nine more recruits, that will bring our numbers up to full strength."

He said goodnight and turned to leave. His nephew had obviously been chosen as the spokesman, and said, "What happened between you and the captain, sir?"

"Nothing for you to worry about," he said dismissively and then added, "Just that we reached a compromise about some padding – Ruben can tell you about that, but as I say, keep the chat short." He slipped out, and quietly closed the door, bolting it from the outside.

All eyes were then turned on Ruben, and someone said, "Come on, Ruben, tell us what happened."

"Nothing more than the sergeant said, really," answered Ruben. Then he elaborated by saying, "I was sent out of the room and the door was closed, so I couldn't hear what exactly was said. But I'm sure you all heard the arguments before that, when the door was open. However, they both seemed happy with what they had agreed, I am to wear a leather jerkin as well as the chains, and the leather jerkin will have padding to protect my shoulders from the chains chafing."

This all seemed an anticlimax, as they had all been expecting a fight between Captain Uglis and the sergeant, in fact one of the boys was already taking bets on who would win a fight. He had said that as Captain Uglis had originally been a Babylonian Guard he would undoubtedly beat the sergeant. Even if he was a little bit older and out of condition, he still had a lot of experience and weight on his side. The majority of the boys, who were led by the sergeant's nephew, held an alternative view. They maintained that the sergeant was younger and fitter and although smaller in build was still very strong, and as they liked him they were definitely on his side. But now it appeared that there would be no fight and that Ruben would still be handicapped, which would stop him winning everything, so their attention died away.

Latich was the only one who said anything more to Ruben as he quickly undressed and slid under his blanket. Latich turned towards Ruben and whispered, "Surely there must have been something more important than just that?"

"Not really," said Ruben, but then added, "Well, I suppose there was quite a lot, but nothing about their dispute, and anything else can wait until later, perhaps when we're alone. I promise you I will let you know everything then. After all, you're my mate." At that point the lamp went out and apart from a few whispers, all conversation died as they all went to sleep after what had been an arduous but interesting day.

True to his word, the boys were not woken early but were woken late, and had plenty of time to get up and wash themselves, before they had to parade outside their barrack hut. The sergeant introduced nine new recruits who had just arrived that morning from the towns around Babylon, to the west. He told the nine new boys to join the parade and then asked Ruben, "How are your shoulders, lad? Slip off your shift and let's have a look." Ruben slipped off his shift; the sergeant walked over to him and peeled off the dressings.

"Wow," said one of the new boys, as he stared with horror at the sores on Ruben's shoulders. "That's what they must do if you don't follow orders. They must beat you, shit, I bet that's painful."

Sergeant Tryone ignored this comment, and asked Ruben, "How do they feel now, lad?"

"Not too bad, sir. They seem to be healing up and drying out," he answered.

"Well, let the air get to them, but keep the shift on over them and make sure it stays clean and they don't get infected. The sores should scab over, and after a while the scabs will drop off. But if they start weeping or bleeding again come and see me immediately."

He then addressed the whole platoon and said, "I will take you over to the main mess hall in a minute while I show the new boys where to put their gear, and they can then join you for some breakfast. After breakfast I will meet you behind the barrack hut and we will continue the fitness and stamina building exercises." He dismissed the boys, whilst he showed the new lads the barrack hut. As the lads filed off towards the main mess hall the topic of conversation was the weather and how it had changed overnight. From being dry and sunny it was now humid and there were a lot of clouds building up in the sky. Some of the lads said that summer was coming to an end and the wet season was starting and it would very soon rain and gradually become cooler with the approach of winter.

When they returned to the rear of the barrack hut the Sergeant announced that training would continue as before, but with the addition of rock climbing exercises and lessons in how to use small ladders to get over walls quickly. They then started much of the work that they hadn't done two days before.

Ruben soon realised that there were only two other main contenders for first place in the exercises. Firstly, if it was a simple race, where none of the competitors had to carry anything, the only one who could give him a close race was Latich. Secondly, when it came to lifting heavy things there was one other lad who was fairly short, but well built and strong. But if there was anything that combined both disciplines, he was unchallenged. However, this only lasted for the next four days, because on the fifth day the leatherworker came over to the platoon as they paraded first thing in the morning. He went to Sergeant Tryone with Captain Uglis, who called out Ruben from the ranks. "Here you are, Ben Uriah. Put this on." He held out the jerkin to Ruben who put it on and found it to be a good fit. "How does that feel? Is it strong enough?" said the captain, thumping Ruben on the shoulder with his huge fist.

Ruben managed not to collapse under the blow, which he noted, with quiet pleasure, must have hurt the captain's hand as he winced and rubbed it.

"Yes, it feels fine, sir."

"Right, you little sod, see how you get on with the chains now," he said as he handed the heavy chain back to Sergeant Tryone.

The sergeant clipped on the chain and the leatherworker showed him how to feed it through the loops that he had made to keep it in place, and once again Ruben realised that his winning days were over. The jerkin together with the heavy chain wound around and across the shoulders, gave him a weird, monstrous, top-heavy look. Not only did he look top-heavy, but also the weight of the whole assembly was daunting. However, he made no complaint and returned to his place in the ranks.

When they started the exercising, it was indeed hard work and he always ended up bathed in perspiration. Surprisingly he was never last in any of the exercises, but always, certainly for the first week, amongst the stragglers. However, as the days wore on, he slowly became used to the additional weight and as his muscles grew visibly, he improved his placing positions until, after about five weeks, he was finishing in the top ten once more.

As the rains came and the weather became cooler, the jerkin became more bearable heat-wise. It was well constructed so that the chains never chafed and he was not at all impeded. After about eight weeks he finally finished first again over a difficult obstacle course, and he could see the pleasure in Sergeant Tryone's eyes as he won the first race whilst being handicapped.

He had also grown considerably during that period, not only in height, but also in extensive upper body and leg muscles. In fact, all the boys had built up their strength and stamina considerably. They were pleased when Sergeant Tryone told them that in the next few days they would be moving on to weapon training. However, they were all a bit disappointed when they were given their first weapons and discovered that these were all made of wood. When this was queried, Sergeant Tryone explained that apart from getting used to the weight (in fact, metal ones were even heavier), it was important that they should not inflict any injuries on one another, or even on themselves, (by misuse). Purely as a demonstration, one of the boys was given full armaments, and found it all extremely difficult to carry, let alone use effectively. They were told that eventually they would carry, apart from the standard sword and shield, specialised weapons – if they showed any particular skill. These specialised weapons included: a double-headed axe (that was called a syblis), the javelin (a good javelin thrower would carry three), and lastly the bow and arrow (the bow was fairly short, but was of sheep's horn that made it heavy) and a quiver full of arrows that was a considerable weight.

The first training was with the sword and shield. For hours on end you could hear the whack of wood against leather that covered the shields, punctuated by the occasional shout of pain when a blow had not been either parried or stopped by the shield. They were all surprised at how tiring this was. They normally went to bed with aching limbs and more than a few bruises that had been sustained in their practise sessions.

Ruben had not been able to reflect on the strange situation that had brought him unwillingly into the army. This was due to constantly being surrounded by all the other recruits and never being allowed the time and solitude that would allow him to think back. The reason for this was quite obvious. If the new recruits could always be kept busy and always be striving for greater achievements, they were far less likely to become depressed, homesick and attempt to run away.

They always seemed to be training, despite the weather conditions. They had even run obstacle courses and fought with their wooden swords and shields in the pouring rain while almost knee-deep in mud. There was one day, during the heart of winter, when it was really cold outside and the rain was lashing down, driven by a bitingly cold wind that blew from the mountains in the north. The wind was so strong that it almost blew people off their feet and it was starting to weaken the barrack huts that had not been finished with clay. Their own hut had fortunately now been daubed with clay over the wickerwork and it was a lot warmer inside, as the wind could not penetrate. They had all been issued with extra blankets and were often allowed to build a large fire outside. They would then put large stones into the fire and these could be brought inside the hut, thus providing them with some heating. Admittedly this was not very much, but it did make a small difference, and that was a considerable privilege.

The cold wind and the lashing rain had made it impossible to carry on outside, so they were told to go back into their barrack huts and keep warm. The sergeants instructed them to pile up the mattresses at one end and told them to do some physical exercises just to keep warm. After a while they were all warm and some of the lads were allowed to sit quietly while the others got on with their sword practise a few at a time. It was whilst Ruben was sitting quietly that he thought about the sword he had discovered and retrieved from the half submerged boat in the marshlands.

The swords that they were using were only short swords, about the length of a fully grown man's forearm, and would normally be worn in a scabbard attached to the belt. The sword that was now in Simeon's floating reed house was different. That sword was one of the larger type normally carried on the back, and it was only an accomplished fighter who was allowed such a sword. Indeed Ruben had seen a large sword such as that owned by Captain Uglis and kept in his office. This thought jerked his mind back to Simeon's wonderful house and all the splendid things that he had seen and learnt about from the amazing old man of the marshes. He thought of how wonderful it would be to see his own sword again, of how superbly sharp it was and of the beautiful jewel encrusted pommel of the sword. His mind wandered back to the treasured museums that Simeon had made. He recalled how Simeon had taught him the way to see the colour of the air that surrounds a person, depending upon the mood that he is in. He remembered that Simeon had told him that he had a gift for this, and tried briefly to use the technique that Simeon had taught him. Try as he might, he looked at people through half-closed eyes, but nothing happened. Everything still looked the same. Then he remembered that Simeon had told him that he had to be calm and patient, and to be in tune with nature and the words of The Creator – whoever that was.

Somebody shook Ruben by the shoulder and he was brought back suddenly into the here and now. He looked into Sergeant Tryone's face, which was stern. "Were you daydreaming, Ruben? That is something that you should not do. I called you three times and got no response. Do not let it happen again, otherwise I will demote you from being a patrol leader," the sergeant said, chastising.

"Oh, I am sorry sir, it won't happen again, I promise," said Ruben feeling embarrassed and contrite. "What do you want me to do?" he enquired.

"It's your turn. Now I want you to fight me, and to see how quick you are. Take off the jerkin," the Sergeant ordered.

Once he was without the jerkin, Ruben was surprised at how fast he could move, and so was the sergeant. He seemed to have plenty of time to be able to parry all the attacks with his sword. This enabled him to move into a good position so that he could take a downward thrust on his own raised shield, whilst he advanced, leaving the sergeant's stomach open to his own sword thrust. "Got you, you're dead," he said proudly. He could see that the sergeant was taken aback, but played along and collapsed in a heap.

Laughing, the sergeant got to his feet and turned to the rest of the platoon who were all surprised at what had happened, and he said, "That was quite deliberate. It was a good opportunity for me to show you how not to get killed by leaving yourself unguarded, by throwing everything into an attack." Ruben was astonished by this, because he felt sure that the sergeant had not seen the killing thrust that he had delivered. But sensibly, he said nothing and just grinned with the sergeant as if they had worked it all out beforehand.

The sergeant looked out of the door, turned back and said to the boys. "The rain has stopped now, even though it is still blowing a gale, and it is dark outside. You had better go over to the mess hall and see what you can get for dinner." As Ruben put down his sword and shield, the sergeant passed him his jerkin and quietly whispered in his ear, "Follow the others out and say that you have left something behind, then come back here for a quick chat." He then busied himself in tidying up all the weapons and then in putting out the sleeping mattresses ready for the night.

Ruben did as instructed, and was not overly surprised when the sergeant said, "You actually beat me, fair and square. You moved so fast that I completely underestimated your ability. Either someone has shown you how to fight or you just have a natural talent – which is not surprising, as you seem to be a natural soldier in many respects. I must thank you for playing along with me as it would have been embarrassing otherwise." He continued, "As you know, we are planning to put you in for the Babylonian Guards at the end of your provisional training, but that is still quite a long time away. Now it is coming up to six months that you have been training, and I am due for a few days off. I am planning to spend a few days with my uncle whom you may have heard is Commander Schudah in Lagash, which is where I believe you come from. I am going to ask the captain if I can take you with me, as I am often allowed to take one of the boys to help carry my belongings. But say nothing about this to anyone. Now hurry back to the others."

Ruben did as he was told, and had a lot to think about. Did the sergeant know that he already had met the commander, and if he knew that, what else might he know of Ruben's history? The same things that he was thinking about earlier flashed into his mind, about Lagash, and where the merchant Mutek had gone. Why had Mutek not been able to prevent him being put in the army? And what had happened to Ishmala, the dumb yet wonderful man who had killed the evil Captain Gershnarl? His mind was in a whirl as he got back to the rest of the lads who had sat down with their meals. He was pleased when Latich called him over, and said, "I have got a dinner for you over here, so sit down and tell me what the sergeant wanted."

Ruben was startled that Latich had realised that he had gone back to talk to the sergeant. He bent down over his meal and whispered to Latich, "You are not meant to know that, and I really can't tell you anyway. It is all terribly confusing and I am not trying to be secretive about things." Apologetically he added, "Look, I will tell you as soon as I can."

****

Captain Uglis sat in his office, deep in thought, drumming his fingers on the table. The previous day some orders had arrived via a messenger, who had not even waited for a response. Those orders had come from

Commander Schudah, informing him that he wanted to see his nephew Sergeant Tryone, whom he knew was training Ben Uriah. The order went on to say that Schudah wanted to see the sergeant on the his next half year's leave, and that he was to bring Ben Uriah with him. The reason was that Commander Schudah had discovered quite a lot of the background information concerning Ben Uriah, all of which had been entangled with the deals of the late Captain Gershnarl. As Captain Uglis had been involved with Gershnarl and he knew that this was common knowledge to the commander, he felt sure that this posed quite a threat to his position. He had told Sergeant Tryone that he was requested to go to Lagash for his next few days' leave, but nothing more.

The sergeant had come to his office a few moments earlier and requested to take Ben Uriah with him. Naturally he considered that it all looked rather dubious, and that at least he would not receive any accolade in the recommendation of Ben Uriah for the Babylonian Guards. At worst it could even threaten his own captaincy, as he and Gershnarl had been mixed up in some shady business in the past, and he was most concerned that the whole situation was buried. The problem that faced him was how to get rid of Sergeant Tryone and the boy. He went over to the wall where a map of the surrounding district was attached. He had heard from one of his scouts that there had been some bandit activity just north of their camp. He thought of how he could send the sergeant with Ben Uriah back to Lagash, by way of an area where they could be intercepted and killed by a band of brigands. He had contacts amongst all the brigands, and so he knew whom he could choose for the job. Having worked out his plan, he told the guard outside his office that he was going for a walk out of the camp, as he needed some exercise. The guard should tell no one about his absence, with the threat of having the guard flogged if any word of his absence was reported. This was a trick that he had learnt from Gershnarl; it was by far the best way to keep everything quiet. He slung his large bronze sword over his back, giving the appearance that he was going for a walk out in the desert, where he would have plenty of room to swing the heavy weapon. He quietly slipped out of the camp and trotted along the track to the north until the camp was well out of sight. He came to a stunted tree, withdrew the large sword and in a few mighty blows cut the tree down. He then went and found a large flat stone, which he brought over and placed on the stump, onto which he placed a round pebble that he took out from his pouch. This was a pre-arranged signal, between himself and the brigand chief, that he needed to see him immediately. Satisfied with his work and knowing that the brigand chief would come and seek him out as soon as he had seen the signal, he went back to the camp.

It was two days later when he was called by one of the sergeants, who reported that there was a merchant at the camp entrance, selling goatskins, who had asked to see him. The sergeant expected that Captain Uglis would send the man away and was surprised when he told him to take the merchant into his office, where he would soon join him. He came back to his office as soon as he could, went in and carefully closed the door behind him. He went over to the merchant, who was the brigand chief, and greeted him warmly, asking him about his wives and all his children, in the customary Bedouin greeting, before getting down to business.

He told the brigand chief of his plans to get rid of the sergeant and the troublesome boy, and where and when the deed should be done. He stressed that although the sergeant was not big, he was pretty tough and that the boy with him was a young trainee who was large for his age. It would take three or four of the man's best men to be sure that they did the job properly, and that the element of surprise itself was not enough to overpower them both. After haggling about the cost of the job, the captain agreed to pay eight pieces of silver, half before the job and half after it had been completed. They then said their goodbyes and the captain went out of his office, shouting at the man and saying he was a thief and a rogue to charge so much for those things, and he had better not come here again. This he thought would be adequate cover for his rather strange behaviour in seeing the merchant in the first place. He then went back to his office and sent for Sergeant Tryone. After a while there was a knock on the door and in answer to this, he bellowed, "Enter." Sergeant Tryone stood before him.

"Ah Tryone, it is about your leave for the next few days, starting tomorrow," he said. "I want you to make a short detour on your way back to Lagash. You are to go by the area where we normally take the boys swimming and camp training, and tell me if there is any sign that the spring has dried up. I have received reports that it is not flowing properly and is on the point of drying up. This story may not be correct, but as you know the area better than anyone else, you can give me an accurate report. Oh yes, and if I don't see you before you go, have a good leave and give my compliments to the commander."

The sergeant left Captain Uglis' office in a state of perplexity. The captain hardly ever wished anyone a pleasant leave and normally treated leave with annoyance that anyone should be so privileged. He was also aware that there had been a lot of speculation in the officers' mess about his seeing the Bedouin merchant, which again was totally out of character. Between all his fellow recruitment sergeants there was a general belief that Captain Uglis could not be trusted at all. All the sergeants knew that Captain Uglis did not really run the training camp at all, but that they did all the work and simply reported to him. They even used to take his orders and then make their own arrangements, as they knew that he would probably forget exactly what he had ordered. Therefore, everything he did and said was treated with suspicion. They all knew of his shady dealings and his involvement with Captain Gershnarl, whose death was considered by everyone to be good fortune. The sergeant was not unduly worried about the next few days, but his concern had been heightened by the unusual behaviour of Captain Uglis. Additionally there was that strange business about his absence the other afternoon, that was in fact common knowledge amongst the sergeants, and, he was fairly sure, was even known to the recruits. Bearing all this in mind, he considered that it would be wise not to leave first thing the following morning, but in fact go tonight. That would also give him the whole day in Lagash, rather than spending half the morning getting there.

He went back to where his platoon was training, in combination with the platoon that they would train with over the next few days that he would be gone. He had told all the boys in the platoon that he was taking Ruben mainly because the commander had asked him to bring him back to clear up some difficulties concerning Gershnarl's death, that was now common knowledge. When he arrived back outside their barrack hut, where they had assembled alongside the other platoon and were waiting to be addressed by another sergeant, he called Ruben over to stand beside him. He said, "There has been a change of plan." Ruben's face fell so he quickly added, "Don't worry, my leave is still going ahead, but I will want to leave tonight, after lights-out and when everyone should be asleep."

"That is all right with me, sir, but what do I tell the other boys? What time would you like me to meet you, and where?" enquired Ruben, with a quizzical expression.

Sergeant Tryone said, "Meet me straight after dinner and tell anyone who asks you why and where you are going, that we are going on an overnight errand for the captain."

He knew all the boys would understand this, that they would ask no further questions. He then went and talked to the other sergeant about what both platoons would be doing during his absence. After this he went back to his own quarters and prepared his equipment. He had also taken out from the stores a brand new sword scabbard and belt, together with a shield for Ruben, even though only soldiers who had finished all their training were normally allowed to wear equipment outside of a camp. All his kit fitted into a small knapsack that he would carry on his back, and he would only carry the one shield with his own sword already in its scabbard. He laid out two winter cloaks and two helmets that he had also taken from the store. He then went to speak to the people who would be on guard duty that evening.

As he expected, Ruben turned up promptly after dinner, wearing his jerkin and with no equipment at all. The sergeant took him to his quarters, where he buckled on the sword and gave him the shield to carry on his arm. He said, "Tell nobody about this, as you are not meant to wear equipment. If anyone asks us when we are outside the camp, which I doubt, because you look big enough to be a young regular soldier, but leave the talking to me."

"Thank you, sir," said Ruben, almost at a loss for words. "I feel like a real soldier now," he said, holding himself very straight.

"Just make sure that you behave like one," said the sergeant.

He then explained to Ruben that they had to go to check on the water from the spring, beside the place where they had been to the sea only six months earlier. It was late, and the camp had become a lot quieter as all the platoons were now in their barrack huts. Sergeant Tryone clipped the dark red cloak round Ruben's collar and put the helmet on his head. He stepped back and admired his own handiwork. He nodded and said, "You'll do." He then fastened his cloak over his knapsack, put on his helmet and led the way out.

## 5
## A BRUSH WITH DEATH

The brigand chief left Captain Uglis' office in a state of amused contentment. It had been so easy to extract far more money than the job normally paid. He had known Captain Uglis for quite a few years, but previously he had always seen him with his fellow conspirator, Captain Gershnarl. His dealings with Gershnarl were on a completely different scale. You couldn't trust that bastard at all. He was a devious sod, and quite capable of betraying any confidence and renege on any agreement, if it suited him to do so. All the brigands had now heard of his demise. In many respects it was good news, but it also made life more complex, in that they normally operated outside the laws that the Babylonian army had to keep. However, on the few occasions that he had worked for Captain Uglis, quite illegally of course, it had been child's play. Captain Uglis was a simpleton, although he thought he was clever. When he had previously worked with Gershnarl, he had simply been Gershnarl's strong right arm, even though Gershnarl himself was powerful. But dealing with the two of them you had to really watch your step, and always check behind you and look out for any possible traps. These days, however, it was easy. Normally the going rate for a simple assassination was just four pieces of silver, or six at the very most. But to charge eight pieces of silver for a sergeant and a boy who wouldn't even be armed, was a good deal.

Mind you, he heeded Uglis' warning that the sergeant was tough and that the boy was large for his age. He therefore thought the best way to do the whole thing was to get two of his best men and go along with them himself as the third person, to make sure the job was done properly. Additionally, he could easily pay them two silver pieces each, which would keep them happy, and then he could claim the further four pieces of silver himself.

His name was Shaleem, and he went away a very happy man, thinking of the two best men that he would choose to accompany him. He thought about this as he skirted back north of the training camp to their hideout. He had deliberately taken two days before going to see Uglis, to give him the feeling that they were not in the immediate vicinity. Now he reached a single tree beside the small ravine, which was only a short distance away from the felled tree that acted as a signpost to the initiated.

He gave a shrill warbling whistle and stood in the open with his arms outstretched. One of his men appeared from behind a boulder and beckoned Shaleem to enter the ravine, whilst the men returned to sentry duty. Shaleem went over to where the rest of the men were sitting around a fire that was well out of sight and burned with no smoke, which would have given their presence away. He went over to two men and beckoned to them to come and join him. Crossing the clearing to his second in command, Shaleem told him that he and the other two were going to do a job for the fool Uglis.

"It would bring in some useful money. You, Abdul, take the rest of the men to our main camp just east of Souza. We shall meet you there in three or four day's time."

One was of average build, yet fairly short; the other was a large man with a full black beard. The two men grabbed their weapons, which were a weird assortment of daggers, swords, cudgels and a spear. Together they trotted along after Shaleem. As they returned the way Shaleem had come, he explained what they had to do and how much each would receive. Naturally they were delighted at such a large payment for what would be an easy job. But the chief warned them not to be light hearted about it; he explained that it would be worth their while to make sure all was done efficiently. In this way they would get plenty of other well-paid work. He said that it would be sensible to get to the place early, to check on the lie of the land and work out how best to do the job quickly.

By the late afternoon they had reached the shore on the Inferior Sea and soon found the fresh water spring. They collected a large pile of rocks, which they dumped in the bed of the stream. This produced many rivulets that ran down the beach in about six different places, which nearly all soaked into the sand. They went just to the east of the area behind a low hummock, where they could be out of sight and out of the wind. Shaleem told the small man to light a fire and prepare something to eat from the provisions that they had brought with them. He then explained to the big man that it would be his job to spear the boy first and get him out of the way. The basic plan was that he should attack the boy, kill him with the spear and then run off leaving the sergeant to pursue him. Shaleem and the other man would then surround the sergeant, whom they could then kill at their leisure. They ate a quick meal and sat warming themselves by the fire as they passed round a goatskin of wine. They watched the embers of the fire die down and wrapped themselves in their fur cloaks. They had just fallen quiet before going to sleep, when they heard a noise. Keeping quiet they crept up to the top of the mound and peered over to try to find the source of the noise. It was coming from two soldiers who were examining the rocks that they had dumped in the streambed. One of them they identified as a sergeant by the zigzag patterns on his cloak, which showed up under the flickering light of the torch that he carried. The other was a young soldier, not a boy, because he wore a soldier's cloak and helmet.

Although they weren't exactly as Captain Uglis had described, they were investigating exactly as he had predicted. Shaleem rationalised that if they were not the two who were meant to arrive in the morning, their presence made the possibility of the other two not arriving certainly substantial. Therefore, he considered the most sensible thing to do would be to carry out his plan as if they were the two to be killed, then wait to see if anyone else turned up in the morning. If the other two arrived as expected they could then carry out the job as planned. Doing away with these two would be no real problem. Additionally, he justified to himself, he could then demand even more money from that fool Uglis. He signalled to the others that they should carry out their plan immediately.

****

Sergeant Tryone and Ruben left the camp, unchallenged by the guard, and walked down the track towards the Inferior Sea. Ruben could remember the start of the journey from his first week in the army. But on that occasion, it had become very hot after a while and it was then that the chain started to chafe and his memory from then on was clouded due to his discomfort. However, the sergeant knew the area well and could easily pick out the route by moonlight. In fact, he could have found the route easily even if he had been blindfolded. Thus, when the moon disappeared behind some clouds they were still able to continue their journey. It was very cold and they were glad of the warm winter cloaks that were lined with dark curly wool, taken from the mountain sheep found to the north. They kept up a good pace and only exchanged a few words, as by walking briskly they kept themselves warm. They paused briefly, at the same point where the sergeant normally stopped, and Ruben remembered the area, as the ring of stones in which the sergeant had made a basin was still visible. They had a drink of water from their leather water bottles and the sergeant said they should get to the freshwater stream fairly soon. It would be easy to find out exactly what was happening, in order to make their report, and they could then continue onwards until they reached Lagash.

They set off at their brisk pace once again, and were soon in sight of the Inferior Sea. The sergeant stopped and made a small torch from a piece of wood, surrounded by a piece of cloth that had been soaked in oil. This he lit with some sparks that he generated using his tinderbox. They then went to look for the fresh water stream, and within a few moments had discovered where it had been flowing. They followed the watercourse back to where it had been dispersed due to the rocks. It was now running in a lot of different pathways down to the sea. The sergeant called out,

"Well this seems to be the cause of the problem. For once it appears Captain Uglis may have been correct. Anyway, let us move the rocks so that the stream returns to normal." They were about half way through their job, when some sixth sense made Sergeant Tryone look round to where Ruben was moving one of the large rocks. He saw a large man with an enormous black beard rush down from the rocks at Ruben. He shouted out to Ruben, "Look out! Behind you," as the brigand was armed with a large spear. But his warning came too late and Ruben half looked up when the spear was thrown from only ten paces away. The lad was flung back by the force of the blow, which must have hit just to the left of his heart. He was thrown to the ground with the spear sticking out of the cloak, which it must have passed through before piercing his chest.

Automatically, the sergeant charged at the brigand, drawing his sword with the horrible knowledge that due to his miscalculation the boy had been killed. The brigand saw him coming and started to run off. The sergeant felt with a sick heart that it was the least that he could do, to either bring the rat to justice and certain execution, or to kill him if he fought. The man had not run far when he turned and drew his own sword. As Sergeant Tryone advanced he heard the sound of swords being drawn from their sheaths behind him. The sergeant wheeled around and knew that he was surrounded. They had obviously walked right into a trap that had been planned beforehand. Tryone grinned ruefully to himself.

"I will take some of the bastards with me, anyway," he muttered, and charged the larger of the two men behind him. They were surprisingly good swordsmen and apart from inflicting a few slight wounds upon the two men, it was not long before the third man joined them and he was hard pressed, with his back to a large boulder.

The clash of bronze on bronze, together with the grunts of fighting men, made Ruben open his eyes. He felt as if he had been caught between the hammer and the anvil, which he had seen many of the metal workers use when they were shaping swords. He had been extremely fortunate, as the large bronze head of the spear, after passing through his cloak had been stopped from spearing him by the chain that had caused him so much difficulty. Although he had been thrown onto the ground by the sheer force of the throw, he had simply been badly winded and rendered temporarily unconscious when his head struck a rock. Clambering groggily to his feet, with the spear still hanging from his cloak, he quickly surveyed the scene and worked out what had happened. His head throbbed and he was still trying to recover his breathing as his rib cage felt battered like a drum. He was burning with a righteous zeal to avenge himself. He withdrew the spear from the jagged gash in his cloak and unsheathed his sword. Gasping deep lungfuls of the cold night air, he strode over to within twenty paces of where the battle raged. The sergeant was tiring, and Ruben could see that it was only a matter of time before the brigands finished him off.

"Oi! Why not make it a fair fight and include me?" he boldly challenged as the stupefied faces of all three brigands gawped at him, and the sergeant stared with astonishment and great relief. Ruben rammed his sword into the earth before him, transferred the spear to his right hand and hurled it with all his strength at his original attacker. "I believe this belongs to you," he said as the spear flew from his hand. The large man with the black beard stood confounded. The spear struck him right in the centre of his stomach and penetrated until his spine stopped it. The brigand tottered backwards and fell over on his back with the spear shaft pointing at the stars, with his lifeblood spilling into the sand. The other two brigands had not moved, and pulling his sword from the earth, Ruben rushed at the nearest brigand, the small man, who just had time to recover his wits and defend himself. It was then a more even fight, but the brigands were no match for the highly skilful sergeant and the still enraged Ruben. After a few moments, the small man dropped his sword and fled in terror. Seeing the dead come to life had been too much for him.

Sergeant Tryone, who now fought with renewed vigour, knocked the blade from Shaleem's hand and had him at his mercy with his sword point at Shaleem's throat.

"Disarm him, and tie his hands behind his back," he ordered Ruben, who appeared at his side. Ruben did as instructed. He pulled the knots as tight as he could and saw Shaleem wince with pain. The anger and excitement that comes with battle suddenly left Ruben and he sank wearily to his knees. The sergeant made Shaleem lie face down on the earth and lashed his ankles together with the dangling cord that Ruben had taken from his waist to tie his hands. He resheathed his own sword and went over to where Ruben was kneeling, still in obvious pain. He saw the deep marks the spear had cut into the chain, and understood what had happened. He unclasped Ruben's cloak, and unclipped the heavy chain, which he unthreaded from the jerkin, whilst he said, "It is a good job that you were still wearing the chain." Replacing the cloak he made Ruben comfortable. He then took the heavy chain over to the struggling brigand chief and firmly wound it round the ropes that bound him, to ensure that he could not get out of bondage.

Sergeant Tryone realised that Ruben was physically and emotionally worn out. After all, they had come a long way tonight; he had almost been killed and was severely bruised. Additionally, he had killed a man. The first time a soldier killed another man in battle was a traumatic experience. He therefore collected some brushwood, and soon had a small fire burning. He said to Ruben, "We will have a short break here, allowing you to rest, before we continue to Lagash with our captive."

****

Commander Schudah had unearthed an enormous amount of information concerning the shady dealings of the late Captain Gershnarl. It was surprising how much information had been exposed, that was previously kept quiet by his men due to the fear of possible reprisals by the captain. There had also been a frightening number of deals with the Bedouin brigands, which held more than just a rumour of the complicity of Captain Uglis. However, nobody knew anything about Ruben Ben Uriah, with the obvious exception of the late merchant Mutek. And that was only on Ruben Ben Uriah's say-so. When he enquired, via the Council of Merchants, concerning Mutek, there was no evidence that he had employed the boy. Some of his servants had said they had seen the boy on a few occasions, and believed he had worked for another boat builder who lived in Nippur, which was upriver from Lagash on the way to Babylon.

What concerned the commander was the evidence concerning the dealings that Gershnarl had had with the brigands. This was far more important than the matter of one boy, who by all accounts was getting on very well and would have to go into the army soon, even if he was underage when he was first enlisted. But the dealings with the brigands could also lead to complications, as the border with the Persians was highly unstable. There had already been a number of border skirmishes and as Lagash was the nearest command post to the border, it was his responsibility to make sure everything was safe. He was also aware of the importance of keeping the trade route open with the east, as it was this that the Persians would try to interrupt. The danger was that if the brigand chiefs sided with the Persians, they could wreak havoc with disruptive border skirmishes that could disguise a full-scale attack on Lagash. His thoughts were interrupted by a knock on his door. His aide entered and told him that two soldiers had just arrived and brought with them, under arrest, Shaleem – one of the most notorious brigand chiefs in the area. The aide informed him that the two soldiers were outside, and one of them was his nephew, Sergeant Tryone.

In a state of bewilderment and delight, Commander Schudah leapt to his feet and shouted, "That is wonderful news! Don't just stand there, man, send him in – the sergeant, I mean. And make sure Shaleem is securely locked up in the guardhouse, with two wide awake guards on him." His aide rushed out of the room to do as he was ordered, and showed Sergeant Tryone into the commander's office.

"Well, well, this is a pleasant surprise. Particularly as you have brought one of the brigand chiefs that we have been after for a long time. But I wasn't expecting you so soon. You must have left the training camp very early this morning."

"Well, last night, actually, sir," said the sergeant as he came in the room, took off his helmet, and warmly embraced the commander. "The ruffian and two of his accomplices tried to jump us."

"And you saw them off," interrupted the commander. "That is excellent news. Good for you, my boy."

"Well, it wasn't quite as easy as that, sir," said the sergeant, as he moved slightly uneasily on his feet. "It was my companion who really did exceptionally well, sir."

"But I thought you were bringing Ruben Ben Uriah in to see me," exclaimed the commander.

"Yes, that's who I mean by my companion, sir," explained the sergeant.

"But they told me you came in with another soldier," said the commander with a puzzled frown.

"Yes, I did sir, he is outside – Oh! – I completely forgot that he was still in uniform. I am sorry about breaking the rules, sir. But it has been rather a long night. If you sit down, I will try to explain."

"I think we had better bring the boy in here first, Tryone," said the commander. "He may well be recognised and that would leave both of us with a lot of explaining to be done."

So Ruben was called in and smiled shyly at the commander. "Good morning, sir," he said. "I am sorry that I am in uniform, but the sergeant and I completely forgot about my disguise."

The commander looked at him with astonishment. "Well, who would have believed it. I very much doubt if anyone recognised you. But you had better take the helmet and cloak off, and say no more about the uniform. Now Tryone, let's hear the story. Right from the beginning, if you please."

The sergeant gave a full account of the events from the time they left the training camp, explaining why he had given Ruben the cloak, helmet and sword. He was careful to explain that nobody in the training camp knew of Ruben's disguise, mentioning that he could well pass for a young soldier. He then gave a detailed account of the events of the night, making sure that Ruben received the praise that was due to him.

The commander looked at Ruben as if seeing him for the first time and muttered, "Well done, well done indeed." After a pause for thought, he said, "I bet you are both tired and hungry, but stay here and I'll have some food sent in to you. When you have finished that, you had better go to my quarters for a well earned rest."

Ruben had taken off the helmet and cloak, which he folded neatly and put in the corner. He was about to sit down next to Sergeant Tryone, when the sergeant stopped him and said, "Let me have a look at that bruise."

Ruben slipped off the jerkin. "It's not that bad, sir," he said. However, when he slipped off his shift, the sergeant's eyes widened with wonder at how he could be so dismissive about such an injury. The bruising was indeed very severe, and the muscles covering his ribcage were all the colours of the rainbow.

The sergeant said, "I will get some liniment to put on that, but not until we have eaten. It smells pretty vile, even though it does do a good job."

Sergeant Tryone and Ruben both tucked in with a vengeance. Neither of them had realised how hungry they were after their long walk and the battle with the brigands. During the meal the sergeant spoke to Ruben. "I think we may have placed the commander in a rather difficult situation. I could be given a special award, or possibly even promotion for what we have done. But there is nothing that can be done to reward you for what you did."

"Oh, that was nothing," exclaimed Ruben.

"What do you mean?" laughed Tryone. "I think my life is worth more than nothing. After all, I was facing certain death, had you not intervened."

Ruben flushed a bright pink and stammered, "I, I didn't mean that, but I don't want any reward. I am not proud of having killed anyone, even though their attack on us was cowardly, and their intention was to kill us. But I don't really think we should just kill people without giving them a chance."

"Listen, Ruben," said the sergeant very seriously. "I fully appreciate what you mean, but regretfully, particularly when you are in the middle of a battle, it is a question of kill or be killed. You simply do not have time to ask questions. When you are a soldier, there are many things that you have to do without question. And nobody, not even your enemy, despises you for it."

Ruben looked at the sergeant quizzically, and finally said, "Yes, I suppose so, but it just doesn't seem fair."

"Fair!" laughed the sergeant. "My dear Ruben, very few things in this life are fair. I think it is sensible to realise that, and just make the best of what you have. You have many gifts and those that make you a natural soldier shouldn't be wasted. Surely it is not wise to waste a gift?" There was a long pause while his words sank in, then he said, "Come on, cheer up, and let us go to the commander's quarters. They are rather splendid. I am sure he will not object if we have a bath, and I will then get some liniment to put on your bruises. I'll have to stand you outside in the breeze then, because you will be rather smelly," he chuckled.

So they did as he had suggested. The commander's quarters were indeed grand, and a servant filled up the sunken bath with hot water, which they could both sit in without touching one another. The sergeant then wrapped a towel around himself, told Ruben to dry himself off and disappeared for a short time. He returned with a stone jar full of extremely pungent, oily liquid, which he liberally smeared and rubbed into Ruben's chest. "This will make you feel as if you are burning, but it's worth the discomfort because it heals quickly." Ruben soon realised that he was perfectly correct, his bruised ribs now felt as if they were on fire, and the smell was powerful. The sergeant led him to a small bedchamber beside the bathroom, and told him to lie on the bed. He then covered him with a fine cotton sheet and a couple of blankets, until only his face was showing. He laughed and said, "That will keep the smell inside. Now, you try to get some sleep." And as he walked quietly away, he heard Ruben's deep, easy breathing and saw that his eyes were tightly closed and realised that he must have been exhausted.

The sergeant did not feel tired himself, even though he had been physically weary. But the bath had revived him and he was still buoyed up with confidence after the pleasure that his uncle had shown following their arrival. He poured himself a goblet of wine from the polished metal jug on the table and sprawled out on the large pile of cushions. Just then, his uncle entered the room.

"No, don't get up," said the commander, waving him down. "I will join you, and you can tell me all about that rather splendid leather jerkin that the lad was wearing. My goodness, hasn't he grown! It is not even a year since I sent him to your training camp." The commander filled a goblet of wine and reclined, facing his nephew and looked at him enquiringly.

"Oh, yes, the jerkin," chuckled the sergeant. "It was made by Habib, our leatherworker, mainly to protect him from the chafing that those chains caused. That toad, Captain Uglis, ordered the chain. Mind you, it did save his life last night, but does that forgive the injustice?"

"No, it doesn't," answered the commander. "And I agree with you that Uglis is a toad. In fact he is little better than that bastard Gershnarl. But I will talk about that in a short while."

The sergeant looked at him with a puzzled expression. But before he could question the commander about Captain Uglis, the commander spoke, holding up his hand to stave off the interruption. "But the jerkin itself is very good quality, and on its own it is heavy. Now I think, even if that wasn't the intention of Uglis, it has helped build up the boy. I have hardly seen someone change so much in such a short period."

"Yes, I know what you mean," said the sergeant. "But surely you are not going to suggest that we make all the boys wear them? Apart from which, that one was made especially out of soft goatskin where it touches the parts of the body that it protects, and it's graded to the hard sun-baked, uncured crocodile skin. Habib went to great trouble making it, as a special favour. To be honest, sir, I really like the boy. He has guts and he is basically very kind, yet possesses, as well as his many abilities with weapons, a strong will to win and not be beaten. That in itself is a rare gift."

"Oh, yes I agree. I'm not suggesting that they all have special jackets, but I think a heavy crocodile skin jerkin could be made for boys that we wish to train up for the Babylonian Guards. It will single them out and could even be considered a worthy prize to strive for," answered the commander. "I think I will have to take a trip to see this leatherworker of yours. Habib, did you say? He sounds a resourceful sort of character and we will try to do a costing. Now, you enjoy yourself here for a couple of days, and then I will come with you back to the training camp and see this Habib." He raised a warning finger. "You must tell no one of this, but I already have enough evidence to nail Uglis, so I will come to arrest him. But I also need to interrogate Shaleem and then make a public display of his execution. It will send ripples through all the brigand bands. They will learn that they do not trifle with the Babylonian Army."

He finished his wine with one long draught, stood up and said, "Help yourself to anything, my boy, but don't bring too many women back here. Remember, you mustn't slur my reputation." He winked and then went out.

\*\*\*\*

The commander sat in the cell facing Shaleem and was virtually on the point of giving up the interrogation. Shaleem had determinedly sat there and constantly denied even that his name was Shaleem, despite the fact that he had been recognised by many people whilst imprisoned. The commander tried for one last time. "So you deny your name is Shaleem, and insist that you know nothing about the activities of the brigands?" There was a long silence, with the man facing him not showing any movement in his face. The commander continued. "Have you nothing to say about the attack that you carried out against two of my sergeants, the ones who brought you in early this morning?" There was another long silence, after which the commander got to his feet and said to the guard by the cell door, "Send for the sergeant of the Babylonian Guard, together with the executioner. Even if he won't admit to who he is, I am still going to have him executed, simply because I don't like the look of the rogue. I feel sure the Sergeant of the Guards can devise some suitable target practise for his men."

The guard let the commander out of the cell, locked the cell door behind him, and then rushed off to the Babylonian Guards' quarters. He soon returned with a tall young sergeant, who had only recently been promoted.

The commander said, in a loud voice to ensure that the prisoner heard him, "Ah, Sergeant Belthezder, I am sure that you can devise some form of long distance javelin and discus throwing practise for your men. We have a common bandit that nobody will miss, whom you can tether to a long rope. Make sure that none of the Guards are particularly good shots, but make sure they finish him off eventually."

He then started to walk away, but paused in mid stride when he heard the cry of, "You can't do that! I demand a trial!"

Retracing his steps Sergeant Bel dragged the man unceremoniously from the cell by the heavy chain that still bound his wrists behind his back. "Oh, yes, we can, and we will! You see, no one really knows who you are, Shaleem, and nobody will miss you anyway." Sergeant Bel dragged Shaleem to the edge of the compound, where the lashing beam was situated, where Mutek had been flogged to death by a whip of scorpions. He secured the loose end of the chain, and paced off fifty steps, where he drew a line in the hard earth with his sword. He then called over an armed guard and borrowed the man's javelin. Without even running up to the line, he hurled the javelin at the nervously waiting Shaleem who saw it coming and ducked, flinging himself to his right. The javelin flew directly to where he had been standing and stuck in the ground, with its shaft quivering. This was all too much for the brigand chief, and he shouted out to the commander who was standing near to Sergeant Bel, watching the proceedings with a certain amount of pleasure. "What do you want me to tell you?" he screamed in terror.

"I don't want you to tell us anything, except to admit that you are Shaleem," answered the commander.

The casual manner in which it had all been done was too much for Shaleem, and he now begged for his life and admitted that his name was Shaleem, but claimed that everything he had done – particularly trying to kill the two soldiers, had been on the orders of Captain Uglis.

"That's more like it," said the commander as he walked over. He spoke a few words into the sergeant's ear and came over to where Shaleem was now on his knees. "You are nothing but a dirty thief and a murdering blaggard, Shaleem, and nothing you say will make much difference in that you are going to die today. However, it is really up to you. Your death can be slow, painful and ignominious, if you continue with this charade of silence. But, if you confess to your crimes, you will be publicly executed swiftly and with dignity. Frankly, I don't give a damn what you decide."

Shaleem chose the latter, and went meekly to the commander's office and made a full confession. The commander had even called in a scribe to write down the full list of misdemeanours. It was a long and appalling list, and Shaleem realised that he had been extremely fortunate to have lived for as long as he had. He was taken out that evening to the public town square, where a large crowd had gathered to see the execution. Before Shaleem could even look at his accusers his head was severed from his body by the huge, whistling axe wielded by the masked executioner.

****

It took another few days for the commander to sort out most of the outstanding business and send a report of his intended imprisonment of Captain Uglis. This report went with the request for a martial trial that would have to be in front of a general from the Babylonian Guards, as many of the alleged misdemeanours were performed whilst Uglis was in the Babylonian Guards. Finally, a party of about forty people set out from Lagash, led by the commander who was standing proudly in his chariot, in his full regalia. A party of at least twenty men from the Babylonian Guards followed him, under the command of Sergeant Bel, his original sergeant having been promoted to captain, to replace the vacancy left by Gershnarl. The party also included Sergeant Tryone and Ruben and a variety of personnel who served the commander.

Ruben was delighted to find himself marching along beside Sergeant Bel, who had deliberately moved beside him and chatted to him like an old friend. When Ruben asked him about the interrogation of Shaleem, and about the various reports that had been circulating, the sergeant grinned and told Ruben that his speciality was in javelin throwing, which was why the commander had used him to intimidate the brigand chief. Ruben told him that he was being trained for the Babylonian Guard after all, so that Bel's prediction could well come true. Sergeant Bel also admired the jerkin that Ruben wore, and said that there was a rumour that all boys being trained up for the Guards may well wear similar crocodile skin jerkins. Ruben told him the full story behind it and then went on to compliment Bel on his promotion to sergeant. Bel said that he had been fortunate in being in the right place at the right time, with no one available to take Gershnarl's place. His previous sergeant had filled that position, so his promotion was inevitable. However, this made him the youngest sergeant in the Guards, which was indeed a considerable honour.

The morning was bright and cloudless, and the weather was getting warmer as spring arrived. Although the mountains to the north were still cloaked in snow this would not last for long with the warm wind blowing northwards from the desert in the south. Sergeant Bel asked Ruben how much longer his training would take, to which Ruben replied that he did not know. The sergeant told him that he had been informed that the garrison at Lagash was possibly going to be strengthened. After which, a small force of Babylonian Guards may well be sent just north of Sousa, where there had been quite a few border skirmishes. Nobody seemed to know whether there might be serious fighting with the Persians, or if it had all been just a local uprising caused by the Bedouin brigands. Anyway, what this effectively meant was that they would need some more recruits in the not too distant future. At this point their conversation had to be halted, as they had arrived back at the training camp. Ruben could not help considering how quick and easy the march had seemed, in comparison to when he had been brought out from Lagash the previous year. Ruben only had a brief moment to say goodbye to Sergeant Bel, as the tall sergeant was called by the commander to go with him into Uglis' office. Sergeant Bel in turn, patted Ruben on the back and said, "Cheerio lad, see you soon," and was lost to sight as Ruben went back with Sergeant Tryone to his own barrack.

****

Captain Uglis was sitting in his office, and had been wondering why he had not heard that the assassination had been completed. But he was not worried, because there had been no word from Lagash to give him any hint that things had gone wrong. So when the guard came in to say there was a large party arriving from Lagash, he thought that this was something else, on completely different business. He had come out of his office and was standing waiting to greet the commander, who he immediately recognised. He did not even see Sergeant Tryone and Ruben leave the detachment of soldiers and make their way to the barracks. He was taken by surprise when Commander Schudah, accompanied by Sergeant Bel, stood directly in front of him, not bothering to acknowledge the guard's salute or even say a word of greeting. With a serious face, his eyes staring straight and emotionless above his straight lipped unsmiling face, the commander simply said, "You are under arrest, Captain Uglis, for various serious offences concerning your dealings with the Bedouin brigands. In particular your intended assassination of Sergeant Tryone and Ruben Ben Uriah, which I am pleased to inform you was unsuccessful. All of these offences have been listed and you will be taken for trial on the charge of high treason." He ordered the guard away, turned to Sergeant Bel and said, "Lock him in his office, where he should be manacled and guarded by your men until we leave in a few days' time. I have other business here, as well as ensuring that the training camp continues uninterrupted."

Sergeant Bel placed a strong arm on Captain Uglis' shoulder and pushed him backward into his office. The still puzzled captain almost fell over his own feet. Although he was a big man, he knew he was no match for Sergeant Bel, who was a well-muscled young Guardsman, stronger and fitter. Apart from that, he was still in a state of shock, and the sergeant had twenty of the Babylonian Guards under his command. The sergeant bound Uglis' wrists with a leather thong behind his back, and pushed him down until he was squatting on the floor. He then tied his feet together with the captain's own leather bootlaces, and commenced searching the room for any sharp weapons. He took Uglis' short sword from his belt, together with his large sword that was hanging on the wall. He also found a handful of other potential weapons that could have been used to free the captain. With this bundle of weapons, he left the still stunned captain sitting on the floor and went out. He barred and locked the door behind him.

In the meantime, Commander Schudah had gone in search of the leather worker, Habib, who he found hard at work repairing equipment. The commander came straight to the point, after introducing himself and, pacing up and down, he began, "Now Habib, you will undoubtedly remember the special jerkin that you made for Ruben Ben Uriah, following the request from Sergeant Tryone. What I would like, and do remember this would have to be cheap, are some leather jerkins made out of the heavy uncured crocodile hide for boys who are going to be trained for the Babylonian Guard."

"Are they going to be to protect the boys from chains?" enquired Habib, immediately warming to the task.

"Oh no," replied the commander. "They would be decorative and heavy enough in their own right."

"So they wouldn't have to be lined with soft leather?" Queried Habib, half to himself. "In that case the job could be done quite easily, but obviously it depends how many you would want."

"Probably about thirty, to start with," replied the commander.

"Let me see," said Habib, rubbing his chin thoughtfully. He wandered down the workshop, muttering to himself all the time as he looked into all the shelves and checked on various skins. "I will want probably about four large crocodile hides and I think I can make up the rest with supplies that I already have."

"That sounds fine," responded the commander. He indicated to one of his servants. "Tell this man exactly what you need, and I will see if it's financially viable."

He then left the leatherworker's hut and went to the main mess hall, which was the largest building in the camp. He called over to one of his other servants and told the man to find Sergeant Tryone, and tell him to meet him in the main mess hall as soon as possible. The man scampered away to do as instructed. Meanwhile, the commander went over to the cooks and enquired if they had enough food to supply his party. Having assured himself that by staying at the camp for a couple of days he would not deplete their food supplies, he was pleased to find Sergeant Tryone waiting for him.

"Now Tryone, what I would like to do is this. Please tell me if it would cause a lot of difficulties." He paused before continuing. "I would like to appoint you as captain of this camp, but as you are a relative of mine, I will need to get special permission to do that. In the meantime, do you think that the training camp could continue under the direction of the sergeants all working together?"

Tryone laughed. "It has been working like that ever since Uglis took over, sir."

"Really? As bad as that, was he? So obviously that would be quite suitable."

"Without a doubt, sir," said Sergeant Tryone, smiling with pleasure at the prospect of being in charge.

"Good, that's settled then. Now I would like you to assemble all the sergeants out by Uglis' office, whilst the boys are having their midday meal. Oh yes, and find Sergeant Bel for me please."

He left the main mess hall and was wandering back to the captain's office, where he met Sergeant Bel.

"I understand you were looking for me, sir?" enquired the sergeant.

"Ah yes," said the commander. "I want you to find somewhere to lock up Uglis, and you can then pack all your men in one of the spare barrack huts. I am afraid they are unfinished, but that should not hurt big strong healthy Guardsmen," he chortled.

"I know just the place to put Uglis," smiled the sergeant. "It is a rather smelly latrine. But it is on its own, and will be easy to guard. And I can certainly billet my men. How long do you think we will stay, sir?" he asked.

"I just need long enough to make sure everything is running

smoothly. I won't really be happy until we get Uglis back in Lagash, so we will only be staying for a couple of days."

Uglis was taken from his office and securely locked in the latrine, allowing the commander to use his office, which had a small bedroom attached to it. Having contented himself that all his men had been safely billeted, and all the trainees were in the main mess hall eating their midday meal, he went back to the office, where all the training sergeants were waiting. He got them to squeeze into the office and perched himself on the desk before addressing them all.

"I understand that you have been running this camp yourselves since Captain Uglis was appointed. That is not how it should be done. However, I am going to ask you to keep doing it like that for the time being. My intention is to have Sergeant Tryone take over the camp; he is after all, the senior sergeant. As you know, he is my nephew, so I'm having to get special permission for that appointment, which may take a while." He paused, looking around the assembled faces to see if there were any questions. As there were none, he dismissed the sergeants and told them to simply tell all the trainees that Captain Uglis was being replaced. He then said, "Before you go back to the training, I want you all to select a few boys from each platoon who you think may be good enough for the Babylonian Guard. They will then be trained up specially and I want them ready by the end of next summer, not this year, but next year. Is that understood?" Having no questions put to him, he dismissed the sergeants. They had all been surprised at his calm efficiency and attention to detail. They soon realised that this was not simply what made him a good commander, but it was a family trait. Sergeant Tryone possessed a similar efficiency.

Having received full details of what was needed by the leatherworker in the way of crocodile skins, as well as having made sure that everything was back on an even keel, he took his party back to Lagash, complete with Uglis in chains behind the chariot and surrounded by Babylonian Guards. Uglis had tried on two occasions to escape, but not being very resourceful, his attempts had been easily thwarted. Sergeant Bel was also a happy man, as this mission had been accomplished to everyone's satisfaction. He was also pleased at the possible prospect of a new detachment of Babylonian Guards joining them in the not too distant future.

****

Life in the training camp continued as before, with the exception of the new platoon of trainees. From Sergeant Tryone's platoon, Ruben was obviously one of the chosen few, but everyone waited with baited breath to see whom Sergeant Tryone would select to join him. No one was really surprised that the sergeant's nephew was chosen. Apart from being a favourite with the sergeant, he was skilful with weapons and fairly tough. Ruben was not surprised that the other strong lad was chosen, but was delighted that Latich was also chosen to wear the crocodile jerkin.

Sergeant Tryone had just received a message saying that he would be appointed to captain, and was moving into the captain's office when there was a knock on his door and the guard came in.

"I have Ben Uriah outside, sir, requesting to see you, but he won't tell me what it's about. Can I show him in?" asked the guard.

"Yes, send him in," replied Captain Tryone.

Once the door was shut behind him, Ruben said, "I am sorry to trouble you, sir, but I have what may seem a rather strange request."

"Come on then, lad, out with it. After all, I can only say no!" he grinned.

"I was wondering if I could have the chain back to wear. It has a special significance for me, and in a strange way I quite enjoy the challenge of being handicapped," he requested.

The sergeant looked at him for a while, and then slowly smiled. "Here you are, Ruben. I have been expecting the request, as I have got to know you over the last half year." He laughed, and produced the chain from the drawer of his desk. "Before you go," he said. "We are experiencing some difficulties in obtaining crocodile skins. As you know the marshes, and Ur in particular, do you know anywhere that we could buy the necessary hides?"

Ruben thought for a while, and then replied, "I do remember that there was a man who is specialised in catching crocodiles, and I believe that he had a shop near to the inn where I was staying. But I was only there for a for about eight days, so I don't know the man's name."

"That's good enough to go on," said the captain. "We can get a messenger to start from there." He was about to dismiss Ruben when he noticed the boy looking at him expectantly. He looked up and said, "I cannot send you, so don't even ask."

"I understand, sir. I fully understand and I wasn't going to ask, but would it be possible for you to send a message to someone for me?" he requested.

"As a special favour, Ruben, so don't tell anyone else. Is it to a special friend, or even a member of your family that you have not mentioned before?" asked the captain.

"Just a friend that I made at the inn. She works there," he replied.

"I see," laughed the captain. "You young scoundrel. Sending

messages to your girlfriend is hardly army business. All right Ruben, just this once, so tell me what you would like to say."

Ruben flushed bright pink, and said, "It is to a girl called Lialah. Tell her that I am well, and ask her to tell her Uncle Simeon that I will not forget everything he taught me, and that I hope to return to see him as soon as I can."

Captain Tryone stared at Ruben. This was indeed a strange message; obviously there was an enormous amount that was not being mentioned. He eventually said, "All right Ruben, I will do that for you." He thought about asking about who this Simeon was, but as Ruben said nothing more and shifted uneasily on his feet, he thought that he had better not ask. He told Ruben that the message would go the very next day, and dismissed him.

The next day the message went off with a trusted corporal, whose main job was to negotiate for large crocodile hides. The corporal returned about five days later with a pack mule loaded with the requested crocodile hides. When the captain asked him about the message, the corporal said that he had delivered the message, but that there had been no reply. The crocodile hides were soon made into leather jerkins, and it was all done well within the budget that had been set. Very soon the new platoon of lads who were to be trained for the Babylonian Guards were issued with the new jerkins, and their training began in earnest, under the direct supervision of Captain Tryone.

He had quite forgotten about the strange message as the days lengthened and midsummer passed. The hottest time of the year was over and it was beginning to cool down now, much to the relief of the new trainees, who had been nicknamed the Crocs. They were all doing surprisingly well, and seemed to wear the new jerkins with immense pride. Captain Tryone was standing watching the Crocs finish an obstacle course, which was inevitably won by Ruben, despite the chains. He never seemed to stop growing. The captain was just thinking that he would be as tall as Sergeant Bel, or possibly even bigger, when a messenger came up to him holding out a scroll of parchment. He said that a passing merchant who was on his way to Sousa had delivered the message. Tryone unrolled the scroll, which was addressed to the officer in charge. The script was in bold handwriting, written in a curious style. It asked him to tell Ruben that his treasure was safe. His silent friend and Simeon awaited his return, and that Simeon's niece sent her love. It was signed with a large S, and there was another line after that which said: "Remember the works of The Creator and look after his creatures", This was unusual, particularly the last line.

Captain Tryone sent for Ruben, and returned to his office in a state of bewilderment. When Ruben arrived, he asked him if he could read. Ruben told him that he knew some of the letters and a few easy words, but that he had not been taught properly. The captain explained that he had received a scroll from Ur, which told him that his friend was well and looking forward to seeing him. However, the captain did not tell Ruben everything the scroll had said. He did not understand it himself, but told Ruben that he would keep it for him. Also, that if Ruben wished to learn to read and write, he would try and arrange it, but it would have to be done in addition to the normal training. He dismissed Ruben, and retired that night in a disturbed state. He had come across unorthodox and strange beliefs before. They always confused him, and what was more, they confused the minds of young soldiers. Ruben was one of the most natural fighting men that he had ever trained, and despite the basic rule that allowed any form of religious belief to be held, he did not want the boy's natural soldiering abilities to be disturbed. Admittedly, he could always fall back on the basic credo that it was none of his business. However, because he was conscientious and wanted the boy to succeed, he did not want him to fill his head with strange ideas.

# 6
# THE CROCS

As their third winter approached, it was decided to let the new platoon train with real weapons, rather than wooden ones. These weapons were of the standard army issue and weight, but they were not sharp, for the obvious reason of not inflicting fatal injuries. However, a blow from a heavy bronze sword, even if it was not sharp, could easily break bones or injure ligaments or muscles. Therefore, the training officer had to be particularly vigilant. They got the boys to work in pairs of fairly even abilities to ensure that there were not too many injuries. None of the boys was ever without one or two bruises, but this taught them to respect one another and the tools of their trade.

After a few weeks the boys were encouraged to take up at least one weapon in which to specialise. Many of them were good with several weapons, so it was difficult to decide on which one they would choose. Ruben was one of these, particularly because of his stature; he could wield an axe, use a long sword, and throw a javelin or a discus well. However, as the thought of using his long sword was always in the back of his mind, he opted for the large sword. Not being content with this, Captain Tryone also wanted him to be a javelin thrower, which Ruben also enjoyed doing. That was also Sergeant Bel's main weapon – and Sergeant Bel was his undoubted hero. Because Ruben specialised in two weapons, he had to work for a long time every day. In addition to this, true to his word, Captain Tryone announced one day that if anyone wished, they could attend reading and writing classes. These would be held late in the evening, after all the weapons were locked in the armoury. Quite a few boys decided to try this out, mainly because you could not be promoted any higher than a sergeant if you could not follow written instructions. Some of the boys, even though they had elected to try this, found it difficult and dropped out, particularly if they had no previous experience. Fortunately for Ruben, as his uncle had been a boat builder and had used plans, he already knew some of the basic letters and techniques. He enjoyed the evening classes, as they exercised the mind rather than his physical abilities, which by the end of the day were well used.

Ruben also found that mental exercises stopped his mind from wandering away from soldiering, as once the basic principles of reading and writing were accomplished, they always worked on army exercises, such as the number of weapons needed, the numbers and weights of rations, and even on more complex ideas of strategy, which Ruben found exciting.

One evening in the middle of winter they were introduced to working with maps. Ruben found this easy to understand as he had used maps before, and he became involved in a complicated discussion with the teacher when the lesson ended. When the other boys went out to the main mess hall to get some supper he found himself alone with the teacher and they continued their discussion. The teacher suddenly saw how late it was, and asked Ruben to return the maps to Captain Tryone's office. Happily agreeing to this chore, he scooped up an armful of scrolls and went over to the captain's office. He knocked on the door and waited until he heard the reply of, "Enter." He then went in with the maps and found Captain Tryone sitting by the small hearth, eating his supper with a goblet of wine. When the captain saw that it was Ruben, he relaxed and said, "Just dump the maps on my desk, Ruben." Turning his face towards the fire he called over his shoulder, "Have you eaten?"

"No, sir," replied Ruben looking up and adding, "I had better hurry back, otherwise there will be nothing left."

"You will probably find there is nothing left now anyway, but you are welcome to join me, I have plenty," invited the captain.

"Thank you very much, that's very kind of you, sir," said Ruben. He laid the maps tidily on the desk. The captain got another plate out for Ruben and was putting out some food for him. As he finished tidying up the maps Ruben's eyes fell to the open drawer of the desk and saw an unusual scroll that was open at the end and he could not help noticing the large S in an unusual script. His mind immediately flashed back to that occasion in late summer almost a year and a half earlier when the captain had told him about the scroll from his friend and had said that he would keep it for him.

Ruben quietly shut the drawer and came over to where the captain had filled up his plate. He sat by the fire and tucked in to his meal. The captain couldn't help noticing the sudden change that had come over Ruben – from being his polite chatty self he was suddenly withdrawn. In an attempt to restore the situation, the captain asked, "How did you get on with the maps?"

After a brief silence, Ruben seemed to wake out of his reverie, and said, "Oh, I am sorry, sir. Yes the maps, they were fine. I had no difficulty in understanding the maps at all. In fact I have used a map before. The one that I remember very well was when I was going to Ur. The map had previously been folded, and the path that I needed was right on the fold and it wasn't clear at all."

To keep the conversation going the captain said, "But you found what you were looking for, did you?"

"Yes, but I had temporarily lost my way because I took the wrong road, as the map was unclear." He smiled reflectively. But of course this simply made him think back to the sword and he went on eating in silence.

The captain became rather concerned, so he stopped the boy from eating and said, "Is there something troubling you, Ruben?"

"Well, yes, there is, sir, actually. You see, I saw that scroll from my friend Simeon, the one that came almost two years ago. The one you said that you would save for me. I was just wondering what it said. Could I possibly have a look at it?"

"I see," said the captain. "Oh, nothing that I didn't tell you. It's basically an acknowledgement of your message. But don't worry, I will give it to you, later on." He tried to make his voice sound normal and conversational. "How are you getting on with the javelin? Do you think you can challenge Sergeant Bel yet?" The commander hoped that talking about Sergeant Bel would stop him thinking about the scroll with the strange message.

"I'm getting on really well, sir. I don't know how far Sergeant Bel can throw the javelin, but I bet it's a long way."

"Oh, yes," said the captain. "The commander told me that when he used Bel to intimidate Shaleem, he threw the javelin at fifty paces without even running up. And it was quite casual, from what I understand."

"Gosh!" spluttered Ruben, half choking on the goblet of wine that the captain had given him. "I'm not that good yet."

Realising that this ploy had worked, the captain said, "Well, you keep practising, because I want you to be able to at least challenge him, when you finish your training at the end of the coming summer."

"I didn't realise it was so soon – how quickly the time seems to have gone," exclaimed Ruben.

"Yes, I'm afraid the commander has set us quite a task. But if you continue your hard work, I'm sure you'll be ready," said the captain encouragingly.

"I'll do that, and thank you very much for the meal, sir. It was most welcome." Ruben put down his plate. "Good night, sir, and thanks again."

"Good night, my boy," said the captain, with sincere relief.

This had certainly cured Ruben's curiosity regarding the scroll, as he had no reason to disbelieve Captain Tryone. On the contrary, he trusted him implicitly and knew that the scroll would be given to him when he had mastered the art of reading. But he knew that at the moment he would struggle trying to make out the strange characters. Anyway he now had a definite ambition: to try to reach the fifty pace mark for throwing the javelin.

The very next day, after all the standard practise, when they were allowed to practise with their specialised weapons, Ruben took out three javelins from the armoury. Apart from there being nobody to pair up with to use the large swords, he decided to measure out fifty paces and see how near to the bank he could hit. He found that it was a question of throwing the javelin at a certain angle in order to achieve maximum distance. If he threw it too low it would drop to the earth and stick in with more force than was necessary. If he threw it too high it would fall and stick in but with all the effort being used in throwing it high. However, he could get the angle right by visualising the target person about so many paces above where he would be, which depended on how far away he was. In this way he could get the javelin to go the required distance with it retaining enough force to penetrate the target. He was surprised to realise that he could manage an object at forty paces, using a reasonable run before letting fly. But when he thought about a fifty pace throw without running up, it must mean that Sergeant Bel would be able to throw something like seventy-five or eighty paces, which simply had the effect of heightening his esteem of his hero.

He realised that the sergeant in charge of arms had been watching him and called him over to ask him what he was doing. Ruben explained that he was trying to throw the javelin as far as he could and he had heard that someone else had been able to throw fifty paces without running up. The sergeant asked him how many paces he could throw without running up. Ruben said that he did not know, but he would soon find out. He tried and was delighted to realise that it was only just a little bit shorter than the forty paces that he had originally managed with a run up. The sergeant of arms was becoming very interested in what the boy was trying to do. He gave him a few hints and lessons, which developed into a complete training session on javelin throwing. Ruben learnt that using a run up was important, but you had to stop the run and use the forward momentum to throw the javelin. By doing this he was putting all the forward momentum of his body behind the throw. It took quite a lot of practise, but by the end of the afternoon he was throwing the javelin up to the sixty pace limit. He wanted to continue, but the sergeant of arms told him that it was impossible to continue that form of exercise for too long as he could easily put undue strain on certain parts of his body. The sergeant of arms said that he would help him by working out a schedule to do a certain amount each day, and he would then evaluate his progress. He had also learnt during the morning's sword practise, that it was far easier to kill an opponent with the point of the sword in a forward lunge or thrust, than in a large sideways swipe. All in all he had learnt a basic principle: that a ing soldiers had shown no sign of panic. The brigand chief was about rally his men, some of whom still stood undecided, when another elin whistled very close to his head. That made his mind up and he lowed his men into the rocks where they gradually melted away twards, away from this devilish band of young soldiers.

The band of ten trainee soldiers waited, nervously watching the rocks, they feared that the brigands might be rallying for another attack. But en no attack came, Ruben told them to keep a close eye on all the rocks ile he went out to retrieve his two javelins, one of which still had a ear of blood on it. He wiped this off on a sod of grass and checked ound to ensure that it was safe. He made his way back to the small band, ho were all excited at their easy victory. They had just stood down and ere talking excitedly about vanquishing a brutal larger force of brigands hen Ruben realised that the other arrow that was shot in the air probably eant that they should dash over to the other group in order to give aid. e quickly ordered the band back into order and was about to command em to dash off to where the other arrow had been seen, when Captain ryone came running hard with a drawn sword, followed by the other wenty trainees.

He asked Ruben what had happened and received a concise report aying that the attacking brigand force had decided against pressing home heir attack when the small force of soldiers stood their ground and fired pon them. Ruben mentioned nothing about his own javelin throwing that had wrought such havoc. The captain congratulated him and all his party for standing their ground and apologised for being late in arriving. Ruben said, "Well, I realised that you would be quite a while, when I saw the other flaming arrow that was fired in the sky."

The captain explained. "I am sorry about that. There was a mix up, and it should not have been fired."

"No problem, sir, it is just that we feared we might be needed, and we've only just got ready to set out again."

As all the boys chatted to one another about what had happened, the captain said that they could all have a short break, as he was still breathless. He called to his nephew and asked him which of his bowmen had fired the arrow. Given the boy's name, he called him over and was about to tell him off for causing what could have been a fatal accident.

Ruben, who was standing nearby talking to Latich, came over and said, "Don't be too hard on him, sir, I am sure that one of my lads might have done same the thing. It is really the person commanding the group who must take responsibility." This was an accusation against the captain's nephew and a deep silence fell over the whole gathering, as there was a lot of tension in the situation.

great deal of weapon training was in technique rather than just strength.

He talked to Latich that evening over supper, about this whole principle. Latich said, "Well, I fully understand and to a large extent I probably agree with you. But I find if I fight just by parrying your blows, it makes my arms ache, because you put so much force into each stroke. So that in itself must be important."

Ruben looked puzzled and said, "What do you mean?"

"I mean in tiring out your opponent," answered Latich.

"Oh, yes. So it is really a combination of using strength and technique," said Ruben decisively.

They had also been taught to concentrate their efforts on areas that needed a lot of improvement. Latich had asked Ruben to help him build up his upper body strength, so he and Ruben had started exercising without weapons. This they did by pushing or pulling their own weight up and down, in a series of laying flat on the ground and pushing themselves up with their hands, or hanging from the branch of a tree or a doorway beam, and pulling themselves up and down. They found that by counting the number they did each day and gradually trying to increase it, everyday was showing a great improvement. They not only felt fitter, but they looked stronger as it seemed to build up muscles that showed much more. They soon got into the habit of exercising first thing in the morning, and last thing at night, before they collapsed into a deep, exhausted sleep.

The winter soon passed, and one morning the captain said, "I have been informed that there are some brigands in the area. Before I get one of the new patrols to go out to the seaside for their camp training, I want the Crocs to go on a route march with weapons, to ensure that the area is safe." This caused a great deal of excitement, as they had previously been forbidden to carry weapons outside the camp. They had spent a lot of time marching round and round the interior of the camp's perimeter, carrying their weapons. Doing each lap at a different pace: one lap marching, another lap trotting, another lap marching, with the occasional lap thrown in when they used to run flat out. This had been hard exercise, as they were carrying full weapons and the whole perimeter of the camp was a large distance. But the whole aspect of doing a route march, with full equipment, outside the camp really made them feel like soldiers. The captain's motive had simply been to scare off any small bands of brigands. They were, therefore, fully equipped not only with weapons, but each with a bronze helmet and leather breastplate, which was buckled over their shifts and under their crocodile skin jerkins. The only difference between this form of dress and full uniform was that their shifts were a variety of colours and very few of them wore short kilts. Even those who only wore one that denoted the family that they came from, as opposed to the dark red army issue, or even the purple of the Babylonian Guards. There was still quite a lot of pent up excitement as they were fully equipped and readied to set off. The captain split them into three groups. He said there were three different routes down to the camping area, one that circled round to the left, that being the east side and one going round to the right, that being the west side. He put his nephew in charge of the party going on the west side, and put Ruben in charge of the party going on the east side. He said, "I will give you both a short head start and then I will come along with the third group directly towards the Inferior Sea."

"What happens if we see any brigands?" said one of the lads, rather excitedly.

"I doubt if you will," laughed the captain. "I am sure if there are any in the area they will slink away when they see that you are armed, like the jackals that they are. But if you do see anything you are to fire a smoking arrow straight in the air. And if anyone sees an arrow like this, everyone should head for it." He ensured that each party had one bowman with an ox fat soaked cloth tied around an arrow, which would burn with black, oily smoke. They were all buzzing with excitement now. Although the captain felt it was fairly safe, he kept a serious expression so that they all felt this was the real thing.

The captain ordered them into ranks and marched them out of the camp. He took them for a few moments, until they were out of site of the camp. He drew his nephew and Ruben to one side and said, "You see the shadow cast by that small tree," pointing to a small jacaranda tree that was just coming into bloom, with the onset of summer. He placed a flat stone a little way from where its shadow lay. He said, "Both take your parties at a fairly fast pace. When that stone is touched by the shadow from the tree, I will set off with my party down the main track and hopefully we will arrive at the Inferior Sea at the same time." Both Ruben and the captain's nephew realised that they did not have a long start, so they both set off with their parties at a fast trot, with the sun shining on the bronze helmets and their armaments clattering. The captain gave them slightly longer than he originally said he would, but it was not long before he led the third group at a good pace towards the Inferior Sea.

The captain's party had just passed the normal halfway stage, when to their left a smoking arrow soared into the sky. He halted his excited party as he was rather surprised. Although he had received reports of brigands in the area, his information had led him to believe that there were only parties of two or three strong. A small party of brigands of that size would certainly keep well away from ten fully armed trainees. He was about to order his party to go in the direction of the smoking arrow, when another arrow went up to their right. This was most peculiar, but he had to make a

quick decision on which party he should go to assist.
was slightly stronger in bowmen and as arrows might l
bay, even though they were not sharply pointed, he
direction to where his nephew was. He said to his grou
fast as you can and make plenty of noise as we go." His
excited trainees almost bumped into his nephew's band,
no brigands in sight. He breathlessly asked his nephew w
a flaming arrow.

His nephew apologised and said, "I am sorry, sir, bu
bowman got it wrong. He thought he had to fire it in ackn
the first arrow."

Ruben's party had seen the band of brigands, w
surprised. Ruben had instructed his bowman to fire a s
although the brigands had not initially seemed like they
attack. The warning arrow had changed their ideas. The
twenty strong and well armed. Their leader guessed tha
young soldiers was only half their number, but if he had gue
that the smoking arrow would bring more troops, his p
doomed. He therefore told his men to attack the small
brigands drew their swords and knives, Ruben saw the othe
to his right climb into the sky. He realised that they coul
immediate aid and that all his boys looked towards him as the
warrior. He ordered his lads to stand fast and not to run into
they would be hunted down in ones or twos, and killed.
correctly that the brigands didn't have any weapons except sw
and cudgels. Out of his ten lads, four of them were bown
ordered them to shoot directly at the brigand leader. None of
struck home, which was possibly just as well as they were not 
the brigands felt they were being attacked by a fearsome part
soldiers. They did not recognise the strange crocodile skin j
possibly thought that this was a new and skilled party, as
immediately attacked. However, they knew there was no alterna
fight. They gathered their courage and followed their leader,
drawn his broad sword and was waving it like as scythe. Rube
only person in his party with a deadly weapon, as the javelins
pointed bronze heads. He waited as his bowmen reloaded new
notching them to their bowstrings. He then hurled one of his three
directly at the brigand chief, who led the charge of his men. The
brought him down, badly gashing his thigh and, as four more
whistled amongst the other brigands, most of them turned and f
the rocks. Seeing their chief brought down by the javelin and tryin
to his feet, with blood running down his leg, had been too mu

The Captain felt trapped. He wanted, out of family loyalty, to support his nephew, but he knew that Ruben was right. He had also overheard some of the other boys talking about the javelin throwing, and that it had been the deciding factor. So he did not try to support his nephew and rebuff Ruben. He therefore quietly said to Ruben, "Yes, you are probably correct. I will have an inquest into it later. But first we must check out the whole area, and then continue to the Inferior Sea."

Accordingly, he got the boys to fan out on either side of the track and they made their way to the Inferior Sea, ensuring that the area was quite deserted. Just as they reached the sea one of the boys on the outskirts of the party called out, "Come and have a look at this, sir." The captain told the other boys to remain where they were and went in the direction of the shout. When he reached the point where the boy had called, he recognised the area as being the place that he and Ruben had fought against the brigands just over two years previously. The boy was agitated and was pointing to a skull and a few scattered human bones lying around a spear shaft. The skeleton was all that remained of the brigand that Ruben had speared. The vultures and other carrion eaters had made short work of the body that they had not had either the time or the strength to bury. The sight made the captain realise that this could easily have been both himself and Ruben. He took the boy away from the spot and called the other lads together down by the sea. As it was now about the middle of the day, he instructed the boys to make a small campfire and eat the food that they had brought with them. Whilst this was being done, he backtracked to the site where the bones were scattered. The brigands had obviously returned to the spot and stripped the corpse of any weapons, money and jewellery. However, as the spearhead was badly buckled, notched and burred, they had left it. It was typical of their sort that they had not bothered to cover what remained of the body, but had let the carrion eaters finish off the corpse. Although the captain was not a particularly religious man, he considered that all the variety of gods that were worshipped may have some significance, but had never thought deeply about the subject. He was aware however that the scene of a skeleton could be quite distressing, as it was in the normal custom for bodies to be buried. He therefore dug a shallow grave and quickly covered the bones and skull. Apart from anything else, this act of being alone gave him time to reflect upon the situation in which he had been placed, where he had promised an inquest. He realised that the inquest was more of a re-examination of his own principles that was at question. He knew that he had been a good training sergeant and so far his captaincy had progressed smoothly, but he realised that he had been over generous to his nephew in the past and until now this had not been questioned, although it had obviously been talked about behind his back. One of the main reasons for his show of favouritism was that he had promised his brother, when his brother was dying, that he would ensure that his nephew was well looked after. He had always been loyal to his promise, but now realised that in some respects he had been over zealous, and that was not doing the boy any favours. Having completed his self-appointed task, he returned to the camp that the boys had made. Here he was delighted to see that a small group of lads had started a fire and were sorting out the provisions. The small stream had been dammed lightly to make a place where water bottles could be refilled. It was not really warm enough for swimming or washing in the water. In fact, everything was running remarkably smoothly and he soon became aware that it had all been done under the direction of Ruben, who had automatically slipped into the role of leader. The rest of the day was uneventful, everything was in order down at the camp training ground and there had been no sign of anyone else in the area on their march back to the main training camp.

As he had promised, he called an inquest into the events of the morning shortly after they arrived back at the camp. He firstly spoke to the lad who had shot the arrow into the air when no signal had been required. He pointed out the error to the boy and said that it had been a foolish thing to do, which could have proved fatal, and that in future he must always check any action like that with his commanding officer. However, he did not impose any penalty on the boy, who went away relieved, after promising not to make the same mistake again. He then sent for his nephew and explained, with a stern expression that he had never used previously when addressing the boy, that his actions were not those of a potential leader. He also told him that he had incorrectly shown him preferential treatment in the past, but as the boy was now old enough and capable of maintaining his own position he would no longer receive any special favour. He then dismissed his nephew and sent for Ruben. He told Ruben that he had been perfectly correct and that the matter had been sorted out. Then he changed the subject, and said, "You didn't tell me about your excellent javelin throwing. I also understand that you have been practising throwing long distance. How far can you throw now?" he asked.

"About sixty-eight paces, sir," said Ruben proudly. "And I seem to be able to increase every time I throw."

"So, you think you can take on Sergeant Bel yet?" asked the captain.

"Well, I'll certainly do my best, sir," Ruben replied.

"Well, you have roughly sixty days," said the captain. "I have decided to bring forward the date for your graduation trial, to try to please Commander Schudah."

Ruben left the captain in a state of euphoria. The whole day had been highly successful and he now had sixty days to improve his javelin throwing and then take on the famous Sergeant Bel. He went to bed that night with grim determination, and a plan that he would immediately put into effect to improve his distance. He also considered that as the date for the trials had been moved closer, it would probably mean that everything else had to be hurried along, so that he would get little chance for additional practise. He would go to bed in state of virtual collapse every evening from now on.

****

The following day, when their normal weapon practise was over and he had spent a short time practising with a large sword, Ruben went over to the sergeant of arms who had been giving him the javelin training, and asked, "Sergeant, do you have any heavier javelins?"

The sergeant looked at him with surprise, "No, Ruben, all are standard issue. Why do you ask?"

"Well, I was wondering if by using a heavier javelin, it would build up my strength so that I could, after a while, throw a normal javelin even further," Ruben replied.

The sergeant of arms laughed and he said, "You seem to have developed the idea from wearing those heavy chains of yours. But I don't really think it would work with javelin throwing. If you used a heavier javelin it might increase your stamina and throwing power, but it would adversely affect the balance, which is crucial, so I don't think your idea would work."

"Oh dear," said Ruben. "I now have only sixty days, and I was hoping to get to the eighty pace mark by then."

"I am afraid that there is no way, except practising, and you mustn't keep practising when you're tired," said the sergeant. "But I tell you what I will do. If you come first thing in the morning to have a few throws, then do a few more in the normal afternoon session, I will make one javelin available in the evening."

Ruben was delighted with the suggestion and said, "Thank you very much, sir, that will be a great advantage." He then took his javelin and was about to begin his normal practise when the sergeant came up to him again.

"Look, Ruben, I think it would be a good idea to leave your jerkin off. You will find you will be able to get a faster run up," he advised. This sounded sensible, so Ruben followed the suggestion and placed his jerkin beside the javelin racks. Much to his surprise he was able to throw well over the seventy paces mark. The sergeant also advised him that throwing over seventy paces would be a waste of time, simply because an enemy that far away would have plenty of time to dodge out of the way. The sergeant said that fifty paces was the maximum distance for target practise, but if they increased that to seventy paces nobody else would be well practised at that distance. After spending another long training session, the sergeant said, "Off you go now, but come back after supper just before your evening reading and writing lessons. I will have a target set up for you, with one javelin that I can arrange to be left out."

Ruben picked up his jerkin, which still bore the heavy chains, and dashed off to his next discipline, putting on the jerkin as he ran. He was now well used to the weight and it did not bother him. This next discipline was another extra item that had been included in their daily routine. This was a special obstacle course, which they had to negotiate with full kit. It included jumping over low walls, swinging on a rope over an imaginary chasm and crawling underneath a large patch of thorn bushes – this was called the assault course. All the boys then went for their supper, during which Ruben had told Latich that with all the extra training that had to be completed, he felt that they would have to give up their evening and morning exercises, otherwise they would just be too exhausted. Ruben was surprised when Latich readily agreed to this suggestion. Latich said, "I am glad you suggested that because to be perfectly honest it was all getting a bit too much for me."

Ruben laughed. "Well, you're not the only one. With all the extra training we're going to have to do you'll find you'll build up plenty of strength anyway."

It seemed no time at all before Ruben was back throwing the javelin in the darkening sky where the sergeant of arms had placed a dummy target figure between two lit torches at the seventy pace mark. As Ruben left the javelin-throwing site and dashed off to his evening reading and writing class he noticed that stars brilliantly lit the evening sky. They seemed so close you could almost pick them from the sky, where they hung like bunches of grapes.

The teacher of the reading and writing class was waiting for Ruben as he ran up to the door with an apologetic grin. He panted, "I am so sorry if I kept you waiting, sir, but our deadline has been brought forward so we're all trying to get in as much practise as possible."

"That's all right, young man," said the teacher, who was a newcomer to the camp. He had been brought in from outside the army for this class and he was actually a philosopher and an astrologer by profession. He was interested as Ruben asked him about the strange phenomena of the bright stars. The teacher said that it was a sign that meant that they were going to have a very hot, long, dry summer and muttered something else, almost under his breath, about this being a portent of something that was happening away to the west, probably an important birth. He said to Ruben, "Yes, I have heard about the captain's decision to speed up your training, but that means each lesson will have to be slightly longer if we are also to finish at the same time. You are not really late. I too was looking at the stars. I wasn't particularly waiting for you, but now you're here we must get on." That evening the class went on longer than normal, and all the other lights were out when they retired to their barrack huts. Everyone was mentally and physically tired and with hardly a word spoken they all crawled into bed and were soon fast asleep.

This situation continued day after day. All the training was speeded up but nothing was left out. The lads worked hard and an excellent camaraderie had built up in the platoon, with everyone striving to reach his maximum ability in his chosen areas. Obviously for a few of the lads, like Ruben, who had chosen more than one weapon to specialise in, it meant very hard work indeed. But Ruben was the only person with more than one specialised weapon who was attending the reading and writing class. The philosopher had been perfectly correct in his weather forecast as it turned into one of the hottest and driest summers that Ruben could remember.

One day during breakfast in the main mess hall, the captain announced that the well in the camp was running low, so everyone would have to be careful with the amount of water that they consumed. He asked if anyone had any experience of wells and their workings. He was hardly surprised when Ruben said that he knew a little about wells. He explained that there might be a blockage to the watercourse where the well had been dug. The captain had come to realise that apart from Ruben's many physical attributes, he was also a very bright lad whose natural curiosity had made him learn a lot about all aspects of life.

"How and when did you find out this information, Ruben?" The captain asked.

"When I was staying in Ur, Captain, they had a well that had remarkably clear water, not at all like the ordinary brackish water in the marsh lands, and I made enquiries and spoke to the person who built it," explained Ruben. "You see, most wells are dug to find underground streams and it might be a situation of our stream drying up, due to the weather. But it could also mean that the stream has been blocked."

"I see," said Captain Tryone. "And how do we find out the cause?"

"Well, someone has to go down and see," answered Ruben. "And I'd like to offer myself, sir."

Most of the others had lost interest in the matter, and returned to their breakfast and the events of the day. But as this was an important matter, the captain agreed to lower Ruben down the well to see if there was anything that could be done. On their way out to the well they saw the leatherworker going towards his workshop. The captain called him over and asked if he had a leather sling that they could fit onto the lowering rope in place of the wooden bucket. Habib said that he had the perfect item. So whilst he went to fetch it, Ruben and the captain made their way to the well where Habib soon joined them. With his strong hands and fingers, Habib quickly detached the wooden bucket and attached the leather sling. He and Captain Tryone held the winding handle of the drum around which the rope that now held the new sling was fastened, which lowered the end of the rope into the well.

Once Ruben was comfortably seated in the sling he called down, "Lower away," and was soon descending into the well shaft. It was the first time that Ruben had been down a well and it surprised him how cool it was below ground level. After what seemed an awfully long descent, his feet went into the muddy water, but it only came up to his knees before he was standing on the squelchy bottom. He could see very little, coming from the bright sunlight, but after a while his eyes began to adjust to the dark. Gradually he could see the sides of the well and he could just make out deliberate gaps that had been left in the brickwork. Groping around with his hands he reached into one of the gaps and felt some stones that seemed to move slightly when he pushed and pulled at them. He crawled back up the well shaft and said, "Pull me up."

He was glad to be on the outside once again, as he it was cold down at the bottom of the well. "I really need some light down there," he said to the two enquiring faces, as they looked at him. Captain Tryone called to one of the soldiers and asked for a torch to be brought, which was lit and given to Ruben. He once again descended into the dark, damp depths. When he reached the bottom this time he managed to wedge the torch into a gap above the water line. This enabled him to use both hands to free the rocks, which were blocking the gaps in the well shaft. He shouted back up that he needed a bucket and a small trowel.

During the time that he waited, as he looked up at the small blue circle of light above him, he thought about the astrologer who must spend a lot of his time looking at the stars at night time. He thought of the muttered comments about the possibility of an important person being born in the west. That was where his father had gone, and was where he was hoping to follow. All his original plans started flooding back to him. Those ideas had only been held in check by all the activity of late, and he thought of Simeon and of his beautiful sword, that he believed was still on Simeon's wall. However, his thoughts were soon interrupted when the bucket arrived, together with the trowel. Using both hands he could pull out the larger rocks, which he put into the bucket. He used the trowel to fill up the bucket with smaller stones that were also blocking the flow of water. The bucket was finally full, but Ruben was very cold, so he called up to be raised. The small party of people around the top of the well were shocked to see that his teeth were chattering with the cold. They took the bucket from him and eased him out of the sling where he sat on the hot dry ground, gradually warming up. He told the captain that he thought he was correct in that stones had been washed down from the mountains and were blocking the bottom of the underground stream. Normally it would not be a nuisance, but because the level of the stream had dropped drastically, they were the cause of the blockage that had stopped the water. He said that he thought another couple of bucketfuls needed to be cleared out.

Before he could say that he would go down again, Habib said, "It must be easier to lower me down, I must be a lot lighter than this great lump." He pointed at Ruben. "And he needs a break." Before Ruben could even respond, Habib climbed into the sling, grabbed the bucket and said, "Lower away." Very quickly after that there was a shout to pull the bucket back, which was again full of stones. These were emptied and the bucket was lowered again. After another short time the command came up to raise Habib. He was soon at the top of the well with the bucket half full of stones and a couple of trowelfuls of mud. He was also cold, but said the water was running again now and there should be no further problems. Just then Captain Tryone was called away on urgent business, but said as he hurried off, "Well done, both of you. I'll be leaving the clearing up to you men, and then you had better get back to your work." Ruben was left chatting to Habib as he warmed up. All the stones were piled up and everyone else gradually went away. The two left the wellhead and Ruben picked up the leather sling and walked with Habib back to his workshop, chatting away quite happily. Habib was saying to Ruben that most of the camp should be grateful for what they had achieved, but this had not really occurred to Ruben as the main thing on his mind was how to get back to his initial plan of following his father's footsteps. He toyed with the idea of running away but almost immediately discarded it. He was enjoying the army and felt that if he ran away now he would be deceiving many of his new friends. It did occur to him that if he needed at some time to get away, the first thing that he would want to do would be to go and see Simeon, not only to ask Simeon's advice, but to retrieve his sword. Thinking about the sword, he thought about the scabbard that he had made. Although it was a good scabbard from the materials available, a proper metal and leather scabbard would be better. An idea sprang into his mind and he said to Habib, "A friend of mine is keeping a special sword for me. Would you be able to make a scabbard without seeing the sword?"

Habib frowned and said, "That's a strange request. And to be quite honest I've never even tried." He thought for a while and then said, "I suppose I could, but I would have to know the exact dimensions and also the exact weight."

Not put off, Ruben asked, "If I gave you the exact size and weight, would you make me a special scabbard? I would be very happy to pay for it by doing any extra work for you."

"It is not the money, Ruben. To be honest I would be happy to do it for free, but can I not see the sword?"

"It would be difficult for me to retrieve it, but I might be able to get all the information that you need," suggested Ruben.

"Fine," said Habib. "Presumably you need to keep this all quiet. There must be a good reason, so I won't ask why you need to be so secretive about the sword."

"Great, thanks Habib, I'm not sure yet how long it will take, but I will try to get you the measurements, the weight, and possibly a drawing of the sword." Ruben was delighted by this offer and as they had reached the workshop, he gave the sling back to Habib, said goodbye and rushed off to where the Crocs were training.

That evening, Ruben made a special request of the philosopher, at the reading and writing class, about wishing to send a message to someone in Ur.

The philosopher replied, "Yes, I will help you do that, but it will have to be after the normal lesson has finished. I have to go into Lagash tomorrow, so I could send it off for you. I know a man who often goes to Ur on business."

After the lesson had finished, when the other lads had all left the room Ruben came up to the philosopher and said, "I hope you don't mind, sir, but I pinched an old piece of papyrus and I have penned in what I would like to say in the message."

"That is well done indeed, young man," said the philosopher. "I certainly do not mind and am glad that you have attempted to write yourself – let me have a look to see what you have done."

Ruben handed him the scrap of papyrus on which he had written in large childish writing the message to Simeon. "I am afraid my writing is not very good yet and I am not sure if I have used all the right characters. The message is to a man called Simeon, but should be sent to his niece, who is a girl called Lialah who works in the inn at Ur."

The philosopher studied the writing and said, "This is quite good.

Admittedly you have made a few mistakes, but I can put that right for you. In fact, I will write the introduction. You can then write the message and I will finish it off." So that is what happened. Ruben was pleased with his work and delighted that the philosopher had agreed to help. The philosopher said that if he got a reply, he would pass the reply directly to Habib. Ruben again went to bed late that night, but very contented.

\*\*\*\*

The report that Commander Schudah read was the first glimmer of hope that he had received for the last several days. It was a report from Captain Tryone about their incident with the band of brigands, mentioning that the party led by Ruben Ben Uriah had stood their ground whilst being heavily outnumbered. It also reported that Ruben's javelin throwing, combined with the archery from his bowmen, had driven off the brigands. The report requested, due to the increased bandit activity in the area, that he might allow the Crocs to carry normal weapons when outside the camp. The report stated that Captain Tryone believed that the Crocs would be ready for their trials by midsummer. All the other news that he had received referred to increased bandit activity and border hostilities. That morning the commander had received more reports from his scouts that the Persian Army was manoeuvring a large force just northeast of Sousa.

In his last report to Babylon he had mentioned that it looked as if there may well be a direct attack from the northeast towards Lagash, and that the new city walls that had been started almost two years earlier had still not been finished. He remembered that when Captain Tryone had visited him and he had ordered his captaincy, what both he and Ruben had mentioned about the foundations when they had left the town. Although many towns were walled, Lagash had never had a wall, because it was still very much in the growing stage, and until two years ago everything had been very peaceful in Sumer. But as Lagash was a vital trading point right on the entrance to the Euphrates it was important that it stayed in Babylonian hands. One of the other recent reports that he had received informed him that he was being sent two further battalions from the army to quell any border invasion. This was in addition to the two battalions that he had received several years ago when there had been all that sad business about a protest from the Council of Merchants of Lagash, which had led to the imprisonment and death of Mutek. He also had a small force of the elite Babylonian Guards, but most of these should be kept in reserve to defend the city.

His lieutenant aide came in, after briefly knocking on the door, to inform him that all the captains were waiting in the conference room to discuss the plans that he was shortly to implement. The commander rose from his desk, picked up his helmet, and followed the lieutenant out of the room. On the way to the conference room they discussed exactly how they would billet the two new battalions that they would receive shortly. They arrived at the conference room and the commander took his place at the head of the table. He removed his helmet and said, "At ease gentlemen. Make yourselves comfortable as this could be a long meeting." They all sat down and made themselves comfortable, and then turned their enquiring faces towards him.

"As you all know, there is a potential threat from the Persians who are mustering their forces northeast of Sousa." He waited for this information to fully sink in. "I am expecting two further battalions within the next few days. That will give us over five hundred fully trained army soldiers, plus a small force of Babylonian Guards. Now, as soon as the two new battalions arrive from Babylon they will be readied to march northeast with one of our existing battalions, which will still leave the city well defended. I want these battalions, led by a small force of the Babylonian Guard, to attack the mustering Persian forces. Attacking, as we know, is often the best form of defence."

The general discussion went on for the rest of the morning. When most of the decisions regarding placements, provisions, weapons, equipment and personnel had been exhausted, the commander finalised by saying, "When the two battalions of the army march northeast towards Sousa, I will come with the Babylonian Guard assessor to inspect the new platoon that has been training for the Guards. It is quite possible, if the assessor agrees, that the new platoon could go with the other Guards." He looked directly at the Captain of the Babylonian Guards. This man had been the previous sergeant who had served under Gershnarl and had been promoted to captain after Gershnarl's death. Commander Schudah continued, "You will have to remain here with most of your men, to arrange any potential defence. I will send one platoon of the Guard under the direction of Sergeant Belthezder, who has been specially requested to attend the trials of the new platoon. What I propose is this: Sergeant Belthezder will be made up to lieutenant and will require one of the new recruits to be made an acting sergeant of the new patrol, who will be the first new recruits to the Babylonian Guard. They will be allowed to keep their crocodile hide jerkins. I suppose that is purely hopeful speculation, as we do not know what the outcome will be, although Captain Tryone appears fairly confident in the new recruits' abilities. I would have to send a new platoon into action straight from the training camp, which would mean that I would have to get them to swear the oath of allegiance to the

King, which I am empowered to do, but it is most unusual."

There were nods of agreement all round the table, with the exception of one of the older captains who said, "Sergeant Belthezder is very young, even for a sergeant. Are you sure that promoting him to acting lieutenant would be a wise move?"

Commander Schudah frowned at the captain, "I know Belthezder is young, but I have every confidence in him. And it is about time that we had younger senior officers in this Babylonian army of ours if Babylon is going to become a great country."

This was a forceful putdown and the captain it was aimed at blushed accordingly, as he was a lot older than the commander himself. After a long pause during which the air again seemed to be laden with the possibility of immediate action, the commander said, "If there are no further questions, gentlemen, that will be all. You all know what you have to do, and there is no time to be lost. You are now dismissed."

When the room had emptied the commander turned to his lieutenant aide and said, "Let us go and inspect the walls that are being built. They should have been finished at least three moon cycles ago by their own estimate. I often think we should use slave labour, like the Egyptians do."

"It's about time you got tough with them, sir," exclaimed his aide. They then set off to do a tour of the new walls that were nearing completion. One of the reasons why the walls had taken so long, was that they included an extension into the river, which would form the outer shelter to a man-made harbour. Additionally, the walls were very thick and had a platform below the ramparts for the defending soldiers to shelter and access. They met the builder in charge of the works, who was an Assyrian and had worked in many areas since leaving his homeland. He realised the commander was here to enquire about the delay, so he went with his excuses all prepared. "Ah, Commander," he smiled ingratiatingly. This only had the effect of making the commander even more annoyed than he had been. "I have to inform you that my men are going sick with the hot weather, so it will be at least another two moon cycles before all the work can be finished."

"I am bloody well fed up with your excuses," said the commander. "All I get from you is excuse after excuse. From what my men tell me your workers just loaf about in the sunshine. Damn it man, don't you realise the urgency? We could be under attack within ten days, and if we are, you will be standing outside the walls and you can use your excuses on the Persians."

This wiped the smile off the builder's face. He thought at first that the commander was joking, but when he saw no hint of a smile he realised that it was said in deadly earnest. He stammered, "B-b-but, my men work as hard as they can!"

"Enough of your pathetic babbling. Any more of your excuses and I'll have you publicly flogged, like the damn scoundrel that you are." After shouting these words at the builder, Commander Schudah turned on his heels and marched away with his lieutenant aide beside him, leaving the builder quaking with fear after this outburst.

This had the desired effect. The work on the walls quickly reached completion. During those next ten days the two new battalions of the army arrived by ship, coming down the river from Babylon. They were quickly provisioned and joined by the other battalion from the town and were sent northeast to Sousa, to await the arrival of the small force of Babylonian Guards, who would spearhead their attack on the Persian forces. The large platoon, led by Sergeant Bel, was made ready to go to the training camp with the commander. They now just awaited the arrival of the assessor, and on midsummer's eve he arrived. He was a semi-retired general, who wore the purple plumage of the Babylonian Guard and arrived on a magnificent white stallion with his two companions, who had had great difficulty in keeping pace with him, a fact which was evident by their exhausted expressions and their steaming horses.

"It is good to see you, General," said Schudah, with an outstretched hand.

"It is good to see you again, Schudah," said the general and shook the commander's hand vigorously.

"Come in for a meal that has been prepared," said Schudah as he retrieved his tingling fingers. Even though the old general was now semi-retired, he had not lost his vitality and was still as strong as an ox.

The commander led the way into his own dining room where a pleasant meal awaited them. He told the general that they would eat and he was welcome to spend the night and that they would leave first thing in the morning for the training camp, where the new recruits were preparing for assessment.

"Excellent, Schudah! As you know I don't like to be kept waiting – even though these young pups," and here he pointed to his two companions, who both wore the purple dress of the Guards, "are very puny, like all the kids these days." The two exhausted Guardsmen with him smiled sheepishly. They had ridden for two days since leaving Babylon, which was normally, a five-day journey. "But tell me about these new recruits. They sound very interesting, particularly with the crocodile skin jerkins. I believe that this was your idea. I think it's a nice touch."

So the commander told the general the full story behind the crocodile jerkins, mentioning Ruben and Uglis (Uglis had now been tried, found guilty and was in chains in the citadel in Babylon). He also mentioned that he believed that Captain Tryone was planning to test the young man's javelin throwing against that of Sergeant Belthezder, who had recently won the army championships.

"This young man sounds interesting," said the general. "I look forward to meeting the lad – he must be pretty good for a sixteen-year-old."

"That's just the point," explained Schudah. "We are not really sure how old he is – he may even be younger. But apart from that, although he was picked up in the marshes at Ur, he claims that he came from Lagash. His parentage is not clear and he certainly doesn't look as if he comes from this area. Anyway, he is a nice lad, very polite and fairly intelligent. I think you'll like him. Captain Tryone thinks that he is a potential leader."

They chatted amiably for a while after the evening meal, which was consumed with a couple of pitchers of wine. The general's two assistants made their excuses and went for a full night's sleep, which they certainly looked as if they needed. However, the general produced a flagon of Arrak.

"You will hopefully join me for a nightcap, Schudah," said the general as he poured the clear spirit into two goblets, without even waiting for an answer.

"Well, only the one, General," said Schudah, whose mind was already fuzzy with the amount of wine that he had drunk. He had the feeling that he was not going to get much sleep that night and would probably be suffering in the morning. The general was reputed to be a man of vast excesses – yet he was probably quite capable of being stone cold sober in the morning. The evening continued well into the night and it was a long time before the commander could get off to bed, and when he walked from the room he had difficulty keeping his balance.

Early the next morning the platoon of Guards, with Sergeant Bel in charge, lined up ceremoniously, as they waited for the commander. The general appeared on his large white stallion, full of high spirits and without showing any trace of the previous night's excessive drinking. The party was then joined by Commander Schudah, standing in his chariot, holding on with both hands and looking very much the worse for wear. "Forward," said the general, automatically taking charge of the party and leading them up the road at a fast pace northeast towards the training camp.

The fast pace was maintained the whole journey, which at first was something of a nightmare to Commander Schudah. The general in the lead was followed by his two assistants and then came Sergeant Bel leading the platoon of Babylonian Guard, running at a fast trot. Schudah followed them in his chariot. Fortunately, no one saw him throw up over the side, after which he felt better. The breeze created by the forward momentum helped revive him and when they arrived at the camp, he did not look too unpresentable.

Captain Tryone had been forewarned of their visit and the entire camp had paraded in the late morning sunshine. The air was still and there was not a cloud in the sky. It was going to be a very hot day. Everyone was on parade and the camp was looking smart, with each platoon lined up behind their appropriate training sergeant. The Crocs were lined up behind Captain Tryone, and they all looked smart in their crocodile skin jerkins. They were all wearing white shifts that they hoped would soon become the purple of the Babylonian Guard. Ruben had taken the chains off his jerkin and stood at one end of the front row, perfectly erect at attention. He had continued to grow and was now half a head taller than everyone else in his platoon, even Latich who, standing beside him, looked small in comparison, due not only to Ruben's height, but also because he was a well built young man. The general trotted into the camp on his white stallion with the Babylonian Guards behind him, and when they reached the parade square shouted, "Halt," at which point they stopped and snapped to attention. Many of them were still panting and they were visibly soaked in perspiration. As the general dismounted from his horse, Sergeant Bel came up to him, but had to jump aside as Commander Schudah's chariot drew up in front of the general. The commander was in charge of all the proceedings and therefore felt that he would exercise his command. Drawing the chariot to a halt he said to the general, "Thank you for leading the party, General, I will take over now." He turned to Sergeant Bel and said, "Let your men refresh themselves at the well, providing that it is acceptable for Captain Tryone."

Captain Tryone marched forward and said, "Good morning, Commander. Presumably the General is here to assess the Crocs for conscription into the Babylonian Guards." Without hesitating he nodded in recognition of Sergeant Bel and said, "Refresh your men at the well, Sergeant." He turned back to Commander Schudah and said, "Would you and the General like to take some refreshment inside, sir, or would you prefer to have something brought out, and then get on with the assessment?"

"I'll take over now," said the general, feeling the commander had put him in his place. "No, we will have refreshment brought out, Captain, so that we can get straight on with the assessment. I am not a man who likes to be kept waiting."

Drinks were soon brought out to all the senior staff. The general downed two mugs of millet beer, without seeming to even swallow. Captain Tryone said, "May I allow the other lads to stand down, sir?"

"Certainly. Allow them to stand at ease, Captain, but I don't see why they should not watch the exercises."

Realising that there was a problem over who was in command, and with the knowledge that the commander should really be in charge, and would soon reassert his authority over the proceedings, he said, "Some of the boys are only twelve, sir, and it is extremely hot. They are not soldiers yet, and are under my command. I therefore intend to allow them to sit down and watch the exercises if they wish to."

Before the general could answer, the commander said, "Quite right, Captain. I think that is an excellent idea."

Realising that the odds were totally against him, and that he would be met with further rebuttal if he pursued areas that were outside his remit, the general decided to stick to the task in hand. "I see," he said. There was a long pause. "Right! Let us start with the assault course, with all the lads wearing full kit." One of his assistants came over to him, and whispered something in his ear. "Oh yes!" He turned to Captain Tryone and said, "Will you introduce the boys to me? Allow my assistants to give them all a number that should be marked on their tunics, together with their initials. This will aid my assistants who will record their progress."

In this manner the trials got under way, with all the Crocs given a number, which was written with charcoal on their shifts, beside their initials. The general scrutinised the boys as each was introduced and gave them a long hard stare – trying to intimidate them. Fortunately they had all been forewarned of this, so that it had little effect. The general noticed when he came to Ruben that he hardly had to look down at him. The boy's eyes were almost on a level with his own. He said to Ruben, "I have heard quite a lot about you, young man. I hope you live up to expectations."

"I will certainly do my best, sir," replied Ruben, looking straight ahead and focusing his eyes on the middle-distance.

After they had all been numbered, they dressed in full kit, including their specialised weapons. They were asked to complete the assault course twice. At the end of this they were all panting and sweating profusely.

"Right, this time you will be timed," said the general. And the boys had to complete the course again, this time setting off in threes. The measurement against them was how long it took the sand to run through a tiny hole in a glass bowl that was produced for this very purpose. They all achieved this under the prescribed limit, which was three bowls full of sand. Next came the ordinary sword practise, in which they were paired off and had to fight one another, with the occasional individual being asked to fight one of the assistants, who was a highly skilled swordsman. His sword was razor sharp, unlike their own, but if he developed an opening, which happened in most cases, he only made a small wound on his opponent rather than deliver a fatal blow. Gradually the wounded became more and there were only a few sword fighters left. Ruben was one of these and had been fighting against the expert swordsman for quite a while, escaping injury, until the general called for a halt. They were ordered to have a short break for refreshment. But they were soon on their feet again, running around the perimeter fence with full kit. Despite the fact that they had been well trained, this was a gruelling exercise as it was carried out right in the middle of the day when the sun was directly overhead. Four of the boys collapsed with exhaustion and were carried off into the shade, their attempts to be Babylonian Guards ended.

Eventually they came to a stop and the general ordered them to undertake special weapon training. This started, to Ruben's great relief, with the bowmen. They had to shoot at a target fifty paces away; the target was the picture of a man. They had to hit the target with at least four out of five arrows. Next came the large sword practise, where they were paired off again. Occasionally the expert swordsman would take someone's place. Again Ruben found himself pitted against this man who was as fast as anything Ruben had ever seen. More by luck than judgement he managed to stay unscathed and was not drawn into making a thrust when given an easy target, which he knew would leave him open to a counter-attack. Eventually this ended and the expert swordsman actually congratulated Ruben, much to his surprise, as he felt that he had been well outmatched. Next came the discus throwing, during which Ruben had a well-earned break. Finally came the javelin throwing, when a target of a man was set at fifty paces and they were expected to hit the target with one out of their three throws. This Ruben found easy, and sent his javelin straight through the dummy's chest. This was much to Captain Tryone's delight, and even Sergeant Bel gave a low whistle of approval. At long last all the training exercises were over and the adjudication was finished.

Just before the results were announced, Commander Schudah called out that they were having a special challenge. This was against the army's javelin champion, Sergeant Bel of the Babylonian Guard. He then handed over to Captain Tryone. The captain said to Sergeant Bel, "We have all heard how splendid you are at placing three javelins in a man-sized dummy set at fifty paces. Would you accept a challenge from our own champion, but this set at seventy paces?"

Sergeant Bel obviously could not refuse, and although he knew he could easily throw this distance, he had never attempted to hit a target at that range. The target was set up at seventy paces, and a great hush fell over the crowd of onlookers. Sergeant Bel came forward, took a javelin and threw after taking a reasonable run up. The javelin hurtled through the air and just caught the dummy figure on the shoulder, twisting it around. Tremendous applause greeted this fine effort. Ruben stood forward and launched a huge throw, which almost brought him to his knees after all his efforts that day. He closed his eyes, as he could not bear to watch as he thought he had thrown the javelin too high and had missed. A tremendous cheer broke out from all the training camp as the javelin neatly took off the dummy's head. The first person to congratulate Ruben was Sergeant Bel, who said, "Well done! That was a mighty fine throw. Even though I hit the target my throw was not as accurate. I can see that I am going to have a great deal of difficulty retaining my championship next year." Ruben was so surprised that he could only smile happily when pounded on the back.

The tumultuous applause was quickly diverted as a horseman came galloping into the camp from the northeast. The horseman galloped into the camp and headed straight for the group of officers. He hardly reined in and positively vaulted out the saddle, neatly landing on his feet. He rushed up to Commander Schudah. He was a corporal of the Despatch Corps and had ridden hard all the way from Sousa. Sergeant Bel held the exhausted horse's reins. The poor animal was foaming with sweat and exhausted almost to the point of collapse.

The corporal, who was now in front of the commander, briefly saluted and said breathlessly, "Begging your pardon, sir, but my captain had no time to write a report. He sent me to inform you that both battalions are under fierce attack from the Persians, and are having difficulty containing them. He requested reinforcements, and if possible the Babylonian Guards."

A heavy silence fell on the group of officers and onlookers. Nobody had expected this. The first person to speak was the general, who said, "I know it is your decision Commander, but I suggest that I take the platoon of Babylonian Guards under the command of Sergeant Bel, together with the Crocs that have passed the trials. That will enable you to dash back to Lagash, possibly sending the reinforcements from there, and send an urgent despatch to Babylon."

"For once, I think, you are right, General," said the commander. "But the Crocs have not yet taken the Oath of Allegiance to their king and country, which I feel I should do first."

"Damn it man, this is an emergency. Every minute we delay is vital. The Oath is only a formality, and can be taken later."

Captain Tryone interrupted, "I think that is sensible, sir. It also gives me a chance to evacuate the camp."

This forced Commander Schudah to give agreement. He gave orders for the Crocs to be uniformed as Babylonian Guards and to carry regular weapons. While this was done he told Captain Tryone to gather up all his important papers and evacuate the camp, and then to march the recruits back to Lagash.

The general said to his assistants, "All the assessments are to go back to Babylon, but one of you can do this. Take them, together with my stallion, which is far too valuable to risk in battle." He said to the expert swordsman, "I think you can come with me. You would be of more assistance in the battle."

There was great excitement amongst the Crocs. From being trainees they were suddenly the elite Babylon Guard, and were marching to war.

# 7
# ESCAPE FROM VICTORY

The large platoon of Babylonian Guards lined up outside the camp. They were about fifty strong with the previous corporal now promoted to acting sergeant. Alongside them stood the Crocs, resplendent in their new Babylonian Guards' battledress, very consciously preening themselves and admiring their own finery. They were the first entirely new platoon in the Guards, as new conscripts had previously joined existing companies. Sergeant Bel was now acting lieutenant and was in total command of the force. He was theoretically acting under the general, but as the general was semi-retired, he really should not have been with the party. But nobody dared to have the effrontery to accuse the general of being too old to fight for his country. Indeed, he was still a powerful man and he still had plenty of energy for fighting. Whatever he may have lacked in common sense, by virtue of age and the ravages of drink, he certainly did not lack experience.

As the Crocs required a sergeant, there was some discussion between the general and Acting Lieutenant Bel about taking one of the younger corporals from the existing platoon. But as Lieutenant Bel correctly said, any outsider did not know the strengths and weaknesses of the lads under his charge. Therefore, much to his surprise and delight, it was decided to make Ruben an acting sergeant. He knew his platoon well and took the charge he was given seriously, as he knew all the young Guardsmen looked up to him as an experienced warrior. The general called them all to attention and was about to set off towards Sousa, when Habib, the leatherworker, rushed over from Captain Tryone's office with a small goatskin satchel. He said to the general, "I am sorry to have to stop you, sir, but Captain Tryone asked me to bring something over for young Ben Uriah."

"Well you had better give it to him," snapped the general in an irritated manner.

Habib trotted over to Ruben and handed him the satchel. "There is a scroll inside that comes with the Captain's compliments. He says that you know what it is. The satchel also holds something from me, with my best wishes and hopes that it will fit your sword whenever you manage to collect it. It should fit perfectly, as your friend sent a full-scale outline. It is a long sword and not as wide as the standard issue and is of a rather unusual design." He lowered his voice and added, "If it is bronze, you will have to be careful that it does not snap. But I have a sneaking suspicion that it may be one of the new swords that are made from iron, and has come from the east." He said the last few words very quietly so that only Ruben could hear.

"Hurry up there," demanded the general. "We have a war to go and win." And with that command he turned the small force towards the northeast and marched them down the road towards Sousa.

The Crocs were excited at the prospect of battle and had forgotten their exertions of the day. Even those who had been slightly wounded in the sword-fighting trials, had had these wounds patched up and disregarded their discomfort. There was a lot of whispering amongst the ranks. Since the general was well out of earshot at the head of the column, Ruben said nothing to quell the high spirits of his new platoon.

At the start of the march, Ruben wanted to look in the goatskin satchel to examine the scroll that had come two years previously from Simeon. The scabbard had been made by Habib to fit the sword that was still in Simeon's floating reed house. However, he realised that to do so he would have to stop, which was totally out of the question. He secured the satchel to the javelin holder on his shoulder and managed to put it to the back of his mind. Fortunately, this was not too difficult as he had plenty of other things to occupy his mind. The general kept them marching at a steady pace, but had the sense to not over-tire the force.

By the early evening they could see Sousa, nestling in the foothills, which led to the mountains in the north. The general was faced with the decision of whether or not to march straight into the battle that they could hear raging in the distant town. He halted the company and called to Lieutenant Bel, so that they could decide on the best strategy. Lieutenant Bel considered that the best way was to attack immediately, but not to press too far forward. That way he felt the Persians would fall back, thinking that a whole battalion of the elite Babylonian Guards had joined the battle, and would break off their attack on Sousa for that day. This would give them all a chance to regroup. He hoped reinforcements would be sent from Lagash the next morning. This was agreed and an attack formation was worked out. It was decided to integrate the battle-hardened Guards with the newly trained platoon, on the basis of two experienced Guardsmen to one of the freshly conscripted young lads. The plan was for the bowmen, and then the javelin and discus throwers to punch a hole in the front ranks of the Persian army. This would open the Persian ranks and the swordsmen would then forge a breach. However, it was vital that they should push no further than the outer walls of the town.

The company then fell in, positioning themselves in the planned strike-force formation. The general, followed by Lieutenant Bel, the experienced swordfighter and Ruben, led them. As they neared the town, the general increased their pace to a slow trot. He galloped forwards himself, drew his sword and demanded that the greatly relieved defending troops in front of him, defending the town square, make a space for their advance. As the defenders stood aside, the Guards filled the space, firstly with their bowmen firing directly into the front rank of the Persians. The bowmen then stood aside as twelve javelin throwers filled their place and sent twelve javelins hurtling into the disorganised Persian ranks. A gap was forced open and more arrows, javelins and discuses rained down on the first and second ranks. The attack was then reinforced by the swordsmen who, much to everyone's surprise, were led by the general, chopping his way through the ranks like a harvester reaping corn. The Persians immediately fell back, as the rumour spread that a large force of the Babylonian Guards had joined in the battle. The fighting became confused, but the Persians soon retreated out of the town. Lieutenant Bel called for a halt as they reached the outskirts of the town, as previously decided. However, he was alarmed to see the old general charging after the fleeing Persian soldiers. Someone seized his shoulder from behind. It was Ruben, and he said, "Let me go and bring him back, sir."

Knowing that he would have to stay to discipline his force, he said to Ruben, "Very well then, you go after the General, and bring him back as quickly as you can."

"Certainly, sir," replied Ruben, slipping off his large sword from his back and handing it to Latich.

Lieutenant Bel picked up one of the previously thrown javelins, handed it to Ruben and said, "You have used all your javelins, so this may come in handy."

Ruben rushed forward, nimbly jumping over the dead and dying and soon reached the general who had chased two of the fleeing Persians into a barn on the outskirts of the town. Ruben reached him as he went in; his eyes alight with the fury of battle. Ruben grabbed him by the shoulder and said to him, as if addressing a runaway child, "Come back, sir. We have to get back to the others." The general swung round and looked uncomprehendingly into Ruben's eyes. They stared at one another for a few moments.

Eventually the light in the general's eyes dimmed and he said, "Oh, yes, of course," and walked back as meekly as a child. One of the fleeing Persian soldiers had set fire to the straw covered barn, and this was now fiercely ablaze. As Ruben pushed the general out of the blazing barn, one of the timbers holding the roof collapsed, striking him on the back of his helmet and then bounced into the burning building in a cascade of sparks. Ruben had not had time to see the danger, and the impact of the blow knocked him unconscious to the ground. The general returned to

Lieutenant Bel who was ordering a defensive wall to be built out of rubble and existing brickwork. The general had quickly regained his old ebullience, "That will see the rascals off. That will be the last we will see of them tonight," he said to Lieutenant Bel.

"Yes sir, well done," was all that the busy lieutenant could reply. He asked the general to summon the captains of the defending force so that a co-ordinated defence could be organised. It was not until the general had walked off that the lieutenant wondered where Ruben was. However his mind was soon full of other matters as all the questions from the defending force came his way. Where to put the wounded, how to treat them, should the dead be buried, was there anything to eat, could they now have a rest? The general reappeared with a couple of captains from the defending army battalions. They decided to extend the built-up defensive wall and to patrol it with soldiers wearing borrowed Babylonian Guard helmets. This would give the Persians the impression that there had been a larger force of Guards than just the two platoons that had arrived in the nick of time. This was organised. Then the lieutenant had to busy himself looking after his own men and, of course, the Crocs. It was well into the night before Lieutenant Bel found out that only two of his men had been killed and three were slightly wounded. None of the Crocs had been killed but two were wounded, and one of those quite seriously. The other problem was that Ruben was nowhere to be seen and nobody knew where he was. In fact, Lieutenant Bel had been the last person to see him, except for the general. When Lieutenant Bel questioned him all he received in reply was a troubled expression and a vague comment about the heat of the battle and a brief conversation with one of the new boys. Lieutenant Bel went back to the makeshift walls and could see the litter of dead and dying outside the walls, spreading back to the Persian ranks which were now just on the other side of a small wadi. Could Ruben be lying out there either dead or dying? Much though he wanted to find the answer, it was far too dangerous to send a search party out as they would be within bowshot of the Persians and there were still a few glowing fires amongst the debris and enough moonlight to give a clear shot.

****

Commander Schudah, having given Captain Tryone orders to clear the camp and march the trainees back to Lagash as soon as possible, wheeled his chariot round and set off for Lagash. The only one accompanying him was the horse rider who was one of the general's assistants, who had all the records of the trials to take back to Babylon. The horseman also had the general's white stallion, which cantered along beside them at an easy pace.

The commander arrived in Lagash just as it was beginning to darken in the east. He swept through the gates with the horseman and the general's stallion following him in close order. He was pleased to note that all the walls were now complete and well manned, with the Captain of the Babylonian Guards waiting to meet him just inside the large gateway. He briefed the captain to send out half a platoon of Babylonian Guards to usher in the trainees that Captain Tryone would bring back from the training camp. Having done that, he continued up to the barracks and called to his lieutenant aide, as he jumped off the chariot platform before it halted.

"I want to see all the captains as soon as possible. And get me a scribe. I will be waiting in the main conference chamber." The scribe was the first to arrive, and he soon had him writing a report. It told of the emergency situation, which had arisen whilst the training session was being completed. He told of the attack on Sousa and the action that he had taken in sending a platoon of Babylonian Guards with their newly trained soldiers who had passed the test for the Guards. He went on to report that he would send a further battalion to try to save Sousa, but that Lagash needed urgent reinforcements – possibly a whole regiment of Babylonian Guards, as well as two further battalions of fully trained soldiers. No sooner was the report finished, read back and the ink powdered, than he gave the scroll to the Despatch Corps sergeant with explicit instructions that it must get to Babylon as soon as possible.

The commander was joined in the conference chamber by all the available captains, to whom he related the happenings to date. He asked how each captain had deployed his men and charged them with reducing their numbers by one third, so that almost a complete battalion could be sent to reinforce Sousa. This still left the city well defended, but he knew that they would not be able to hold out for very long unless they received reinforcements. His captains left him with the promise that they would find enough men to form a makeshift battalion, but that it would not be until first thing in the morning that this battalion could set out to reinforce Sousa.

****

Ruben awoke in the early dawn light with a splitting headache, and it was getting worse. His helmet was wedged down tight and he had to reach up and gradually work it loose, until it finally came off his head with a dull plop. After a short while the headache seemed to decrease and he became aware of his surroundings. He was lying outside the now burnt out barn, almost below a stone drinking trough. It shielded him from the sight of his own front ranks that were behind the makeshift walls. The low stonewalls of the burnt out barn also shielded him from the Persian front ranks that were on the opposite side of a small wadi about fifty paces beyond the barn. There were quite a few corpses lying in the immediate vicinity, and there was still some moaning coming from fatally wounded men, calling out for their mothers or loved ones. Rolling onto his back, Ruben manoeuvred himself into a sitting position with his back to the drinking trough and took a closer stock of his own situation and predicament. As his head cleared he checked over his body for any wounds, and was pleased to find that he was unscathed. Even his head, which was still aching, had not been cut at all. He inspected his helmet and was pleased to find that the purple feathers of the Babylonian Guards, although slightly singed, were still all present and easily identifiable. There was, however, a large dent in his bronze helmet that was also deeply scored by the timber that had given him a glancing blow. Fortunately, the leather padding to the helmet had absorbed a lot of the impact, which was why his head had not been badly hurt. Looking around and taking stock of his exact location, he realised that it would be rather foolhardy to attempt to move into the open. In the half-light of dawn, he was within bowshot of both opposing forces, who might shoot before trying to recognise their target. As he looked around he realised that he had been carrying his empty javelin case, upon which the goatskin satchel was still secured. With nothing better to do he opened the satchel and took out a magnificent goatskin sheath, which was neatly folded. It even had a flap that went back over the handle of his sword that would protect it from wind and rain, as well as keeping the magnificent hilt out of sight of prying eyes. After inspecting the sheath, he took out the scroll from the satchel and began to read Simeon's message. He reread the part that assured him that his silent friend and Simeon were awaiting him, and wondered if this meant that Ishmala was alive. They had kept his treasure safe. He also read the exhortation to "look after the works of the Creator." He thought deeply about this and felt his eyes prickle with the build up of tears, as he looked around him at the carnage that was indeed the work of men. As the sun climbed into the sky and it grew hotter, the stench of decaying bodies grew more and more pungent as did the activity of flies, which gathered on the corpses. A few carrion crows that were pecking at the dead were soon joined by bold vultures, despite the attempts of the soldiers on both sides to shoo them away by hurling rocks at them. It was a grisly thought that in some respects the battles of mankind made life easier for some of the works of the Creator. But as quickly as this thought had occurred to him he dismissed it, as it was not the message that

Simeon wished to convey.

Realising the difficulty that he might have in regaining the safety of his own side, the thought came to him that this might be an ideal opportunity to sneak away, without deserting his friends or fighting other people with whom he had no quarrel. The sun was now high in the sky, and he wondered what both sides were now planning. He realised that the Persians were probably preparing for another attack, when he heard from behind him the cheer that greeted the reinforcements from Lagash. This, therefore, put the idea of further conflict into a possibly remote category. But there was still no movement from either side. He found it relatively easy to slake his thirst, as the animal trough above his head was still full of water – even though this water was luke warm and rather unpleasant. The day wore on, yet there was still no activity from either side, although he realised that there must be a lot of discussion behind the lines. He remembered that he had not sworn an Oath of Allegiance, and this reassured him that he would not be breaking an oath if he quietly disappeared. He therefore found himself hoping that evening would come and he would get a chance to slip away unobserved.

His hopes seemed dashed by a sudden blare of trumpets, the warning of a deputation coming forward from his own side. From his position he could see, without being seen, as the general and Lieutenant Bel, dressed in the purple of the Babylonian Guard, together with three battalion command captains in the bright red of the Babylonian Army, came forward under the white flag of truce. His side had not come to negotiate any form of surrender or peaceful settlement, but demanded the immediate withdrawal of the Persian forces from Babylonian soil. The deputation gave the Persians until midday the next day to move back to behind their own border in the mountains, or to be wiped out by the avenging Babylonians. The deputation went back, to another blare of trumpets, as it seemed that the answer was not immediately forthcoming. Ruben waited and there was still no activity on either side. He realised that he had not eaten for twenty-four hours, but the thought of food soon diminished as he watched the carrion eaters feeding on the decomposing bodies that littered the area. Eventually it started to get dark, so Ruben decided that if he was going to make a move it was now or never. At the time of gathering darkness, when the light is fading and everything is in the shadows and the light plays tricks with people's eyes, he made his move. Leaving the javelin case, but fixing the goatskin satchel to his sword belt, he crawled forward around the barn and kept on going, moving from behind one piece of debris and then to another, he gradually made his way down to the wadi. He was pleased to find that the dried up watercourse was fairly steep sided. This made it far easier to avoid being seen by either side. Crouching low, he made his way following the watercourse, which headed in a southerly direction, skirting the buildings around Sousa. Once he was out of hearing distance of the town he straightened up and broke into a trot, still heading in a southerly direction. The wadi turned towards the southeast and he could hear the sound of a small stream, which joined the wadi. The stream turned once again towards the south and he realised that this stream became the one that led down to the Inferior Sea, emerging at the camp training ground, where he and Sergeant Tryone had fought the brigands a couple of years previously. He soon heard the sound of the waves lapping against the shore and he reached the Inferior Sea just as the moon rose into a clear, star-studded, night sky. He walked along the shore, heading towards Lagash, and found a small boat that had been pulled well above the high water mark, where it was attached to some rocks. The boat belonged to his old training camp, where it was used in the summer for fishing and occasionally rescuing trainee solders. He realised that this was his means to make his way to Ur, without having to go through or bypass Lagash.

\*\*\*\*

The demand from the forces now defending Sousa from the Persian army, was the idea of Lieutenant Bel, as it reinforced the idea that Sousa was strongly defended. When he had marched out with the General and the battalion captains, he kept his eyes searching amongst the surrounding bodies for any sign of Ruben or any Babylonian soldier. But he had seen nothing except dead Persians who were being eaten by the flies and the carrion birds. By nightfall there had still been no answer from the Persians and he wondered whether or not they were going to see if the demand was a bluff, which it most certainly was. If that was the case, he was not sure what would be the next move. Whether or not they should stay defending Sousa, which was quickly running out of food, having to feed over a thousand extra people. But if they left the town and retreated back to Lagash, they would be leaving the townsfolk to the attacking Persian soldiers, who would not hesitate to rape, plunder and pillage the town. Not that this worried him, it was not his decision anyway, but one that had to be made by the battalion captains – if they had the nerve to override any decision made by the semi-retired general, as was their right. Lieutenant Bel was fairly certain that he could do little more that day, but as he wandered off towards the room that he had commandeered for himself as an office and bedroom combined, he started to wonder why they had had no information in advance of the Persian attack. He realised that in the days when Captain Gershnarl and Captain Uglis had been round, they had organised a complex system of informants. Admittedly, many of the enterprises that the informants were involved in were extremely dubious, so cutting them off was correct. It did, however, mean that there was no flow of information concerning movements outside the army. He therefore summoned a couple of his Guards, who were locals of the area. He told them to borrow some ordinary clothes from the townsfolk, discard their uniforms and disappear into the night, going out to encircle the Persian army and, masquerading as simple shepherds or Bedouins, try to find out what was happening. They must return first thing in the morning and tell him what they had learnt.

He was woken first thing in the morning by the two scouts who he had set out. The information that they gave him was excellent; it appeared that the Persians were moving away northwards. They had started moving in the night; the estimate was that there were close on four thousand troops. His bluff had worked. From the information he was given, the entire Persian army would have left by mid-morning. Armed with this piece of information, he hurried to spread the news to the general and the battalion captains.

They were delighted at his news and impressed at learning of the initiative he had used to gather the information. He then went to the makeshift wall and looked out to watch the last departing groups of Persian soldiers. After waiting for a while to make sure that everything was clear, he led out a small party of Guardsmen to check for any Babylonian soldiers amongst the dead. He himself went straight in the direction that the general had gone, when Ruben had pursued him. He came to the burnt out barn, but could see no sign of any Babylonian dead in the area. This mystified him. He had given orders for the Persian bodies to be stripped and stacked in funeral pyres, which would later be torched. He was about to leave his men to the grisly task when he spotted, lying beside a water-trough, a brand new javelin carrying-case. It was Babylonian and must have belonged to Ruben. He was more perplexed than ever as he lifted up the carrying-case and noticed the marks on the strap where something had been attached. Then he remembered the interruption at the trainee camp, from the leather worker. The man had given a small satchel to Ruben, who had attached it to the javelin-case. He picked it up and walked back thoughtfully. The best thing would be to have a talk to the leatherworker and to Captain Tryone, to see if he could shed any light on the matter.

It was after midday when two and a half battalions, plus the two platoons of Babylonian Guards left the town, marching southeast back to Lagash. They left behind them a couple of hundred soldiers, approximately half a battalion, to tend the funeral pyres and ensure the civil order of the town was maintained. It was well after nightfall before they reached Lagash. He ordered his men to go and eat in the mess hall and went in search of Captain Tryone and the leatherworker.

****

Ruben noticed that the tide was out and had just turned, so he decided to rest until the tide came in. He could then row down to Lagash aided by the outgoing tide and enter the Euphrates on the next incoming tide. He untied the boat and dragged it down the beach to just below the high water mark. He climbed into the boat, made himself comfortable, and was soon asleep.

He was awoken by the shifting boat as the incoming tide started to lift it from the sand. He fully awoke and jumped into the shallow water. With a few heaves he pulled the boat into deep water. He jumped aboard again and started to row out to sea, as darkness was beginning to be chased away by the new day. Keeping the boat a few hundred paces out from the shoreline, he rowed at a leisurely pace in a southeast direction, towards the city of Lagash. He knew that it would take the best part of the morning, but he was in no great hurry, as when he arrived he would wait until the incoming tide, which would help him as he entered the river. Sensibly he had filled his water bottle from the stream before he had boarded the boat. He was now beginning to feel hungry, as he had not eaten for at least a day and a half. Looking about he noticed a small net in the boat that had carelessly not been taken back. This, however, was to his advantage. After checking that there were no large holes in the net and that the weights on one side and the floats on the other side of the net were all securely fastened, he threw the net overboard and pulled it back in, hoping to find a small catch. Regrettably the net was still empty, but as he had plenty of time, he rowed a little further out and tried again. All in all it took him six or seven casts of the net in slightly different locations before he managed to catch anything. Even then he had only caught a very small fish. Oh, well, he thought to himself, it is probably better that I went in to the army, than tried to be a fisherman. However, one fish was better than nothing and he might have a bit of luck later when he entered the river. It was now becoming hot, as the sun rose higher in the sky. Realising that he was now even further from the shore, Ruben started to row in earnest and soon had the boat moving along at a reasonable speed. He kept this up, taking a sip of water occasionally. He did not find that rowing was hard work, but as his hands were unused to the oars, he found that his palms had started to blister. Fortunately he could now see Lagash in the distance.

How different it all looked now that the city walls were complete and the new walls extended into the river to make a harbour for the large ships that came from the east to dock and unload the cargoes. He was glad that he had rowed further out into the sea than he had originally planned, as he did not want to be seen from the shore. As it was just before low tide, he thought he would have a further attempt at fishing, before he started to enter the river, as rowing against the out-flowing current would be very hard work. He noticed a commotion in the water to his right, where the surface was broken by the dorsal fins of dolphins that had herded some small fish. This was indeed a golden opportunity and too good to miss, so he rowed the boat over the area. This time, when he cast the net into the sea he retrieved it with six reasonable sized fish inside it. This was indeed good fortune and he could imagine how tasty they would be when cooked over an open fire. Unfortunately, this made him hungrier than ever, and he could hardly wait until he could get ashore and cook his catch. By now the tide had started to turn and he rowed directly upriver, keeping well away from Lagash. The blisters on his hands had burst and every stroke was painful. Trying to ignore the discomfort, he started to row more towards the southern bank attempting to find the inlet that Ishmala had rowed into a few years previously. He must have missed the small inlet, as when he looked to his left, he had rowed well past Lagash.

He was not surprised that he had missed the inlet, as he remembered that it was well concealed. So he rowed on, despite the discomfort of his hands, knowing that he would soon reach the inlet where the half submerged pirate boat lay, where he had discovered his sword. It seemed to take a lot longer than he remembered, but eventually he found it. With great relief he rowed passed the half submerged wreck to the small sunny beach, where he gratefully grounded the boat and stepped ashore. He rinsed his bleeding hands in the water, despite the pain caused by the salt. He knew that this would keep his hands from getting infected, and that they would then heal quite quickly.

The first thing that he did was to take his catch of fish up to the shelter of the small trees, under which he had woven the original scabbard for his sword. He soon gathered enough wood from the trees and using the tinderbox, which all soldiers carry as part of their basic kit, he soon had a small fire burning, over which he grilled the fish. Chopping off the heads and the tails off the fish, but did not bother to skin them. He was so hungry that he almost burnt his mouth by eating the fish before they had a chance to cool down. This he washed down with the last few mouthfuls of the water from his now empty water bottle.

He considered whether or not to go on and he then remembered the boat. He was concerned that if he left it where it was, he could be traced easily. Therefore, he decided that the best thing to do would be to sink the boat. Taking off his clothes and armaments, Ruben slipped back into the water. He returned with a couple of large stones that he had brought up from the riverbed. He placed these into the boat and dragged the boat back down the sandy beach and into the water. It did not take him very long to fill the boat, by rocking it from side to side; allowing the water to splash over the gunwales after which it gradually sank out of sight. He went back up the beach and allowed the dying rays of sunlight to dry him, before he dressed again. He then inspected the dent in his helmet. Peeling back the leather interior, he found that he could tap out the dent by using the hilt of his dagger. Although it was now getting dark, he thought that he would be sensible to travel on and get to the small family who had given him shelter before. So he set off once again down the old caravan route that would eventually lead him to Ur.

Ruben knew that he had quite a distance to travel, so in the gathering dusk he broke into a trot. Although it had been a long day in the boat, he had not been tired out by the exercise, and his legs felt as if they could do with a run. After all, he was now superbly fit. The blistering on his hands was not serious, his left hand being worse than his right hand, due to the sword and javelin training, which had callused his right hand. He wore his helmet, as it was easier than carrying it. He covered the distance in a surprisingly short period, but it was still completely dark and the moon had just risen when he saw the small dome shaped huts just to the left of the track. He could see a lamp burning in one of the huts, so he went over and called outside the doorway. "Hello there, is anyone at home?"

"Yes," came the reply. "Identify yourself, and come in," uttered a querulous voice.

Taking off his helmet and stooping through the doorway, Ruben entered. "I am here on the King's business," he said, knowing that nobody would question him any further.

"Oh, do come in, sir. Can I offer you a drink?" asked the old man, half rising to his feet. "Please sit down."

"Yes, but I will only take a drink of water and possibly fill my water bottle, before I continue my journey to Ur," replied Ruben.

"Are you sure I can offer nothing more, Sergeant?" asked the old man. "Please help yourself. There is a full pitcher of water just by the doorway. My son is in the Guards, and it is quite a long way to Ur, if that is where you are heading."

The old man had noticed the badge of rank on Ruben's tunic and was very polite. As Ruben expected, he did not ask what business he was on, but he did ask him if he came from Lagash. Ruben informed him that he had not come from Lagash, but from Sousa, where there had been a battle with the Persians. Ruben felt quite safe giving this correct information, as news of the battle would soon reach most parts. But, he told the old man, there was no danger, and he had come as he knew the area. The old man was sitting beside his wife, who was lying on her bed and was not looking very well.

"How long has your wife been ill?" Ruben asked the rather disturbed old man.

"For the last ten days," came the reply. "But at first she just seemed very tired and weak, and we were going to see the old man of the marshes – he is a great healer, and his floating house is at Ur this time of year. But I do not think that she has the strength to make the journey now." The old man looked distressed, as he looked at his wife with great affection, holding her hand as a tear rolled down his face. "I do not know what to do. She has never been so ill before and I cannot carry her." This was said purely as a matter of fact and not as a plea for assistance.

"I will stay the night, sleeping in one of the other huts and we will see how she is in the morning. If she is no better, I will carry her to Ur," said Ruben.

"But I can't ask you to do that," said the astonished old man.

"You haven't asked me," replied Ruben. "The matter is not open for discussion, it is really no problem. If I continued to Ur tonight, I would arrive too late to do anything anyway. It is the least I can do for a fellow Guardsman's father. I will be in the next hut. Make sure you call me if she becomes any worse." So saying, Ruben left the old man who was too astonished to speak and he just cried out of relief.

The plight of the old man had moved Ruben. And it solved his problem of where to stay the night. Apart from telling him that Simeon was in Ur, which greatly excited him, he was only repaying the kindness of a few years previously, which he could hardly mention.

****

Lieutenant Bel soon found both Captain Tryone and the leatherworker Habib, who were getting together in their temporary quarters. The captain spoke as he came in, and said, "I understand that you seem to have frightened the enemy away, Lieutenant. Have you heard how the general is crowing about it as his own personal victory?"

"Yes," said the lieutenant, sitting down on a seat, which Habib provided for him. "Crazy old sod, he is damn lucky to be alive. But I think that his life has cost us the life of one of the best recruits that we had ever seen," he said dejectedly, removing his helmet and accepting the goblet of wine that was pushed towards him.

"What do you mean?" queried Captain Tryone, with a puzzled frown.

"The old bugger went chasing after the fleeing Persians, and I let young Ruben go after him to bring him back. Now I think the Persians captured the boy. At least that is what I think may have happened," he said tiredly.

So the story of the battle, according to Lieutenant Bel, was told. He told Captain Tryone about what Habib had given to Ruben, which Captain Tryone knew nothing of until now. He had asked Habib to pass the scroll on to Ruben, before they left. The captain told the two men roughly what was on the scroll, and said that he thought Ruben may have taken this opportunity to disappear and would be a long way away by now.

"By the gods," exclaimed Lieutenant Bel. "I think you're right, the cunning little scamp."

"Not so little," said Habib. "He is a lot bigger than me, and he is still growing. I bet he will be as big as you, Lieutenant, or possibly even bigger. Best of luck to him, that's what I say."

"And there is nothing that we can do about it," chuckled Captain Tryone, "The General would not let Commander Schudah have the boys swear the Oath of Allegiance, so he hasn't broken any rules."

"Yeah, he's a bright kid, all right," laughed little Habib. "Led you a merry dance."

"I think the best thing that you can do, Lieutenant, is to mark him down as a casualty of battle, and be glad for the boy. After all, you may now keep your javelin throwing title next year. Because if he were around you would have great difficulty in keeping it," said the captain.

"Yes, I suppose you're right," brightened up Lieutenant Bel. "Well, let's have a drink to wish him well, wherever he is." So they refilled their wine goblets and drank a toast to Ruben, and went on to discuss the crazy antics of the old semi-retired general, as no harm had really been done.

\*\*\*\*

As the sky was beginning to pale to the east, Ruben came out of his hut. He went directly to the other hut, ducked through the doorway and noticing that the old man was asleep, went directly over to the elderly patient to check on her condition. She still looked grey and not too well, but she was awake and whispered, "Are you the young man who came last night?"

"Yes, old mother, and how are you feeling this morning?" he enquired.

"Much the same, young sir. I am sorry that I cannot get you some breakfast," she offered apologetically.

"Do not be silly," smiled Ruben. "What I want to know is if you feel up to making the journey to Ur, to see the old man of the marshes and see if he can cure your illness."

"But I cannot walk," replied the old woman with a puzzled expression. "And it is at least a morning's walk away."

"You are not going to walk," commanded Ruben. He went over to the old man and woke him up with a gentle shake of his shoulder. Ruben asked him to prepare for the journey. He asked the old man whether he had a litter on which Ruben could lay his wife.

"No, I have nothing like that," answered the old man, as he got a few belongings together. "But I can help you build one. It will not take long if we dismantle one of the beds."

"Wait a moment, my friend, and let me see how heavy your wife is." Leaning over the old lady and squatting down, Ruben placed his arms under her and lifted her like a child. He was surprised how light and frail she was. He turned to the old man and said, "Do not worry about the litter. She is no weight at all." He carried her outside and made sure that she was comfortable in his arms and wrapped a blanket around her, to protect her from the cool morning breeze. He asked the old man to fasten his helmet, as he had his hands full. He was surprised to realise that the old man hardly came up to his shoulder. He remembered when he had passed this way a few years previously that the old man had been slightly taller than he was then.

They started the journey and despite his burden, Ruben had to regulate his pace to the speed of the old man. He realised that this would make the journey a lot longer, so he turned to the old man and said, "Tie your bundle around my neck, so that you have nothing to carry. Now just you follow at your own pace, old friend."

"Why yes, young sir, you are very kind. I will try to follow as fast as I can," he said apologetically.

It was then easy for Ruben to lengthen his stride, as he wanted to get as far as possible before the sun started to heat everything up. Checking occasionally that the old lady was in no distress he hurried along, as the ground began to rise under his feet, and they rose above the mist that still hung over the marshes. As he continued in a southwesterly direction, the sun was beginning to beat down upon his back and to burn off the mist from the surrounding marshlands. He could now see Ur in the distance.

****

Commander Schudah was reading Lieutenant Bel's list of casualties, when there was a knock on his door and his lieutenant aide came in and said, "Sorry to trouble you, sir, but I have the senior metalworker outside who is demanding to see you on urgent business."

"Well you had better show him in," said the commander in a rather irritated manner. "And while I am seeing him, you can ask Lieutenant Bel to come and see me."

The metalworker was excited and launched straight into what was on his mind. "We seem to have discovered how to make the new metal called iron into a stable, very hard and strong metal, that is ideal for making armaments as it is far stronger than bronze. It also keeps its edge for longer. As you know we have been working on this for a long time. What we have to do is melt it to a high temperature and mix it with certain quantities of charcoal and…" The commander cut him short.

"I am sure you know what you are talking about, but you have lost me already. I do not really need to know the details yet. It certainly sounds excellent news, but what is so vital? At the moment I am very busy."

"But the metal comes from the mountains in the north, right beside the Persian border. And the mines must be protected. So can you send me lots of soldiers? If we can equip our army first, we will be in a strong position." This all came out in a crazy jumble of words, as the man was excited. The commander told him to cool down, but it was important, very important.

After a long pause, he smiled at the man and told him that due to the importance of this find he would definitely send him as many soldiers as possible to defend the area. He then asked him to come back later in the day, by which time he would have sorted something out. The man's excitement was infectious, and he found himself smiling as Lieutenant Bel came in.

"Ah yes, Lieutenant, I was just reading out the casualties list. It is very good, so few either dead or injured. But I was very sorry to see Ruben Ben Uriah's name on the list. He will be missed, a very sad loss. I know you were friendly with him. What exactly happened?"

"Well actually, sir, when we attacked, we found the old general was right in the front waving his sword about, like a man possessed. Right in the front rank he was, so I with the expert swordsman on my left and young Ruben on the right, we kept in front of him. The expert swordsman killed many Persians the young Ruben certainly kept up with us, but when we reached the agreed limit, the old general went charging on. I let Ruben chase after him to bring him back. That was the last I saw of him, the old general came back alone," he said, shifting uneasily.

The commander mistook this for sadness and said, "Never mind Lieutenant, you mustn't blame yourself. But if you're ever in that situation again let the old goat kill himself – to be honest he is a real pain in the arse. We lost the wrong man, but don't worry, you did very well and I am requesting your Lieutenant's appointment to be made permanent."

\*\*\*\*

As Ruben neared the town and could make out the different buildings, he could also make out Simeon's floating reed house moored beside the river. It was slightly different from when he had last seen it, as it now had a new small dome shaped hut at the other end of the reed mat, although the palatial building looked unchanged. He was now very thirsty and sweat ran in a great stream down his back. He considered going via the inn for a jug of beer to quench his thirst, when the old lady coughed, and moved restlessly in his arms.

"Not much further now, old mother," he said and forgot about his thirst, changing direction to make straight for Simeon's floating reed house.

As he began the slight descent towards the river he noticed that a group of people was standing outside the inn, looking at the unusual sight of a single Babylonian Guard carrying a person down to the floating house. In front of the group of the people was a pretty young woman who watched his every step intently.

His attention was directed back to the floating reed house, as the hunched figure of Ishmala came out of the new hut and looked in his direction. The large black figure then hurried back into the palatial building, and the bright green turbaned figure of Simeon appeared at the doorway. Realising that Ishmala would not recognise him and would still be extremely cautious of any Babylonian Guardsman, he suppressed a smile and thought that Simeon would also not recognise him. Putting on a stern expression he continued down the bank and stepped on to the floating reed mat. He stopped then as Simeon came forward, fixing him with those piercing blue eyes and said, "What have you brought for me to look at this time, Ruben?"

# 8
# SIMEON

The whole element of surprise was lost, but beneath those bright blue eyes Simeon's face beheld Ruben with a wide friendly smile. It was catching, and Ruben smiled back just as broadly, his eyes on the same level as Simeon's. "It is all right Ishmala, it is an old friend. He would not hurt you, and I think you would like to meet him. I am sure he wants to meet you," he called back over his shoulder. The old lady coughed and Simeon immediately became business like. "Bring your burden in here," said Simeon, turning and walking back into the main building. "Lay her on the small bed beside the wall, and tell me what you can about her infirmity."

"I am afraid I know very little," said Ruben. "This is an old lady who lives along the river, with her husband who is still on his way, but she can tell you more about her illness and with your leave I will return to help her husband along." Ruben took off his helmet, as well as the bundle that belonged to the old man and laid them aside, standing back from the bed to give Simeon plenty of room. He turned to find Ishmala standing right behind him, his face lighting up in a huge grin of recognition. Ruben found that he still had to look up into the large smiling black face, as he only came up to Ishmala's chin. He found that the breath was squeezed from his lungs, as he was clasped in a mighty embrace from the huge man.

"Ishmala can come with you," said Simeon without even looking up. "He can carry the old man."

They turned to leave and noticed as they walked out of the building, that the crowd from the inn had followed Ruben to the side of the river. The pretty girl in the front of the party gave a shout of recognition and leapt on to the floating mat and threw herself into Ruben's arms, smothering his face with kisses.

"I thought it was you right from when I first saw you, but how big you have grown in four years!" said Lialah.

"I am not the only one," said Ruben, holding her at arm's length. "You have grown into a very beautiful young woman." They stood blushing at each other, but moved off when Simeon called out, "You will have plenty of time to renew your friendship later, but now you have a job to do."

"I will come with you," said Lialah, hardly louder than a whisper, "And bring you up to date as we go."

"That sounds great to me," said Ruben. "But first let me have a drink of water, before I drop."

After Ruben had slaked his thirst with a couple of mugs of the cold spring water, Ishmala, Ruben and Lialah set off back down the caravan route looking for the old man. Lialah walked between the two men, with her arm around Ruben's and her other hand holding Ishmala's. During the short period that it took them to reach the old man as he came wearily along, Lialah talked the whole time. She told Ruben of how Ishmala had escaped from the crocodile and had been helped out of the water by Simeon. He had laid in a fever for about three moon cycles, due to the deep wounds in his leg, which had been infected. Simeon had nursed him, changing the bandages and dressings every day, but the wound seemed to get worse and the smell was quite overpowering – which was why Simeon had built the small hut for Ishmala. Eventually Simeon had found a special floating flower and from its leaves he had made a hot poultice, which had cured the infection and saved Ishmala's life. Even then it had taken him the best part of a year before he could walk again and recover his strength. He still walked with a slight limp, but it did not seem to worry him. Anyway, he now lived with Simeon in the floating house, but kept to his separate hut. He was a tremendous help to Simeon because he could push the raft off any part of the marsh where it had caught in the reeds or on the mud banks, as well as helping Simeon in his role as a doctor to the people of the marshes. Lialah still called Simeon, Uncle S'meon, which Ruben found very endearing. Lialah chatted all the way, which was rather convenient for both Ruben and Ishmala, as it would take a long time for Ishmala to explain everything in sign language – apart from which Ishmala enjoyed Lialah's company almost as much as Ruben did.

When they reached the old man, Ruben told him that his wife was now safely with Simeon, whom the old man also called S'meon. Ruben insisted on helping Ishmala carry the old man back to Simeon's floating reed house, by making a seat for him on their interlocked hands. This meant that the old man could also put his arms around both their necks, leaving Lialah to walk behind with a supporting hand on his back and her other hand still entwined in Ruben's arm. During the journey back she went on to tell Ruben how pleased Simeon had been to hear from his captain, and that they had eagerly awaited his return. By this time they had almost reached the reed house again. Lialah was still chatting to Ruben about some changes in Ur, caused by the order for crocodile skins for the army – asking him if his jerkin was one of them. He had just told her that his jerkin had started new recruits for the Babylonian Guards wearing the crocodile skin jerkins, when Simeon told Lialah to cease her constant babble and to go back home to collect her bags. Ruben gave

Simeon an enquiring glance, which made Simeon ask, "Hasn't she told you yet?" When Ruben shook his head Simeon merely smiled and said "Oh well, no doubt she will inform him. But now I must get back to my patient. Your room is as you left it."

Simeon went back to talk to the old man who was sitting beside his wife. Ishmala had gone back to his hut at the other end of the reed mat, so Ruben went to the room, which he had occupied before, where his helmet had already been placed. He was delighted to see that his sword was still placed above his bed, still in the reed and rush scabbard that he had made for it. The hilt was just as he remembered it, with dark leather binding which felt comfortable in his hand. The pommel still had the large lapis lazuli stone that was surrounded by small fragments of a clear stone, which caught the light, so that it shimmered and sparkled in the sun, which he could see through the window grill. Lifting it down from the wall, he drew the sword from the scabbard and gasped in wonder. It was not the dull grey that he remembered, but was now a shining silver blade, which was very sharp. Someone had obviously spent a long time cleaning and polishing the blade. He unfastened his own sword and removed the leather satchel that Habib had given him. This contained the goatskin sheath, which he now tried out. It fitted perfectly. As he was now experienced in the art of sword fighting, he could tell that the balance of the sword was ideal and he could easily wield the sword with one hand. He also found his old knapsack with his other few possessions, like the small knife, the tinderbox and a few coins that Mutek had given him. All of this had also been carefully cleaned and obviously well guarded. He puzzled at this for a while, remembering Simeon's dislike of warfare and anything connected with it, then decided that this must have been the work of Ishmala. He laid out everything neatly on his bed. He unlaced his crocodile skin jerkin, which he added to his possessions, then he stood back to admire them. He thought that it was not a great deal to have accumulated in four years, but then remembered the vast number of things that he had learnt in the army, all of which would help him on his quest. Hearing a noise outside he left everything where it was and stepped outside his room. Lialah had returned and was listening to Simeon, who said, "Now my dear, I know that you want to talk to Ruben, but that must wait as I will need peace and quiet with my patient. So I will be most grateful if you can send Ruben out to talk to Ishmala and get on with preparing the evening meal, as I will not be able to do it myself."

"But of course, Uncle S'meon. But where should I put my bags?"

"I don't really mind," said Simeon. "I suppose you will be sharing Ruben's room, if he can put up with your incessant chatter," he chuckled.

Overhearing this conversation, or rather command by Simeon, he started walking towards the doorway that led out on to the floating mat, but stopped beside Lialah and Simeon and stood to attention, thumped his chest in a salute, then walked on outside towards Ishmala's hut. Lialah said nothing, but put her bags in his bedroom and then went into the small kitchen to start preparing the evening meal. Ruben continued to Ishmala's hut, where he sat down facing Ishmala, and began talking to him and asking if it was he who had polished the sword and had kept everything of his so clean and tidy. Ishmala nodded and explained in his own sign language that he had spent a long time cleaning the sword with grape juice and fine white sand. He had then polished the sword with a special wax that was made by one of the small insects that flew around the marshlands. They continued to communicate most of the afternoon with Ishmala showing Ruben the large scars where he had been attacked by the a huge crocodile. Then he listened as Ruben told him about the main things that he had done and learnt at the training camp. He was about to tell Ishmala about how he had left the battle at Sousa when Lialah came over and said that Simeon required his assistance. Strangely she then stayed talking to Ishmala, while he went to see what Simeon wanted him to do.

As he entered the main building, Simeon handed him his jerkin and helmet and said, "I would like you to take the old man up to the inn and ask the innkeeper to give him a room for the night, which I will happily pay for." So Ruben put on his helmet and jerkin and led the old man out of the building and up the bank to the inn. He spoke to the innkeeper, who looked exactly the same as he had four years ago. The innkeeper did not recognise him and he thought it best not to even try to explain that he had stayed at the inn before. The innkeeper said that he was very happy to give the old man a room for the night and he would not charge anything for either the room or an evening meal. He also said to Ruben that he had great respect for S'meon and for a Guardsman, which he quickly corrected himself to say Sergeant, when he noticed the insignia on Ruben's tunic.

Leaving the grateful old man, Ruben went directly back to give the good news to Simeon. When he entered the main building of the floating house he was amazed to see Simeon kneeling next to the old lady with his hands resting on her head, with his eyes closed and his face quite rigid, with beads of sweat standing out on his brow. He quietly walked back to where Ishmala and Lialah were talking and asked Lialah in a quiet voice, "What is going on?" Lialah told him that Simeon was healing the old woman. How he did it was a complete mystery, but he required them not to interfere. She also told him that afterwards Simeon would be very tired, so that they would have to wait until he had rested before they ate their evening meal.

Eventually, Simeon appeared at the doorway, beckoning them to return. He looked totally drained, which gave him a haggard appearance. He said, "Will you please give the old woman a drink, and excuse me while I go and have a lie down?"

The old woman was sitting up and said, "What happened? I remember going to sleep as I felt so weak, but now I feel a lot better and am thirsty and hungry." Ruben gave her a drink of water, while Lialah warmed up some broth that Simeon had prepared earlier, which she then gave to the old woman, saying, "You must rest now and you can get up in the morning." The old woman obeyed her without question and was soon fast asleep.

Lialah told Ruben to get the table laid for their evening meal and to call Ishmala. When Ruben came back with the large Nubian, Simeon had returned and looked a lot better for having a short rest. While Lialah was serving a most unusual vegetarian meal, Simeon said to Ruben, "We will be leaving Ur tomorrow morning, when the current takes us out into the marshlands. The old woman will then be able to return home with her husband, and we will be travelling across the marshes to a town on the eastern side, where I have promised to take Lialah. However, I am not sure how long it will take. That will depend on the current and if I am delayed for any reason by the Creator."

"Why are you taking Lialah away from here?" asked Ruben. "She has not told me anything about this." He looked enquiringly at Lialah, and then at Simeon, waiting for one of them to explain to him.

Eventually Simeon said, "Her mother has arranged for her to go and work in Babylon, as she feels Ur is not the right place for her to live. It is now a quiet and uninteresting town for a young woman." He then continued, "Now if you, Ruben, are still intent on following your father's footsteps, to try and trace his whereabouts and find where Abraham led many tribes thousands of years ago, you will need to go in the same direction. But you can make your mind up about that on the journey across the marshes. That will be your decision, and I have let Lialah share your bedroom. But it is important," and he raised a warning finger looking at both of them, "that both of you understand that if Ruben decides to follow his destiny, then you must part."

Ruben understood what he meant, as despite being in the training camp, he was no stranger to sexual attraction and where it ended, or life began. In the training camp, he had been one of quite a few of the lads who had often sneaked out at night (this was done with the knowledge of the commanding officer, provided that all who went returned). The midnight outing was to a Bedouin brothel that often camped nearby.

During the meal, which Ruben found unusually tasty and remarkably varied, particularly as there was no meat or fish, the conversation continued, as Simeon told him about some additions that he had made to his museums, which he would show to Ruben in the morning. He told Ruben that the marshlands were moving further to the south and that it was possible that the old caravan route may well be used again, allowing Ur to regain its importance.

When they had finished the meal, Lialah and Ishmala gathered the plates and took them outside to be left for the insects to clean – which Ruben remembered was Simeon's usual habit. Lialah and Ishmala then went into Ruben's bedroom and started rearranging things, while Ruben continued his conversation with Simeon. There was so much that he wanted to ask him, but firstly he asked him about the healing, what he had done and how he had done it. Simeon told him that it was a form of healing where he drove out the illness by placing hands on the person who was ill. He said that it was a gift that he had developed and came directly from the Creator. When Ruben asked him if he was the only person with this gift, he said that quite a few people could develop it. It was similar in many respects to the art of seeing the colour that surrounds a person, which Ruben had discovered earlier. He then asked Ruben if he had used the technique that Simeon had taught him previously. Ruben said that he had only tried once, but that it was difficult as there were always plenty of other people and a lot of things going on that disturbed his concentration. Simeon said that it was not the time or place for this principle and that it could not be easily adopted, when people were thinking about killing one another, but that Ruben may be able to relearn the art, provided that he could concentrate his mind on pleasant things.

At this point Lialah and Ishmala returned, Lialah kissed Simeon on the cheek and said, "Goodnight Uncle S'meon," then she turned to Ishmala and did the same, wishing him pleasant dreams. She then ruffled Ruben's hair as she walked past and told him not to sit talking all night.

Simeon began telling Ruben that he now allowed Ishmala to eat fish, as Ishmala had pointed out that they were not warm-blooded creatures unlike people or other animals. So Simeon had allowed this, providing that Ishmala ate in his own hut. Which made Ishmala laugh, he pointed to his stomach, which he then rubbed and pointed to his mouth then rubbed his stomach, indicating that he really enjoyed eating the fish. He then flexed his arms, showing his enormous biceps and again patting and rubbing his stomach, indicating that the fish he ate gave him strength. This made Simeon laugh and he said, "You do not need to eat fresh fish or any flesh from one of the Creators creatures to make you strong," Ruben said. "But surely, the Creator also made the plants that grow, and they are living things."

"Yes, Ruben," responded Simeon. "But they are a necessary part of the food chain, and they regenerate themselves anyway."

"Yes, Simeon," replied Ruben. "But surely large fish eat small fish as well as insects, so it cannot be totally wrong to eat other animals."

"My dear Ruben, I do not deny that for one minute, but there are many things that I cannot rationalise, it is simply that I do not see the need to eat other living animals when I can live quite well by eating plants."

Simeon then asked Ruben how he had become a Babylonian Guardsman, and risen to the rank of sergeant so quickly. Ruben told him that it was only a temporary appointment, made when he graduated, and it was all because he was required to lead a platoon of new recruits to the battle at Sousa. He then went on to tell of how, when he had been knocked out and woke up, being cut off from his own troops, that he had managed to slip away unnoticed. He then discovered the boat at the shore of the Inferior Sea and had rowed back past Lagash. He had then come ashore by the pirate ship, and had sunk the boat to avoid discovery. Ishmala thought that this was great fun, laughed merrily and patted Ruben on the back. Ishmala stood up, put his hands beside his head which he then tilted to one side, indicating that he was going to sleep, he smiled at both his friends, turned and went to his hut.

Ruben was about to ask Simeon more questions, but was interrupted by Simeon who said, "I am sure you have many questions, if I am not careful you will get me talking all night. I remember that last time you went to sleep while I was talking. But now I need my sleep, apart from which Lialah told you not to be up too late." With that they both went to bed.

Ruben was surprised when he went into his bedroom to see that it had all been changed round and that where the old bed had been, there was now a double bed. His belongings had all been neatly tidied up and placed on a shelf by the wall. Lialah was in bed, but not asleep. She said to him, "I thought you were never coming. Once you start talking to Simeon you never stop."

"Hark who's talking," he chuckled, whilst he got undressed. "This is a pleasant surprise," he said. "But I must warn you that as Simeon correctly surmised, I will be following my father's footsteps and trying to find my true homeland. It is only fair to warn you that, despite your charms, I will be leaving you in Babylon."

Lialah sighed, and said, "I thought as much, but we can enjoy one another's company whilst we can." So saying she lifted the sheets, inviting him to join her. He realised that she was wearing nothing and quickly finished undressing and slipped in beside her. She was warm and pliable in his hands, and she put her arms around his neck and huskily whispered in his ear, "You seem to be all covered in hard muscles, did you do nothing but hard work with the men in the training camp?"

"Not all the time, we did occasionally find female company, if that is what you are trying to find out," he said smiling, and returned her passionate kisses. He made love to her tenderly, fully enjoying the warmth and softness of her body, after which they spoke quietly for a few moments, until she went to sleep in his arms. He realised that his journey across the marshes was going to be most enjoyable, but knew that it would be but a brief interlude before he started once more on his quest.

The next morning, he awoke as the day was beginning, slipped out from beneath the sheets and quietly left the sleeping Lialah and went through the main building, stopping briefly by the old woman to check that she was sleeping soundly. He came out onto the platform, just as Ishmala came out of his hut and gave him a large smile. He said to Ishmala, "I am going for a swim, is that what you intended to do?" Ishmala nodded agreement, and the two men dived over the side of the raft into the mist-shrouded waters, knowing full well that there was no danger of crocodiles in the early morning. Ruben was a good swimmer, but despite his fitness he was still no match for Ishmala, as the large black man went for an early morning swim most days. They swam around, laughing and splashing one another for quite a while. And then reboarded the floating mat just as the sun was beginning to burn through the mist.

Ruben re-entered the main house with a towel around his waist and was greeted by Simeon, who was talking to the old woman. He could hear Lialah moving around in the kitchen and went to say good-morning. She came over and gave him a kiss and said, "As you brought no clean clothes with you I have brought some of my older brother's old clothes. They might be a little small, but get dressed anyway because I think S'meon wants you to take the old woman back to her husband as soon as we have had some breakfast." This he did, and found that she was correct about the clothes, which only just fitted and were very tight across the chest, shoulders and biceps. Lialah laughed at him when she came into the bedroom and told him not to worry, as she would make them fit by adding a small insert to the clothes. As they would be out in the marshlands for the next several days, it would not really matter, but they must buy him some new clothes when they got to Babylon.

They all sat on the floor around the small table eating a light but tasty breakfast, made from an unusual type of reed barley mixed with asses' milk and a large type of watermelon. Ruben decided that Lialah was a good cook and handy to have around, as well as her other obvious comforts.

After breakfast, Simeon asked him to take the old woman, who now seemed fully recovered and had joined them for breakfast, back to join her husband at the inn. He was pleased to be accompanied by Ishmala who had three eels that had been caught overnight on a fishing line attached to the end of the floating mat. Ishmala had indicated to Ruben that he did not want to eat the eels, but was taking them up to the town. Ruben took the old woman into the inn to be welcomed most gratefully by her husband, who could not thank Ruben enough, a fact which Ruben found rather embarrassing. After checking with the innkeeper that there was nothing owing, he bade them farewell and went in search of Ishmala. He found him just coming out of a new shop that had been opened by the man who caught the crocodiles, as his business had improved due to the demand for crocodile hides from the army. He was carrying a small cured crocodile skin that was a dark green colour. When Ruben asked him what it was for, Ishmala pointed to where Ruben would carry his sword, indicating that it would look good on the goat skin sheath and that it was his gift to Ruben. Ruben thanked him very much and told him that he had already been too kind, but Ishmala dismissed this by indicating that crocodiles were bad animals, but that their skins were useful. Ruben could fully understand Ishmala's dislike of crocodiles, particularly as one had nearly killed him.

When they got back to the floating reed house, they found Simeon untying the raft from the large stakes that held it to the riverbank. They both helped Simeon in this task and then stepped aboard the floating mat and Ruben was again incredulous at how Simeon knew that the current would take them out, which it did.

Simeon told Ruben that they would travel west to Larsa, then cross the caravan route where it was normally floated, then travel north to Uruk and finally northwest to Kish, which was the western side of the marshlands. From there he could take Lialah to Babylon, which was less than a day's walk away. Babylon was meant to be an amazing city that was dominated by the citadel where the fabulous Hanging Gardens were to be found. Ruben thought this was exciting because it was from there that his quest really began.

****

Commander Schudah was delighted by the swift response to his request for more troops, which were being despatched as soon as possible from Babylon. They would come down river to dock at Lagash and he would send them immediately northwards with the senior metalworker to Sar-e Pol-e Zohab where the new ore was taken out of the ground and smelted into iron, which could then be manufactured into weapons. If these weapons were as good as the few that had been captured from the pirates who had come from the east, they would make a fantastic difference. That difference would give the Babylonian army a great advantage, but rather than raise hopes that may not materialise he had sworn the senior metalworker to secrecy, with the promise of large amounts of the money that would pour into Lagash as the main trading post. He was extremely pleased that the army had held on to Sousa, and that the Persian army had moved back to the north into the mountains, but felt sure that there was a sound reason for this, far more than the crazy old general claimed. He seemed convinced that he had frightened them off.

The new troops arrived the very next day, in three boatloads and, much to his delight, they included another small company of Babylonian Guards, and the lieutenant in charge of this small company also carried confirmation of Lieutenant Belthezder's appointment. Some of the Babylonian Guards would be sent northward to the mines with the other soldiers, and he would integrate some of the new platoons with them. He was also rather pleased that the new trainees were to be allowed to keep their crocodile skin jerkins. All of this added to his prestige as a city commander, rather than a border town commander. As soon as he had been told that Sousa was safe, he had sent Captain Tryone back to the training camp. Much to his relief, because all of these young trainees were getting in everybody's way, apart from which the young ones were not very disciplined.

A few days later he received a request for a new small boat from the training camp, as the previous one had been stolen. He wondered who would steal the rowing boat, because it was painted bright orange and it would be a major job to repaint the boat so that it was unnoticeable. He remembered the day when the general had come back earlier. One of the lookouts on the harbour walls had reported seeing a small brightly coloured boat being rowed up river, by the far bank. But when he had heard the report, he had dismissed it as being unimportant, and as the sun had been very bright that day, he had thought that it had been a mistake. Anyway, he had far more important things to worry about, so he simply approved the request from the training camp, and passed the order out to the man who had taken over Mutek's boatyard. The man had not only taken over the boatyard, but he had taken Mutek's daughter as a wife. This was the daughter that he was rather fond of himself, but he had resigned himself to never taking a wife. His job kept him busy, even though he had quite liked the idea of having children – particularly if they had turned out like young Ruben – who he then remembered as being reported missing from after the battle at Sousa. It was a shame, as he had been a nice boy, but possibly he was not cut out for fatherhood. Still there was no point in daydreaming, he had far too much to do, and he had been very successful so far in his life anyway.

His musings were interrupted by a knock on the door, and when he called out "Enter," Lieutenant Bel came in.

"I am sorry to trouble you, sir, but I thought it would be best to let you know that the general has just left for Babylon. He asked me if he could take one of the new Crocs who could read and write back with him. He left his expert swordsman in exchange, as the man requested to come back to see more action. I sent him off with young Latich, who has been promoted to corporal – if you remember he was a good friend to young Ruben. But when Ruben disappeared or was possibly captured or killed, he seems to have lost confidence in himself."

"Yes, that's fine, Lieutenant, thank you for letting me know," said the commander, "Oh yes, and would you like to join me for dinner tonight, as I would like to discuss some new ideas with you?"

"Thank you very much, sir," said the surprised lieutenant. "I would be delighted to accept."

\*\*\*\*

After they left Ur, Simeon spent most of the day with Ruben, showing him around his four museums, which contained everything that could be found in the marshlands. The first had a few additions to the plants and flowers, and in particular Simeon pointed out the leaf from which he had made the poultice, which had healed Ishmala's wounds. The next room that held all the insects only had one addition, but Simeon pointed out the small wasp that made the wax that Ishmala had used to polish Ruben's sword. The room full of birds' feathers did not have any additions, but Ruben still found it fascinating. He pointed to many of the feathers and asked what type of bird they had come from and realised, according to Simeon, that the marshlands were a stopping place for many of the birds that flew from the south every spring. The same birds would then return after the summer. In the last room, Simeon had a great addition of fish, which had been found by Ishmala as he was a very good swimmer and could stay underwater for longer than Simeon could. Because of this he had been able to see a lot more fish, and the whole underwater world was more complex than Ruben had thought possible. Additionally there were some fish, which Simeon said proved to him that the marshlands were moving further south. These fish would only be found where the water was much warmer all year round.

The rest of the day was spent in conversation about various plant and animal life that had been started by looking through the museums. That evening they had gone to bed early and Ruben had said to Lialah, in the quiet dark after they had exerted themselves in passionate lovemaking, "I think Simeon is amazing in the way that he knows so much and can tell so much by even tiny changes."

"Yes, and when he keeps referring to the Creator, presumably he means there is one person who made everything, do you think that's true?"

"I really couldn't say," replied Ruben. "But it's certainly a new concept, and in many ways it seems a lot more sensible than having lots of separate gods."

The next few days were quiet. With the raft drifting along through the marshlands, the sun blazing down during the day, but with the mist rising from the marshes in the evening, which was quite a relief as it was cool and made it far easier to sleep. Simeon told them that they should arrive at Larsa on the following day. That afternoon he found Ruben sitting at the back of the house, quietly watching all the animal life around him.

"Are you trying to compose your thoughts so that you can see the colour surrounding people?" inquired Simeon, looking hard at Ruben, fixing him with those bright blue eyes.

"Yes, that is exactly what I'm doing. At times I'm sure you can read my mind," challenged Ruben.

"You are not the first person to say that," said Simeon. "But it is not a question of being able to read anybody's mind, but simply observing them closely."

"Oh," exclaimed Ruben. "I didn't mean to be rude, but that's the impression I often get."

"Do not worry, my boy," said Simeon, placing a reassuring hand on Ruben's shoulder. "Now tell me, did you have to kill anyone while you were in the army?"

"One person," said Ruben. "But that was when I was attacked when I was out one night with my training sergeant. But it was not really deliberate. After all, he thought that he had killed me." And Ruben related the whole story of the fight with the brigands. "But apart from that, at the battle in Sousa everything happened so quickly." He then told Simeon about when he had fought alongside Lieutenant Bel and the expert swordsman.

"So it is possible that you killed some of the Persians in the attack at Sousa," said Simeon. "But as you say, that was all happening quickly, so you cannot be sure." There was then a long silence, before Simeon spoke again. "But that was before you went after the old general, which was in itself an act of kindness. I do not suppose that you will be judged too harshly."

"I do not know what you mean by being judged, Simeon," said Ruben, with a bewildered expression.

"I am not totally sure myself," responded Simeon dismissively. "But it may take you a while before you can order your thoughts to be in harmony with the thoughts of the Creator."

"But you think I still will be able to see the colour that surrounds a person, depending upon what they are thinking?" asked Ruben, brightening up. "Because it is such a wonderful thing to be able to do. I remember that I was doing it in Ur without much difficulty. But then it suddenly disappeared when I heard that Captain Gershnarl was at the inn and – well, I'm sure you know the rest. About me throwing mud at the captain when he was about to hit Lialah, but then of my being caught and Ishmala suddenly appearing and killing the evil Captain Gershnarl."

"It is not for us to judge whether someone is evil or not," explained Simeon. "Because we do not know the full circumstances that have affected the other person."

"But everyone says that he was evil," protested Ruben. "Surely you know what he did to my father and mother?"

"All too well, my boy. But it is not my job to judge," explained Simeon. "Perhaps he was evil, and Ishmala was carrying out a just execution, but that is not for me to say."

"I am sorry Simeon, but I do not think I really understand what you are trying to tell me," said the still bewildered Ruben. "Perhaps I am being not very intelligent. But changing the subject slightly, did you know my mother? And if so, what was she like?"

"Yes, I knew your mother very well, and she was more beautiful than any woman that I have ever seen. She was even more beautiful than Lialah, although not dissimilar, except that she had beautiful golden hair," said Simeon with a misty look to his eyes, almost as if he was about to cry.

"And was my father a brave person, as Mutek told me?" continued Ruben.

"It is not for me to say whether or not he was brave, all I can tell you is I think he always tried to do the right thing, but he often had difficult decisions to make," said Simeon. "And I was sorry to learn that Gershnarl ordered Mutek to be lashed to death, I can understand for that reason alone why Ishmala killed Gershnarl."

Simeon sat with Ruben in companionable silence, watching the wildlife of the marshlands as the floating raft drifted along towards the west and the sun sank into a wonderful sunset. Everything around them seemed to be gold and the final rays of the sun turned the water into burnished copper. Lialah called them in for dinner just as it was beginning to get dark and the mist was starting to rise from the water.

That evening, Simeon and Ruben were both silent, each occupied with his own thoughts. It was a very quiet evening meal. Lialah had just collected the plates and was putting them outside, when Ishmala touched Ruben's arm and beckoned him to follow him out to his hut. Ruben followed Ishmala and watched him as he set out his fishing line that occasionally caught eels overnight. As Ishmala was throwing the line into the water, he and Ruben froze like statues as they saw the snout of a small crocodile that was following a duck with a line of chicks following in its wake. The small crocodile was about to snap up one of the chicks when Ruben noticed the pole beside him that Ishmala occasionally used to push the raft clear of reeds or mud-banks. Without thinking Ruben picked up the pole and hurled it like a javelin, it struck the crocodile on the back of its head. Although it did not really injure the crocodile, particularly as it was not pointed, it made the crocodile miss its target. There was then a great commotion in the water then, as the duck flew into the air rounding on the beast, trying to distract it from attacking the chicks, which quickly disappeared into a bed of reeds. Ishmala thought this was very funny, heartily clapping and patting Ruben on the back.

Lislah came over to see what the fuss was all about, so Ruben told her what he had done and said that he would now have to try and get the pole back. Lialah told him not to be silly, because at this time of day the crocodiles were active and that there would be no difficulty in getting a new pole when they reached Larsa. She had to take Ruben indoors to stop him swimming after the pole and asked Simeon to make sure he wasn't so silly in future. Simeon asked what all the fuss had been about, so Ruben told him about throwing the pole at the crocodile to stop it eating the chicks. Simeon said that they ought not to interfere with the marshland creatures, because each one was important in the whole life workings of the marshlands. Ishmala was still laughing about the incident; he'd disagreed with Simeon and indicated that all crocodiles should be hit with poles. He also indicated that Simeon was getting old and a bit crazy. To which Simeon laughed and said, "This crazy old man is going to bed."

Later that night Lialah asked Ruben what he and Simeon had been talking about that afternoon. He told her that he had asked him about his parents and repeated the gist of the conversation. He also asked Lialah if she had ever seen a person with gold coloured hair, as most of the people had dark hair, like hers. She said that if his mother had gold hair that was why Ruben's hair was lighter than everyone else's in the area. She also said that a person's hair and eye colour depended very much on that of their parents. Ruben then asked her how long she had known Simeon.

"All my life, at least, I met him when I was small, but I have only really known him personally for the last six years," she explained. But then added, "It is strange, because my memories of him when I was young, were that he was very old and quite small. But you know how often things seem different when you are young, but I clearly remember that I think he didn't have bright blue eyes. Your eyes are just the same, you know."

"You contradicted yourself then," laughed Ruben, teasing her and then continued. "I think your memory is at fault, anyway, how old do you think Simeon is?"

"I really don't know," she answered. "He is one of those people who may be really old, but you can't tell as he is so darkened by all the sun and living out in the marshlands." After agreeing that Simeon was ageless, they went to sleep in each other's arms as they often did.

They arrived the next morning at Larsa, just as Simeon had predicted. Larsa was simply a marshland town that was built on a slightly higher mud flat than the surrounding marshes. This meant that it was virtually an island, particularly in the rainy season when the caravan route was completely underwater. The small town was entirely built from reed houses, some of which were extremely ornate in the way that the weaving had been completed. The whole community gathered when Simeon's floating house came into sight and there was quite a demand for information about what was happening in other places. There were also a few sick people who were waiting for Simeon's doctoring skills. While Simeon was kept busy seeing those people, Ruben had a good look around the town that was little more than a village. Just to the north of the town the ground rose slightly higher, where there was a dense woodland area. Ruben thought that this was as good a place as any to try to find a new pole, to replace the one that he had hurled at the crocodile the previous evening. He therefore took his large sword in its sheath, careful to ensure that the ornate hilt was hidden under the flap, which he still did not want to draw attention to, and went in search of a small tree. The area was densely covered with saplings, some of which looked quite suitable. However, when he leaned on the saplings some of them were flexible and it took him quite a while to find one that was made of a harder wood. He was then faced with cutting it down, and as there was virtually no room to swing the sword, he had to cut the sapling by using a sawing motion. This type of motion normally blunted any sharp instrument, but he was pleased to see that the blade was still as sharp as when he started. Having cut the sapling, he realised it was far longer than the original pole, by just over two full spans of his outstretched arms. He therefore chopped the end off about half a span over the original length, as he thought that this additional length may be an advantage and not difficult for a man of

Ishmala's size to use. The length that he had chopped off the end was not a great deal taller than he was himself and it tapered to the end where it split into small branches on which there were leaves the form of which he had not seen before. He then took the pole and the end back to the floating house.

He showed the new pole to Ishmala, who was truly delighted. The pole was comparatively heavy, but Ishmala indicated that the additional length was an advantage. Seeing Simeon was still occupied, he went into the room of plants and was delighted to find that this was not one of the plants in Simeon's museum. He therefore cut off the end and left it in the museum to see whether Simeon would know what it was.

Lialah had been sent out to get some more food, and Ishmala was trimming off the bark of his new pole, so Ruben thought he would join Ishmala and trim off the bark of the smaller length, which he hoped would make a javelin, as it was about the right size. He had returned the large sword to his bedroom and was using his small bronze knife to strip off the bark. The wood under the bark was white and damp at first, but quickly dried in the hot sun and turned dark. Just stripping the bark had blunted the small bronze knife, and when left to dry the wood seemed hard and less flexible. Ruben was just showing Ishmala his javelin and said that it really needed a metal end, which was sharp and would also give it slightly more weight at the front, which would help it fly up in a straight line, when Simeon came out of the house, having seen one of the people that was sick. Ruben told him about the javelin and the pole, and insisted on showing Simeon the leaves that he had found on the top end of the sapling. Simeon confirmed that he had not seen this plant before and that it was probably a harder wood that normally would be found much further south, which was additional proof that the marshlands were moving farther to the south. Ruben did not think that the position of places could change, but did not say anything about this. Simeon then lifted the javelin and showed Ruben that it only just floated in the water, and said that if he put a heavy metal point on the front end, he had better not throw it in the marshes as it would sink far beneath the surface. Simeon took Ruben ashore to go and find Lialah, so that he could help her bring back the food that she had gone to buy. He walked along with Ruben, leaving Ishmala who was still trying out his new pole. Simeon wanted to go and visit a special place behind the town. They soon found Lialah, who was glad to see them as she had a lot of provisions to carry. Ruben helped her with this, which brought a few strange looks from some of the men in the town, as it was customary for the women to do this work on their own.

Simeon said that he would meet them later back at the reed house but he wanted to leave that evening to enable them to reach the place where they should cross the caravan route the next morning, so that they could then travel to Uruk. They went their separate ways, as Ruben had no difficulties with carrying the provisions that Lialah had bought. On their way back to the reed house, Lialah told Ruben that she had been a long time because she had been caught up in a conversation about the weather. Ruben said, "I thought that the weather here hardly ever changes."

"Generally that is true," said Lialah. "But according to what I was told, the wind will blow down from the mountains in the north and we are in for a storm."

"But surely the storm will not affect us too much if we stay here. Because Simeon told me that he has been through many storms without much damage being done to his house," Ruben replied.

"Yes," said Lialah. "But I understand that it may be difficult to get up to the point where we should cross the caravan route. Do you think that we ought to let Simeon know?"

"Yes, we most certainly should. What we will do is get the provisions back to the reed house, then if you start preparing an early dinner, I will go and get Simeon back," said Ruben.

They soon arrived back at the floating reed house and Ruben told Ishmala what he was going to do. Ishmala agreed that this was a good idea, so Ruben ran off in the direction that Simeon had gone. As he ran through the town, he noticed that many of the people were making sure that everything was secure and that nothing was left outdoors. Ruben found Simeon on a rise, just before the woodland area where they had been earlier. This was the place where the people from the town buried their dead. He saw Simeon standing beside a small pile of stones, which had been placed to show that someone had been buried there. Simeon did not see him coming, as he was standing with his eyes closed. Seeing him like this Ruben slowed down and then walked quietly up to Simeon and touched him lightly on the arm.

"I am sorry to trouble you Simeon, but Lialah was told that we are due to have a storm, which certainly seems correct as everybody in the town is making sure that everything is secure. But she also told me that it may mean we have difficulties in crossing the caravan route, unless we get to the crossing before the storm strikes"

Simeon said, "You did the wise thing in coming to let me know. Let us hurry back to the house and get under way so that we can reach the place before nightfall."

So they hurried along, although Simeon did not run but walked very quickly, and Ruben found it easier to jog along beside him. While they were travelling back, Ruben asked whether the town would be safe. Simeon told him that the storms only came down from the north and that the rise in the ground around the woodland area often served as a good windbreak that protected the town. Ruben asked him whose grave he had been visiting, but Simeon answered dismissively, saying that it was just an old friend. Ruben was rather puzzled by this, as he felt sure that he had seen the hame Simeon cut into one of the stones, but he said nothing.

In a short while they reached the reed house, and were soon inside where Lialah was ready with the evening meal, even though it was still the afternoon. As they ate in silence it was quiet outside, without a breath of wind. When they entered the house Ruben had looked at the sky, which was totally cloudless, and he wondered how people could predict a change in the weather without any obvious sign. A hasty meal was soon consumed and rather than leave the plates outside, Simeon told Lialah to give them a quick wash and then store them away. Simeon came out of the house just as Ruben and Ishmala were untying the floating house from the mud flats on which Larsa was built. Using his new pole Ishmala pushed them away until they were again caught in the current that turned the raft in a northerly direction.

Simeon told them that the caravan route ran to the south of them and soon turned towards the north. Hopefully they would intercept the caravan route where it dipped down below the surface of the marsh, thus allowing the raft mat to cross over. The sky was darkening in the east, as the sun sank in the west towards the marshlands, but this evening there was no sunset of spectacular colour. Simeon pointed to the northern skyline where they could just make out some clouds in the distance. He told them that it would be quite a race to the crossing point before the storm struck. Ruben asked him what would happen if they did not reach the crossing point in time, to which Simeon replied, "In that case we will be driven on to the caravan route and probably be blown to pieces." Ruben thought he was joking at first, because he said it without any emotion or concern. And when asked if he was serious he simply said, "It is in the hands of the Creator, it is for him to decide our fate."

They still drifted northwest, but as Ruben watched the clouds in the distance, they grew as they rushed southwards in the gathering dusk. They could see the slight rise to the west as the caravan route came into sight where it crossed the marshes. Ishmala stood ready with the pole to make sure that they did not run aground. Just as Ruben could make out the dip to the northwest, it was blotted out by a squall of rain, at the same time as the wind struck the house. The waters of the marshland seemed to be whipped into small waves and the progress of the raft stopped, as the wind pushed it southwards, although the current seem to continue pushing northwest.

## 9
## REPAIRS ON THE FINAL DRIFT TO KISH AND BABYLON

Ishmala stood at the forward end of the raft and found that he could just reach the bottom with the pole. Pushing on the pole he then walked down the raft so that it moved north into the wind, which was soon joined by a lashing rain. Ignoring this, Ishmala came to the end of the raft and drew out the pole and then ran back to the front end of the raft and repeated the exercise. As he slowly walked past the house, Ruben shouted to him above the wind and rain that they should take it in turns, so that Ishmala would not tire out too quickly. So this time when Ishmala reached the end, he drew out the pole and threw it to Ruben who repeated the procedure. However, it had now got dark and Ruben knew that there was still a long way to go. On the next pass, Ishmala pointed to the caravan route, which was visible as the waves were whipped into it in a white foam crashing into the bank. Ishmala grabbed his arm and pointed to the large reed rope that was used to secure the raft to the bank. Before Ruben realised what he was indicating, he had picked up the rope, tied the end in a loop, which he passed over his shoulder and jumped off the side of the raft.

Ruben realised what he was doing then, as the water only came up to his waist, and he waded ashore through the boiling foam. Ruben grabbed the pole, which he rammed into the water by the back and pushed with all his strength to stop the raft running aground. As he stood straining, Ishmala began to walk along the caravan route, towing the floating house towards the north as Ruben held it away from the shore where the waves were breaking. Both men were almost at the end of their reserves of strength when the caravan route dipped below the level of the water. It happened so quickly that Ishmala was almost up to his waist when he realised. At that point, the rope that Ishmala was pulling went slack and the reed house nearly ran onto the last edge of the caravan route that was still above water level. Fortunately, Ruben had just seen this in time and had jumped overboard and was trying to keep the house from grounding.

He was fighting a losing battle and the floating house was beginning to crush him, when suddenly the weight was eased as Ishmala added his enormous bulk to the struggle. Finally the whole raft was through the gap and into calmer waters, with Ishmala and Ruben being dragged along and eventually struggling aboard. No longer caught in the current, the floating house drifted along southwards, being blown along by the wind. Ishmala and Ruben went round to the doorway of the house and stared inside, each grinning at the other as they had prevented a disaster. A delighted Lialah made them sit down and prepared a hot herb drink, which Simeon had been mixing. Even he looked up appreciatively at them both and said, "You certainly deserve this, we would have been blown to pieces if we had run aground."

Ruben said, "Do you mean that we have altered the fate prepared for us by the Creator?"

"No, my boy!" replied Simeon. "The Creator gave you both the strength and wisdom to use it correctly, which prevented the disaster."

"Do you mean that it was all planned?" asked the incredulous Ruben. "If so, he has a funny sense of humour."

They all laughed at this, as no one knew what else to do. Simeon said, "We will now have to wait until the storm blows itself out, but we will be safe, so you can all have some well earned rest." They then went to bed, with Ishmala sleeping in the small bed in the main room. It had turned colder, but the house stood up well. Although the constant pressure of the wind and rain made the walls occasionally buckle under the buffeting of the wind, they soon sprang back to normal and although the rain never came in, its constant hammering was disturbing. It was nice to be tucked up in bed with Lialah, listening to the howling wind and lashing rain, and although Ruben was physically tired, the noises from outside kept him awake. He finally dropped off to sleep even though the storm's fury had not yet abated.

The next morning they awoke to perfect calm, and looked out the door to inspect any damage that had been done to the reed house. The basic structure of the house had weathered the storm without any major damage, but there was quite a bit of remedial repair work to the reed weaving. Most of this was simple, but the more intricate parts had to be left to Simeon. The basic mat was firm, but it was littered with various flotsam from the marshes, with the occasional dead fish washed on board. Ishmala's hut was still in one piece, but was twisted out of shape, and this required a lot of work to put it back in order. Simeon asked Ishmala and Ruben to dive under the raft and inspect the base structure for signs of damage. Ruben did not understand what the base of the structure was, but Ishmala seemed to, so he dived over and followed Ishmala when he was underneath the mat of reeds. Ishmala pulled aside some of the wet reeds revealing a basic wooden frame, which after a while Ruben realised was in the form of an elongated A. This had an additional base that was parallel to the middle horizontal, which formed a rectangle. All the angles of the rectangle were braced with diagonal struts and the whole base was latticed with stiff reeds. Inside this and overflowing it was the living reed mat, which had been covered by a loosely woven carpet of rushes, but as the reeds grew through the carpet the basic appearance belied its solid base structure. Some of the base structure was lashed together, but the ropes that were used had been covered in a sticky black substance that seemed to be water-resistant. Having tackled this with Ishmala, Ruben climbed back onto the platform while Ishmala went back to resecure some of the lashings.

Ruben asked Simeon where the black sticky substance came from and was fascinated to learn that there was a large area to the south of the marshlands where there were pools of this substance, out in the desert. Simeon told him that it was something made by the Creator and there were apparently other places further south in the desert, where this also occurred – it would also burn, but when it did, it made a dirty dense black smoke, so that it was not much use for cooking. It did however have some good qualities, like being unaffected by the water and actually sealing some of the logs so that they did not become rotten by being constantly in water. Ruben asked Simeon when he had found this, as it could be used in caulking some of the ships rather than having to boil up animal bones and animal hooves, which was normally done, not only in the caulking paint, but also in the glue that shipbuilders used. Simeon told him that this was already done in many places where this substance was found, but that transporting it was not easy. Not for the first time, Ruben wondered how Simeon had come to know so much, but he thought it better not to ask.

Ishmala returned to the surface and when he had clambered aboard he informed Simeon by signs and gesticulations that one of the main horizontal beams to the frame had been split. It should be replaced or reinforced as soon as possible, but that they were in no immediate danger. Simeon considered this and then said, "We can make temporary repairs when we get to Uruk. That will suffice for the time being." They would then go on to Kish, as lifting the house and the mat out of the water to make a complete repair would take longer.

Ruben then asked Simeon exactly where they were. To which Simeon replied, "To be honest, I know roughly where we are, but not the exact location, I think we have been blown quite a long way off our previous course, so it may take a while before we arrive at Uruk." Apart from a few other reed beds and the occasional stand of rushes there was nothing in sight. The sun was sinking towards the western horizon, and they realised that the repair work and inspection had taken most of the day. Simeon told them that the currents in this part of the marshlands were not so strong and that it was fortunate that Lialah had re-provisioned their food supply just before they left Larsa.

Simeon then went indoors to help Lialah prepare the evening meal.

While he was inside, Ishmala took Ruben by the arm to where his javelin had been secured and indicated that he had the perfect piece of metal that would make a sharp end. He produced the old knife that Simeon had given him when its handle had broken off. It was the old one that Simeon had found near the wrecked pirate ship that had come from the east. The knife was more of a dagger, as it was sharp on both sides. Using Ruben's small bronze knife that he had to resharpen on a stone very often, Ishmala cut a slot in the large end of the javelin and shaved down the sides where the javelin had been chopped off the end of the pole. He then put everything down, went into his hut and came out with a bag of sand. From the bag he took out a large flat stone over which he placed a handful of sand. He then placed the knife on top of it, which had started to have the small brown flowers appear on the side. He scooped some more sand over the knife and took another small stone out of the bag. This stone was not heavy and seemed to have a lot of small holes in it, and then much to Ruben's fascination he sprinkled some water over the sand and began to rub the sand over the blade with the light stone. Gradually the blade of the knife had the brown flowers rubbed off and the metal became shiny, which Ruben realised was what he had done to his sword blade. He said to Ishmala that he understood what he was doing and offered to take over. Ishmala happily agreed to this, and while Ruben rubbed away at the knife to make it shine, Ishmala went back into his hut and came out with a length of fishing line. This he tied about a hand's span from the slotted end of the javelin in a tight knot, he then waited while Ruben cleaned the end of the knife that was to go into the slotted end. He then took the knife blade and placed it into the slot, where it fitted neatly. He then wrapped the fishing line tightly right up to the end that he tightened off. The fishing line had been wet when he started and now he left it to dry in the dying rays of the sun as it sank below the horizon in another glorious sunset. Then they left their labour as Lialah called them in for dinner.

While they ate another plant meal, Simeon asked Ruben where he had learned to read and write, producing the scroll that had been sent to Lialah at the inn in Ur. Ruben was delighted that Simeon had kept the scroll and told Simeon about the reading and writing evening classes that Captain Tryone had started at the training camp. Simeon said that as they now had more time on their hands, he would continue helping Ruben with the writing. Ruben was pleased with this idea, as he knew that his own writing was still not very good. After dinner, when Lialah was putting the plates outside, Ishmala took Ruben back to where they had left the javelin end to dry. The end had dried and the fishing line had shrunk making the binding, which held the blade extremely tight, but the brown flowers were beginning to form on the metal again. Ruben was rather dismayed at this, but Ishmala shook his head and laughed at him. Ishmala easily rubbed the brown flowers away as they had only just began to form, and took the javelin with the puzzled Ruben following him into the kitchen where, much to Lialah's surprise, Ishmala took some cooking oil and poured it over the blade. Ruben remembered that this was effectively what he had done when the brown flowers had began to appear on his sword, only he had used a paste of dates and olives, which was virtually the same as cooking oil. Ruben then smiled in understanding, and Ishmala indicated that Ruben should finish cleaning the blade so that it shone and that he must then sharpen it. Ishmala then indicated that he would coat the blade in the wax that he had used on Ruben's sword so that it would stay bright and shiny. They were then hustled out of the kitchen by Lialah, as she wanted to finish tidying up.

Ishmala and Ruben then went back outside where it was now dark and the mist was beginning to cool everything down and they put all their things back in Ishmala's hut. Then they returned to the house to join Simeon, who was fixing the new branch of leaves that Ruben had put into his museum of plants. Simeon said that the plants had probably been brought as a seed by one of the returning birds, who must have stopped at Larsa on the way back north in the spring. As they came out from the plants museum, Simeon asked Ruben if he had played any games while he was in the army. Ruben told him that some of the soldiers who were instructors at the camp, used to play a variety of games in the evening in the mess hall. But that the new trainees had to go to bed and that the lights soon went out after they were in bed. So although he had seen the games, he had not actually played them. Simeon asked him if he would like to learn a few games, saying that it might be an advantage. Leaving the lamp on the small table, Simeon went in his room and returned with a pile of small clay tablets. He then put these down on the table, and began to teach the other three how to play some games. Ishmala shook his head and indicated that the games were very bad. Simeon said, "They can be very bad Ishmala, you are perfectly correct, but that is only when they are played for money. They can be played without using money, so that people neither win nor lose, and when they are played like that, they can be good fun and very instructive."

"Have you ever played any of these games for money, Simeon?" asked Ruben.

"Yes Ruben, I am afraid I have. But as Ishmala said, it is not a good thing to do. You should either not know how to play and decline any invitation to do so, or if you do know how to play..." Here Simeon frowned and raised a finger, then added, "I must warn you, that if you do play you should do so for fun and not for money."

Ishmala indicated that he did not want to know how to play, he was rather tired as he had been busy all day, so he would go to bed, he waved good night to Ruben and Simeon, kissed Lialah goodnight and disappeared out of the door.

Simeon then said, "Ishmala is sensible not to get involved in these sorts of games, perhaps that is the best thing to do. But it is common for soldiers to play these games, so I do not think that it would be dangerous to show you something about them, as they can be instructive and fun."

Simeon then spread the clay tablets in front of them and showed how each was different, in either the symbol or number of symbols that it displayed. Simeon told them that there were a few games, some of which were simple and some more complicated. He produced a small wooden cube, each of its six faces showing a different mark. It could be thrown and it then tumbled and came to a stop with one face pointing upwards. He told them that when playing games that used this small wooden cube, the game depended on which face was shown. This of course was something that could not easily be predicted, resulting in the game being one of chance, or opportunity, and these games were often played for money.

Then Ruben said, "This sounds fascinating, but extremely difficult to follow, could you show us how to play a simple game so that we can learn how to play. Possibly we can then learn more later?"

"Certainly," said Simeon. "I was about to suggest the same thing."

He laid out about forty of the small tablets with the symbols facing upwards. He pointed to each symbol and gave it a name, but he said, "Do not worry about remembering the name, just remember what the symbol looks like." Showing that there were two identical tablets, he then turned all the tablets over so that the symbols were hidden, he also moved some of them around.

"Okay," he said. "Let's start with Lialah, now each person has to turn over two tablets and see if they are identical. If they are the same, that person then picks up the tablets and puts them next to himself, or herself. That person then has another try, until they are unsuccessful, but then the tablets they have turned over remain where they are, but are turned face down. Then it is the next person's turn."

Lialah tried without success, then it was Ruben's turn, he tried, but was unsuccessful, but the first tablets that he had overturned had the same symbol as one of the tablets that Lialah had overturned. Ruben could not remember exactly where it had been. It was then Simeon's turn, and he knew exactly where they both were and turned them over. As he did this, he then said, "You have to keep watching closely and try to remember exactly where things are." As his first attempt was successful he then had another try, which did not work, so it was then Lialah's turn. This time she was lucky and turned over two tablets that were identical, but was not lucky on her second try. The game progressed with the number of tablets left on the table becoming less. Eventually there were four tablets on the table and it was Ruben's turn. He had remembered the place of two tablets, but these were not identical, so he turned over one of the other tablets that matched one of the others. The final two tablets were also identical. This made his final score five pairs. Lialah also had five pairs, but Simeon had ten pairs.

Ruben said, "I enjoyed that, but obviously we were easily beaten by you Simeon."

"I would have been surprised if you had beaten me," laughed Simeon, "As you are new to the game, yet I have played it before – sometimes on my own. But as you can see it can be good fun. But if you do play these games you must make sure they are played just for fun, and not for money. But it is now late, so I suggest that we go to bed." They all agreed, Ruben and Lialah said goodnight to Simeon and went to bed.

When they were in their bedroom, Ruben had taken off his shift, which he had not put on until that evening. When he had been inspecting the damage to the raft, he and Ishmala had been consistently in and out of the water.

Lailah then said, "Ruben! Your back, it is very red, does it feel sore?"

"Not really sore," explained Ruben. "But it does feel hot." He turned around. "Just feel that," he invited Lialah. She put her hands on his back, which to him felt refreshingly cool.

"Yes, I see what you mean, I think I will use you to cook things on," she joked. "Seriously, I am going to put some of Simeon's special ointment on your back, you will find that it makes it more comfortable. But you must promise not to rub it off in the night." So saying, she left the room and returned with a large stone jar. From this jar she took out a handful of oily white cream-like liquid, which she rubbed into his back, neck and shoulders.

"Ah, that's nice," said Ruben, enjoying the sensation. "Don't stop. You can continue rubbing anything that's hot." As he turned around, he took her in his arms and pulled her to him.

She blushed, but did not push him away. "That was not what I had in mind," she exclaimed. "If you are outdoors all the time tomorrow, you must either keep rubbing some ointment into your back, or wear a light shift. You are not like Ishmala, his skin cannot burn."

"Even your skin is darker than mine," he said whilst he undressed her. They then made passionate love, as she kept him on top of her with her legs locked around his waist. She made him lie on his chest that night, so that his back had a chance to allow the ointment to soak in. She asked him drowsily, "Why is the skin over your shoulders so hard? It looks as if there are two old wounds. What happened?"

So he told her all about having to wear the heavy chain, under the orders of Captain Uglis. "It was not the weight that I objected to, but the chafing that the chain caused. It wasn't me who complained to Captain Uglis, it was Sergeant Tryone – who was later appointed to captain. It was he who ran the training camp, and before they made him captain. He had an argument with Captain Uglis that resulted in the crocodile skin jerkin that was made for me by Habib the leatherworker. He was a nice man, little Habib," he mused, reflecting on the kindness of the man, and remembering the day when they cleaned out the well. "He was a good friend of Captain Tryone and it was he who made the goatskin sheath for my sword, which Ishmala wants to cover with a small dark green crocodile hide."

Lialah snuggled beside him and drifted off to sleep. He started remembering his days in the army training camp and the games that the training soldiers often played. When he was thinking about the games and how good Simeon was, he remembered what he had been told about his father by the merchant Mutek. Mutek had told him that Uriah had been a brave man – "an argument with Uriah at the gaming tables". These words suddenly echoed in his head as if Mutek was standing beside him and speaking into his ear. Was it possible that Simeon was Uriah, surely not – he argued with himself. But if that was possible, so many other questions were answered. He considered whether or not he should confront Simeon with this, but then remembered an old saying, 'Do not awaken the sleeping crocodile because his smile conceals a lot of teeth'. Remembering this, he finally dropped off to sleep.

The next morning, the raft continued its slow journey through the marshland, which seemed hardly to change in this area. It was another beautiful day with the sun shining brightly from a deep blue clear sky. He asked Ishmala to show him the split log in the base structure, which needed urgent repair work. Ishmala agreed to this and they swam under the raft and Ishmala showed him the log in question. It seemed a small crack that was covered by ropes that lashed it to the other beams, but when Ishmala pushed and pulled the beams, Ruben could see the movement that should not be happening. As they clambered aboard the raft again and sat down, continuing their work on Ruben's javelin, Ishmala indicated that it was perfectly safe whilst they were travelling along quietly, but that it would not stand even a mild blow and certainly not a major impact with a sandbank. Ruben then said, "What we need is another couple of long poles, like the one I cut. We could then lash them to either side of the split beam, I am sure that would suffice, what do you think?"

Ishmala nodded his head in agreement and indicated that it was a good idea.

Quite unexpectedly the peace of the day was then shattered. Lialah shouted, "Ruben, what did I say last night?"

"Oh dear," said Ruben. He then looked at Ishmala and said, "Sounds like I'm in trouble." Then to Lialah he replied, "To wear my shift, or let you rub some more ointment into my back." Lialah came over with the jar and said, "I said you were to rub the ointment into your skin, not me!"

"Yes my darling, but you do it so nicely." He then turned his back towards her.

"Oh, very well," sighed Lialah and rubbed the ointment into his back and shoulders. Ruben sighed with relief and evident pleasure. This exchange had Ishmala shaking with silent laughter, he thought it so amusing that he had to stop working and decided then to go for a swim.

Ruben had virtually finished the javelin, which he then coated with wax, not just the blade, but the wood as well. This was because the wood was beginning to get dry and he realised that it could start to splinter. The final effect was satisfying, the wood seemed to glow the colour of burnt honey and the small metal blade glinted in the sunlight.

Simeon was now sitting outside as well, surrounded by pieces of parchment, pots of ink, brushes of various sizes and a drawing board. He called Ruben over and said, "You wanted me to help you with your writing, so here I am."

"Great, thanks Simeon," said Ruben delighted by the new challenge. "Tell me what to write and you can then tell me how to improve."

They started with a short sentence, which Ruben wrote to Simeon's dictation, and when he had finished Simeon said, "The first thing that you need to do is to alter the grip you have on your brush. It is not a javelin or a sword, but a delicate instrument. You hold it between your thumb and first finger – like so." Here he showed Ruben exactly what he meant. From that time onwards, Ruben's writing became a lot clearer, and he was so pleased with the new skill that he had learnt that he spent most of the day writing to Simeon's dictation. Towards the end of the day, Ruben said, "I think it would be a nice idea if you told me the names of everything in your museums. I could then write those names, which you could put beside the items, that would enable any visitor to learn about the marshland flowers and animals."

"Now you are reading my mind," laughed Simeon, his face lighting up with a large smile and his bright blue eyes positively twinkling. So that was how the next few days were spent. They were probably the most enjoyable days that Ruben ever spent, the weather was lovely and the company was great, in fact they all spent a very enjoyable time together.

It took them over five days before they reached the dip in the caravan route, which they had been blown through by the storm. The following day, true to Simeon's prediction, they arrived at Uruk. The town was similar to Larsa in that it was built on a mudflat, but it was larger than Larsa and the mudflat rose to the north into a large wooded area where there were some large trees. These trees marked the end of the mudflats as they were rooted in firm rising ground, where the caravan route came up from the marshlands, as this was a spur of solid ground that extended south.

Leaving Simeon to the inevitable number of people who required his doctoring skills, when he said he would be fine with Lialah's assistance, Ruben and Ishmala left the floating reed house, then made their way North through the town and up to the high ground in the North where the large trees were located. It did not take them too long to find a couple of large saplings that, although not the same wood as the pole Ruben had previously cut, seemed sturdy enough. As there was plenty of room to swing his large sword Ruben was about to cut the first sapling, when Ishmala put a restraining hand on his shoulder. Ruben turned and looked enquiringly at Ishmala, wondering why he had stopped him. Ishmala indicated that if Ruben had just hacked down the sapling in that direction its top branches would have become entangled with those of the surrounding saplings and it would be more difficult for them to free it. He then took his own knife out and marked the sapling, which was actually more of a small tree. The marks that he cut in the tree indicated to Ruben that he should cut about a quarter of the way through the tree on one side. Then Ruben should come around to the other side to cut the tree slightly higher up, which would make it fall in an easier direction for them to work on. Ruben complied with the instructions and although there was not as much space for him to swing his sword when making the second and deeper cut, the small tree soon fell in the direction that Ishmala intended. Ruben was about to start trimming the branches that grew out from the small tree, when once again Ishmala put a restraining hand on his arm. This time Ishmala cut around the branches that he wanted to cut off, a few of which were a finger width from the main trunk. He also showed Ruben the best way to cut these branches, which required far less effort, because it meant cutting in the direction that the branch had grown. The couple of places where branches were not trimmed directly close to the trunk, left small notches, which Ruben realised were for securing the lashings. Ishmala seemed quite content to allow Ruben to do most of the hard work, even though he could have easily done it more quickly himself. Ruben appreciated this as he enjoyed the work, but realised there was a lot more to cutting and trimming than just wielding a sharp instrument. They soon had the first pole trimmed to size. Ruben then let Ishmala walk amongst the other saplings and small trees until he found another suitable one. Once again he indicated and marked where Ruben was to cut this small tree, a task that Ruben soon accomplished. Although it had taken longer than Ruben had originally anticipated, he felt satisfied with the work, as he had learnt a great deal about cutting down trees.

When they returned to the raft, they were pleased to see that all the people who needed Simeon's doctoring skills had now departed, and Lialah had re-provisioned the floating house. Simeon said hello to Ishmala. "I would like you and Ruben to carry out the repair work immediately so we can get underway, as it will take us a couple more days before we arrive in Kish. It is not far, but as the current is weak we will have to rely more on the wind to blow us there. Will the repair work take long?"

Ishmala shook his head in response, and indicated that they could do the work before sunset.

Ishmala and Ruben therefore set to work immediately. Ruben noticed that Ishmala had already left four lengths of rope to soak, so that when they tightened them they would not stretch again and wear loose. They had to reposition the raft out from the bank, so that they had enough room in which to work. Ishmala tied the four ends of the ropes to various notches and then left them on the side of the raft whilst he and Ruben jumped over the side to where they were waist deep in water. Ishmala positioned the sturdy saplings in the appropriate places, which Ruben noticed with interest, were ideally shaped – in particular the notches for the lashings. He did not realise that Ishmala had measured out everything in such detail beforehand. They started lashing the two poles on either side of the split log. At each turn of the lashing rope, which was kept taut, Ishmala lay back in the water with his feet on the pole, pulling the lashing tight with all his weight. The result of the repair work was one large beam that was extremely rigid. The raft did not flex under their combined efforts as it previously had. In fact, Ruben had to admit that Ishmala was remarkably talented in boat and raft building. He then remembered that Ishmala used to work for Mutek, so he now knew how he got his knowledge of construction.

Once they had clambered back on board, they pushed the raft away from the bank and set off on the final leg of their journey across the marshlands. As the sun sank into another glorious sunset, they drifted slowly along, pushed along by the light breeze.

****

Latich was pleasantly surprised and enjoyed his new position as one of the old general's assistants. The confirmation of his promotion to Corporal had been ratified at the same time as his new appointment. He travelled with the general to Babylon and tolerated the general's leg pulling and heavy drinking, which was a small price to pay for the honour that went with the position. As he had not specialised in any particular weapon, but had excelled in the reading and writing classes, he was ideally suited for the job. His only regret was in losing his good friend Ruben, who had disappeared in mysterious circumstances during the battle at Sousa. Nobody had seen him in the battle and it was highly unlikely for a retreating army to take captives, but no trace of his personal belongings, or his body, had been found on the battlefield. Except for the javelin holder that had been found by Lieutenant Bel. His disappearance was all the more unbelievable due to his amazing ability with weapons, his remarkable strength, stature and courage. He had been more than an ordinary friend, as he had also been of great assistance in helping Latich to become one of the elite Babylonian Guards, the wearer of the coveted purple uniform. He had journeyed to the fabulous city of Babylon with the general, but found that, as the general was in semi-retirement, he had periods of long inactivity, and would offer his services for additional guard duty at the Citadel in Babylon where he was billeted.

This Citadel was a truly remarkable building. As well as being a prison, a fortress and a palace, it was where the fabled Hanging Gardens were situated. They covered the entire north and west side of the citadel itself and streamed down from the very top in a spectacular series of terraces right down to the river Euphrates running at the bottom of the Citadel. The gardens were watered by an ingenious system of buckets that were attached to ropes that led all the way up to the top level where they tipped over and emptied the contents before descending to the river. This ingenious device was driven by a huge treadmill that was operated by prisoners placed under guard in the Citadel. The trough where the buckets emptied themselves was on the top terrace of the gardens. The water ran down a series of irrigation canals that kept the plants well watered. Latich had on one occasion seen the massive bulk of Uglis working on the treadmill, under the constant lash of the overseers. Although Latich had no liking whatsoever for Uglis, who had repeatedly picked on him, he felt that this was an unhappy end for anyone, particularly someone who had been a wearer of the prestigious uniform. But it did serve as a strict reminder that nobody was above the law or the rule of the King in this harsh but great country.

Whenever he was on occasional guard duty, Latich tried to ensure that he was in sight of, if not inside, the magnificent gardens. He was told that the gardens were the idea of the previous King, and had been a gift to one of his beautiful wives – who was apparently a remarkable woman with golden hair. He caught occasional glimpses of the apparent offspring of this fabled woman, and they were indeed very unusual and wonderful to behold. Bearing in mind that most people in the area, like himself, were dark of hair, which was normally curly.

He had made a few friends in the Babylonian Guards, but no one who would be a bodyguard and shield as Ruben had been. However, his uniform itself was prevention enough to deter most intimidators.

As he had become friendly with and was fascinated by the work of the librarian who worked in the palace's library, he often volunteered for scholastic duties, particularly with maps and scrolls, which most Guardsmen would not touch. Recently, when doing such a duty, he had been asked to take some scrolls to another part of the palace, where he had seen the visiting king of Assyria, the tyrant Tiglath-Pileser. He had looked as Latich had anticipated. He was a large powerful man with long hair and his beard plaited in ribbons, and Latich could well imagine him sitting down to a meal of human flesh, as he was reputed to eat his enemies. The presence of this monster in the Citadel had put everybody on edge, mindful of his or her own purpose and making sure that everything was kept in perfect order.

Whenever he could, he would spend long periods looking at the maps of the area, particularly at Assyria, which was to the west and north of Babylon, and further west, where there was supposedly another sea. He often wondered what sort of people lived in this place, and what they were like. It was reputed that an ancient kingdom called the Hittite Empire had been situated to the northeast of this sea. And, that beyond that there was another great civilisation amongst the many islands and another mountainous country north of that sea, which had been torn apart by internal battles where many heroic deeds and other wonders had been performed. But this great civilisation had been in conflict and internal strife, which meant that it was no longer a country to be feared. Such as Assyria, or even his own kingdom of Babylon.

It was two days after Latich had seen Tiglath-Pileser, who was still in the Citadel, when a messenger dashed into the library asking for Corporal Latich. The messenger boy was only a few years younger than Latich himself and was evidently surprised that a corporal of the Babylonian Guards could be so young. Trying to hide his surprise, the messenger said, "I am sorry to trouble you, sir, but there is an old general who has just arrived at the Citadel, who is demanding your presence."

"Where is he?" demanded Latich.

"He was on his way through the barracks," answered the messenger, and then continued, "But he asked me to have you meet him outside the Royal chamber, where he has been summoned by the King who is in conference with the King of Assyria."

"I had better be on my way. You will lead me to where I am to meet the General," ordered Latich.

Following the messenger through various passages and up and down marble stairs and through arched corridors of dressed stone, they arrived in an antechamber, outside two huge bronze doors, where the general was waiting for Latich.

"And about time too, you young scoundrel," boomed the general, giving Latich a playful pat on the back. This was delivered with such force that it almost sent him flying. "You realise why I'm here?" asked the general.

"No, sir, I have really no idea," answered Latich. "I did not even know that you were in the Citadel until the messenger found me. I can only presume you have been requested to see the King."

"Yes, that is correct, to see the King and that great oaf, the cannibal Tiglath-Pileser, if what they say is true," he laughed. Without further ado he asked the guard outside the bronze doors to announce their presence. Their arrival was communicated through a small hatchway and the large bronze doors were swung open as the general was announced. The doors were covered with engraved pictures of battles and each one was hauled open by three slaves as they were so heavy, but they swung open on silent greased hinges.

The King was a pleasant looking man of average size, but stood erect and looked regal in fine white linen, which was trimmed with gold. Beside him stood the large ape like figure of Tiglath-Pileser, his plaited beard and hair hanging in greasy strands onto his bare shoulders and hairy chest. His large bear-like arms were festooned with bangles and his huge hands were covered with ornate rings of many different metals.

"Ah, General," said the King. "I have been telling the King of Assyria about our Babylonian Guards, and of course, how good they are. As you are the main assessor, I thought it best for you to answer some of his questions."

Speaking in a surprisingly squeaky voice, Tiglath-Pileser said, "Do you think that your men could beat an equivalent Assyrian force?"

"Without doubt, sir," responded the general. "Without being rude to your Majesty, just two platoons drove back the Persian army at Sousa, and they were terrified to engage us in further battle," was his proud boast.

"If they are all like that little wretch behind you," said Tiglath-Pileser with a malicious grin, "I very much doubt it. I could blow him away like a leaf in a gale."

"He is a poor example, your Majesty," explained the general, "He is purely chosen for his ability as a scribe. But I can have, with my King's permission, two of the men who led the assault on Sousa here in under a week. They are a fine example of what the Guards are like."

"Umm. Yes, I'd like to see them, I'll take them back to Nineveh with me, so that we can train our men as well as yours."

"Yes, I will agree to that," said the King. "So let that be written and accomplished." This was an order to his own scribes, who immediately started writing the order. The King then turned to the general and said, "When they arrive, I want you to go with them and you can take your scribe with you."

\*\*\*\*

Ruben had been for his normal early morning swim with Ishmala and had returned for breakfast, which he ate with Simeon and Ishmala, as Lialah was still in bed. He then went outside again with Ishmala and was pleased to see that it was another glorious day as the sun had now burned off the early morning mist. As usual, he and Ishmala did some exercising to ensure that he retained the fitness that he had become used to when in the army. He had started arm wrestling against Ishmala, knowing that he would never be capable of winning against the huge man. But it certainly kept his arms strong and possibly improved their strength. His hands seemed tiny when held in Ishmala's enormous hands, and the wrestling was futile against arms that were like tree trunks. Ishmala would not really push his arm down until he felt that Ruben had had enough, but held his arm upright while Ruben exerted himself trying to flatten it. Ruben was again not wearing a shift and his pale skin had now turned a golden brown. However, he thought that he had better once again cover himself with Simeon's ointment, and went in search of Lialah.

He found her still in bed and he sat on the side of the bed and ruffled her hair, saying, "Come on sleepy head, it's not like you to lay around in the mornings."

She opened her eyes and looked at him and said, "I am sorry, Ruben, but I do not feel very well this morning. I did get up for a little while, but I was sick, so I went back to bed."

"When did this start?" he asked looking most concerned. "You seemed perfectly well yesterday evening. Have you told Simeon?"

"No, I did not want to worry him," she replied. "I am sure there is nothing to worry about, to be honest I have not been feeling well first thing in the mornings for the last few days."

"Are you sure that you don't want me to tell Simeon?" asked Ruben. "I am sure that he could cure you, he seems to be able to make everyone else better."

"No, please don't bother him, he will only be worried about me, it really is nothing." With that she got up saying that she was already feeling better and had Ruben come in for some ointment to be rubbed into his back and shoulders. When he confirmed that he had, she dressed and rubbed the ointment into his back and also confirmed that she now felt a lot better.

Ruben went outside the reed house to where Simeon was sitting surrounded by his ink brushes and parchment. He said to Ruben, "Are you going to help me finish off the work that we started for my museums?"

"Most certainly, Simeon," answered Ruben. "We have almost completed the names indicators."

Just then Ishmala came over, and using his usual sign language, asked Ruben if he could borrow the goatskin sheath for his large sword. Ruben soon returned with the sheath and gave it to Ishmala, asking why he required it. Ishmala just smiled at him in response, took the sheath and disappeared into his hut. Ruben shrugged his shoulders, realised that he would soon find out and went back to work with Simeon. They continued for the rest of the day in companionable silence, broken only by the occasional question or instruction. Their work was virtually completed when Lialah called them in for supper.

The evening meal was uncooked, but was nonetheless enjoyable as the plants were cold and crunchy. When Ruben asked how Lialah managed to keep them cold, she took him into the kitchen and pulled out a door in the floor where a large waterproof goat skin sack dropped into the water below the raft. "That is quite incredible," said Ruben, "Simeon seems to have thought of everything."

They went back into the main part of the house, where Simeon had just returned from putting the dishes outside. He told them to sit down and began to speak. "Tomorrow evening we will probably arrive at Kish. Our journey will then be over and Ruben, you should take Lialah to her aunt's house, who has promised her somewhere to stay and work. It is not in Kish, but in Babylon, which is less than a day's walk north. You have only to walk up a large hill and at the top you can look down to where the river Euphrates runs along, past the great city. Whilst you are there, do try to look at the wonderful Gardens in the Citadel, they are as fabulous as they are reputed to be." He was about to continue when Ishmala came into the room from his hut. He was concealing something behind his back.

With a flourish, Ishmala produced Ruben's sword sheath that he had covered with the dark green crocodile skin. It was a magnificent piece of work, which even Habib would have been proud of. Ruben realised that it would look good when worn and would contrast well with his crocodile skin jerkin. He was deeply touched by Ishmala's kindness, particularly as he had nothing to offer in return.

Simeon broke the awkward silence by saying, "Let me tell you about the Hanging Gardens which you will see in Babylon. They are part of the Citadel itself and cover the entire north and western side of the building. The Gardens are beautiful, full of exotic flowers and amazing vines that cover great archways and corridors. They run in a series of terraces that start right at the summit of the Citadel with the final level being right down beside the river. The Gardens are entirely man-made with an enormous amount of imported soil that was brought up onto the terraces that were built specially. The entire structure is wonderfully laid out where there are small secret arbours. The Gardens are kept watered by an ingenious system of irrigation canals that are fed from water that is transported up from the river itself."

Simeon went on to explain what sort of flowers they would see in the Gardens, which seemed to tumble down from the Citadel in marvellous cascades of deep red, purple, lilac, orange, white and gold. He continued for quite a while with a faraway dreamy look on his face.

"How do you know so much about these Gardens, Simeon?" enquired Ruben.

"I was one of the workers, well actually, an overseer to the slaves who carried out a lot of the work. But I think I have talked enough for tonight and we should all go to bed now, as tomorrow is our last day on this voyage. I hope we will see some of the fisherman who are based in Kish." Here he turned to Ruben and said, "I hope you have recovered enough Ruben, to re-enable yourself to see the colour that surrounds people." He stared hard at Ruben, those piercing blue eyes of his seeming to penetrate Ruben's soul. He then said goodnight to them all and disappeared into his bedroom.

The next morning after breakfast, Ruben and Ishmala were arm wrestling when Ruben sat back and said, amid his laughter, "It is absolutely ridiculous, I will never be able to beat you Ishmala, you are far too strong for me." He then saw a fishing boat, which true to Simeon's prediction must have come from Kish, which was just over the horizon to the northwest. Jumping to his feet, he ran into the reed house to fetch Simeon. Simeon was in one of his museums and just finishing placing the labels that he and Ruben had finished the previous day. Dragging Simeon by the arm, Ruben said, "You are perfectly correct, there were some fishermen just over there," where he pointed. "That is a peculiar boat, it is more like a raft."

"Yes Ruben," said Simeon. "You see, around here the marshlands are calm and the water is fresh. Therefore the fish that they tend to catch are far smaller than the fish that are found nearer to the sea. So the boats they use do not need high sides as there is seldom more than a ripple on the water." He then led Ruben to the nearest point on the reed mat, from where they could clearly see the fishermen, and he told Ruben to sit down. "Now, do you remember what I instructed you to do last time, about how to look at them and try to think what they are trying to accomplish?" Ruben nodded his assent and looked at the fishermen with half-closed eyes. There was then a long period of silence.

In hardly more than a whisper, Ruben said, "Yes, I am beginning to see a smoky blue aura round each man." He then went on to describe how the colour changed as the fishermen moved around and began to catch fish, and how the aura around each man changed colour and size according to his state of mind. Additionally, when one man became more excited and dominant, his aura seemed to swallow up that of the other fisherman. Ruben then opened his eyes wide and turned to look at Simeon, who in turn was smiling at him. They were then both laughing with pleasure. Ruben had regained his ability. Simeon told him that it was just a question of being in harmony with nature, to be at one with the Creator. He then told Ruben to keep working at his regained ability and he must try to ensure that he never lost it again.

Ruben sat for the rest of the day watching all the fishermen, as the reed house gradually drifted past more and more of the strange fishing crafts. He then detected that the raft was moving faster than previously. When he looked around to see why, he realised that Ishmala was using the pole to propel the raft along, as the water here was very shallow. He looked again at Ishmala through half-closed eyes and could soon make out the pale blue colour that surrounded the huge man, who was content in his work. He watched until the sun began to sink into the west and the mist began to form above the water. It was getting dark and he could just make out the light of Kish in the distance when Lialah called him in to dinner.

That evening Simeon produced a flagon of a special drink that he said would help make the meal a special occasion, as it was the last meal that they would share together. They normally drank water with their meals as Simeon and Ishmala never drank wine or any alcohol. Simeon told them that this was not a wine, but a special type of cordial that had been made from watermelons. It was light gold in colour and Ruben remembered that he and Ishmala had drunk a similar cordial all those years previously when Ruben had first met Ishmala, who had rowed him across the river from Lagash when he had started travelling to Ur in search of Simeon. The cordial had the effect of brightening up everybody's spirits, which had sunk when Simeon said that this would be the last meal that they would share together. Ruben knew this was probably going to be true, as he was prepared to take Lialah in to Babylon and then continue on his quest westwards, and it was doubtful that they would all meet again. Lialah then asked Ruben if he would wear his uniform the following day.

"I do not think that would be wise," he said. "You see, I am not really supposed to be here and it might lead to people asking questions that can not easily be answered honestly. I think it would be far better for us just to travel as friends, or even pretend that we are brother and sister."

Lialah laughed at this. "Don't be silly, we do not look remotely similar. People would never believe such a ridiculous story!"

"I am afraid that Lialah is correct," said Simeon. "Tell nobody anything unless they ask, and even then give only the briefest information. Once you start telling lies, you often get deeper and deeper into difficulty. But surely you will take your uniform with you, because it may often come in handy to still be a Babylonian Guard."

"I have brought an extra large bag with me," said Lialah. "You can put everything in there, even your sword, jerkin and helmet, there will still be plenty of room for the clothes that we will have to buy in Babylon."

"I do not see what is wrong with these clothes," said Ruben.

"Apart from being too tight and not fitting, they are shabby. I will not walk along with you," laughed Lialah. "But pretend you are nothing to do with me and I shall walk on the other side of the road. Apart from which, you need a haircut, you look like a wild man who has come in from the desert."

Ishmala thought that this was funny, as he did with all their little arguments, and was grinning broadly when Simeon asked him to come with him out of the reed house. Nobody else had noticed that they had drifted on to the bank at Kish, so Simeon required Ishmala's assistance to secure the raft on to the bank. While they were doing this Lialah made Ruben sit on the floor while she combed and cut his hair, which he noticed from the pieces that fell on his lap, had turned a lot lighter in the sunshine. After a while Simeon came back and told them that they were secure by the bank and that he had sent Ishmala up to the local inn to tell of their arrival, so that the message could be spread that he would be free to see anyone who required his doctoring skills in the morning. He then said, "I will go to bed now, because tomorrow will be a long day for me, I also suggest that you also get an early night, so that you can start on your way first thing in the morning." He was about to go in to his bedroom when he turned around and said to Ruben, "Remember, my boy, if you are ever in doubt about which way to go, look to the works of the Creator, he will show you the way to go, as he did with Abraham all those thousands of years ago." He then said his final good night, told them to pack their bags ready for an early start and said that he would see them in the morning.

Ruben awoke as the sky was beginning to pale, only to find that Lialah was already moving around in the bedroom. He quickly got dressed and asked her if she was joining them for breakfast. She said, "I am not hungry and will skip breakfast as I am to finish off packing and tidying up in here before we leave. I suggest that you go and eat a good breakfast before we leave."

He went through to the main room and joined Simeon and Ishmala, where he filled himself up with plenty of wheat cakes and maize porridge, which he ate with fresh asses' milk that Ishmala had managed to acquire from the town. All three of the men ate in silence, each one occupied by his own thoughts and seeming reluctant to finish. Eventually, Lialah came out of the bedroom with two large bags. The largest bag was Ruben's and contained his uniform, crocodile skin jerkin, helmet and large sword as well as a few other odds and ends and a couple of changes of clothing. But even then it was still half-empty, although it weighed far more than Lialah's bag. Ruben was already wearing his thick belt with his short army sword, but many people frequently wore these swords, so it did not automatically mark him as a soldier. Simeon had woven a dark brown cover, which when wrapped around the javelin, made it look more like a staff that a journeyman would carry.

The three of them went out onto the floating reed mat and noticed that on the riverbank there was already a small crowd of people waiting to see Simeon. So he quickly bade them a fond farewell, telling Lialah that he hoped to see her fairly soon, even if just to convey a message back to her mother that she was faring well. He held Ruben firmly by the hands and said, "Try to remember everything that I have taught you and I am sure that your quest will meet with success. You are far better equipped for the journey than your father was when he set out." And he then pressed a purse into Ruben's hands and said, "That is for the journey and some of the clothes you will have to buy. Make sure you get some warm clothes because summer is coming to an end, and when you travel up the river into the mountains it may turn very cold. Do not continue too far into the mountains, but head west." Ruben had a quick look into the bag, which was full of gold coins, and he gasped with a sharp intake of breath.

"There is ample money in here Simeon, you have been very generous, you have been more than a father to me," he said choking on the words.

It was then Ishmala's turn to give them both a huge hug, which left them both breathless. Ishmala indicated that he had enjoyed the last few weeks immensely and his heart would always be with them.

Ruben said to him, "Take care of that crazy old man and don't go fighting any more crocodiles." Which made Ishmala laugh.

"Goodbye, dear Ishmala," said Lialah. "Keep Uncle S'meon safe." She then took Ruben's hand and with moist eyes stepped off the raft and up the bank into the town without daring to look back.

They continued walking through the town, neither saying anything to each other. The town was small and they soon reached its outskirts and started the long climb up the hill, which Simeon had warned them about. After a while Lialah put her bag down and Ruben could see that there were still some tears in her eyes. Believing that she was still feeling sad at leaving the floating reed house, he said, "They will be all right, my dear. All good things must come to an end and we now have the wonders of Babylon before us."

"I am not sad Ruben, I am just not feeling very well," she said.

Ruben said, "Oh I am sorry, is it the same thing that you were suffering from previously? Will you be all right or shall we go back?" He then put down his own bag and sat beside her, putting his arm around her shoulder.

She turned and smiled at him saying, "No, I will be all right soon, it is nothing to worry about."

After a little while, she said she was feeling better and that they could go on. As they both stood up, Ruben picked up her bag as well as his own and he gave her the staff to lean on, informing her that she should only lean on one end, as the other was really the sharp end of the javelin. They toiled on up the hill, which was not only very steep but also seemed to be endless. Lialah needed to rest often, as it was quite a climb. They were well away from Kish now, which had disappeared far below them and they looked southeast out over the marshlands. The sun was now high in the sky, and it was very hot struggling up the hill, although Ruben seemed to thrive on exercise. When they had just come over a rise, Lialah groaned to see that the road still led on upwards and she said: "S'meon just said this was a long hill, not a mountain – I am sorry Ruben but I don't think I can keep going without another rest."

"That does not matter, we have plenty of time, although I would like to get to Babylon so that we can have a good look around this afternoon. Why don't you have a rest with the bags if I put them down here, while I go and see how much further we have to go." Lialah readily agreed to this suggestion, and as Ruben put down the bags and went running up the hill, she was amazed at his energy and endurance.

In a short time he was back beside her and said, "The top of the hill is not far and there is a wonderful view of Babylon from the top." He wanted to take Lialah up immediately as he was very excited, but she said, "Let me rest a little longer."

"No, I can't wait," he said, and before she realised what he was doing, he had slung both bags over one shoulder and snatched her up in his arms like an infant and started carrying her up the hill. She giggled and put her arms around his neck and gave him a kiss. And as he walked on she said, "I don't know what I would do without you."

"Just stop fidgeting and we will soon be at the top." It was then that he realised how difficult it was going to be to leave her in Babylon. He had not realised how attached he had become to her, as her rich dark hair felt soft against his cheek and it framed her beautiful oval face. But they were soon at the top and he set her down, where they both stood and stared with awe, looking at the magnificent view of Babylon that stretched below them on the far side of the river Euphrates. It was dominated by the Citadel that rose majestically above the town where its large balconies were supported by ornate pillars of white marble that stood out starkly against its golden roof that shone in the harsh midday sun.

## 10
## THE HANGING GARDENS

The order arrived at Lagash within two days of it being written. It had been sent by boat, which had been rowed non-stop down river from Babylon. The boat was a small rowing boat that was manned by six slaves, four of whom were constantly rowing with one oar apiece, with the other two resting and changing places occasionally. The river was only tidal up as far as Nippur so that it was far quicker coming from Babylon by boat than returning that way. Lieutenant Bel was annoyed when Commander Schudah passed him the urgent summons to go to Babylon with the expert swordsman, whom he had just promoted to sergeant to replace Ruben Ben Uriah. Abzher was his name and he was a great favourite amongst the Crocs, which was why he had been chosen.

Lieutenant Bel had integrated the Crocs into the entire command of Babylonian Guards stationed at Lagash, and was still shaping them into a more effective and efficient force than they had previously been. His Captain was more than happy to leave the day to day running of the command to the capable Lieutenant. The captain had plenty of other work to do, organising the defence of not only Lagash, but also Sal-e Pol-e, that mined iron and produced the new weapons that had started to arrive daily in Lagash.

Lieutenant Bel went to break the news to Sergeant Abzher, who was drilling the Guards outside the barracks. When Lieutenant Bel gave him the news, his face fell and he said, "I thought I was free of the old sod, by the gods, what on earth does he wants with us? I suppose that I had better go and pack a few things. Do you know how long we will be away?"

"I really have no idea," said the lieutenant. "I believe from the order that we have to accompany the old general with the Assyrian King back to Nineveh. But don't pack a lot, it is far better to travel light and if we need more clothes the bloody Assyrians can provide them. We will leave at midday, I will meet you outside the stables."

They rode hard that afternoon and arrived at Nippur, where they stayed overnight at an inn, as Lieutenant Bel had no intention of camping on this ridiculous assignment. The local innkeeper asked them about the new weapons that he had heard about, and if there was any chance of acquiring any – which he obviously intended to sell to the highest bidder, which probably meant that they would end up in the hands of brigands. Lieutenant Bel said with a perfectly straight face, "I don't know what you are talking about, we only have the standard issue of bronze weapons and we would certainly not sell anything anyway."

"Suit yourself," grumbled the innkeeper, as he handed them platefuls of cold food and jugs of beer. Lieutenant Bel leaned over his dinner and whispered into Abzher's ear, "Commander Schudah particularly asked me not to mention anything about the new weapons. But I suppose the word has already got around."

"Yes, I think it's far better to keep quiet for the time being. Apart from which, we do not want to get involved in any shady dealing. The very fact that we were approached is a legacy of that old bastard Gershnarl. Did you ever meet him?" said Sergeant Abzher.

"Meet him," echoed Bel. "I served under him and watched the old git as he was crushed to death by an enormous servant of one of the merchants in Lagash, a nice fellow who Gershnarl had flogged to death. The whole business was incredible, I will never forget it."

So they spent the rest of the evening in quiet discussion, not so much about events in the past, but of their hopes for the future. They were both young men who were good and capable soldiers, each an expert in his own field. Both men had already made significant progress in the Babylonian army and they both had ambitions for the future. After another couple of jugs of beer they went to bed, having informed the innkeeper that they would be leaving first thing in the morning and required an early breakfast.

****

Ruben and Lialah walked down the hill to the river Euphrates where there were plenty of boatsmen offering to take them across the wide river for a few brass coins. As Ruben had only a purse full of gold coins, that were worth far more than they were being asked, Lialah paid the ferryman for the passage.

Having arrived in Babylon, Ruben suggested that rather than go straight to the relative's house where he was to take Lialah, they could stay at an inn in the city and take some time looking around and buying the clothes that he needed. Lialah agreed to this suggestion without hesitation, as she had no desire to be parted from Ruben so soon.

Having agreed on what to do they went in search of a respectable place to stay. As they walked along, Lialah gripped Ruben's hand tightly, particularly when he received admiring glances from any of the other young girls that they passed. There were quite a few people who noticed them and obviously this large, well built and good looking young man with fair hair attracted considerable attention. Similarly, Ruben shielded Lialah from any of the admiring looks of interest that any young men gave her, and there were many, as she was attractive and remarkably pretty. Having rejected several inns, they finally settled in a tidy and pleasant looking Inn that was more expensive than the other places, but as Ruben had plenty of money, he considered it a sensible investment. They then went to leave their possessions in the room that they had paid for, before going to explore parts of the city.

They ventured out into the markets, where there were crowds of people and many traders haggling for goods. Lialah found it intimidating, as she had come from a small town in the marshlands. However, Ruben was more used to large markets having been in Lagash and Nippur, he enjoyed haggling for all the items that they had to buy, even though it meant that buying took a lot longer. He soon realised that the best tactic to apply when you wanted something was not to seem interested in buying it and make a derisory offer. They had to leave one stallholder as the merchant saw Ruben's purse when he opened it and realised that it was full of gold coins. So this was another lesson that they learned when haggling for wares. By the end of the afternoon they had purchased most of the things they thought Ruben would need, as well as buying some food to eat. But they realised that if they wanted to buy fresh fruit they needed to get to the market first thing in the morning, as it went off in the heat and stifling atmosphere, which was full of strange aromas of spices and incense, apart from the unwashed bodies and animal dung, that attracted vast numbers of flies and other insects and small animals.

Back at the inn they examined all their purchases and were quite content with the afternoon's expedition. They then went downstairs to the main eating area where they ate a pleasant meal; Ruben ate vast quantities of nicely cooked meat, which he had missed as Simeon only ate vegetables. They spent most of the evening talking to the innkeeper and his wife, who were kind people. They knew the marshlands fairly well and they had heard of the mysterious doctor and of his unusual healing powers. As Simeon had advised, they did not tell of their direct background, but listened to the other conversation, which needed little prompting. They then retired to their bedroom where they discussed what they would do the following morning.

Although, when the morning arrived, Lialah was not feeling very well, so Ruben said that he would go out himself to find out where her relative lived and the sort of work that she would expect of her. When he came downstairs, the innkeeper's wife inquired where Lialah was. So Ruben told her that she had not been well the last several days, particularly in the mornings and that he would be most grateful if she could look in and see Lialah. After eating a hearty breakfast he asked the innkeeper the location that he had been given where he was to take Lialah.

The innkeeper frowned and said to him, "Why do you want to go to this area of the city, particularly as you have such a lovely young woman with you?"

Ruben simply said that, "I was only casually interested, as a friend mentioned it to me." He was surprised when the innkeeper winked at him and laughed. Ruben grinned back, but said nothing and went outside. He wandered down to the river and accidentally came into the area that he was looking for. He was dismayed to find that it was an area well frequented by soldiers, and his further enquiries soon confirmed that the area was full of brothels. Ruben firmly decided that he would not let Lialah into the area, even if the job intended for her was not prostitution, which he feared could easily be the case. Working in such an area, which was full of lecherous and often drunken soldiers, was no place for Lialah. He decided that he would try to find her a better job and made his way back to see how she was.

When he arrived back at the inn he found Lialah was out of bed dressed and she said she was feeling a lot better, but she was pensive. She told him that the innkeeper's wife had been to see her on Ruben's request. She said, "It was very nice of you to be so concerned. The innkeeper's wife asked me a lot of questions, about how long we have been sleeping together and other very personal matters. I think we had better have a talk."

"I think that is wise," said Ruben. "I also have some disturbing news to relate."

"Perhaps you had better tell me what you have discovered?" she asked.

Ruben sat down and said, "This relative of yours, how well did you know her and do you know what job she wanted you to do?"

"I have only met her once, and that was about two years ago, but I really don't know what she did or, in fact, what she wanted me to do."

"Well, the area she lives in is full of prostitutes and a lot of undesirable people and I do not want you to go there, I think it far better to try to find work elsewhere."

She sat down beside him on the edge of the bed and took his hands in her own. "What I have been told may well affect any job that I may seek. I honestly did not intend this to happen, but I have been expecting the news that I have to give you."

Looking perplexed, Ruben asked her to tell him, because it seemed to be important, and to get straight to the point.

She said, "I believe I am going to have a baby."

Ruben was speechless, but eventually said, "I cannot be your husband, I must go on this quest, even though I am very fond of you and were things different, I would be very happy to have you as my wife."

Lialah threw her arms around him and burst into tears. Kissing her tenderly on the forehead Ruben held her in his arms and said, "There must be a way out of this, perhaps I had better take you back to Simeon."

"No, don't do that, he will only be angry with me, he did advise me of the risk that I was taking. That is why I did not want you to tell him about me not feeling well in the mornings," she sobbed. "And I can hardly go back to Ur, there is nothing for me to do there, and with an extra mouth to feed, my mother would not be pleased."

"This is not only your problem, my darling, but also mine. There is not much point in crying about it, what is done cannot be undone. I am sure we can work something out, so cheer up and let us go out and try to see the Hanging Gardens."

"Oh, Ruben, you are so kind and understanding, can you not take me with you?" asked Lialah.

"I would not take you on such a journey even if you were fit. It is a long and difficult road that I have to travel, I have no idea of what hardships lie in my path, it is certainly no place for a woman."

She stood up and went over to rinse her face and while she was getting ready to go out, Ruben said, "They tell me that the king of Assyria is in the Citadel, visiting our king, so there has been a lot of pageantry."

"Will we be able to get into the Gardens at the Citadel?" asked Lialah. "I would imagine that they would not let anyone in, particularly if the king of Assyria is there."

"I had not thought about that," replied Ruben.

"Why don't you wear your uniform? We might to be able to get in that way," suggested Lialah.

"Well, I don't really want to let people know that I am a supposed Guardsman here, but I could take it with me in a small bag," Ruben replied.

So they left the inn with Ruben carrying his uniform in his small satchel. They walked through the streets until they neared the Citadel. He stopped by an alleyway and he suggested that Lialah walk past the Citadel and have a look to see if people were being allowed in to see the Hanging Gardens or not. This she did and was back shortly. She said, "They are only letting in soldiers, or people who have urgent business." He said that he could put on his uniform and they could try to think of an excuse to enable them to enter, but that it had better be unquestionable, as it would only draw attention to them otherwise.

"Suppose you tell them that you were asked to bring me in to work in the Gardens?"

"You don't even look like a gardener, apart from which you are a woman and far too young to do that sort of work," said Ruben laughing.

"But I could say that you have come to play with the king's children, because I heard that they do play in the Gardens."

They agreed that this was a good idea, and thought that it was worth a try. Ruben quickly slipped on his uniform and helmet, and then set off purposefully towards the entrance with Lialah following dutifully behind. He reached the gate and the guard on duty was fortunately a young man and a lot smaller than Ruben. Ruben stopped as the guard saluted him and told him that he had brought Lialah to play with the royal children. The guard said, "I am sorry, sir, but I have to ask you for the tablet that you were given on your way out."

Fearing that there would be the sort of check, Ruben had already prepared a story and said, "I am sorry, but the other young guard was busy when I went out and I did not have time to wait for a tablet," Ruben bluffed. The young guard did not want to anger this young Babylonian Guard sergeant, who he thought was probably telling the truth, so he said, "That's perfectly all right, sir, it's just that we have to be careful, what with the visiting king and his entourage." Ruben and Lialah were just being passed in when there was a small commotion outside the entrance. As he looked around two horsemen rode up to the guard. They were both large men and dressed in full Babylonian Guard uniform. They had obviously come a long way, as the horses were snorting and breathing hard. The leading horseman leant down and handed the guard a scroll, which was obviously his admission order. The guard snapped to attention, saluted and gave quick directions, then ushered them through. Fortunately Ruben and Lialah were standing in the shadow as the two horsemen rode past them, because it was Lieutenant Bel and the expert swordsman. Luckily they turned left into the stables, and Ruben felt sure that the gardens were straight ahead around the back of the buildings, so he and Lialah hurried past. They continued straight ahead and came to where another pathway crossed the one they were on, here they could either turn left or right, or even go straight ahead up a broad flight of steps. They chose the latter as they could see a square archway covered in vine leaves at the top of the steps.

They went up the steps and emerged on to a wide grass pathway that cut straight across from the archway. About fifty paces to their right there was a solid wall where another large wall ran diagonally across the path and carried on down the Gardens, which they had come right into. This wall was covered in hanging vines that were in flower that was of bright yellow changing through amber to gold. The pathway, which they had stumbled across, was on the side of one of the large terraces. To their left the path led away out of sight and turned the corner, back to the left again.

They walked arm in arm along this pathway in silent wonder at the riot of flowers that burst from amid the lawns and surrounded the trickling streams of water that kept everything cool and fresh. As they walked along, the terraces to their right fell away down to the river far below them. From their left the Gardens seemed to cascade and tumble down in a living blanket of flowers, vines, bushes, shrubs and small trees, which were all covered in a mass of different blooms. The Gardens were truly magnificent. Simeon's poetic description, although it had sounded extravagant at the time, hardly seemed to do them justice. Ruben realised that they could easily lose their way, as they did not know the layout of the Gardens. He therefore told Lialah to try to memorise certain bushes and plants so that they could find the way back. Ruben was so intent on trying to memorise their way that he did not notice the young Babylonian Guard who was walking along in front of them, until Ruben almost bumped into him. Fortunately Lialah grabbed his arm to stop him. She whispered in his ear, "That young soldier in front of us is wearing a jerkin like yours."

"Yes," replied Ruben. "And I know him very well." Much to Lialah's surprise, he shouted to the young soldier. "Where do you think you're going, Corporal Latich?"

Latich visibly jumped into the air, he had seen the large, fair-haired Guardsman who was carrying his helmet and was walking arm in arm with an attractive young woman, but he had not realised that it was Ruben. Firstly, because Ruben was meant to be either dead or being held by the Persians. Secondly, Ruben was not wearing his crocodile skin jerkin, his hair was lighter and neatly trimmed, plus he was well tanned from his time in the marshlands. Apart from that, Ruben was the last person that he would expect to see in the Gardens. He had supposed that this Babylonian Guard was strolling along with his young female companion, admiring the gardens, as he was doing himself, not his old friend.

Recovering, he turned around and snapped to attention, as the other Guardsman was a sergeant, he still did not recognise his friend and said, "I am sorry, sir, but I am off duty and was just taking a walk." He noticed that the sergeant had not returned his salute, but stood grinning at him. The voice had sounded familiar, and there were not that many people in Babylon who knew him by name. Suddenly, he realised who it was, and stood open mouthed, hardly believing his eyes. Eventually he stammered, "B-b-b-but Ruben, where on earth have you come from?"

"I was just doing the same as yourself, we obviously have a lot of catching up to do."

The two young men embraced each other warmly, and both started speaking at once. Then they both laughed. All this time Lialah was watching in bewildered astonishment. Ruben then introduced Lialah, saying, "This is Lialah." He then turned to Lialah and said, "This is Latich, who is a very good friend of mine, we were at the same training camp together. He then turned to Latich and asked if there was anywhere quiet and secluded where they could talk.

"Just around the next bush there is a small arbour with a seat in it that we can use."

There was a small arbour just as Latich had said, into which they all squeezed and found that they could see out without being noticed, and any conversation would be muffled by the surrounding bushes. Just then a small child came into view chasing a wooden ball that was rolling along in front of the infant. They were not sure who it was, or in fact whether it was a little girl or boy, but it was obviously one of the royal children. Ruben turned to Lialah and said, "Well, what are you waiting for, you were brought to play with the children," he laughed. So Lialah went after the child and started playing with the ball where they could see her. She was soon joined by a group of other children and seemed content playing with them.

Latich turned to Ruben and said, "Before we start all our news, where on earth did you find that beautiful girl?"

"She is an old friend of mine from Ur, and I have been travelling with her ever since I went there after the battle at Sousa." He then told Latich of what exactly happened at Sousa and of how he got cut off from his own side and had taken the opportunity to disappear. He explained how he had found the boat, rowed past Lagash into the marshlands. He then asked Latich what he was doing here in Babylon. Latich told him that he was now working for the old general and he told Ruben that it was an easy job, particularly as the old general was semi-retired.

"But of course," said Latich, "the old man is absolutely crazy, and half the time his head is spinning like a chariot wheel, due to his constant drinking. But we are now waiting for Lieutenant Bel and Sergeant Abzher, who of course you would not know – he's the expert swordsman who came to the assessment, I am sure you remember fighting against him. Well, he joined us in Lagash and the lieutenant promoted him to your old position. Then he sent me to replace him. We are now waiting for their arrival, and will then go back with the Assyrian King to Nineveh, because the old general said that they are a fine example of the Babylonian Guards, rather than myself, whom the king considered pathetic. He's a big, fat, ugly brute, who is horrible." They continued talking for a long time, bringing each other up to date and laughing at various aspects of each other's stories.

Latich then looked up and said, "Goodness me, that's him there, talking to your girlfriend. The king has being trying to interest him in one of his sister's children, but the odious brute does not like golden-haired women. He far prefers our native girls, like your Lialah. You had better watch him so that he doesn't take her from you."

"My dear Latich," laughed Ruben. "I know you think I am good with weapons and am strong, but I am in no position to challenge a king."

"Yes, I see what you mean, but you have to do something, she looks as if she needs rescuing. I am not kidding when I say he is horrible, he even smells horrible," said Latich.

"I think you are probably right," said Ruben. "I think the best strategy would be for me to go and try to get her away. But then you come along and say that Lieutenant Bel and Sergeant Abzher have just arrived, which they have as I saw them come in. If we go down that flight of steps behind them, is it easy to get out again?"

"Oh yes, the Gardens are perfectly symmetrical, just go along until you find another flight of steps, which you can come up back to this level. But before we go, tell me where you are staying in Babylon, so that I can reach you if I need to," requested Latich.

Ruben told him where they were staying and Latich said that he had seen the place, so that if he needed to he could always leave a message. Ruben then put on his helmet, which had the effect of making him look taller and older than he was. He then left the shelter of the arbour and went to where Lialah was desperately trying to get away from the king of Assyria. She was very glad to see Ruben coming towards them as this horrible, big, smelly man with his long hair and beard, plaited in greasy strands that hung down over his hairy chest and shoulders, was attempting to put his arm around her waist.

Ruben came up behind Tiglath-Pileser and said, "I am sorry your Majesty, but I have been sent to take the young woman back." The Assyrian king turned around immediately, as he did not wish to be interrupted, and stared directly into Ruben's bright blue eyes, that returned his aggressive stare. The king realised that this Babylonian Guard was as tall as he was lean and strong and looked as if he could handle himself.

But not to be put off, the king said, "I haven't finished yet, you impudent pup, just who do you think you are to speak to me without my permission?"

Not to be put off so easily Ruben replied, "I was only doing my duty, sir. The young woman has other duties to perform."

"I don't give a damn, you impudent scoundrel," said Tiglath-Pileser. "Any more of your bloody cheek and I'll cut your tongue out." He put his hand on the hilt of the large sword that hung from his waist.

Fortunately, the Babylonian king's niece, who was about the same age as Lialah and had joined in the game with the children, spoke out in a frightened voice, "The king has forbidden anyone to draw a weapon in the Gardens!"

Realising that he was a visitor and not in his own country, the Assyrian king let go of his sword and said, "But I can still knock some manners into this bastard."

Ruben caught his bunched fist in its backward swing. His arm-wrestling with Ishmala had increased the power of his wrist and arms, and he had the Assyrian king in a vice-like grip. "I would not try that your Majesty," said Ruben without raising his voice, but holding the king's aggressive stare, with his piercing blue eyes flashing like summer lightning.

The situation was diverted, as Latich came hurrying towards them calling out as he came, "I am terribly sorry to interrupt your Royal Highness, but the lieutenant and the sergeant of the Babylonian Guards that the old general sent for, have just arrived in the Citadel."

Swinging round to face this new interruption, Tiglath-Pileser let his arm drop as Ruben released his grip, and said, "Is there no limit to the interruptions that I must endure from these purple clothed vermin. Are you young bastards not given any teaching about waiting to speak until I address you? I will obviously have to speak to your king about the insults I have had to endure this afternoon. I am sure he will allow me to administer a fitting punishment on you both. I still have not finished with this young woman," he said, turning to Lialah. But to his astonishment she was no longer there and neither was Ruben. He turned a complete circle but still could not see them and was about to speak again to Latich, when two other large Babylonian Guards flanked Latich on either side. The taller of these two men was taller by half a head than the king of Assyria.

"Can we be of assistance your Majesty?" said the tall lieutenant. "We have ridden here from Lagash, and were summoned to attend your Lordship," said Lieutenant Bel.

"Where in bloody Hades have they gone?" demanded Tiglath-Pileser, as even the children and the other young woman had retreated.

"Who do you mean, sir?" asked Lieutenant Bel.

"Everyone, particularly that other soldier in purple, with the attractive young tart," grumbled the king of Assyria. "These bloody gardens are bewitched!" he said, walking away in a vile temper.

"What was all that about?" enquired Lieutenant Bel, turning to Latich.

"I really have no idea, sir," lied Latich, and told him that he had only just arrived. "There were some children playing here, but other than that I have seen nobody," Latich exclaimed, hoping that the lieutenant had not seen Ruben.

Ruben and Lialah had run off, Ruben quickly dragging Lialah, dashing over the soft springy grass, which quietened the sound of their running feet. Lialah's feet seemed to hardly touch the ground as Ruben dragged her along down the flight of steps and along the lower terrace. It was not until they were well out of sight that he dared to look back. Realising that their flight was unnoticed and they were not being pursued, he stopped and they sat down behind a bush, allowing Lialah to get her breath back. After a few moments of heavy breathing, during which she was unable to speak, she finally said, still gasping, "Thanks Ruben for saving me, but did you have to run so fast? Try to remember I am not as fit as you are and I am carrying your child, even though it does not show yet."

"Sorry, my dear, but I daren't let Lieutenant Bel see me. I think we are safe now, so you rest here while I go and check the way ahead." Checking that she was hidden from view, he then cautiously looked around and trotted off. He was soon back and said, "It all appears safe now." He then asked if she was ready to continue, and after a pause she nodded her assent, but said, "But please don't run." He helped her to her feet, gave her a kiss and led her away out of the Gardens. When they were outside the main gate, he ducked into an alleyway and changed out of his uniform. They then went back to their inn. When they were back in the safety of their room, he asked her who the other pretty girl with the golden hair was.

She said, "That was our king's niece, he has been trying to get the Assyrian king interested in her, but fortunately for her he does not like golden haired girls, he says they are unnatural, she told me that he far prefers girls like me."

"I wonder if our king would do a swap," teased Ruben.

"Oh you beast," said Lialah throwing a cushion at Ruben. "He is really horrible, I would rather die than go with him."

"Even that can be arranged," said Ruben advancing menacingly.

"I shall turn you in as a deserter. I will tell that nice Lieutenant Bel that you forced yourself on me and ask his protection."

"We will see about that," said Ruben, suddenly swinging her up in his arms and dumping her on the bed, where he made passionate love to her, which she feebly resisted then joined in with equal vigour.

****

Lieutenant Bel, Sergeant Abzher and Corporal Latich went back to the barracks discussing the strange behaviour of the Assyrian king. Latich informed them that he had seen a dark haired Babylonian girl playing with the royal children and the king's niece, who had been seen by the lieutenant and the sergeant as they approached. Luckily neither of them had seen Ruben or Lialah. Latich deliberately told them nothing about Ruben's appearance that afternoon, so that he could deny knowing the other Babylonian Guard if the Assyrian king brought up the subject, as he felt sure that he would. They all agreed that the Assyrian king was a nasty person and both Abzher and Latich agreed with Lieutenant Bel that Tiglath-Pileser was only good for target practise. They all thought it a great joke when Latich said, "Even Lieutenant Bel's well aimed javelins would not penetrate his obnoxious smell."

That evening they were invited to the king's dinner, where Tiglath-Pileser said to the king that his Babylonian Guardsmen might be good soldiers, but they could do with a lesson in manners and that they should not speak to him without him first addressing them. He then went on to tell the king that he wanted the dark haired girl who was playing with the children. Also that he wanted the young Guardsman who had resisted him to be punished. However, the king had been most annoyed that the Assyrian king had shunned his niece, as he had had an enormous argument with his half sister about offering her to Tiglath-Pileser. Even though the king had eventually won, by using his authority and saying, "If I want to give her to someone else, she has no choice in the matter." So he simply informed the king of Assyria that he did not allow such people to play with the royal children, so Tiglath-Pileser must have made a mistake. This only annoyed the Assyrian king, who slammed his fist on the table and demanded that a search be made. Not wanting to upset his guest, the king said that he would have a search made in the morning. But as he had plenty of other urgent matters, he would be grateful if the Assyrian king left for Nineveh within two days. The Babylonian Guards who had come especially for that purpose would escort him.

Tiglath-Pileser was affronted by this dismissal and said to Lieutenant Bel, "What's all this I hear about Lagash having a lot of the new metal weapons that have come from Sal-e Pol-e?"

Glancing at his king, who gave a small shake of the head, indicating that he did not want the news to be confirmed, the lieutenant said, "If we had such weapons, your Majesty, we would be wearing them."

"Are you calling me a liar?" bellowed the Assyrian king.

"No, I am just saying that your information is incorrect, Sir," said Lieutenant Bel, keeping his voice level.

"Insolent pig!" roared Tiglath-Pileser. "Address me as your Majesty and lower your eyes. Bloody filth," he shouted, spitting out a mouthful of food as he marched out of the hall. The others finished their meal amid quiet conversation and gradually drifted away after taking their leave of the king.

Just as he was about to leave, the king called, "Lieutenant Belthezder, a word with you please." He then thanked the lieutenant for not saying anything about the new weapons, then asked him not to stay long in Nineveh, but find out the extent of the strength of the Assyrian army. He should then hurry back and if things got difficult he was to kill Tiglath-Pileser and get away as quickly as possible, without endangering his own life.

\*\*\*\*

Latich had left the dinner as soon as he could slip away unnoticed, and left the Citadel to advise Ruben of what had happened. He arrived at the inn and went over to the innkeeper and asked if Ruben was around, giving a quick description of his friend.

The innkeeper said, "Yes, he is in the back room, with my wife and some other friends. Please feel free to go and speak to him if you wish."

Ruben saw him enter and beckoned him over. Latich shook his head and indicated that Ruben should join him. When Ruben came over, Latich said, "I need to speak to you urgently and in private."

Seeing he was agitated, Ruben pointed to an alcove that was empty and said, "Let us go and sit over there and you can tell me what is troubling you."

Latich told him about the Assyrian king's behaviour at dinner, and that he had demanded a search for Ruben and Lialah, which the king of Babylon had reluctantly agreed to carry out first thing in the morning. He went on to say that they would be safe until tomorrow, but they would be wise to leave the city first thing in the morning.

"I see," said Ruben. "Where do you think would be the best place for us to go?"

"You would be safe back in the marshlands," said Latich.

"No," said Ruben. "Lialah would never agree to that, if anything, I think we should go upriver."

"Anywhere out of the city," said Latich. "But in a couple of days we should be leaving with the Assyrian king and going directly to Nineveh, which is roughly in the same direction."

"Well, not exactly," corrected Ruben. "Nineveh is more north, on the River Tigris. What is the next town upriver?" Ruben enquired.

"Well, you could leave by the southern gate and cross the river, as if you were going into the marshlands, then follow the river. As you know, there is a loop around Babylon and you can follow it around to the north and then follow the river, as if you had left by the northern gate." Latich fully explained the plan that had come to him.

"That sounds like a good idea," said Ruben. "But what is the main town in that direction?"

"Well, there is another small town, but that is entirely on the northern bank, which means you would have to cross the river again, and that would mean using a ferryman, so your passage would not remain secret. But if you go to the next town, which is Zohab, which is on both banks, that would be safe."

"We will do that then," said Ruben standing up. "This is probably goodbye, I may not see you again, but at least I have a chance this time to say goodbye and wish you well." They embraced, and Ruben said, "Very many thanks for the timely warning and your loyal friendship."

Latich said, "My help today was nothing compared to all the help you gave me in the training camp, I will never be able to fully repay you."

Ruben was about to leave, when he turned back to Latich and said, "If you get a chance, when you come back from Nineveh, you can tell Lieutenant Bel all about me and give him my regards."

Ruben went back to Lialah and when there was a break in the conversation, he whispered into her ear that they must leave, so she should say that they had a long day tomorrow, meaning they needed to go to bed. Lialah did as she was requested and they left the room. As soon as they were outside she said to him, "What was all that about?"

"I will tell you soon, now I would like you to go up to our bedroom and prepare to leave early in the morning." With a surprised look on her face, she left and went upstairs. Ruben went over to the innkeeper and said they would be leaving very early, but he was not to worry about getting them anything to eat, and he checked that everything was settled up. He then followed Lialah upstairs.

When they were back in their room he told her why they had to leave Babylon and that they would leave the way they had come and give the ferryman the impression that they were going to Kish.

"We will then double back and follow the river and keep to the southern bank and then head for Zohab." He went on to say that he would have to take Lialah with him for fear of her safety, but it would not be wise to go too far before trying to find somewhere that she could stay.

"If at all possible we will find somewhere in Zohab, but let us not worry about that yet, the important thing is to get out of the city."

Lialah was more than happy with this arrangement, even though she would have liked to stay in Babylon for a little longer, but the prospect of being with Ruben was preferable. As they went to bed, after preparing everything for the morning, Ruben lay in bed wondering why the sudden recollection of Miriam, whose parents had treated him like their own son, had come to him. Thinking hard about this it was probably because he had thoughts that Miriam might be the right kind of girl for Latich, she would possibly restore the ability that he had once shown in himself, and with the thought of his friend, he went to sleep.

When he awoke it was still dark, but he could sense that morning was not far off. He rose and woke Lialah and said they had to get going. By the time they had washed and dressed the sky was beginning to pale in the east. Very quietly they left the Inn and they had soon walked down to the river, where some of the market stalls were being set up. Here Ruben bought some food. They soon found a ferryman who was just getting his boat out and was pleased at this early morning trade. Ruben gave him the brass coins to pay for the trip across the river; the ferryman started rowing and asked, "Where are you off to so early in the morning?"

Ruben said, "We have to meet someone in Kish before noon, so we thought we had better leave early."

"A journey for me first thing in the morning is a good omen," said the ferryman with a smile, as he rowed them swiftly through the quiet river. He soon had them on the far bank and they left him. After walking for a couple of hundred paces, Ruben stopped by a small grove of trees and said to Lialah, "We will sit down here and have some breakfast." As Ruben sliced the bread with his bronze knife and cut up the juicy watermelon, Lialah decided that she was hungry after all, and Ruben was delighted to see her eat first thing in the morning. It was a good sign that she was getting over her early morning sickness, even though her pregnancy did not show yet. Ruben knew that she would soon start to thicken up around the waist and as soon as that happened it would not be wise for her to travel long distances. When they had almost finished eating, they noticed that the ferryman who had brought them over had picked up another wayfarer and had set off rowing back to Babylon. Realising this was a good opportunity to double back, they waited until the ferryman was virtually out of sight halfway across the broad river, then they picked up their bags, and headed upriver, moving diagonally towards the riverbank where they would be shielded from view by the tall rushes. The sun was now high in the sky and they walked along keeping to the riverbank as it gradually turned north. Lialah suddenly grabbed Ruben's arm and pointed through a gap in the rushes. Here they could see the entire western side of the Citadel and it was indeed a marvellous sight. The wonderful golden rooftop of the Gardens seemed to cascade down the terraces in glorious colours that were beautifully mirrored in the calm waters of the river below them. They stood in wonder for a long time looking at this spectacle. It was a superb feeling that only the previous day they had been in these magnificent gardens, and had looked down to where they now stood. The spell was eventually broken as a galley rippled the water as it was rowed upstream. They moved on upriver, keeping out of sight of the occasional boats that passed them by.

When they stopped for lunch, Lialah asked, "How far do you think we have to go?"

"I am not sure," replied Ruben. "But I believe we will pass another town on the north bank of the river, quite a way before we come to Zohab, which is twice as big as the town on the northern bank. But as I have not seen a map I do not know how far it is, and we may have to camp out for the night."

"That sounds rather military, Ruben," said Lialah pulling his leg. However, it should be very cool down by the river."

"I think," said Ruben, "that it would be best not to camp by the river, because of the large number of mosquitoes."

"We never had any problems in the marshlands," said Lialah, surprised at Ruben's concern.

"I know," replied Ruben. "I am not sure why, but Simeon seems to have some strange power over all the creatures in the marshlands, it is as if they respect him, they never worried us when we were in his floating house. But whenever I have slept right beside the river, the only way to ensure there is no problem is to light a fire, the smoke tends to keep them away. If we did that it would only draw attention to us. So we had better make camp a little further up the valley."

They walked on for the rest of the afternoon, and Ruben was surprised that Lialah neither complained, nor asked him to carry her bag, even though they were in no hurry. Shortly before sunset they could just make out on the far bank the outskirts of the small town that Ruben had spoken of. At the same time Ruben noticed a clump of trees a short distance up the side of the valley to their left. He pointed this out to Lialah, and said, "I think that would make an ideal campsite. They soon were at the trees, which were in fact situated in an ideal position, from which they could see quite extensively over the river. Ruben quickly selected a small tree with a fork in the branches just below shoulder height, where he put down their bags. Taking his large sword out of his bag, he cut down a small sapling. Lialah watched him at work and was surprised at his speed and efficiency, as he made a bivouac by propping the sapling in the fork of the tree with the top branches resting on the ground. He then made a small tent like structure by spreading a blanket over the sapling, which he secured by placing large stones at its edge. He then cut some bracken that was growing nearby, which he laid on the ground inside the structure. On this he placed another blanket, he then looked at Lialah and said, "Try that for comfort."

She lay down on the soft yet springy blanket. "Oh yes, that's fine. But where are you going to sleep?" she asked mischievously.

"Any more of your cheek, and it will be on top of you," returned Ruben.

That night they ate most of the bread, cheese and cold meat that he had bought at the market, before spending a quiet night lying cuddled together in the bivouac.

\*\*\*\*

The search that the king instigated revealed that there had been two strangers in the Gardens as Tiglath-Pileser had said. However, further investigation revealed that the mysterious couple had been staying in one of the local inns, but they had now left and were believed to be headed for Kish, in the marshlands. When this information reached the Assyrian king he was extremely annoyed, as he had relished the thought of adding the dark haired girl to his harem as one of his concubines. He said as much to the king of Babylon and virtually implied that their treaty rested on this girl being found and sent to him in Nineveh. With those instructions, not realising how insulted the Babylonian king had been, he then left with his retinue and the old general with the three accompanying Babylonian Guards, by the northern gate. They did not cross the river but rode northeast along the bank with the intention of going through the northern part of Zohab. Here the town was on both sides of the river, where another tributary ran into the Euphrates. There was a complex system of ferries that crossed both the tributary and the main river, but it did have a few houses on the northern bank, with a good ferry over the river. Tiglath-Pileser had arranged to meet some of his informants who had come from Sal-e Pol-e, who had told him about all the new weapons that were being sent to Lagash.

Latich was both surprised and concerned about this strange turn of events, as he had previously informed Ruben that Zohab would be perfectly safe. Latich's anxiety must have shown on his face as Lieutenant Bel said to him, "What is troubling you, Corporal?"

In an attempt to hide the real reason for his concern, Latich answered, "I have never been outside my own country, Lieutenant, and from what I understand, the Assyrians are hardly ideal hosts."

"I agree with you there," said Lieutenant Bel, and added. "We must all be on our guard and be sure we stay together."

They were not travelling fast, but certainly quicker than if they had all been on foot. The Assyrian king rode in a chariot, which they kept well clear of because it had vicious looking blades that extended from the wheel hubs. His retinue travelled either on horseback or in two large oxen-drawn wagons that tended to slow the party down. The old general and his accompanying Guards were also on horseback, which Latich had only just mastered. His previous journey from Lagash to Babylon had been something of a nightmare, which had left him extremely sore for the next few days. He rode between Lieutenant Bel and Sergeant Abzher, who were both accomplished horsemen, and they kept an eye on him and an occasional steadying hand. The old general kept prancing all over the place on his restless white stallion, getting on everybody's nerves and often riding dangerously close to Tiglath-Pileser's chariot. They kept travelling until they came to the northern part of Zohab, where lodgings had previously been registered, much to the Babylonians' surprise.

## 11
## THE ROUTES CROSS

Ruben and Lialah woke when the sun was up and already heating up the air inside the bivouac, which was beginning to get rather uncomfortable. They walked down to the riverbank, where Ruben decided to go for a swim. Lialah contented herself by rinsing her hands and face in the cool water and sat on the riverbank swinging her feet in the river, while Ruben went for his swim. She was watching some ducks that were slightly down river from where she was sitting. They were amusing to watch as they bobbed up and down, occasionally putting their heads under water and swimming down and returning to the surface, where they shook the water from their plumage. She was so intent in watching them that she didn't see something under the water that suddenly grabbed her leg and began to pull her into the river. She was waist deep in the water before she realised what had been pulling her in. Ruben rose out of the water laughing, "You thought that you were going to be eaten by a crocodile, didn't you?"

"Well, you certainly had me worried," she retorted. "That was a beastly thing to do, at times you don't deserve someone to look after you. And how am I going to get my dress dry now that you have completely soaked it."

"You, looking after me, That is a good joke!" said Ruben, moving behind and holding her around the waist and slowly pulling her underwater. They rose in a flurry of bubbles, streaming water and laughter. Ruben helped her back on to the bank and said, "You will soon dry out once we start walking. We still have a fair way to go before we get to Zohab."

"All right, let's get going then," said Lialah, and then added in a more serious tone, "I hope you realise that you will have to stop doing daft things like that soon."

"Yes, but you look nice like that," said Ruben admiringly.

She glanced down and saw that her thin cotton dress clung to her body, and seemed to be transparent as it displayed the fine shape of her breasts. "And you can stop leering at me, you are as bad as the Assyrian king," she said

"Possibly, but not as smelly," laughed Ruben. They walked up to the campsite, which they soon cleared and put everything back in their bags before setting off.

Eating the remains of their food for breakfast as they walked along, Ruben began telling Lialah that he knew little about the way that he had to go and even less of the sort of people who lived in the lands that he had to cross. This led to their discussing the sort of position that they needed to find for Lialah, so that Ruben could leave her without having to worry about her and the baby. They could reach no agreement by the time that they could see Zohab in the distance. It had not been as far as Ruben had feared and it was about the middle of the afternoon when they arrived in the town. The town was on both sides of the river, but as the main trade route ran along the northern bank, they were advised to cross by the ferry, where they would come to a respectable inn. The main ferry was fairly complex, as another river flowed into the river Euphrates from the north and although this river was only small it was deep and fast flowing, so it had no crossing points for the main trade route. Therefore the ferryboats ran in three directions, directly over to the north bank or to the northeast bank below the river that flowed into the Euphrates. The other route went along the northern bank, avoiding the turbulence created by this faster flowing tributary. They took the ferry directly across and soon came to a respectable looking inn.

Putting their bags down, Ruben walked up to the innkeeper and asked if they could buy an early dinner. The innkeeper said that he already had a guest who had the same request, so they were welcome to join him. He showed them in to the back room of the inn where there was a merchant who was washing his well-travelled feet. The merchant was drying his feet by the time they came over and were introduced as fellow travellers who came from the same area that he came from. He introduced himself as Dathram and seemed a pleasant and talkative fellow. He said that he had walked down beside the river with his pack animals and was heading for Babylon, having come all the way from Great Egypt. There he had joined a caravan, which he had now left at Ashkilon, which was about four days' walk upriver, by the border with Assyria. He explained to them that he had travelled a long and difficult journey from Egypt to trade his goods in Babylon for things that had come from the east. Ruben told him that he had come from Lagash and had been in the marshlands south of the great river. But he and his companion, who had come from that area, were heading in the direction that Dathram had come from.

As Dathram looked at him with keen interest, he asked which was the best way to go and what sort of people he would encounter on the way. Dathram told them that he and his companion should go up the river through Ashkilon, where they would see the first cataract, then in to Assyria, but to keep beside the river as far as Neath, but then to turn west across the river before the route took them on to Nineveh, saying that the road was long and difficult, but that he had made the journey four times in the past.

Ruben asked him what sort of people lived in these countries. Dathram replied, "You must be careful when you are travelling in Assyria, because the Assyrians are a hard and cruel people. They will easily rob and deceive you, although some of the people can be kind, it is best not to trust them. Further southwest than Assyria there is a strange land where there are many tribes of different types of people. Generally the land is called Canaan, where the people often worship strange statues of a god called Baal – this god has many different names, and often demands human sacrifice. Canaan's border with Assyria often changes, so you cannot be sure which country you are in, but I understand that the tyrant king Tiglath-Pileser wants to move his border southwest across Canaan to the sea. But as there are many different tribes in that area, he will have to fight many battles. Now, to the north of Canaan there is the old Hittite Empire, which is now in pieces with lots of small kingdoms, each of which has its own ruler, but there is little of value there so try to avoid it, it is also very mountainous. But if you turn south and travel beside another sea through Canaan you will find a lot more tribes. They always seem to be fighting one another so there are a lot of battles to avoid. Here you must be careful with who you meet, some of the people that live there can be nice, but always be on your guard and do not trust anyone unless you feel sure about them. Further down the coast you find an old sea faring people, who are often called Philistines, and their main capital is Gaza, on the coast. They are also warlike, again, be careful of them. But if you pass through there you will eventually come to Great Egypt, the land of the Pharaohs. They are civilised and have marvellous cities with great palaces – that is where I do a lot of trade."

Lialah interrupted. "What is a Pharaoh?" she asked, unable to retain her curiosity.

"A good question, my dear! I suppose he is a king, but they say he is also a god, or at least becomes a god. I think that is right, but it is all mysterious and is part of the Egyptian religion. They seem to have as many gods as we do. All beliefs are strange and I find it best not to get involved, but always try to respect other people's beliefs," said Dathram.

"Well! That sounds interesting, I bet you could tell many stories about your adventures," said Ruben.

"Yes, my young friend, I certainly can," said Dathram. "I could tell you stories all night long, so it's best not to get me started," he chuckled.

Dathram was a large man, although slightly shorter than Ruben. He was broad and looked as if he could take care of himself. He had light brown, curly hair that was flecked with grey. It needed cutting, and apart from a few days' stubble he was clean-shaven. He had a broad, open face that broke into a smile easily and dark brown eyes that were set well apart and were friendly, warm and considerate. He asked them to excuse his appearance, as he needed a wash and a change of clothes.

"But first I must check my animals, and then eat and get some rest." He stood up and said, "Come with me, I could do with someone who is strong, as I have to unload my animals."

Ruben and Lialah followed him out of the back door of the inn to the stables, where he had locked up his pack animals. There were four large mules, each one carrying a heavy burden. He started unloading the animals, passing each item to Ruben as he went. There were many heavy cases, some of which were locked chests that were very ornate. There were some long, heavy, curved poles that looked like logs, but on inspection they were not poles, but these things were wrapped in dark cloth, each one was as tall as Ruben was himself. Ruben put them down where Dathram pointed. Lialah watched with wonder and much interest, she was so fascinated by the large log things that she asked, "What are they, Dathram?"

"Those, my dear girl, are ivory, each one is a tooth, but I have never seen the animals that they came from. As you can imagine, they must be huge," Dathram explained.

Eventually the job was done and Dathram said, "Thank you very much, young man, you have been most helpful. I still do not know your name, and I am still not sure why I trusted you. Because all these things are very valuable – and will hopefully make me a rich man, when they are sold. I have spent my whole life working for the money that they cost." He looked at Ruben intently, and smiled at Lialah. "I think it is because of your lovely friend, and also your bright blue eyes. I once met a man who had eyes like yours, back in Babylon a long time ago. He was working for the old king on the Gardens that were being built on the Citadel. It is funny, but I can not remember his name, but he was honest and a nice man."

"His name was not Simeon by any chance?" asked Ruben.

"No, I do not think so," replied Dathram. "I am sure it will come to me soon." He paused, deep in thought, his brows wrinkling. "Yes, his name was Uriah, it is strange but he also asked me all about the things that I have been telling you, and much more as well," he laughed.

"I think that was probably my father!" said Ruben.

"Well, well, it could well be, so how is he?" enquired Dathram.

"I am afraid I do not know for sure," replied Ruben. "You see he left me when I was just a baby, in rather strange circumstances."

"By all the gods ever worshipped, what a strange coincidence. Now what is your name? I can't keep calling you Son of Uriah, can I?" questioned Dathram.

"I am Ruben, and my companion is Lialah," said Ruben.

"Well, my young friends," said Dathram, putting his arms on their shoulders. "Let us go and eat, for I am starving. We can talk while we eat, it is safe to leave my treasures here, they are locked up and the innkeeper is an old friend of mine."

They left the stables, Dathram locked the door behind him and they returned to the inn, where the innkeeper had put down a table, laden with food. They ate their meal, Dathram listening to Ruben's story, which was told without him mentioning anything about being in the army, going on to say that he had met Lialah, whom he had previously met when he came back to Ur, and they had been travelling together since then. He told Dathram that he had been taking Lialah to Babylon, where they had been in the beautiful Gardens in the Citadel, but they had met the aforementioned Tiglath-Pileser who had taken a fancy to Lialah, so they thought it was wise to leave the city.

Dathram laughed and said that he was not surprised, because from what he had heard the Assyrian king was not very nice, and once he got tired of a woman, he often had them killed and rumour had it that he ate their flesh.

Lialah shuddered. "How horrible," she said. "I think we did the right thing to leave the city."

All the food had been eaten, Lialah eating one plateful, while Ruben ate three, and Dathram, five.

"When you have been to Egypt," said Ruben, directly addressing Dathram, "did you ever hear about the sons of Abraham trying to establish a New Kingdom?"

"Yes," answered Dathram. "Apparently there is an old city north of a fabled salt sea, called Jericho, that was captured by a strange tribe who came out of the desert, they are now at war with the Philistines and the other tribes in Canaan. They have a strange belief in just one God and they claim that he has given them that land. They call it Judea, and I believe that they called themselves Israelites."

****

The old general was extremely annoyed that the lodgings that the Assyrian king had procured simply afforded one large room for all four Babylonian Guards. It was most uncustomary for a general to share the same room with his lower ranks, particularly with a sergeant and a corporal. He complained loudly and bitterly to Lieutenant Bel, who agreed with him that it was indeed an indignity, particularly as they were still in their own country. He took the general by the arm and steered him to a quiet corner of the room. He asked the general to sit down and sat down himself, saying, "I am very sorry about this, sir, but I think there is something far more important that we must speak about."

The old general looked indignantly at the lieutenant and said, "I do not see what is more important than this damned outrage, but I will hear you out."

"I know that you theoretically outrank me, sir, but you are semi-retired and our king did inform me that if things looked bad we were to abort the mission." He deliberately did not tell the old general exactly what the king had charged him with, as he knew that the old general would be affronted by the lieutenant having to make such important decisions, that were, to say the least, rather dramatic. He said, "As we came in I noticed the senior metalworker from the mines and workings at Sal-e Pol-e, who must be working in collusion with the Assyrians. Do you remember Tiglath-Pileser's outrageous behaviour at dinner shortly after he asked me about the new weapons?"

"Yes, I most certainly do," boomed the general. "The insolent pig actually spat out the excellent meal, and marched out of the room. I have seldom seen such behaviour."

Lieutenant Bel kept speaking in a low voice and tried to calm the old general down by saying, "I think we are all in agreement with you, sir, but the important thing is that we are receiving new iron weapons in Lagash, the king knows this but does not want the word to spread until we are all fully equipped with the new weapons. Because it will give us a tremendous advantage over the Assyrians, and there will be no need for the treaty."

"By the gods, I see what they have been playing at," said the old general. "We must arrest that traitorous dog and put him in chains, and march him back to the Citadel to work the treadmill."

"Just so, sir, but remember, at the moment we are vastly outnumbered by the Assyrian king's retinue. We cannot do anything yet, but neither can they, provided that we all stay together."

"I see, but what do you have in mind?" enquired the old general.

"Well, what I propose, is that we send young Latich back to Babylon with an urgent message to the king, informing him of what is happening and that the metalworker be arrested on his return to Sal-e Pol-e. And that a full company of troops should meet us at Ashkilon."

"That's a damn good idea," said the old general. "He would not be much good in a fight anyway, so until then we will stay together, and then catch the whole bloody bunch of scoundrels." He jumped to his feet and clapped the lieutenant on the back.

Just then there was a knock on the door, it opened without invitation and an Assyrian messenger said, "The king demands to see the tall lieutenant."

Before they could stop him, the old general was at the door. He thrust the messenger outside shouting, "Bloody wretch! Wait until you are asked to enter, you can tell that greasy pig that we will all come when we are ready," and slammed the door. "The sooner we can get away the better," he said.

Trying not to laugh, but grinning at the other two, Lieutenant Bel stood up and said, "You are right, sir, but let's not make too many enemies, let's all go together, but please let me do the talking." And then said in a whisper to Sergeant Abzher, "Try to keep the old boy out of trouble, gag him if necessary." Then they all left, going to where the messenger took them.

They came to a large room where Tiglath-Pileser stood behind a table that had some new weapons on it. Lieutenant Bel recognised these weapons as some of the new iron issues that had come from Sal-e Pol-e.

"What do you think these are, Lieutenant?" demanded Tiglath-Pileser, picking up one of the short swords and thrusting it into the table top, which almost collapsed and left the sword blade shuddering upright, well embedded in the table top.

"Very nice, your Majesty," said the lieutenant, firmly gripping the sword and pulling it free with apparent ease. "Where did these come from, your Majesty?"

"Don't play innocent with me, Lieutenant, you know where they come from," shouted the king of Assyria. "Do not lie to me, you know they come from Lagash, if you lie again I will cut your tongue out."

"That would not be wise," said the lieutenant in a calm, cold voice that carried implied menace. "You cannot expect me to disobey orders."

"Get out you, scum," roared the Assyrian king.

Without a word they all turned and walked out.

As they left the room, Lieutenant Bel noticed the messenger who had summoned them earlier, he was hanging about outside, obviously listening to what transpired. As he tried to shrink into the shadows, Lieutenant Bel grabbed him by the arm and demanded that they be brought their meal, which they would eat in their room, together with some wine. When they got back, he asked Latich if he had sufficient materials to write a letter. Latich nodded the affirmative and Lieutenant Bel told him to get them out, but not to let the messenger see what he was doing when he returned with the food.

"Now, first thing in the morning I want you to take the message that the general and I will dictate, directly to Babylon. It will be addressed to the king, and you should take it directly and put it in his hands." Latich got out a black scroll and his brushes and ink, but was careful to keep them behind his back when the food was brought in. The servant left, telling them that they only needed to put the empty plates outside when they had finished. The old general immediately helped himself to a goblet of wine saying, "I need this, and when it is finished we will send for another flagon."

Lieutenant Bel said, "Begging your pardon, sir, but I think it would be sensible if none of us drank a lot tonight as we must all be on our guard."

Before the old general could say anything, Sergeant Abzher reinforced what the lieutenant had said by adding, "He is correct, sir, we dare not trust anyone outside this room, not even the innkeeper and his staff, as they are all being paid by the Assyrians."

"Traitorous bastards," growled the old general emptying his goblet in one swig. "I suppose you are right," he reluctantly agreed.

They ate their food in comparative silence each one thinking about their immediate future. When they had finished, they put the empty dishes outside the room as requested. Lieutenant Bel then stationed Sergeant Abzher by the door to check on any movements outside, to ensure that they were not overheard. He also checked that there was no one outside the windows, listening to what was going on inside. Being sure that nobody knew what was going on, he asked Latich to sit down and to write as he dictated. The message started, 'To his most Royal Majesty, the King of Babylon. This message is written in Zohab on the evening after we left the Citadel and its contents are for yourself only, and are of prime importance'. Latich wrote quickly in a neat hand, with just the occasional check on words that the lieutenant dictated, with occasional interjections from the old general. The message was brief and to the point. It explained that the senior metalworker from Sal-e Pol-e had informed the Assyrians that they were producing the new weapons. Whether or not any of these were yet in Assyrian hands was not definite, but that he should be arrested and made to talk. It then went on to say that they would try to continue along the north bank of the river and on to Nineveh, but should they be intercepted at the border, he would then try to fulfil the king's orders, as events had indeed turned out badly. He got Latich to re-read the message and confirmed with the old general that it was satisfactory. He then stamped the message with his seal, and requested the old general to do the same. When all this had been finished it was getting late, and he insisted on moving all the beds to the centre of the room, where they would sleep fully dressed and with one person keeping a vigil, to be replaced at suitable intervals. The only one that he insisted not to be woken was Latich, who was extremely grateful for this courtesy, and slept soundly until morning.

Their night had been undisturbed and Lieutenant Bel was wondering if he had overreacted, when there was a knock on the door, this time it did not open until they responded. It was the same servant from the inn, who entered with a tray of light breakfast. Putting the tray down he said, "As soon as you have eaten, the king requests the pleasure of your company outside as he wishes to make an early start."

This complete change in behaviour took them all by surprise and they ate their breakfast warily, unsure of what awaited them. They soon finished their breakfast, collected their few possessions and went outside, expecting to find their horses. However, in this they were incorrect, the king of Assyria welcomed them most politely, and much to their dismay said, "I have already sent the wagons and the animals to the ferry, down by the Euphrates, to avoid the tributary that flowed in from the north. We will now walk down to the riverbank and await its return."

This was something that they had not anticipated, and Latich looked enquiringly at Lieutenant Bel, wondering how he was going to get away. Lieutenant Bel walked beside him down to the river and whispered in his ear, "As we get on our horses, and out of the town, start pretending that your horse has become lame, or has a stone in its hoof, and fall back behind the party. When I give you a nod, travel as quickly as you can back to Babylon, and give the message to the king." He added for good measure, "You must get the message back, even if I call you back just ignore me, it is absolutely vital. Is that clear?" asked the lieutenant in a quiet but clear voice.

"Yes, that is perfectly clear, sir," responded Latich.

\*\*\*\*

It had been a warm evening and had clouded over, although the clouds were high and it did not look as if it would rain. Ruben and Lialah had decided, with the innkeeper's agreement, to sleep on the roof. Ruben had woken and risen early while Lialah was still sleeping. He was sitting on the small wall on the side of the roof, looking around the town, trying to spot any early morning people walking around on their particular business, through half-closed eyes, trying to make out the colour that surrounds them. This he had been trying to do most days since he had regained the ability to do so under Simeon's instruction when they had been in the marshlands. During such quiet moments, he was quite successful and had been watching some people who had been down by the river. It was obvious that they had been checking on some fishing lines that they had left out over night, quite deliberately, in an attempt to catch fish. The position that he was in gave him an excellent view over the town, down the main street to the ferry. His interest was caught by the early arrival of the large ferry that docked and unloaded two large ox-drawn wagons and about ten horses. They were on their own except for a couple of handlers. But even his sharp sight could not make out the markings on the wagons, or on the horse blankets. Even though some of the horse blankets were the familiar purple of the Babylonian Guards. His interest was aroused and he watched with great anticipation to see who was on the ferry when it came back upriver. As although the river was not as wide here, it was still wide enough to be unsure of what was on the far bank. He did not have long to wait as he could soon see the ferry returning. Still watching through half-closed eyes there seemed to be a large aura of many vivid colours around the ferry that came upriver from the north bank around the turbulence caused by the tributary. Indicating a large number of people, all with strong feelings, from the green of uncertainty to the orange of surprise, the bright red of anger to the maroon of hatred. As the ferry unloaded he could make out a chariot and much to his dismay, the great bulk of Tiglath-Pileser on the chariot.

At first he was unsure of what to do, but then he realised what must have happened and providing that they kept well out of sight, they were in no immediate danger. He went over to where Lialah was still sleeping and woke her up, informing her that he had just seen her admirer. She woke and amid the drowsiness of early morning, she said, "What, I mean, who are you talking about?"

"Your secret lover," jested Ruben. "He has just come for breakfast. Come and see, he has just come over the river."

Rather unsure of what he was talking about, she followed him over to the side of the roof. Following his pointed finger, she could make out the shape of the Assyrian king. "Aggh," she gasped. "That horrible brute, you can almost smell him from here. What is he doing and why is he here?" But before Ruben could answer, she drew back from the side of the roof and said, "We must get going!"

He put his arms around her shoulders and held her close to him. Kissing her head that was buried against his chest, he said, "Do not worry, my precious, I do not think that we are in any danger and he will not ever touch you as long as I am alive. So come down, but tidy up, whilst I will try to see what is happening."

Lialah dressed herself properly, and quickly packed her bags. She came over to where Ruben was standing watching what was happening down beside the river. It was at least two hundred paces away and she was amazed at how keen his eyesight was as he could make out most of the people and what they were doing. He told her that Tiglath-Pileser was in his chariot leading the party up the road towards them, but only at a walking pace, as the others were walking along leading their horses, with the ox carts following. He pointed out, in the middle of the party the tall figure of Lieutenant Bel, who walked with Latich, Sergeant Abzher and the old general.

****

A strange feeling of being watched came over Lieutenant Bel, although he was used to being watched, it was a standard thing for people to stare at the elite Babylonian Guards, with awe and dread, even more so for Lieutenant Bel as he was a striking figure, tall and well muscled. But this was slightly more than the normal feeling, that produced an uncertainty in his mind and he often looked up at the nearby window openings and rooftops to see if he could see who was watching him. As he was unsuccessful, he decided that it must be his over anxious nerves playing a trick on him, so he started thinking about how to get Latich away.

At the top of the main street they turned right, passing a pleasant looking inn, which was all locked up. They headed northwest out of the town, and they had just passed the final buildings when the Assyrian king said that they could now all mount up and they could travel faster. He had simply made an exhibition of himself, which was purely based on his own barbaric pride, as he enjoyed the terror that his passing struck into the mortal souls who had the temerity to watch with dread fascination.

They all moved off, the four Babylonians keeping close together. Just a little further along they branched off the main road and headed north, rather than heading straight on which would eventually lead them to Ashkilon. This was much to the surprise of the Babylonians. They suddenly realised that the Assyrian king was taking a direct route through deserted scrub country straight for his own border. Lieutenant Bel nodded to Latich, and according to his earlier instructions Latich began to fall behind the rest of the party, and as if trying to rectify his problem Lieutenant Bel also fell back. Regrettably the Assyrian king noted this, and shouted back, "What is going on there, I need everyone to keep up a good pace."

"One of our horses seems to be having difficulty, your Majesty," returned the lieutenant.

"Let my horse expert have a look," ordered the king. One of the men on the ox wagons jumped down and ran over and started looking at the hooves of Latich's horse. Latich had himself dismounted and after the man had looked at the front hooves, declaring them to be in good condition, Latich told him that the problem seemed to be with the hindquarters of the horse. Lieutenant Bel had also ridden over beside Latich, dismounted from his horse and feigned an interest. Just as the expert picked up the horse's final hoof and was about to declare that it was in excellent condition, Lieutenant Bel struck him a sharp blow on the back of his head with his bunched fist. This had not been seen by anyone except Latich and as the man sank to the ground, Lieutenant Bel looked at Latich and nodded his head, mouthing the words, "Go, run like the wind!"

Latich ran like he had never run before and was fully two hundred paces away before the lieutenant shouted, "Oi, come back Corporal."

Wheeling around, Tiglath-Pileser shouted, "What in Hades is going on back there?"

Helping the stunned man to his feet, the lieutenant said, "I am sorry your Majesty, but the little blighter has run off."

"Couldn't face it, eh?" snarled the king of Assyria. "So much for your Babylonian Guards. Let him go Lieutenant, he was a disgrace to you, you will manage quite well without him," all the time thinking that he would be one less to dispose off when the time came. So he turned his chariot back towards the northwest and ordered the party forward.

"But he has the plans for the training schedule, your Majesty," explained the old general, looking concerned. "We will most certainly chastise him when we return," he continued seeming to accept the situation. The expert horseman was helped back onto the ox cart, groggily saying, "What in Hades did he hit me with?"

"I didn't see," lied the lieutenant. "Probably the hilt of his sword."

"Make sure you give the bastard a good whipping from me, I was only trying to help," said the man rubbing the back of his head, which felt very sore indeed.

The king kept them riding all day before stopping. They realised that he had come well prepared for this diversion, with plenty of food, tents and blankets for all the party. The three Babylonians pitched their tent slightly away from the others, and ate their meal in some agitation, trying to decide what to do. All three of them agreed that Tiglath-Pileser had planned the whole journey and that they would be met at the border by a considerable number of Assyrian soldiers. Leaving the general for a moment, both saying that they had to answer nature's call, Lieutenant Bel and Sergeant Abzher went behind a clump of bushes. Lieutenant Bel said, "We will have to act within the next day, otherwise we are dead men. So keep close to me and be ready to act as soon as I give the word."

\*\*\*\*

Latich ran as if the Cerberus, the hound who guards the entrance to Hades, was behind him. Even when he entered the town he did not slacken his pace as he thought he heard the sound of hoof beats behind him. This he may well have done, but if so it was another horse, and no one in pursuit from the Assyrian king's party. Just as he ran towards the inn where Ruben and Lialah had been staying, he saw the side gates that led from the stables being opened. Realising that this was an ideal refuge for him to recover his breath, he dashed inside the opening gates straight into Ruben. Both were astonished, but much to Latich's gratitude, realising that he had been running from something or someone, Ruben closed the gates behind him and allowed him a chance to recover his breath. Lialah and Dathram, who were standing beside the mules that Dathram had repacked with Ruben's assistance, were equally surprised. Dathram had prepared to leave early as he hoped to get to Babylon in a single day.

Once Latich had recovered his breath, he grasped Ruben by the arm and breathlessly said, "This is my lucky day, you are just the person I need to speak to. Both to warn and to ask for help."

"What are you running from Latich? Who is chasing you?" asked Ruben, wearing a puzzled frown.

"The Assyrian king's party, did you notice if anyone saw me?" questioned Latich.

Ruben opened the gates, and had a brief look around. "There is nobody in sight, and I feel sure that nobody saw you. Now will you tell me what this is all about?"

The words tumbled out of Latich in an incoherent stream, and seeing three bewildered faces before him, Latich took a deep breath and started his story in a more appropriate order.

"I am running from the king's party, under explicit instructions from Lieutenant Bel. I am carrying a scroll that has to be taken to our king in the Citadel, and I am so sorry that I told you Zohab was safe," he blurted out. He then went on to tell them about Tiglath-Pileser's change of route and how he had displayed the iron weapons that were now being made in Sal-e Pol-e and been sent to Lagash. He told them in whispers about the treason of the senior metalworker and then Lieutenant Bel's veiled message. He added, "I am not sure what he is going to do, but I am sure that it is dangerous and if there is anyone who can help him, it is you."

Ruben was in a considerable dilemma. He needed to get Lialah to safety, he wanted to help the lieutenant, but he wanted to continue on his quest and he wanted to follow Simeon's advice and not get involved in mortal combat. He paused, looked at Lialah, then at Dathram and finally back at Latich. He said, "This is indeed a problem that I hadn't bargained for. Leave me alone for a few moments, while I make up my mind what I should do." He walked away from the group into the half empty stables, wondering what was the correct decision. After a few moments, when he was lost in thought, he returned to his companions who were talking quietly by the gate. He said to Latich, "You must go directly to Babylon, I suggest that you travel with Dathram, you can look after one another, I am sure that he will be glad of your company. He also has important things to get to Babylon. You should cross the river and travel along the southern bank. Although it may be longer it will certainly be safer. Now, much though I would like to help the Lieutenant, I have promised to protect Lialah. She is carrying my child. The Lieutenant must fight his own battles, I have no allegiance to Babylon and though the Assyrian king revolts me, I have no quarrel with him or his country, providing he keeps his hands away from Lialah. I am no longer a Babylonian Guard; to suddenly appear would take a lot of explaining, besides which, my path lies in a different direction." His mind finally made up, all the pleading looks from Latich simply hardened his resolve. Lialah was of course pleased, by not only his assurance of her welfare, but by the admission of him being the father of the unborn child that she was carrying. Dathram was also pleased at having a Babylonian Guard escorting him, even if that Guardsman was hardly typical of his sort, his very presence would deter any would-be robbers.

He said that they had all better get on the way, so he returned to the gates, which he opened, bidding Dathram and Latich farewell. Saying to Latich, "I will be following the direction the king's party took so they will have to pass me first, I will guard your rear." Then adding to Dathram his thanks for the information about the route that he had to take, he wished Dathram well saying that he hoped that he would sell his wares and make a handsome profit. He then pushed them out into the street, urging them on their way. He suddenly remembered an earlier promise he had made and called Latich back. "When all this is over, will you do me a final favour?" Without waiting for a reply he continued, "Will you deliver a message for me to my uncle's daughter in Nippur, telling her that I am well and now fully committed to my quest?" Meanwhile, Lialah had picked up their bags and giving him his bag and staff, they also started out and went northwest in the direction of the Assyrian king's party.

They followed the road rather than following the river, as they had been informed that the riverbank was often boggy and difficult underfoot. Particularly if it had rained in the mountains to the North, which the innkeeper believed may have happened last night. This was a sign that the summer was coming to an end, they were now in harvest time, but there were often brief thunderstorms before the rains started in earnest.

As they walked along, Lialah said, "Latich seems to believe that you can stop the entire Assyrian army."

"Yes, I am afraid so," he said. "He has a misguided belief in my ability. I suppose it is nice to be held in such high regard, but of course it is untrue, but I only said that to reassure him. I am not that good, I might be if I practised and fought in a lot of battles like the Lieutenant and Sergeant Abzher, but that would of course mean killing a lot of people – of that I have no wish, apart from which I am not particularly special."

"You are very special to me," said Lialah, holding Ruben's hand and giving it an affectionate squeeze. She then transferred his hand so that it was around her shoulders, allowing her to snuggle close beside him. They walked on in silence for a while and then Lialah said, "While you were in the stables making up your mind, Latich told us that the Assyrian king had wanted me taken to him. But that he did not think that our king was going to comply with his wish, so that I should not worry. Do you think there is any danger?"

"Probably not," answered Ruben. "But it will be as well to keep out of sight for a few days, until we are sure," he reflected. They walked on and after a short distance Ruben stopped and looked at the grass beside the road on which they walked, which was dusty and firm, as there had not been any rain for quite a while. He put down his bag and staff and walked about the area examining the ground carefully. He then said, "The Assyrian king turned off here and has gone in a northerly direction, I think he has headed straight for the border of his country. You see, the grass springs up again after wagon wheels and horses' hooves, but the tops of all the taller grass and plants have been cut off," he explained, pointing out the telltale signs. "Tiglath-Pileser's chariot has passed this way, I can think of nothing else that would leave such marks."

"Well I think that is a good thing for us," said Lialah. "I feel a lot safer with him out of the way."

Later that day, roughly about the middle of the afternoon, they came through into a small town, where Ruben bought some food and a goatskin full of fresh water and after he had made these purchases he said, "The cloud has broken up and the sun has come out, so I think it is going to be a nice night. Therefore I think we would be wise to sleep out of doors, possibly in one of the fields where they have cut the wheat into stacks, which we can sleep under, is that all right?"

"Yes, I enjoyed the other night when we slept out," she replied.

After a drink and eating some food, they continued on their way. Since leaving the small town they had seen nobody on the road. They were just about to walk off the road down the valley to where they saw some stacks of wheat, which the harvesters had recently cut, when they saw a small party of people coming towards them. "Leave the talking to me," instructed Ruben.

"Good afternoon," called out Ruben in a pleasant voice. "How far is the next town?"

"The next town is Mulch, and we left it this morning so you have a long way to go if you wish to stay at the inn there," came the reply from an elderly man, who was leading a donkey and a couple of women and a few children.

"Can you tell us how far Zohab is?" asked the elderly man.

"I am afraid that it is possibly too far for you to go tonight," replied Ruben. "But there is another small town just a little further on, and I am sure that you should be able to find lodgings there for the night."

"Oh that is good," replied the elderly man. "Because the children are very tired."

"Have you seen any other travellers today?" asked Ruben.

"No young man, you are the first people that we have seen all day," responded the elderly man. "Although we did see a small cloud of dust, possibly a party of horsemen and wagons away to the north," he said pointing towards the sinking sun.

"Yes, they passed us in Zohab very early this morning," returned Ruben, but added no further explanation. "I am sure you will get there by nightfall, provided that you do not tarry for too long," said Ruben casting a warning glance at Lialah, who was already giving the children some water to drink.

"Thank you, you and your young companion are very kind," said one of the women.

"You are very welcome," said Lialah, smiling at the children. "Off you go, and take care."

They watched them go and as they disappeared from sight, Ruben said, "You must be more careful, particularly as we get nearer the border with Assyria. Remember what Dathram told us!"

"Yes, I know, but the children were so sweet," explained Lialah.

"Crocodiles always smile, but they also bite," laughed Ruben. He then led Lialah by the hand down the valley to where the wheat was stacked in sheaves, which they quickly rearranged into a neat little tent. Sitting down by the tent, they ate some of the food and chatted about the strange events of the morning. They were wondering what was happening away to the north and also discussed of Latich and Dathram, feeling confident that they would have reached Babylon during the day. They then crawled into their makeshift tent and Lialah was soon fast asleep, curled up next to Ruben. He lay awake for a while wondering whether he had made the correct decision, feeling concerned about the Babylonians in the Assyrian king's party.

# 12
# THE CAUSE OF WAR

Latich and Dathram made good time; they kept up the brisk pace that they started with, after crossing the ferry from the north bank directly to the southern side of the Euphrates. Keeping to the south of the river on the main road, rather than going down and following the river, which was the way that Ruben and Lialah had come. The main road ran higher up the side of the valley and was more direct, as it did not meander at all but ran in a straighter southeasterly route. About mid-morning they could make out the small town on the northern bank, but they did not stop even for something to eat, but kept to their fast pace, which Dathram said he often maintained. As far as Latich was concerned, it was rather like a route march and as he had no kit to carry he had no difficulty in keeping going. Apart from which, he felt that a mere merchant could hardly better him, but Dathram's heartiness was a great comfort as he was still agitated. They soon fell into easy conversation, as Dathram was interested in Ruben's history, which Latich told him about in great detail. That did not take very long, as Ruben had seldom talked about himself, even to his closest friend. Dathram soon realised that Latich held Ruben in high regard and spoke of him as a great hero. He told Dathram about Ruben's excellent javelin throwing, saying that if he were still in the army he would be the greatest javelin thrower of all time. Dathram was interested in the quest that Ruben was on. He found it easy to get Latich to tell him all about their training together, and how Ruben had befriended him and helped him to become a Babylonian Guard.

By the early afternoon they could make out the distant city of Babylon, which was dominated by the large Citadel whose golden roof glinted in the rays of the sun, which now broke through the clouds. Looking towards its northern and western sides where the fabulous Gardens were layered in many terraces, stretching from the golden roof down to the banks of the river. This was indeed a wonderful spectacle. Dathram told Latich that every time he had returned from the west he had noticed how the Gardens flourished, and was interested to learn about the treadmill, which carried up the water from the river itself to run many sparkling streams that kept the gardens so well watered.

Travelling further on, they came to the main junction where three roads met. The road that came from Kish, that was in the marshlands to the south, the route that led into the wilderness and finally into Canaan, and their own road that followed the river from Ashkilon that was in the northwest. These three routes met where they turned north to the main route that led down the valley to where ferrymen offered transport across the river to Babylon. Although they had passed a few people going in the same direction as them, or travelling towards Zohab, the road had not been busy. However, there was a constant stream of travellers coming from and going to Babylon. Dathram and Latich turned left down the valley towards the ferry. Latich said that he would be able to commission one of the special crafts as he was on the king's business. Dathram said to him, "If you can get me into the Citadel where I can offer my goods to the royal household, I will treat you to a special dinner tonight." Latich assured him that he would be able to get Dathram into the Citadel and agreed to the bargain.

He then added, "I hope to be able to take you up on your kind offer, but if I am ordered elsewhere, will the offer still be open for a later date?"

"Most certainly, my young friend, your company has made the journey interesting." So the bond was made, this being the start of a long friendship.

Down at the ferry, Latich once again found his uniform a great advantage as people stepped aside to allow them to pass in front. True to his word, Latich called out to one of the special ferries that were larger and had either two or even four strong oarsmen, who quickly rowed them across the wide river, where they made their way directly to the Citadel.

At the gate they were stopped, but when Latich produced the scroll he was carrying with the official seal indicating that it was for the king personally, he was ushered through. He gave the guard an explanation that he had travelled with Dathram from Zohab, and that Dathram was carrying valuable treasures for the king's household. Accordingly he, Dathram and the mules passed through into the Citadel. Dathram would not leave the mules unattended due to the valuable cargo that they carried. A courtier escorted Latich to the royal chamber where he had previously met the old general, where he waited outside the large bronze covered doors.

He would not part with the scroll, but informed the courtier that he had been instructed to hand it directly to the king. The courtier left him for a few moments, then shortly returned and asked Latich to follow him into the royal chamber. The king was in conversation with two generals from the army and the commander from Ashkilon. This commander was a nephew of the king and was a frequent visitor to Babylon, but on this occasion had arrived with disturbing news of unrest and menace from the bordering Assyrian army encampment.

The king broke off his conversation and spoke directly to Latich, saying, "I believe you have an urgent message for me." As he took the scroll from Latich he said to him, "I half expected this and by virtue that they sent you I imagine that this is bad news." He said this while he was breaking the seal and reading the scroll. His lips hardened into a thin line and the room became quiet and heavy with tension. "Damn that greasy barbarian," he raged. "It seems as if he has had spies working for him." He then turned to Latich and said, "Did you get away last night?"

"No, your Majesty," replied Latich. "I did not manage to get away until this morning, after we had crossed the river on the ferry at Zohab."

"You did well to get here in one day," said the king. "Does anybody else know about this accursed business, except of course for the old General, Lieutenant Belthezder and Sergeant Abzher?"

Latich knew that he must not say anything about Ruben. "Well your Majesty, the only person who may know something could be the merchant who was leaving Zohab at the time I escaped. So I brought him into the Citadel with me on the pretence that he can display some of his goods to your household." The lie came so quickly to Latich that it was out before he realised what he was saying. He was then prompted by the king into telling the assembled high-ranking soldiers the details of his escape. He was quick to commend Lieutenant Bel, and said that the three remaining Babylonians were ensuring that they stayed together.

The king said, "You have done very well, my boy, your name is Latich, I believe," he said, putting an arm around Latich's shoulder. "Now young man, as you have been a party to what is happening I am going to trust you with more details and then another journey, are you up to that?"

"Yes, your Majesty," replied Latich, eager to please and feeling proud of himself, by being praised in exalted company. "Do you think it would be possible for the merchant to display his wares, which he is keen to do?"

"I think it is a sensible idea and will complete the ruse," said the king. "You think quickly, young man, so serve me well in this matter and you will be well rewarded." He then gave an order to his courtiers, to show the merchant to his wives and their maidservants where he would be allowed to exhibit the items that he had brought.

With Latich still at his side, the king turned back to the assembled company and reread the scroll aloud. One of the generals gave a sharp intake of breath and asked what had been the orders that were referred to. The room went quiet and it felt very hot and oppressive. After a considerable pause, the silence was broken by the king who said, "The orders that I gave the Lieutenant were that if the situation became bleak – which it undoubtedly has – he was to kill the Assyrian king. But only if there was an opportunity to do so without endangering himself." There was another long silence while these words sank in. There was a cough, eaking quiet words into the horses' ears, he managed to bring all three ck to the pile of equipment, which he began to fasten. At the same time, ticing the retrieval of the horses, the lieutenant and the general picked burning brands from the fire, which they used on the Assyrians' tents.

The flames rose quickly on the dry material just as the sun rose above e eastern skyline. Positioning himself outside Tiglath-Pileser's tent with is javelins at the ready, and the old general keeping watch on the other nts to make sure that the lieutenant wasn't assaulted from behind, he aited for the Assyrian king to emerge. He waited while he could hear the houts of the other Assyrians, hastily abandoning their tents. Unfortunately his wait was in vain, as the Assyrian king had, fortunately for himself, left his tent a few moments earlier in order to relieve himself. He was standing, urinating copiously beside his chariot, which was attached to the hobbled horses. He heard the commotion in the encampment and despite the large amount of alcohol that he had drunk the evening before, quickly realised what was going on. Although he was bare-chested, he was still armed, and he unhobbled the horses and jumped onto his chariot.

The sound of the chariot made lieutenant Bel realise that his quarry had already left. He swore, but then joined the old general in hacking down the emerging Assyrians. They were soon joined by Sergeant Abzher, when they became aware of the thunder of hoofs as the Assyrian king came back in his chariot and charged directly at them. Standing his ground whilst the old general and Sergeant Abzher ran for their horses, Lieutenant Bel threw the first of his three javelins at the figure in the charging chariot. The Assyrian king ducked and swerved at the same time, as the javelin flew within a hand's span of his head. But even the swerve of the chariot still left the lieutenant having to dive out of the way of the deadly sword blades that stuck out from the wheel hubs of the careering chariot.

Lieutenant Bel rolled over and rose to his feet and went over to join the others who were mounting their horses. Lieutenant Bel had retrieved his two remaining javelins and ran towards his horse. He was unsure whether they should ride back to freedom or pursue the Assyrian king. There were, however, five unharmed Assyrians who had now armed themselves and were coming at the three Babylonians. At that moment the old general charged after the racing chariot, brandishing his sword and yelling curses at the cowardly king. Sergeant Abzher dismounted and engaged the nearest Assyrian in a sword fight. Another of the Assyrians fell with a javelin sticking through his torso. Keeping his remaining javelin, Lieutenant Bel was about to join the sergeant, who killed the Assyrian he had engaged, but he stared in horror as the Assyrian king's someone shuffled around and there were a few murmurs. The king held up his head to silence any forthcoming interruption, he continued, "I realise that I was asking the impossible, but Lieutenant Bel is courageous and resourceful, and if there is one person who could possibly succeed in such a suicidal task, it is he."

After a short pause he continued, "This will of course shatter the agreement with Assyria. Possibly, it will lead to several border skirmishes and unrest, if not open warfare." There was another pause, which was broken by the commander of Ashkilon, the king's nephew. His name was Mithrandir.

"If it does lead to open warfare, Ashkilon will bear the brunt of any Assyrian attack. It is vital that I be sent immediate reinforcements," he said.

"Quite so, Commander," said the king. "I am proposing to send as many forces as the Generals can supply. I will also pull back some of the Babylonian Guards who have been deployed at Lagash and Sal-e Pol-e. This will of course weaken our defences in the east, but I do not think there is any great danger from Persia to the north and most of the problems from the east come from a small pirate force, rather than large organised armies."

"I am sure that we can gather together ten battalions," said one of the generals looking quizzically at his counterpart. "That is excellent," said the king. Then turning to Latich, he said, "I would like you to take a message to Commander Schudah, who is at the moment at Nippur. Will you do that for me, young Latich?" he asked, and without waiting for a reply he added, "But of course that would be straight after dinner. I know that will mean travelling overnight, but the road is good and safe, so I suggest you go and get some rest." The king then turned back to the generals to discuss where the troops were to come from.

Feeling superfluous, and realising that he had his orders and was dismissed, Latich made his way back to the barracks. He had only gone a short part of the way when Dathram hailed him.

"You have opened the door to vast treasures, I cannot thank you enough," laughed Dathram, his smile spreading from ear to ear. "Dinner tonight will be the first of many treats." Before Latich could interrupt he continued in telling him that the royal household had been delighted by everything that he had brought and that he was sure that he would be appointed as the main royal merchant in charge of all the trade with Egypt. "And what is more, my young friend, this position comes with a residence here in Babylon, as well as a residence in Memphis in Egypt."

"I am sorry, Dathram," said Latich. "I am indeed very pleased for you. But I cannot join you tonight, as I have to go to Nippur straight after dinner with the king."

"Just as I feared," sighed Dathram. "This whole business is obviously complicated. Oh well, you can join me at any time, you will always be welcome in any of my houses," he chuckled.

"I will probably be back within a few days, but while I am in Nippur I must look up an old friend of Ruben," he explained.

"Ah yes," said Dathram. "I wonder how he and his young woman are getting on."

"I am sure that Ruben and Lialah will be all right, it is Lieutenant Bel, Sergeant Abzher and the old general, that I am really concerned about," replied Latich.

\*\*\*\*

Returning to their tent, Lieutenant Bel and the sergeant discovered that the old general had moved all their equipment into the centre of the tent.

"Whatever are you doing, sir?" enquired Lieutenant Bel.

"Making sure that we are not murdered in our beds," replied the old general, adding, "I know you think that I am well past it, but I am not completely gaga yet, just remember. I was not made a General for nothing, and I was fighting these dung-eating barbarians before you two were off your mothers' tit."

"Oh, yes," said the bewildered lieutenant. "Do you think that they will surprise us in our beds, sir?"

"I wouldn't put it past them," stated the old general. "Apart from which, I have a good idea that you are planning something, and I suggest that the sooner we move, the better."

Realising that he should not forget the old General's position and that he was still a formidable warrior, Lieutenant Bel told him that they had not worked out any plans yet, but he was probably correct.

"We certainly did not mean any offence by excluding you, sir," said Sergeant Abzher. "Do you have any suggestions?"

"Ah, that's better," said the old general, "We must work together – as a matter of fact, I have."

"Very well, sir," said an encouraged Lieutenant Bel. "What do you have in mind?"

They then all sat in the centre of the tent, having checked that there was no one in sight when they looked out of the tent's flap, and discussed what action they should take, and when. The old general, Lieutenant Bel soon realised, had a very good idea of exactly where they were, and that in another day's fast travelling, they would reach the Assyrian border. He

suggested that Tiglath-Pileser had all this previously p
was a high probability of an Assyrian force meeting th
border or even before it. Lieutenant Bel informed the ol
had the same feeling and that all they had planned was
immediate action. The old general pointed out that it wou
particularly as they were heavily out-numbered, to strike
"That way, we will catch the scoundrels off guard." Whil
came to realise that all this made good sense, he added, "I
to strike first thing, just before dawn. They will still be grog
wine that they have been drinking, and that is the best tin
advantage."

"I think that's perfectly correct, sir," said the lieutenar
would be a good idea for you and I to stand on guard whilst
retrieves our horses."

"That will be a pleasure," said Sergeant Abzher, drawin
pointed dagger and testing the edge with his thumb, smiling
"It has been quite a while since I used stealth, but I am sure
back to me easily."

"As soon as you get the horses, the General and I will set
tents and the general can cover my back while I spear the Assy
said the lieutenant. They then carefully went over the plan aga
detail, trying to discover any weakness in it, and having fo
although they knew it was highly risky, they went to bed ful
with their weapons in easy reach. They were soon asleep as
tired, having ridden a long way that day after the early start in
well as assuming that tomorrow would probably be even busier.

Lieutenant Bel awoke while it was still dark, but his body c
him that there was only a short time before sunrise. He woke t
two and they soon reassembled their equipment and went out of tl
to find that the sky in the east was getting lighter. The Assyrian ter
quiet, but the embers of the large campfire around which they h
sitting the previous evening were still glowing. Motioning the o
leave their belongings in a pile, Lieutenant Bel indicated that S
Abzher was to go round to where the horses were tethered, whilst
the old general went over to the fire to prepare for the next stage
plan. Nodding his assent, the sergeant moved quickly but quietly a
behind the guard who was only half-awake, supposedly guardin
horses against theft or predatory animals. The sergeant crept behind a
one silent motion had his hand over the guard's mouth whilst his d
went up under his ribs to pierce his heart. The only sound was the
thump of the guard's body as it hit the ground. He wiped his dagger o
dead guard's cloak. Silently, the sergeant untethered their three horses

chariot raced towards his charging pursuer. The old general must have forgotten about the deadly sword blades that extended from the chariot's wheels, but his magnificent white stallion had not, and hastily leapt above their scything motion. Unfortunately, this unexpected leap unseated the old general who fell backwards from his leaping horse directly into the path of the vicious spinning sword blades. Although mortally wounded from the deep crescent shaped gouges gushing blood from his body, the old general rose unsteadily to his feet and with his ebbing strength threw his sword directly at the Assyrian king. Tiglath-Pileser had stopped his chariot and was looking around; he ducked under the flying sword that would have removed his head as it was flung with such force. He smiled with glee and he wheeled his chariot around to come back and finish off the staggering old general. In his excitement and lust for blood, the Assyrian king had left his side exposed, it was only a brief glimpse, but long enough for Lieutenant Bel to hurl his remaining javelin with deadly accuracy, at only thirty paces distance, at the Assyrian king. Tiglath-Pileser died as the javelin smashed into his bare flank beneath the left armpit, crashing through his ribs and into his black heart with the point just bursting from where his right nipple had been, in a welter of blood. The chariot came to a stop with the horses blowing hard, just in front of the old general, who sank to his knees as his lifeblood soaked the ground. Lieutenant Bel ran over to the old general and was kneeling down as he was joined by Sergeant Abzher, who had just finished off the remaining two Assyrians who had the temerity to fight on against the highly skilful and accomplished swordsman. The old general looked up and his tortured, bloodstained face broke into a smile, he croaked out with his dying breath, "Got the bloody scoundrels." He died and did not hear, as did the lieutenant and the sergeant, the sound of hoof beats as a departing horse was lashed into a gallop, and the remaining Assyrian fled northwards towards his own country.

Looking at one another, neither the lieutenant – or the sergeant had the energy to be worried about the fleeing horseman. The lieutenant said, "He will spread the news, but it would have been impossible to have kept it secret anyway." The fight had only lasted for a short time, but the sun was already beginning to warm the air and flies were beginning to settle on the dead and dying. As he looked up, the lieutenant saw the circling vultures that would soon be feeding greedily on the corpses. The lieutenant said to Sergeant Abzher, "Let us wrap up the body of the old general and try and get him back to the embalmers. We can then tidy up the corpses, and finish off the dying men and build a funeral pyre, as they died an honourable death."

Tearing up the tents in which they had spent the night, as it was the only material left unburned, the lieutenant and the sergeant soon had the old general's body securely wrapped enough to keep everything except large predators away from his now decomposing body. Working as swiftly as they could, so that they could be on their way as quickly as possible, they made a pile of the dead Assyrians, a few of which were initially still alive but beyond assistance, so they slit their throats, in a form of mercy killing. They threw as much brushwood and dried grass onto the pile as they could easily gather. They then set fire to the pyre adding the glowing embers of the previous evening's campfire. The funeral pyre also included Tiglath-Pileser's chariot, which had a stout wooden frame that burnt quite fiercely. Using the tent poles and the leather harnesses from the other horses, which they allowed to run free, they made a litter that was attached to the old general's white stallion. They then mounted their own horses and rode south from the smouldering remains towards the distant river where they hoped to encounter the next large town upriver from Zohab. This was Mulch, the very town that Ruben and Lialah were headed for.

The two Babylonian Guards were exhausted by their labours, which had begun immediately after their fight, which although it had not lasted long required an immense amount of skill and strength. They were both bloodstained and covered with minor wounds and badly in need of rest and something to eat. They only had one full water bottle and a half-full goatskin of rather sour wine, which Lieutenant Bel said was only fit for bathing their wounds, particularly as it was the rough wine that the Assyrians used to drink. They rode for the rest of the morning, leading the old general's horse, which towed the litter with his wrapped corpse on it. The wrapping was now soaked in blood on which the flies were constantly settling.

They stopped during the heat of the day, and lit a small fire near the wrapped body where the smoke managed to keep the worst of the flies away. They were just a little way from the side of the valley in which the great river Euphrates flowed towards Babylon. They drained the last of the water and bathed their wounds in the wine, deciding to press on despite the clammy heat, mainly because they needed to find rest, food and shelter. They eventually crested the final hill and looked southwards across the wide valley of the Euphrates to see to their southeast the small town of Mulch. With great relief they turned their horses in that direction and began riding towards their destination, where they knew there was a small garrison where they could commandeer a boat as well as getting some assistance, before recommencing their journey back to Babylon. They discussed the matter at length, both trusting that Latich had returned back to Babylon to alert the king to the impending problems with Assyria.

They also discussed the man who had escaped and realised that it was the Assyrian horse expert that Lieutenant Bel had knocked out, allowing Latich to escape.

"I should have hit the bugger a damn sight harder," sighed Lieutenant Bel, with disgust at his own folly.

"If you had, there might have been immediate reprisals," said Sergeant Abzher, "So there is no point in berating yourself."

They soon rode into the small garrison at the western end of the town, and were surprised to meet one of the senior captains, who had left Babylon the previous evening and was headed for Ashkilon. He was fully aware of the events related by Latich and was delighted to hear the news that the Assyrian ogre had been killed. He told the two dismounting Babylonian Guards that they had completed a virtually impossible task. Also he said that he would commission a boat to take them directly to Babylon, where the king would be highly pleased. Additionally, he informed them that he would also arrange for the old general's body to be sent downriver immediately, but they had better wash and eat before they left. Feeling grateful that a senior officer now made decisions, Lieutenant Bel almost collapsed in the washhouse and allowed himself to be undressed and washed by servants. All this took place as Ruben and Lialah walked into Mulch's east end where they found an inn in which to stay.

\*\*\*\*

Lialah was delighted when she and Ruben entered the inn at Mulch. Ruben spoke to the innkeeper, and requested board and lodgings for at least one night for himself and his young wife. When they went to their room to wash and have a rest before dinner, as it had been a tiring day's walk, she said to Ruben, "That was the first time you have referred to me as your wife, do you really mean that?"

"Oh," replied Ruben. "It was probably the weather affecting my clear thinking." He jested whilst he took off his shirt and said, "It is so hot and sticky, I am sure that we are in for another storm."

"Don't change the subject," responded Lialah. "I know it is hot but I am sure that was not affecting your reasoning."

By way of an explanation Ruben said, "Well, you are beginning to show signs of your pregnancy, so I'm just trying to stop idle gossip."

"So you have no intention of marrying me," she said, rather disappointed.

"I never said that!" Ruben exclaimed. Seeing her disappointed look, he came over and put his arms around her and kissed her on the head, holding her close to him with her brown curly hair pressed firmly against his chest. He explained, "I have not clearly thought this out, but I do have to go on this journey as I have already explained many times. It is a hard and difficult path that I must follow, that was confirmed by Dathram, so perhaps I would try to find somewhere for you to stay and have the baby, while I go on the journey and then return for you. You see, I have no wish to lose you, you know that you mean a lot to me."

With tears in her eyes she said, "Thank you Ruben, you know I will always wait for you, I have always loved you and always will."

"Now cheer up my little sweetheart, and we will finish washing and you can have a rest before dinner, whilst I want to have a look around town to see if I can get any news."

Leaving Lialah to rest, Ruben strolled out of the inn and wandered through the town down to the riverbank. He went to talk to the ferrymen, which was a good source of gaining news. Just as he was approaching the jetty, one of the imperial fast riverboats was rowed downriver, propelled by four powerful oarsmen. On board the craft was a magnificent white stallion beside a large bundle that was swathed in clean bandages. He knew that this was the old general's horse, and it was not difficult to guess that the large bundle was his dead body. Obviously something had happened, but the very fact that his body was being sent back to the embalmers for ritual burial was in itself a good sign. He then sat down and chatted to the ferrymen who were not busy. They told him that there must be something going on, as a fast craft had passed them heading for the garrison a little further upriver mid-morning. It had obviously come directly from Babylon and there were eight powerful rowers who looked exhausted, so they had been rowing overnight. There had also been, in the late afternoon, a large galley full of soldiers who were going further upriver to Ashkilon. They told him that Ashkilon was at least a day's fast journey by river, or three days' walk away. Apart from that, one of the men there told him that his younger brother was in the army and stationed at the garrison. He was on duty today, but he had arranged to meet him and he was sure that he could gain a lot more information, which he would be happy to pass on tomorrow. Thanking the man most graciously for the information, Ruben gave the man a few coins and promised to return in the morning for further news.

He then noticed a few fishermen who were nearby. They had just moored their boat and were unloading their day's catch. Ruben was surprised at the size of some of the fish that were mainly found in the sea, but did occasionally swim upriver to Nippur, and he was surprised to see that they had come as far as this. He went over to the fishermen and asked about their catch and how often these large fish came upriver. He was interested to learn that these fish travelled upriver every year about this time and could even be found leaping up the first cataract that was above Ashkilon. He became involved in a detailed discussion about the various types of fish that they caught. He found that the knowledge that he had gained from Simeon about the behaviour of fish was of considerable value to him in this discussion. They chatted for some time and then the conversation turned to the change in the weather, the fishermen thought that it would soon rain and the wet season would begin in earnest.

Just as he was about to leave, Ruben saw another craft being rowed downriver and stood watching. Although the boat was not close to the riverbank his eyes met those of the tall figure standing in the stern of the boat. The tall figure was freshly dressed in full uniform and was unmistakably Lieutenant Bel. Although nothing was said by either of them, Ruben felt sure that he had been recognised. However, the craft did not stop and hurried on its way southeasterly towards Zohab and Babylon where it was obviously headed. Feeling much relieved in his knowledge that the lieutenant had not met the same fate as the old general, he turned and walked back towards the inn.

He joined Lialah who was much livelier, and looked extremely attractive in a new dress of pale lilac that complemented her dark hair and light brown skin. She had purchased the dress in Babylon. He said, "You look beautiful. I feel very proud to take you to dinner."

"Thank you, husband," said Lialah. "Come here and I will brush your hair, it is looking tangled again."

As he came over and sat down obediently, he said, "I have some interesting news to relate. I found out quite a deal of information down by the ferry, and then I saw Lieutenant Bel being rowed back towards Babylon." He then went on to tell her of all the things that he had seen and heard. He told her that there seemed to be dramatic events taking place. He also told her that the weather would probably soon break and that rather than travel on foot through the pouring rain they would be advised to stay at the inn until they could get a boat to take them to Ashkilon. But it would also depend on what sort of news they heard, which he would learn tomorrow.

As Ruben had promised, he returned to the jetty the next morning and found the ferryman who had promised more news of what had been causing the increased river traffic. The man was talking to another ferryman and looked rather glum. However, his face broke into a smile as he saw Ruben and beckoned him to come over and join them. Ruben's friend said, "I was just telling my mate here about the news that I learnt last night. It seems that the two Babylonian Guards, the tall lieutenant and his sergeant, who took one of the king's fast boats downriver yesterday evening, had managed to slay the Assyrian king's entire retinue, including Tiglath-Pileser himself." Ruben looked surprised, as was indeed everybody else who heard the story, although he knew more than most of the lieutenant's fighting skill and strength. Even though many people doubted the story, Ruben knew that it was probably quite correct, as he had seen for himself the evidence of the dead old general's body and Lieutenant Bel being rowed down river headed for Babylon.

He said, "Well, if you heard it from your young brother and have seen the craft taking the two Babylonian Guardsmen yourself, it must be true."

"Sounds like a tall story to me," said the other ferryman, laughing mockingly.

"I have seen the lieutenant fight," said Ruben. "And believe me, he is formidable." He was feeling annoyed at having the story doubted.

"There you are," said the first man.

"Well," said the doubter. "And where did you see him fight?"

"At Sousa, if you must know," replied Ruben. "I fought alongside him." Ruben said this without realising that he had talked himself into a corner that would take some explaining to get out of. The two ferrymen men stared at him in amazement.

"Then you must be a Babylonian Guard," said the first man. "Are you on leave, because according to my younger brother, all leave has now been cancelled."

"No," said Ruben. "I am a mercenary." The lie came out automatically before he realised the consequences of what he was saying.

"By the gods, I can well believe it, you look like a soldier, but certainly not a Babylonian," said the first man. "I suppose that is why you are so interested in what is happening."

"Well, yes. But I have no wish to become involved any further, I simply want to get to Ashkilon and then pass on through Assyria into Canaan and the countries beyond," explained Ruben.

The two ferrymen looked at each other in bewilderment, the first man saying, "You must be bloody mad, all this means that there will now be a war with Assyria, and Ashkilon will bear the brunt of the fighting. The only people going up there will be soldiers, but there will be plenty of folk coming downriver to get away from the fighting."

"But if I get there quickly, I can surely get through before the trouble starts," said Ruben enquiringly.

"Well possibly, but nobody will take you there, and it rained a bit last night and looks like it is going to do so a lot more, so it wouldn't be a nice walk, unless you want to walk through the pouring rain for three days," he was told.

"You could buy old Zak's boat. He has been trying to sell it for ages," said a newcomer to the conversation, who had overheard most of what was being said. "It is a good boat, even if it is rather old, if you like I'll take you to him," said the man, hoping to be rewarded for his assistance.

Seeing this as a means of escape and possibly the only realistic solution to the problem of getting to Ashkilon quickly, Ruben agreed to the suggestion, slipping the man a few coins. He was taken immediately a few streets away, slightly downriver from the ferry jetty. His new guide told him that Zak, the man to whose house they were heading for, had previously been a ferryman but had given up the work as he was now getting too old to row people across the river. They soon came to his house, where the boat was moored outside. Whilst his guide knocked on the door, Ruben had a quick look at the boat. It was old but as the man had said, it was in good condition. As Ruben had previously worked as a messenger boy for his uncle who was a boat builder in Nippur, he knew what to look for and the common defects that could often be hidden.

The door opened and an old man came out, he had a weatherbeaten face and although he now stooped, he still had strong arms and hands that were well callused by his trade. He said to Ruben, "I understand that you are interested in buying my boat."

"That is correct," said Ruben. "I need to get to Ashkilon with my young wife. I have been looking at your boat and although it is fairly old it does seem about the size that I need. What price are you asking?"

"About fifteen gold pieces," said Zak.

"That is far more than it is worth," said Ruben. "I have not even inspected the hull, but there are quite a few defects with the hard wood fittings." These he pointed out.

Realising that he could not cheat this young man, Zak said, "All right then, but twelve gold pieces is my lowest price."

"Let's take her out on the water," said Ruben. And before Zak could protest, Ruben grabbed hold of the thwart by the stern post, swung the boat around so that it was pointing across the river, and lifted the back of the boat, walking backwards so that the prow rested on the side of the river. He asked the other man to help him to lift the boat fully clear and turned it over. The planking on the bottom looked fairly sound and was well painted, but when Ruben closely inspected a couple of planks, he pointed out where minor rot was beginning to show. He said, "Admittedly the rot is not bad, and it would still serve my purpose, but you are asking far too much. I will pay no more than eight gold pieces." He and Zak haggled for quite a while and finally agreed on ten gold pieces. Zak seemed happy at the deal, as he had hardly expected to sell the boat easily. Ruben was also happy because the boat had a canopy at the back where

Lialah could shelter from the rain, apart from which, he felt sure that he could get the money back as Ashkilon would be full of people who would be trying to get away. Agreeing with Zak that he would take the boat first thing in the morning, he paid him the money. He then walked back to the inn to tell Lialah what he had negotiated.

He met Lialah on his way back to the inn. She had been out in the town market place, where she had bought some fruit, which they could eat for a light midday meal. She said quite breathlessly as she took hold of Ruben's arm, "The whole town is abuzz with news that the Assyrian king has been killed, but there will now be war with Assyria. Do you believe that two men could kill all those Assyrians as well as that horrible beast?"

Holding her hand, Ruben said, "I think every word of it is true. Lieutenant Bel and Sergeant Abzher are a formidable team. I told you what I saw last night, and I now have received the same information from the ferryman who I spoke to yesterday, he confirms the story and has heard the same from his own brother who is in the local garrison."

"But what are we going to do now?" asked Lialah.

"We are going to go upriver to Ashkilon as fast as we can," said Ruben calmly. "We will then try to get past Ashkilon before the trouble starts." Lialah looked at Ruben in amazement, he had accepted everything so calmly and was beginning to tell her about the boat that he had bought, and that they would start off first thing in the morning and hope to get to Ashkilon in a couple of days.

She said, "But can you row that far on your own?"

"I would like to meet a man who could stop me," said Ruben firmly. She knew then that his mind was made up and to try to stop him would be useless. She therefore listened to the rest of his plans, understanding that she had to get enough food together for the journey and that they would be leaving first thing in the morning.

When they got back to the inn and went to their room to eat the fruit that she had bought, Ruben told her about his having to tell the ferrymen that he was a mercenary and had fought beside Lieutenant Bel at Sousa. She said, "Well, you did fight beside Lieutenant Bel at Sousa, but what is all this about a mercenary? I do not even know what a mercenary is."

"Well, that's easy," said Ruben. "A mercenary is a soldier who fights purely for money, or what he can get from the people that he kills. I happen to know that our army does occasionally use mercenaries."

"Does that mean you can wear your uniform again?" she asked.

"That is just the problem. I can certainly wear weapons," he said thoughtfully. "But I cannot wear the Babylonian Guard uniform. The only mercenaries I have seen wore a grey or black uniform."

"Well, that is easy, after we have eaten, I can go out again and buy some blackberries, there are plenty at this time of year, and a black cockerel, so that we can use the feathers in your helmet. I can then dye your uniform, while you replace the plumes in your helmet with the black cock's feathers," she explained, adding that it would be something constructive to do and that the uniform would be ready by the morning.

When they had finished their light meal, Ruben went to see the innkeeper and told him that they would like to stay one more night, but would be leaving very early the next morning. While he was doing this, Lialah went back to the market, where she bought the necessary things to change his uniform into that of a mercenary. On her return they went to work, Lialah making the dye with the berries, which she pounded to a pulp then added water, which she boiled and finally added Ruben's uniform's shift and kilt. While she was doing this, he prised out the purple plumes from his helmet and replaced them with black cock's feathers, which he sealed in the helmet with melted wax.

The following morning dawned grey with low cloud cover, heavy with expectant rain. It had been a warm and humid night. Ruben and Lialah rose early and ate a light breakfast, which Ruben had already arranged with the innkeeper. Lialah was wearing another new dress that she had bought in Babylon. The dress was loose around the waist, which was why she had bought it, knowing that it would hide her pregnancy, which was now beginning to be noticeable. Ruben was wearing his re-dyed black uniform, complete with the crocodile skin jerkin and his normal bronze sword and dagger in place. The story that he had given the ferryman, about him being a mercenary and having fought at Sousa, which was still talked about as an amazing victory, accorded him more courtesy than he had previously received.

Leaving the innkeeper with a far larger payment than was required, Ruben and Lialah left the inn, with Ruben carrying his bag and his large sword in its crocodile hide scabbard in full view. Lialah carried her own bag as well as Ruben's helmet with the black cock's feathers. They went to Zak's house via the marketplace where some, but not all of the stalls were being set up. Lialah had previously requested from the stall, which sold fresh unleavened bread, that they would require a few flat loaves and they also purchased some goats' cheese, as well as a large goatskin filled with water, and some grapes.

Zak was ready to meet them outside his house by the riverbank. He had not heard the news of the impending war with Assyria when he had sold the boat to Ruben; he was therefore all the more pleased at having made the sale. Although he knew that Ruben would have no difficulty in selling it to people wanting to leave Ashkilon, there would be no demand for anyone wishing to buy boats in Mulch. He assisted Lialah into the boat and helped her stow the bags and provisions, also showing her how to erect the waterproof canopy, as he said he was sure that it would rain very soon.

He waved a friendly goodbye as Ruben quickly rowed the boat away from the bank and into the main channel of the wide river.

"How long do you think it will take us, Ruben?" asked Lialah.

"I am not really sure yet," he replied. "This boat was not built for fast travel, although it is a good boat and will get us there safely. But I am not sure how long it will take me. All I know is that the fast messenger craft managed to do the journey in one day."

"But they have at least four oarsmen," said Lialah. "And they are normally large and strong oarsmen."

"Are you implying that I am not strong enough?" said Ruben accusingly.

"Oh no, most certainly not, but four of them and with a craft that is designed for speed must be a lot quicker," said Lialah.

"We will ask the ferrymen as we pass them," returned Ruben. "We are just coming up to the main jetty."

As they came alongside the main ferry jetty, Ruben saw the man who had given him all the up to date news and he called out to him, asking him how long it would normally take to row a boat like the one he was in to Ashkilon. The ferryman replied that it would normally take two days, but perhaps longer, as it depended on the person who was rowing. Ruben thought about this and pulled away at an amazingly fast pace.

"You are not going to keep that pace up for long," said Lialah warningly.

"The only thing that will slow me down," responded Ruben, "is if I get blisters on my hands, as I did when I rowed from the sea near Sousa past Lagash on my way to Ur, before we met for the second time."

"Best of luck," called a friendly voice. "They will need all the help they can get in Ashkilon." It had come from the garrison that they were passing. One of the soldiers standing on guard duty by the jetty had recognised Ruben as a mercenary. Ruben replied to this with just a friendly wave. He was wondering how best to protect his hands from getting blistered. His arms were strong from all the exercise that he had done on the reed raft with Ishmala in the marshlands, and well up to the task. His hands were strong and not soft due to the sword fighting and javelin throwing from his days in the army. But he knew that, as he was not used to rowing, his hands would blister in certain places. He asked Lialah if she had any bandages or material that she could tear into strips, and when she said that she had, he pulled the boat over to the riverbank where they briefly stopped. He asked her to bandage up his hands very tightly, particularly across the palms, around the base of the thumbs and the base of his fingers, where he could feel the beginning of soreness.

Just then two large galleys came into sight, both heading in the direction that they were going. These galleys were packed with soldiers, wearing the bright red of the Babylonian army. Allowing them to pass, Ruben then pulled out again and tried to keep up with the galleys. He was doing a good job, but they gradually increased the distance between them and his small boat. At about midmorning it started to rain, at first lightly, but a cold wind from the east sprang up and the rain became heavier. He stopped briefly to ensure that Lialah managed to get the canopy up to keep herself and their belongings dry. He told her to start preparing something to eat, as he resumed rowing. He kept up his fast pace even though the galleys had disappeared far into the distance, but was pleased to note that the bandages had stopped his hands becoming blistered. He stopped for a rest when he thought it was about midday, although he was not sure as the heavy low cloud totally obscured the position of the sun. Lialah had prepared something to eat, and told him to come back into the canopy. He dried himself down, with her assistance, and they sat down together eating the bread, cheese, melon and grapes that she had prepared. He ate at least three times as much as she did and was soon back at the oars again. She was stunned by the way that he kept such an incredible pace. She knew that he was very strong but did not realise the amount of stamina that he possessed. She even had to insist that he took a break a bit later in the afternoon, just as the first of many craft came downriver from Ashkilon.

As the first boat passed them, Ruben called out, "How far is it to Ashkilon?"

"It is at least a day's travel for you, as you are rowing against the current," came the reply. "We left there first thing this morning." Theirs was a reasonably long craft that was fairly new, and even though it was fully laden, it did have two sets of double oarsman. Apart from which, it was going with the current and therefore was making fast progress.

"And how far to Mulch?" came the question over the water.

"You should reach there by late evening," replied Ruben.

Lailah was quite dispirited by this news, but Ruben's reaction was simply to pull even harder on the oars. The old boat had never been rowed so hard before and it started to creak and judder with every stroke. Lialah called through the pouring rain, "I think you had better slow down Ruben, otherwise this old boat will break up!"

"No, she will be quite sound," he replied. "It is just that this boat is unused to hard work, and she is complaining," he grinned. The rain really lashed down, turning the water into a bubbling maelstrom. He called out through the driving rain, "I am sorry, my dear, but can you bail out while I keep rowing." She obediently came out from beneath the canopy and started bailing the rainwater that was almost ankle deep, covering the bottom of the boat. Almost immediately, Lialah was as soaked as Ruben, but fortunately this very heavy rain soon gave way to a lighter drizzle. Lialah began to shiver with the cold, so Ruben told her to go back beneath the canopy to dry off and put on some dry clothes.

"But what about you?" she asked as she hurried back and started to comply with his request.

"I am not cold," came the reply. "In fact I am very warm, the rain is quite refreshing and washes away the perspiration, so do not worry about me," he laughed.

He leant back pulling on the oars again, bracing his feet against the specially designed footboard to get maximum strength into each stroke. He could dimly make out the shape of another galley, also full of soldiers, which was following them. He thought that he would try to keep ahead of this galley, and for a while managed to succeed in his effort. But slowly the galley came abreast of him and began to pass them by. The captain of this large galley, which had twenty oars either side, each one being operated by two slaves, called out to him, "You are making excellent time my friend, but I bet you will not reach Ashkilon before dawn."

"What is the wager?" responded Ruben.

"Five gold pieces," called back the captain, amid cheers from his own men.

"You will lose your money," responded Ruben.

This was met with peals of laughter, and lots of ribald remarks from the soldiers on deck, particularly when they saw Lialah changing her dress in the canopy at the stern of the boat. Ruben followed the galley for some considerable time, but it gradually pulled away in to the gathering dusk. Lialah then called to him, "Ruben you must come and eat, you must be exhausted! After all, we hardly need money, and there is no point in half killing yourself."

"All right, little one," called back Ruben. "But I am not going to let those cheeky dogs get away with their remarks."

Lailah had prepared some more food, which Ruben hastily demolished, telling her that the exercise was good for him, even though his muscles were beginning to ache severely. It had now stopped raining, although the cloud was still low, and he looked a peculiar sight as the dye had run slightly, leaving dark lines down his arms and legs. The bandages around his hands had begun to wear loose, so he asked Lialah to re-bandage them.

Despite Lialah's protest, he returned to the oars and was soon pulling hard again trying to make up for lost time. In a state of disbelief at his stamina, Lialah gradually fell into a doze, being lulled into sleep by the creak of oars and the swish of water passing beneath the hull. She awoke around midnight, as the lights and bustle of activity by the riverbank at Ashkilon fully woke her. They moored their little boat just behind the galley, just as the first pre-emptive attack by the surrounding Assyrian army tested out the defences of Ashkilon.

# 13
## SAVING ASHKILON

At midnight, the riverbank jetties at Ashkilon were normally quiet, but tonight there were people everywhere. The whole place was in uproar. There were people trying to get aboard boats, others haggling over the price of the fare, there were people trying to take valuable items with them that the boatmen refused to carry because of their weight; there were soldiers disembarking from the large galley, there were soldiers trying to establish order and beyond that there was the distant sound of battle. The sound of trumpets, the clash of bronze, the shrill blast of whistles and the screams of the attacking Assyrians intermingled with the cries of wounded and dying men. There were people running everywhere with lit torches. Everything seemed to be in chaos. Ruben tied up the boat at an available stake on the southern bank. He then said to Lialah, "I will try to find out what is happening. It is vitally important that you stay here."

Lailah was both frightened and extremely disorientated by having woken to this terrifying experience. Particularly coming from a quiet marshland town, the experience of large cities was new to her. The hustle and bustle of Babylon, which was a friendly city, had been exciting, but this was something else – it was as if she had not woken, but was experiencing a nightmare. She wished Ruben hadn't run off, but knew that he had to find out where to go and what their next move was going to be. From the crowds on the riverbank, she was suddenly aware of someone stepping on board their boat. Reaching down, her hand closed around Ruben's staff. Before she could realise what was happening she had picked up the staff and was wielding it at the man, screaming at him to get off. He was caught by surprise and looked up as she lunged the staff at him. The end of the staff hit him on the shoulder and as it was not a solid staff, but Ruben's javelin wrapped in a blanket, the end that had hit him was the very sharp, bound-on knife blade. He reeled back in alarm with a small cut on his shoulder and fell back into the river. Although this had prevented him boarding the boat and kept other people away, it of course drew everyone's attention to the area and there was soon a large crowd standing back from the girl in the newly arrived boat, who was behaving like a wild and terrified animal.

Fortunately the crowd was soon parted by a large, tired and strangely streaked young man with blond hair, who was followed by a sergeant who had been trying to establish order when this young mercenary had virtually ordered him to assist.

"It's all right Lialah, I am back," said Ruben holding out his hand and saying, "Give the staff to me, collect up our belongings and come ashore." Feeling gratefully relieved, she handed him the staff and then their other belongings and almost ran off the boat into his already laden arms.

"Oh, Ruben, I was so frightened, why are there so many people and what is going on, there is so much noise and activity. I didn't know what I was doing when I pushed that man into the river," she said all in one breath, the words tumbling out so that he had difficulty in understanding her.

"Despite all my efforts, it appears we have arrived too late," he sighed. "But the sergeant will tell us where we can go for the remainder of the night."

As the sergeant and a couple of his men who had followed him were breaking up the crowd and re-establishing some order, a small portly merchant grabbed hold of Ruben's arm and asked him if it was his boat. This man was agitated, but strangely reminded him of Mutek, and had the sort of face that would normally wear a smile far more easily than the nervous agitation that it now possessed.

"Is this your boat, sir?" he enquired and without waiting for an answer, said, "I will buy it from you, here is a bag of gold coins, that will cover the cost."

"Thank you," said Ruben, looking down at the large bag of gold coins. "But this is too much, I don't need all this."

"Please take the money," said the merchant. "You have answered my prayers."

Ruben had to stand Lialah aside, together with their baggage, so that he could intercede with the sergeant and his men. Telling them that the boat had now been bought by the small rotund merchant, who had a wife and two children, whom he was now helping onboard the boat.

There were also two slaves who carried a few possessions. These they stowed onboard as the merchant, his wife and the children seated themselves beneath the canopy. The two slaves squeezed onto the rowing bench and with one oar apiece soon had the boat in the river pointing downstream. Shouting his thanks to Ruben, the overloaded boat quickly disappeared into the night, being rowed back in the direction that it had only recently come from. The sergeant, who now had the crowd in some order, turned back to Ruben and said, "Follow me, sir, I know just the place where you can go for the remainder of the night." Dutifully Ruben shouldered his large bag and with his staff in one hand and with Lialah gripping tightly to his other hand, he followed the sergeant into the deserted streets, well away from all the commotion by the riverbank and the noise of battle by the city walls. The sergeant soon led them to a quiet inn, where he had to call the innkeeper from his bed to open the door.

Retaining bolts were slid back and the door was slightly opened. When the innkeeper saw who it was, he allowed the door to swing fully open. "Don't tell me the bloody rats have broken through already?" grumbled the innkeeper.

"No, we are fairly sure that this attack is only probing for weakness," said the sergeant.

"What do you want with me then?" demanded the innkeeper. "It's hardly time for a chat, Mustala!" he said sardonically.

"I have brought you some custom, Uncle," said the sergeant.

"Oh, well, that's different," said the innkeeper, his frown quickly changing to a smile. "Show them in, man, I haven't got all night."

Ruben and Lialah were hastily ushered into the inn, with the innkeeper shutting the door behind them.

"I am sorry, but I have nothing to give you to eat my friends, but I do have plenty of comfortable beds," said the innkeeper, obviously delighted with new business. "You look as if you need a good night's sleep."

"We most certainly do," said Ruben. "And I would be most grateful if you have any hot water," he requested.

"That, I can manage," said the innkeeper. "I will just show you to your room first and then I will go and get it." He then rounded on his nephew. "Well done boy, go now, and thank you for bringing them." He then tried to hustle the sergeant outside to the other two soldiers, who were still waiting in the street.

"Hold on a moment, Uncle, I must speak to your new guest before I go."

Thinking that the sergeant was going to ask for payment, Ruben put his hand in the bag of gold coins that the merchant had given him, as he was quite willing to part with one for the help that they had received. But he found that his arm was checked as the sergeant placed a hand on his wrist.

"No, I do not require payment, sir. In fact, I was looking for you," said the sergeant.

"What for?" enquired Ruben, surprised.

"I had been sent by Commander Mithrandir, who has the unfortunate job of being in charge of this besieged city," explained the sergeant. "You see, we were on the galley with him, and it was he who told the captain to bet five gold coins that you would not arrive before morning."

"Oh yes, I remember," said Ruben, his face breaking into a broad grin.

"He was amazed that you did arrive so quickly, in fact, so were we all. Now if you would be good enough to come to the barracks tomorrow and ask for me, I am Sergeant Mustala," said the sergeant, holding out his hand to give Ruben's hand a firm shake. "I will take you to claim your five gold coins, I am sure that the Commander will also have some work for you," he said smiling. He slipped quickly past his Uncle and out in to the night, to join his two waiting men.

The innkeeper rebolted the door and then escorted his new guests to another room, which seemed pleasant. The innkeeper said, "I will not be long and I will soon return with some hot water."

Slipping his shift off, Ruben said to Liaah, "Will the dye continue to run when this shift gets wet?"

"It should not have run anyway," said Lialah apologetically. "I probably put too much dye in the water, but it should be all right now. Anyway, your kilt has not run, probably because it was made of wool and flax, but the shift was made from cotton. I suppose you will want to wear them tomorrow?"

"Yes, I think I have to," replied Ruben. "As I am marked as a mercenary, I am sure this Commander Mithrandir will have some duties already planned for me."

At that moment, there was a knock at the door. "I have brought your hot water, sir," said the innkeeper, waiting until Ruben called him in.

Ruben went to the door and relieved the innkeeper of the pitcher of hot water. "

"Just leave the pitcher outside, sir, and would you like me to call you in the morning?"

"Yes please, but not too early," said Ruben with a smile.

"That's perfectly all right, sir, I will give you a call around mid-morning with some breakfast. Goodnight, sir, and thank you again for your custom, as you can well imagine, you are the only guests here at the moment.

"What a nice man," said Lialah, as the door was closed.

"Yes," responded Ruben. "And by the way, he spoke to Sergeant Mustala, it seems that Ashkilon must be well defended, so we can sleep safely in our beds."

"But you'll now have to fight as a mercenary. What do you think you'll be doing?" she asked.

"I really have no idea, let us take tomorrow as it comes. I will just wash this dye off and collapse into bed," he said with a yawn.

The next morning the innkeeper called them as promised. Ruben was still asleep, but woke to Lialah's shake, got out of bed and dressed. They ate the light breakfast that the innkeeper had brought them, which consisted of a pleasant tasting river eel, a few olives and some wheatcakes, served with asses' milk that was just beginning to turn sour.

After breakfast, Ruben and Lialah counted out the money that the merchant had given them. There were over thirty gold pieces in the bag and when Ruben added that to the money that he had left, he found to his surprise that he still had over fifty gold coins. He said, "And do not forget, that today I will be given more. But do not go mad and spend it all while I am out, but pay the innkeeper for last night and say that we hope to be staying for a few days, but do not commit yourself until I return."

"Do you think it is all right for me to go out?" asked Lialah.

"Probably it is fine," replied Ruben. "But check with the innkeeper and do not go far, we are in a strange city, right by the border and I don't want anything happening to you." Having said that, Ruben adjusted his sword belt, slipped on his crocodile skin jerkin, which he laced up, and slung the large, heavy sword on his back. "Let me go and see what the day holds," he said, putting on his helmet and ducking through the doorway.

Lialah felt very alone when he had left, but busied herself by tidying up the bedroom and then, taking some money and the empty dishes, went in search of the innkeeper.

She found him talking to a woman who, she supposed, was his wife, in the kitchen of the inn and paid him for the previous night's stay and said that they hoped to be able to stay longer, but this would depend on what Ruben might be asked to do. She then asked if it was safe to look around outside and perhaps go for a short walk.

The innkeeper said, "Yes, but do not go too far and keep well clear of the river, as I understand it is still chaotic down there. I believe that the Assyrians sent a couple of fire boats down river last night and that may be the way that they will try to get into the town."

"Do you think that they will get in?" asked Lialah, sounding worried.

"Not really, young woman, the city has vast walls and is well defended, with the promise of even more soldiers being sent," he replied assuredly.

"I will probably go out shortly," she said. "But I will not be gone for a long time." She left the innkeeper and returned to their room. Making sure that she had Ruben's small bronze knife on her belt, she also picked up his staff and left the inn for a walk around the immediate vicinity.

By making a few enquires, Ruben soon found his way up to the main barracks, which were by now overcrowded. Further enquires soon led him to Sergeant Mustala.

"Ah good, I am glad you're here," said the sergeant. "If you would be good enough to follow me, I will take you to Commander Mithrandir." He took Ruben through the barracks and into the adjoining palace. He went to the main chamber, where a guard stopped them. He exchanged a few brief words with the guard and they were soon ushered in.

Commander Mithrandir was standing by the main table, overlooking a map of the city that was attached to the table, discussing defensive arrangements with four captains from the army. He looked up as the sergeant came in with Ruben and said, "Ah good, I have been waiting to meet you and give you the five gold coins that I owe you, you certainly broke the record for a single oarsman to cover the distance from Mulch under a complete day. I was told in Mulch, when we stopped to leave reinforcements at the garrison there, that you had fought alongside Lieutenant Bel and Sergeant Abzher at Sousa." He smiled warmly and continued, "I am pleased to tell you that the king promoted them both, they are now Captain and Lieutenant accordingly. I hope they will be arriving soon, in charge of a new battalion of Babylonian Guards. Would you do me the honour of fighting alongside them again?" he asked as he gave Ruben five gold coins. "I do not even know your name, young man."

"Ruben Ben Uriah, Commander," said Ruben, and realising that he could hardly refuse he said, "That will be a pleasure, sir, I will look forward to their arrival."

"That is good, very good indeed. They should be arriving in a few days. We can then strike back at the besieging Assyrians. That will give them something to think about," he chuckled and then continued, this time to Sergeant Mustala. "I will want all the Guards billeted separately from the army. All the officers can stay in your uncle's inn, Mustala, you can tell him that he will be paid accordingly. I am afraid you will have to commission some empty houses, probably move a few citizens around, to keep all the Guards together. I will leave that in your capable hands, Sergeant."

"By your command," said the sergeant, thumping his chest in salute. He then turned on his heel and left the room.

"You can join us, young Ruben," said the commander. "If you have any comments do not be afraid to speak out."

This caused a lot of muttering from the assembled captains, who eyed the newcomer with distaste.

"I must object, sir," said one of the captains.

"Really," said the commander. "And what is your problem this time Britzeldah?"

"Well, he's a bloody mercenary and we don't know him yet," said the grey haired and grizzled captain. "Apart from which, he's only a boy!"

"And a very big boy, and probably twice the warrior that you are, Britzeldah. Now, the lad has dashed here to help us, he fought with Lieutenant Bel at Sousa, which as you know was a remarkable victory, and I trust him, so I will not stand for any more dissension," said the commander, raising his voice above the muttered agreements from the other Captains. "Your dislike of everyone outside the ordinary army, which even extends to the elite Babylonian Guards, is legendary, and I will have none of it in my presence," he said warningly. "We have a difficult and demanding job to do, remember the whole of Babylon is relying on the defence of the city. So it is important that we work together as a team, is that understood?" He glared around the room. There was a long silence and he eventually continued. "Now where were we, oh yes, our problem really lies in the defence of the river, which cuts the city in half, the problem being that the river is so wide it will take a long time to get reinforcements from one side to the other and also to stop the Assyrians sending down fire ships or even attacking by boat. Has anyone got any ideas?"

"I still like the idea of creating a small island in the middle of the river by sinking a couple of galleys," said Captain Britzeldah.

"Keeping them defended would be even more difficult than leaving the river open," said another captain.

"I don't like the idea of wasting our ships," said another.

"We should have built two large towers, one on each bank, as I suggested six months ago," said another.

"We haven't got time now," said the commander.

"Do we have a heavy iron chain long enough to go over the river?" asked Ruben.

They all stared at him. "Possibly. Why do you ask?" said Commander Mithrandir.

"Well, sir, if we could stretch a chain, or possibly two, just below the surface of the water, from either side of the city walls, that would stop any fire ships or other boats getting into the city," suggested Ruben.

"And if we have one, how do you propose getting it over to the other bank, or can you fly?" sneered Captain Britzeldah.

"Surely we can row it across?" protested Ruben, not easily being dismissed by the captain.

"It's a nice idea, but it would be difficult as the Assyrians have lots of small craft that they can use to intercept it. You see, once a boat is out of bowshot range, we are likely to lose it. Unfortunately, so many of our small boats left to take people away, we are largely outnumbered in small boats," said the commander.

"Well surely someone can swim across," persisted Ruben. "Drawing a rope behind him, that can then be attached to the chain, which could then be pulled across."

"He would get shot full of arrows for his trouble," laughed Captain

Britzeldah, enjoying his teasing.

"No, under water," said Ruben, not being put off, but blushing none the less.

"Unfortunately," said Captain Britzeldah with a perfectly straight face, "none of our fish are that intelligent." He collapsed guffawing at his own joke.

All the other captains joined him in the jest, thinking Ruben silly to suggest such a crazy idea.

"I will do it," said Ruben quietly.

"Do you think you can?" enquired the commander.

"I am sure I can, sir," said Ruben defiantly. "Once that has been done we can build a bridge, using moored galleys and other craft to support a floating bridge that will get our troops across quickly."

A hush fell across the room, and all eyes looked at the young man.

"If you are confident that you can do it, we will give it a try and then proceed from there," said Commander Mithrandir. "You have a lot of guts young man, it's the best idea yet that anyone has come up with, and we will give it a try. I will get the chain made, by joining every other chain we've got if need be, so if you would be ready by nightfall, we will meet by the southern end of the city wall."

Ruben returned to the inn, to discover that Lialah had returned briefly with the request for a bowl, which the innkeeper's wife had provided. She had then left saying that she would be back shortly. Ruben explained to the innkeeper that they would be staying for a little longer, giving the innkeeper a couple of gold coins as payment in advance. He explained that he was to join the Babylonian Guards when they arrived and hoped that he would be able to stay on at the inn, where all the officers from the Guards would be billeted. Much to his surprise, the innkeeper had already been informed of this piece of news, by his nephew, Sergeant Mustala. The innkeeper asked him, "How many officers would there be?"

"I am not sure exactly," said Ruben, thinking out loud. "You see, it is going to be a new battalion, now normally there would be the captain, two lieutenants and eight sergeants. I should imagine that some of them would be quite happy to share a room. But you had better set aside a large room for the captain, as he will probably use it as an office as well."

"I understand that they should be arriving in a couple of days. That is very good news," said the innkeeper, obviously delighted at the thought of renewed business. "I'm always happy to put up Babylonian Guard officers, as they are always smart and tidy, apart from which they are not noisy and do not get involved in fights, unlike their men, who always seem to get into fights with the ordinary army," he explained.

"That is why the commander wanted the Guards all billeted

together," said Ruben. "You see the rest of the army feel that they get better treatment, which I suppose is true."

Lialah came in then, forcing a break in the idle chatter. "You are back far sooner than I expected Ruben," greeted Lialah brightly. "Did they not have anything for you to do?"

"No, just the opposite," replied Ruben. "I will have to return later. Let us go to our room and I will tell you all about it."

"Just before we go," said Lialah, with a restraining hand on his arm. She turned to the innkeeper and said, "Will your wife object to me doing some washing later?"

"I'm sure that will pose no difficulty," said the innkeeper in reply.

Ruben then led Lialah back to their room, and noticed that she was carrying a bowl full of blackcurrants.

"Where on earth did you get those and what do you intend to do with them?" enquired Ruben.

"I found them growing wild, a few streets away on some waste ground. I am going to make some more dye, and dye a couple more shifts for you, as you will no doubt need them," she told him, and then asked, "Well, what exactly happened?"

"For a start we will be staying here," he explained, and then proceeded to tell her all about the Babylonian Guard battalion that would be coming, under the leadership of the newly promoted Captain Bel, and that he was to join them. She listened quietly as he went on to explain about what had happened in the palace that morning. He then told her of what he had volunteered to do that night.

She gave a sharp intake of breath and said, "Oh, Ruben, why did you volunteer for such a dangerous job?"

"Well they were being rude and teasing me," said Ruben, trying to justify himself. "I certainly hope they can fight better than they can discuss tactics. Otherwise the city will be lost. But if I can do this thing, we may be able to survive until Captain Bel arrives." Then he paused and added, "Anyway, no one else will do it."

"You sound very patriotic," said Lialah. "I thought you were not keen on fighting for Babylon?"

"Well, it seems I have no choice," said Ruben. "Apart from which, they are a lot more civilised than the Assyrians. But anyway, I have volunteered now, so it must be done. However, your dye has given me an idea."

"I have not made it yet," said Lialah.

"Will it wash off me, if I dye myself?" he asked, ignoring her facetious remark.

"Well yes, but not immediately, and it will take quite a bit of scrubbing with hot water," replied Lialah. "But why do you want to dye yourself, I prefer you just the way you are," she giggled.

"If I dye myself, like Ishmala," he explained, "and if you dye a pair of shorts black as well, I should be safer in the water tonight."

She left Ruben, who said he would have a lie down to conserve his strength for the night's swim, and went off to the kitchen with the blackcurrants, taking a couple of shifts and a pair of shorts that they had bought in Babylon, saying that she would be back soon with something to eat, as he would have to go out before dinner that night.

Ruben lay on his bed and thought about what he was going to tell Captain Bel. After discarding a few ideas, he decided that it would be far easier to tell him the truth, particularly bearing in mind that Latich may have already spoken to him. He was not worried about swimming across the river underwater, as he knew that he could cover the distance only coming up for air four or five times. But wondered how deep the water was and how fast the current would be. He was almost asleep when Lialah came in, with a tray loaded with nice things to eat and a large bowl of steaming hot, black dye.

She said, "I have dyed the other things, they are hanging outside in the sun to dry, now, strip off and dye yourself, even your hair, and do not sit on anything until you are completely dry."

"Yes, your Majesty!" responded Ruben, getting off the bed. "Am I allowed to eat while I dry off?" he asked, bowing as he did so.

"As long as you do not walk around and leave a lot of black footprints for the new cleaner, who is me!" she told him.

"You do not have to work," he said frowning at her.

"I know that, but it will give me something to do as well as helping the innkeeper when the Babylonian Guards arrive. Anyway, it's none of your business, you Nubian slave, just do as you are told." She laughed merrily.

"Ishmala was not a slave, he told me that he was when Mutek bought him. But because he was so loyal, Mutek made him a free man. So I don't want any more of your cheek, or you will end up with a black bottom," he warned as he continued rubbing dye onto himself.

At dusk, the time when it becomes difficult to distinguish everything clearly, Ruben quietly left the inn and quickly made his way towards the meeting point, where the city was stopped beside the river. He went on his own, fleeing from shadow to shadow. This was despite Lialah's wish to accompany him; he had refused her company, saying that it would be too dangerous for her to be on her own. Even though she had argued that she would not be on her own, that he could introduce her to Commander Mithrandir who, she was sure, would look after her. But Ruben was particularly obstinate on this occasion and said that she had to stay at the inn. Although he trusted Commander Mithrandir, he did not trust the other soldiers, particularly those like Captain Britzeldah, who he thought was a coward and a cheat, or at least not trustworthy. Very few people, if anyone, noticed that he had black skin, all they saw was a large man in a black uniform, with a green crocodile skin jerkin. He was armed, but only with his short bronze sword, as he knew that he would have to undress and leave his possessions. He arrived by the water's edge, below the large wall that jutted out into the river. There were stone steps leading down into the water, so he positioned himself above this in the shadow of a buttress on the side of the wall, upon which he could hear the soldiers patrolling above. He did not have long to wait as the captains arrived, all talking about him and what he was attempting to do. One of them said he was a brave lad, but he was committing suicide just because Captain Britzeldah had laughed at him. Captain Britzeldah said, "No, I bet he won't even show up. I have seen a lot of these big kids, they are all the same, scared shitless when it comes down to it."

Ruben just smiled to himself, keeping hidden against the wall, waiting for Commander Mithrandir. After a few moments there was the sound of horses and an approaching chariot. The chariot drew to a halt and Commander Mithrandir jumped down. "Right then, I have brought everything with me, it's in the chariot. I have been fortunate, I spoke to the captain of the galley in which I returned from Babylon. He produced two long anchor chains that have been made from the new metal so are even stronger than the bronze ones. I have also brought the rope long enough to do the job. When it is across, I have arranged for a team of oxen to stretch it taught, they are waiting on the northern bank. Now it seems that all is quiet out there, but I believe the Assyrians may be getting ready to send some fireboats down river," he informed them, looking from one to the other, to see if anyone had anything to add. Then he looked behind him and said, "The sooner we get started the better, now where is young Ruben?" Captain Britzeldah was about to open his mouth when a large dark figure stepped out from the shadow by the wall.

"I have been waiting for a while, sir," he said. Captain Britzeldah's mouth dropped open, but before he could speak Ruben said, "I was just listening to the captains." His bright blue eyes glared at Britzeldah, who took a step backwards, as his eyes seemed to see his very soul and mock him.

"By the gods," said the commander. "You have dyed yourself black. That is a cunning move, where did you learn that trick?"

"From a Nubian, but he didn't need to dye himself because he was black anyway, sir," replied Ruben.

"Well, it is a good idea," said the commander, glancing around at the captains, most of who smiled with him. "Now, let us get down to the job in hand. If you strip off, Ruben, and put your clothes in my chariot and tie one end of the rope around your waist, then commence your swim. I will pay out the rope behind you, whilst the captains can secure the ends of the chains firmly to the wall. Now, when you get across behind the wall on the northern bank, which juts out like this side, you will find steps like these. At the top of the steps you will find a team of oxen with Sergeant Mustala and his men, you can see them here." He pointed to the far bank, where a flaming torch was being waved beside the wall. "They will take the rope from you and attach it to the oxen. We will have connected this end to the chains, which can then be pulled across. With the weight of the oxen heaving on the chains, the dip will be minimised, so they hang just below the surface." He explained the plan that he had worked out, which sounded to Ruben to be foolproof.

Ruben removed his helmet and undressed down to his shorts, folding his clothes as he went and putting them in the chariot. Securing the rope around his waist, he took off his sandals, added them to the pile and walked down the steps into the water. When it came half way up his chest, he ducked beneath the surface, acclimatising himself to the change in temperature. He then resurfaced and filled his lungs with air, before diving deeply into the river, the dark rope snaking down behind him. He was surprised at the strength of the current, which was far stronger than he had anticipated, mainly because of the jutting out walls, which compressed the river, but also because the river here was only a short distance below the first cataract, which was hidden from view just above the bend in the river – this of course, Ruben knew nothing about. He soon realised that he was being swept down river and had to redirect the angle of his swim, so that he was heading more up stream. It was far harder than he had anticipated and after resurfacing for the fourth time, he could see that he was still under half way across. He was using his own peculiar style, which he had used all those years ago when he had swum into Lagash. This did not make any splashing and because of being dyed black, he was not noticed by either his own Babylonians, or the Assyrians. The Assyrians had a few small craft just cruising around in the middle of the river, out of bowshot from the walls. Not even they spotted him as he took another deep breath and ducked beneath the water again renewing his efforts. After what seemed an eternity and resurfacing for air at least another ten times, his strength was beginning to ebb, but he could finally make out the steps by the far wall. As he was preparing for the final distance he could see a few of the Assyrian fire ships being torched and made ready to be floated down river. He swam on as fast as his remaining strength allowed and finally reached the northern bank, and dragged himself up the steps to collapse into Sergeant Mustala's arms.

The astonished sergeant did not at first realise who he held in his arms, but as soon as he saw the rope around Ruben's waist he realised who he was holding. Lowering Ruben gently to the ground he tried to undo the rope, but the knot had tightened with the drag of the long rope and the cool water. Realising that speed was essential, he quickly cut through the rope with his dagger. Calling his men to aid him, they began to haul in the rope. It became very heavy as it began pulling the chains across, so he brought down the team of oxen, which he soon had harnessed to the rope, and then led them up beside the wall.

Ruben's breathing was now becoming regular and he sat up to watch the progress. He groaned as he realised that the fire ships were quickly approaching the rope towing the chains. The weight of the chains dragged the line taught far below the surface of the river. This would mean that the fireboats might pass over both rope and chains, or if not, they could snag against the rope and illuminate the scene. This would give one of the Assyrian small boats time to row out, cut the rope, ruining the plan and all his hard work. Knowing that he must try to prevent this, the urgency made him call up his deep reserves of strength and he rose to his feet and dived back into the river, swimming powerfully out towards the fireboats. He knew that he was splashing in his urgency, but hoped that his colour would obscure him as a target. He reached the first fireboat as a few arrows whistled and splashed into the river around him. Diving under the side, he swam under the boat and managed to turn its keel and pushed it into the path of the other fireboat. The two boats collided in a shower of sparks, which temporarily slowed their progress down river. He surfaced quietly and saw the approaching Assyrian craft, which had shot arrows at him. Fortunately they did not see him, but a soldier was leaning out of the prow and had noticed the rope as it surfaced from the river where it towed the heavy chains. Ruben dived again and swam on a collision course to intercept the boat. He surfaced just under the prow beneath where the soldier was pointing. The man was so excited and calling back to the other soldiers, he did not see the black arms that came out of the water and dragged him over the edge of the boat. Ruben did not have the strength to fight the man, but his bronze breastplate and other protective battle-dress soon dragged him under the water. In their attempts to rescue their colleague the boat stopped as they tried to fish him out of the water, by which time the end of the emerging rope was within bowshot of the soldiers on the northern wall. Ruben swam quietly away beside the fireboats, which drifted downriver, but caught on the chains as they came out of the water by the northern bank and became taut. Exhausted, Ruben also felt himself being pushed against the chains, which he clung to as he slowly dragged himself back towards the southern end of the wall. The only person who had witnessed everything, and what he had not seen he had guessed correctly, was Captain Britzeldah. Realising that he had misjudged the gallant young mercenary, he leapt into the river and helped Ruben ashore. Very soon Commander Mithrandir and all the captains were leaning over the exhausted Ruben, whose head was pillowed in Britzeldah's lap. Amid the congratulations, Ruben gasped out to Commander Mithrandir that he must send out a galley, just down river from the chains, which would be safe from the fireboats, but would have enough bowmen to shoot any Assyrian who realised what was holding back the fireboats and prevent them cutting through, or breaking, the chains, which would obviously take them a very long time. He then lapsed into exhausted sleep.

The commander ordered one of the captains to have a galley equipped with bowmen and to be rowed within bowshot of the chains in the middle of the river. The Assyrians had no large boats to challenge one of the large galleys, which would now be safe from the fireboats. fire obviously being one of the major threats to wooden galleys.

Captain Britzeldah picked up Ruben's exhausted body and with Commander Mithrandir's assistance laid him in the chariot, which they walked beside back to the palace. Ruben gradually awoke from his sleep of sheer exhaustion, as he warmed up in front of a large fire that had been lit in the palace's main chamber, where he had been laid on a couch. His eyes opened to find the concerned grizzled face of Captain Britzeldah peering over him.

"He is back with us, Commander," called the captain.

"Fine, that is excellent, now, if you get some of this hot broth inside him he should perk up," said the commander. "The young have amazing powers of recovery, he will soon be thinking clearly again and I want to know what his ideas were on this floating bridge that he talked about."

Ruben was soon sitting up and had redressed back into his uniform, but had not replaced his jerkin as it was very warm in the room, even though the fire had been left to die down. Having had his own personal physician, who had been responsible for the restoring broth, check Ruben over, Commander Mithrandir asked Ruben about his idea for a floating bridge.

"Well, Commander," began Ruben, trying to give a sensible description of his earlier idea. "How many galleys do we have here at the moment?"

"Five at present," replied the commander. "But there should be two more arriving shortly with more reinforcements. Oh yes, and then that of the Babylonian Guards."

"Well I think the five galleys moored in a line with a few smaller crafts, would be enough. This would support a laddered planking walkway that we could use to move troops quickly across," Ruben explained.

"Yes, I think I understand what you mean," said the commander. "Let me call one of our boat builders and a couple of the galley captains to discuss this idea."

Eventually, the plan was complete, and it was still well before dawn. It was decided to have the galleys in place immediately, armed to keep the Assyrians from finding out what was stopping their fireboats from coming downriver. Also, work was to commence on building the walkway that would eventually span the entire river. The meeting soon broke up with all the different captains going their separate ways with different orders. The plan was to have the five galleys in line, bow to stern, just downriver from the chains, within close bowshot or javelin range of them, to prevent the Assyrians tampering with the chains. By morning, the Babylonians knew that the Assyrians would see the protruding ends of the chains, even though the ends would be safe as they were right below the city walls and could be easily defended from above.

Ruben was left alone with Commander Mithrandir whilst the others went about their allotted tasks. The commander said to Ruben, "You may as well go back to your inn and go back to bed."

"What about you, sir?" enquired Ruben, as he got up from the couch and put on his crocodile skin jerkin. Reaching for his helmet, he was about to leave the room when Commander Mithrandir replied.

"Do not worry about me, it is my duty to ensure the defence of the city, so I doubt whether I will be able to get much sleep until the next reinforcements arrive." He looked tired but managed to notice, and said half to himself, "Where have I seen a jerkin like that before?"

"I believe all the new Babylonian Guards wear them," said Ruben, without offering any further information.

"I suppose you got it from Sousa!" said the commander. "It is superbly made and is a remarkably good fit." He paused for a moment deep in thought, suddenly remembering, and said as he recalled the occasion, "Ah yes, the young Babylonian Guard who came back to Babylon with a merchant had a similar jerkin, however, I am sure his was not as well made." Ruben was on the verge of telling this pleasant man the truth, when the commander seemed to dismiss the subject and said, "I will accompany you out of the palace."

Ruben said, "If you are going down to the city wall by the river to check on the work, may I come with you, sir?"

"Yes, by all means, if you are not tired," said the commander. So the two of them walked down to see what was happening by the river.

The galleys were being rowed out and one galley was already in the centre of the river, where it had been shooting at any Assyrian boat that had come near the two fireboats, which had almost burnt out and were on the point of sinking. Unsure of what had stopped their first two fireboats, but believing that it was some curious obstruction in the river that they had regrettably caught on, the Assyrians sent more fireboats drifting downriver towards the galley. The chains stopped these too, and there was soon a line of fireboats in the centre of the river that could not proceed down past the chains. The other galleys were soon moored into position and it was obvious that laddered wooden planking could easily breach the distance between the five galleys and the shore.

It was now getting light and the commander was just complimenting Ruben on how the plan had worked, when one of the army captains came up to the commander and told him that his lookouts on the city walls had noticed the Assyrians preparing to attack the City walls on either side of the river at the same time.

"This is just what I feared," said the commander. "I only hope that our divided forces will be enough to contain them."

At that point, Lialah arrived looking desperately for Ruben. When she saw him she ran into his arms and embraced him, saying that she was unable to sleep for fear of what he had been doing. A rather embarrassed Ruben introduced her to Commander Mithrandir. They made a peculiar sight, this attractive girl clinging onto the large young man who was still half coloured with blotchy black dye. Ruben then asked the commander, "Will it be alright if I return to fetch my sword, so that I can help out with the defence of the city, sir?"

"If you feel up to it, young Ruben, I am sure an extra sword could be put to good use," said the commander. "Have you got any preference as to who you fight with?" said the rather surprised commander.

"If I may, I would like to fight with Captain Britzeldah, just to prove that I can fight as well as swim," said Ruben.

"All right then, young man," said the commander. "You will find him on the northern city walls just the other side of the river, where the main Assyrian attack will come. I am sure that he would be pleased to receive your assistance."

Telling the commander that he would return soon, Ruben left with Lialah still clinging to his arm, walking in the direction of their inn. As they went, Lialah said, "I am not letting you go back like that, you really must have a good wash to remove most of the dye."

"I am sure that the Assyrians won't object to being killed by someone dirty," he exclaimed. "In fact, it should make them feel more at home."

"Do you really have to go back?" she enquired.

"It will help the defence of the city if I do, as well as proving my own ability. But do not worry about me as we have the advantage, so there should not be too much to do," he said reassuringly. Although he hoped that there would be some fierce fighting, so that he could equite himself fighting with his large sword that he had not yet used in battle. They soon reached the inn and Ruben went straight to their room, while Lialah went to see the innkeeper to request some hot water. She returned with a full pitcher to find Ruben had stripped off and was trying to wash himself with cold water.

She said, "You are silly, you will never remove the dye like that. Now just stand still, and I will rinse you down with hot water with some herbs in it and I will give you a good scrub." Ruben found the experience surprisingly pleasant and was pleased to see that most of the dye came out. He soon redressed and put on a clean shift, all the time complaining that he smelt like the bushes in Babylon's Hanging Gardens.

Lailah laughed and said, "If the Assyrian soldiers are as vile smelling as that horrible king of theirs, you will not even need your sword. Their king hated those beautiful Gardens, probably because they smelt so nice."

"Their dead king," corrected Ruben. "That is what this whole business is about."

"It wouldn't happen if women were in charge!" retorted Lialah. "All these wars are silly."

"You sound just like your old Uncle Simeon," laughed Ruben. "Now you have a good sleep and stop worrying about me, what with my magic sword and this smell, they will probably all run away." He then kissed her, put the sword on his back, grabbed his helmet and slipped quietly out of the room. When he was in the street, he put on his helmet and broke into a trot as he was eager to get into action with the sword that he had never tried out in earnest.

He soon reached the site of battle, after boarding a small boat that was taking other soldiers across to the northern bank, where, to his astonishment, the Assyrians had already managed to gain the top of the wall and fierce fighting was taking place. Running up the steps whilst he drew the large sword from his scabbard on his back, he reached the top of the wall just in time to be confronted by a fierce, powerfully built Assyrian who was leading the assault. This fearsome opponent had just brushed aside two defending Babylonian soldiers and came at him yelling curses and shouting, "Out of my way, boy."

"You must remove yourself," replied Ruben, standing his ground. "It is you who trespasses, so you remove yourself or I will."

The Assyrian laughed, baring his yellow and blackened teeth and swung his large bronze sword in a sideways sweep directed at Ruben's head. Ruben did not duck, but parried the blow with his own sword, which not only stopped the blade, but cut into it, completely absorbing the impact without the normal jarring sensation that Ruben expected. The Assyrian drew back his blade and swung again, from the other side, which Ruben again parried with remarkable ease. Another few blows were met with even stronger resistance and Ruben was moving forwards as the smile on the Assyrian's face vanished. Ruben's sword was unscathed whilst that of his opponent was notched in three places and had begun to lacerate. The Assyrian had never met resistance like this, admittedly this unusually uniformed young man was large, but this strange shining sword had met his own blade with unyielding power that was now forcing him backwards. He was now parrying Ruben's blows and saw to his horror that his own blade was shredding under the impact. He was not quick enough to parry the next pointed thrust, but felt sure that his own bronze breastplate would turn the blade. He watched in horror, as the blade seemed to pass through his breastplate as if it were made of thin material, and his lips parted in a shriek as the blade cut through flesh and bone to pierce his heart. As he died and was pushed over the wall, Ruben advanced towards two more Assyrians who had been watching the conflict. As they attacked in unison their blades were both swept aside, one of which was almost severed and the other was deeply notched. One of them slipped to his left and was impaled by the Babylonian soldiers rallying behind Ruben, while the other tried to return to the ladder, which he had ascended. He was unfortunately pushed forward by the next Assyrian trying to get off the ladder onto the battlements, this act being his undoing, as Ruben's next thrust took him through the guts. Tearing his blade free from the screaming and dying man in a shower of blood and torn flesh, Ruben continued the upward swing of his sword, which the Assyrian on top of the ladder met with his shield. The horrified soldier saw his shield split and Ruben's sword bit into his arm. His arm was flung upwards, the shield went spinning away and he fell back onto the next soldier trying to climb up behind him. Ruben reached the top of the ladder, which was now empty although there were three soldiers still coming upwards. Holding his sword in one hand he grabbed the top of the ladder and gave it a sharp twist and pushed it sideways so that it fell from the wall.

The immediate area around Ruben was now free from Assyrians and reoccupied by Babylonian troops. He turned to the man beside him, who was a sergeant in the bright red of the standard army uniform and had followed Ruben to regain that area of the battlements. The man said to

Ruben, "I am afraid that I don't know you, sir, but I certainly am glad that you are on our side."

Smiling his acknowledgement, Ruben asked, "Where is Captain Britzeldah?"

"He will be where the fighting is heaviest, a little further along the wall, sir," replied the sergeant.

"Make sure that all future attacks never get off the top of the ladders," instructed Ruben and went to his left looking for the captain.

Britzeldah was indeed in the heart of the battle and was being hard pressed on both sides by Assyrians who had reached the top of the wall. He was surrounded by bodies from both forces and was engaged in a swordfight against three Assyrians who had him surrounded. Whilst he was fully engaged with two attackers on one side, the remaining Assyrian was about to plunge his sword into the captain's unguarded back, when his own helmet burst asunder as Ruben's bright blade cut cleanly through it. The blade continued through and cut deeply into the flesh and bone of his skull, enough to kill the man instantly. Captain Britzeldah had known that he was on the point of being killed so was surprised to glance back at the dead body, which toppled over with his blood and brains oozing over the battlements in a gory mess. Realising that he had been saved gave him the renewed strength to push away one of his attackers and catch the other with a blow to the throat. The man he pushed aside was soon engaged in mortal combat with Ruben and to his horror saw slithers of his own sword being cut off as it met Ruben's superior blade. In his terror the man jumped off the battlement to impale himself on the swords of his own soldiers down below. In the temporary lull Britzeldah said, "By the gods, am I glad to see you. I thought I was a dead man then, but now with your help we can clear the top of the wall." This was soon accomplished, with both Ruben and the captain instructing the defending soldiers on how to prevent the Assyrians getting onto the wall by attacking the top soldier as he tried to cross from the top of the ladder to the battlements.

Ruben then asked Britzeldah, "Where are all the bowmen and javelin throwers?"

"They are all down on the galleys with the Commander," said Britzeldah, sadly shaking his head. "We have only a few spearmen up here, but they have only the knowledge to stab with the spears."

"Bring some spears to me," ordered Ruben.

Four spears were soon produced and stacked against the battlements. Ruben picked one up and although it was not flighted as well as a javelin, he hurled it with deadly accuracy and power at an attacking ladder where it skewered the leading soldier who pulled the ladder down as he died. Ruben then said to Captain Britzeldah, "Will your men follow my leadership in your absence?"

"Most certainly, my young friend," said Britzeldah. "Particularly now they have seen you fight."

"Good," said Ruben. "You must go yourself to the commander and tell him that he cannot have need of all the bowmen and javelin throwers, they should be distributed along the walls." Then Ruben took another spear and stepped towards a ladder that had come up from the Assyrian attackers below. Again it found its mark and another ladder toppled over.

The captain shouted to his men to obey Ruben's instructions and ran down the steps off towards the river. The work on the walkway and the galleys was nearing completion. Commander Mithrandir asked him impatiently, "Why have you left your post? I have to assume the north wall is safe."

"For the moment it is," said the captain. "But sir, you really must send us some bowmen and javelin throwers, most of them aboard the galleys seem to be idle. There is ample work for them on the walls. To be honest I am fortunate to be alive, I was rescued in the nick of time by Ruben. Never have I seen a sword so superbly wielded, and what a sword it is, bright as the noonday sun and of incredible strength. Apart from that, I have never seen spears thrown with such power and accuracy."

Realising that his concern for the safety of the river had severely jeopardised the walls by removing too many bowmen and javelin throwers, he ordered Captain Britzeldah to take a third of them to the north wall. Calling Sergeant Mustala, he ordered him to take half the remaining javelin throwers and bowmen to help on the southern wall. This left himself a third of the original force to deter the Assyrians from trying to get down the river past the chains. This was about correct in number and he realised that his error had nearly caused the defeat of the city. He then felt how tired he was as it had been over two days since he had last slept. His thoughts of his bed were quickly dispelled as a messenger came up and said, "Two reinforcement galleys have just been sighted coming up river, sir."

"Thank goodness for that," he exclaimed. He then walked down the almost completed walkway to the riverbank where the two galleys would be moored. He watched the two galleys, which were packed to the brim with fresh soldiers all ready for action. He watched them being expertly moored and as soon as the gangplank was in place he went on board to meet the captain of the first galley. He advised him to divide his men and send half to each side of the walls to replace the dead and the exhausted soldiers who could return to their barracks for a rest. He then went aboard the second galley and informed the captain of the galley to send his men to the barracks, where they would be needed in gradual replacement. As he was about to leave, the captain of the second galley said, "Excuse me sir, you will be pleased to learn that the Babylonian Guard galley should be here first thing in the morning."

Feeling that he could safely get some sleep, he turned his tired footsteps towards his palace and bed. He was about to enter the palace when he was called from behind, and he turned to see that it came from Ruben, who was blood splattered and also looking weary as he half carried the limping Captain Britzeldah. The captain had an arrow piercing the meat of his thigh. But fortunately it was not bleeding very much, but leaving a trickle of blood down his leg. Ruben said, "I think you had better get a physician to cut out the arrow head, as it appears that the Assyrians are using barbed arrows, which they are now shooting at the defenders on the walls. You see, we have forced back the attackers from the base of the walls by using the bowmen and javelin throwers."

"Yes, I will certainly send for my best physician," said the commander. "If you would be good enough to bring him into the palace we can then get him patched up."

"It is not that serious, I hope I will still be able to be in charge of the defence of the northern wall, sir," said Captain Britzeldah.

As Ruben helped the captain into the palace and delivered him into the arms of the waiting physician, the commander who was right behind him said, "I have had excellent reports about your timely arrival at the north wall. You will also be pleased to know that Captain Bel with a complete battalion of the Babylonian Guards should be arriving first thing in the morning. Now I suggest you also return to your inn, inform the innkeeper of the anticipated arrival of his guests, and get yourself some rest."

Ruben thanked the commander and promised that he would get some rest, and left the palace heading in the direction of the inn. He was most surprised when on his walk back, a few soldiers in the street stepped aside for him and saluted his passing, politely saying, "Good evening, sir!" Further up the street others smiled at him and went out of their way to be polite and friendly. He was given a bunch of grapes and patted on the back by another soldier, who said, "We are most grateful to be able to fight alongside you, sir." He soon reached the inn where he was met by Lialah who was concerned by his appearance.

She said, "I thought you said it was going to be easy, and it would be not much to do?"

"Yes, that is what I honestly believed," he replied, and then explained further. "However, all is safe now and reinforcements have arrived. I hope there will be time for me to have a wash, and can you rinse the stains out of my uniform, before we have dinner? I am hungry enough to eat a team of oxen."

"You look worn out," said Lialah. "Come with me and let me clean you up." She led him to their room where he took his large sword off his back, whilst she unlaced his jerkin, which she took over to the jug of water and basin and wiped it clean with a damp cloth. "Take off your shift and kilt," she ordered. "I will rinse them out and leave them to dry. You can wash yourself and then we will just be in time for dinner."

He agreed without rancour, but then took out his sword and began to inspect.

"You haven't time to play with your toys," she said angrily. "We are going to dinner like civilised people."

He shrugged, put the sword back in its scabbard and put it under the bed, but then said, "I will have to resharpen and polish the sword before we go to bed." He sighed, took her hand and let her lead him out of the room.

When they sat down to dinner with the innkeeper and his wife, Ruben told the innkeeper of the anticipated arrival of the Babylonian Guards. Then, much to Lialah's annoyance the innkeeper and Ruben talked about the battle all through dinner, although he made small part of his own involvement in the fighting. However, the innkeeper had already been informed of his prowess and leadership. On their return to their room Lialah said, "I thought you promised uncle S'meon not to kill people."

"I can hardly be a mercenary and avoid battle," he retorted. "Apart from which, you were the one who encouraged me and made my uniform."

"Don't blame me!" she shouted, and stamped in rage.

"Don't get upset, little one," he smiled gently, put his arm around her shoulder, and kissed her. "I am only looking after you."

"I know," she said in a small voice. "I am sorry I was angry, but it's all so sad having to kill other people."

"I do agree, but I am not in a position to offer alternatives," responded Ruben pausing reflectively. He picked her up and gently laid her on the bed. "Now you get into bed, and I will join you very soon."

He then retrieved his sword, took it out of the scabbard, and washed and dried the blade as he inspected it. He was delighted to see that it had no damage and it only needed a little resharpening. He found this was quite tiring on his fingers, as he had to lean with all his weight behind the sharpening stone before it made any real impression, as the blade was so hard. Finally he was satisfied and repolished the blade using the wax stored in a stone pot that Ishmala had given him, returning the blade to its scabbard, which he also cleaned, before slipping it beneath the bed. He undressed, reminding himself to wake at dawn, and was asleep in Lialah's arms almost before his head touched the pillow.

## 14
## THE COST OF VICTORY

One of the windows in their room faced the east and was brightening as Ruben awoke. As he wished to meet the Babylonian Guard galley when it arrived, he quietly slid from beneath the covers, careful not to wake Lialah, dressed himself, putting on his now dry shift and black kilt, grabbed his jerkin and large sword, which he put on his back, and taking his helmet, he quietly left the room. He was just lacing his jerkin as he met the innkeeper by the front door.

"Good morning," said the innkeeper. "You are about early this morning."

"Yes, but do not talk so loudly as my wife is still asleep," he requested. "Would you be good enough to tell her when she wakes and makes her appearance, that I have gone down to the river to welcome the Babylonian Guards. After meeting them and reporting to the Commander I shall probably bring them straight back here."

He left the inn and hurried down to the riverbank, where much to his surprise a new galley had already arrived and was just finishing being disembarked. After a few enquiries he was directed to the palace, where he found the commander welcoming the new arrivals. As he entered the main chamber the commander noticed him and beckoned him over. This was the moment he had been dreading, and had wanted out of the way in private. But he found himself being introduced to Captain Bel and Lieutenant Abzher by the commander who said, "I believe you have already met Ruben as he fought beside you at Sousa."

Captain Bel nodded his agreement and held out his hand with an easy smile saying, "Hello Ruben, it is good to see you again." There was however a great deal that needed explaining, which Ruben could detect from the captain's eyes, which met his at almost the same level.

The captain's quizzical look was broken by the commander, who said, "Young Ruben was responsible for swimming across the river with the chains, it was his idea to bridge the river with the walkway suspended by the floating galleys that has now been built in place."

"Do not forget his brilliant swordsmanship and spear throwing," interrupted Captain Britzeldah. "Show them your sword Ruben, my men are calling it 'The bright flame from the east'."

Ruben produced his sword, very glad that he had cleaned, sharpened and repolished the blade so diligently the night before, but still felt like an exhibitionist, placing it on the table for inspection.

There was a low gasp of astonishment. "May I hold it?" asked Lieutenant Abzher.

"Certainly, sir," replied Ruben.

Lieutenant Abzher lifted the sword by its dark red leather bound grip, which contrasted superbly with the bright blue lapis lazuli stone on the pommel, set amid sparkling small stones of rainbow colours, saying, "It is not only beautiful, and worth a fortune, but it is so well balanced it makes even our new iron weapons seem clumsy."

"It cut through bronze as if it were papyrus," said Captain Britzeldah.

"Perhaps," said Ruben, "your new weapons need not be so heavy. They are probably fashioned like the old bronze ones."

"I think you may be right there," said the lieutenant. "We may have to work on that, once we have put them to the test."

"Anyway, you seem to be quite a celebrity," said Captain Bel, still with the enquiring look on his face. He then leant close to Ruben and whispered quietly in his ear, "You have a lot of explaining to do." He then said in a louder voice, "You and I have a lot to catch up on, but it can wait until later." Captain Bel then turned to the commander and said, "I presume that the city is now quite safe, sir. But needless to say you would like us to break the siege."

"Quite so," replied the commander. "Although it is not a real siege, as we can be supplied by river. I have a map where our lookouts have marked the rough positions of the encamped Assyrians." He then gestured to the table, which held the map on which the river was shown. It also showed the city and the surrounding countryside in fairly large scale. Ruben could see the position of the first cataract that was just up river from Ashkilon, but obscured from view by a bend in the river.

"May I take the map to my quarters, commander?" asked Captain Bel.

"Yes, most certainly Captain," replied the commander, adding, "How long do you think it will take you to work out a plan?"

"I think the sooner we strike the better, so we should work out a strategy by midday," replied the captain. "And then strike just before dawn tomorrow."

"Excellent, that really is fine news," said the delighted commander. "Now I will let you go to your quarters, I have billeted you, men separately from the main barracks. You will be staying with your officers at the inn where Ruben is staying, so I'm sure he will take you and your officers with him." The commander then rolled up the map, which he presented to Captain Bel, who thanked him for his courtesy and promised to return with details of their strike just after midday. They then left the palace and followed Ruben as he led them towards the inn.

Falling into step beside Ruben, Captain Bel said, "As soon as I am settled in my quarters, I will send for you. Apart from catching up with your story, I need to know where the strong and weak points are in our defence."

"Most certainly, sir," replied Ruben. "Do you know anything about why I am here?"

"I know a surprising amount," replied the captain. "Latich told me a lot of your story, and that it was you in the Hanging Gardens. Apart from which, I saw you at Zohab when I was aboard a craft travelling down the river to Babylon."

"Yes," laughed Ruben. "I was certain that you recognised me, that was shortly before I bought one of the old ferry boats and we rowed up river, but arrived here just when the Assyrian attack started. You see, I had hoped to pass through Ashkilon before the trouble started."

"So you still want to go on this quest?" enquired the captain. "Latich told me all about that, but there are still some parts of your story that I am unsure of."

"I will certainly tell you all that you wish," said Ruben. "But we are just coming up to the inn, which should be all ready to accommodate you and your fellow officers."

Ruben introduced the captain to the innkeeper, who took over and took them to their rooms. Ruben was pleased to realise he had correctly judged the number of officers who were in the party. He then went to his own room to tell Lialah what had happened, and to apologise for having left her at dawn. When he went into their room, he was pleased to see that she was up and dressed. She was looking extremely attractive, as was so often the case these days. She was eating some fruit that she had prepared as a light snack, which looked very appetising, particularly as he had missed breakfast.

"I do wish you would tell me in advance of your plans," she said, chastising. "Only it is very distressing to wake alone and realise you have gone, especially as I do not know where or why."

"I am very sorry, my dearest," said Ruben, humbly apologising. "But I was not going anywhere dangerous and as you can realise, I wanted to meet Captain Bel, to ensure that there was no great difficulty in my having left the Guards at Sousa." He told her that he had been too late anyway and had met everyone at the palace, going on to explain about the events at the palace and of the name Captain Britzeldah had given his sword. There was a knock at the door, which when opened revealed Captain Bel.

The captain said, "I would be grateful if you can come to my room, Ruben, and would you be good enough to ask your wife to request that the innkeeper send us some wine and a couple of goblets." Ruben quickly introduced him to Lialah who said that it was a pleasure to finally be introduced to him, as Ruben had often spoken about him, and that he was very handsome and she would bring the wine herself. He said, "I am delighted to meet you Lialah, and you certainly are as attractive as Latich and that odious wretch, the Assyrian king, said that you were. Indeed, you had to be something special to pinch one of my most promising young Guardsmen." He then turned to Ruben and said, "But come along Ruben, we have work to do." He then left, going back to his own room, with Ruben following closely behind.

When they were both seated in his room at either side of the table on which the map was unrolled, the captain said, "Do not worry, my friend, there is no problem about your leaving the Guards. But I would like to know exactly how you left Sousa, only Latich did not have a chance to tell me about that, if he ever knew." So Ruben told him exactly what had happened at Sousa and of how he left the battlefield undetected by night, his journey down to the sea, of finding the boat, which he rowed into the marshlands and sank, to ensure that he could not be traced. He then offered to pay for the boat. But the captain laughed, and said, "My goodness, that is an incredible story. You have more than covered the cost of one small rowing boat by what you have done here at Ashkilon."

"Thank you very much, sir," said Ruben.

"And that is another thing," said the captain. "You can stop calling myself and the other officers, sir. Remember you are now a mercenary, to whom seniority means nothing. You must just call me Bel, like all my other friends, or just my rank."

Lailah then knocked on the door, and when it was answered came in with the wine. As she put the goblets on the table in front of both men and filled each from the pitcher, which she carried and then set on the floor, Captain Bel said to her, "I am particularly glad that the Assyrian king did not get his hands on you. We must keep all our flowers here in Babylon." She blushed at the captain's kind remark, saying that he was charming and a pleasure to serve. She then departed, with their thanks. The captain then asked Ruben which was the strongest wall. Ruben told him that he had only fought on the northern wall, as the fighting had been fiercer there, due to it being closer to the Assyrian army's encampment. But he believed the north wall was probably stronger, as it was higher than parts of the southern wall, due to the proximity of the hills on the southern bank of the river.

"That is worth knowing," said the captain. "Now would you go and ask the two lieutenants to join us. They are in the room to your right."

"Yes most certainly, um, Bel," and then Ruben paused and shuffled his feet rather awkwardly. "I did not actually leave the Guards to be with Lialah, but we met at Ur, where we had previously become good friends."

"Yes, I remember now," chuckled the captain. "But it is always wise to tell women that they are very important. Remember that for future reference," laughed the captain.

Ruben went next door and returned with the two lieutenants. On re-entering the captain's room, Ruben said, "Do you still need me, Captain?"

"Yes please, Ruben, if you could bring two more chairs and two more goblets, as we should share this excellent wine." They were soon all seated around the captain's table, each with a goblet of wine that the captain himself filled from the pitcher. Pointing to the south wall on the map the captain said, "I believe that the Assyrians may well put all their forces into one large attack, just here above the palace, as it appears that this is the city's most vulnerable point. That being the case, they will have to ferry most of their troops across the river. Can you check with the lookouts on the wall, to see if they are moving more troops to the south bank, Ruben?"

"Yes, I can do that, as I know the lookouts by now," Ruben replied.

"In that case, we will attack their base camp on the north bank," said the captain. "If I am not right, we will simply redirect our attack to the party on the south bank. But I think I will be proved correct."

"Will it mean a great difference to our plans?" enquired the lieutenant, who was new to Ruben, but had been introduced shortly before as Lieutenant Jezraal, who was a specialist bowman.

"No, not at all, Lieutenant," said the captain. "Our basic plan will be identical, but simply on the other side of the river. Either way we will be attacking the smaller force and will attack just before dawn, hopefully with the element of surprise. Do not forget that although we have a full battalion, we will still be largely outnumbered. But as you know, that is so often the case."

"Are you going to use the same strategy that we used when we killed the Assyrian king and his retinue, when we were with the old general just west of Zohab?" enquired Lieutenant Abzher, adding, "That is hardly original, sir."

"No, not really," said the captain. "The idea will be similar, but remember, the Assyrians have no idea that there are any Guards here, which was why I demanded the galley to row through the night. So we should not have been seen and they will not be expecting an attack so soon." Ruben was surprised to hear this criticism coming from the Lieutenant, speaking to his captain more as an equal. However, Captain Bel did not seem perturbed about the criticism. Ruben soon realised that the captain encouraged all his officers to voice their thoughts.

"The plan I have in mind," the captain was continuing, "is similar, but as we have Lieutenant Jezraal and his bowmen, I intend to use them to outflank the Assyrian force, and then to shoot at them from the northeast. Half of the arrows are to be lighted brands, to set fire to their tents and equipment. Is that all right with you, Jezraal?" He looked enquiringly at the lieutenant.

"That sounds fine, sir," replied Lieutenant Jezraal, adding, "Particularly if the ground is soft, which will muffle our footfalls."

"You need have no worry about that," interjected Ruben. "It seems very green, and there was another light shower of rain last night. The only problem that we may have is if the rain really starts, which is indeed a possibility, which would nullify the effect of the flaming arrows."

"Yes, that's a good point," said Captain Bel. "In which case do not use flaming brands. The effect will still be good, if not so dramatic." Pausing for thought, he then continued. "After each bowman has released ten arrows, and I want a signal flaming arrow sent directly into the sky at that time, we will attack with javelin and sword from the east. Then the bowmen will retreat around to cover our rear. Is everyone happy with that?" He looked enquiringly from face to face, and seeing no dissent, he continued. "Ruben, you can fight alongside me as I want to see that wonderful sword in action."

"Abzher and I will go and brief the sergeant, sir," said Lieutenant Jezraal.

"Hold on Jez, let's drink to that," said Lieutenant Abzher. So they finished the pitcher of wine drinking a toast to the plan, which they all thought suitable.

Captain Bel then said to the lieutenants, "You go and brief your sergeants on the plan, but instruct them to keep the details secret. Then send them to their men and instruct them to have their men rested and fully equipped, ready for action at midnight. Tell them that no purple uniforms must be seen on the city's walls. We can then all meet down by the floating bridge. I will make a few notes for the commander, but before I take the plan to him I will see you for a midday meal with the innkeeper, which will be ready shortly."

As the two lieutenants left his room he turned to Ruben and said, "You had better tell Lialah that we will be going into action shortly after midnight, but you will be with me, so she should not worry. But tell her that she must keep well away from the south wall tomorrow morning. Then could you please hurry down to the lookout on the walls by the river, and ask them to keep a watch on all that is happening upriver."

When they met for a midday meal at the inn, much to Lialah's surprise and delight, Captain Bel insisted that instead of serving she should join them, seated between Ruben and himself. He talked to her and Ruben about the Hanging Gardens and all about flowers, on which subject she was surprised to learn that he was very knowledgeable. He also knew a lot about the marshlands, as he had a brother living in Larsa whom he visited whenever possible. He was fascinated to hear about Simeon's floating reed house in which they had travelled from Ur to Kish, and mentioned that he had heard that people had said the marshlands were moving further south. Ruben told him that Simeon believed that this was happening and told him about the tree that he had made his javelin from, whose leaves indicated that it came from a tree that was new to the area.

Captain Bel said, "I would like to see this javelin of yours. Does it have a large bronze point?"

"No, it is an iron knife blade that had a broken handle," Ruben explained, "which I lashed to the javelin."

"Presumably it is fairly light?" enquired the captain.

"Yes, it is," replied Ruben. "I will show it to you after the meal," he added eagerly.

"It will have to wait until I have returned from seeing the commander," said Captain Bel. "But I shall look forward to seeing it later this afternoon."

After the meal, when Ruben and Lialah had returned to their room, she scolded him, saying, "Trust you to turn the subject around to talking about weapons."

"That was accidental," said Ruben defensively. "Apart from which, javelin throwing is an interest that we both share."

"You soldiers are all the same, but I suppose you will never change." She sighed, but then brightened up. "Can we go for a walk around the city walls this afternoon?"

"After the captain returns," replied Ruben. "I am sure it will be safe."

Shortly after they had been talking about Captain Bel, there was a knock on the door and when Ruben opened it, the man himself was there. Ruben asked him to come in and went to where he had the javelin still wrapped in a blanket, which made it look like a staff. The captain was impressed by its lightness and balance. He bet Ruben three gold coins that he could throw the javelin further than Ruben. Ruben said he would willingly take him up on the bet and gladly take his money.

The captain laughed at Ruben's confidence and said, "After we have seen the Assyrian dogs off, I will give you a javelin throwing lesson that you will never forget, you cheeky scamp." He then left them to go for their walk around the city walls, advising them that it was quite safe at the moment and he would be grateful if Ruben could check what was happening upriver by asking the lookouts. He also said that although there should be no Babylonian Guards on the walls, it would be as well if Ruben could make himself clear to the enemy, so that they would not expect his collusion with the Babylonian Guards.

Ruben and Lialah left the inn and walked to the eastern end of the southern wall down by the riverbank. They then climbed up the steps to the top of the wall, and walked to the west along the battlements. There were a lot of soldiers on the battlements who nodded and saluted Ruben as he passed with Lialah clinging to him tightly, as if to say, this is my man, he belongs to me. The battlements passed over a stout wooden gate, which was studded with large bronze nails and secured by a huge stone buttress. This buttress could be moved aside, but only by two men pushing on its counterbalance. They soon reached the western end of the wall and Ruben asked the lookouts what had been happening up river.

The lookout replied, "There seems to be quite a lot of activity upriver, sir. We believe that the Assyrians are moving more troops to the south bank."

"Thank you," responded Ruben. "I think they will probably attack the south wall in a concerted effort tomorrow morning around dawn."

"Yes, sir, that certainly seems possible," said the lookout.

Lailah and Ruben then went down the steps to the riverbank and walked to the floating bridge. As they walked onto the bridge the guard at the end saluted Ruben. They saw that at every ten paces there was a bowman keeping watch upriver, and if the Assyrian boats came within range of their bows, it was fired upon. As they walked on, Lialah asked him what had given him the idea for the bridge. He told her that it was probably a combination of being on Simeon's floating reed house, his uncle being a boat builder and him seeing some children leaping from log to log in the marshlands in Uruk when he and Ishmala were repairing the raft. They continued across the bridge and then walked northwest back to the city wall on the northern bank. When they walked up the steps to the battlements, Sergeant Mustala, who trusted that his uncle was treating them well at the inn, greeted them. They told him they were being treated extremely well, not only themselves, but also all the Babylonian Guard officers had complimented his uncle on the comfort of the inn. They reached the part on the battlements where Ruben had rescued Captain Britzeldah and he pointed out the blood from the battle that had not been completely washed away. They continued all the way around, over a similar gateway to that on the southern wall, and at the end of the wall beside the river on its northern bank, they found a ferryman to row them across to the southern bank for a couple of brass coins. The walk had taken all the afternoon, and the sun was beginning to set in the west as they returned to the inn.

On entering the inn, Ruben went straight to see Captain Bel, whilst Lialah went to their room. On reaching the captain's room, Ruben was about to knock, when the door opened in front of him and Lieutenant Abzher stood in the doorway and said, "We were just talking about you. Have you got any news about what is happening upriver?"

"Yes, that is what I came to tell the captain," Ruben replied. The door was then fully opened and he was ushered inside. "It appears that you are perfectly correct in your assumption, Captain. The Assyrians have been moving troops across the river most of the day, so I mentioned to the lookout that they were probably planning an assault on the south wall early tomorrow."

Captain Bel smiled. "Just as I anticipated," he grinned. "It is simply a matter of knowing your enemy. Just like their old king, they always go for the weakest, and never look over their shoulder. Thank you Ruben, for the information. Now do not bring your new javelin tonight, as we will have no time for retrieving any weapons, like javelins or arrows. We have plenty to spare and I will be able to provide you with three, I hope we will be able to collect them when the Assyrians leave with their tail between their legs, like the dogs that they are."

"Will I see you downstairs for dinner this evening, Bel?" enquired Ruben, the captain's first name now becoming easier.

"Probably yes, but it is wise not to eat a large dinner before going into action, as it often tends to make you drowsy," said the captain advisedly.

"That is perfectly correct," added Lieutenant Abzher. "There is nothing like a little hunger to sharpen the senses."

"I will remember that," said Ruben as he left them, returning to his own room.

When he came in he noticed that Lialah was wearing another of her new dresses and looked quite stunning. Noticing his look, she said, "Do you approve?" twirling round for his inspection.

"Yes, my dearest." He came over and gave her a kiss. "You look most attractive, as always, but tonight's dinner will not be a grand affair, as we have to go into action later tonight. So none of the Guards will be eating a large meal and alcohol will not be drunk, after which most of the officers will retire to their rooms in order to have a rest."

Her face fell. "But the captain will be there I trust?" she enquired.

"Oh yes," he replied, adding, "You are rather fond of him, aren't you?"

"Well yes, he is nice, but you are still my favourite," she said, blushing coyly. "Anyway, if you have a wash, I will brush your hair again. It is such a mess." He submitted to her request without argument, and they then went to dinner.

During that evening, the dinner was a quiet occasion; all the officers seemed to be preoccupied with their own thoughts. Lialah tried to brighten the conversation and asked Captain Bel when the next army championships were to be held, and would he be trying to defend his javelin throwing title.

The captain said, "Oh, it will be quite a long way off and I had not really thought about it, but I suppose I will. I doubt if there is anyone good enough to give me a serious challenge," he said, grinning at Ruben.

"No doubt you will retain your title, but only because I will not be at the meeting," responded Ruben, quite nonchalantly. However, apart from this light-hearted exchange the meal passed in a sombre mood. The men drifted off one by one to their rooms. After a while even Captain Bel took his leave, apologising to Lialah as he went, saying that the men were often very quiet before going into a battle. But he said, "That is a good sign, as overconfidence is a great danger. But do not worry; I am sure everything will work out fine. Ruben will be at my side tonight and I will not let him do anything foolish." He winked at Ruben as he left the room, returning to his own quarters.

Ruben only picked at his food and then pushed the plate to one side and left the room with Lialah, going back to their own room. Once inside she said to him, "You normally eat twice as much as everyone else. Why is everyone so worried?"

"It is not that people are worried, they are just cautious. Whenever you go into battle there are a lot of things that you cannot predict or allow for. Particularly during a night action. There is always a lot of confusion and it is only sensible to remain calm and clear headed," he explained.

Lialah shivered and said, "I have a premonition that something terrible will happen."

"Do not be so silly," said Ruben. "Since when have you started having premonitions? I am sure it is just the quiet atmosphere that is making you concerned. Tonight should be easier than yesterday and the day before. Attacking is always easier than defending and we have the element of surprise on our side. So do not worry about us, remember what the captain said, he really is an excellent soldier." Ruben took off his jerkin and sword belt and lay on the bed.

Lialah lay beside him and put her arms around him, saying, "I cannot help being worried, it is only natural to be concerned about someone you love."

Her closeness and the warmth of her body began to arouse Ruben and he ended up making extremely passionate but tender love to her. As he covered her nakedness with a single cover, he saw that her pregnancy was beginning to show. Her breasts, always well proportioned, were now beginning to enlarge and the nipples darkened and became more pronounced, apart from which her waist was beginning to visibly enlarge. She was soon breathing evenly in her sleep, so he quietly rose from the bed, dressed in his black uniform, laced up his jerkin, put on all his armament and quietly left the room, extinguishing the oil lamp.

He met Captain Bel on his way to the front door. The captain gave him a javelin holder with three of the new javelins suspended from it. He slung this over his shoulder as he went outside into the cool night air. The night was moonless and heavy with cloud although it remained dry. Captain Bel asked the lieutenants if the sergeants had gone to fetch their men, and confirmed that they had instructed them their passage was to be silent and unlit by torches. They then made their way down to the floating bridge to where all their men were assembled. As they walked along, Captain Bel turned to Ruben and asked, "Have you felt the weight of these new iron pointed javelins?"

"Yes," said Ruben. "They certainly seem a lot heavier than the old bronze ones."

"Yes, that's correct," said the captain. "I always find that it is best to hold them slightly nearer the sharp end when you throw them. That way they tend to fly better, but of course you have to use a lot more force."

"That's a very good tip, I will certainly bear it in mind," said Ruben.

When they had reached the floating bridge, and Captain Bel had checked that everyone was present, he started to usher the men in single file across the floating bridge and through the silent streets of the northern bank up towards the main gate in the city walls. Apart from the occasional muted wishes of "best of luck" that came from the soldiers who were keeping watch on the river, the passage was quiet. When they reached the city gates in the northern wall, the captain called the two lieutenants and Ruben to his side. He told them Lieutenant Jezraal would take two thirds of the bowmen and proceed directly from the gates in a northerly direction until they reached the trees just beside the main road that ran parallel to the river. Once there they would proceed in a Northwesterly direction to encircle the Assyrian encampment beside the river. The remainder of the battalion would proceed alongside the city walls until they reached the river. Here they would leave the remaining bowmen to cover their retreat after the attack. He and the rest of the men would then creep quietly beside the river until they were within fifty paces of the Assyrian encampment.

Lieutenant Jezraal and his party quickly and noiselessly left the main party, moving stealthily towards the trees that were just a dark outline to the north. They were soon swallowed up in the darkness. Captain Bel waited for a short period and then led the rest of the battalion westwards along the city wall, until they could just make out and hear the gurgle of the river in front of them. Here again they waited completely unnoticed by even the soldiers patrolling the wall above. Then moving stealthily parallel to the river, but keeping away from the bank lest anyone blundered into the water and made a commotion that would alert the Assyrian guards. They could soon make out the Assyrian encampment, with its guards standing beneath lit torches, and a few of the sleepless Assyrians who were still sitting by campfires drinking rough wine. They stealthily approached to within hearing distance of the all night revellers. They then lay or squatted on the damp grass, and it seemed to Ruben, who was becoming impatient, that they had to wait for simply ages. He was beginning to get stiff and the night sky to the east was showing the first signs of the approaching dawn. When across the river and nearer to the city, horns began to blare and the sound of a large assault being mounted against the city was distinctly heard. At almost the same time there was the sound of the thwack of arrows striking resistant flesh and bone and the startled cries of pain, and then flaming arrows were seen curving down into the Assyrian encampment. When they struck their intended targets, which was considerably often, tents and other equipment were soon ablaze. More arrows flew in to the awakening Assyrians, bringing anguished cries of pain from the dying and injured men. Further flaming arrows rained down on the encampment, bringing confusion and uproar, which increased and intermingled with the sound of battle coming from behind them. Eventually a flaming brand hurtled directly skyward to arc in a parabola and fell into the confused tumult that was previously a well-ordered encampment. On that signal, Captain Bel leapt to his feet and sent his first javelin hurtling with devastating accuracy into a confused guard who was trying to make up his mind what to do. Immediately Ruben and the others followed the captain's example, not only hurling javelins, but also attacking with drawn swords, cutting down the bewildered Assyrians. Ruben's final javelin was hurled into a burning tent where scrambling figures were trying to arm themselves. It struck its intended target and the man sprawled backwards onto his companions. Drawing his sword and charging beside Captain Bel he swung the sword at an Assyrian shield that was raised in defence. The sword split the shield and continued until it met the flesh and bone of the arm behind it. There was a yell of pain and Ruben withdrew the sword only to plunge it point first into the agonised defender. Suddenly there was an anguished cry of recognition, the Assyrian expert horseman had been in the camp and recognised Captain Bel.

"Fly friends, run while you can, the king's slayer is amongst us."

Another shout of, "and the bright flame of the east" soon joined this. The carnage was great and the blood of the dead and dying soon darkened the ground. The slaughter had been brief but extensive and the attack on the south wall of Ashkilon had been called off as boatloads of Assyrian troops rowed back to the flaming encampment. Captain Bel called off the attack at that moment, and Lieutenant Jezraal and his bowmen joined the retreating Babylonian swordsmen. Arrows that were shot from the remaining bowmen just to the west of the city covered their retreat. Captain Bel and his retreating Guardsmen were soon back below the city walls and amid great shouts of triumph that came from the soldiers high up on the battlements. The sun was rising high above the city and they could now see the devastation they had wrought. Also it showed the startled faces of the retreating Assyrians from the south of the city, where they were hurrying back to their boats in order to row to the aid of their colleagues.

\*\*\*\*

Nozgrarot, Tiglath-Pileser's cousin, led the Assyrian army as Tiglath-Pileser's only male children were not yet old enough to bear arms. The chains across the river had frustrated this general, and the floating bridge, which had prevented an assault downriver by small crafts that he had planned in addition to attacking the walls. His original attack on the north wall had only just failed. Now, as the south wall was far easier to assault, he had decided to put all his forces behind one massive attack, which he felt sure was going to succeed. Even though the Babylonians in Ashkilon had received reinforcements, these had been from the ordinary army, and none of the Babylonian Guards, who were renowned for their ferocity. He believed that all the Guards were elsewhere protecting their borders. He knew that the plan lacked originality, but felt certain that it would succeed. Thus allowing his men the opportunity to plunder the city, capture the galleys and open Babylon's back door.

Nozgrarot had been taken across the river to personally supervise the attack just before dawn. Although he realised that the Babylonians were probably ready to meet his attack, he did have one new weapon that they had not previously encountered. The Assyrians had now trained large numbers of discus throwers, which the Babylonians had previously never faced. Even though they may have faced the occasional discus, this weapon had never been used en masse. He felt sure that constant bombardment of the battlements would allow his forces time to scale the walls. His troops would attempt to scale one wall in many different places. This would surely deliver the city into his grasp, despite fierce resistance from one powerful mercenary whose very presence seemed to terrify his men. His troops were now ready for battle, so as the trumpets blared their challenge, his troops advanced with the shields held high, interlocking against the arrows that they knew would rain down from the battlements. He had previously looked back across the river to see his base camp was all quiet, and now looked forward to feasting at Commander Mithrandir's table and of making his wives into his whores.

He kept his discus throwers back until they were within easy distance of the battlements. He was prepared to sacrifice some of the vanguard of his army to get close. He was met, firstly by a duel of bowmen, which his troops lost, but still advanced over their fallen. And then by javelin, which they also lost, relentlessly advancing, heedlessly trampling their own dead and dying. He had just grabbed a discus, he himself, he was a big man and was an expert with the weapon, when one of his captains pulled his arm. He turned to see the signal arrow as it rose high in the sky before plummeting into his already devastated base camp. He had no alternative but to call off the assault and race back to rescue his essential belongings. In a bellow of rage he hurled the discus at the battlements. He soon realised that the cheering that was coming from the battlements, were really jeers at his own folly. He then joined his own troops in their race back to their boats.

****

Lialah awoke while it was still dark, she knew that there was still a long time before dawn and she thought back to yesterday. After her initial disappointment concerning the dinner in the evening it had worked out to be a pleasant evening and she had slept very well after their lovemaking. But where was Ruben at the moment, and what was he doing? This naturally worried her, making the prospect of returning to sleep quite impossible. After lying awake for some considerable time, she heard movements from elsewhere in the building. Realising that someone else, probably the innkeeper and his wife were awake and active, she got out of bed, quickly dressed and left the room in search of company. The innkeeper and his wife were in the kitchen, preparing a large breakfast, which the captain had ordered for their return. As she came into the lighted room, the innkeeper said that he was not surprised to see her.

"I can well imagine that you were unable to sleep, due to your young man being involved in everything that is going on. My wife and I were just talking about you. You have probably come to realise that I am a man of plain speaking, so I will come straight to the point that I wish to raise. As soon as this battle is over, and it certainly looks as if the Babylonian

Guards will see off the Assyrian dogs, Ashkilon will once again be busy. There will be a lot of people returning, plus a lot of other visitors, which is always the way after battles. Now we understand that your young man is pledged to go further into the west, but no doubt you do not wish to go with him, bearing in mind your pregnancy." She was about to reply, when he put up his hand to stem her protest. "I did not notice it, myself, but my wife did. You women seem to have a way of communicating without speaking," he chuckled. This was a long speech for him, as he was normally quiet and only spoke out of necessity and was certainly not a gossip. Continuing, he said, "What my wife and I were wondering, was if you would like to stay with us, obviously working whilst you can. You see, my wife realised that you must have worked in an inn before, as you know what to do. Then you can have your baby here in Ashkilon, waiting until your young man returns or makes plans for you to join him." Pausing to allow this offer to register with her, he then said, "It will be doing us a favour as a pretty girl like you is always popular with the guests." He looked at her smiling, but feeling slightly embarrassed – it had taken him a long time, as well as a lot of prompting from his wife, to make the offer.

"Oh gosh, that is such a surprise," she said. "I really don't know what to say. It certainly is a kind offer and could well be the answer to a problem that we have been reluctant to discuss. But would it be convenient if I do not say yes immediately, as I would like to discuss the idea with Ruben first?"

"Yes, my child, that will be fine!" said the innkeeper's wife.

During the latter part of this conversation, the sound of battle had penetrated from the south wall, followed by lots of cheering from the battlements. All three of them went outside into the early dawn to try to work out what was happening.

"It sounds very much like a victory to me," said the innkeeper. "I shouldn't wonder if the Babylonian Guards will not shortly be returning." Unable to retain her curiosity, Lialah walked in the direction of the south wall, completely ignoring Captain Bel's advice. She came to the corner from where she could just see the steps leading to the battlements of the south wall. She turned the corner just as General Nozgrarot's hurled discus flew over the battlements and came spinning to earth, where it struck her a glancing blow on the head. A glancing blow from a heavy discus hurled with considerable force, can be destructive. It knocked her out and she collapsed on the ground. Captain Britzeldah, who was on the battlements, being transferred from the north wall due to his injury, saw exactly what happened. He had instantly recognised Lialah as Ruben's wife. As he was concerned for her well-being, he limped down as quickly as his heavily bandaged leg allowed, and lifted the unconscious girl. He was pleased that she was still breathing evenly and that the discus had not cut her head in any place, and he hoped that she was only temporarily stunned. Nonetheless, he thought it better to take her directly to the best physician that he knew, which was of course in the palace. He carried the unconscious girl in his arms and walked straight into the palace. There he met Commander Mithrandir, who also recognised Lialah and was equally concerned and told the captain to lay her on the couch, while he sent for the physician, asking Britzeldah, "What on earth happened?" As soon as Britzeldah informed him what had occurred, but assured him that he considered it not serious, the doctor arrived so that Captain Britzeldah had to repeat the entire story of the incident. The physician confirmed what Britzeldah had said and completely agreed with him, saying that she would wake up fairly soon with an intensive headache, but apart from keeping watch over her there would probably be nothing seriously wrong.

The officers of the Babylonian Guard then returned, entering the room, very pleased with themselves, full of mutual congratulation and speaking of their exploits, which had devastated the Assyrian encampment. Captain Bel came to attention in front of Commander Mithrandir. "Mission successfully completed, sir," he said smiling, and then continued, "with comparatively few losses, just two dead and three wounded, sir."

"That really is very good, Captain," said the commander, "and by the sound of the cheering on the walls and the hasty Assyrian retreat from the south wall, it sounds like you inflicted some serious damage."

While this exchange was going on, the other officers were chatting and milling about in the room. Suddenly Ruben spotted Lialah lying on the couch and rushed over to where she lay, and held her hand, kneeling beside her just as she awoke, blinking her eyes and holding her head in her other hand saying, "What happened, where am I, why is my head so painful?"

"I have no idea," said Ruben, hastily looking around for someone to give him details of why she was there.

Captain Britzeldah came forward and said, "She was knocked out by a flying discus near the south wall." Looking rather relieved that she was now awake, he went on to explain. "It may have been the last weapon that was used in the battle, but it was purely by accident that you were hit, and fortunately it was only a glancing blow."

"But my head pounds so savagely," groaned Lialah.

"You will be all right, my dearest," said Ruben, looking much relieved and adding, "Lay still for a while, the pain will probably ease shortly."

"But Ruben, I have such exciting news to tell you," she went on, ignoring her discomfort. "The innkeeper and his wife have asked me to stay at the inn, where I can have the baby. Isn't that wonderful?" She said this and then lay back and closed her eyes saying, "You can now go on your quest." Finally adding in a barely audible whisper, "I hope you find your father." Her head then slowly sank back on the cushion as if she were asleep.

Still holding her hand, Ruben said, "I think I have already found him." To which there was no answer. He then thought her asleep and so did the others in the room except for the physician, who noticed the tiny trickle of blood coming from her ear and that she had stopped breathing.

All the talking had ceased and everyone was gathered anxiously around the couch. The physician said, "I am afraid she has gone. That blow to her head must have caused internal bleeding."

"No, she cannot be dead," protested Ruben severely. "She is just asleep, I will take her back to the inn." And with that he started to lift her off the couch, but was restrained by Captain Bel, who had to use all his strength to stop Ruben from lifting her, and gently laid her back. Ashen faced, Ruben walked out of the palace, returning towards the inn. Captain Bel hurried after him and fell in beside Ruben as it began to rain. As they walked along, Ruben said, "It is all right Captain, I know the way."

Captain Bel turned to look at Ruben and thought at first that he was crying, but soon realised that his eyes were dry and it was the rain on his face, not tears. The captain then left Ruben to walk back to the inn, as he had to return to the palace to complete his report to the commander. On his return, he found that Lialah's body had been taken by the physician to the embalmers, under orders from the commander to preserve her body. Captain Bel then finished his report and with his officers returned to the inn, all in a far more sober mood.

As they entered the inn, the innkeeper greeted them saying, "I have a special breakfast already prepared for you, I am sure that you must have a good appetite, so please go and eat without worrying about having to clean yourselves up."

"That is very considerate, and we certainly will take you up on your kind offer," said Captain Bel, ushering his officers into the dining area. He himself took his place, but noted the absence of Ruben.

Lieutenant Abzher also noticed the empty place and said, "Would you like me to go and invite him to join us?"

Thinking about it, the captain said, "No, I think we had better leave him for the time being, to mourn his loss. If he has not appeared when we have finished, I will go and see him myself." They all tucked in with relish and renewed appetites and had soon finished off all the food. Captain Bel then said, "You have all done very well, so you can now go and catch up on some well-earned sleep. But be ready again by nightfall, in case we are needed again." He followed them out, but rather than going to his own room he went along to Ruben's.

He knocked on the door, but met with no answer so he knocked again, equally in vain. He therefore opened the door quietly and went inside, only to find the room empty, except for Lialah's things, and a note on the table that was weighed down with a large number of gold coins. In bewildered amazement he read the message that was addressed to him. It told him that Ruben had now gone on his quest and was sorry that he could not wait and say goodbye. The money was to pay for Lialah's embalming and transportation down river, where her body should be weighted and sunk in her beloved marshlands. But if Commander Mithrandir said that the money could come from his service as a mercenary, Captain Bel was to inform him that he should have been fighting for them as a Babylonian Guard – so his services need not be paid for. It finally went on to request that Captain Bel should please supervise this request, and he was sorry that he would not have the opportunity to out-throw the captain in a javelin contest. It was just signed with a large R. Cursing himself, the captain picked up the letter and the money, threw a cloak over his shoulders and hurried down to the palace.

\*\*\*\*

On his return to the inn, Ruben hastily packed his bag; he quickly wrote the letter to Captain Bel, which he weighed down with approximately two thirds of his remaining money. Leaving the inn quietly by the back door he made his way through the empty streets to the east end of the south wall. It was now raining heavily and there were few soldiers on the battlements at this end of the wall. Gaining the battlements, he moved along the wall to where it was about three times his own height, where he lowered the heavy bag and his staff on a length of rope that he had tucked into the bag. It quietly reached the ground and he jumped down after it, landing noiselessly like a cat on the wet ground. This was unnoticed by any of the soldiers, the majority of whom were nearer to the western end of the south wall.

He walked on, having retrieved his bag and staff, and headed in a southwesterly direction before turning again towards the west, keeping parallel to the river, but almost out of sight of the city walls, which were often obscured by squalls of rain. Then he walked northwards to the riverbank, hardly noticing the large number of dead Assyrians that littered the battlefield. Their blood had been washed into the river, where it had attracted some of the large crocodiles, which had boldly come ashore to drag some of the already putrefying corpses back to their lairs, where they would feast later on the rotting meat.

He could just make out the far bank where the remaining Assyrians were stowing their equipment onto their last unburned carts, which were then drawn northwesterly in the direction of Nineveh. He noticed the large man sitting on a black horse. It was General Nozgrarot who had a large plaited beard, very much like that of the now dead Tiglath-Pileser and who looked directly at him. It seemed that they were barely ten paces apart, despite the mighty river flowing between them, and the large man shook his fist at Ruben, before turning his horse to follow the remnants of his bedraggled army. With a heavy sigh, Ruben turned upriver to where the first cataract fell tumbling down the cliff. He then walked northeast, looking for somewhere to scale the cliff, the top of which was almost hidden in the low cloud and spray from the falls.

# 15
# "SKREE"

Captain Bel reached the palace and shook the rain from his cloak. It looked as if the rain had now started in earnest and that in itself would put a stop to any further attacks from the Assyrians, if indeed they had not already left. Leaving his cloak in the hall and entering the main chamber, he came face to face with Commander Mithrandir.

"Back so soon?" asked the commander. "I thought you would be catching up on some sleep."

"Indeed I should," said the irritated captain. "But I think you should read this." He handed the letter, complete with the money, to the commander, telling him, "Ruben has left the inn and this farewell note is all that I found."

The commander read swiftly. "Presumably he has not been gone long?" he asked.

"Not for very long, sir," replied the captain. "Although I doubt if we could find him in this weather."

"No, I think you are correct, apart from which I don't really think that we should go after him," said the commander. "But with regard to the money, we cannot accept it, it is the least we can do for him. I would do that for any of my command."

"And I will certainly carry out his wishes," responded the captain.

"But can you fill me in on what you know of him?" asked the commander. So both men sat down and the commander ordered a couple of goblets of wine, as this was obviously going to be a long tale.

The captain told him everything he knew about Ruben, right from the time that he had caught him at Ur. He told of how nobody could verify Ruben's age, but even he was unsure himself, although he was sure that he had not yet been twelve years old, and too young for the army. He went on to finish the story, which took the rest of the morning. He finished by saying, "To be honest, I still think he has not finished growing, and I think if it came to it he would probably out-throw me in a javelin contest."

"Yes, he certainly is a remarkable young man. To be fair, he saved the city. He and Lialah were indeed a grand pair, and it is a very sad day for him. But, we have our jobs to do. I have a city to govern, and you have a battalion to command," said the commander, adding, "I do not think that it is a story that ends here, and I believe we may hear more of him."

"I certainly hope you are correct, sir," responded the captain.

They were interrupted at that moment, as another soldier walked over to the commander. "Excuse me, sir," said the intruder. "But the scouts that you sent out to reconnoitre, have just returned," he explained. "Would you like to see them now?"

"Ah, yes please, we have almost finished and I am sure that the Captain would like to hear their report as well," came the reply. As the soldier walked away to bring in the scouts, the commander turned to Captain Bel and said, "My lookouts informed me that it looked like the Assyrians were moving away. So I sent out a couple of scouts to check on this information, to ensure that they have completely withdrawn."

Two scouts walked over, looking as if they had only just returned, as they were soaking wet and mud spattered. One of them said, "It is as you expected, sir. They appear to have completely left, they loaded their equipment into their remaining serviceable ox-wagons shortly after midmorning and appear to be headed back to Nineveh."

"Presumably you followed them?" enquired the commander.

"Yes, sir, for quite a distance and they showed no evidence of returning," said the scout.

"Very good," responded the commander. "You can now return to the barracks to clean up." He then turned to Captain Bel and said, "Just as I had hoped. You see, the ground that they were camping on will soon become flooded as the waters come down from the mountains and the river level rises."

As the scouts were leaving the room, they had a brief exchange of words, and one of them turned back to the commander. He said, "There was something else, sir, we were fairly sure that they were led by General Nozgrarot, who was the last to leave, and he seemed to be shaking his fist at someone on the south bank. Now, we are not sure as we were under cover in the trees and it was quite a long way off, but we think it may have been the mercenary who fought with us on the walls, and then with the Guards."

"Yes, that is quite possible," said the commander. "Thank you for that observation." Turning back to Captain Bel he said, "Well I should imagine if that was Ruben, which certainly seems a possibility, he is probably well away by now."

"Yes, and it appears that you may not be requiring our services any longer," the captain observed.

"That seems probable," replied the commander. "But I would be grateful if you could stay for a few days, just to be sure."

"That I will be happy to do, and if I may, I will send my men out to patrol the area, as it is unwise to leave them unoccupied," said the captain. Standing up, he said, "I will now go back and get some sleep, but will return later this evening to discuss how we proceed with the search."

"That is excellent, Captain, I will send an urgent message to the king to inform him that it looks as if the city is now safe," he said smiling. "But this will only be a preliminary report, and if it is confirmed, will you return to give him further details?"

"Of course, that sounds ideal, sir, but I was wondering if you are going to mention anything about Ruben in your report," the captain asked.

After a long pause, the commander said, "I think not. There may be a few questions to answer later, particularly about the chains and the floating bridge, which I should like to, but we will tell the king about Ruben only if he asks."

"I think that is wise, Commander," said Captain Bel. "News may well spread, but we will say nothing unless we are asked. After all, you know the king far better than I do," he said smiling, as he took his leave and returned to the inn.

****

Ruben had to walk for a considerable distance towards the southwest before he found a place to attempt to scale the cliff. Even then his first two attempts ended in failure, as about half way up he ran out of hand and foot holds, and was faced by an unblemished slab of rock. However on his third attempt he was fortunate enough to find a way round this smooth face and could then see his intended route to the top. It had by now almost stopped raining, there being only fine drizzle. He was soaked through and his hands had many minor abrasions. He began tackling the last pitch when a large boulder that he was about to put all his weight on came away from the face revealing a narrow cleft. From that cleft a pair of bright yellow eyes stared indignantly into his face, and an alarming cry of "Skree!" issued forth.

Fortunately, Ruben was well secured, standing with both feet well astride, otherwise he may well have lost his footing in alarm. As it was, he peered back into the gloomy recess of the cleft and could make out that the eyes only moved slightly, as they came from a baby eagle that was wedged into the cleft. He guessed that the bird may have been on its first solo flight, as there were still traces of infant down on its bedraggled plumage, when it was probably caught by a squall rain and blown into the cleft in the cliff face. The bird was well trapped and could not move itself, but he realised that any attempt to free the eagle would probably result in being attacked by the viciously curved beak and the strong sharp talons.

He realised that he could not free the bird, which may be unable to fly and would need to be carried to the top of the cliff. This he was unable to do whilst carrying his bag and staff, without possibly injuring himself. He looked directly into those bright yellow eyes and said, "Wait a short while, little friend, and I will soon return to help you." The eyes blinked back, almost as if saying that it understood, and remembering the exact spot, Ruben continued his climb to the top of the cliff. Putting down his bag and unwrapping the blanket around the javelin, Ruben slung the rolled blanket around his neck and retraced his climb down the cliff to where the bird was trapped. On reaching the place, he unwrapped the blanket, into which he intended to wrap the baby eagle. He then proceeded to carefully release the bird from where it had been wedged. On his touch behind the head, obviously out of reach of the hooked beak, and with his other hand covered by the blanket around the talons, gradually easing the bird, it did squawk and struggle but without resisting, as if it realised that it was being aided. He soon had the bird free and wrapped with its wings folded as neatly as possible in the blanket, with just the eagle's head protruding. He secured the blanket with a leather thong in a sling around his chest where the eagle's beak could only peck at the stout crocodile hide of his jerkin. Very soon he had regained the top of the cliff, and in the remaining light of the late afternoon, he retrieved his bag and javelin and walked back along the cliff top to where the distant falls could be heard.

It had now stopped raining and the dying sun broke through the cloud to the west, as he reached the top of the cataract. It was a magnificent sight as vast quantities of water fell like a vertical river down the cliff-face to crash into the churning river below. This was almost obscured by the spray that rose to the top, where he stood on the bank, looking back down towards Ashkilon, which now seemed like the model of a city. He said to the bird, "We will walk along beside the river before we find somewhere to camp for the night. I hope I will be able to catch a fish and I can then have a look at your damaged wing." He had noticed that the baby eagle had a damaged wing when he wrapped it in the blanket and tried desperately to remember the bone structure of a bird's wing that he had seen in Simeon's museum of birds. Although it contained no eagles, as they were hardly ever seen over marshlands, he knew that most wings would be of similar bone construction.

He strolled along the riverbank, thinking that if he could immobilise the bird's wing, leaving the baby eagle unable to fly would certainly end its life, in either starvation or being food for another predator. He would then have to look after the bird while its wing mended itself, as all broken bones do when allowed. He walked along amid rocky outcrops with small trees and bushes, as the dying sun set above the river, spreading a reflective sheen from the water, brightening the area, bathing everything in a soft yellow light. He finally came to a small inlet where he could make out the shapes of large fish floating just below the surface. This seemed a good place to spend the night, as only fifty paces away there was a rocky outcrop with a large overhanging crag that would give him shelter. Taking his bag and javelin to the rocky outcrop, he placed them on the ground and untied the sling in which the eagle was suspended from his chest. It appeared to him that the eyes no longer looked fierce, but seemed to look appealingly at him. As he laid the baby eagle beside the bag, from which he took out a length of fishing line that he tied to the end of his javelin, he said to the bird, "I will be back soon, with some fish that we can eat. I think I will call you by the name that you gave yourself, Skree."

Hurrying back to the river inlet, because the sun was very quickly disappearing below the river and he only had a few moments of the daylight remaining, Ruben positioned himself at the edge of the inlet looking down to where he had seen the large fish. It was no longer where it had previously been, and as he frantically looked around, shielding his eyes from the dying rays of the sun, a ripple in the water to his right caught his eye, as a large fish moved to where it had spotted an insect alighting on the surface of the water. With the javelin held ready in his right hand he took careful aim, at a point just behind where the insect had touched the water. He waited until the dark shadow of the approaching fish was about to try to swallow the insect in one quick movement raising itself out of the water. He hurled the javelin, which had the fishing line tied to the end, and was delighted to see the javelin penetrate the fish just behind its jaws. There was a tremendous commotion in the water as the fish, which was twice the length of Ruben's outstretched arm, disappeared below the surface of the water and with its final dying movement tried to swim away to deep water, with the javelin still firmly embedded in its head. Ruben quickly stood on the fast disappearing fishing line and was almost pulled off his feet by the strength of the fish. Ruben swiftly grasped the line and began to pull the dying fish towards him. The line initially cut into Ruben's already grazed fingers, which made him wince, but he firmly retained his grasp and the fish was soon lying just below him, now quite dead from the javelin, which still protruded from its head. Leaning down onto his knees he pulled the javelin to where he could hold it just before it entered the fish; he then stood up, pulling the fish out of the water. The tail of the fish brushed the ground even when he held it up to his chin. "What a monster this is!" he declared, thinking that he and Skree would not starve for a couple of days. As he removed the javelin and the dead fish was beginning to change colour, he remembered that it was one of the large fish that he had seen caught at Zohab and previously the same type that came from the sea and were occasionally brought ashore in Lagash. This confirmed what the fisherman in Zohab had told him, that they swam up river and somehow up the cataract. Contemplating this seeming impossibility, he carried the dead fish over his shoulder, returning to the outcrop of rock in the now darkening landscape to where he had left his bag together with the baby eagle.

His return was greeted by a squawk from the baby eagle, whose appetite was heightened by the smell of the fish, which Ruben threw on the ground in front of the bird. Realising that the eagle would be unable to eat whilst wrapped in the blankets, he considered what his next move should be. The eagle would be able to eat the fish raw, but obviously, Ruben preferred his fish cooked. What came first, freeing the eagle, or lighting a fire? He knew that lighting a fire was going to take quite a while, as he doubted whether he would be able to find any dry wood. He decided that the first move should be to free the eagle. Taking the stout leather thong he began to unwrap the blanket to free the bird's talons. This he did carefully to expose only one foot, which on its own could not claw him. Binding the leg with at least three turns of the thong, he secured this to a boulder, which would prevent the bird from trying to fly away. He then carefully unwrapped the bird, immediately standing back, allowing the bird, to stretch its wings and move freely. The baby eagle flapped its still wet wings and hopped around trying to take off into the air, but was unable to do so because of the broken wing and the confinement of the thong. Even in the gathering dusk, Ruben could clearly make out the damaged wing, which Skree soon stopped attempting to flap. Drawing his large sword from its scabbard on his back, Ruben chopped the head off the fish and threw it within easy reach of the eagle. He had by then decided how to go about building a fire, and walked away in search of firewood, looking for a small half dead tree that he had seen earlier. Fortunately the moon rose as he started out, shedding its pale silvery light over the area, which made it easier to find his bearings and he found the tree that he had previously spied. With his large sword the tree was soon felled, and he noticed that the surrounding scrub contained small pieces of fluff on the spiky brambles. Knowing this had come from the fleece of one of the mountain sheep, he plucked off the strands of fluff realising that they would make good kindling material. He dragged the tree back to his camp beneath the overhanging crag and was pleased to note that the baby eagle was still tearing scraps of flesh from the fish head, which it quickly devoured. Using his large sword he chopped the small tree into reasonably handy lengths. Although the surface of the wood was very wet, the inner part and the heart of the wood were quite dry, with little sap as the tree was mainly dead. Putting away his large sword into the scabbard, he withdrew his small bronze knife and sat on a boulder near to Skree and started to shave thin strips from the heartwood. The baby eagle looked at him tilting its head to one side as if to say, 'What on earth are you doing now?'

"You will soon see, my little friend," said Ruben in reply to this imagined question.

Working diligently on the shaving, Ruben had soon whittled down three lengths of wood into a large pile of almost dry shavings. Using a handful of them above the strands of fleece that he had plucked from the thorn brambles. And with this kindling material, he managed to light a fire, which he gradually built up, eventually using the damp wood. The fire naturally alarmed the eagle and it hopped behind the boulder to which it was secured, occasionally peering around the boulder to see what Ruben was doing. This greatly amused Ruben who hoped that Skree would soon become used to fire. He started grilling large steaks from the fish over the fire, which although burning fairly well, was also sending out a lot of smoke. Realising that this could be an advantage, he cut lengths from the fish that he suspended in the smoke so that it would dry and flavour the fish for future consumption. The warmth from the fire soon dried out Ruben's clothes that were beginning to feel uncomfortably wet and cold in the cool breeze that was blowing down from the north.

His meal was soon ready, and until then he had been so preoccupied with establishing the camp he had not realised how hungry he had become. He therefore tucked in to the large steaks of grilled fish as he sat on the boulder, having removed his crocodile hide jerkin. He was pleased to see that the bird had ventured from behind the boulder and was stretching his wings to allow the warmth from the fire to dry his feathers, even though he did not venture very close. Having finished his meal, Ruben stacked the remainder of the logs that he had cut right at the back of the overhanging crag, to ensure that they did not get wet from further showers of rain. He then realised how tired he was as he had been a complete day without sleep. His thoughts went back to the inn at Ashkilon, and it was then that he felt so very sad about the death of Lialah. Trying to put such thoughts to the back of his mind he went over to his bag and extracted his blanket that was comparatively dry, even though most of the contents of the bag had become damp due to the torrential rain. Wrapping the blanket around himself he lay down on the almost dry ground by the dying embers of the fire where he was soon fast asleep, joining the eagle who was standing nearby.

He awoke early in the morning as the grey sky, heavy with rain, was beginning to brighten, but still looked as if it was ready to give him another cruel soaking. In that moment before rising he felt stiff, the grazes on his hands were hurting and his mind flew back to the comfort of Ashkilon and Lialah's warm embrace. It was then that the tears began to fill his eyes, which he tried to brush angrily away, but eventually he gave in and allowed them to flow, as if he was washing away his grief. He was soon brought back to reality by the cries of the baby eagle coming from behind the boulder. Rising to his feet and feeling annoyed with himself at his neglect, he went to find the eagle pathetically trying to straighten its damaged wing, where the broken bone had slightly overlapped and was obviously causing considerable discomfort. Getting the blanket, which had previously wrapped the javelin, he soon had the eagle immobilised and the talons and beak unable to claw or tear at him, by folding them in the blanket. He had previously decided how to immobilise the broken bone, which obviously had to be set before it would mend properly.

Leaving the immobilised bird wrapped in the blanket he quickly went over to the fire and blew the embers into a small blaze, which he fed with some of the now dry wood. He then left the campsite and carrying his helmet as the only convenient container, he ran across to a boggy area near the inlet in which he had caught the fish the previous evening. Here the wet ground was red muddy clay, which he put into his helmet, using scoopfuls of mud gathered with his bare hands. He then had to run across to the inlet, where kneeling down he washed his hands as best he could. Returning with the helmet full of muddy clay, he picked up the eagle and went to work trying to set the broken bone, saying to the bird, "I am sorry, Skree, but this is going to hurt." The bird looked fiercely at him as if to say, 'Well get on with it.' There was a lot of squawking and he had to hold the bird as firmly as possible, but still managed to get fairly badly clawed and lost a chunk out of a finger. But he had straightened the wing as best he could, then using a couple of twigs that he placed either side of the bone, he covered the whole area with large daubs of clay, which he took from his helmet. Much to the eagle's terror, he then took it squawking to the fire where he held the broken wing fairly close to the blaze even letting it scorch some of the bird's feathers. But it performed the necessary task of making a hard cast that kept the wing immobilised. Even though Skree was still squawking in desperate protest, he started to carefully fold the wing and securely wrapped the eagle in the blanket, but this time leaving the talons and head completely free. He then returned the bird and secured it with the thong on its leg, which held it close to the boulder under the shelter of the overhanging crag. He took a pace back to admire his handiwork, and put a log on the ground for the eagle to perch upon, where it indignantly made a lot of noise and pecked at the restraining thong. Ruben sucked the blood that welled from his pecked finger, and said to the bird, "You can make all the fuss you like Skree, but if my work is correct you will soon be able to fly again. But if not, my little friend, I will have to kill you because you will die anyway."

Suddenly becoming aware that the breeze had freshened, and distinctly held the smell of approaching rain, he realised that he had only a short while to gather more firewood and ensure everything was well protected from an approaching storm. Hurrying about the campsite, he hastily put everything beneath the overhang, and slipping on his jerkin and large sword, went in search of another tree. There were quite a few of these small trees in the area, where the rocky ground offered little in the way of nutrients or soil in which to firmly root themselves. Therefore they were somewhat stunted, and often half dead by the end of a hot dry summer. This was to his advantage and he had soon cut down a couple more of the trees, which had a chance to dry out in the breeze before it again began to rain. Ruben had only just returned to the shelter of the overhanging crag, before the heavy drops of rain became a downpour, which was buffeted by the wind that smacked against the overhanging crag. Ruben had chosen his campsite well, as the overhang pointed to the south, which gave quite a large area protected from the rain, which was coming from the north.

When he had dragged the two trees into the shelter, he began to cut them up and add them to the pile of now dry wood, pausing occasionally to throw a few more logs on to the fire, which kept it warm and cheerful. Realising that he may have to stay where he was for a few days until the weather abated, Ruben wondered if there were further improvements he could make that would make it more comfortable. He had noticed that there were many loose rocks and small boulders in the area, and thought that if he could bring these to the overhanging crag, he could build small walls making the site more like a cave. Knowing that getting his clothes wet again would mean that he had even more clothes than those that were already in his bag, that would require drying out, he decided that the best thing to do would be to run out into the rain without any clothes, knowing that if he kept active he would not get cold. So he undressed and laid his clothes in a neat pile, keeping on just his stout leather sandals, which gave his feet some protection. He ran out into the pouring rain and began collecting stones and boulders, some of which had to be rolled back to the overhang. This kept him busy, but being active was better than sitting watching the rain and it kept him warm, even though he was getting soaked. He had finally built the small walls to the shelter, which he bonded with more of the clay that he collected from the area near the inlet. He was muddy and soaking wet as he stood naked beside the fire, admiring his handiwork. Chuckling to himself, thinking that Lialah would have been almost correct in describing him as a wild man, he slipped off his sandals and ran back outside and dived into the river to wash away all the mud and perspiration. The river was colder up here, but he was surprised at the amount of fish and small reptiles that he saw, realising that some of the fish were babies that would probably get washed over the falls and would eventually reach the sea.

Climbing out of the river a few moments walk further upstream, Ruben began to trot briskly back to the shelter through the rain, which had not eased at all, when just on his left he noticed some blackberry bushes that still had a large number of ripe berries. Thinking that this would be a good supplement to the fish, he quickly gathered a couple of large handfuls, as well as filling his own mouth a couple of times. He then hurried back through the rain to the shelter where he was extremely grateful of the fire by which he stood warming himself, after depositing the berries on a rock at the back of the shelter, which was now more like a cave and totally protected from wind and rain. He had placed some of the berries on the ground beside Skree who still looked at him indignantly, as if saying, 'So you're back then and you didn't get washed over the cataract, which is a shame.' However, when presented with the berries Skree seemed to look friendlier towards him, as if deciding that he was not so bad after all.

Whilst he was squatting in front of the fire, which he had built to a roaring blaze as he now had plenty of firewood, he began to feel quite dizzy and had some difficulty in focusing his eyes clearly on the fire. He also felt very sleepy in the warmth and lay down on the blanket and found himself dozing off to sleep. But this was unusual for him, although not totally surprising, as people often have a short sleep during the early afternoon. This was of course more the custom in the summer, when people slept during the hottest part of the day. When he awoke shortly afterwards his head was aching as if he had been drinking some particularly rough wine. He then looked over to Skree who had eaten the berries and was looking rather strange, as if he also could not focus clearly. He realised that the over ripe berries had already started to ferment, and that Skree had unwittingly become slightly intoxicated. He thought that this was immensely funny as the bird fell off the perch, landing on his back. He started to unpack his bag and hang the damp clothes out to dry in the now warm shelter. It was still raining and looked as if it would continue for the rest of the day, so he was glad that he had spent a busy morning making the shelter as comfortable as possible.

\*\*\*\*

True to his word, Captain Bel returned to the palace in the early evening, with his plans to send out scouting parties around Ashkilon, to ensure that the Assyrians had completely left. These plans, which Commander Mithrandir approved without question, involved nearly all the Babylonian Guards being sent out later that night, providing the weather kept dry, as it had now stopped raining. They would return later on the next day having thoroughly searched the entire area. If all was clear they would then wait for another day before returning downriver to Babylon.

Captain Bel returned to the inn, where he instructed the two lieutenants and all the sergeants about how to go about the search, saying that if they came across any stray Assyrians they knew what to do. This of course meant putting them immediately to death, as taking prisoners was something that the Babylonian Guards very seldom did when in battle. The plan was put into effect as the rain had not restarted, and it was not until mid-morning the following day that the parties of Guardsmen began to return, confirming that the Assyrians had indeed left. Although a few straggling wounded had been put to the sword even though they had shown no resistance and had pleaded for their lives.

A storm had now started and everyone was quite content that Ashkilon was safe, and life started to return to normal. The next morning also dawned grey and bleak with the rain still coming down heavily. Under Captain Bel's leadership the Guards left Ashkilon on the galley that had rowed them upriver. The galley already carried the mummified body of Lialah in a solid wooden sarcophagus, and Captain Bel had a complete report of events to give to the king when they arrived in Babylon.

The large galley made quick time on the return journey, as they were travelling with the river in full spate. They stopped briefly the next day in Zohab, where many of the original townsfolk from Ashkilon had fled and they were delighted to hear the town was now completely safe and that they could make plans to return. The galley then rowed on and reached Babylon early the next morning, where it moored amid the cheers of the many townsfolk who had turned out, despite the atrocious weather, to cheer the soldiers who had saved the frontier city.

As Captain Bel left the galley, making his way towards the Citadel amid the cheering throng, he was amazed at how the news of their victory had preceded them. On entering the Citadel, Captain Bel refused the offer of being allowed to clean up before going to see the king. He therefore walked in to the royal chamber and felt very aware of his unwashed and untidy dress. However, ignoring some of the whispered comments he went straight up to the king and handed him Commander Mithrandir's report. With this he said, "Ashkilon is now completely safe, your

Highness, we have driven the Assyrian dogs back to Nineveh after killing at least one third of their army, which was completely routed."

"You have done superbly well, Captain, there are many who doubted your ability to lead a whole battalion, but I happen to agree with Commander Schudah about having a lot of younger senior officers in our army. I will read Commander Mithrandir's complete report at my leisure, but I did of course receive his interim report, together with the rather strange request for additional galleys. He briefly mentions a floating bridge that used the existing galleys. But can you tell me why they were not attacked by fireboats sent downriver by the Assyrians?"

"It is all in the reports your Majesty, but the floating bridge was protected by chains that were spread across the river from the end of the north city wall to the start of the southern wall. This was already done before we arrived and I must admit it was ingenious. However, I am sure that on reading the commander's report he will give you far more detail about its construction."

"That is fine, Captain, thank you once again and now I will allow you to go and have a much needed wash and change," he smiled, wrinkling his nose. But then added, "I am holding a celebration dinner tonight. You and your Lieutenants will of course be the guests of honour." With that, Captain Bel was dismissed from the royal chamber, and made his way back to the barracks.

Dinner that evening in the Citadel was a splendid affair, Captain Bel and both his lieutenants were wearing new uniforms, that had been specially provided and they had washed and dressed with meticulous care. There must have been nearly one hundred people seated in the chamber, but pride of place had been reserved for Captain Bel, and Lieutenants Abzher and Jezraal. They were of course seated at the right hand of the king and the food was truly excellent. After the meal, which consisted of many courses of a tremendous variety of selection, and while most people were enjoying subdued conversation, the king turned to Captain Bel and said, "This afternoon I read in detail Commander Mithrandir's report, but there is something that seems to be missing. As you probably know, Commander Mithrandir is one of my relatives and I know him very well. It would therefore come as no surprise to you that I can easily tell when he is withholding information. Can you tell me whose idea it was to put the chains across the river and build the floating bridge?" But before the king allowed Captain Bel to answer he added, "I have also heard that there was a formidable mercenary who was fighting for us, can you shed any light on this?"

Captain Bel realised that word of Ruben's presence had already reached the king's ears and trying to deny that he had been in Ashkilon would be unwise. He therefore felt that it would be far safer, particularly for his career, to tell the king the truth.

"There was a young mercenary there, your Majesty. He is indeed a formidable adversary; he is certainly as good with a javelin as myself and with a large sword as Lieutenant Abzher. I believe it was his idea about the chains and the floating bridge, but these were done before we arrived. He was the same person who Tiglath-Pileser had been arguing with in your Gardens. He had in fact fought beside me at Sousa and he had previously been a Babylonian Guard. It was his young wife that the Assyrian king wanted you to give him as a concubine, but regrettably she was killed in the battle by accident, and I now have her mummified body aboard the galley, which I have promised to bury in the marshlands from where she came."

"Thank you, Captain, for your honesty. But where is this remarkable young man now?" enquired the king.

"We are not sure. All that I can tell you is that he has left Ashkilon and has probably followed the river northeast and is now out of the country," answered the captain.

"What a shame," said the king. "Well let us leave it at that, Captain. Experience has taught me it is well to leave some mystery, otherwise stories will only be invented anyway."

The king was then interrupted and his attention was diverted elsewhere. Captain Bel breathed a sigh of relief, and the rest of the evening passed without further difficulty. But when the captain stood up to take his leave of the celebration, the king turned to him again.

This time he said, "Oh Captain, I am sending you back to Lagash with the battalion that is now yours to keep and command. Commander Schudah has requested that you be returned to control the city, so you can leave whenever you like. I would however be most grateful if you could do me the favour of taking my new envoy to Egypt when you go. His name is Dathram and he wishes to go downriver to Nippur, with young Latich who I have now assigned to him. They are sitting at the end of the table over to the right," he said, indicating with his head to the large man sitting with Latich at the end the table.

As he left the assembly, Captain Bel stopped by Dathram, holding out his right hand to Dathram and placing his left hand on Latich's shoulder. "Hello Latich," he said and then turned directly facing the large man to whom he had extended his right hand, "I am pleased to meet you, sir, the king has asked me to provide you with passage downriver to Nippur."

Dathram took the offered hand, and with a good firm grip, said to the captain, "I am delighted to meet you, Captain, if you can tell me where and when you wish to take us on board, we will meet as requested."

"I would like to leave the day after tomorrow, so if you could be ready to leave shortly after dawn by the docks I will happily enjoy your company on board," said Captain Bel, smiling broadly.

"That is splendid Captain," said Dathram. "There will just be myself and Latich. We will meet you as requested."

Latich had been trying to interrupt ever since Captain Bel came over and could finally restrain himself no longer, blurting out, "Did you see Ruben in Ashkilon, Captain?"

"I will tell you about Ashkilon on the trip downriver," replied the Captain noncommittally. So saying, he left.

****

It was two days before Ruben could venture out again as the storm had continued relentlessly. It was only then for a brief foraging trip to restock with additional firewood. However, the day after dawned bright and clear, even though it did not look as if it would stay that way for long. He then went in search of one of the mountain sheep, the spoor of which was evident all over the area. A large flock had obviously passed this way in the rain, comparatively recently, judging by the fresh droppings.

Ruben had taken his javelin, intent on a change of diet, as although he had not yet exhausted his supply of fish, he thought that a change would be a good idea and he could also look for some edible roots as well as more berries. He soon spied several mountain sheep, which had strayed from the main flock, but they were extremely jittery and it took him four attempts to stalk one of these sheep until he was within about fifty paces. He decided that even a short run up before loosing the javelin would panic the animal, resulting in a wounded sheep charging around with his javelin protruding from it, making recovery difficult. He tried to get a little nearer, crawling on all fours from rock to rock until he came a little closer, but there was still a large area without cover between him and his prey. He knew that he would either have to risk a long throw, or abandon this attempt. Looking at the sky, he saw that the rain clouds were beginning to gather ominously and he would soon run out of time. As the sheep was looking the other way his foot moved a large stone, but luckily it did not make any noise. Thinking quickly he picked up the stone and hurled it well above the sheep so that it landed with a clatter at least thirty paces the other side of the animal. The sheep immediately bolted straight towards Ruben where he was crouched behind a boulder. As he stood up the young sheep swerved to one side revealing a brief broad side view, which he took advantage of, hurling the javelin, which hit the sheep just behind the shoulder where it penetrated to the heart.

Feeling very proud of himself, he soon had the dead sheep over his shoulders, but he had quite a long way to run back to the shelter before the rain gave him another soaking. Having just made it in time, he decided to return in the rain to where he had seen some edible roots. He did not want to get his clothes wet again, as he had only just finished drying out all his other gear, which was now repacked in his bag. He quickly undressed and ran out into the rain, shortly returning with the roots.

That afternoon he butchered the sheep, cutting it into large steaks that he grilled on the fire as well as leaving long strands of lean meat to dry in the heat of the fire, that could be eaten at a later date. That evening he dined on tasty grilled mutton with roots that he baked in the embers of the fire, and afterwards filled himself with fresh cherries that he had come across when collecting the roots. He was surviving well, but was keen to start again on his journey, even though it would mean that he had to carry Skree, as he reckoned it would be a further ten days before the wing had a chance to mend. Unfortunately due to bad weather, it was another two days before he could risk continuing his journey.

The morning that he set out was dry and bright; the previous evening had seen the last of the storm clouds. He left the shelter almost reluctantly, with a pile of dry wood tucked neatly at the back of the man made cave that he hoped could shelter future travellers. He set out on his journey carrying his bag and javelin with one hand and with Skree perched on his shoulder where his talons could not penetrate his crocodile hide jerkin, which Skree now condescended to do, as the eagle was now on good terms with him. This was not really surprising, as the bird had learnt to trust him to provide plenty of food, which it now would even take from his hand.

Walking on the southern bank of the river he was clearly making good progress travelling further into the mountains. However, the main caravan route was on the northern bank of the river, but he remembered Dathram's warning about not going too far north, particularly with the approach of winter and he did not want to go anywhere near Nineveh. He therefore considered that he should try to make a new passage on the southern bank and he had hoped he would soon reach civilisation. Later that day when he had almost given up hope, he came in sight of a small town on his own shore, but a small river that lay between him and the town halted his progress. This river was not particularly large, but would nonetheless require either a long detour or swimming across. He saw some fishermen near the northeast shore. He hesitated before hailing the fishermen, as he was not sure whether he was in Assyria, Persia or even Canaan. He was unsure of what reception awaited him and checked his dress to ensure that there was no identifying mark showing where he had come from. Fortunately he was still wearing the black uniform of a mercenary, had his large sword on his back and was carrying his javelin, which identified him clearly as being a soldier of fortune. Even his Babylonian helmet had been knocked out of shape and now had all the plumage torn out by Skree, who had been offended by the black feathers and subsequently plucked them out with his beak. Deciding he was in no great danger he called out to the fishermen and was pleased to see that they quickly rowed over to him. He politely greeted them and asked, "What town is that over there and would you be good enough to tell me which country I am in?"

"The town is Thrax and nobody really knows whether it is in Assyria or Canaan, because the border keeps changing, although we normally consider everything southwest of the main river is in Canaan. But the town governs itself and nobody really cares who says they are in charge of the area as they never contribute to our welfare," the fisherman explained at considerable length.

"Can you ferry me across? I will gladly pay the fare that you charge," Ruben asked.

"We will happily take you with us for free," said the same man, who was obviously in charge.

Ruben climbed aboard, but as he did so both men kept well away from him and the man who had yet to say anything suddenly asked, "That bird looks bloody vicious, what on earth is it wearing?"

"That is my eagle," said Ruben. "He is quite tame and will not bite, but has a damaged wing at the moment."

The fisherman grinned, but still kept his distance and started rowing across the small river, then back along the southern bank of the Euphrates. He still kept a watchful eye on the bird and this large well-armed and dangerous looking mercenary, who could obviously kill both men and take the boat if he so desired.

Fortunately, the man in charge was far more friendly and sat rowing nearer to Ruben and started a conversation.

"Have you travelled far, friend?" he enquired. "We do not get many visitors in these parts."

"I have come from Ashkilon in Babylon, where there was a big battle, which you may have heard about," Ruben replied good-naturedly, warming to the fisherman.

"Yes, we heard that the Assyrian army was well beaten," said the fisherman. "Were you in that battle?" he asked.

"Well, I saw some of the action," replied Ruben, saying nothing about who he had been fighting for.

"We were talking about it earlier," said the fisherman. "And I was saying to my younger brother here, that it was a good job the Assyrian army were thrashed, they are insolent pigs and it is sensible to keep clear of Nineveh these days."

"Yes, that is what I have heard and advice I will keep," responded Ruben.

"So where are you going? If you don't mind my asking," enquired the garrulous fisherman.

"I was hoping to pass through Canaan to the far sea," Ruben informed him. "Does the town have an inn or anywhere to stay?"

"Well, not really, there is an inn of sorts, but it is only a gathering place for folk to drink, they don't offer accommodation," came the reply.

The boat then ran aground near the town and all three men waded ashore. Ruben put down his bag and perched Skree on his belongings, before turning back to assist the two fishermen in dragging the boat ashore. Ruben lifted one side of the boat clear of the ground, while the two brothers struggled with the other side. "You are certainly a strong fellow," said the older fisherman. "If you are looking for somewhere to stay, you are very welcome to stay with us, if you don't mind sleeping in the boathouse."

"That would be splendid, and I will happily pay for my lodging," said Ruben gratefully.

"Well I am sure that we can work something out, if you are not in a great hurry you can earn your keep, as we have some building work that needs finishing before winter, and you look just the sort of strong handy person we need," said the older brother.

"That would be most convenient, as I am in no great hurry, and I will be happy to accept your kind invitation," said Ruben gratefully, holding out his right hand saying, "My name is Ruben Ben Uriah."

"I am pleased to meet you Ruben, my name is Andreas and this is my younger brother Stephan," said the older brother, shaking Ruben's hand.

# 16
## KINDNESS RETURNED

Ruben was glad that he had made friends with Andreas and Stephan, who had offered hospitality that he readily accepted. He now remembered roughly the position of Thrax, recalling the maps he had studied. He would move on upriver to Nafrath, that being definitely in Assyria, and then across the constantly changing border to Timon, which was surely in Canaan. They left the boat where they had put it on the riverbank, and walked to the nearest house, which was where the brothers lived. Andreas was giving Ruben a potted family history all the time that they were walking, which made Ruben realise that Andreas was garrulous to the point of being tiresome. He briefly glanced at the younger brother, who returned his glance with a gesture of mock despair.

They entered the small house, which Andreas had already told Ruben had been the only home that they ever had, initially living with their parents who had been killed a long time ago when Thrax was part of another kingdom, subjugated by the invading Assyrians. The house was very small, consisting of just two rooms, the first of which was the main living, cooking, and eating area, the second being the brothers' bedroom. The boathouse was an annex to the main building, but only had room for the boat and a workbench, although this was the part of the building that was being extended, to which Andreas had previously referred. Ruben deposited his luggage, weapons and stood his eagle on the workbench, perched on a large piece of wood.

"Will your boat be all right if it is left outside?" enquired Ruben.

"Oh yes," replied Andreas. "It is often left out during the nights, only requiring shelter in the winter, which is why we must finish the extension."

The work had only recently commenced, with two large columns that would eventually support a heavy wooden beam, which would take the weight of the roof of the extension. Most of the materials for the building were stacked outside and looked as if they had been there for quite some time. Stephan finally managed to get a word in among his brother's constant chatter, explaining to Ruben that because there had been such a large demand for fish recently, they had been unable to complete the construction work themselves. Much to the brothers' delight, Ruben informed them that he would be happy to complete the work on his own, so that they could continue fishing, as they were apparently the only fishermen in the town.

As Andreas was explaining to Ruben in considerable length and laborious detail, he was suddenly interrupted by his brother who said, "Andreas, it is your turn to cook tonight."

"Oh yes, so it is," agreed his elder brother. "Perhaps you will explain to Ruben what we wanted." With that he left Ruben with Stephan and returned to the main living area to prepare the evening meal.

"I am sorry about my brother," apologised Stephan. "He is so talkative, he drives people crazy, but he is well meaning and kind as well as being a good fisherman."

"Please do not apologise," said Ruben laughing. "We all have our faults and his kindness is obvious. Anyway, I am fairly sure that I know what you require and with your agreement, I would like to build it without instruction."

"That you most certainly have," said Stephan. "But do you mind telling me where you learnt about building?"

"My uncle, for whom I worked before I became a soldier, was a boatbuilder, and most building requires similar principles."

The next day Ruben started work whilst the two brothers went fishing, collecting the fish from the night fishing lines that they had just finished setting when Ruben had hailed them from the southeastern bank. When they returned around mid-morning with a creditable catch, they were amazed at Ruben's industry. Ruben had already placed the large wooden beam onto the columns, and dug the foundation trenches for the walls, into which he had placed the foundation stones. Between these he had erected a framework using a triangular pattern of smaller timbers temporarily lashed together. When Andreas asked about this, Ruben said to him, "Triangular supports are stronger than vertical uprights, so that you do not need such heavy timbers to support the roof."

Realising that they had found an ideal worker, Andreas was extremely satisfied and said to Ruben, "We are off out again and will not be back until late afternoon. Is there anything you require before we go?"

"Not for me, but may I request one of the eels you caught overnight for my eagle?" asked Ruben.

"Yes, most certainly," replied Andreas, but before he could request one from his brother, Stephan had already produced one of the still wriggling eels from the basket, which he handed to Ruben.

Extracting his small bronze knife, Ruben quickly chopped the head off the eel, which he offered to the eagle. Skree, who held the body in his talons and began to tear at the flesh with his hooked beak, took this with great relish. Watching Ruben's efficient movements, Stephan said, "Why do you use a bronze knife? Because, although we use bronze, we noticed that your other weapons are made from iron…"

"The bronze knife has sentimental value for me," Ruben explained, "It was given to me by an old friend who is now dead." He then continued with his building work, leaving the brothers to return to their fishing.

\*\*\*\*

General Nozgrarot rode back into Nineveh at the head of just over half the original army with which he had set out. Apart from losing one third of the army in the battle at Ashkilon, further casualties had plagued the retreat. He had lost many to dysentery, cholera and typhus plus the other typical diseases that tend to afflict large numbers of people travelling in unsanitary conditions. He had to be honest, the retreat had become a rout, and this made him the laughing stock of Assyria, which had the effect of making him even more ill tempered than usual. It had possibly obliterated his chances of securing the throne after his cousin's untimely death. However, he was not going to give up the possibility of securing the position for himself that easily, but it demanded some extraordinary form of face-saver. He knew that he could correctly claim that the Babylonians now had iron weapons but he still needed another scapegoat, on whom he could pile the blame.

As he rode through the quiet streets of the city it became evident that no one wished to welcome back what remained of the bedraggled army that he led. A sly man with a pinched face and a sallow complexion rode up beside him. This man was slightly wounded, with a grazed leg that had been inflicted by a collapsing tent in the burning base camp. He had stolen a horse from his captain when the captain had died from his festering wounds and disease.

"Begging your pardon, General," whined the sly man. "But you remember that large mercenary who you shook your fist at when we left the camp just outside Ashkilon?"

"What of it?" demanded the irritated Nozgrarot, not even glancing in the man's direction.

"Well, he never went back to the town, but continued up river," said the sly man, hoping for some reward. But the general simply grunted and continued riding on without even acknowledging him. However, still hoping for some reward, he rode just a couple of paces behind the general who was now deep in thought.

There could be something in this information, thought the general, reasoning that the mercenary must have already been paid and was probably looking for other battles and more money. But, as Babylon was at war with Persia, he could hardly fight for the Persians. Therefore he would probably try to pass through the south of his own country to enter

Canaan, where there was always lots of money to be gained by a mercenary. Now if this mercenary was in the country, and if he could be detained, it might be possible to bring him to Nineveh in chains and that would give Nozgrarot the scapegoat he needed. He knew there were a lot of ifs in this half-chance, but he had nothing to lose so it was worth a try.

The general summoned back the source of this information calling back over his shoulder, "Come here you miserable worm. How did you learn this information?" Noticing the man's lack of rank said, "Where did you get that bloody horse?"

"I saw the man myself, General, while I was guarding your back as you left the battlefield. The horse was given to me because of my wounded leg by my captain, as a reward for my fighting so bravely," lied the sly man, riding back beside the general.

Not easily deceived by this crook, Nozgrarot asked, "What is your name, worm?"

"Ratarz, General," came the prompt reply.

"As you are obviously a reliable man and a good soldier, from this moment on you are now Sergeant Ratarz, and as you have seen this mercenary and will doubtless recognise him again, you can select ten of my finest troops and ride south in search of the bastard, then bring him back to Nineveh in chains."

This was not the reward that Ratarz either wanted or expected, the whole aspect of riding southeast towards the border was the last thing that he wanted to do. Me and my big mouth, he thought to himself, next time I get a chance, I'm leaving this bloody army.

And so it was that he led a small party towards Nafrath in the southeast.

Nozgrarot went back to brooding, this wasn't much to go on but at least it was an effort that he could be seen to be making. Apart from which, little sneaky cretins like Ratarz infuriated him.

****

The weather at Thrax had been remarkably good after the initial storms that heralded the beginning of the wet season, before the onset of winter. This had allowed Ruben to complete the building work, whilst the brothers went fishing every day to meet the additional demand for fish. When Ruben had been finishing off the work, he had noticed that Skree was becoming fidgety and realised that it was time to take the immobilising mudpack off the eagle's wing. He realised that this was the moment of truth, because if the wing had not mended correctly, the bird would be unable to fly. If that was the case, he had better kill the eagle and release Skree from the cruel fate that would follow.

When the building work was completed and had been admired by both Andreas and Stephan, he asked if he could have a bowl of warm water and if they could possibly help him to hold the eagle, which had grown considerably even in that short space of time. Andreas said, "We will be only too glad to help, just tell us what to do."

"It is simply a matter of securing his head and his talons, while I remove the blanket and wash off the clay holding his wing," explained Ruben.

"If I hold the head," said Andreas, "while Stephan holds the talons, will that be sufficient?"

"I am sure it will," replied Ruben. "But you had better hold firmly, as he is a strong little fellow."

They took their places either side of Ruben, holding the eagle while Ruben unfastened the securing blanket, amidst alarming objectionable squawks from Skree at this most undignified situation. Ruben then started to soak the clay, whilst stopping the other wing from flapping. Ruben was surprised at how easily the clay came away, without even turning back into mud, but breaking into pieces that fell off the feathers. All three of them then took the bird to the doorway and at Ruben's signal, they all let go and withdrew a few paces. The eagle kept up the squawking and started flapping its wings whilst running around, more like an agitated chicken. Although there appeared to be nothing wrong with the bird's wing, it seemed unable to take to the air, despite their combined efforts in chasing it and trying to get it to take off. After a while it became apparent that Skree considered this to be some sort of game, whilst the three men were all becoming more and more agitated and frustrated. Skree was seemingly thoroughly enjoying this game, as he had become used to running around on his legs and was very adept at avoiding the waving arms and kicks that were aimed at him. A basket of fish had been knocked over in the commotion and Skree grabbed hold of a fish with his talons, but this of course made it unable to run. As Ruben closed in on the bird it gave its wings a mighty flap and to his surprise rose into the air. It dropped the fish and was soon swooping around, realising what its wings were for. They left him to eat the fish and fly around, while they went indoors for the evening meal.

Stephan was serving the meal that he had cooked, it being his turn, whilst Andreas and Ruben sat talking. Andreas said, "Why do you not train the eagle to kill for you?"

"That was not my intention when I tried to mend the wing," said Ruben, "Apart from which, I would not know how to go about it."

"Oh, I thought you must have been used to birds," said Andreas with complete surprise.

"Not really," said Ruben. "I simply found the eagle when I was climbing into the mountains and it seemed worth trying to mend its wing."

"How remarkable," exclaimed Andreas. "But I think you will now have a tame eagle who will not leave your side."

"Why do we not go into Thrax this evening?" asked Stephan, joining in the conversation. "There is an old man who is often at the inn who used to train hawks when he was living in Nineveh."

"That is an excellent idea," said Andreas. "We were going to celebrate the completed building work anyway." Having agreed on this they washed up, tidied the room and all went out, leaving Skree who had returned to sleep on his perch in the now completed boathouse.

It was only a short walk to the town inn, as the brothers' house was just on the outskirts of Thrax, which was not a large town. The inn was, as Andreas had previously said, more of a meeting place than a conventional inn, as it did not offer accommodation. Andreas was the first to enter the Inn, with Stephan and Ruben in close order behind him. Although Andreas still did most of the talking, Ruben preferred to talk to Stephan who he liked and from whom he received more concise and informative replies.

They all sat down at a small table and were greeted by the Innkeeper who came over and asked what they would like to drink. Andreas introduced Ruben and requested three mugs of millet beer, which they drank in preference to the Assyrian rough wine. Andreas was telling the innkeeper that they were celebrating the completion of the building works, which Ruben had been doing on his own.

"I was wondering who was doing the work," exclaimed the innkeeper. "The supply of fish has been good recently, so you two must have been out every day, but I was told that work was being done to your house."

"And a very fine job it is," replied Andreas. "We found ourselves a very efficient workman." As the drinks were poured, Andreas started to introduce Ruben to most of the people present, in his normal talkative fashion.

Whilst he was talking to one person, praising Ruben's ability, Stephan pointed out an old man in the corner, saying, "That is the old hawk trainer from Nineveh." He asked Andreas if he would excuse them, which was convenient, as Andreas had become involved in telling someone in great detail what Ruben had been doing.

Leaving his older brother, Stephan took Ruben over to the old man and offered to buy him a drink.

"No, allow me," said Ruben producing a gold coin, which more than paid for a round of drinks. "I hope you do not mind the intrusion, sir," said Ruben addressing the old man. "But I wish to seek your advice with regard to training a tame eagle that I have."

The old man's face lit up when he asked, "Do you know what type of eagle it is? Because, all eagles are difficult to tame, as they are normally considered too wild and savage."

"I don't really know," admitted Ruben, and so went on to describe the bird.

"It sounds like one of the golden eagles that are normally found in the high mountains," said the old man with incredulity. "Would you mind telling me how you came to tame it?"

"It was quite easy really," explained Ruben. "I found it as a baby with a broken wing, which I successfully mended." He told the complete story to the old man who was intrigued and said that he had never heard of anyone mending an eagle's wing before.

"The problem I now have," said Ruben, "is how to train it to kill, as it still relies on me to throw it food. Have you got any ideas on how to go about training it?"

"It should not be that difficult," said the old man, and he began telling Ruben the means that were used to train birds to kill for their owner. Ruben became so involved in the conversation that he did not realise that Stephan had been called away for a short time.

The evening came to a close when the innkeeper asked everyone to leave as it was by then very late and a lot of alcohol had been consumed. The evening had been most enjoyable for everybody; they all went their separate ways swearing lifelong friendship and saying that they must all meet again, although nothing was arranged. The brothers walked home chatting to Ruben, and asking him what he had learned from the old bird trainer. Ruben explained that he had been given quite a few ideas how to train it to kill for itself. He went on to tell them, "I do not really want to keep it to kill for me, but I can't leave the bird on his own, otherwise it may well die and that would defeat the initial work of saving its life. It may then leave me when I descend from the mountains, or even before, if it decides to – although I like the bird, I do not wish to keep it captive."

"Oh yes!" said Stephan, suddenly remembering something important. "Did you notice the stranger in the room who called me over?"

"Do you mean the tall thin man who came in when you and Ruben started to talk to the old bird tamer?" asked Andreas.

"Yes, that is right," replied Stephan. "I did not realise you noticed."

"I know you always tell me that I'm very talkative," laughed Andreas. "But that does not mean I do not see everything around me.

Anyway, that was not a total stranger, he is a frequent visitor."

"Yes, I suppose you are right," returned Stephan. "Anyway, he asked me about Ruben, as he had not seen him before." He then turned to Ruben and said, "He came from Nafrath and he told me that there was an Assyrian sergeant with some troops who were asking about a large mercenary, and if anyone had seen him."

"Do you have any idea of how many men there were?" asked Ruben.

"The man did not say exactly, but I believe it was only a small patrol, probably of about ten or fifteen at most," replied Stephan. He then continued, "But nobody from Thrax would betray you, as everyone hates the Assyrian army. Have you any idea of how long you will be staying? Not that we wish to be rid of you."

"That is perfectly correct," added Andreas. "You are more than welcome and can stay for as long as you like."

"Thank you very much," said Ruben gratefully. "But I really must start moving before the onset of winter. If I may, I would like to stay for another few days while I train Skree to kill without my assistance. After which, I shall resume my journey, I am sure that avoiding the patrol should not be difficult, and after bypassing Nafrath I will soon be in Canaan, however, I will never forget your kind hospitality and friendship."

The next day, Ruben commenced the training that had been recommended by the old hawk trainer. This consisted of tying dead or almost dead animals, like fish, mice or even rabbits when Ruben could catch them, to a length of fishing line, then pulling the bait along in front of Skree so that he would pounce on the bait. This exercise seemed to work well and Skree obviously felt that this was a good game. Soon Ruben was running quickly dragging the bait and Skree was able to dive on the prey from high in the sky. Skree soon became good at this.

On the third day of the training, a young lad happened to pass by. The lad carried with him five plump pigeons that he had killed with a slingshot, which he was clearly very adept in using. He asked Ruben what he was doing, as he had never seen such strange behaviour before. Ruben explained what he was trying to do and when he saw what the lad carried, asked if he could buy a couple of the pigeons. The lad offered to give him the pigeons, if Ruben allowed him to watch, but Ruben insisted on paying for two of the birds from the lad. It had been necessary to keep Skree hungry during the exercises, allowing him only a couple of mouthfuls of the prey when he caught it. As he wasn't sure that these birds were suitable prey for an eagle, he threw him one of the dead pigeons. Skree began to tear it apart, swallowing large chunks of the fresh meat with obvious satisfaction, looking at Ruben as if to say, 'Why haven't you fed me my favourite meal before?'

"Right Skree let's see you catch one," he said, fastening the end of the other pigeon's wing to a long length of fishing line. He twirled it around his head, causing the dead pigeon's other wing to extend as if it was flying. He was delighted when Skree managed to take the bird in mid air, despite his attempts to vary the speed and height of the bait. He then considered that the training was complete and announced to the brothers that he would be leaving the next morning.

Accordingly, he appeared after a hearty breakfast all packed and ready to go, wearing his crocodile skin jerkin, his large sword slung over his shoulders, and with his short sword and dagger on his belt. He had taken to wearing the small bronze knife strapped on the outside of his right calf, just below the knee. He had abandoned his dented, damaged helmet and was deliberately not wearing his black uniform, but wearing a light blue shift and kilt instead. Cramming his already bulging bag with a couple of days' food that the brothers had kindly prepared, he took his leave of them, promising to visit if he was ever in the area again. Then with his large bag and a javelin in his hand, and with Skree circling overhead, he set off towards Nafrath, which he had been told was a couple of days' walk upriver. He had also been told that Nafrath was built on an island around which the Euphrates flowed in a variety of small rivers, with many of the rivers being bridged. Timon, in Canaan, was well southwest of the mountains and should be considerably warmer. Ruben considered that, with luck, he might be able to reach the area in less than seven days. It was now quite fresh, so he broke into an easy trot to kept himself warm.

\*\*\*\*

Sergeant Ratarz was enjoying his new job. He had selected some tough troops, but had been careful to ensure they were not intelligent men and would simply carry out his instructions without question. He had been allowed to keep the horse, or at least not asked to return it, although his patrol of soldiers were on foot. They had left a trail of devastation in their wake, being extremely brutal to people wherever they passed on their way, questioning them about the mercenary whom nobody had seen. Ratarz was sure that people had told the truth, but he delighted in using his power, exercised by his men, to threaten, beat, terrify, burn and even rape these simple mountain folk who denied having seen this person.

His soldiers had become undisciplined in their dress and often used appalling language when addressing these courteous folk. They were a disgrace, even to the hard regime they represented. They had just left

Nafrath, having caused a terrible commotion at the town's main inn, where they had drunk large quantities of rough wine, assaulted many of the townsfolk, as well as raping the innkeeper's daughter and serving girls. The town people had been so angry at this behaviour that they had got together a small group of vigilantes who were intent on revenge if they returned. However, Ratarz had no intention of returning, as he had already decided after visiting Thrax, which was the next town downriver, that if the mercenary had come this way he was now a long way away and that they had missed him. He therefore intended to have some more fun at Thrax and then return northwest, hopefully deserting from the army whenever the chance arose.

They left Nafrath early that morning, crossing to the southern bank of the Euphrates and continued southeast along the river towards Thrax. Although they were undisciplined in dress and in general behaviour, they were still a formidable fighting force and struck terror into the hearts of any unlucky travellers who were unfortunate enough to encounter them. Sergeant Ratarz was about to call a halt and make camp for the night in the lee of a large rocky outcrop, when he spied a small party of travellers coming up from Thrax. Ratarz had seen the party before they saw the Assyrians, this was because he was on horseback and therefore could see further ahead. He thought that this would be a good opportunity to have more sadistic fun and called his men off the road, telling them to shelter behind some rocks.

The party consisted of two men, three women and two children, all of whom were looking for somewhere to shelter for the night after leaving Thrax early that morning. They had made fast progress despite the children, who had to be carried some of the way. Ruben, who came running along behind them, hailed the party of travellers from behind. "Hello friends," he called out, as he recognised one of the men who had been at the inn when he had been talking to the old hawk tamer. "If you are travelling to Nafrath, may I join your party and possibly help carry the children?"

The older of the two men replied, "By all means, we could certainly do with your assistance, but we were about to stop for the night. So do not tarry if you wish to press ahead."

"That is fine with me," said Ruben, pointing to the outcrop of rocks about one hundred paces in front of them. "That would be an ideal place to shelter for the night as it will be out of the wind." He paused for a few moments and then said, "That is strange, I am sure I saw something move up there."

"I didn't see anything," said the younger of the two men. "But I am sure you are right and if something did move, we will soon see it when we get there, it may be a stray mountain sheep."

"You may be correct," said Ruben. "But I believe there is a party of Assyrian soldiers in the area, so let us check before we go."

"And how do you propose we do that?" laughed the older of the two men.

"No problem," said Ruben as he looked up in the air to where Skree was circling overhead. "Skree," he called, "What is in those rocks?" Skree called pointing. The eagle flew above the rocky outcrop and started diving down with outstretched talons, although it swirled in flight to avoid an arrow that flew close. Nobody in the party of travellers, except for Ruben, whose keen eyes missed little, had seen the arrow. Ruben immediately called Skree back. "If that is a mountain sheep, it has learnt how to shoot an arrow," he said, smiling grimly.

Skree came winging back to perch on a small stunted tree just beside Ruben. The women moved the children back behind the men, being rather cautious of the eagle. Ruben said, "I think we have company," and then addressing the men, he asked, "Are you armed?"

"I am," said the younger of the two men. "But my older brother carries no weapons."

"Take my short sword," said Ruben, handing him the hilt of his short iron blade. "Now all stand behind me, we need to get them in the open." He picked up his javelin in his left hand and selected a round rock that fitted into the palm of his other hand, and after a run of no more than six paces, hurled the rock at the outcrop to land well above where the arrow had come from.

"By the gods!" said the older of the two brothers, who had never seen such a powerful throw.

The rock landed with a clatter and it disturbed other loose stones, which started rolling. Those small stones soon disturbed the larger rocks and boulders; even Ruben was amazed as the whole side of the outcrop began to slide in an avalanche towards the river. Suddenly figures started appearing from behind boulders, desperately trying to escape. Soon the rumble of falling rocks became a roar as a large section of the outcrop tumbled into the churning waters of the fast flowing river. As the roar died away, a hush fell over the area revealing five Assyrians who had escaped the avalanche. Despairing cries of men were heard from the river, but even those were cut off as the men were drowned in the boiling tumult.

"Well, that has increased the odds in our favour," said Ruben advancing, thinking it best to attack now, before the Assyrians came to their senses.

After only a momentary delay, the Assyrians, led by a burly soldier, came forward in a rush, yelling curses, intent on avenging the loss of their comrades. Their charge was immediately halted, as the burly soldier fell backward with a gurgling cry of agony, as his lifeblood flowed into the soil around the javelin that protruded from his throat. Ruben had stood his ground even though the other two men had retreated another few paces, and he had felled the first attacker with an instinctive throw of deadly accuracy. He immediately seized the opportunity to advance and in one swift movement had reached over his shoulder to draw the large sword from its scabbard. As he lifted aside the flap and drew out the sword in his right hand the stones sparkled and glittered, around the large blue lapis lazuli pommel. This complemented the bright flash that came from the blade itself that Ruben swept in a continuous movement.

"Aahiee, it is him," cried out one of the shocked Assyrians, turning to run. "The bright flame of the east." His other three companions soon joined him to race back the way they had come.

All that could be heard for a few moments was the sound of running footsteps, but then it was quiet except for the noise of the river. Before the other men had fully recovered their senses, Ruben automatically took charge of the situation and began telling people what to do. He instructed the women to take the children over to a grove of trees and one of the men to find a suitable area where they could make a shelter among the rocks. He instructed the other man to find wood and prepare a fire so that they could have something warm to eat and drink. In the meantime he went over to the dead Assyrian, withdrew his javelin, and took the man's weapons from the body before throwing it into the river.

On his return to the party, he was pleased to discover that they had found a reasonable shelter and the men had already started a fire over which a pot was slung warming some broth.

Ruben addressed everyone, "I am sorry that I started issuing orders, I automatically acted as if I was in the army again," he said apologetically.

"Please do not apologise, we owe you our lives and are most grateful. It is our good fortune that you came along when you did." This was said by the older of the two brothers, who Ruben had recognised from the inn at Thrax.

"Well it was me they were after," explained Ruben. "So you may have been safe if I hadn't been here."

"Maybe, but you can never tell. So thanks anyway. Now before we continue, let us introduce ourselves. My name is Harad," he held his hand out to Ruben giving a firm handshake.

"Ruben Ben Uriah," said Ruben in reply, as he shook Harad's hand.

"This is my younger brother Joself, he and his, um, wife, Tasmin. They have just visited us in Thrax and we are now accompanying them back to Nafrath where they have been living for the last six months." He then continued, but Ruben had looked at Tasmin and the rest of the words fall on deaf ears, because Tasmin looked almost identical to Lialah. The only difference that he could detect was that her hair was of a dark brownish red with a golden tinge, as opposed to Lialah's very dark brown. But it fell in identical loose curls to hang just over her shoulders. She also seemed to Ruben to have a similar stance and the same mannerisms. He then realised that Harad had introduced his wife and his children, as well as his and Joself's mother, but none of these names Ruben could recall.

Trying desperately to pay attention, without looking at Tasmin, who reminded him so much of Lialah, Ruben managed to pick up the basic story that Harad was telling him. The main fact that Ruben grasped was that Harad and his family, the two young children being his own offspring, were going back to Nafrath to stay in Joself's house, while Joself and Tasmin journeyed on to Timon. "What a strange coincidence," said Ruben. "I too am going to Timon, which I believe is in Canaan."

"That is correct," said Harad. "It lies just beyond the Empty Sector."

"I have heard nothing about an Empty Sector," queried Ruben, looking quizzical.

Harad laughed. "I am not surprised, it is all new, but if you help us finish setting up the shelter, we will tell you all about it over dinner, perhaps you can travel with Joself and Tasmin."

"Oh yes," exclaimed Tasmin, delighted. "I would like that." And turning to Joself she said, "Don't you think that that's an excellent idea?"

"Well, I'll think about it," said Joself reservedly, having noticed Ruben's interest in his wife.

Having made a reasonable shelter for the night, with a separate sleeping area for the women and children, they all sat around a pleasant meal that Harad's wife and mother had prepared. Ruben added the food that he had brought with him and they all ate their fill while swapping stories of why they were travelling. It seemed that Joself and Tasmin had been staying with Harad and his family, who were now going to Nafrath where they would stay in Joself's house, while Joself and Tasmin travelled to Timon on urgent business.

The two children, both young boys of about five and six, gazed at Ruben with awe. He seemed to them to be some sort of god who had been sent down to protect them from the wicked Assyrians. This large, powerful and mighty warrior, with his own magnificent and clever eagle, was their special guardian. This same belief seemed to be held by Tasmin, much to Ruben's embarrassment and Joself's obvious dislike.

Ruben thought it would be best to change the subject of conversation, so he said to Harad, "Perhaps you would like the Assyrian weapons, as I do not think it is wise at the moment to be unarmed."

"Well, all right, but only until we get to Nafrath. You see I do not like wearing weapons and using them is even worse, I do not understand why people cannot live in peace," protested Harad.

"You are possibly right," said Ruben. "It would be nice if there were more people like yourself, but in my experience there are too many occasions when you need to be armed."

"That is what I keep telling you," said Joself, admonishing his older brother. "Particularly when you have the responsibility of a wife and children, as well as our mother!"

"Where did you get your wonderful sword, sir?" piped up one of the children. This brought an annoyed glance from Harad.

"This was a special present from the gods," said Ruben to the child, whilst winking at his father. "Given to me when I was a small boy, only a few years older than you, but I had to find it as it was hidden deep in the river, way over to the east where the river flows into the sea."

"And have you had it ever since?" gasped the boy.

"Oh no," said Ruben. "A special friend of mine looked after it, when I was sent into the army and taught how to use it."

"And did the gods give you your special jerkin and your eagle?" questioned the boy, taking the opportunity to move closer to Ruben and touch his jerkin.

"The eagle, yes, but the jerkin was made for me when I was in the army," explained Ruben. "It is made from the skin of one of the great big crocodiles that you find downriver." Here he made a large grabbing motion with his hands, imitating a crocodile's jaws, scooping up the boy, amid howls of merriment from both the children. They were soon both sitting next to Ruben, who was telling them wonderful stories about fish and animals that lived in the river and the sea.

Much to the children's frustration their mother told them that they must go to bed, but they would not leave Ruben's side until he had promised that they could walk with him the next day if they did what their mother wanted.

"You obviously like children," said Harad. "It is surprising considering your trade. They hardly go together."

"I suppose not," admitted Ruben. "But being a mercenary was to a large extent accidental. I was caught up in the war with Assyria by misfortune."

The men were soon sitting alone around the fire as the women went to bed soon after the children. Ruben saw his opportunity and spoke to Joself, who seemed annoyed that Tasmin had given Ruben a kiss goodnight as well as himself and his brother.

"Your wife is very attractive," said Ruben. "But my friend, I am not interested in her, as she is your woman, my fascination simply stems from the fact that she is almost identical to my late wife."

"And what happened to your wife now?" asked Joself.

"She was killed in the battle at Ashkilon," said Ruben meeting Joself's eyes in a steady look above the fire.

Joself looked down and mumbled his apologies.

"Oh, I too am most sorry," said Harad, and after a pause added, "but I think we had better try and get some sleep, as we still have a long way to go tomorrow."

"Yes, I agree," said Joself. "But do you think we had better take turn in keeping watch?"

"Certainly," answered Ruben. "But I am not sleepy so I will keep first watch, and then wake you." The two brothers were happy with this, so saying goodnight they wrapped themselves in their blankets and were soon asleep.

Ruben found it difficult to sleep, as the very presence of Tasmin reminded him so much of Lialah. He did not think that he was jealous, even though he had to admit that Tasmin was extremely attractive, her unusual hair colour made her even more striking than Lialah had been. But it was not desire that he felt, simply the cruel bereavement of her untimely death. He thought he had got over his loss, but realised that having had Skree to worry about and then being busy when he was in Thrax, had managed to keep his mind from reminiscing. Still, he was now able to think of Lialah with deep affection and he knew that it was simply a matter of time before he could finally get over her death. Even so, he knew that he would have to speak to Tasmin and request that she stop being too familiar with him, as it obviously annoyed Joself and that was not a sensible thing to do. The more he thought about it, the more he felt sure that Tasmin seemed to be doing it almost deliberately. He therefore decided to speak to Harad in the morning, as there was something strange about their relationship. Why had Harad paused before saying that she was Joself's wife? This was not the only question that he needed an answer to; he also could remember Dathram saying nothing about this Empty Sector that Harad had referred to.

It was a calm and quiet night, there had been a pink glow from the sunset in the west the previous evening, giving the promise of a fine dry morning. As he was not tired and could not sleep he went for a walk along the river to check that the path by the rocky outcrop was still passable. This was the case, even though it was a bit of a scramble over the rocks, but the route was passable even for the children. He found as he went further up the river that the water here was a lot calmer, and as the sun was just beginning to rise he slipped off his clothes and went for a quick early morning swim.

******

Ratarz had been extremely fortunate, although he had been knocked unconscious by a falling rock; he had not been swept away in the avalanche as many of his men had. His horse was lying dead and was half buried by rocks, together with the body of that stupid bowman, who had shot the arrow at the eagle. It was that which had alerted their presence to the large mercenary, who was the last person that Ratarz had wanted to meet. He was now wide awake, badly bruised and hungry, but lay still, checking himself for broken bones. Having decided that he could still move, he slowly raised himself and looked around to see what had woken him. Then he could see that large bastard in the river below him. He kept well out of sight as the mercenary came out of the river, dressed himself and went back around the rocks to where he must have camped with the small party from Thrax.

Considering his predicament, Ratarz made, for himself, an unusual decision. He had noticed the bow and arrows that were lying near to where the dead bowman was half buried. He had decided to wait until the bloody arse that had caused the landslide with that lucky throw, would pay with his life. He picked up the bow and arrows and even though he was not a good shot he was quite definite that he could kill the bastard if he got close to him. Deciding that the party would come past him, he selected a large boulder to sit behind while waiting and then shoot him in the back as he walked past.

He did not have long to wait, as the party assembled itself quickly, once they were roused by the mercenary on his return. He could hear them deciding to start moving early before stopping for some breakfast, because of the need to travel with plenty of breaks in the journey for the children. Ratarz carefully positioned himself so that he would only have to fire from a few paces away. Very soon the first of the party came past; they were so incredibly close that he could not miss. Eventually the large mercenary came past with his large bag and javelin in one hand and helping a small boy to leap over the rocks with his other hand. As the bastard was wearing a stout crocodile skin jerkin, he took careful aim at his neck, which he felt sure he could hit at such close range. He pulled back on the bowstring and was about to loose the arrow when a shrill screech assailed his ears and there was a rush of wind as the talons of the eagle tore at his head. The arrow flew wide of its intended victim and he was so desperate in trying to free his hair from the vicious claws, that he stumbled in rising to his feet and fell down the rocks into the river. As he could not swim he was soon drowned in the raging current.

It had all happened so quickly, the cry of the eagle, the arrow whistling past Ruben's head, the twang of the bow and the desperate cries of the assailant as he tumbled down into the river. By the time Ruben had swung round putting himself between where the arrow had come from and the party, all he could hear and see was the splash. It did not take him long to realise what happened, his attacker was by then being whipped away down river so quickly that any chance of rescue was remote. Not that he felt inclined to try to save someone who had just tried to kill him, so instead he shouted his thanks to Skree for saving his life. The rest of the small party gathered around the children and Harad, who had been in the lead, asked him if he was all right and what had happened.

Ruben told him what he knew, but then sensing his opportunity to speak to Harad on his own, he asked the boy to walk with his Uncle Joself, and the party should hurry along while he and Harad checked there were no other survivors intent on revenge.

The party was soon heading northwest, whilst he and Harad checked amongst the rocks. They soon found the dead horse and the dead bowman and were quite definite that this shot had come from the only survivor, who was now dead himself. As they hurried after the party, Ruben asked Harad to tell him all about Joself's relationship with Tasmin.

"I have to be honest with you Ruben, it is all rather strange. Joself came back last year from Canaan saying that he had won this woman from a Canaanite trader in a game of dice. He told me that she was his for a year, but if he wanted her for longer, he would have to pay sixty gold pieces. That, as you can well imagine, is a lot of money in these parts."

"What a strange way to go about obtaining a wife," commented Ruben.

"Well, perhaps it may seem so to you, but it is fairly common in Canaan. Unfortunately Joself has only managed to get fifty gold pieces, and he is travelling to Timon to try to negotiate to keep her," Harad explained.

"Do you approve of his choice?" asked Ruben, feeling shocked.

"Well, it is not really up to me," said Harad. "But personally she is not my choice. Oh yes, she is pretty all right, but not much good at the important things, like cooking and making a home, mending, and organising the house. But Joself says that he loves her. To be honest, I don't think she really cares for him. I don't mean that in an unkind way you understand, but she doesn't seem to want to settle down, and often seems to want other men, as I am sure you have noticed," he said with a shrug of his shoulders. "I am only his older brother, he won't listen to me, he thinks I'm daft and unrealistic, but I want him to be happy, so I say nothing. You never know, she may turn out all right in the end, but I somehow doubt it," he shrugged again.

There was a long pause as the two men walked along, each deep in his own thoughts. Eventually, when they came in sight of the party, which had stopped for breakfast, Ruben said, "What about this Empty Sector that you were going to tell me about?"

"Well, it all happened earlier this year, I believe it was in the spring. A friend of mine was travelling with a few male companions into Canaan when they came across some bandits who had attacked a small caravan. This caravan was carrying salt and that strange yellow rock that burns, which had come from a place near the fabled salt sea away to the south. The bandits had unsecured all the salt and yellow rock and were arguing over what to do with these goods, when my friend and his companions attacked them. The containers of the goods became broken in the fight, which was stopped by a sandstorm. Everything in the area was covered in a layer of salt and yellow powder, so nothing grows there now," he chuckled merrily. "I know it all sounds bizarre," he said, wiping away the tears of mirth, "but that is how it happened. It is not a large area, a small plain, between the foothills to these mountains and the hills of Canaan, where Timon is situated."

They now joined Joself and the others in the party for breakfast. Harad said to Joself, "I was just telling Ruben about the Empty Sector," he laughed, "and all about how it became like it is."

"Did he believe you?" asked Joself smiling. "Because it is true, Ruben. It will probably revert back once it has all been washed away, but it now makes a good boundary because no one lives there and nobody wants to own it."

"I think I'll believe it when I see it," said Ruben cautiously, just in case they were pulling his leg.

They soon moved on again, the children delighted that their hero was back with them, with his magnificent eagle that was circling high above them. They took it in turns to walk with him, and at every stop that was made, they sat with him and he continued to tell them wonderful stories about strange places, unusual people, huge men and ugly men, of training in the army and of battles, enormous boats and beautiful cities with wonderful gardens. He was of course only telling them the story of his own life, perhaps slightly embellished, but it was told with such excitement and conviction that it sounded incredible but true. By the end of the long day's walk they were both asleep, Ruben carrying one of the children and Joself carrying the other. This was just as well, as it prevented them from seeing the grizzly sight that was awaiting the party as they crossed the bridge and entered Nafrath.

# 17
## THE EMPTY SECTOR

As they entered the town an appalling spectacle met their eyes, in addition to the putrid stench of death that assaulted their nostrils. Nafrath was a walled town and as they entered by the southeastern gate, four corpses swung from the crossbeam of the entrance gateway. They were unmistakably the four Assyrian soldiers who had retreated from their attack on the party when their leader had been killed by Ruben.

"What sort of barbarism is this?" demanded Ruben, as he handed back the sleeping child to Harad's wife. Taking immediate control of the situation, he instructed Joself to hand over the other boy to his mother and told Tasmin that she must quickly take all but the men to her and Joself's house, where the women and children should stay, until joined by the men. He then told Joself to find anyone in charge of security for the town, as there was no one about, and it seemed unnaturally quiet. As the women left, shielding the eyes of the waking children, woken by the foul smell and being naturally inquisitive, Ruben asked Harad for his assistance. Dumping his gear and removing his sword belt, he drew his dagger and handed it to Harad, telling him to pass it to him when requested. He measured off ten paces, turned, and running to just below the crossbeam, launched himself into the air and caught the crossbeam where the four corpses were hanging. It was obvious that their death had not been a quick one, but that of slow strangulation, causing horrible contortions of the face, whilst the victims had been stoned to death. Hanging from the beam with one hand, Ruben asked Harad to pass him the dagger, which he used to sever the rope from which the nearest corpse hung. The body fell with a dull thud on the ground, which was littered with stones that had been thrown. Moving hand over hand along the beam with his dagger held between his teeth, Ruben had soon cut down all four corpses; he then passed the dagger back to Harad and dropped lightly to the ground, landing like a cat. Harad was astonished at Ruben's agility, he would not have believed that such a large person was capable of such acrobatics, but of course Ruben was superbly fit and still young. He and Harad were just on the point of straightening out the corpses, when they were interrupted by one of the town's officials who had come with Joself.

"Hey, what do you think you are doing?" said the official.

"That is just what I was going to ask you, by doing such a shameful thing!" countered Ruben crossly.

"They were guilty of grievous crimes against citizens of this town," said the man righteously.

"Of that, I have no doubt," said Ruben. "But they are Assyrian soldiers, and I would not like to be in your position when word of this gets back to Nineveh."

"But the whole town took part in the execution," said the official pompously.

"That does not mean that news of the treatment will not get back to the commanders who sent the soldiers here in the first place, apart from which, such behaviour is most uncivilised," said Ruben indignantly.

"And just who do you think you are?" asked the official, puffing out his chest. "I am an elected member of the town's authority, so do not tell me my job, or I'll have you thrown out of the town."

"You can if you wish, because I have no desire to stay in such a place," said Ruben. "But not until I have dealt with these dead bodies, after all you are only asking for disease to spread by leaving them hanging like they were."

He walked away from the man back to one of the corpses, while asking Joself to get a spade and Harad to bring him some firewood and oil. They both obeyed, leaving the astonished official by himself. He soon disappeared.

The two brothers did as they were requested, bringing Ruben what he needed. He quickly dug a shallow grave into which he threw the four corpses, covering them with firewood, which he liberally drenched with oil and then lit the pyre, as was the standard way to deal with the dead, following his army training. As the flames died down, Ruben covered the hot embers with the earth that he had dug out of the ground.

This was just outside the town wall, where the gate had been left open, and nobody stopped the three men as they walked back to Joself's house, through the unusually quiet and now dark streets. The women and children were delighted with their return and quickly produced a much-needed meal. During the meal the children wanted to know what had happened to Ruben's eagle.

"They don't like towns, eagles like open spaces and high mountains where they live." he told them. "We will probably see him tomorrow."

"I thought we were going to stay here?" questioned Harad.

"I do not think that would be wise," stated Ruben. His statement was confirmed by Joself, who hastily nodded his agreement.

"Well, where now?" asked Harad looking from one to the other.

"I think it would be best if we all leave by the southwest gate tomorrow, I will travel on with Joself and Tasmin into Canaan as originally agreed. But you should come with us, and then double back, keeping well clear of the town and travel home to Thrax," said Ruben.

"You see I believe word of what happened to the soldiers will get back to Nineveh, and reprisals against the town will follow."

"I agree with Ruben," said Joself. "After all, I know these people and they are not like the good honest folk of Thrax. I have decided to move on, I may return to you in Thrax, but it all depends on what happens in Canaan."

"What of my opinion?" demanded Tasmin.

"Quiet, woman!" said Joself decisively. "You will for once do as you are bid." The rest of the meal passed in silence, the women and children leaving the men to make their plans on their own.

The following morning they rose early, and over breakfast Harad advised the women exactly what they had planned. Harad's wife and Tasmin would go shopping to obtain plenty of food to take with them. "Simply enough for three or four days' travel," he said.

"But when are we going, and are we all travelling together?" asked his wife.

"I am just coming to that," he informed all the enquiring faces, particularly those of the children, who seemed excited by the idea of this new journey.

"Whilst our wives are shopping they should make it known that we are all travelling together. Joself and I will go out trying to find out as much information as we can about what happened yesterday before we arrived. Joself will also tell the house merchant that he will be leaving and will probably not be coming back." As he said this there was such excitement that he had to hold up his hand to demand silence. He then continued. "Mother will stay here with the children and Ruben help her to leave everything tidy and to pack all we can carry." This announcement was met with shrieks of delight, it excited the children, the prospect of being with their hero was unbelievable. He once again had to tell them to keep quiet and then continued. While he was out he expected them to be good boys and do everything they were told by their grandmother and Ruben. They immediately quietened down and gave their solemn promise.

He carried on. "Once we are back, we will leave as soon as possible taking the southwestern gate and its bridge, go across the southern part of the river, travel as if we were going to Canaan. But then, when we are well beyond the town we will split into two parties. Mother, we and the children will travel back, keeping well away from the town and head back to Thrax, which we should reach in two days. Joself and Tasmin will travel as originally planned with Ruben to the Empty Sector and eventually to Timon."

This was met with cries of disappointment. But the children were soon calmed by Ruben who said, "Come along, boys, we have lots to do."

He made them stand in a line next to him, thumped his chest in salute and said, "We are at your command, Grandmother."

This greatly amused Harad and trying not to laugh he said to Joself and both wives, "Let's get going then, we all know what to do."

Harad's mother was very organised and they soon had everything tidied up and the bags packed just inside the front door. Ruben had taken two small bags and with a few light pieces of wood, he made two small frame knapsacks for the boys to carry, with laced cord that he used for straps. They then had to wait for the others to return, so rather than just sitting around waiting, Ruben showed the boys how to travel, walking with the minimum of effort and told them, "It is up to you two lads to make sure that you and your family arrive home in Thrax in good time without being noticed." The boys both listened intently and did everything that they were told.

The eldest boy then said, "I am going to be a soldier when I grow up, just like you."

"It is not all fun, excitement and winning battles," he said. Then continued to explain. "Being in the army often entails very hard work, hurting and even killing people is not a good thing to do. So often you do not know what you are fighting for and why. You have to hurt others. It is far better to be kind and help other people."

"But why do you do it then? You are so clever in everything you do," asked the boy admiringly.

"My life was planned out for me," said Ruben. "And I was built to be big and strong, but sometimes I wish that I did not have to fight other people."

The door then opened, and the others came back, having completed all the shopping and their other tasks.

"Great," said Harad, looking around and noticing everything was packed and ready to go. "The girls are just dividing up the provisions and we can then set off. Joself and I discovered much disquieting news, it would appear that some people who took part in stoning the soldiers, can not now be found, additionally, many of the decent people kept well away from what was happening yesterday. Joself and I believe that news may already have been taken to the nearest Assyrian army base. So it would appear that you were perfectly correct, Ruben, the sooner that we start the better."

Shouldering their burdens, they all filed out of the house, the children being keen to show their parents their knapsacks, which Ruben had made for them, to allow them to carry some of the load. Obviously this was only a small amount that was light in weight, but it made the children feel grown up and that they too were helping. One of Joself's neighbours, an elderly and pleasant man came out of his house, to say that he was sorry to see Joself go, as Joself had been a good neighbour and helped the old man if he needed assistance.

Joself replied saying, "I will miss you too old friend, but I may be back and if I am passing I will certainly drop in to say hello. Now you take care of yourself and be sure to keep well away from any Assyrian soldiers who come around. If they ask where we went, be honest with them and tell them that with our friend, this large mercenary," and here he indicated Ruben, who was wearing his black tunic and kilt, "we are heading to Canaan, across the Empty Sector."

They all waved goodbye and set off towards the southwestern gate and its bridge. They travelled in procession with Harad and Joself in the lead, followed by the children proudly carrying their knapsacks, Ruben came next in line, fully armed with his large bag and javelin held in one hand and the largest holdall that held all the food and cooking equipment. The three women came next in line, which was customary, although they normally carried most of the burdens, but in this case most of the heavy things were carried by the men. They had been following the stream that ran into Nafrath and then on to enter the Euphrates, this stream they had previously crossed and then followed to Nafrath. Just here there was a crossing ford, when the stream came down from the northern side of a small hill that was directly in front of them. If they crossed the stream here they would be leaving what was definitely Assyria and be in the area that seemed to be under no king's command. It would have been easier for Harad and his family to leave here, as they were well clear of the town, and follow the path southwards and then turn back to the northeast and journey to Thrax. Harad and Joself had been discussing this when Ruben called out to them to stop here.

Harad turned back to Ruben and said, "Oh, I am sorry Ruben, I had forgotten that you were carrying most of the heavy equipment."

"It is not the weight that has made me call a halt," said Ruben. "But I wish to make a reconnoitre," he explained. Then putting down his heavy bag and the holdall, he said to them, "Wait for a few moments, as I will not be long." Then leaping across the ford, he ran up the hill at an amazingly fast pace. Then they looked up and could see two eagles circling above the small hill that Ruben was climbing. When he reached the top the two eagles flew to meet him. One of the birds was obviously Skree, but none of the party had any idea where the other bird had come from, also it was of a slightly different plumage.

Ruben had reached the top of the hill only slightly out of breath, as the two eagles flew to meet him. Skree landed as usual on his shoulder, protected by his jerkin. The other bird perched on a small hawthorn tree.

Ruben stroked Skree's feathers at the back of his head, which he knew the eagle liked.

"I am glad you have found a companion my feathered friend, I suppose you will now wish to fly further into the mountains and make a home," Ruben asked. Skree squawked as if to reply in the affirmative. "However, there is one job I would like you to do for me before we part, as I must now leave the mountains." Skree glared back at him, as if to say 'Why do you want to go there, it is hot, dry and dusty.' At least that was the meaning that Ruben took from that glare.

"I am sorry my friend, but that is the way I have to go, but will you do one last favour for me?" Skree looked at him and cocked his head one side. Ruben looked all the way around and could see a party of horsemen riding to the ford coming from Nafrath in the North. "I will leave you now and go back to take my party to the eastern side of this hill, where I will take two others and travel to the southeast. We will then send the others with the two small boys back to Thrax where we lived when your wing was in the clay bandage." This he said whilst using sign language and pointing. "What I would like you to do is to make sure that the two small boys arrive home safely, will you do that for me my beautiful friend?" Skree gave a single squawk in response and flew into the air, followed by his new companion. Ruben then turned and ran down the hill, leaping from rock to rock and using his javelin to balance his fast descent.

While he was on the hill, Joself said to Harad, "By Hades, what is he doing?"

"I really have no idea," replied Harad. "He seems to be gesticulating and looking about."

"No Father," said one of the boys, "he is talking to the eagles." Harad looked at his son, as if seeing him for the first time.

"By the Gods!" said Joself. "I do believe he is right. Anyway he is coming down the hillside now and we will soon know."

Ruben reached the ford, and was soon back with the party and said, "We must continue on this side of the stream to the other side of the hill, where we can re-cross the stream where there is another ford and disappear down the northeastern side of the hill." As they all looked surprised he added, "You see, there is a party of Assyrian soldiers coming after us from Nafrath and I think we can be out of sight before they arrive here. Only, meeting them on our own would not be a good idea." He picked up his equipment and hurried the party along, this time sending all the party in front of him as quickly as they could go.

The lad who had said to his father that he was talking to the eagles, dropped back beside him and asked, "You were talking to the birds, weren't you, sir?"

Ruben smiled at the boy and said, "Yes, my lad, I was asking them to look after you, and make sure you arrive back to Thrax safely." The boy gazed up at him with wonder.

"Do they understand your speech, or do you talk in their language?" asked the boy.

"Well, I think they understand, but I use a lot of sign language that I learnt from my Nubian friend, the man I was telling you about the other day," responded Ruben. "But do not tell your parents, because they may not believe. Grown up people often do not believe things that seem easy to young people, mainly because they cannot do it themselves. But we really must hurry along now, so I want you and your brother to run on ahead until you come to the ford." The boy ran on and Ruben could hear him say to his brother that he would race him to the ford, and the two boys dashed off in front of their parents. The rest of the party hurried along as quickly as they could, all the time being encouraged to move faster by Ruben. Regrettably, Harad's mother was short of breath and began to fall behind. Ruben put down his large bag and the holdall, carefully positioning them behind a small boulder so that when seen from a distance they were not easily recognised. Much to the old woman's surprise, he said, "Hold on, Grandmother, I will carry you." Before she could protest, he picked her up in his arms and chased after the two boys, finally overtaking them just before they got to the ford, where he had already put their grandmother down.

"You will have to do better than that lads," he said whilst regaining his breath. "Even your grandmother beat you." The two boys were just on the point of protesting as it was not a fair race as grandmother had not run and was carried by Ruben, but they were cut short as Ruben directed them across the ford, which only came up to their knees. He hurried them up, asking the boys to take their grandmother behind a large pile of boulders that were a short way ahead. The rest of the party came along gasping for breath, but Ruben relentlessly hurried them across the ford.

At this point Tasmin said, "I have hurt my ankle," and looking at Ruben, pleadingly asked him if he would carry her.

"I cannot carry you all," said Ruben, knowing full well that there was little wrong with her ankle. "I will take your bag and you will have to manage as best you can." This interchange was heard by Joself, who said nothing but was glad at the outcome. They all made the shelter of the rocks just in time, before the horsemen reached the lower ford. Ruben lifted one of the boys onto his shoulders, where the boy could look out between gaps in the rocks and tell them what was happening. The lad said that the party was of eight soldiers all on horseback, they stopped at the ford and had a quick look around before travelling back to Nafrath. Ruben waited for a while until all the party regained their breath. He then told Harad to take the party on around the hill until he could see the road that led south from the ford at which the horsemen had stopped. He then left the party to move on while he went back to collect the two bags that he had left.

He moved cautiously at first, but when he saw that all that could be seen of the horsemen was a cloud of dust in the distance, he ran in the open to retrieve his bags and then strolled back after Harad's group. They had stopped in a convenient place where they could overlook the road without being seen, also from where they could hide if required. As it was approximately the middle of the day they decided to stop for a light meal, before splitting up and going their separate ways. The women prepared the lunch and also divided up the food, Harad and his wife taking the minor portion of the remaining food, just enough to last them and the boys for two meals, as they hoped to reach Thrax in under two days. Ruben thought it was interesting to note that Tasmin's walking ability seemed to have miraculously cured itself. He went and sat with Joself and mentioned this. Joself seemed resigned to his wife's philandering, but realising that Ruben would not take advantage of this situation pleased him.

"Thank you for refusing to carry her, Ruben, she was just up to one of her old tricks again," he said.

"Why do you put up with it?" enquired Ruben.

"I really wish I knew," he said with a deep sigh. "But the fact is that I do love her, and I really think that she does care about me."

"So you intend to go ahead with your plan to try to negotiate to buy her," he enquired, still a little incredulous at the idea.

"I know it sounds crazy, but I don't suppose you have ever had any difficulty in attracting beautiful women," he said.

For once, Ruben felt awkward. "No, you are right there, and in the big towns there is never any shortage of available females, although I am not the type who just uses women for pleasure," he admitted.

"But you haven't had great difficulty either," said Harad joining in the conversation. "And after all, there is a lot more than good looks to look for when seeking a wife."

"Yes I know, we have had this conversation many times," responded Joself. "But I can't get her out of my head."

Their conversation was interrupted as Harad's wife brought some food over, which they ate, and soon it was time for them to get going again. There was a cry from above and they looked up to see both eagles circling high in the air above the road.

"The road seems clear and the eagles want us to get going," said Ruben to Harad. "So let's say our goodbyes and start travelling." The two boys did not want Ruben to leave them and he felt almost the same way. "I am sorry boys but I must travel on, but the eagles will make sure you get home safely, always keep looking up, they will ensure that you keep to the right road and warn you of any danger," he told them, with an encouraging smile.

"But will you ever come back?" asked the older boy.

"I do not know, boys," replied Ruben, forcing himself to smile, even though he felt sad at leaving them. "Now I am relying on you both to always be kind to animals, and eagles in particular, and also to look after your father and mother."

"Yes, sir," both boys replied, returning the salute in thumping their chests, as Ruben had done. He then turned and picked up his bags and started walking off slowly, whilst Harad and his wife said their goodbyes to Joself and Tasmin. He was soon joined by Joself, with Tasmin walking between the two men, which although pleasant, did hinder fluent conversation between the two men. They continued walking southwesterly, continually moving away from the mountains as the scenery gradually changed and it became noticeably warmer. Even though it was not yet winter it was hotter than usual for the time of year and the air seemed dry, with a faint acrid smell that was rather unpleasant, particularly after the cool fresh air of the mountains. Ruben remarked on this to Joself, as talk about the weather was a safe subject to discuss.

"That is the Empty Sector," said Joself. "Apart from nothing growing there, it smells obnoxious and all the standing water in the area is undrinkable, unless you want to go raving mad," he laughed. "It is therefore important that we fill our empty water containers before we cross from one of the unpolluted springs."

"How far is it from here?" asked Ruben.

"We still have more than a day's journey before we come to the edge and it is best to make the crossing in one long march, without having to stop," said Joself decisively. "I was therefore going to recommend that we stop soon, so that we reach the Sector the next evening. Then we can camp by the edge and start early the next morning."

"Although you are the guide, and know the country far better than I," said Ruben, "would it not be a good idea to keep going while it is still light, as it is not even near the end of the day, just in case there is any pursuit from Nafrath?"

"But that would mean that we will not reach there sometime before noon tomorrow," exclaimed Joself, questioningly. "Surely we would not want to cross during the hottest part of the day?"

"There is no rule that we cannot rest, before going on during the late afternoon and evening," replied Ruben.

"No, I suppose not," said Joself. "But it would mean that we will not reach Canaan until night-time."

"There is nothing wrong with that," cut in Tasmin scornfully. "I know where we will be welcome."

"Well, if you are prepared to go on," asked Joself. "But I thought your ankle was painful," he sneered.

"Well, it seems all right now," she laughed at him, obviously intending to mock him and start an argument.

Sensing a possible altercation, Ruben said, "I think it would be best to press on to make as much distance between ourselves and Nafrath as possible."

They walked on in silence for some considerable time through a quiet wood that consisted mainly of birch trees, whose leaves were turning to gold and copper before joining those that had already fallen.

"Is there any wildlife in this area?" Ruben asked Joself.

"There used to be small deer," replied Joself. "But they are rare since the Empty Sector came into being."

"Well, if you two keep to the main path," suggested Ruben, "I will scout over to the right of you, which would be down wind of any animals. You never know, I may be able to provide us with fresh venison tonight."

"Oh, what a lovely idea," said Tasmin. "Can I come and watch how you hunt?"

"I do not think it would be a good idea," laughed Ruben. "There is no time for talking as I have to move quietly, and quickly. So I suggest that you two go on ahead and I will join you later." As this idea seemed a good suggestion to Joself, who took Tasmin's hand and urged her onwards, it left Ruben alone, for which he was most grateful. He had realised that they needed to be alone to talk, apart from which he had noticed something move away to the right out of the corner of his eye. He put down the bags beside one of the trees and stood very still with his javelin in his right hand, intensely watching the area where he felt sure that he had seen something stir.

He watched Joself and Tasmin walk out of sight and waited for a while after he could no longer hear them. Then he smelt the strong musk of deer and saw a small fawn move out from behind a thicket and move slowly away, grazing on some of the leaves that were still green. He quietly followed the animal to within about fifty paces away. He knew he could hit the fawn from that distance and possibly kill it, but was unsure of whether it would be a clean, swift kill. The fawn then turned to look him directly in the eyes, it obviously did not recognise him as an enemy and its large honey coloured eyes were gentle and very trusting. He lowered his throwing arm and felt very guilty. They did not really need the meat as they had brought plenty of food that would last them until they reached Canaan. His words to the two small boys echoed in the back of his mind, mocking him. 'Be kind to animals,' was what he had said and he also remembered Simeon's words, 'Take care of the Creator's creatures,' which made him feel hypocritical. The small fawn slowly walked towards him and he squatted down as the animal came over to smell him and lick his fingertips. He suddenly remembered the dark brown sugary sweets that Harad's mother had made for the boys, which they had shared with him. He fished around in his pockets and fortunately found one, which he offered to the fawn, saying, "Try this, little fellow." The sweet was a great success and the little animal nosed around his pockets to see if there were any more. He stroked and patted the fawn as it unearthed a remaining sweet from his pocket, when there suddenly came a low barking call that Ruben realised must have come from the fawn's parents. It pricked up its ears and turned its back on him and trotted back into the thicket, towards where the call had come from.

Ruben stood up, and feeling rather foolish, picked up his javelin and walked back to where he had deposited the bags. He picked up the bags and walked along the path that Joself and Tasmin had taken, although he did not walk quickly as he was not in a rush to catch them up. It was late afternoon by now and the sun slanted in through the half empty branches of the trees, casting attractive autumn shades all around. He once again began to wonder about all the lovely things around him and was surprised when he realised that he could see Joself and Tasmin a few hundred paces ahead of him. They had not seen him and were for once talking earnestly, walking hand in hand. He stood for a moment and looked at them with half-closed eyes and unexpectedly, he could make out a faint blue aura around them. He had not lost this gift that Simeon had taught him. He thought that all the fighting and the people that he had killed in Ashkilon, apart from the bitterness he felt over the death of Lialah, had ruined his ability to see the colours that surround people, but he again remembered Simeon's words, 'You must be in harmony with the Creator.'

He watched his friends move on and after a while hurried up to join them, feeling both elated and mystified that he had regained the ability that he had thought he had lost forever.

"Did you not have any luck?" asked Joself.

"No, I could not get close enough," lied Ruben. "But we do not really need the meat so I'm sure that we will manage quite comfortably."

"But if you could see it, surely you would be able to hit it as you have strong arms?" enquired Tasmin.

"My dear girl, there is a lot more to it than just throwing and hurting something," said Ruben, going on to explain. "It is wrong to wound something and then let it die from loss of blood, after a long chase. If you have to kill something you should kill it swiftly, do you not agree Joself?"

"Oh yes," said Joself, surprised at being consulted, but then recovering and saying, "Yes, my dear, Ruben is quite correct, it is unkind to let the animal suffer."

They walked out of the eaves of the wood, and it was now beginning to get dark. "Let us carry on just a little further, to that small clump of trees on the next ridge, that would be a good place to camp for the night, as we will not be approached from behind without easily spotting those who may come looking for us," Ruben suggested.

"Yes, I think that's a good idea," agreed Joself. "Do you think it will be safe to light a fire?"

"It should be," responded Ruben. "Providing it is not too large and the light can not be seen from the east."

They were soon on the other ridge, and whilst Tasmin gathered some dried wood to make the fire, Ruben and Joself set about constructing two bivouacs. Ruben made sure that Joself and Tasmin's sleeping area was well away from his own and that he looked back towards the east, so that he would be alerted by any sound of pursuit. They ate a substantial meal, which mainly consisted of unleavened bread, goats' cheese and smoked meat that they had brought from Nafrath. This was uncooked and the fire was simply used to make a hot sweet herb drink that was common to those from the mountains, but entirely new to Ruben. It was strangely invigorating and very warming. Ruben asked Joself about this saying, "That is a pleasant drink, where does it come from?"

Joself said, "It is made from dry leaves that come from a bush that grows in the area, and the dried leaves are mixed in hot water with sugar. It is very pleasing and easy to carry, as you only have to worry about the leaves and sugar, providing that you have a water container to heat it in. We find it useful, particularly in the winter, as long as you have a small clay pot to heat the water, you can even use ice or snow instead of water in the winter."

"Are there any traditional drinks common to Canaan?" Ruben asked Tasmin, wishing her to take part in comfortable conversation.

"There is a strong alcoholic drink called Rahki," she told him. "It is made from fermented olive skins, when they have extracted the oil. It is a clear liquid and goes milky white when mixed with water, but it is strong and should be drunk with care."

"I think I have heard of it," said Ruben. "Is it sometimes called camel juice?" he asked.

"Yes, that's right," laughed Tasmin. "That is the name that some of the merchants give to it, but it is only served in the temple on special events, at feast times or other celebrations, according to local custom."

"And what exactly did you do in Canaan, before you met Joself," enquired Ruben.

"Oh, well, I originally used to work in the temple, but then I was bought by a merchant and it was from him that Joself won me in a game of dice," she explained quietly, seeming reluctant to elaborate.

"And what sort of work were you engaged in at the temple?" persisted Ruben; very interested as this was an unusual situation.

"Oh, just serving at special occasions and helping the priests with other minor jobs," she said, trying to dismiss the subject. "Now let me have your plates, both of you," she ordered. She tidied up and took everything down to a little brook that started as a spring, which bubbled out from the bottom of the ridge.

"That is the first time that I have seen her tidy up," exclaimed Ruben, looking at Joself enquiringly.

"It is the subject," returned Joself. "I have never been able to gain a suitable answer as to what her duties were in the temple. You see they have many strange customs and it is difficult to bring her to talk about them."

"I hope you did not mind my asking?" Ruben enquired.

"Not at all, Ruben. And thank you very much for leaving us alone this afternoon, we had not spoken properly about the future for some considerable time, it made everything a lot more straightforward and we seem more settled now."

"Well I am glad of that," said Ruben. "But now, if you'll excuse me, I would like to go and rig up an early warning system to alert us if anyone is following our trail."

He left Joself and returned to where they had come out of the wood, and found a few sturdy saplings that were growing either side of the path. He bent them over and entwined the tops at about knee height along the path, so that anyone coming that way in the dark would walk into them, making the saplings fly back. This, he hoped, if someone set it off, would wake him. He then returned to the ridge that he had left and was pleased to note that Joself and Tasmin had retired for the night, although it was not late and as they were in no rush – they had not planned on an early start in the morning. He was glad of his own company as he had a lot to think about. So he crawled into his bivouac and lay on his back, just as the moon rose, casting a silvery light across the area between himself and the wood. Although he did not feel sleepy, for the first time in a long time he contentedly lay down and thought of the strange events of the day. He was unsure of how long he lay there, but eventually he drifted off to sleep, even becoming used to the faint unpleasant smell that came from the

Empty Sector.

He awoke with a start, as a swoosh came from the wood, immediately followed by the drumming of hoof beats that retreated into the distance. He was instantly awake and watched the edge of the wood for a few moments, but nothing emerged and the quiet of the early morning returned. He cautiously came out of the bivouac and crossed to the eaves of the wood, where he had set his early warning system. The saplings had sprung back to being upright and he inspected the ground to see what had set it off. He chuckled to himself, the ground was marked by the cloven hoof prints of a deer, which must have set off his early warning device by accident, there were no other prints in sight. He even laid down and put his ear to the ground to listen and try to detect the noise of any movement. It was so quiet that he could hear the steady rhythm of his own heart. Straightening up, he walked slowly back to his bivouac, which he dismantled, then redressed himself and repacked his bag. He went to the other side of the ridge to where they had set up their small fire the previous evening and started preparing breakfast, whilst making plenty of noise to wake the others.

Joself came out of his bivouac still yawning and said, "You are up early, Ruben."

"I was woken when my early warning system was set off," he explained. "But there is nothing to worry about," he hastily added, noticing Joself's concern. "It was activated by one of the forest deer and I am sure that there is no one following us. Having woken up, there seemed little point in going back to sleep and as we had an early night yesterday I see no point in hanging around. With the additional time we can carefully obliterate all signs of our having been here, which should guarantee we are not followed."

"That sounds like a good idea," said Joself. "We will join you in just a few moments." True to his word, both he and Tasmin came out of their bivouac shortly. Tasmin giving him a hand to prepare a light breakfast, whilst Joself dismantled their shelter. They then quickly finished the meal, Tasmin cleaning up and repacking the bags whilst Ruben and Joself checked the area to ensure that there were no obvious signs of their having camped there.

Joself said, "Either I am becoming more used to the smell of the Empty Sector, or it is less strong this morning."

"I think the latter is correct," judged Ruben. "Although it is not really noticeable yet, I believe the wind has changed to the southeast, which probably means that we are going to have some even warmer weather."

Having packed everything and rechecking the area, they set off, following the brook, which Joself said ran into the Empty Sector and where, before it became polluted, they could fill the water containers and stop during the hottest part of the day before their final march across the Empty Sector.

"What was it that you said yesterday, Joself?" enquired Ruben, "About, if you drink the water, you go raving mad?"

"Well, I have never seen it actually," said Joself. "But I believe that drinking the water can have that effect on either man or beast." Ruben considered making a joke of saying that Tasmin should try it out as she was neither, but being unsure of how the jest would be received, he thought better of it. The journey continued in amiable silence until they turned a bend in the brook that they followed, which had now become a stream. Here there was a small waterfall, which tumbled over a slab of rock, where it fell into a pool surrounded by date palms forming a small oasis right on the edge of the Empty Sector.

The sight was dramatic; it was unreal, almost unbelievable. Had Ruben not been expecting it he would have had difficulty in believing his eyes, it was just as Joself had explained, the sight was really quite incredible. There was nothing growing there, just a few dead trees and plants lying around that had not already been buried in the sand or burned by fire, either accidentally or on purpose. It was a complete wilderness, a miniature desert. But it was not that large as Ruben could quite easily make out the hills on the far side, they were bluish grey in colour and covered by trees. The whole area was a natural depression, but rather than being full of vegetation, lakes and wildlife there was nothing, it was as if a giant had crushed everything under foot. Small flurries of fine powder were occasionally whisked up by the wind, although the wind was very light. The flurries were of fine sand that was made from salt, the yellow rock powder and ash from fires. The name Empty Sector suited it very well, it was, in fact, one of the first man-made ecological disasters. Although they did not realise it at the time, it was only temporary and would revert back into a pleasant valley in a few generations.

Ruben stared aghast at the strange spectacle before him. Eventually he said, "You were perfectly correct Joself, it is exactly as you described, I would not believe it unless I saw it with my own eyes, in fact I still have difficulty in believing what I see. Please forgive me for doubting you, but I feel sure you can imagine my scepticism."

"That's all right Ruben," he said placing a hand on Ruben's shoulder. "I myself still find it shattering. You see, I remember it when it was a green and pleasant valley, full of lakes and plenty of animal life. Now, although it does not seem far across, it often takes far longer as you often have to go round marshy areas that were lakes. Anyway, I suggest we wait under the palms during the heat of the day, refill our water containers from either up here or the waterfall, but be sure you do not drink the water from the pool below the waterfall as it will be contaminated."

Tasmin was staring, just as Ruben had. "Isn't it frightful, although the little pool down there looks very inviting."

"Yes, my sweet," said Joself. "It is safe to bathe in but be sure you do not drink any of the water, unless of course it comes straight off the waterfall."

Joself led the way and all three of them scrambled down to the small oasis where they deposited all their equipment.

"I am just going for a quick walk around, to see if there is anything to see, if you see what I mean," smiled Ruben, pleased with his own wit. He then walked off, while Joself and Tasmin started cooking a meal and refilling the water bottles. Ruben returned just as the food was ready and said, "A little further out across the depression there are some unusual tracks, I think they belong to a large animal, or should I say animals, as it appears there are quite a lot of them. From the prints, I believe they are some form of dog, or a large cat which hunts in packs, is that possible?" he asked, with a puzzled frown.

"I know of no such animal," said Joself.

"You may not," said Tasmin sharply, suddenly reverting back to putting her husband down. "They are probably a form of vicious dog that sometimes comes up from the south into Canaan, they are called Hyena. They are only seen occasionally, but they are ferocious and will attack and kill almost anything. They do not normally attack people, but I would rather not be on my own if they are here."

"I do not think you have anything to worry about, you are safe with me," said Joself.

"So you say, but I would prefer to rely on Ruben," she returned, dismissing him and smiling at Ruben.

This conversation set warning bells sounding in Ruben's head, he had thought that Tasmin's desire for him had passed, but it appeared not to be the case and it seemed that they were back to where they had started. Ignoring the smile, he went to sit beside Joself and said, "How long do you think it will take us to reach the far side?"

"I would like to leave fairly soon," said Joself. "So that we can reach Canaan by early evening, or at least not too late at night. If we can start as soon as the heat dies down, we will then still have plenty of daylight to cross the worst area."

"Presumably this side is more difficult to cross?" enquired Ruben.

"Yes, most certainly," replied Joself. "You see, most of the streams and lakes were on this side, so we will have to be careful not to get trapped in any bogs, but once we are halfway across the going becomes a lot easier."

"That sounds fine with me," said Ruben, smiling and relaxing beside Joself and helping him to finish tidying up. He took out the small bronze knife from its sheath, strapped just below his knee, and began to resharpen it on the stone, which he kept in his pocket for that very purpose.

"Do you keep all your weapons sharp and ready for action?" asked Joself conversationally.

"Yes I do," replied Ruben. "I suppose a lot of it comes from my army training, but it is a good habit. Although the new iron weapons do not need so much attention, they keep their edge for a lot longer."

The two men sat talking about how they had spent their formative years and Ruben was interested to hear how Joself had learnt to become a fur trapper, catching animals for their pelts, as his father had done before him. It appeared that although he had kept up the family business, his older brother disliked the work and now grew vegetables for a living, despite the poor soil around Thrax.

"As long as he's happy," commented Joself. Standing up he said, "It is time we got going." He turned and was about to call to Tasmin, but looked at her with surprised annoyance. "You have chosen the worst possible time to get wet!" he said reprovingly. "You will have to change, as I want to get going."

"This dress will soon dry, if I leave it out in the sun," she said defending her action. She was waist deep in the water of the pool and was heading for the waterfall. "I am just going to rinse off and I will then change."

"Knowing you, that will take forever," he responded, showing his frustration.

"Why don't you go on in front and carry all the bags for a change, rather than leave Ruben to carry everything?" she said mocking him.

"I think I will do just that," he replied decisively. "But you and Ruben must hurry along after me and be sure you do not keep him waiting." He turned away and walked back to where Ruben was sitting under the palms.

Despite Ruben's protestations that he could easily carry his and the large bag, Joself seemed determined to carry it and said, "I will be all right Ruben, it will help me leave a firm trail, but make sure you do not wait for too long before you start to follow. If you have not caught me up by nightfall I will start retracing my footsteps." He then turned, picked up everything he could carry and commenced the journey. Ruben watched him go with disappointment, he was now faced with having to hurry along Tasmin, which he knew was going to be difficult.

After watching Joself trudge away fully laden with as much as he could manage, Ruben allowed what he considered was ample time for Tasmin to get out of the pool and changed. This he based not on his or any man's normal dressing speed, but on the time that it used to take Lialah to get ready, being fully aware that women normally took far longer. His thinking of Lialah and his often repeated requests for her to hurry up, brought a fond smile of remembrance to his face. He then rose, checked that his equipment was in order and called to Tasmin, "Are you ready yet?" trying to keep any degree of exasperation from his voice.

Her voice came back from beneath the waterfall, "I am just coming, will you be a dear and pass me a towel."

Thinking that she was fully dressed but simply had wet hair, he walked over to where she had left her bag near the waterfall and called out, "Where exactly are you?"

"Just here," she answered, stepping straight out from beneath the cascading water, completely naked. The act had been so deliberate and she made no attempt to hide her nudity from his gaze. His eyes automatically travelled to her heavy wet breasts that glistened with droplets of water, which also sparkled on the dark hair at the base of her softly rounded stomach. Her lower abdomen was not as flat and graceful as Lialah's had been before her pregnancy, and there was a line of small creases over her stomach below her large rounded breasts. Realising that he was staring at her, she huskily and provocatively said, "Do you like what you see?"

Recovering from shock, Ruben averted his gaze and passed the towel saying, "Of course I like you, you are very attractive, but you are also trying to seduce me, and frankly I have no desire for you as you are a friend's woman and not my own. Now will you please get ready as it is well past the time that we should start after your husband." He held out the towel to her, turned on his heel and walked back to the grove of palm trees.

She soon came to join him, fully dressed with her damp hair drawn back from her head and tied with a leather thong. "I'm sorry Ruben," she said, placing a cool hand on his forearm. "I thought you would be like most soldiers and would not miss the opportunity of a tumble under the palm trees. I really am quite good in these things!"

"Well I am afraid you misjudged me," he retorted, angrily brushing her hand off his arm. "Were you not married, it might be a different matter, but as it is, I am not interested. Did your husband not tell you that my initial reaction to you was simply that you looked remarkably similar to the girl who was carrying my child? She was killed in the battle at Ashkilon."

"Oh, I am sorry, Joself never told me," she said, sincerely

apologising. "But I'm all packed and ready to go now, so let us get moving after Joself."

"Great," said Ruben rising to his feet. "Follow me, try to walk over my footprints and not over Joself's tracks. I will be setting a quick pace, so try to keep up, but if it is too fast just let me know." They hurried along, the late afternoon sunshine casting long shadows, but it did mean that Joself's footprints were more clearly visible even in reasonably firm ground. It appeared that Joself had taken a few re-corrected turns. As his tracks were occasionally retraced over which he had scored a line in the soil with an arrow pointing in the correct direction that they were to follow. Occasionally these led through slightly marshy ground, but the indentations were not too deep, even though Ruben's own footfalls made deeper impressions due to his heavier weight. The first part of the journey was made in silence and Tasmin kept up the pace that Ruben set. When Ruben decided to call a brief halt for them to take a drink of water, he realised that Tasmin was sweating profusely and breathing very hard, although she had not complained. To relieve the oppressive atmosphere that had descended upon them, he decided to try to probe her about her past.

"I could not help noticing that you have had a child," he mentioned conversationally. He knew about the marks on her stomach that had been caused by a previous pregnancy, as the prostitutes when he had previously gained his experience, had such markings. On speaking about this to Lialah, she had told him about the marks that were left when the skin had been stretched. He had also noted the tiny lines around the corners of her eyes and that the roots of her hair were darker than the reddish gold that her loose curls were normally coloured, which indicated the use of certain dyes.

Tasmin was shocked by this casual remark, and asked, "How do you know?"

"By the marks on your body," replied Ruben. She was silent for such a long time that Ruben looked at her to see if she had heard him correctly, and was surprised to see that there were tears in her eyes. "It is often better to talk about things, rather than keep them secret. So I suggest we walk on slower this time allowing you to talk about it if you wish."

"Yes, I think that is best," she said in a voice that was just above a whisper, and they walked slowly on. "You see, before Joself met me when I had been bought by a merchant, I previously worked in a temple and as well as minor jobs helping the priests, a lot of the time I was used as a temple prostitute."

"Yes, that figures," said Ruben, who had heard many incredible stories about Canaan and the strange gods that were worshipped. "But what happened to the child?"

She was quietly crying by now, "They took it as a sacrifice to one of their gods," she sobbed.

Ruben was horrified, but tried to keep his voice even when he said, "I understand now, but do not talk about it if it is painful to remember." She was about to reply when he put a hand on her shoulder and pointed to the footprints that they were following. They had suddenly lengthened, which was a sure sign that Joself had been running and all of a sudden those prints were joined by many animal tracks like those that Ruben had seen earlier.

As they looked at one another, a howling chuckle came from the direction the footprints led, followed by a human cry.

# 18
# OF HEALING LEAVES AND SANCTUARY

Ruben and Tasmin exchanged horrified glances, they were unsure from how far away the cry had come, but it was obvious that Joself was in difficulty and great danger. Searching around, Ruben noticed a couple of dead trees that were half charred. He dashed over, pulling Tasmin with him, dumped his bag on the ground and said to Tasmin, "Try to start a fire, then wait until I return or call you." With his javelin in his right hand, he sprinted in the direction from which the cry had come, it was of course in the same direction that the tracks led, so he had no difficulty finding Joself.

He arrived on the scene to see that Joself had previously discarded the bags that he carried and was now backing away from the pack of snarling hyena, which were foaming at the mouth and seemed to have been driven as mad as rabid dogs. He was slashing at the occasional animal that came near but he was vastly outnumbered and hemmed in on three sides. He was screaming at them, not so much out of terror, although he was obviously frightened, but out of hatred that would normally drive them off. He had realised that he was backing into some marshy ground and he was already up to his knees in glutinous mud.

One of the beasts was preparing for a spring at him, and due to his restricted movements caused by the mud he would have fallen prey to those large snarling jaws. Ruben had already seen the danger and hurled his javelin directly at the beast just as it was about to spring into the air. The javelin struck just behind and below the shoulder and, as it was hurled with tremendous force, smashed through bone and pierced the animal's heart. Thrown sideways by the javelin, the hyena's blood spurted out from the wound and this distracted the other beasts, which turned on the dead animal and tore it to pieces. Some of those closing in on Joself had minor injuries caused by his sword. After hurling the javelin, Ruben reached over his shoulder and swept his large sword from its sheath, using this in one hand, with his short sword in the other. He was soon amidst the pack of hyena, slashing indiscriminately left and right with his long sword and stabbing any animal that came within reach of his short sword. Eventually Ruben had killed five of the snarling, enraged hyena, but even then the remainder of the pack still showed plenty of fight. Now Ruben was beginning to tire, but had miraculously escaped any injury from those viscous snapping jaws. Suddenly the remainder of the pack began to flee away from the outraged shouts of Tasmin as she ran up hurling brands of fire. A much-relieved Ruben said, "Thank you for disobeying my orders!"

She had no time for his sarcastic appreciation, but said, "You must help Joself, he seems to be sinking into the bog and he is hurt." Ruben could see this for himself when he turned round, Joself was almost waist deep and he had small bites that he had not been able to avoid. The blood was oozing from a few small wounds and running into the quicksand adding to the mess that sucked him down.

When Ruben started into the bog to try and reach Joself, his own weight soon had him knee deep in the mire and it was with substantial effort that he managed to free himself. "We need a rope up," he called to Tasmin.

"We haven't got one," she replied. "And to make a rope from pieces of material would take too long."

Ruben looked desperately about him, "Are there any trees around here?" he asked.

"There is nothing growing," answered Tasmin. "But if you hold my hand, I may be able to reach him."

"But surely you will sink into the mire?" said Ruben.

"No, I do not think so, as I am far lighter than you. Here, take my hand, there is no time to argue."

Ruben stood with his feet in a wide stance and reached out as far as he could above the bog. Tasmin ran lightly around him and grasped his wrist leaving his hand free to grasp her wrist, her feet only slightly sinking below the surface. She stretched out her other hand and called out to Joself, "Give me your hand." She just managed to interlock her fingers with her husband and immediately called to Ruben, "Start pulling as hard as you can."

This Ruben did, his own feet sinking a little before he managed to get some purchase. He then pulled with all his strength and at first felt nothing move. He realised the strain on Tasmin's shoulders must have been immense; he was amazed that she did not cry out. Then, slowly at first, they began to move towards him, allowing him to back off even further and pull Joself completely free. Joself lay in an exhausted heap, smeared with blood from his own wounds and with mud from the mire, which clotted his tattered clothing.

Tasmin was also exhausted and needed time to recover from the immense strain on her shoulders, although she still did not complain. There was a small fire where Tasmin had laid some of the burning brands.

"I will be back in a moment," called Ruben over his shoulder, as he ran back in search of their equipment. He soon returned with his own and Tasmin's bags complete with a goatskin of clean water. By this time Tasmin had recovered and was kneeling with Joself's head in her lap, speaking words of encouragement and endearment to him. Ruben gave her the water saying, "Use it sparingly to bathe his wounds, which should then be temporarily bound, we must then move away from this accursed place before the hyena return. While you are busy binding Joself's wounds, I will gather all our remaining equipment." He left them by the small fire and commenced collecting items of clothing and baggage that had been scattered over quite an area. He managed to retrieve his javelin from the torn and dismembered carcass of the hyena. In his search of the area he occasionally caught a glimpse of the remainder of the pack, which had been drawn back by the smell of blood.

Eventually he had found most of the gear that they had started out with. He then turned to Tasmin and said, "We must move on as quickly as possible, is Joself capable of walking?"

"I do not think so," she replied. "He seems delirious and has lost a lot of blood."

"I can carry him over my shoulder, but it will not be a comfortable ride and that leaves nearly all of the equipment," he said thinking aloud.

"Well, let's get going then," Tasmin said to Ruben. "I will bring as much as I can manage."

Before leaving, both he and Tasmin took a small drink of water, leaving a couple of mouthfuls for Joself on the journey. He hefted Joself onto his back, having removed his large sword, which he slung around his neck, and had to ask Tasmin to pass him his javelin, which he was loath to leave, apart from which, he considered he may well need it again before the night was over. He was surprised to see that Tasmin had collected almost everything else as well as a firebrand that she considered necessary. Ruben commenced walking as quickly as he could under Joself's weight. Once again he was surprised to note that Tasmin managed to keep up with him without complaining.

They seemed to keep going for most of the night, which in truth was not the case. The moon had now risen and they could occasionally see a pair of eyes watching them, but whatever it was never came too close. Ruben knew that if he put Joself down, he would never have had the strength to lift him again, and it became an enormous effort to simply put one foot in front of the other. His mouth was so dry that he could not speak and it was only by the mere fact that Tasmin kept walking as well, that he kept going. They were under the trees at the side and had started to climb before Ruben realised that the crossing had been completed. He leant unsteadily against the bowl of a tree and gratefully lowered Joself to the fern covered ground, and then lay exhausted next to the inert body. Tasmin stumbled along behind, finally releasing all the baggage and crawled forward to cradle Joself's head in her lap. Eventually she croaked, "He is still breathing, can you light a fire please, Ruben?" she requested through cracked lips. "I believe I can also hear running water, there must be a stream nearby, can you also bring some water?"

Ruben could hardly believe what he was hearing; the fact that she could still keep active was unbelievable. But somehow he managed to stir himself and did as she requested. He first went in search of the stream, which was no more than fifty paces away, and he drank deeply himself before he filled the empty goatskin with cool clean water. As he walked back to Tasmin, he felt his strength returning and he insisted that she drink before attempting once more to attend to Joself. He lit the fire that gave her some light with which to work on redressing Joself's wounds. As she took off the first and largest blood sodden binding around the main bite in his shoulder, she gave a sharp intake of breath, as the wound was oozing an evil smelling discharge of pus and blood. She did her best, with Ruben's concerned assistance, to clean the wound with warm water and to redress it, by tearing up one of her dresses. As she worked on her semiconscious husband, he gave the occasional groan and mumbled incoherently. All the wounds were as bad, giving off the same vile smell with an unpleasant discharge. "I am afraid that the wounds are very badly infected," she said. "It must have been something from those animals."

"Yes, but it has reacted so quickly," said Ruben. "I have never seen anything like it." He did not want to alarm her, but he remembered one of Simeon's patients in one of the marshland towns, an elderly woman who was bitten by a wild cat, she had died, despite all Simeon's herbal remedies and powers of healing. The old marshland doctor had said, "When you get that smell of putrefaction, there is very little you can do."

"There is an old woman, some people say she is a witch, but she is reputed to possess magical powers and I believe she lives in these woods. Will you stay with Joself while I go and search for her," she said, drawing her feet under her and rising unsteadily.

"Unless you know your way very well, why not wait for a short while, as it will be light before long, apart from which you must be exhausted and you badly need some rest," he suggested.

"I suppose you are right," she said almost reluctantly, wearily sitting down again. "But I do not think I can sleep."

"Well, I can," he said yawning. "And when it is light, I will help you search the area."

"No, you cannot do that," she explained. "The old woman I seek is called Messuda, she lives on her own and is reputed to eat young men." However, she found she was talking to herself, as Ruben was fast asleep, lying beside Joself with one hand on the hilt of his large sword, as if he was a guard who had temporarily closed his eyes.

He awoke well after sunrise, to the sound of Joself murmuring and moving from side to side, whilst in a delirium. He was sweating profusely and the bandages were once again soaked through with the evil smelling discharge. Ruben rubbed the sleep out of his eyes and sat up looking around for Tasmin, but she was nowhere in sight. He hoped that she had gone in search of Messuda, and trusted that she had not gone through another miraculous change and decided to leave them, but tried to dispel the thought as quickly as it had occurred to him. He blew some life into the fire and added some more wood and put a container of water on to boil, so that he could change Joself's dressings again. Whilst he started the work, swabbing out the wounds as best he could, using very hot water, he noticed Tasmin's bag beside him, which seemed to confirm that she would be back. He took another of her dresses, which he tore into bandages, apologising to her as if she was present. But before redressing the wounds, an idea came to his mind. Leaving Joself for a short time, he ran over to the stream where he found some large leaves growing beside the water and pulled them from the ground. He tore them into small pieces as he hurried back and made them into a poultice. This he had seen Simeon do, and although he had no idea of the plants that he used, he hoped that they might have the right properties and not be poisonous. He knew the risk that he was taking, but considered that Joself would probably die anyway, so believed the gamble worthwhile. He soaked the poultice in hot water before he applied it, saying to the ashen faced Joself as he bound it up, "This is either a kill or cure treatment my friend, let us hope it is the latter." As he finished redressing all the wounds, having used the poultice only on the main area, Tasmin came running back down through the trees.

"Ruben, I have found the witch, Messuda, you must stand back behind me while she inspects Joself's wounds," she said pulling him to his feet and pushing him away, shielding him from the old woman who followed her.

Ruben was not sure what was happening to him, Tasmin's grip on his arm and her voice was so urgent, that he complied without rancour. He strained to look past Tasmin at the old woman, but Tasmin kept moving in front of him and he then remembered some of her words the previous night, before he had fallen asleep. Something about her being a witch, but he could remember no further details. Eventually he stopped trying to look past Tasmin and simply listened to what she said. She spoke in a harsh cackling voice, her words grating on his ears.

"Who put the herb poultice on?" the old crone demanded.

Tasmin was temporarily shocked, as she had not seen Ruben apply it. While she was in shock, Ruben moved out from behind her and said, "I did, is there anything wrong with it?"

"Bah Larkslip, not much good, but won't hurt," she crowed, spitting in the fire but still not looking up. "Bloody 'erb med'cine ain't got no power."

"I know a marshland doctor who would disagree with you," said Ruben looking straight at her. Tasmin gave a small gasp and tried to drag him back, but was too late.

The old witch looked directly at Ruben, her face half covered by a black cowl. Black undefinable eyes stared out at him from wrinkled eye sockets either side of a sharp wart covered nose. Thin wisps of white hair jutted out above those merciless eyes. Her walnut brown face creased into a wide grin, with filthy stunted and broken teeth she cackled, "Hah, plenty of meat there."

Ruben moved back, as if struck in the face. But Tasmin stood in front of him and boldly said, "I only asked to see if you could help my husband," she explained.

"You said nothing about bringin' me an' me sisters some food," said Messuda in her harsh cackling laugh. "But this one will die anyway, there ain't nothin' I can do to save him, even if I wanted to." The old witch drew a curved dagger from her black robes. "It will cost you five gold pieces to stop me cuttin' 'is throat now," she cawed, pricking Joself's skin below the left ear, allowing blood to well up and trickle down his neck, ready to draw the dagger across and sever his throat.

Ruben could see his javelin at least fifteen paces away and knew that he would not be able to cover a fraction of the distance between himself and this evil old hag, before she could kill Joself. There was also something that warned him against even moving in front of this witch.

"I will give you the money, but please don't hurt my husband," Tasmin pleaded, rushing to where she had put Joself's purse. She took out five gold pieces and threw them behind the old woman. Messuda rose to her feet, backed away, and picked up and inspected the money.

"I will be back before sunset to take the body," Messuda cackled, pocketed the coins and disappeared into the trees.

Tasmin knelt over Joself, sobbing. "I was only trying to help my dearest and it has all gone hopelessly wrong."

"What are you talking about?" muttered Joself opening his eyes for the first time and blinking in bewilderment. Tasmin was as surprised as Ruben, who stared at them both, not fully appreciating what had happened. However, he finally came to his senses and looked enquiringly at Joself. "Yes, I feel a bit better now," Joself said quietly. "But my arms and legs still ache and I have been asleep for a long time."

"How about your shoulder?" enquired Ruben.

"Oh, was that hurt as well?" responded Joself, trying to rise, but giving up the effort, which was obviously too great.

"Just lie still while we attend to everything," ordered Ruben. He kicked the fire back into life, and added some more wood and refilled the container to boil more water. Tasmin looked enquiringly at him from a face that was tear stained, lined with worry and looked exhausted from lack of sleep.

"Come with me," Ruben told her, handing her the now empty goatskin. "We are just going to get some more water," he called to Joself over his shoulder and took Tasmin by the arm. "While you were away, I redressed Joself's wounds and put on that herb poultice, what did she call it? Ah, Larkslip, I believe she said. It was made with boiling water poured over the broken leaves, and I believe it is working. Now, the heat of the poultice will have gone cold by now, but if we renew it and deal with the other wounds the same way, we will then have a few hours left in which to leave before Messuda returns. By the gods, that old witch frightens me, even more than the entire Assyrian army."

The effect that this information had upon Tasmin was most dramatic, she immediately brightened up, dried her tears, began working efficiently again and refilled the goatskin whilst asking Ruben how he knew about Larkslip. He told her that he had seen some plants growing by the stream, which had a bright yellow vein to the leaves. These had reminded him of some plants that an old marshland doctor had used, but it was more luck than knowledge in knowing about their healing properties. He found the roots and broken stems of the plant that he had used and searching about found some more of them.

"Oh, you are clever," she said happily, carefully picking them. "They must work," she confirmed smiling. "Because Joself said he did not know of the wound to his shoulder and that was by far the worst."

"Yes, our luck has changed," he said in agreement with her, "But we have to work quickly. Now, I will take the goatskin back and start undoing the bandages on the wounds while the water is boiling. Can you collect as many leaves as you can and join me in a few moments?"

She quickly returned, her hands full of the leaves of Larkslip. "I don't think there are any more, at least not in the immediate area, do you think this will be enough?" she enquired.

"I am sure that will be plenty," he answered, and pointed to where he had moved the original poultice. The wound had started to heal at the edges and there was only a tiny amount of pus left, that being a brighter yellow in colour with none of the smelly brown discharge.

"I think one more poultice on this main wound, plus smaller ones on the other wounds, will be plenty, the wounds can then be allowed to scab over and heal naturally."

"Yes," agreed Tasmin nodding her head. "I am sure you are right. I will take over now, so that you can start building a litter, and we can move him out of here." Making sure that Tasmin had plenty of dressing materials and adequate hot water and crushed leaves to finish the job, he turned his mind to building a litter on which Joself could lie, realising that he would have to drag this himself as well as carry some of their bags. He began selecting saplings that were sturdy yet springy, about twice his own height. These he lashed into an oblong with a couple of sturdy cross struts, using bark that he had stripped from one of the larger trees, grateful that his large sword and his other weapons were not bronze and still retained their edge, and making a mental note that all his weapons needed cleaning and resharpening. Then finding a fibrous creeper that was climbing one of the older trees in the woods, wove a loose lattice in which Joself would lie. He also made, using wider twists of the creeper, two loops, which would slip over his shoulders, so that he could drag the litter still leave his hands free. He worked quickly, keeping an eye on Tasmin and watching the sun gradually sink towards the western horizon. Tasmin had finished bandaging Joself's wounds, this time each with a hot poultice, after which she still had a couple of the Larkslip leaves left, which she carefully wrapped with the remains of another of her dresses that had been torn up. She repacked her bag, then helped Ruben lay Joself onto the litter that he had built, which also had enough room for the large bag that contained all their cooking and eating equipment, including a couple of goatskins full of clear water.

"That's about it then," said Ruben, refastening his sword belt and slipping his arms into the shoulder straps of the litter. "You lead off," he instructed Tasmin. "You are the guide", He picked up his large bag in his left hand and his javelin in his right. "Start moving off," he ordered. "But make sure you choose paths that are wide enough and not too narrow to allow the litter through."

They walked to the top of the long slope that skirted the side of the depression, which they crested just as the sun began to set. They had reached a clearing at the summit before they re-entered the wood, which they saw ended about halfway down the next slope.

"Do you know where the old hag lives?" Ruben asked of Tasmin.

"No, I found her wandering in the woods," she replied. "But I believe that she lives with her two sisters over to the north," pointing to the right along the crest of the hill. Ruben half closed his eyes and tried to imagine the old witch going where they had just come from. Almost immediately a dark area seemed to emanate from the trees, moving diagonally from where Tasmin had pointed towards, where they had stopped after crossing the Empty Sector, which now was almost entirely in shadow, except the far side from where they had started their crossing just over a day previously.

"Let us hurry on," urged Ruben. "We have not long before she finds that we have left. Our tracks will be easy to follow and we must get clear of the woods and over the solid ground where she will have difficulty following."

Tasmin plunged down the other slope carrying the remainder of her and Joself's gear. Noticing that Joself was now awake, Ruben asked him, "Are you all right Joself, I hope that the ride is not too bumpy?"

Smiling faintly, Joself said, "No, I am fine, Ruben, if the jolting becomes too great I will call out."

"If you do call, please do so quietly," he requested. "We will probably be followed, so there is a need for speed." He then started after Tasmin, keeping up a good pace but trying to keep the litter running along as smoothly as possible without jerking or swinging it from side to side. They were making good progress and the trees were thinning out and Ruben could just make out through the trees the edge of the wood.

Just then a harsh cry came from behind them, "You won't git away, I'll soon 'ave yer." Messuda cried out after them from the top of the ridge.

"Let me try to delay her," requested Tasmin.

"No way, let us keep together, there is safety in numbers and I am sure that we can make it," returned Ruben in a commanding tone. He speeded up, saying to Joself, "Hang on in there, my friend." Very soon he and Tasmin were running side by side and had emerged from the woods onto some rocky ground that had little vegetation. He realised that the bumping litter must have been uncomfortable, but there was no protest from Joself who must have guessed the need that urged them on. There was a clump of bushes about one hundred paces away to their left and this was what Ruben was heading for, despite the strain where the loops were chafing the tops of his arms and shoulders. Tasmin was also struggling along, her breath wheezing in her throat and she had to grab Ruben's arm to save herself from falling, there were also a few muffled gasps from Joself. However, they just reached the clump of bushes behind which they threw themselves, before looking back. They could just make out the dark shape of the old witch, who came out of the woods looking left and right to try to see which way they had gone, as the ground was too rocky to leave clear tracks.

They were peering through the bushes and realised that although they were safe for the moment, they were still too near for comfort, being just over one hundred paces from Messuda but less than sixty paces from the edge of the woods. Ruben whispered to Tasmin, "Can you find me a stone or a piece of wood to throw?"

"Do you think you can hit her from here?" she replied, frowning at him while speaking just as quietly.

"Possibly," grinned Ruben. "But that was not what I had in mind. What I am hoping to do is to try to divert her attention so that we can get well clear of her."

"Oh, I see," she whispered back, looking all around and eventually pulling out a piece of wood just about as long as her forearm, which she passed to him, asking if it was suitable for his needs.

"That's perfect," he said, accepting the offered wood and weighing it in his hand. Then, when Messuda was half turned from them and inspecting the ground in the dying rays of the sun, he stood up and hurled the wood at the nearest of the trees. The piece of wood flew in a flat trajectory turning slowly end over end, landing just inside the line of trees with a muffled thud.

"Wha'zat," cried the old crone, wheeling around in the direction the sound came from. "Tried to double back on me did yer, but I'll 'ave yer now," cackled the old witch, disappearing back into the trees at the spot where the piece of wood had landed.

They listened intently for a moment, hearing the occasional rustle as she looked around for them. During this brief period it had become darker, as the sun had sunk below the next ridge. Ruben whispered to Tasmin, "Let us try to steal away quietly." They left the clump of bushes, trying to keep it between them and where Messuda had disappeared, going as quietly as they could. Tasmin led the way and made sure that there were no obstacles in their path, or anything that would make a noise. They kept going and gradually the ground began to rise, and although Tasmin kept looking behind her she saw no sign of pursuit. They sped up their progress and by the time they had reached the crest of the next ridge, the moon had risen and they were sure that they had escaped. As Ruben started down the next slope he said to Tasmin, "How far do we have to go until we come to the next town?"

"I am afraid that is still quite a long way off," she said with a sigh. "But I believe there may be some remote houses in the area." They had not gone much further when they saw some lights in the distance, as they approached they could see the light belonged to a large villa. Considering that this may be a good place to seek refuge, they pushed tiredly ahead, Tasmin saying, "Leave the talking to me."

As they neared the villa it became clear that this was no single dwelling place as it was extensive. It consisted of several buildings that were mainly on only one level, but they were interjoined by covered walkways around large courtyards that were all well illuminated by flaming torches set in wall brackets. They intersected the gravel parkway leading to the main doorway, which was slightly open. Tasmin stuck her head around the door and called out, "Hello, is there anyone there?"

Almost immediately an answer came back. "Yes, I will be with you in a moment." There was then only a short delay before a smartly dressed soldier came to the door. A soldier he certainly was, but his uniform was unusual and neither one that Ruben nor Tasmin had seen before. "Can I be of assistance?" said the soldier, who was not young, as there were flecks of grey in his hair, despite his youthful step and unlined face.

"We seek lodging for the night," said Tasmin.

"All weary travellers are welcome here," greeted the soldier, gesturing them to come in. "Are there only the two of you?" he asked, yet quickly corrected himself. "Ah, the third is hurt I believe, or is he ill?"

"Something of both, I regret to inform you," said Ruben as he pulled in the litter and slipped the loops from his shoulders, pleased to be free of his burden.

"No one is turned away from the house of Coronus, particularly if they need medical aid," said the soldier. "My name is Druselus, and I am the door warden to his house," he said in a kindly tone.

"Do you by any chance have a doctor here," enquired Tasmin.

"My good woman, you could not have come to a better house, if your injured friend requires treatment, I can easily arrange for that," said Druselus. "Can you give me details of his injuries and sickness," he continued in the same kindly voice.

"He is my husband," Tasmin corrected him. "And he has been sorely wounded."

"If I may interrupt," said Ruben hastily. "He was badly bitten by savage hyena in the Empty Sector, over to the east about a day previously."

"He is still alive, I see," said Druselus with considerable surprise. "I think we had better get him to the doctor without delay. If you take one end of the litter that you brought him on, I will take the other and lead the way."

It was so much easier to carry Joself in this fashion than it had been for Ruben to drag him over the rough rocky hillside, the pathways were also of course smooth and brightly lit. They left their bags and Ruben's javelin where Druselus had indicated, telling them that he would take them to the bedrooms that would be set aside for them. He led them around a couple of courtyards along the torch-lit walkways and soon they were in an ante-chamber to what seemed like a well equipped and tidy surgery. Druselus asked Tasmin to knock and open the door, and he and Ruben walked in, and on the doctor's orders, who had been tidying up and replacing some stone jars full of different coloured crystals and powders on the shelves, laid Joself on the examining table. Druselus spoke quietly to the doctor before speaking to Ruben and Tasmin. He told them that the doctor would look after Joself and redress his wounds, but would require more information from them both. He then said, "I must go and inform my Lord Coronus that you are here, he may well wish to speak to you." He said this whilst looking directly at Ruben. "I will be back shortly and will ensure that rooms are made ready for you and that your baggage has been attended to." Before Ruben or Tasmin could ask him anything about where they were or why they were being treated so well, he departed.

The doctor was a short rotund little man with a jovial face, who reminded Ruben of Mutek, and he wasted no time in asking who they were or why they were here, but simply about Joself's injuries and how they had treated him. Joself was either asleep or unconscious, although he was breathing quite naturally and did not show any signs of the fever that he had suffered from previously. When the doctor undid the dressing he was delighted to see that the wounds showed little sign of the purulent discharge and were already healing.

"This is a most unusual thing," he told them. "Are you sure the wounds were inflicted by hyena in the Empty Sector and had been driven wild by the contaminated water?"

Ruben was about to answer when Tasmin told him that the animals had definitely been hyena, as she came from this area and had seen them previously. She also confirmed that they were acting savagely, quite unlike their normal behaviour, and said that if it had not been for Ruben who had killed many of them, Joself, who was her husband, would have been torn to pieces. She then related the complete story of how they had been delayed, obviously omitting the reason, and saying that they had found Joself fighting off the pack, but that he had been trapped in a bog from which they had dragged him. The doctor then asked her about the poultices that he had removed and what had been in them. She told him that they had been Ruben's idea and at that point she stood back allowing Ruben to continue the story.

"I believe the plants are called Larkslip and it was merely good fortune that they have healing properties. I myself am no doctor," he explained. "But where I come from, which is away to the east in Babylon where the marshlands join the river Euphrates, there was an old marshland doctor who I helped and he used a similar looking leaf on animal bites."

"I still have some of the leaves," interrupted Tasmin, telling the doctor that they were wrapped in her baggage.

"I would like to see," said the doctor. "But for now I will redress the wounds with only a soothing salve as they do not seem to be infected." He immediately commenced this, using clean dressings and bandaging neatly. "However," he continued as he worked. "I feel I must warn you that in cases that we have previously dealt with, if the patient survives the bites from any animals in that area, they are often affected in the mind or in other ways and are unable to work as they previously did."

This information had a profound effect on Tasmin, her initial pleasure at Joself's recovery vanished and her eyes filled with tears as she clasped his hand. The doctor quickly added, "I am only mentioning that it may happen, not that it will. The problem is that we know so little and the Empty Sector has only recently come into being. It is not at all definite that this will happen, and I am only trying to prevent any future distress, it may well be that your husband will be unaffected as he has shown remarkable powers of recovery so far, possibly thanks to your friend's poultices." He placed a comforting hand on her arm, smiling kindly at her.

At the same time, the door opened to be filled by Druselus who said to Tasmin, "A room has been prepared for yourself and your husband just across the corridor and a single room next door is being readied for your friend." Turning to Ruben he said, "With the doctor's agreement, we will place your friend in one of the beds and my Lord Coronus would like to speak with you, young man, I am sorry that I forgot to ask your names," he apologised.

Ruben and Druselus were about to lift the litter when the doctor said, "Would you be able to carry him without the litter, as that will have to be burnt."

Tasmin was about to object, when Ruben said, "It doesn't matter Tasmin, doctors are fussy about these things, it was only hastily built and has served its purpose." Picking up Joself like a child and turning to Druselus he said, "It can be left here, if you would like to show me the way I will carry my friend. I have carried and dragged him this far, a few extra steps will not be a burden and I would like to finish the job."

Although he said nothing, Druselus widened his eyes in admiration of the younger man's strength and tenacity and, recovering his poise, led the way into the bedchamber that had been prepared for Tasmin and Joself. As he led the way, Tasmin said to him, "I am as much to blame as yourself for not introducing us, my husband is Joself and our young companion here is Ruben, who as you can see is very strong and is a mighty warrior",

Druselus replied, "That I can see," and as Ruben laid Joself on the bed that he indicated, he said to Ruben, "That I believe is why my Lord Coronus wishes to speak with you, young man." He told Tasmin that if she needed anything, she had only to sound the gong that hung outside the bedchamber door. He then led Ruben out, who, before he left, smiled brightly at Tasmin, congratulating her on the effort that she had put in the past two days and in leading them to this excellent place.

Druselus led Ruben along the corridor and around another courtyard, which had a fountain splashing into a large pond where Ruben could just make out the shape of golden coloured fish, or that is the colour they appeared in the torchlight. Realising this was an opportunity to question Druselus, he asked, "Where exactly are we?"

"Do you not know?" replied Druselus with a surprised expression.

"I am afraid I have absolutely no idea," admitted Ruben. "Save that we are in Canaan on the east side of the Empty Sector. But I have never been this way before and am a stranger to the area. Additionally, can you tell me who Coronus is and what uniform you wear?"

"Which question shall I answer first?" laughed Druselus. "I will tell you a little about him and you will learn the rest in good time." They had reached the main part of the establishment and Druselus showed Ruben down a wide hallway, speaking as he went. He told Ruben that Lord Coronus was in fact a Greek general whose family had settled here after the Trojan wars. Coronus had also been a counsellor to the Assyrian King and had helped in the training of some of the army. However, he had resigned his position when their previous king, Tiglath-Pileser used the treaty with Babylon as an excuse to build up his army whilst secretly raiding the caravans that came from Egypt, blaming the raids on Canaanite bandits. They had reached the end of the hall and Druselus tapped on a small door that stood beside the main doors. He went halfway inside and spoke to another soldier sitting beside a desk, then returned and knocked loudly on the main door at the end of the hall. After waiting for an answer, which came quickly, he opened the door, gesturing to Ruben to remain where he was, and went in to speak to Coronus. After a while, during which Ruben looked around the palatial hallway decorated with ornate woven wall hangings and bronze ornaments on pedestals, Druselus came out and asked Ruben to enter.

Coronus must originally have been an imposing figure, almost as tall as Ruben, but was now elderly and leant heavily on an ebony cane as he rose to welcome his guest. He waved Ruben to a chair and sat down himself, asking Druselus to bring in some refreshment. His hair and beard were as white as snow, which contrasted with his well-tanned face that looked younger than he probably was. His clear grey eyes looked keenly at his guest and were widely spaced above a generous mouth, which often smiled, or so Ruben imagined due to the deep laughter lines that his beard did not hide.

"Good evening Ruben, I have been expecting you for some time, I apologise for not shaking your hand, but my hands can not stand much pressure these days." And he held up his right hand, which was covered with scars and was more like a claw that he had difficulty bending.

Ruben was surprised by this greeting and said, "Thank you for your kind hospitality, and it is I who should apologise my Lord. I am not really in any fit state to sit in your fine house, as I have not had the chance to wash or change into more fitting attire. Also, my weapons are badly in need of attention, as the last couple of days have been rather demanding. But why did you expect and await my arrival, as I had no foreknowledge of meeting you?"

Coronus held his eyes in a long steady gaze before answering, and then with a faint smile he said, "Presumably Druselus has told you a little about me?"

"Yes, sir!" replied Ruben. "But not a great deal, mainly about your previous position and history, but not of your current situation."

"I can tell you that here in Canaan I am entirely a free agent, I am answerable to no man, and own this house and all who work for me, which as you can imagine allows me considerable local prestige." He paused, holding up his hand silencing any interruption, and then continued. "I had been informed by my old contacts in Nineveh, that the Assyrians were hunting for a large mercenary passing through the southern part of Assyria. After the battle at Ashkilon where their General Nozgrarot was defeated, and blamed the defeat on the presence of a powerful mercenary, who fits your description. I was immediately interested, as although I have no dealing with Assyria now, I trained Nozgrarot and though I have no personal liking for the man, I do respect him as a soldier and a fine discus thrower. There was then no news from Assyria and we thought you had passed through. However, a few days ago some of my men had heard a commotion in the Empty Sector and on surveillance reported your presence, but also that of the witch, Messuda." He grinned at Ruben's look of surprise, before continuing. "Personally I do not believe that the old hag possesses any real magic, her main weapon is fear. The simple folk in this area are frightened of her, therefore they will do as she commands."

"I can understand that," said Ruben during a convenient pause. "But I would not like to put her to the test. There is something evil about the old crone."

"I must admit that I agree with Ruben," said Druselus, who had unobtrusively brought in a tray with three goblets of wine and had sat in on the conversation.

Ruben was grateful for this, as it made the atmosphere more congenial and less formal.

"Possibly," mused Coronus. "Anyway, we do not have to worry

because she sticks carefully to her own boundaries and will come no further west than the crest of the next ridge after her woods, so she should be no further trouble to you. Anyway, you have given her the slip and your departure was observed by my men. So that is how we knew of your coming. Does that answer your question?"

"Yes, most certainly, sir," replied Ruben. "But," he quickly continued, "I would still like to know what exactly you do here and what staff you have, if I may be so impertinent?"

"Of course, my boy," chuckled Coronus. "Basically I am retired, yet because I am wealthy, I find pleasure in keeping this fine house as a place of rest or retreat for those in need, particularly soldiers like you. But I have no affiliation to anyone, so let me warn you; the room next to your room could be given to your enemy if he came to this door. Nobody is turned away; the only rule is that the peace of this house is maintained by all who stay."

"I understand, my Lord, and will happily comply with your wishes," said Ruben, rising to his feet and bowing low.

"Oh, do sit down, there is no need for formality," snapped Coronus, dismissing Ruben's polite gesture, but with an amused twinkle in his eye. "Now, what I would like, before I dismiss you, is to see that magnificent sword that we have heard so much of," he said, indicating the long sword, which Ruben had slipped off his shoulder and stood beside the chair when he had sat down.

"I am afraid it is not particularly clean or as sharp as I like to keep it," explained Ruben.

"That I fully understand, being an old soldier myself," said Coronus. "But I would still like to see it, with your consent."

Almost reluctantly, Ruben rose and withdrew his sword from its scabbard, which was accompanied by a low whistle of admiration from Druselus. Ruben laid the sword on Coronus's lap and as he did so he said, "I am at your service while you provide shelter for myself and my friends, my Lord."

Deeply touched by this tribute, and by the beauty of the sword, which if anything was enhanced and denoted itself as a fighting man's weapon because of the bloodstains on it, Coronus was temporarily speechless.

"That is a magnificent weapon," said Druselus in little more than a whisper.

"Thank you, Ruben," said Coronus. "I accept your kind offer and the courtesy with which it was made." His clawed right hand closed on the grip, as if the sword reawoke the muscles in his hand. "It is well balanced and as Druselus said, is a magnificent blade. Now, I will trouble you no longer, take back your blade, but remember that you're now in my service and from what the doctor has told Druselus, could indeed be for up to ten days. Go now to eat and rest, Druselus will give you your orders in the morning."

Ruben took back the sword, re-sheathed it and thumped his chest in salute. He left the room without another word, following Druselus and wondering what his duties would comprise.

## 19
## NEW POSITION, NEW CHALLENGES

Waking early, as dawn began to lighten the sky with an ominous red tinge to the clouds, Ruben was keen to learn exactly what he had let himself in for. He vividly recalled his meeting with Coronus, his new Lord, and his return with Druselus, who had given him an idea of the layout of the extensive villa and where the guest dining area was. Druselus then accompanied Ruben back to his own quarters, after sharing a late supper with him, and was amazed by his enormous appetite. He laughed to himself recalling Druselus saying that they would have to order extra food, as they had not anticipated feeding an army. He had then paid a social visit to Joself and Tasmin and was delighted to find that Joself was awake and saying that he felt a lot better, but was still very tired and was being treated well by Tasmin, who had cheered up remarkably. He then returned to his room and having previously requested a bowl of hot water, he used this to clean all his weapons. Having completed this long overdue task, he then spent further time in resharpening and re-polishing before finally retiring to bed. He had slept well and this morning was trying to recount the number of days since he had slept in a proper bed, as he did not consider his time in Thrax as sleeping in a real bed as it was like camping.

Putting aside these thoughts, he had come to the main eating area where he was to meet Druselus for breakfast and learn of his new duties. He had been served a large breakfast and was halfway through when Druselus joined him with a cheerful, "Good morning, my friend, I trust you slept well?"

"Very well, thank you," replied Ruben. "I was just trying to remember when I last slept in a proper bed."

"Life is like that, particularly when you are in the army," said Druselus. "I remember one campaign when I was almost two years on the move by day and sleeping rough by night." He paused for reflection and then said, "Mind you, it makes you value comfort more."

"Indeed, it most certainly does," observed Ruben. "And I hope I will enjoy my stay here?" he probed, while searching Druselus' face.

Druselus laughed. "Yes, I believe you will. I am sure your new duties should be to your satisfaction and well to your liking, as well as being comparatively easy."

"Let me be the judge of that," responded Ruben. "Now, put me out of my agony and tell me just what I have let myself in for?"

"It is quite obvious really," answered Druselus, deliberately drawing out the suspense.

"For you, it must be," rallied Ruben. "Come on Druselus, just what have you got lined up for me."

"Using your skills, to our advantage," came the reply. Druselus was obviously enjoying this game of cat and mouse. Finally, seeing Ruben was becoming agitated, he decided to relent. "We need some help training a new platoon of boys who have been sent here from the Greek island from which the Lord Coronus originally comes. They are only a few years younger than you and have to be taught how to use weapons." He saw Ruben's face light up and added a cautionary word. "You will be working directly under me, as obviously we have no knowledge of your ability to train. You see, being good with weapons does not mean that you will be a good teacher, although I am sure you remember your own training and are aware of that fact."

"Most certainly, I remember so many occasions when we were taught how to fight in certain ways, but when questioned, we were told, 'do it that way because I tell you', not because of a particular reason, which would have made sense." Ruben tried to explain, the words tumbling out in a confused rush as his boyish enthusiasm took over.

"Yes," laughed Druselus. "I know what you mean. Well, let's see if you can do any better. We start as soon as we have had breakfast, or should that be as soon as I have had breakfast, and you have had ten breakfasts," he said laughing merrily.

Very soon Druselus was leading the way through the courtyards out to the back of the villa where there was a small training ground. This was in active use, but neat and well tended with dummy targets and an obstacle course to one side. Ruben could see a barrack hut, very similar to the hut that his platoon had used when they were based in their training camp near the Inferior Sea. It was less than two years ago when he had left, marching at the front of his platoon, leading his troops into their first battle at Sousa, but it now seemed a lifetime ago as so many other things had happened since. As they neared the hut he saw that it was not barred, so he assumed that there was no danger of any of the boys trying to run away. But then he remembered that they had been sent here from a distant island and would obviously not wish to run away in an unknown land. Druselus reached the door, and pulled it open and marched in with Ruben following close behind. There was an immediate scurrying of feet as the young recruits lined up beside their beds. And proper beds they were, not just sleeping mats like the one that Ruben had used. In fact, as Ruben looked around the hut, he noticed that it was larger and better provisioned than where he had trained, his scrutiny was immediately cut short as the boys came to attention.

"Good morning, sir," said one of the boys, speaking to Druselus. "Are we still going to start our weapon training today?" This was said with eager anticipation that clearly showed on all the young faces.

Ruben remembered how keen he and his companions had been when they were told that they were due to start learning how to use the tools of their trade.

"You most certainly are," said Druselus as he walked along looking into the young excited faces, with his hands clasped behind his back. "However, time is short as we only have until next spring before you have to return to Cyprus. Therefore, we shall not be following the normal training pattern, but will use bronze weapons." He allowed a few excited whispers to break the silence, without reprimand, to let the gravity of his words sink in. "They will of course be unsharpened, as we do not want any blood spilt, or limbs removed accidentally."

A few sniggers gave way to outright laughter as one boy, obviously the platoon comedian, stood with one leg held behind his back, acting as if the lower half of his leg had been cut away.

"You may well act, young Cornelius," smiled Druselus. "But if our new expert hits you with even a blunt sword, your leg will come off." At that remark everything became quiet and all eyes fixed on Ruben. He was suddenly aware that he was the expert referred to and quickly composed himself not to share in the jest. He also realised that although only a few years older than most of the boys, he was considerably larger than Druselus, let alone any of the boys, some of whom were only half his weight. "Yes, boys, we are indeed privileged to have with us the hero of Ashkilon, I am sure that you have heard some of the tales, so be sure not to antagonise him."

Ruben was then aware of the position that he was now in. He certainly did not feel like a hero and whispered to Druselus, "Steady on, I am only here to help with the training and not to keep your doctor in business." This took some of the awe from the atmosphere and it felt like he had returned to his normal size, after seeming like an immense figure, a god amongst mortal men.

"Anyway, boys," said Druselus, "if you go over to the armoury, you will be issued with your normal weapons and we will meet you there in a little while."

As the boys hurried out of the hut, Ruben said to Druselus, "That was a bit strong, I now have an enormous reputation to live up to."

"Like your appetite," grinned Druselus. "I think you will find that that is an advantage my friend," commented Druselus. Taking Ruben by the arm and leading him outside, he asked, "Would you like to take over for a brief introduction?"

"Yes, I think that would be a good idea," responded Ruben. "It will allow me the opportunity to set the record straight, as I do not want to be regarded as a great figure, simply as a good soldier." This was said as they followed the boys across the training ground and went towards another hut, but this one had a securely locked door. As they walked towards the hut the wind began to blow harder, removing some of the remaining leaves off the trees, and as they felt a few drops of rain, it turned noticeably colder.

"Is there anywhere indoors that we can use?" enquired Ruben. "Only I think that we are in for some rough weather."

"I believe you are correct in your prediction, yes, we can use the gymnasium," replied Druselus.

"You are well equipped," said Ruben. "The only indoor gymnasium that I have seen was in the Citadel in Babylon."

"Yes, we are well equipped, but I did not know you had been to Babylon," said Druselus with wonder. "Tell me, are the Hanging Gardens truly magnificent?"

"Absolutely, they are quite breathtaking," replied Ruben honestly. But then in his turn asked, "Is Rhodos a large island, and are there many islands that belong to Cyprus?"

"Yes Ruben," answered Druselus. "Cyprus is one of the largest islands, at least that is the main town on the north end of the island, which is separately ruled, as are most of the islands. Although they are mainly allied to the kingdom of Greece, but Cyprus has two other main cities, the largest of which is called Lindos and it is apparently very beautiful.

"But Greece and its islands are full of such wonders, many of which I have seen. Our tales will have to be told in the evenings, for there is a lot that you can tell me as indeed there is a great deal that I can tell you. Our Lord Coronus can tell even more. I believe that he was a lad who served for a while under King Odysseus and have heard from his own lips tales of his adventures when returning from the Trojan wars. Now, most of the boys are from families of great lineage and all have a military background, which is why I have no great worries about their using heavier weapons than usual to start with. I am sure that most of them have already used swords and shields, so will be accustomed to their weight."

"I am glad that you told me as it will make a tremendous difference," said Ruben. "Are we just starting with the ordinary swords and shields?"

"Yes, that's right," replied Druselus. "I believe many of the boys have decided to specialise in one additional weapon, but we need not worry about that yet."

"Right, now you have no more surprises for me, I trust?" asked

Ruben.

"No, of that you have my word," laughed Druselus. "I will leave it up to you now." They had just arrived at the armoury to find that all the boys had now been equipped with swords and shields. Druselus held up his hand for silence and when this had been achieved he said, "Will you all please make your way to the gymnasium, as the weather looks like it is going to turn wet, not that I am worried about you lot. But the armourer will not want any weapons returned that are soaking wet."

Whilst Druselus was organising the boys, Ruben slipped into the armoury and asked the armourer if he had any old shields that he would not miss if they got badly beaten up. The armourer thanked him for his courtesy, as he told Ruben, "I have a couple at the back that I am going to have replaced, so take one of those if you wish. So many other officers would not even bother to ask."

Ruben thanked him and hurried to join Druselus as he shepherded the boys along to the gymnasium, which they entered and turned to face Druselus, who said, "I will now hand you over to our expert."

Ruben realised that Druselus had deliberately not introduced him by name, which allowed him to use any name or rank that he wished to be referred to by. Taking a deep breath he commenced, "Now, boys, whilst I am instructing you, if you have any questions please raise your hand, rather than waiting till the end, as you may not remember correctly and we will become confused," he said clearly, with no sign of nervousness. "I suggest you simply call me Sergeant, which is the rank that I once held before I became a mercenary."

Immediately a hand shot up, and he looked enquiringly at the boy. "Which army were you in, Sergeant?" asked Cornelius.

Ruben recognised the platoon comedian and realised that this was his first test. "Why do you ask?" he responded, stalling for time.

"Just a polite enquiry, sir," answered Cornelius.

The boy was quick, thought Ruben as he decided to be honest so as not to be easily caught out. "The Babylonian Guard," he remarked casually, "I believe I was the youngest soldier to hold such a position." A low gasp was heard around the gymnasium, as the name was highly respected throughout the known world, even Druselus looked at Ruben with renewed respect. Ruben allowed a pause before continuing. "Now, if that has satisfied your curiosity Master Cornelius, I would suggest that you sheath your wit as it is obviously keener than your sword."

Subdued laughter brightened all the faces, except for Cornelius who coloured brightly.

Ruben thought that now he had put the lad down he must quickly restore his honour, otherwise he would make an enemy. "Now, you all have standard swords and shields and the shield, is primarily not a weapon but a defensive barrier, which is of course important, but for the first part we will concentrate on using swords. But before you put your shields away, if I may I will demonstrate an important fact." He then produced the beaten up shield that he had obtained from the armourer and placed it on the ground. "Now, for this demonstration I would like an assistant," and before anyone could offer their services he looked at Cornelius and said, "Perhaps you will oblige me, Cornelius?"

The boy came forward with considerable apprehension, obviously worried about being made to look a fool. "Thank you, young man," continued Ruben conversationally. "Now, let us swap swords, but be careful because my sword is very sharp and although it is about the same size as yours, it is a lot heavier."

They exchanged weapons, Cornelius finding that the sword that was offered to him, hilt first, was brighter than the bronze sword that he had given to Ruben. Additionally, he could see that it was honed to a very sharp edge on both sides, quite unlike the bronze sword that he handed to Ruben, which had a pronounced, rounded edge. He was so fascinated by the fine edge, that he ran his thumb over it to test its sharpness when he believed no one was watching. He was horrified to see the blood well up from the fine cut that he had inflected by only a light touch. Fortunately the cut was on his left thumb and as he was right-handed, he held his left hand behind his back so that Ruben would not notice. Ruben had placed his shield on the floor with the dome side upwards and was squatting down beside it. "Now, boys," he was saying, "if this bronze shield is used to stop a heavy blow from a bronze sword it will not break," at which point he brought down the bronze sword in a swift and heavy blow, far harder than any of the boys could deliver. As he had predicted, the shield withstood the blow, although it was heavily dented. "Now, if it is used to stop a blow from my sword," he paused and turned to Cornelius. "If you would be good enough to do the same thing?" he asked.

Cornelius now felt that he would be made to look very silly indeed, as he knew that he would not be able to hit with such devastating impact, but also knew that he could not refuse. He brought Ruben's short sword down, using as much force that he could muster and was amazed and delighted by the result. The sword had hardly dented the metal, but had cut through the outer layer of bronze, exposing the stout leather backing. Cornelius stood back in surprise, the blow had not even jarred his arm as he had been expecting, and his ears at first did not recognise what Ruben was saying.

"Well done, my young friend, that was indeed a mighty blow," said Ruben, taking back his own sword and handing back the bronze blade to

Cornelius. "Just be sure to bind your thumb with a clean cloth," he said in a whisper as he patted Cornelius on the back and directed him back to the other boys.

He could see Cornelius glowing with pride as he returned to his place and then held up the shield, bending back the sides of the cut that Cornelius had made, so that the leather backing was clearly visible. "Now, my weapons are made from iron and not bronze, and that, my friends, is why the Babylonian army, with one full battalion of Babylonian Guards equipped with iron weapons, won the battle of Ashkilon. Now I do not want to hear any more talk of heroes, the Babylonian Guards with whom I fought are simply very fine soldiers." Ruben breathed a sigh of relief, and thought to himself, well, so far so good.

Ruben was just returning the bent and broken shield to the side of the gymnasium, when he looked across to Druselus and he saw that Lord Coronus had come unnoticed into the room. He looked quizzically in Druselus' direction, and was waved on by a please continue signal. Again, he addressed the boys in a clear voice, "We will now continue with just the swords, so you can stand the shields against the wall behind you." As soon as this instruction had been carried out he continued, "When using your sword, you can use it to stop any blows that are aimed at you as well as using it to try to injure or kill your opponents. Please notice that I use the word opponents, as you will not always be fighting a single person in a one-to-one encounter. But that is what we are going to do in our training. I am now going to demonstrate the standard five attacking strokes and perhaps Druselus will be kind enough to act as my opponent," he paused as Druselus came forward. He then said once more to the boys, "Do not worry, I will not chop him up." This brought plenty of laughter from his attentive audience. The standard strokes were demonstrated to the boys by both men, with Ruben finally dismissing Druselus with a kindly, "Thank you, sir." Turning back to the boys he said, "I would now be grateful if you would pair off and practise these moves, take it in turns to attack or defend. First with no particular force, until I have been amongst you and adjusted your moves. When I give you the individual agreement you can start whacking each other, and I want to see you sweating with effort."

The boys paired off and they started the moves as Ruben went amongst them, correcting and advising on angles and direction and occasionally re-pairing partners so that they were all equally opposed. Once he was finally happy that each boy had a suitable opponent and that they had mastered the basic moves, he said, "Now let us see work, and you will keep going until you drop from exhaustion." The gymnasium soon reverberated to the sound of swordplay, as the practise continued in earnest. He stood watching and keeping his eyes on the action, and gradually moved over to where Druselus and the Lord Coronus were speaking.

Druselus stepped forward and said above the noise, "Please be still until I say continue." He waited until the noise had quietened and all eyes had turned his way. "The Lord Coronus will now have a brief word," he said, moving backwards to allow his place to be taken by the tall white-haired figure.

Coronus spoke in a clear, commanding and powerful voice obviously unused to being questioned. "I see that you are being trained extremely well. I am more than happy for this to be continued until dinner this evening. This will be served in the main hall, when I will address the entire household."

"Continue," called out Druselus, who turned to Ruben as Coronus left the gymnasium. "He was exceptionally pleased with your training methods and the demonstration about the new iron weapons. He also thought that your handling of young Cornelius was superb, and so did I. He is a clever lad, but can be a terrible nuisance if he wants to be difficult. But I think we may now see a change in him," he said, while still considering the boy's behaviour.

They kept the boys hard at work until the bell sounded for the end of the day's work, by which time all the boys were very tired but happily returned all their weapons to the armoury and then went to wash away the dirt and grime after the long tiring day, proudly showing off their bumps and bruises, Cornelius displaying his small cut where he had felt the sharpness of Ruben's sword, but praising his teaching methods, ability and strength. Additionally he would not hear any criticism aimed at Ruben without effective verbal retaliation.

Druselus went with Ruben, discussing the day's training, towards the guest quarters and told him that there would now be ample time for them to wash and change clothes before the evening meal. He left Ruben with the promise that he would come back and accompany him and his companion to dinner, if Joself and Tasmin wished to join the entire household who would be entertaining some local friends that evening.

Ruben knocked on the door before entering to see how his friends were. He was surprised to find that Joself was out of bed and walking, albeit with difficulty. When they heard about the dinner that evening, they agreed to come and were very interested to hear of Ruben's successful day's work in his new temporary position. Then going into his own room to prepare himself, wash and dress in clean clothes, he was surprised yet pleased to see that everything was tidy in his room and all his clothes had been washed. It therefore did not take him long before he was ready for the evening. On their way to dinner with Druselus walking alongside Joself and giving him an occasional steadying arm, Ruben, who walked beside Tasmin, asked her who had washed his clothes and tidied his room.

"That was me," she said. "I hope you don't mind?"

"Most certainly not, particularly if you don't want anything in way of payment, which you won't receive anyway," he said laughing.

"Oh no," she replied. "It was simply that I had plenty of time on my hands as Joself was sleeping most of the day."

They soon came to the main hall and found that places had been laid for them at one end of the top table.

They stood behind their seats as the room gradually filled with the entire household, all the guests, members of the household including Lord Coronus' small detachment of soldiers and the platoon of boys who were being trained. The top table consisted of Lord Coronus in the centre and Druselus on his immediate right. Next to Druselus came Ruben with Tasmin and Joself. On the Lord's left were a couple of local dignitaries, the nearest man wore a gold torque, like the one that Ruben had seen Mutek wearing, so Ruben supposed that he was a leading merchant. Next to him was a man in a flowing robe with an unusual tall hat, which he did not remove, so Ruben imagined that he was a priest of some sort. On this man's left there were a couple of elegant women who seemed to be well known by everyone and completely comfortable in the surroundings. At a right angle to the top table were three long tables with occupants on both sides, the platoon of boys on one table, other guests of the house on the middle table and the small detachment of soldiers plus other members of the household who worked at different jobs on the third. The only people missing were the cooks and serving staff who were obviously otherwise engaged. Ruben estimated the total number of people at between ninety and one hundred.

Before everyone seated themselves, Lord Coronus spoke to the gathering, saying, "I have called this impromptu gathering to celebrate the arrival of some guests," at which point he waved to those on his right. "Additionally, as it is a local feast, we have the local head merchant from Timon together with his high priest, as well as our neighbours from across the valley," here he waved to those on his left. "Apart from that, I have called you all together as today I witnessed a demonstration of something that we have all heard rumours of. This I will speak of in detail later, when we have eaten, as this thing will, I believe, make a dramatic change to the world. But let us now enjoy the closing year's feast, which I will ask the local high priest to bless."

The man in the flowing robe with the strange hat was very small, as even with his unusual attire he only reached Coronus' shoulder, so therefore he stood on his chair and made a strange incantation, after which everybody sat down and the food was served. Ruben was about to ask Druselus a question, but was directed to Tasmin as she kicked his foot.

"What is it?" he asked in a confused whisper.

"Please keep between me and the high priest, lest he recognises me," she whispered and immediately turned to help Joself.

Ruben was momentarily confused, but suddenly everything dropped into place in his mind as Druselus said, "I thought you were about to ask something?"

"Oh yes, I am sorry, I was temporarily interrupted, but everything is all right now. I was going to ask what form of worship is practiced in Timon?"

"Oh, some weird barbaric belief to a local stone statue called Baal, a very strange thing it is too, I would steer clear of it if I were you," he said quietly, obviously keeping his eyes well away from those of the high priest.

Ruben asked little, but noticed much. He did as Tasmin had requested and kept the strange little man from seeing her, but noticed on more than one occasion that the high priest was trying to look past him. He had small beady black eyes, not dissimilar to those of Messuda, and he wondered if there was any connection.

The meal was a good one, and Ruben realised that Coronus must indeed be very wealthy, as it seemed from what he had said he had called this feast without prior warning. Yet the food was fresh and had suddenly appeared and the more he considered it, the stranger it seemed. However, they were nearing the end of the meal and the speech, or speeches, after the meal might shed some light on how it had happened. He thought he could guess what Coronus was going to talk about and he waited with eager anticipation for what was to come.

He listened intently as Druselus stood up and clapped his hands until all heads were turned his way, he then asked for silence and sat down again, leaving Lord Coronus to speak to everyone. "I trust that you will forgive me if I do not stand, as what I am going to say may take some time," he began in his strong commanding voice. "Firstly, I would inform you that this feast was actually planned to be held five days from now, yet as the high priest from Timon and its leading merchant were visiting this afternoon, I decided to bring the feast forward after witnessing this morning's demonstration. The boys in the training will recall the event most vividly, but I am sure that many of you have little idea of what I am going to talk about." He paused as there was general muttering from the main hall. He waited until all was again quiet, before he continued. "For many years now we have all become familiar with a heavy metal that is dug from the mountains, called iron. Although this metal is at times hard and even brittle, it can also be soft and bendable like copper. A great deal of time and money has been spent trying to learn how to make it more stable, so that it can be used instead of bronze, as it is far cheaper and very common, as deposits have been found in many places. There have been rumours that the secret has been discovered and new weapons have been made. But this morning I saw a demonstration of these new weapons that we believe are now being made by the Babylonians. The method that is used will not, I believe, remain secret for long and very soon this new metal will change all our lives. Does everybody understand me?" he asked and waited, looking around as many heads nodded in agreement. "Personally, I think it is a good thing that the secret may be shared so that no single country will dominate everybody else. And we must be quick in helping others to develop and use this metal not simply for conquest, but in day-to-day use."

There was a general hubbub of conversation as everybody turned and spoke to those sitting near them. A stooped and wizened man rose from the central table to speak.

"Friends," he said in a softly spoken, but wise voice. "The Lord Coronus has spoken with great wisdom. We must help in the spreading of this new knowledge. I believe that it is every scholar's duty to mankind to improve the situation of his neighbour." He then sat down to much applause and conversation, some of which was not in agreement.

"Well said, Ripotle," said one loud voice.

"Hear, hear," said another.

"As long as the Assyrian threat is curbed," said another.

"I disagree entirely," another voice responded.

Druselus stood up, after being prompted by Coronus, and called for silence. "This is not a debating chamber, nor is it a marketplace, here the Lord Coronus decides the aims of his house. Here we are strangers in a foreign land, our actions must be peaceful and not antagonise our hosts," he said, calming all the voices.

Lord Coronus then rose to his feet and bracing himself against the table, drew himself to his full height, spread his arms wide and said, "My good people, did you not hear that I said 'may be shared', which is pure hypothesis. It is not up to us to influence the destiny of mankind. When I started this house, it was created as a sanctuary for rest and also as a training ground for young soldiers, because that is the position I previously held in Greece and I enjoy doing that which I am good at." He remained standing but there was such command and majesty in his voice that everyone remained silent. "We must keep to our principles and I only told you what has happened so that I can consider any changes to our policy." Again he remained upright, almost daring anyone to speak, but again the room remained totally silent. "Now I suggest that you continue your discussions in groups, and if any group wishes to suggest a change in policy, they must elect two people to argue their case for change. I will allow two complete days before I listen to those deputations, which must be put to Druselus before I will even consider them, before the start of day in three days from now," after which he turned, holding his cane in front of him as if he was leading an army into battle, and marched from the room, still holding himself erect by sheer willpower. The silence was maintained for a while, until people began to stir, someone coughed and the spell was broken. Then everybody seemed to be speaking at the same time and people began to move, forming groups, shouting and jostling. Ruben felt a tug on his arm and turned to see Tasmin who whispered urgently in his ear.

"Please go and delay the high priest, while I help Joself out of the room, as he is headed this way," she pleaded, imploring him to do as she requested.

Realising the urgency of the situation, Ruben turned towards the small man in the strange hat and headed straight for him. The high priest tried to step aside but was far too slow and was soon dwarfed by the young man's broad torso.

"Excuse me, sir, but I know very little of your god," said Ruben, waylaying the small man. "Can you tell me more about Him?" he asked trying to look interested.

The beady eyes looked at him. "Who was that woman behind you?" he said trying to look past Ruben.

Ruben blocked his line of vision, "Oh, just my friend," he said hastily. "She is of no importance. Now tell me about this God of yours?" he asked, boldly turning the little man around and directing him to a seat into which he pushed him down, facing away from the direction that Tasmin was leading Joself.

"Excuse me, sergeant," said a young voice at Ruben's elbow. Ruben glanced quickly around and saw Tasmin disappear, and looked back again to find young Cornelius at his shoulder.

"Hello, my young friend," said Ruben smiling broadly. "And how is your thumb, Cornelius?" he enquired, turning his back on the confused high priest, who was completely abandoned as Ruben walked away with the young trainee. He was soon surrounded by the boys, all of whom seemed to have a new question for him. Many of the questions were about the future training and how quickly they would progress to being able to specialise in certain weapons. Most of them knew that he specialised in using a large sword and in javelin throwing. It was only natural that many of them asked to see his famous sword, to which he replied, "All in good time, but not until you have mastered the ordinary sword."

When asked about his javelin throwing, there was the inevitable question of, "How far can you throw the javelin, sir?"

His reply to this was, "Throwing a long distance is hardly necessary, so I do not know. If you are throwing the javelin at an enemy he will be able to take evasive action if he sees it coming from a long way off. That is why we train to throw at a target that is positioned between thirty and fifty paces' distance."

Some of the soldiers joined in the conversation and were interested to know whether Ruben knew anything about how the new weapons were made, to which his reply was always the same, that what he knew about weapons was how to use them and of course, how to look after them. Before he realised, most of the guests had departed and the boys were sent back to have a full night's sleep, as they would be hard at work again tomorrow.

Very soon he was showing the final few people out alongside Druselus, who, when they had left and the door had been closed, turned to him and said, "Your friends did not stay for long after the Lord Coronus' speech?"

"No, I think Joself was rather tired," explained Ruben. "After all, today was his first day up, which quite surprises me, he is making remarkable progress, don't you think?"

"Most certainly, but what I found confusing was, why, after my warning you to steer clear of the high priest, you headed directly for him, steered the little swine into a chair facing the corner and then abandoned him?" he asked with a mischievous grin.

Ruben grinned back and replied, "That was quite deliberate, it was a diversionary tactic, but it is a long story so if you don't mind, I will tell you all about it another day."

"That's fine, Ruben, it is getting late anyway and we must continue with the boys tomorrow, so let us turn in ourselves." And then as an afterthought Druselus asked, "I was told you went for a swim in the lake at the front of the house this morning, surely it's rather cold at this time of the year?"

"Yes, I suppose it is," responded Ruben honestly. "But I have normally started my day with a swim, ever since I was about knee-high," he chuckled, "because we lived by the river, and the only time I did not do that was when I was in the army training camp. It is a very good way of keeping fit, you do not notice the cold if you keep moving."

"Sounds like a good idea, would you mind if I join you tomorrow?" Druselus enquired.

"Certainly not," answered Ruben, "I will give you a call when I get up." With that he went back to his room and was about to enter and go to bed when he changed his mind, and knocked on Tasmin's door.

She opened the door almost immediately and ushered him inside. "Thank you very much for what you did this evening, I dare not meet that terrible man again, you see, he was the one who stole my baby to use as an offering to his god," she explained.

Ruben was horrified and was at a loss for words and simply stared aghast at her.

"Yes, I am afraid it is true," she admitted. "Even though I do not know who the father was and the child was not planned as I was a temple prostitute," she went on to explain.

"Does Joself know about this?" asked Ruben looking at the sleeping man, who had just been tucked in.

"No, I have not told him," she replied. "Do you think I should?"

"Yes, I think you should, but not until he is a lot better," replied Ruben. "I think he should know the full details before, and if, he decides to go ahead with his plan," said Ruben thoughtfully, but was mystified when she began silently crying. "Whatever is the matter?" he asked, not understanding her problem.

"Even if he does want me and decides to go ahead with his plan, I had to give some of his money to the old witch, so he does not have enough to even negotiate," she explained between sobs.

"Of course," said Ruben, slapping his forehead as he remembered. "I had forgotten that." He stood lost in thought for a while and then said, "Try not to worry about it, my dear, there are quite a few days before he will be well enough to travel on. I am sure we will be able to work out something by then," he said, smiling gently at her. "But now it is late, try to sleep, we will have to climb one hill at a time," he said, putting his arm around her shoulders and kissing her on the forehead, then he went back to his own room and went to bed.

He found it difficult to get to sleep as the problem was playing on his mind, so before he could get to sleep he checked how much money he had himself. It totalled just over forty gold pieces and he knew he could easily spare ten or even twenty gold pieces to make the money that Joself needed to buy Tasmin without having to negotiate. He then retired to bed and soon drifted off to sleep with an idea forming in his mind.

The next day, as promised, he called Druselus early in the morning and they went for a swim together. Although Druselus was at least twice Ruben's age, but he had kept himself extremely fit and Ruben noticed that he had no difficulty in keeping pace with him in the lake. As they returned to have breakfast, Druselus told Ruben that where he had lived in Greece was very near the sea, and he too used to go swimming often. He also told Ruben about the sea and said that although the salt made it unpleasant if you drank it, it was easy to swim in. To this Ruben replied, "Where I grew up in Nippur on the river Euphrates, the river was affected by the water from the sea, which altered its depth, they call it the tide. Is the sea in Greece like that?"

"No, not really, but I have heard strange tales of a sea far away where that happens, apparently it lies beyond the pillars of Heracles, whatever they are."

"It is a strange world, there is so much we do not know," said Ruben. "An old friend of mine told me that parts of the world were moving, that is certainly a mystery beyond my understanding."

Their friendship grew over the next few days, particularly when Druselus asked Ruben if he had ever been taught how to wrestle.

"Do you mean, fighting without weapons?" inquired Ruben.

"Well, yes, but it is not quite like that," Druselus explained. "There are many rules about things that you cannot do, like throwing sand into someone's face, or kicking them between the legs."

"What is the purpose of that?" asked Ruben, confused at such a strange idea.

"Well, it is a game, but you can learn a lot from it. If you like I will show you," offered Druselus.

"Do you mean you want to fight me?" asked Ruben.

"Yes, as long as you stick to the rules," said Druselus, laughing.

"Agreed," said Ruben. "But I am a lot bigger than you, and I will easily win."

"Will you now?" questioned Druselus. "Let us have a wager on it if you are so confident."

"If you are so keen to give me your money," laughed Ruben, "I would be a fool not to take it."

Druselus then went through the rules, clarifying about not punching in the face, kicking in the groin, biting or spitting or hair-pulling and all the other tricks that are often used in hand-to-hand fighting. They then decided to have the contest in the evening, away from all eyes that might think that they were fighting over something important.

When the event took place, Ruben attacked, sensing an easy victory, but soon found himself on his back, with Druselus standing over him laughing. This happened time and time again and Ruben realised that his own size and weight were not necessarily an advantage. Druselus told him that in a contest, a person won by so many falls, or a submission, and at the end of the evening he had won eight fights to Ruben's one. When he laughingly relieved Ruben of a gold piece, he said, "Perhaps I should have mentioned that I was the army champion. But if you like I would really like to teach you how to use your weight and incredible strength to the best of your advantage, as when you had me pinned down I had to submit, otherwise you could have broken my back."

"Would you really? I would be more than grateful, Druselus," enthused Ruben honestly, realising it would be to his advantage.

Their daily training sessions, carried out late at night, made their friendship grow stronger, and Ruben found it was going to be hard to leave, as Joself daily became fitter and finally announced that they would soon have to go.

In the meantime, Ruben made sure that Tasmin had informed Joself about her having had a child, which Joself decided did not matter. He also asked Tasmin to give him all of their money, mainly for safekeeping, and spoke to her of his plan. Joself came to talk to him one evening after dinner, by arrangement, to learn what Ruben's idea was. Ruben had also spoken to Druselus about taking Joself to Timon, yet leaving Tasmin at the house where she had already started helping with the cooking and the cleaning. His discussions with Druselus had taken them both to Lord Coronus to seek his advice.

Ruben thanked the Lord most kindly for his hospitality, but informed him that now his friend had recovered from his injuries, due to a large extent to the excellent aid that they had received from the doctor. He went on to say that the time had come where Joself needed to continue his journey to Timon and would the Lord allow Ruben to leave with Joself and then return to stay for a while longer? Additionally, would it be convenient to leave Tasmin in the household, where she was learning many skills and, Ruben hoped, being of great assistance? Lord Coronus looked stern, but all of a sudden he broke into a merry laugh.

"Ruben, my dear lad, you have indeed been a great asset and have more than paid for your stay, and I would be more than happy for you to come back. This house has served its purpose to your friend whose wife has also been, and still is, of great value. But the only one thing in life that will never change is change itself. So I have long been expecting you to come to me to say goodbye. I am therefore more than delighted to learn that you are planning to return when your friend's business has been completed. Now, if you let me know what you have to do, I will do my best to try to assist."

The reason for Joself's journey was then discussed and the Lord Coronus was not in the least, much to Ruben's surprise, appalled at the idea of buying a wife who he had used for almost a year, in fact he seemed to think the idea was quite sensible. He told Ruben, "You could in fact do him a favour and take some of the old bronze armour with you to the market, and see what you could obtain in part exchange." He also advised that Joself should approach the merchant on the basis that the goods he had obtained were already used and therefore the price was too high, in other words, he should try to renegotiate, simply because that is the way that the local people operate. However, he said, "If the merchant is insistent, do not make a fuss, and pay the agreed price, but nothing more. If the merchant does want more, tell him to come and take back the goods, they are at my house and he will have to speak with me." He further told Ruben that they must on no account get into any local squabbles and at all costs avoid the temple and the high priest. The little man, he had been advised, was still annoyed at the way he had been treated, even though he himself considered the whole episode comical.

Accordingly, the next morning Ruben and Joself travelled with a mule on the road to Timon, leaving a lot of equipment behind them. They were travelling light as they expected to be only a couple of days and would soon be back at the house. They were told that they should reach Timon before nightfall and only stay one full day before they returned on the third day. It was late morning when they set out, but they maintained a reasonable pace without stopping for lunch, which they ate on the road as it was now winter and chilly if they stopped moving, and they crested the final hill just as the evening was approaching. Timon was most certainly a strange town to look down on, but it appeared that they had arrived during a period of high importance. They stood looking down on the town, which seemed deserted except for a large crowd who were standing around a statue, outside a spacious building that he presumed was the temple. The statue appeared to be glowing and had arms raised in front of the large triangular body, the arms forming a chute, which led to a vast gaping mouth, out of which flames could be seen.

"It does not look as if we will be able to avoid the temple," said Ruben. "But we had better try to stand at the very edge of the crowd and see what is going on."

"It is either that, or go back," said Joself.

As the two men were standing undecided they were suddenly surrounded by at least twenty almost naked young women and jostled down towards the large crowd, the scantily clad young women laughing and cavorting as they led them towards the seemingly expectant gathering.

## 20
## TROUBLES IN TIMON

Dathram had been very busy since his appointment as the Leading Merchant and Ambassador to Egypt, he had organised his main residence in Babylon and offices in Nippur and Lagash, where most of the trade with the east would be conducted. As he had been delighted with Latich, who had given him the opportunity for an audience with the royal household, which led to this appointment, he had requested the king to appoint Latich as one of his assistants, which released Latich from being a Babylonian Guard, for which he was not really suited.

He had in fact just returned from Latich's wedding celebration feast. The young lad had settled in Nippur with the daughter of Ruben's uncle, the girl called Miriam, to whom Ruben had passed a message via Latich from where they had met in Zohab. Dathram recalled the strange first meeting with Latich when he had been running past the inn where Dathram had met Ruben, and from where he had been about to leave. Latich had run full tilt into Ruben, his old friend from the army training camp, as if the hound Cerberus, was snapping at his heels. Latich had delivered the message and had become very friendly with Miriam, whom he had now chosen as a wife. Latich had fulfilled Dathram's trust in him and was aspiring to become a trustworthy and loyal merchant, under Dathram's direct guidance. He had been placed in charge of the office and warehouse in Nippur, where he was now living with his new wife.

Dathram had been extremely pleased with the way that everything was taking at the Babylonian end of the trade route that he was attempting to build. Having decided to travel back to Egypt himself, where he already had contacts he could trust and from where he could build, he was in fact not over worried about that end of the route. His main problem was that Assyria had completely shut the door leading to the west and down towards Egypt, after the humiliating defeat they had suffered at Ashkilon. Therefore, Dathram needed to find a way to bypass Assyria, so that he could make a success of his new position. He knew that to bypass Assyria to the south was almost impossible, as it meant travelling into a fearful desert and then across unknown lands that were reputedly inhabited by dangerous nomadic tribes. But the route following the river Euphrates northwest and then south into Canaan was perhaps a possibility. After a great deal of consideration and discussion with fellow merchants, he decided to take his problem before the king.

An audience was granted and he found himself once more in the

Citadel, in the main hall behind the enormous bronze covered doors, explaining the problem to the king. "I really need to travel myself to see whether a route can be found, your Majesty."

"Would it help if I gave you an armed escort?" suggested the king.

"No, I do not think that would help your Majesty," replied Dathram. "You see, if I take soldiers, it would be considered an act of war by the Assyrians, but also as intimidatory by the Persians in the north."

"Can you not send someone else? As I do not wish to place you in a dangerous situation," said the king. "I did not appoint you with the intention of putting you at risk."

"Then I will have to resign my position with the trade route not even established," apologised Dathram, sadly shaking his head like a large wounded lion, gesturing an attitude of despair with open arms. "You really ought to let me go," he implored. "As I alone possess the knowledge and have the contacts in Egypt. That is why you offered me this position in the first place and I would dearly love to see the job completed satisfactorily."

"Well, you cannot travel until the spring anyway," said the king, resigning himself to losing the argument. "Something may well develop between now and when you intend to leave, so come and see me before you set out and I will at least give you a token to use as proof of your acting on my behalf." He then dismissed Dathram as he turned his mind to other pressing matters.

Dathram returned to the pleasant house that went with the position, deep in thought as he contemplated how to tackle the journey. He thought that he needed to take a few items to trade and possibly plenty of common gold coinage, which he could offer as sweeteners to places along the road, but felt that he would prefer to travel alone as that way he would not jeopardise anyone travelling with him, apart from which he would not attract as much attention to himself. He felt sure the political situation would not change before the spring, as the Assyrians were not accommodating and a hard people to negotiate with. So he started making plans for one final long and dangerous journey into the west that would either make his fortune and firmly establish his position, or he would die in the attempt. He smiled ruefully to himself as he thought that he had virtually said this same thing before leaving Zohab, when he had departed from Ruben at the end of last summer. He had heard the strange story that Ruben had continued upriver to Ashkilon, arriving just too late to pass through, so he had offered his services to Commander Mithrandir. He had been told how Ruben had performed amazing deeds and then left the city in pursuit of the defeated Assyrian army, when the lovely girl travelling with him had been killed. He wondered, not for the first time, what had happened to the nice, polite, helpful young man, of whom he could believe the stories, as he knew from the brief meeting that Ruben was strong and, according to Latich, highly efficient and skilful in battle.

****

The effect that these nearly naked young women had on Ruben was initially one of surprised delight, but as their cavorting became more and more provocative and seductive, he became embarrassed and annoyed, particularly when he noticed that all these young women had a glazed look to their eyes, and were possibly unaware of what they were doing. As it was very cold and their dress, or what little there was of it, was totally unsuitable, and they must have been very cold. Ruben realised, as the crowd parted in front of him and Joself, that they were jostled to the front of the crowd towards the high priest. The same little man with the shifty eyes and the strange large hat was waiting, as this whole charade was stage-managed. They were expected and had walked into a trap. The young women were obviously acting or performing whilst under the influence of some drug, as they were unaware of their actions, not realising what they were doing. Although Ruben was annoyed, he was aware that the Lord Coronus had distinctly told him to steer clear of the high priest and not to get involved in any squabbles. He realised only just in time that shortly they would be right in front of the high priest, as if they had deliberately made their way to him.

He immediately stood firmly rooted to the spot and clasped Joself by the arm so he too could not move forwards, oblivious to the jostling dancers trying to coax them forward. This forced the high priest to come forwards and greet them, giving him only a slight advantage.

"Greetings, my friends," called the high priest, as he went to meet them. "We are indeed honoured that you have seen fit to join us."

"You are mistaken," said Ruben flatly. "We have no wish to see you or to witness this deliberately planned meeting."

The little man made no denial, but hurriedly said, "You wished to know more about the great god Baal." He swept his hands in an expansive gesture of greeting, encompassing the huge glowing statue.

"That was on a different occasion and in a different place," said Ruben in an uninterested voice. "Come along Joself, we have business elsewhere." He turned on his heel and still grasping Joself's arm, walked away, propelling Joself with one arm and pulling the mule behind him.

"Wait," cried the high priest in desperation. "We have prepared a special festival for you, do join us and take a drink."

As if by magic, one of the scantily clad glazed-eyed young women appeared in front of Ruben and Joself, holding out a tray with two goblets containing a dark brown liquid.

"Do not touch it, Joself," whispered Ruben, pushing Joself ahead to one side of the young woman, releasing his arm, and neatly side-stepping passed the proffered drinks. "They are probably drugged," he continued in his conspiratorial whisper, and they walked away leaving the shocked crowd with the high priest in a tremendous rage.

They were headed back out of the town, but before they reached the edge of the road they made a slight detour to the left where, out of sight from the crowd, an old beggar, without feet, was sitting on the ground.

"Where can we find lodging away from this ridiculous ceremony, old father," asked Ruben, squatting down to the old man and giving him a gold piece.

"Thank you, kind sir," stammered the old beggar, unused to such generosity. "If you go down the fourth street to your left you will find an inn that accommodates travellers."

Following the beggar's directions, they found the inn and were about to enter when there was a howl from the large crowd by the statue of Baal, which they could just see through a gap in the buildings. They watched in mystified fascination as there was a roll of drums and a small bundle was placed onto the outstretched arms of the hideous statue by the high priest, who was standing on a gantry that had been moved into position for that purpose. The high priest stepped back and spread his arms wide, this allowed the small bundle to roll down the outstretched arms that formed a chute to the gaping mouth, where flickering flames could still be seen. When the small bundle dropped into the mouth of the statue there was a burst of flames and a puff of greenish grey smoke seemed to be coughed from the statue, to the cheers of the crowd. Ruben realised with horror that the small bundle had been a sacrifice, in all probability a small child, just as Tasmin had said had happened to her baby. Ruben had hardly believed such a barbaric thing could happen, but now he had witnessed it with his own eyes and stared in horror. He and Joself turned their backs on the scene and entered the inn.

There were only a couple of people sitting with the innkeeper, who rose to his feet as they came in.

"Good evening, friends, can I be of assistance?" he asked.

As Ruben was too shocked to speak and as Joself had not fully realised the horror of what they had just witnessed, he took control and said, "Yes, I hope you can. My friend and I are here on business and would like a room for a couple of nights."

"We have plenty of spare rooms at the moment," replied the innkeeper. "As there is not much business just now." He paused for breath and then continued, "Although there is a ceremony, which you probably realised, but that has only just been arranged, without warning, which is where all the townsfolk are, except for a small number of merchants who are at business in the hall next door." He explained in detail as he led them to a room with two beds.

"This will suit us very well," said Joself.

"You are welcome to join us for dinner," invited the innkeeper, "but it will not be served until late, because the Merchants' Council is meeting and they have ordered dinner, which will be served later than usual," he told them apologetically.

"We will decide shortly, and let you know," responded Joself, and then added, "we have also a beast of burden. Do you have a stable?"

"Yes, just around the back. If you like I will ask my lad to look after him for you," the innkeeper offered.

Ruben had now recovered from the shock, which had momentarily silenced him. Interjecting quickly, he said, "You can leave that to us, sir."

Looking surprised, the innkeeper said, "It will be all right for a while, but do not leave it for long," he suggested, as he left the room.

"That was a strange gathering," said Joself, shaking his head as if trying to rid himself of a bad dream.

"Yes, quite horrible," agreed Ruben, but then went on to say, "It was all stage managed for our benefit, you realise? Someone must have told the high priest that we were coming, and I fear that he is now even more incensed with us, or at least with me in particular. I therefore do not wish to stay here for long, as it may give him another opportunity to seek us out. "

He stood, lost in thought for a while and then said, "Now it may be possible to see if we could conduct our business this evening, say nothing to anyone, and then slip away early in the morning," he said, talking of the idea that had just come into his mind.

Joself readily agreed to the plan, but said, "How do you think that they knew we were coming to Timon?"

"Needless to say someone must have informed the high priest, and that person must work for Lord Coronus, as I cannot imagine Coronus or Druselus passing on the message. After all," said Ruben, pacing the floor whilst deep in thought, "You remember the innkeeper said that the ceremony took place without warning. That means that whoever the informant was, must not have known of our journey until early this morning."

"Yes, that is possible, it also points to only a few people who knew of our journey," suggested Joself.

"Well, whoever it was, it does not really matter now," commented

Ruben. "But we must let the Lord Coronus know that he has an informant working in his house, and we must pass on that information as quickly as possible."

Having decided to go to the Merchants' Hall with the mule, to see if the merchant that Joself wished to contact was there, and also to try to bargain Lord Coronus' arms, they left the inn, informing the innkeeper that they were going to attend to their beast and would be back for dinner later. When they arrived in the Merchants' Hall they found that the meeting was on the point of closure, but had been ushered in by a friendly young merchant who thought they were late arrivals. Ruben recognised one the leading merchants from the dinner at Lord Coronus' house, who was calling for order and was then to close the meeting. Ruben was recognised by the leading merchant, largely due to his size, just as Joself grabbed his arm and whispered in his ear that he had spotted his quarry. The leading merchant called for a temporary halt to business and asked, "Can we be of assistance, my friends?" All eyes had turned to Ruben and Joself, whilst a hush fell on the gathering, which anticipated something of interest.

"Are you still open for business, my lord?" inquired Ruben using a respectful address.

"If you come on business from the Lord Coronus," returned the leading merchant, "then we most certainly are, my friends. What business do you have?" he enquired.

"There are two matters actually, sir," said Ruben. "I have come with some old bronze to sell on behalf of the Lord Coronus, whilst my colleague has outstanding business with one of your fellow merchants." Ruben spoke loudly, with confidence that he did not really possess, but hoped was the best way to conduct business.

His ploy worked, as the leading merchant replied, "I will just close down our initial meeting and then allow you to conduct your business, as the main dealers in old bronze are present. Additionally, the merchant who has outstanding business with your colleague has indicated his desire to trade." The leading merchant then went on to address the crowd. "Referring back to the final item concerning the use of strong drinks as used by the high priest during the ceremonies. Are we all in agreement that it will no longer be allowed?" There was a great deal of murmured agreement amongst the assembled merchants, so their meeting was terminated. However, before the meeting broke up, the leading merchant called to the dealers in bronze, saying, "I believe you have some unexpected business with our friends. As indeed have you," he said speaking to another merchant who had previously raised his hand, indicating that he wished to trade with Joself. He finally shouted above the chattering merchants, "Dinner will shortly be started in the inn next door, as is customary."

The dealers in bronze converged on Ruben, whilst the other merchant came over to speak with Joself.

"Remember everything we discussed," whispered Ruben into Joself's ear, as he went to meet the dealers in bronze and Joself went off to bargain on the other business. This was far easier than Joself had dared to hope. The other merchant was almost surprised to see him and was comparatively easy to haggle with over the price that he had originally demanded for Tasmin.

When Joself said that the goods were already soiled, the other merchant laughed and with a wink said, "Surely, you did not expect a virgin? But she must be good, my friend, otherwise you would not wish to keep her."

"That is true," commented Joself. "Nonetheless, you cannot expect the full amount that you originally requested." They finally settled on thirty gold pieces and both were more than content with the transaction.

Ruben found that due to the possibility of the new metal soon becoming available, there was still a high price for old bronze as it would be melted down and used for other items. So he got a good price for all the old bronze that Lord Coronus had given him. Both men returned with the merchants to the inn, were they found that places had been set next to the leading merchants who wished to talk to them over dinner. Ruben correctly guessed the nature of the conversation, which concerned the final item of the council's meeting. He found himself telling the leading merchant, who was an extremely likeable man, all about the way that they were caught by surprise and jostled to the front of the crowd and greeted by the high priest. Ruben gave a full account of the events of the late afternoon, to which the leading merchant grinned with delight.

"That is an excellent story, and it is clever the way that you managed to turn the tables on the high priest. You see, that is just the way that they work, the crowd is crazed by the drink," commented the leading merchant.

"I believe it is more than just alcohol," said Ruben. "I think that the drink is drugged, so that the people are unaware of what they are doing."

"Ahem, yes," reflected the leading merchant, considering the possibility and accuracy of Ruben's opinion. "Yes that could well be the case. Anyway, we must put a stop to it. I am due to meet with the high priest tomorrow, I can well imagine he will be in quite a rage," he chortled.

Ruben and Joself enjoyed the company that evening, particularly on top of their successful bargaining, but whilst the rest of merchants continued to make merry, they excused themselves saying that they had had a long walk and were now tired, and so retired to their room. Their room was on an extension at the rear of the inn, on the ground level, with just the stables behind the room. Having carefully checked that they were not overheard, Ruben turned to Joself and said, "Do you fancy a night walk?"

Somewhat surprised, Joself asked, "Well, I am not as tired as we pretended, what do you have in mind?"

"Do you remember the tall, slim merchant in the hall?" Ruben asked.

"Yes," replied Joself. "The sly looking one, he took little part in everything but listened carefully to what everyone said, now I think I know what is coming next."

"Yes, you are on the right track," commented Ruben. "You know he did not come to the dinner. I think he has reported our business, and I do not think that we are safe here for the night," he said.

"Well, perhaps not," said Joself. "But I do not see what they could do even if they know our whereabouts."

"You are right again," replied Ruben. "But I would prefer not to cause any problem. As that was the specific instruction from Coronus himself."

"You don't mean that you think we should leave now?" asked Joself in disbelief.

"Correct again!" said Ruben, smiling at him. "But do not worry, because we now have an empty mule coming with us. So if you get tired you can have a ride."

Joself resigned himself to the return trip and they hastily tidied up the room and left some coins on the table to cover their night stay, and slipped quietly out of the ground floor windows. They soon retrieved their mule and were on their way, whilst the merry making was still evident from the noise coming from the inn.

The lights and sounds of the town soon diminished as they crested the valley in which Timon lay. Ruben deliberately led the mule on the grass beside the track, as the ground was stony, where the sound of the mule's hooves clattered on the ground that was now frozen hard in the winter night. Although it was quieter than the pathway, the grass was frosty and crackled under their footsteps, despite the town being out of sight, they still kept beside the path until they were well clear of the area. Ruben then moved back onto the path, which allowed faster travel, even though their passage was far louder. Although it was cold and frosty, there was no wind so they found walking kept them warm. After a while Joself began to stumble and Ruben said, "I think you had better ride, after all it has been a long day and it has not been long since you have been active again.

Put your arms around my neck," he offered and as Joself complied, he lifted him onto the mule's back. "I am sure you will find that better, but wrap this blanket around your shoulders just to help you keep warm, sit back and enjoy the ride, it is a pleasant night and we should hopefully be home in time for breakfast." The road was peaceful and as Joself sat comfortably on the uncomplaining mule, he once again considered himself extremely fortunate in being in company with this large, powerful young man, who never seemed to tire. The thought of getting back and having breakfast with Tasmin, who was now securely his, was a comforting thought and having witnessed that ghastly ceremony in Timon he could now appreciate her feelings towards the high priest of Baal and all he represented.

****

The leading merchant was just on the point of leaving the party and going to bed, when there was a loud hammering on the inn door. It was opened to admit the small figure of the high priest who was dwarfed by four very large slaves who were as black as night and did not speak or understand the common tongue, as they had been purchased from Egypt.

"Where are those two impudent outsiders?" he demanded of the now silent merchants.

"I believe they have retired to their rooms, where they went some time ago. They are probably asleep, and I do not see why they should be woken," the leading merchant countered crossly.

"They desecrated our ceremony," screeched the indignant little man. "I want them imprisoned," he demanded. "Search the inn," he instructed his large servants.

The leading merchant made no movement to stop the search, but said, "You will need more than those four to take them, if everything I have heard about Ruben is correct."

The innkeeper had conveniently disappeared and none of the merchants assisted in directing the four slaves, who were in total confusion. The search was disorganised and chaotic, with disturbed sleepers grumbling at the confusion. When everyone in the inn had been woken and were vehemently protesting, the leading merchant confronted the high priest in a demanding voice.

"Under whose authority do you create this disturbance?"

"The authority of the people of this town, as I am their high priest," responded the little man, knowing that he was on uncertain ground.

"This town is governed by the High Council, of which you are certainly a member, but so am I and other merchants who are present and we have not even been consulted about this," said the leading merchant indignantly. He then continued, "We are also most concerned about the drink that you force on all participants at your gatherings. This afternoon the Merchants' Council decided to have the practice stopped."

"Oh yes," spluttered the little man. "And how do you intend to enforce that?"

"Admittedly you seem to have purchased a large number of these black savages, who obey your orders. We cannot fight them, but we can stop the supply of goods to your temple," stated the leading merchant.

"I, I, I, will lead the people against the Merchants' Council," spluttered the little man.

"In which case, we will ask the Lord Coronus to send a detachment of his personal guard to aid us, I am sure he will agree," was the leading merchant's calm response. "You will now lead your slaves and leave us in peace, as those sought are no longer here."

Knowing that he was outmanoeuvred and had overstepped his authority, or at least had tried to use the power he had been building too soon, the high priest led his large servants back out of the inn, to the derisive jeers of the merchants.

\*\*\*\*

Ruben had kept walking all night and as the sky in the east began to pale with the approaching day, they could make out the outlines of Lord Coronus' house. They led the mule around the side of the house to where the kitchen was beginning to become active. A very excited Tasmin saw them as she was working in the kitchen and rushed out to help Joself down from the mule's back. He was tired and cold as he had been sitting motionless for the last portion of the night, even though Ruben was warm and did not seem to be tired. He instructed Tasmin not to make a scene at their arrival.

"Lead Joself inside back to your room, while I go and find Druselus, but try to keep our arrival secret for the time being as someone knew that we were on our way to Timon, where they had arranged a reception for us." Alarm instantly showed on Tasmin's face, but she was soon pacified by Ruben who said, "Do not worry, everything is all right." Her relief was instant and she led Joself quietly around the back of the house, while Ruben stabled the mule and went to the guardhouse, where he met Druselus.

"Back so soon, my friend. Before you say anything," he said raising a hand to forestall any comment, "we know all about the informer, who slunk back last night thinking he had not been missed. But his absence was noted, even though it was by then too late to inform you. You had better come along with me and tell me everything that happened. Lord Coronus was most concerned and has asked me to conduct a full inquiry. I think the best idea would be for you to tell me all that happened over breakfast, as knowing you, you are probably extremely hungry."

To this suggestion, Ruben laughed. "Yes, as a matter of fact I am rather hungry." Druselus smiled and led the way towards the main eating area, but was halted as Ruben checked his progress.

"Tasmin has just escorted a very tired Joself back to their room, I would like to have Joself in on this. I think it would be sensible to discuss this all together," he requested.

"That sounds a sensible idea," agreed Druselus. "You go and keep them in their room, whilst I bring some food." He then quickly added, "I will try to bring enough, even for you!" He disappeared in the direction of the kitchens, laughing to himself. Ruben was soon ensconced with Joself and Tasmin, whom he had prevented from going to get some food for Joself. Druselus soon reappeared with a well-laden tray.

"Right, you can all start eating and telling your story, but let's just have one narrator," he cautioned.

Ruben took up the story from when they had left the previous morning and continued in an accurate report, with just the occasional nod of agreement or slight elaboration from Joself. When Ruben came to describing the ceremony that was staged for their arrival, complete with a vivid description of the sacrifice, Tasmin gave a sharp intake of breath.

"That is what happened to my baby," she stated in a barely audible voice.

"And you are quite definite that the crowd were all under the influence of something in the wine?" he suggested, looking at both men.

"As certain as we can be," Ruben qualified. "But I am no doctor and we did not drink the wine that was offered."

"I can assure you that that is what normally happened," said Tasmin. "The drink is definitely drugged."

"All right, but we may have to seek further confirmation on that," stated Druselus. "But continue your story Ruben." The story was complete by the time that the breakfast tray was empty, giving Druselus a clear idea of what had happened. "You did well to leave at that point," he added admiringly. "I must now go and report to Lord Coronus." He then turned to Ruben, "Do you have the money that you obtained for the bronze?"

"Yes, it is all here," he said giving Druselus a leather pouch that he had in his jerkin.

"I will now go and report your story, and I suggest that in the meantime you have some rest."

"But I am not tired," objected Ruben. "All I have done is walked to Timon and back."

"Well, stay here anyway," instructed Druselus. "I may shortly need you again."

"May I not go out to help the boys with their training?" Ruben requested.

"If you must, but be sure to be available on my request," stated Druselus sternly, incredulous at Ruben's energy.

After Druselus had left, Ruben made sure that Joself was tucked in bed with Tasmin looking after him and he then went in search of the trainee soldiers. He found the boys at the parade ground where they were continuing their training. He was surprised to find that rumour had spread of his return and incredible stories had already been made up about what had happened in Timon. The story that amused him most was the one that Cornelius was telling, seeking Ruben's confirmation, amidst the laughter of his friends.

"Is it true that you threw the little high priest into his own god as a sacrifice, sergeant?"

"No, Cornelius," Ruben laughed. "But perhaps I should have." He was about to add, 'Because that is what he deserved'. When he was distracted by the sound of hoof beats coming from the front of the house and the challenge of the sentry.

A deputation from the Merchants' Council from Timon had arrived, which included the leading merchant. The deputation was taken into the building where it was asked to wait, which gave Ruben the opportunity to go and see his new friend, the leading merchant.

"I am glad to find you here," said the merchant, whose name was Arthermais. "Presumably you left the inn and came back overnight, rather than going to bed?"

"That's correct, we thought it would be best, rather than risk another disturbance in Timon," explained Ruben.

"You were wise," came the reply. "That annoying little man came looking for you, with four of his apes, but he has overstepped the mark this time. We are determined to bring an end to this disreputable business, mainly for the benefit of the people of Timon, who are normally decent folk. Regrettably, you witnessed an outrageous event when they were all under the influence of drugged wine."

"I am glad that you confirm my belief, needless to say you will confirm my story to the Lord Coronus," said Ruben gratefully.

"That is precisely why we came, we need his assistance to stop the high priest and his bully boys from ruling the town. You see, we can control all the supplies into the town, but we have no weapons or armed force to exercise our power. We were hoping that the Lord Coronus would lend us his small force, do you think that he will help?"

"Well," said Ruben thoughtfully. "He normally tries to take no side in any internal disputes, as he is not a native of this country. But you may be lucky on this occasion, particularly if you confirm the story of our visit, which he is being told about at this moment by the captain of his own household." Ruben suddenly realised that he had given Druselus a rank, and hoped that there would be no objection, but wondered if Druselus did have a rank, and the more he thought about it, the more he thought that he would probably be more than just a captain.

As these thoughts crossed his mind, Druselus appeared, closing the door to Coronus' chamber.

"What have we got here?" demanded Druselus of the guard.

"A deputation from the town, sir," came the reply.

Quickly realising what must have happened, particularly as he saw Ruben talking to Arthermais, he immediately came over and asked the reason for the deputation. Ruben sensibly stood aside and allowed the leading merchant to tell his story. After listening carefully to the story, and having confirmed that this would justify what Ruben had witnessed, he then returned having asked the leading merchant to wait.

As Druselus went in to report to the Lord Coronus, Ruben asked Arthermais, "Are these bully boys armed?"

"Not that I have noticed," Arthermais replied. "Although they may carry daggers, but they are just very large and muscular, but no bigger than you my friend, and I am sure that they would back down against trained soldiers."

"Where do they come from?" Ruben enquired, as he had only seen the large black servants standing on guard outside the temple.

"They have been purchased as slaves and come from Egypt, although they do not originate from there. I believe they come from the lands to the south of Great Egypt, the land of Kush," Arthermais informed him.

"But I thought the trade was done through your council?" Ruben persisted.

"Yes, we've brought them up for the high priest, but they were in chains and were calm and peaceful, giving us no problems on the journey," Arthermais told him.

This gave Ruben an idea and he continued asking Arthermais about the trade with Egypt, and how often they went there. He was told that the trade used to be more frequent than it had been recently, because they no longer dealt with any trade from Assyria. He then told Ruben that they still travelled south, but started by travelling west towards the sea, and would then travel down along the inside of the shore. This was done basically because there were rumours of fighting inland, in between the main sea and inland salt sea where it was very hot.

"Yes, I have heard similar stories from a merchant whom I met, travelling beside the river Euphrates. That merchant said that the Egyptians were keen to trade with the Babylonians, because that was the gateway to the east, where large ships used to come laden with spices and cloth, and that those ships are keen to obtain many of the things that they produce in Egypt," he said, remembering the wonderful things that he unloaded for Dathram.

"Would you be interested in dealing with that merchant, if I could get a message sent to him?"

"Yes, most certainly, if we could bypass the Assyrians we would be very pleased to do business." Arthermais' eyes sparkled with the idea of such a trade. "Do you think it is really possible?" His question went unanswered, as Druselus returned and spoke clearly to the assembled deputation.

"The Lord Coronus will speak with a party of no more than three people. So if you can decide on three people, I will show you in."

As the deputation formed a small huddle to decide on those who would join the leading merchant in his discussions with Lord Coronus, Ruben took the opportunity to have a quick chat with Druselus. "Will you need me for a while, as I would like to check on Joself and Tasmin?"

"No, provided that you come back here after seeing them," agreed Druselus. "I do not think the Lord Coronus will be very long with the deputation, as he seemed annoyed at what has happened to you. Now that has been confirmed I believe that he may well agree to their wishes. So be sure to be back here soon, as I should imagine that he will start giving everyone a new job."

"Do not worry, Druselus," smiled Ruben. "I will be back very soon." He quickly departed and set off towards the guest bedrooms. He soon arrived outside their door, through which he could hear them talking, as he stood quietly.

He knocked on the door and called out, "Is it all right if I come in?" After waiting for an affirmative reply, he went in to where they were both sitting on the bed, obviously having only just risen. "How are you feeling Joself," he asked, although he knew the answer because Tasmin was trying to cover her nudity with a hastily grabbed towel, which was hardly sufficient for the job.

"I feel well enough, thank you Ruben," Joself replied. "Although that long walk showed that I am not yet back to being as fit as I thought I was."

"So presumably you will be staying for a while longer," pressed Ruben.

"Yes, but only for a short time," Joself responded, "as we wish to get back to Thrax where we hope to stay with my brother and the rest of the family. I suppose you will be moving on from here?"

"After a while," replied Ruben. "But probably not until the spring, when the trainee soldiers return to Cyprus," he continued as Joself nodded his understanding. "I was wondering if you would take a message for me that must then go on to Ashkilon. I feel sure that you can find someone to take it down river. I am sure that Andreas and Stephen, the fisherman brothers, will help you, if you tell them the message comes from me and give them a couple of gold pieces that I will give you."

"I will be happy to take it myself," offered Joself. "After all that you have done for me, I mean us," he quickly corrected.

"So, in about a couple of weeks, you suppose," checked Ruben.

"I think that will be about right," confirmed Joself.

"Well, I will ensure that you get safely across the Empty Sector this time," Ruben chuckled. "I will now leave you as I have to return to Druselus, I am sure that you have something to do," he said, rising, and winked at Joself who smiled in return as Tasmin blushed.

Ruben was soon back in the antechamber to Lord Coronus' main rooms, just as the deputation was coming out, but without Druselus. Ruben raised an enquiring eyebrow at Arthermais.

"We were given no direct answer, but instructed to wait," Arthermais stated to the whole room. "Although I am fairly sure that our request will be met, and I do not think we will have long to wait."

They all stood around in expectant groups, talking quietly, during which time Ruben returned to Arthemais' side and said quietly, so that nobody else heard him, "I will have a scroll sent in a few weeks that I hope will reach the merchant that I spoke about earlier. But I cannot promise more than that."

Arthermais nodded his approval and was about to speak when the doors opened and Lord Coronus stepped out, followed by Druselus.

"I am sorry to have kept you all waiting," said Lord Coronus. "But you will all be pleased to hear that I have decided, on this one occasion," here he held a hand up for silence to indicate that this was an unusual event. He continued, "Now this is what will happen." He spoke with clear precise authority and no one doubted that it was a command that would be obeyed exactly. "You must now ride back to Timon, saying nothing to anyone, but begin selecting about twenty young men to be sent here to be trained in the basic use of weapons. They will then act under the Merchant Council's authority." He paused for a considerable time to allow the instruction to clearly register with everyone. "Now, tomorrow, Druselus will lead a small force of about ten soldiers, which is almost my entire command, and they will enforce the Merchant Council's law until the twenty men have been trained. Druselus himself will speak with my authority and take all necessary decisions." There was another brief pause until he continued. "You can now leave, except you Ruben," here he took and fixed his clear grey eyes on Ruben. "I will speak to you in private please." He turned and went back into his main room.

"Off you all go then," instructed Druselus. "We all have work to do." So saying, jerked his thumb at Ruben, indicating that he should follow Lord Coronus.

Ruben was soon sitting beside Lord Coronus, where he had sat on their first meeting. He was surprised to hear what he was now asked. "I would like you to take on Druselus' position, for a brief period. Your main responsibility will be my aide as head of this household and to ensure that the new recruits complete their training by spring, when they will return to Cyprus. You will of course be paid for your services, I know that it will mean leaving your quest aside for a short period, but I think it will be a job that will assist you later on. I, as well as Druselus, have faith in you. Will you accept this request?"

"I offered you my services when I arrived Lord, I would obey it as a command. But as a request I will be more than happy to try to fulfil your faith in me," said Ruben humbly.

Druselus returned quietly to the room and although his presence was noted by Coronus, his level gaze still held Ruben. "Thank you, my boy," was his reply. He then looked at Druselus and said, "You have much to do, you can start by telling Ruben the detail of his new duties. You can now leave me and send Ruben back with my dinner this evening and then report to me shortly before I go to bed."

Druselus walked out of the room and down the hall with Ruben at his side and began explaining about his charge of the household, plus being a personal assistant to Lord Coronus. "He is a special person, who is fair and just, but do remember he is now an old man and can occasionally be short tempered. He does not suffer fools gladly and he is meticulous about his appearance and many seemingly trivial items. You will be acting as his ears and eyes and may occasionally be required to assist him with small nursing duties that he is too proud to ask of anyone else, or for them to know his requirements. You will have to not only wait on him, but report every day of all that happens and be sure to omit nothing, as he is mentally as sharp as the keenest blade and has the eyesight of a hawk. But in return, you will come to know him as a personal friend and he can teach you much as he has lived a full and active life. He has treated me like the son that he never had and I respect him more than my own father. Carry on with the training as you have been, but do not worry, because I will be back periodically to check on how things are going and of course to report about the goings-on in Timon. I will leave the two oldest soldiers with you to act as guards to the house and to help you with some of its running, but you will need to use some of the new trainees to do some of the tasks that are normally carried out by his command. I think it would be more convenient for you to move into my quarters, there is a spare bed in the room so you may as well go and fetch your belongings."

****

Arthermais led the small deputation back to Timon. They were all pleased with what they had achieved, but there was now plenty of organisation to contend with that had to be started immediately. He knew that their going to see Lord Coronus would have been reported to the high priest, but there was nothing that he could now do about it. If they now made ready for the arrival of Druselus and his soldiers, the little man was well defeated, they had moved quickly and must keep the momentum going to ensure that there was no violence, to create unrest amongst the townsfolk. He therefore instructed one of his best merchants to seek out twenty loyal men and to have them come to the Merchants' Hall for the next afternoon, by which time the soldiers would have arrived. He went to the inn that they had used, to seek the innkeeper's assistance in using his inn as a temporary barracks for the soldiers.

The innkeeper was only too pleased to help as he was loyal to the Merchants' Council and was concerned about the strange happenings of late. His own daughter had recently had an argument with her parents about serving in the inn, as she had been offered far more money by the high priest to act as one of the handmaidens of Baal. She was a pretty girl and he felt sure that she would, if she had not already, be taken as a temple prostitute. The inn was set aside for the soldiers' use as it was in a strategically good position, being on the slope of the hill that overlooked the town. It was also next door to the Merchants' Council's chamber, which would make a good garrison for the town as it possessed a watchtower, which made it the highest building in the town, as from the tower all the entrances to the town could be checked.

The high priest had returned to his temple in a foul temper, after the previous night's commotion that he had caused at the inn. He knew he had overstepped the mark and now hoped that if he let things die down for a few days they would soon right themselves and he could continue building up his own prestige. Even his favourite concubine had failed to soothe him and had fled from his bedchamber in floods of tears. His annoyance had flared into anger when he was informed that early in the morning, while he was still in bed, a deputation from the Merchants Council had left the town in the direction of the house of the Lord Coronus. He knew that Coronus had a small force of soldiers, who were the only armed force for some considerable distance due to the close proximity of Assyria, who would send an overpowering force against any show of defiance. But all had been quiet to the east of the town, ever since the Empty Sector came into being. He had posted lookouts on the road to report the return of the merchants' deputation, and his spirits had returned when he heard of the speedy return and he had received reports that they were looking glum. He had supposed that Coronus had sent them back to say what he always said, that the town's business was its own affair, and he would not involve himself as this was not his own country. How often had he heard Coronus say, 'We are strangers in a foreign land'.

The next report that he had received was that the leading merchant had immediately gone into the inn. He chuckled to himself believing that Arthermais had simply gone to drown his sorrows, as the merchants so often had in the past, which had allowed him to build up his own power in the town. He had then instructed that everything in the temple would be open to the main townsfolk, entirely free as if it were a special occasion, but that this would not be advertised, but simply passed on by word of mouth. This of course included the handmaidens of Baal, who would act as prostitutes, either induced by money or drugged wine to service the male population. There was a newcomer to the handmaidens, who he thought he would have train and use as a special incentive for the coming spring fertility rites. He therefore ordered that she remain unblemished, and would be a virgin offered to the most productive wine-grower from last year's harvest, who he already knew. This man was a devotee of Baal, seduced by his own carnal lust and unhappiness at home by his wife's infertility. He would therefore be offered this temptress to lay with for thirty days, which would produce another offspring to be offered to the God.

\*\*\*\*

The next ten days went far too quickly for Ruben who had soon accustomed himself to his new duties. It had seemed strange at first with all the decisions that he had to make and he had surprised himself in how much he had enjoyed his evening sessions of reporting to his new Lord and also in learning the success of Druselus' campaign in the town.

He had risen early that morning and had his breakfast as soon as the cooks were up, having previously been for an early morning run as it was too cold for swimming, there being a light covering of ice over the small lake to the front of the house. He had spoken to the head cook and had received a request to re-provision, which he had agreed and promised to send an order to the town that day. This would prove to be convenient, as Druselus was expected with the party of men to receive basic weapon training. He looked forward to Druselus' visit as everything had been going well and he was proud of how he was managing things. He would also discuss with Druselus the fact that Lord Coronus was suffering more than usual from an old war wound in his leg. He allowed Ruben to actually put him to bed the previous evening. This in itself was an acknowledgement of his own success, but Coronus had specifically requested that the doctor should not be informed, which was disconcerting. He had just been discussing the weapon situation with the armourer as they were not sure what the men from Timon would bring with them. Having just dismissed the armourer, he was surprised to find that Joself was waiting to see him.

"I have just come to tell you that I would like to leave in a couple of days, is your offer of seeing us back across the Empty Sector safely still valid, bearing in mind all your new work?"

"I am sure that I can arrange something," he said, suddenly remembering that he had still not written his suggestions to Dathram. "I am a man of my word, my friend, but I will have to be back the same day, so you must be ready for a very early start."

"That will be fine, in fact, it is a good idea," Joself happily agreed. "We can then get to where we camped on our way here, just before the wood where you went in search of the deer." This jerked Ruben's mind back to the occasion when he went on his abortive hunt, but had rediscovered the ability of seeing the colour that surrounds people when viewed in the special way that Simeon had taught him. He thought quickly and considered that it could be done quite successfully in the way of a training exercise with some of the new trainees, and mentally added it to the list of things he would discuss with Druselus.

"Go and tell Tasmin that we will leave in three days time and I will take eight of the new recruits with me. She is to take breakfast for all of us to eat on the way," he instructed Joself. "I will also have the scroll for you to deliver to Ashkilon."

Joself had only just left when he was told by one of the guards that a party from Timon had been spotted. He hurried to the front of the house and could make out that it was Druselus on horseback, leading the twenty young men for their basic weapon training. It was difficult to wait in a dignified manner and not run out to greet his friend, but his new authority and the dignity that went with it prevented his enthusiasm from overwhelming him.

He welcomed Druselus with a smile and their discussions of where to house the men from Timon and of how they should be trained was soon dealt with, as was the subject of the new provisions required and the question of armaments for the men from Timon. They were just to be taught how to use swords and it was most explicit that they should not wear uniforms, but simply wear a badge of office that would be provided by the Merchants' Council. Having dispensed with those and a few other mundane problems, Ruben told him, as they were walking down the hall to Lord Coronus' rooms, about his bad leg.

"It is probably nothing to worry about Ruben," advised Druselus. "His leg often becomes stiff in the cold weather, but presumably he is all right in himself?"

Having confirmed that his appetite was good, Druselus complimented Ruben on the trust that the Lord Coronus had in him, by allowing Ruben to put him to bed. Ruben then briefly mentioned about his idea of escorting Joself back and agreed that it should be all right, provided that he was back by nightfall and Lord Coronus had no objection.

"That is good," said Ruben. "Now, tell me about the events in Timon. All we have received is the message from you that all was going well and that you would be up today with the men to be trained."

"I suggest you stay with me while I report to Lord Coronus," said Druselus. "That way I will not have to repeat myself."

Ruben did just that, and was surprised to hear such a concise report that left nothing out and in many respects was fairly detailed. It made him realise that his own reporting was, by comparison, clumsy and garbled. He mentioned that very point to Lord Coronus that same evening when he discussed his plans to see his friends off, but was delighted to hear Lord Coronus' reply.

"Do not worry, my boy, you are learning very quickly. Druselus has been reporting to me for longer than you have lived so far. Accurate reporting is an art that only comes with experience, your reports are improving every day. Now, with regard to your trip across the Empty Sector, it is good that you are not having to break a promise and it meets with my approval, but you must plan to scare away the old witch who gave you so much trouble on your way here. I think it would be wise to take at least one person with you across the Empty Sector, but leave the rest on guard duty around bright signal fires."

# 21
## ON THE ROAD AGAIN

The early dawn light had only just begun to lighten the sky to the east, when Ruben, fully armed with his large sword and javelin, plus eight of the trainee soldiers, set out with Joself and Tasmin. All the trainees had normal bronze weapons, which were proudly worn on their sword-belts. They had also started specialising in additional weapons and two of them carried large swords strapped to their backs, whilst the other six carried bows over their shoulders and a full quiver of arrows attached to their belts. Ruben had chosen these six specially, as they were the most promising bowmen, the other two had also proved to be potentially good sword fighters. Each of them carried a small knapsack with a day's provisions inside it, as well as all eight lads helping to carry Joself and Tasmin's equipment. Joself had complained at this and insisted that both he and Tasmin could carry their own equipment, as they would have to do later. However, for this reason alone, Ruben had insisted that the boys carry their equipment, as they would not all be walking the whole day. Ruben himself carried their heaviest bag, the one that contained all their cooking equipment and bedding.

They set out travelling east and had crested the first ridge by the time that the sun hazily shone through the light cloud above the next wooded crest, which was mainly in shadow, and was the area reputedly occupied by the witch, Messuda. Ruben took a careful look from the crest at the opposing slope, particularly at the tree line at its base, in which nothing seemed to stir under the light powdering of snow that had fallen during the preceding night. It was unusual to see snow this far south of the mountains and it was an entirely new experience for some of the boys, as well as for Ruben, who marvelled at the tracks they left behind them. Having assured himself that there was nothing moving on the opposite ridge, he led the party down and towards the tree line at the base of the ridge facing them. At about eighty paces from the tree line Ruben stopped and called for silence, as he once again inspected the bare trees for signs of life. There was a large tree whose bare branches showed some roosting wood pigeons, and when viewed with half-closed eyes Ruben felt sure that he could see a slightly darker aura around the bushes below that tree. He told everyone to put all their equipment on the ground and the two boys who carried large swords to hold the two flaming torches that they had brought with them. He asked the other six, who had bows and arrows, to line up and try to shoot the pigeons when they rose into the sky. Taking careful aim with his javelin he took a short run and released the javelin flying high into the sky towards the trees. It squarely struck the large tree just below the fork in its trunk. The force of its impact sent a shudder up the whole tree as it embedded itself firmly into the tree trunk. There was an immediate squawking and flapping of wings, as the birds rose into the air, this was followed by six twangs, as the six bowmen loosed their arrows. None of the arrows hit any of the birds, which was hardly surprising, as it was a long shot even for a good bowman. However, it did have the effect of waking everything in the area, as the six arrows flew into the woods all around the tree. This included a small dark figure that scurried from under the bushes deeper into the trees, although this was only noted by Ruben as everyone else was watching the birds. Ruben told everyone to remain where they were, whilst he took one of the lit torches and went towards the woods to retrieve his javelin. When he reached the bushes at the base of the tree in which his javelin was embedded, he saw some greasy old blankets and the remains of a fire that had been out for a long time. He withdrew his javelin, and with five or six heavy blows the tree collapsed on the bushes, which he set alight using the greasy old blankets that burnt well.

He came trotting back, chuckling to himself that the old witch had run off and would not be seen again for some considerable time. He led his party to the fire, where he detailed two bowmen and one large sword carrier to stay by the fire. He instructed one of the large sword carriers to spend his time chopping up the tree and all three boys to ensure that this large fire was kept burning until he returned with the others. He also gave strict instructions that they were always to stick together, particularly when in or near the woods.

"There is reputed to be an old witch in the area. You will probably see nobody, but if you do, do not approach them and stay behind the fire with your weapons at the ready."

Then he led the rest of the party up through the woods towards the crest. The fall of snow had not reached the floor of the woods sufficiently to show any footprints, he was therefore uncertain of the direction that Messuda had taken. Resignedly he led the party up through the trees to a low saddle on the crest of the ridge, which was uncovered by trees. From here they could clearly see the bright fire and the three boys working nearby. He paused for them all to eat breakfast, and whilst they ate, he and Joself stepped aside to look down onto the Empty Sector.

They looked down on the large expanse of white emptiness, where not even the boggy areas showed through. They could just make out the far side and the slope where they had refilled their water containers before last autumn's disastrous crossing. The day was brightening with the sunlight showing more clearly through the clouds, which were gradually dispersing although there was not a breath of wind. Joself said, as they looked down on the unusual sight, "I think it has all been frozen to immobility." He pointed to the trees on the descending slope, which were more frozen than those on the slope that they had just climbed.

"I think the wind has been blowing down the valley from the mountains, which has caused greater freezing here. That will make it far less treacherous to walk safely across."

"I believe you are right, my friend, that should make it a far quicker crossing," observed Ruben. "I would, however, like to leave two more bowmen and the other large sword carrier to build another signal fire here to guide our return. I will only take Cornelius and the other bowman with me across the Empty Sector, as they are both good athletes and have been chosen for their proven endurance." They returned to the rest of the party and organised the three to stay behind and light a signal fire. Ruben gave them explicit instructions, as he had with the others concerning the old witch. They redistributed the equipment and set off down the slope and were soon crossing the virgin snow.

They had been walking for a considerable time and were possibly halfway across, when Ruben realised that a warm breeze, coming from the south, had begun to blow. The clouds had completely cleared and the sun shone brightly down on them, reflecting harshly the snow underfoot. The sun had more warmth in it than previously that winter, which combined with the warm breeze, was causing the snow to melt and there were faint cracking noises from the frozen ground. This, Ruben realised, was the ice in the ground melting, which would soon expose the treacherous marshy areas that could easily trap the unwary traveller. He asked them all to speed up their progress and led the party himself by some twenty or thirty paces, as the ground would be more prone to collapse under his weight than that of the others in the party. Thankfully they reached the other side safely, their eyes smarting from the glare of the sun, and they were now sweating in the warmth, after what originally had been a very chill morning.

They were about to eat their lunch when, alerted by the sudden trickling of the waterfall that had previously been frozen, Ruben said, "I think we had better keep our lunch with us and start the return before the ground becomes too soft." He turned to Cornelius and said, "Start off, keeping the distant signal fire as your aim and I will join you in a few moments after saying goodbye to my friends." As the two boys walked away, he took a scroll from beneath his jerkin and handed it to Joself.

"This is the scroll that I have written, you will see it is addressed to Commander Mithrandir at Ashkilon. If you will please ensure that it gets to him, I would be most grateful." He tried to give five gold pieces to Joself, but they were not accepted, as Joself said, "You have already done enough for us, it is the least I can do for you. Goodbye, my friend. If we do not meet again, I wish you every success with your quest. I will leave Tasmin to say her goodbyes, as she has some interesting news to give you." He turned and started heaving their equipment up the bank.

Tasmin then came close, held both his hands, and said, "I am so grateful for the way you have treated me. You showed me the error of my ways and that a man really loved me for what I was. I am expecting his baby, and I would like to name him after you, would you object?"

Completely unprepared, Ruben did not know what to say except, "But you don't know if it will be a boy."

"I am sure it will be," predicted Tasmin defiantly.

"In that case, I would be greatly honoured," declared Ruben. "He will have a good family, with two fine cousins, and do pass on my regards to those boys." He took Tasmin tenderly in his arms and kissed her goodbye. Then, without looking back, lest she see the moistening of his eyes he trotted back after the two lads.

As he came level with them, he realised that the snow had now melted leaving everything with a shiny brown wet sheen that did not identify any boggy ground or even open water. At that very moment, the ground under his feet collapsed and he was suddenly up to his knees in mud. The more he struggled to get clear, the deeper he sank into the mire and had to be dragged out by Cornelius and his friend, who, being lighter, did not break through the upper crust. When they had dragged Ruben to firm ground, he said, "Are you both up to running?" To their affirmative nods he told each boy to hold one end of their bows and he himself took the other. He then said, "We must run together in a line with the bow between us, and be sure to keep a tight grip on the bow, that way we can ensure that no one gets left stuck in the mire to drown in the smelly mud." This way they crossed the distance quickly, pausing only a few times, twice to drag Ruben free and once to drag Cornelius out of the mud. The other boy was of a lighter build and had not once broken through the surface. They arrived safely, but out of breath, all laughing as the danger was now behind them. They ate their lunch and Ruben and Cornelius washed off the mud from their legs and sandals in the stream in which Ruben had discovered the Larkslip leaves that were so helpful in their healing powers. He clearly marked the spot by cutting distinguishing notches into nearby trees, so that a future party coming from Lord Coronus' house could pick the plants for the doctor later on that summer. They went up the hill to rejoin the three lads by their signal fire. When Ruben asked them, they told him that they had seen nobody, but had watched their hasty return across the Empty Sector with great excitement. After a brief pause they went down to meet the other three boys to find that they had also spent a quiet day without interruption from anyone, or so they said. To everyone's astonishment back at the house, they arrived around mid-afternoon with some of their provisions uneaten. To everyone's pleasure, Ruben said that they could have the rest of the day at leisure, whilst he went to report to Lord Coronus.

The following days passed all too quickly, the newly trained civilian force for the town was despatched after their basic training and were fairly soon operating to the Merchant Council's satisfaction. This freed Druselus from his duties in Timon and he was back to take over his role as head of the household. Although Ruben had enjoyed and learnt a lot in that brief period, he was grateful to hand back all the responsibilities that went with the position, in addition to having his friend back, whom he had come to regard like an elder brother. Almost immediately, plans were made to return the lads, who now seemed more like young men as they were more self-assured and confident in themselves. Druselus asked Ruben if he would be good enough to accompany the boys back to the coast to a small harbour called Antioch from where they would sail to Cyprus.

"It is at least five days' march due west, and Arthermais has requested that some of the merchants who will be going to Egypt accompany you. I have already told him that their company will be welcome. But I need someone I can trust with the job and I should imagine that you will be keen to renew your travels." It was more a statement of fact, than a question, and Ruben's compliance was taken for granted. He realised this afterwards, the night before they were due to travel and he had gone to bed, having finally finished his own packing. He realised that he would miss Druselus, but was keen to be on his way again. Druselus had told him that the high priest had recently sent word to Nineveh that arms were being raised in the town due to a local Greek lord, who had in his service a large mercenary from Babylon whose sword was called the bright of the east. If a large war band came from Assyria, it would be far easier to dispel the rumour and remain living peacefully in Canaan if Ruben was out of the way. He also realised that in leading the lads back to Antioch, there would be no one returning and Lord Coronus' involvement in the affairs of Timon could be safely denied. He had benefited greatly by the last unscheduled and unexpected delay in following his original plan to trace his historical roots. In addition to his new friendships, he had been handsomely rewarded for his services. He drifted off to sleep feeling that the completion of his journey was almost in sight, as the land he was seeking would soon be within reach.

The following day had dawned with the promise of the coming

summer, as it was warm and the trees and bushes had bright new leaves and the air was heavy with the scent of blossom. This came not only from the orange and olive trees, but also from the vines and the yellow flowers and the red flowers, which, he had been told, were Mimosa and Pyracantha. It had been a frustrating wait for the merchants' caravan, but this had finally arrived and they set out with the warm sun on their backs, as he left yet another place that he had so happily come to know as home. Their farewell was particularly notable, as Lord Coronus himself came out of the house and stood beside Druselus, lifting his ebony cane in salute, which was a rare and touching gesture.

\*\*\*\*

Another traveller was about to set out, but before noon he was making his way to the Citadel in Babylon to see the king in accordance with his majesty's original request. Dathram knew that the situation with the Assyrians had not altered, so he felt that he was wasting his time, but as the king had requested him to come, and the king was his paymaster, he was duty-bound to obey. He arrived at the Citadel and was escorted to the palace, but found that he had to wait outside the large bronze doors to the main hall as the king was ensconced with another surprise visitor. He was finally called into the main hall where the king was talking to his nephew, the commander of Ashkilon, who was accompanied by a foreigner, who by his dress looked as if he had come from the mountains in the northeast.

Dathram's guess had been correct, the other man was indeed from the mountains and had brought with him a scroll, which was next to the king, whose face brightened up when Dathram entered.

"I have some excellent news that has just arrived, Dathram," announced the king. "It would appear that your visit is not in vain, as I am sure you thought it would be."

"My Lord?" questioned Dathram, as he bowed.

"Commander Mithrandir has brought this scroll. His companion comes from the town of Thrax, which is upriver from Ashkilon."

"Quite a long way upriver my Lord, above the first cataract, well into the mountains," corrected the foreigner.

"It appears," observed the king, "that a friend of yours, who was also a mysterious visitor to my palace last year, has discovered a new route for your journey. If you take this scroll and its bearer with you, you can travel back with him on your journey to Egypt. Needless to say you will extend every courtesy to this man, as I believe he has been travelling for many days without rest." The astonished Dathram took Joself back home with him and ordered his servants to provide Joself with a comfortable bedroom, in addition to a good meal. He also told his servants that he would be leaving for Egypt, with his guest, the next day.

\*\*\*\*

The trip to the coast took the full five days that Druselus had predicted, mainly because of the limited speed of the merchant caravan. Although every day travel started at dawn, they could go no faster than the heavily laden mules, of which there were eighteen. This meant that there were three mules to every one of the six merchants, each also had a servant boy with him. The several towns that they passed on their way each added an extra traveller or two, with additional mules or donkeys. By the time that they finally reached the coast, the caravan was almost forty beasts of burden, ten merchants with their boys, a couple of women, plus various stray dogs. Ruben had been used to caravans in his early days at Nippur, but he had not realised how slowly they moved in comparison to a small party of marching soldiers. To keep the lads active and prevent boredom setting in, he split the party of young soldiers into two groups, one at the head and one at the foot of the caravan. Additionally, he made the lads drop away from the leading group at one hundred pace intervals and walk back down the caravan to the following party, where he sent opposing lads trotting past the caravan to replace those walking back. This way, the lads were constantly on the move and did not have a chance for boredom to provoke silly games or insolent behaviour. Additionally, it gave the appearance of a better-armed caravan than it really was, not that he feared any great danger in Canaan, and it also kept the caravan in good order.

He was pleased when they reached Antioch, and he said goodbye to the lads, many of whom he had come to know very well, like Cornelius. The lads were sorry to leave him, but obviously eager to return home, but they did have a farewell party on the final evening before they were to board the small galley that was to take them across the sea. This seemed enormous to Ruben, as the Inferior Sea at Lagash was small, no more than a large inlet, or so he had been told. Apparently, at the end of the Inferior Sea, there was another large sea, which it was thought was even bigger than the sea he now looked upon. At the party, they presented him with an intricately plaited holder made from small scraps of leather that had been carefully interwoven into a fastening binding that would hold his javelin on his back against his large sword scabbard that had been given to him by Ishmala. He was appreciative of this gift, particularly when Cornelius, who presented it to him said, "All the boys contributed to the work, as we all wanted to give you something to remember us by."

Ruben stood on the shore and waved at the galley as it rowed out to sea, and then turned south to join up once again with the caravan. He stayed with the merchants that night where they camped by the sea, which they would now follow south until the coast gradually turned west and they reached Egypt. That evening he discussed, with the leader of the merchants, which was the best way to travel to the land that he described to them as being an area where a new tribe of people were trying to build a homeland. All they could tell him was to follow the coast south until he came to the shoulder of a large mountain, here he should leave the coast to travel east where there was apparently always conflict.

"Ideal for someone like yourself," they told him. This had upset him, although he said nothing, as he did not want to be considered as someone who always wanted to fight. He thought, I am really a builder, or at least that is how I would like to be remembered', as he did not really like killing anything or anybody.

He lay that night under the stars a little way from the campfire of the merchants, thinking how strange it was that you often had to destroy something before you could build something else. He decided, before he drifted off to sleep, that he would definitely travel on his own now, as he would only be asked to arbitrate in arguments or be asked to protect the merchants from bandits. Apart from which, he was fed up with the dust that the caravan kicked up and the dung from the animals that attracted the large column of sun-birds that were constantly wheeling overhead and dropping on to any remains or dying animals. The next morning, whilst he was not being watched, he disappeared behind some trees and walked away southwards a little way inland from the coast, but still keeping the sea in sight.

For the rest of that morning, he kept travelling quickly, with the occasional glance over his shoulder, to ensure that he was not being followed, even though he doubted that any of the merchants could keep to his pace. When the sun indicated that it was midday, he stopped by a small stream to eat the bread and cheese that he had brought with him. As it was early in the year, it was pointless to look round for any berries or nuts, even though there were appropriate bushes in the area. He could see, in the distance, the dust rising from where the caravan was, so he now felt safe in returning to the shoreline, where there was a more defined path. It was warm in the afternoon sunshine and he decided that he would try to see if there was anything edible in the shallow water for dinner that night, as he had only enough provisions for a couple of meals. Leaving the path and walking beside the edge of the sea, which was not as sandy as the Inferior Sea that he had known so well, he noticed a couple of large flat rocks that appeared to be moving. On closer inspection, he realised that these were animals with large, flat, hard shells; they had many legs and two large claws at the front. When he approached them, they appeared to run away sideways, and although they had many legs, he found it easy to catch them providing that they did not run into the sea. He managed to catch six or seven of these strange animals that he had never seen before, and providing that, when he caught them, he kept his fingers well away from their large pincers, there was no problem. Stowing these animals in a spare bag was not difficult and he then returned to the path, where he kept going to increase the distance between himself and the caravan. The shoreline had not altered much and neither had the scrub covered land. There were, however, a few trees slightly further inland where he thought he would make camp for the night, as the sun was beginning to set and sink below the sea. It was with great delight that he watched the yellow orb of the sun turn pink as it sank below the western horizon, reflecting bright golden dappled sparkling rays from the sea's surface, and turning the sky into wonderful shades of red and orange. He watched the spectacle until the rim of the sun finally disappeared and in the short twilight he went over to the trees, where he made camp for the night. This spot must have been used by a lot of travellers, as there were a few piles of wood that had previously been gathered. Having made a bivouac, he settled down to eat the crabs that he had caught. He had decided they must be crabs, because they were similar in many respects to the crabs in the inferior sea, but those crabs were not so large and used to bury themselves in the sand. He roasted the crabs on a small fire, which he ate with the few remaining provisions that he had brought with him. It was good to be on his own again, without having to worry about anything other than his own survival, which, with all his knowledge of living by the sea and being in the army, was very easy.

 He travelled on, moving southward, living mainly off marine life by the shore, supplemented by the occasional eggs that he stole from the birds' nests that he found in the grass tussocks not far from the path, and also from the occasional roots and plants that he knew were edible. He only saw two other people in the next three days and these he avoided, simply because he wanted to enjoy his own company while he felt at peace with the world. It was later on the third day when he saw the distant mountain, that he had been aiming for, and the ground gradually began to rise inland from the sea. Later in the day, when he was beginning to think about somewhere to camp for the night, he saw, in the distance, a small fishing village below the cliffs that rose from the shoreline, which was turning into the side of the mountain to the southeast. He made his way to the village and waved at the nearest fishing boat that was coming ashore at the end of the day. Feeling quite happy with human company, he asked the friendly fisherman what area this was, and if he could possibly stay anywhere in the village for the night.

"I am willing to pay for my stay," he said, whilst jingling a pouch full of gold coins.

"There is no local inn, but you can happily stay with us, as we have a spare room in the house," said the fisherman, as he jumped down into the surf to pull his boat up the beach. His two companions carried two boxes of wickerwork that were full of the day's catch.

"I will be very happy to join you," declared Ruben. "Can I help you in pulling the boat above the sea, so that it will not get washed away by the tide?"

"The tide?" queried the man. "What are you talking about?"

It wasn't until then that Ruben realised that there was no obvious high water mark, so he asked the man, "Does the water not come up or go down the beach?"

"Not by more than a few paces," replied the perplexed fisherman.

In order to justify his statement, Ruben explained to the fisherman, "Where I come from, away to the east, there is another sea, which alters its position. It can be higher up the beach, or lower down, and it can come up during the night and can wash away a boat that is left there."

"How strange," laughed the other fishermen. "Are you trying to make fun of us?" Fortunately, the original man who had offered accommodation for the night, and who seemed to be in charge, calmed his friends' laughter with a wave of his hand.

"I have heard of this far sea," he told them. "So do not take offence at my friends, we meant no rudeness." The man had noticed Ruben's size and his weapons, and obviously did not want to anger this young man by laughing at him. Ruben had not taken offence, and he simply shrugged his shoulders and helped carry the baskets of fish.

"I took no offence," explained Ruben. "After all, it is a strange world and many people do believe in strange things."

"That is very true, my friend," responded the fisherman. "But thank you for helping with the fish, as well as your offer, I am sure it was well intended. You have come a long way if you have come from the far sea to the east," he continued. "In answer to your original question, I suppose you are still in Canaan, but, let me see, er well, ha ha", he chuckled. "I suppose this land is Canaan. But we are not Canaannites, because our family have lived here for a very long time and were here before most of the tribes in Canaan."

"Who then, or should I say, what tribe, are you?" asked Ruben, feeling confused.

"We do not really belong to any tribe, but we originally settled here and were Amalekites," said the man proudly. "My name is Amos, and my father was called Amal, just like his father before him," he explained.

"So does that make you the leader of your people?" Ruben inquired.

"No, not really, because all the fisherfolk come from different backgrounds, but they have stayed here because the fishing is excellent, as the sea is deep off shore," grinned Amos. "Nobody is really in charge of the village, but we all exist in pleasant harmony."

"So how do you maintain order?" Ruben pressed, becoming more confused.

"We have no order, but we stick together simply because by doing so we maintain our independence," Amos explained.

"I think I understand," said Ruben. "I suppose it means that you get left in peace and do not have to worship the Canaannite Baals".

"Perfectly correct!" smiled Amos. "The only god that we recognise is the god of the sea, Poseidon, who controls the sea and storms."

"I have heard of Poseidon, but who or what is he?" apologised Ruben.

"Well, let me tell you all about it over the evening meal," offered Amos, as they had by now reached their house in the small fishing village. They all went in, leaving the baskets of fish outside, as they all seemed to live in this house. "These are my two sons," explained Amos. "And my wife and daughters will be in soon, and they will look after today's catch of fish. So let us sit down, and while we rest I will tell you tales of the sea and the great sea god Poseidon."

It was a pleasant house, and Ruben gratefully put down all his weapons and baggage, while Amos's two sons tidied up and lit the small fire after offering Ruben some white wine and a seat to listen to their father's tales. They went about their business as if this was an often-repeated situation, which Ruben realised was the case, and settled himself down to listen to Amos's stories. The party was soon joined by Amos's wife and three daughters, the oldest of whom was, Ruben thought, about his own age and a very attractive girl who seemed to be aware of her attributes. She was not slow in displaying her charms in a provocative manner that was ignored by all except Ruben, to whom they were directed.

Ruben thought that he had better make it clear right from the start that he was not going to stay for more than one night and gave Amos a gold coin, which he knew was far more than the normal cost of an overnight stay in an inn, but ignored Amos's attempts to give him some silver coins, saying, "Your kindness deserves just reward."

Eventually accepting the payment, Amos broke off from telling Ruben all the stories of Poseidon, who often took the form of different sea creatures and occasionally created large waves that could destroy towns on the seashore or amongst the islands of Greece, further to the northwest. He asked Ruben where he was heading and when Ruben explained about his quest, Ruben was delighted to hear that they were names for the people whom he sought. It appeared that there was a large tribe of people who had, in Amos's great grandfather's time, appeared from the south and were trying to settle in the land to the southeast. They called themselves Israelites. It seemed that there were quite a few tribes who wanted to settle in this apparently lovely area, so there was often a lot of fighting in this land. It seemed that there were now two main contenders for this land, which the Israelites said was given to them by their God. But the other tribes who were mainly under the rule of the sea-people, who called themselves Philistines, did not accept this. Therefore, there was always conflict between these two tribes, or races of people. They ate their meal, which was a most enjoyable assortment of seafood, but Ruben simply ate, quite oblivious to the taste, as he was so interested by what Amos told him.

"Who do these people say is their god?" asked Ruben, when a suitable pause came in Amos's story.

"That is the problem," said Amos, with a sad shake of his head. "They say their god is the only god and they do not appear to have a name for him, or at least they say his name is secret."

That was almost all that Ruben could ascertain about the Israelites, apart from that the land they occupied lay to the southeast, just beyond the mountain, at the base of which this village lay. Apparently, if Ruben went around the shoulder of the mountain and journeyed southeast for a couple of days, he would finally reach a large lake, from the southern shore of which a river descended down a wide valley and finally came to the fabled salt sea. The only other information that Ruben could gather from Amos was that, in Amos's great grandfather's time, the Israelites had crossed this river and begun their campaign to make a homeland by first destroying what was believed to be an impregnable walled town. Try as he might, Ruben could gain no further information concerning the Israelites' beliefs and their god. This seemed to be a subject about which Amos knew nothing, or did not want to know and was perhaps frightened by. By this time, it was getting late, but the whole family was sitting around Amos and Ruben, who had been chatting by the fireside. Amos sat on one side of the fire, with his wife standing dutifully behind him, resting her arms on his shoulders, while his two sons sat either side of him, cross-legged on the floor, with his youngest daughter sitting on his lap. On the other side of the fire, Ruben had Amos's second youngest daughter, possibly about ten, sitting on his knee, with his eldest daughter draping herself across Ruben's other side, virtually cuddling him. Suddenly, Amos rose to his feet, yawned and said, "Come on children, off to bed, we all have a busy day tomorrow." In response to Ruben's questioning gaze, he explained.

"You all have to dry and smoke the fish we caught today and prepare them for sale to the caravan that is approaching from the north, it should be here either late tomorrow or early the next day." Then, turning to Ruben, he asked, "Are you sure you will not stay on another day, as you could come spear fishing with us?"

"Thank you very much, Amos, but I'm afraid I must be on my way, the information that you have given me tonight is of great interest and I am sure that it will prove to be invaluable," Ruben thanked him courteously.

"You are very welcome, it is nice to talk to someone who is interested in my tales and is such a good listener. So many folk do not wish to know about what is happening elsewhere, they seem only concerned with their own lives." He was dragged away by his wife, who was scolding him for being such a chatterbox. The rest of the family disappeared into their own rooms, with the eldest daughter showing Ruben his own room, which was an annexe on the side of the house. She finally left him with a dazzling smile and a wink, saying, "See you later."

Ruben soon forgot about the girl as he had so much to think about, and decided to leave directly after breakfast to get beyond the mountain and start heading southeast towards the lake, which lay at the end of a very fertile plain, according to Amos. He was lying in bed, thinking about this strange god that the Israelites said was the only god, wondering if there was any possible connection between this god and The Creator, whom Simeon had constantly referred to. Additionally, the old thought that often seemed to return to him, was Simeon his own father? He was wrestling with these thoughts, when the door quietly opened and Amos's eldest daughter slid inside the room, quietly closing the door behind her and then putting her finger to her lips, indicating that she did not want Ruben to make any noise. She was clad in a very light gown that obviously had nothing beneath it.

"Surely your parents will object to this," whispered Ruben, as she came close.

"They probably know and do not object," she confidently told him. "After all, there is no one in this village who interests me. Although some of the other old men would like to get their hands on me, but will not pay the high bride-price my father sets."

"As long as you realise that I cannot stay or take you with me," declared Ruben. "I have a difficult journey ahead of me, I travel fast and am a warrior," he justified himself. "I previously had a young woman travelling with me and she is now dead, killed by accident, when I was unable to look after her."

"I fully understand," assured the girl, slipping out of the gown and into his bed, all in one swift movement.

******

When he awoke he was alone, and heard noises from the kitchen as the household began to stir. He rose and dressed quickly, having doused himself with cold water from the jug that stood inside the door. He joined the family for breakfast, where they all seemed preoccupied in making arrangements for all they had to do later in the day. However, he was greeted with a pleasant smile by Amos's wife who gave him a large plate of breakfast, and told him, "Amos is outside preparing the boats, as he will be leaving shortly." The only person that he had not seen that morning was the girl who had shared his bed during the night. He ate the meal before him and quickly repacked his bags, refastened all his weapons and went out of the house to join Amos.

"I will be off, Amos," Ruben told him. "But before I go, I really must thank you for the information that you gave me last night, I am sure it will prove useful in my quest."

"That is a pleasure, my friend," said the fisherman, looking up at him and smiling. "The money that you gave us is more than adequate for both the information and a good night's rest." It was said with a twinkle in his eye and Ruben felt sure that the fisherman knew what had happened during the night. "My wife is preparing some provisions for you to take on your journey, so I will bid you farewell and wish you all the best," he said, as he extended his hand, which had a firm grip that Ruben returned.

As he left the village, which was still in the shadow from the mountain to the east, he felt energetic and content as he climbed. The girl had never showed herself in the house when he said goodbye, but it had been a good night and he turned his back on the sea sparkling behind him in the sunshine. As he strode towards the sun that rose above the hillside, he realised that he didn't even know the girl's name. He climbed higher and higher, yet the path still went on upwards, not at too sharp an angle, but enough to make it necessary to stop for a few moments occasionally. After a while, he found the ground levelling out. He realised that he was about to turn towards the east and he then looked round to see the village far below, with the fishing boats leaving the shoreline. This stretched away to the north where he could make out, in the far distance, the dust cloud kicked up by the approaching caravan. He was glad to be away from the area and not to meet up with the merchants again, even though the thought of another night with Amos's daughter was quite a temptation. Still, he felt good and was sure that he had made the correct decision not to get emotionally involved. Finally turning his back on the sea he pressed inland around the shoulder of the mountain and set his sights on what he was sure was a small town lying in a fold of the hills to the southeast, which led up to the mountain.

After a while, when he felt quite definite that it was a town, he noticed a single figure coming towards him and thought that this was a good opportunity to discover from this fellow traveller more about the area he was in. As he neared the man he could hear the faint clinging of a bell and he thought the man must be elderly as he was leaning forward and clasped a staff, although he was hooded and kept his head in shadow. He made directly for the man, who suddenly became aware of him and stepped off the road so that he would bypass Ruben. Thinking that this man had noticed his weapons and was afraid of him, he started running to head the man off, calling as he went, "Hello there, please don't be afraid I will not hurt you." The man stopped, realising that he would not be able to escape, and stood in a resigned posture, still with his face in the shadow of his hood and directed at the ground. Ruben could see the bell around the man's neck, which had been making the clinging noise, and he wondered whether there was a reason for this.

"I meant no harm, so please don't run away," pleaded Ruben.

"What do you want of me?" mumbled the hooded figure. "Do you not realise that I am a leper."

"A leper, what is that?" asked Ruben uncertainly.

The hooded figure turned to face Ruben and threw back his hood. "I am diseased and unclean." The words were muffled as they came from a gash in the mutilated mask that was the leper's face.

Ruben recoiled from the horror, but was then overwhelmed by pity. "No, I have not heard of your disease, I am so sorry, is that why you wear the bell?"

"Yes, the people make me wear the bell as a warning device so that they can keep out of my way. But so often I am cursed and they throw stones at me," the leper informed him, not requesting pity but merely stating a fact.

He had never seen a leper before, as the disease was uncommon in the part of Babylon that Ruben came from. "Can I help you in any way?" he offered.

"Well, yes, I am very hungry, if you could possibly provide me with a few scraps of food, I would be most grateful," was the reply.

"Here, take my lunch, I am sure that I can buy something to eat in the town over there," said Ruben pointing to the town for which he had been heading.

"Are you sure?" said the incredulous leper.

"Please help yourself, it is surely the least I can do," said Ruben moving closer to the man, his initial horror turning into interest.

"Come no closer," warned the leper. "The disease is passed on by touch or so they tell me."

Putting the food on the ground in front of the man was all that Ruben could do, and feeling utterly useless, realising that there was little else that he could do, he simply mumbled that he was sorry he could do nothing else, and he turned to walk away. But then remembering that the man would probably know the name of the town, he turned back and asked, "What is the name of the town, my friend?"

The leper was amused by such kindness and by being called 'friend' by this stranger. "The town is called Markret," stammered the leper. "But it is not a very nice place, I would avoid it if I were you."

"Thank you," was the only weak response that Ruben felt capable of saying. He turned again and left the leper to eat the food.

Rationalising that the leper had probably been unwelcome by the town people, Ruben decided that he would try the town out, despite the leper's warning, after all, it was so close and he was now beginning to feel hungry. All the time that he had walked away, yet was in sight of the leper, he felt that he was being watched to ensure that he was out of sight before the leper retrieved the food that he had left. So it was with relief that Ruben turned a bend in the road and kept going towards the town, which he could see through gaps in the trees. Markret was a large town and the road he was on was slightly above the town, which had a road leading down to it a few hundred paces in the distance. Shortly before he reached the crossroads, where he would turn left to go down to Markret, there was a large gap in the trees, which made it easy to see the town before his final approach. He stood looking down at what seemed a normal town, with a busy market at its centre, but sighed as he noticed, on one side of the town market a low building with two large Nubian guards standing with crossed arms, watching the townsfolk. Additionally, behind the building, was another open area with a large stone statue very similar to the Baal in Timon. He groaned inwardly and was wondering whether or not to even risk approaching the town, when a call that was directed at him came from the crossroads. The call came from a group of six or seven men, all carried swords or axes, and were obviously spoiling for a fight.

"Excuse me, but what did you say," called back Ruben, as he had not clearly heard what was said due to the strange dialect.

"We said, 'have you seen a leper on the road'?" came the reply.

"Yes, I passed him a short while ago, he cannot be far, but why do you ask?" queried Ruben, as he walked towards the men. "He is probably eating the food I gave him," he added.

"You gave the disgusting creature food? Are you bloody mad? He is a leper!" jeered a large man, who was obviously their leader. "I suppose you threw him a crust to make sure he removed himself from your path," was the interpretation that the man gave to Ruben's act of charity. "You can join us if you like, we are going to stone him."

"You will do no such thing, you will leave him alone. He has a horrible disease, surely that is bad enough for the fellow?" rationalised Ruben, who hoped to appeal to their better natures. As expected, from this mob of rough uncaring people, they simply laughed at him.

"I will soon drop this leper lover," said a bowman, moving from behind the leader, as he reached for an arrow in a quiver strapped across his back. The man fell dead before he had even notched the arrow to his bow and the others stood aghast, looking at the body, which had Ruben's javelin through his heart.

"We'll roast you alive for that, you swine," said the large leader of the mob, as he drew his sword and led four of the men charging at Ruben.

Rather than back away, Ruben reached over his shoulder and swept out his large sword, which he would use with his right hand, whilst drawing his short sword with his left. The leader's over-handed swinging bronze sword was almost cut in two, as it met Ruben's powerful counterblow and the next instant the sword, or what was left of it, went spinning away into the bushes, as he died on the point of Ruben's next thrust. The iron blade of Ruben's short sword parried the blow from his next assailant, whose bronze blade snapped with the force of the sweep that was met with equal power. His obscene curse was cut off as the point of the sword was thrust into his throat. The third man's charge was halted as his bronze blade was shredded, as Ruben met his downward cut with his large sword and stepped nimbly aside from the fourth man's axe stroke. Unfortunately, the man with the shredded sword, slashed back handed while Ruben was intent on avoiding the axe blow, allowing the shredded blade to score down Ruben's left forearm. This wound angered Ruben and he quickly sent the perpetrator to join his dead comrades by carving through the man's torso with a backhand slice from his large sword. The axeman swung again and his axe rang on the unyielding large sword blade, while the short sword was thrust into the man's chest.

"Come and join your friends," challenged Ruben to the two other men who had not charged, but they both thought better of it, and ran back in the direction from which they had come. This victory had been all too easy, these men were just thugs and were unskilled with the weapons that they had used. Ruben was not proud of the victory, but felt annoyed at himself for allowing the wound that oozed blood from his left forearm.

He returned to where he had dropped his large bag and staunched the blood from his wounded arm with a cloth, and bound a leather thong that he pulled tight around his elbow, which eased the flow of blood. He quickly cleaned both swords and re-sheathed them, before going to retrieve his javelin. This he also cleaned, before picking up his baggage and moving on down the road, making sure that no one was coming up the road that led up from the town, down which the two men had fled. He broke into a loping run, which covered the ground remarkably quickly, and which he could keep up for a long time. The leper had been right, he thought bitterly, as he made plenty of distance between himself and the five corpses.

Forgetting about the hunger that ached in his stomach, he kept going with only one brief rest before the evening closed down around him. There had been no trace of pursuit from Markret and in the last light of the day he left the road for one hundred paces, where he stopped beside some trees and picked some large leaves growing on the ground. Releasing the leather thong from his elbow, he rinsed the wound with fresh water from his goatskin and placed the leaves over the wound, which he tightly bandaged. The wound was not deep, but had been couched from his arm and he was sure that it would leave a scar. He decided to spend the night here and quickly cut a few branches to make a bivouac into which he crept and fell into an exhausted sleep.

He woke in the early morning and thought he heard the sound of someone coming along the road, but when he looked out he spied nobody. Looking around he noticed some mushrooms that had sprung up during the night and these he picked to boil into a soup, which he cooked on a small fire made from an old bird's nest that was in the branches of a tree. This burnt without smoke and he then scattered the ashes of the fire, as well as making sure that there were no traces of his camp. Travelling on, to leave as much distance as possible between himself and Markret, he started walking east again, but kept looking back for a sign of pursuit. Although he never saw anyone, he was sure that he was being followed and could hear the occasional footfall. As he kept going he passed a long line of large trees and slipped behind the second from the end and waited, sitting with his back to the bowl of the tree. It was quite a wait until his pursuer showed, and he was surprised when the leper passed by leaning on his staff.

"Hello, my friend, why are you following me?" asked Ruben quietly.

The leper froze as he had not realised his pursuit had been noted. "I meant no harm," mumbled the figure without turning. "And I can ensure you that I am not being followed."

"Do not worry, I will not harm you, but you still have not answered my question," said Ruben as he rose to his feet. The leper had visibly relaxed, but still kept his face hooded and stared at the ground. "If you feel up to keeping going, perhaps you can tell me why you are following me, while we walk," Ruben suggested.

"I would like that," replied the leper. "If you do not object to my company, for I am unpleasant to look upon."

"You are certainly different," suggested Ruben. "But what is pleasant to some is ugly to others, and the other way round."

As they started walking, the leper said, "You are not from these parts and you are wise beyond your years."

"I take that as a compliment," responded Ruben. "And you are quite correct. Now, answer my question and tell me about yourself." So they travelled on together, the leper telling him that his disease had started only a few years ago and until then he had been a constant traveller, moving from one job to another but always within the same part of Canaan. But now he was not welcome anywhere and had often had stones thrown at him, which was why he had decided to follow Ruben, as he was the first person to show him any kindness.

"That sounds logical," Ruben surmised. "But have you no home or family?"

"None that wants me," replied the leper. He then went on to explain that lepers were always cast away from habitation, as people feared them. "At least, that is what happens in Canaan, and I would now be dead if it were not for you." He continued, as Ruben did not say anything. "To be honest," there was now a catch in his distorted speech, but he kept his head down and doggedly continued, even though he was, as Ruben correctly thought, allowing the tears to start flowing as he spoke openly of what he felt and of his pitiful existence. "I was even wanting to die, but also scared of death. I was eating the food that you had left and overheard your argument with that mob. Nobody has ever spoken such considerate words, let alone fought for me before. So I thought that I would follow you to at least give warning of any danger, as in that way I might repay your kindness."

There was a long silence, which Ruben broke by saying, "Thank you for your honesty, now it is my turn to tell you of my travels and the quest that I am on." He continued to give a brief account of his travels, without elaborating on any of the battles that he had fought or of his military training or of his time in the marshlands. "Do you know anything of the Israelites?" he asked.

"I have heard of such a people, in fact I have heard that they often have truly great holy men who can make lepers clean. In fact, I thought about trying to find them myself," he answered wistfully.

"Well, it seems to me, that we may as well travel together," suggested Ruben, "as indeed you seem to have nothing better to do."

"Are you sure you do not mind?" enquired the leper. "You will not be able to stay at an inn if you are seen in my company?"

"I have had my fill of Cannaanite courtesy," laughed Ruben. "I far prefer your company, and I have no fear of your disease."

They walked on in companionable silence for a while, the leper now standing more upright, even glancing occasionally at Ruben and not worrying when Ruben looked at him, as the large young man smiled at him in acknowledgement of his friendship. They stopped briefly by a small stream around the middle of the day to drink, before continuing. Towards the end of the day, they crested a final ridge and looked down to see, far below them, the sheen of water. They had reached the large lake that Amos had given directions to.

"As we have to make camp for the night, what would you like to eat," asked Ruben.

Surprised at this question, addressed as if there was an enormous selection to choose from, the leper said, "You decide."

"Wait here, my friend, with my baggage," Ruben told him. "There are definitely some goats or small hoofed animals around, judging by the spoor that we have recently crossed," he said as he left his equipment, except for his javelin, which he took as he trotted away. The leper sat down, but did not have long to wait as Ruben reappeared with a small dead goat over his shoulders that he had obviously just killed. They walked to a large cluster of trees that provided good cover and shelter for the night, where they camped and ate roasted goat meat, which was the first proper meal that the leper had eaten in years. That night, the leper told Ruben more about the Israelites, although he knew little to add to Ruben's scant knowledge, and also of the Philistines, about whom he knew considerably more. He also told Ruben that his name was Samuel.

"But I would prefer it if you call me Sam," he requested with a shy smile. "Because before the disease, when I had friends, that was the name that they used to call me." Before sleeping either side of the small fire, Ruben removed the bandage from his arm and inspected the wound. It had dried and had completely scabbed over and Ruben felt that it would heal better in the fresh air. He therefore threw the bandage and the leaves that dressed the wound into the fire, where they burnt brightly.

Early the following morning, while Sam was still asleep, Ruben walked down to the lake and resumed his old habit of having an early morning swim. On his return to their camp, he spotted a spring, which tumbled out of the ground, giving off steam into the cool morning air. On further investigation, Ruben found it to be quite hot, with a curious aroma, he also noticed that the spring tumbled into a pool that he could easily dam into a bathing area. He arrived back, to find that Sam was looking around for him. Having breakfasted on the remains of the goat meat that they had roasted the previous evening, Ruben told the leper about the spring of hot water.

"I have heard something about these hot water springs," said Sam. "They are meant to have healing powers."

"Well, my friend, you," he pointed at the leper, "are going to have a bath, and we will see if there are any healing powers in the water. Now, whilst you are in the bath, which I will make for you by damming the small stream," he instructed Sam, "I will wash your clothes."

Leaving Ruben's equipment neatly stacked behind one of the trees, they both walked down to the stream and whilst the leper stood watching, Ruben begin moving rocks and had soon made a dam that created a sizeable bathing area. The leper looked on in fascination as Ruben worked, heaving around sizeable rocks with ease, the muscles in his upper body rippling like pythons under his skin, which the leper could see had hard skin covering over wounds on his shoulders. The dam was soon completed to Ruben's satisfaction; it was just like being back at the army training camp, he thought.

"That is a fine pool that you have created," remarked the leper. "You obviously know a lot about building by the way that you fitted those stones together," he said in admiration of the dam.

Ruben asked Sam to come into the water, which was about waist deep. "Now undress and throw me your clothes." The leper meekly obeyed Ruben, finding the warm water marvellously refreshing on the blotchy and scaly skin that had not been exposed to sunshine or water for a very long time. As Sam stretched out full length under the water, flakes of skin, lice, nits and other infesting vermin floated over the dam. Ruben, using Sam's staff, stirred his damp clothing around in the pool. He then picked up all the clothes and called to Sam, "Enjoy your bath whilst I take this down to the lake and give them a good wash." After giving the clothes a really good scrub, through the pebbles and stones at the lake's shallows, Ruben found that the washed clothing was tatty and full of holes. Thinking that he would have to obtain some better clothing for Sam, he wrung them out, took them back to the pool and spread them out on the rocks to dry in the sunshine. Whilst he did this he noticed that the scab on his arm must have been washed off whilst he was making the dam and the new skin under it had grown fresh and clear, with no sign of scarring. Wondering about this, he said, "They will soon dry, but stay in the pool for a while. I noticed a small boat on the lake where there were some fishermen, there must be a small village near here. I will go and dress properly and see if I can purchase some better clothing for you." It was said as a statement of fact, rather than as a question, so Sam did not argue, but lay back in the pool enjoying the warm water running over his body. Ruben returned up the hill, dressed quickly, put on his sword-belt and jerkin and trotted off in the direction of where he believed the village would be, after first checking that his large sword, javelin and the baggage were safely out of sight as well as some of his gold coins being in his belt pouch.

Hoping to find that people in the village were more hospitable than the other Cannaanite places that he had visited, he planned how to buy some new clothes for Sam. He would tell the people he and his little brother were travelling, his little brother was tired so he had left him back at their camp, whilst he came to buy him some new clothes, as his normal suit of clothes had been torn in the bushes. As he was trotting along, he was thinking about the words that the leper had used in his praise of Ruben's handiwork, 'That is a fine pool you have created, you must know a lot about building...' Ruben suddenly stopped, as if he had run into a barrier. In a flash, the words Creator, builder, healing powers, coalesced in his mind. He immediately thought of Simeon and looked at his healed arm, then wondered if there were remarkable powers in that water. The leper had certainly looked a lot better when Ruben had left him, he was suddenly keen to return, but as he had already come so far he decided to press on and not return without the new clothes. His guess about the direction of the village was correct, and the people there had a lighter hair colour, more like his own, and seemed taller than most of the Canaannites that he had seen. They were very friendly, accepted his story quite readily and told him that they were really Danites and related to the Israelites that were settling further to the south. This Ruben learnt was further south than Beth-Shan, which was one of the main Philistine towns that lay to the south of the lake.

Ruben realised that he had been away for a long time, as the sun was now high in the sky. Taking the clothes that he had bought, which were of course a lot smaller than his own, he thanked these pleasant people and said he might return if he got the chance. He started back to where he had left Sam and as soon as he was out of sight of the village, he broke into a run in order to get back before Sam started to worry. He had travelled further than he realised and was beginning to tire when he came to the lakeside and started up to where he had left the leper wallowing in the pool. It was now empty and he stood panting and wondering where Sam could be, as the clothes had gone. He noticed that the ground all around the pool was a lot more trampled than it had been when he had left. Additionally, there were wheel marks from what he considered, when he inspected them, had been a chariot. He remembered that Sam had told him that the Philistines used chariots. It was with a feeling of dread that he realised that his friend was probably a prisoner of the Philistines and was currently on the road to Beth-Shan, which was the direction that the wheel marks led. Racing up the hill he soon found his equipment and strapped on his large sword and javelin, thinking, that in order to rescue his friend, he would now have some real soldiers to fight.

## 22
## MEETING WITH SAMSON

Judging by the marks where the chariot wheels had crushed the grass on the hillside, Ruben was certain that the party of Philistines could not be very far away. The party had travelled south alongside the shore of the lake, and rather than directly following their footsteps, Ruben ran up the hill and had a clear view all around. He set off, still running, but conscious of the fact that he was now carrying all his equipment and had already run a considerable distance that morning, so he hoped his pursuit would not be long. Fortunately, he had only been running for a short while when he could see his quarry in the distance. Shielding his eyes from the sun reflecting off the lake, he could make out a party of six soldiers, two of whom were aboard the chariot, which had three captives in tow. He recognised the last of the captives as being his friend, by virtue of his shabby garments and slim build, caused obviously by his poor diet. All three captives were being jostled and harried by the four other Philistine soldiers who were following the chariot that was only going at a walking pace. Ruben suddenly realised that they had not segregated his friend from the others, so were the other two lepers as well? He then noticed that the jostling was effected by hand, which was very strange. Did the Philistines not consider that a leper was contagious, or had he made a mistake and it was not his friend Sam? The party had stopped as the two horses pulling the chariot were being watered in the lake, and the soldiers were talking amongst themselves. They had paused by some large boulders, which Ruben used as an effective screen to cover his approach. He was glad to see that none of the soldiers were bowmen and as he reached the boulders he was trying to work out how to release the captives, and wondering if these soldiers could fight. He was tempted to rush and take on all six, but he thought discretion would be better than being reckless, particularly as they were of unknown ability. Additionally, the soldiers looked fit and were well armed, although their weapons were bronze.

From his vantage point on the boulders overlooking the chariot party, Ruben saw to his right another party of Philistine soldiers, all on foot, but leading more captives. This party was considerably larger, about twenty soldiers with eight or nine captives. The two groups united, with the soldier in charge of the larger party reporting to the soldiers in the chariot. Ruben could not hear everything that was said, but it was obvious that the soldiers were pleased with themselves, as some of the captives were important people. They did not stay long, but were soon underway again, heading directly south, while the shore of the lake curved around to the east to where a river ran from the lake.

As they left, Ruben studied the captives and was surprised to note that one of them was a young woman, and a most attractive young woman who seemed, by the actions of the other captives, of important bearing. She was as tall as most of the men, but not skinny as many girls tended to be, but well proportioned and statuesque, or so Ruben thought. However, the most fascinating thing about her was that her hair was a sort of reddish gold and as far as Ruben could tell it seemed to be her real hair colour, not dyed, as Tasmin's had been, apart from which it was not curly but fell in a straight cascade onto her shoulders. Leaving the shelter of the boulders as soon as he could without being spotted, he made his way, running fast to the higher ground overlooking the party, which he was determined to keep in sight. Not only did he want to rescue his friend Sam, but this girl intrigued him as apart from her hair, she was well dressed and had most unusual eyes, of a vivid green.

Much to Ruben's surprise the Philistines kept the captives separate. The order of march being ten Philistines in front, the new party of captives, which included the girl, then ten more Philistines followed by the chariot, with the three captives tied behind and finally the four remaining Philistines who brought up the rear some one hundred paces after the chariot. This was a long party to watch and follow without being spotted, but it was necessary to keep everyone in view without being seen. Ruben managed by moving slightly higher up the hill to the west of the party. Although their pace was slow they did not stop or have a break until late in the afternoon. At this point Ruben moved closer and was concerned to see the young woman requesting some privacy from the others in the party and the guards, in order to relieve herself. As Ruben watched, three of the guards left the main party and were obviously planning to catch the girl on her own. One glance at the leers on their faces was enough to let Ruben know what they intended. This gave him an immediate dilemma, he would have preferred to await the cover of darkness, but he could not stand by while the girl was raped in the bushes, which provoked him to act sooner than he intended.

With a quick check behind him to ensure that nothing else unexpected was about to happen, he noticed, from his vantage point above the party of Philistines, a large man coming along but obscured from the main party by a bend in the road. He was, in fact, a very large man, with an enormous sword and long flowing hair that hung halfway down his back, plus a beard and moustaches, which covered his face and hung almost to his belt. Thinking that at least this newcomer would divert some attention, he felt easier about going into action. Two guards had escorted the girl from the party to a secluded area behind the rocks upon which he was standing. There was a small entrance to this area sheltered from the path by two small trees, where the two guards stood, allowing the girl to pass through. Around the back of this secluded area, there was only one possible way of escape and here, the three potential rapists had slipped in. One of them stayed in this position to block off any retreat, whilst the other two circled round either side of the area, ensuring that they were concealed from her notice by the bushes. She loosened her gown and disappeared from view behind one of the low trees. However, her position was evident by the sound of splashing, while the two Philistines approached her from behind, grinning at each other. As she emerged from the trees, the Philistines came either side of her and caught her wrists and upper arms. Despite her struggles, they forced her back over a boulder, then one of the Philistines moved around behind her and pinned her arms behind her head, whilst the other Philistine stood above her, raising her gown and exposing her lower body. He was about to expose himself when he was hurled into the bushes by the force of Ruben's javelin, which pierced his heart and stood upright, quivering in his chest. Ruben jumped down into the secluded area, drawing his large sword, as the girl broke free from the man holding her, he had deliberately let go, in order to meet this threat. His drawn sword parried Ruben's attacking blow. As the swords rang, the third Philistine moved out to grab the fleeing girl. He securely held her but made no move to intervene, as his colleague was a fine swordsman. However, he had now met his match, as his sword was gradually being whittled away by Ruben's harder blade, which met every counter thrust with alarming power. The Philistine's sword was turned aside and his frown became a grimace, as Ruben's sword slit open his belly.

"Dagon!" gasped the man, calling on the Philistine god, as he fell to his knees, trying to stop his innards from spilling over the ground. This entreaty was almost unheard, as there was a huge bellow from the road, which Ruben guessed came from the large man who was attacking the whole party. Thinking that he had better try to aid the unknown aggressor, he immediately went straight for the man holding the girl. The Philistine thrust the girl at Ruben and drew his own sword, but Ruben side-stepped the girl and sliced the man's hand off. His cry of pain was cut short as Ruben's next blow cut into his throat and he collapsed in a pool of his own blood.

"Are you hurt?" Ruben asked the girl, whom he held with his other hand.

"No, thanks to your timely intervention," stammered the girl, as she recovered from shock.

Ruben turned to see one of the Philistine guards approaching him with a drawn sword, whilst the other turned towards the melee on the road. Ruben engaged his fourth adversary, but forcing the man back with fierce blows that were all well met, quickly had the man retreating, shocked as his sword was notched whenever it met Ruben's harder blade. He stumbled back as another huge roar came from the roadway, one of the words seemed to spread terror into the man's face.

"It is Samson who is upon us," screeched his fellow guard. But the man's terrified look soon became a death mask of agony, as his chest cavity was opened by Ruben's next crashing blow.

"If you are all right," said Ruben. "I will go and help your friend on the road."

"He will not need your help," she said calmly. "There are only about twenty of them."

Ruben could hardly believe what she said, and asked, "Did I hear you correctly?"

She stood looking at him, with an expression of mild amusement, and said, "Yes, smashing up Philistine patrols is Uncle Samson's favourite pastime."

Ruben looked down into her smiling eyes with a quizzical expression and said, "Your uncle, you say?" Noticing at the same time that her green eyes had flecks of gold in them and that he had been correct about her hair, as the tiny hairs on her arms were of the same colour. Shaking his head, as if trying to wake from a dream, he made his way over to where the guards had been to look down on a site of carnage, suddenly realising that the girl's hand was still in his.

They stood looking between the two trees that formed an entrance to the secluded area, from where they saw the road full of dead and dying soldiers. The chariot was on its side, the two horses still attached and whinnying as their hooves thrashed wildly in the air. The three captives lay sprawled in the dirt, still roped to the back of the chariot on which Samson was leaning. One final push would send the chariot, horses and men careering down a steep slope to the bottom of the valley far below.

Shouting at the huge man, "Do not push," Ruben sprang forward, dropping the girl's hand, running towards his friend Sam. But his plea was ignored and the chariot, horses and men turned over and over until they crashed on the rocks at the bottom, where silence prevailed as all were dead.

"There was no need for that," Ruben snapped angrily.

"Why not?" demanded Samson. "They were Philistine horses and the captives were only Canaanites."

"Rubbish," shouted Ruben. "One of the men was my friend, and horses are not like people, and they have no affinity."

"I will send you to meet them, you impudent stranger, no man questions me like that when I am on the Lord's business," roared Samson, again picking up his enormous sword.

Ruben wheeled around with his sword still in his hand. "You will find me a more fitting adversary," he shouted in reply, standing to meet Samson's challenge.

The girl's cry of, "No, Uncle, he is a friend," was lost, as the huge man charged at Ruben, swinging his sword, as if reaping the corn. Ruben's angled blade should have pushed the sweep over his head, leaving him open to a single lunge. But the power behind the sweep held in Samson's great hands, kept the blade in a horizontal sweep, but rather than knocking the sharper blade aside, Samson's bronze sword was almost cut in two with an ear-piercing screech. The mighty blow had jarred Ruben's whole body, but somehow he had maintained his hold. Samson was amazed his own sword so badly cut, he wrenched the blade backwards to send it into the road, even though it was tightly fixed on Ruben's sword, which went with it. Ruben had never backed down from anyone and, although Samson was only a hand-span taller than Ruben, he was at least twice as heavy. Even though Ruben realised this, he was intensely angered at what had been done to his friend and the horses. He took a pace forward and drew his short sword in a gesture of defiance.

The girl jumped in front of Samson and said, "Spill no further blood Uncle, he saved me from being raped, he is no enemy, but a mighty warrior."

"Stand aside, girl, I will teach this heathen a lesson."

As he was advancing with bare hands, Ruben unbuckled his belt and threw down his short sword, but still advanced to meet Samson in hand to hand combat. Samson charged the two final paces and tried to grab Ruben's hair. Ruben checked his advance and, using all the skill that he had learned from Druselus, allowed Samson's charge to push him on his back. He ducked beneath Samson's grasping fingers and drew his legs up to his chest, under Samson's great body and gave a mighty heave, straightening his legs whilst gripping Samson's great beard. The effect of this sent Samson flying over Ruben and he landed with a shattering crash on his back. Ruben scrambled to his feet and picked up his short sword, blind with anger.

"No!" screamed the girl, as her initial entreaty had been ignored, and she ran to Ruben's side and grabbed his wrist. "Kill me instead," she said, standing in front of Ruben.

Ruben's anger immediately dissipated and he dropped the sword and said, "I am sorry, you are correct, too much blood has already been spilt today." Her hand slipped into his, as they both watched and waited until the huge man rose to his feet.

Much to everyone's relief, Samson threw back his great shaggy head and roared with laughter. "We will finish our game another day, young man, when there are no women to spoil our fun."

\*\*\*\*

At the same time that Ruben had been fighting with Samson, Joself and Dathram stood looking down on the Empty Sector.

"So this is the area that I have heard so much about," muttered Dathram as he gazed in wonder at what had been a fertile and attractive vale full of animal life, but now stood barren with the strange smell of salt and sulphur. "I am glad that my last journey was prior to its making."

"Yes, it is not a pretty sight," said Joself. "I will always remember my last crossing to the east, when Ruben rescued me from the maddened hyena. But we will camp here tonight and cross first thing in the morning."

That evening they sat either side of the fire talking about Ruben.

"Commander Mithrandir speaks very highly of his fighting prowess, for which I can vouch as I have seen it in action."

"I saw a far kinder young man, who with his charming wife was very helpful in unloading my mules," said Dathram.

"Oh yes, he is a grand person, one of the kindest I will ever meet," responded Joself. "Well, tomorrow will see us at the place where I left him, or should that be where he took me," Joself laughed.

The next morning they broke camp early, and after filling their goatskins, they manhandled the mules down the bank beside the palm fringed pool. When they were almost halfway across the area Joself looked towards the far side and saw a signal fire burst into flame. "How strange," muttered Joself. "The last time I looked back I saw the same signal fire, or at least a fire coming from the same place." When they reached the far side later in the morning, they found the reason for the fire, which had indeed been rekindled from the same spot. There was a party of soldiers who had come from the Lord Coronus, to gather the Larkslip beginning to grow. The soldiers recognised Joself, so it was a happy meeting, and after a while they went back with Joself and Dathram to the large villa. The soldier in charge told Joself that they had lit the fire primarily as a warning to the old witch, although she had not been seen or heard of recently.

Their arrival at the house was quite an occasion. Druselus greeted

Joself and Dathram as old friends, asking Joself about Tasmin and imploring him to stay at least one night, before journeying home.

"I will take you to meet Lord Coronus, after you have rested, he will be delighted to see you both as he often talks about Ruben. He will be pleased to hear that the message came to fruition. But I must warn you both that he now tires very easily."

After checking that his mules were well tended and he and Joself had taken some light refreshment, they went with Druselus to see Lord Coronus.

"I am extremely pleased to see you again young man," Lord Coronus said to Joself, as Druselus brought them into his chamber. "Do take a seat and tell me of your travels and the merchant that you have brought with you from Babylon. I am pleased to meet you, sir," said Coronus as he addressed Dathram. "Please forgive me for not standing up as you entered, these sorry legs of mine have seen too many summers I fear. But I hear you are travelling east and then south towards Egypt, the same direction that my other son took earlier this year," so saying, he smiled and winked at Druselus. After a while, Coronus became sleepy and Druselus led them out of the chamber.

"Who did he mean by his other son?" Dathram asked Druselus.

"He was talking of Ruben," replied Druselus. "He often refers to myself and Ruben as the sons he never had," he said, smiling sadly.

Joself only stayed the one night and left early the next morning as he had been travelling hard ever since he left in the early spring and was keen to get home to Tasmin. Dathram stayed for a few extra days before travelling on, with the Lord Coronus' words ringing in his ears, "If you see Ruben, give my kindest regards and tell him that we all remember him, and if he ever wishes to return here, he will indeed be most welcome."

\*\*\*\*

"Tell me your name, young man," said Samson as he draped one huge arm over Ruben's shoulder, giving him a friendly squeeze that left Ruben breathless. "I suppose that I had better introduce you to everyone. This young woman, who insists on calling me Uncle, whom I note you seem very attached to, ho, ho! Perhaps I will give her to you as a wife, if you can afford her. She is really my mortal father's younger son's eldest daughter, but is often in my charge. She is called Naomi and is considered very beautiful, but I cannot see anything in her myself." At this introduction Naomi blushed, but Samson continued without noticing. "Here we have..." he went on to introduce the fellow captives, all of whom were Israelites of considerable importance in their own community.

"Had we not better get back home, Uncle?" asked Naomi. "The Philistine town of Beth-Shan is not far and there might be another patrol or even a larger force along soon."

"That should be no problem for me and my young friend here," replied Samson. "But I suppose it is getting dark and I don't want to have to carry you all home, even if my young friend helps, as I am sure he would carry you on his chest, ha, ha, ha!" He chuckled as he winked at Ruben.

"I had better go and retrieve my belongings if I am to accompany you," suggested Ruben.

"You had better do that. What did you say your name was?" enquired Samson.

"You didn't give me a chance," replied Ruben, smiling in return. "It is Ruben Ben Uriah, and it is your people I have been seeking. I have travelled for a long time since leaving my home in Babylon, away to the east."

When he returned with his large bag and javelin, Naomi handed him his sword-belt, which he put on, sheathing his short sword. She also had retrieved his large sword that Samson had dislodged from his enormous bronze blade, saying, "That is a marvellous weapon, it does not seem to have been damaged at all, despite all its use. And do you know what that beautiful blue stone is in the pommel of the sword?"

"Yes, it is lapis-lazuli," replied Ruben.

"It is the same colour as your eyes," she said, handing him the large sword.

"Thank you," muttered Ruben, blushing in return, as he re-sheathed the sword in its special scabbard before slinging it to his back, attached to the javelin.

"Will you two hurry up and join us," bellowed Samson, "I would like to get going."

"Are you going to leave all the dead lying here?" enquired Ruben.

"The Philistines can clear up their own filth," said Samson, looking down his nose at the already festering bodies, now swarming with flies, littering the road in pools of dried blood, after which he turned his back and led the party in a southwesterly direction, with Ruben and Naomi bringing up the rear.

"Do you normally bury your dead?" asked Naomi as she walked along beside Ruben.

"No, not exactly, although we bury ordinary folk, important people are embalmed before burial, but we normally heap the bodies of enemies and burn them," he replied. "The Babylonians believe in the afterlife, like the Egyptians – well most of them do, those who believe in the old gods, the Sun God being the most important."

"We believe that there is only one god and he will judge everyone who will come back to life again on his return to Earth," Naomi explained.

"That is interesting, oh, excuse me," he apologised, as he put down his large bag and readjusted it, while rubbing his shoulder, which had been bruised in his fight with Samson.

"Carry your bag in your left hand," advised Naomi. "So that I can help you with it, as I have nothing to carry."

"Thank you," he said in appreciation, remembering how he had first helped carry Lialah's jars of water from the well in Ur, and the strange looks that he received, as it was considered that carrying water was a woman's job. But remembering how it led to their becoming friends, which later turned into their relationship.

Misinterpreting his silence, she asked, "Do you miss your friend who was killed?" Her question was met with a puzzled frown and believing he didn't understand her, she went on to elaborate. "The one who was tied to the chariot that Samson shoved down the slope."

"Oh Sam, the Cannaanite," he brightened, following her reasoning. "Well, I haven't known him for very long, but when we met up he was a leper," he then went on to explain in detail what had happened and how Sam had seemed to be cured and finally adding, "I would like to have seen him to be sure."

"I believe the hot springs near Lake Kinneret do have healing powers, but it depends how they are used. Are you a gifted healer?" she asked.

"Not particularly gifted, but I knew someone who was and I learnt a lot of herbal lore from him." He went on to tell her about Simeon, even telling her that he believed that possibly Simeon was his father. She was fascinated by everything that he told her and he kept nothing back, except not speaking about Lialah. It had all come tumbling out as he found this girl so easy to talk to and it was a relief to be able to finally tell someone.

They had walked a long way and for a long time. It was now well into the night and Samson had been asked by some of the party to stop for a while. There appeared to be a dispute about where they were going, a couple of the people wanted to go to Haggan, where they had initially been caught by the Philistines, whilst others, Samson in particular, wanted to press on to Sabasti, where they had originally been going. The argument was that although Haggan was certainly closer, it was now felt to be unsafe as there were obviously some Philistine spies or sympathisers who lived there. But Sabasti, although a lot further, was a safe stronghold where there was an Israelite force under the leadership of one of Samson's captains, a young man called Saul. Eventually it was agreed to keep going south towards Sabasti, even if they had to stop and camp overnight, even though none of them had any provisions.

Ruben asked Naomi, "Why doesn't Samson simply tell everybody what they are to do, he is obviously the leader?"

"He most certainly is," she replied. "But it is not our way. I think at times we must be the most argumentative people, as no one seems to be able to give orders that all other men will follow. Except for women, we always have to do what men tell us," she bridled at this injustice.

"I am afraid it is the same everywhere that I have been, and to be honest it is unjust, as women often have good ideas, but it is simply that they are not as strong as men. But I am considered strange in my ideas, as when back in Babylon I would always carry more than my wife as it was only fair because I was a lot bigger and stronger." He had not originally intended to mention that he had previously lived with someone else, but he rationalised this by thinking that she would have to know sooner or later and it was better that he should mention it.

"Oh, you have a wife," she stated.

"Did have," Ruben corrected. "Unfortunately she was killed by accident in a battle."

She felt strangely pleased by this sad news, but had the grace to say, "That must have been awful, I am sorry for you."

"Thank you," he murmured. "It was over a year ago, I am over the loss now, although she was pregnant at the time and I often wonder what the child would have been like."

"Oh Ruben, I'm so sorry," she said as she held both his hands in hers.

"Come along, you two," bellowed Samson. "Keep up with us."

Ruben picked up his bag in his right hand, and keeping her right hand in his left, they quickly closed up the gap between themselves and the rest of the party.

They travelled until the middle of the night, continuing south and always going uphill. Samson finally called a halt as some of the party had difficulty keeping going.

"We will shelter in the caves here," said Samson, indicating some naturally occurring caves in the hillside. The caves were clean and unused by animals, except bats, for the floor was covered in bat droppings. Samson led the party into one main cave into which they had to wriggle one by one, but as Samson managed to squeeze his bulk through the gap, it was evident that everyone else would have no problem. Samson had lit a torch, which had been deliberately left for the purpose. This illuminated one major cavern, but there were passages leading from the major cavern deeper into the hillside. Samson went among the party, allocating areas for people to sleep. When he came to Ruben and Naomi he said, "If you want to sleep with the wench, her bride price will be one hundred gold pieces."

Ruben was admittedly fascinated by the idea, but thought that if he wanted the girl, for her own sake it would have to be done properly.

"No thank you, Samson, the price is no problem, but I am rather tired."

"Ha, ha, ha!" roared Samson. "Enough energy to fight me but not to take the girl." He turned to Naomi and said, "He is obviously a man of taste, he does not fancy you," and he went away chuckling.

Naomi blushed, and Ruben was immediately at her side talking quietly, "It is not that at all, I like you immensely so far, but we hardly know each other."

"Thank you for your sincerity, please accept my apologies for my uncle, he is very insensitive at times."

Ruben was the only person with extra clothes and blankets and he made a pillow for her, as well as lending her a blanket. Ruben lay down next to her in one of his other blankets and lay awake as Samson extinguished the torch. He could hear the girl's regular breathing beside him as he pondered about the last day, deciding he would find out more about the Israelites and their strange belief in a single god, as well as some of their other peculiarities, before committing himself. But he had to confess that the idea was tempting and the girl was beautiful. Without realising what he was doing, he put his arm protectively around her shoulders and at his touch she cuddled closer to him and slept with her warm body touching his.

Ruben woke with the grey light of early morning slanting through the entrance in the far wall, alerted by the minute sounds of the returning bats. He rose quietly, making sure that he did not disturb the girl, over whom he draped his blanket, and made his way to the entrance. He looked about cautiously, but there was no one in sight. Hearing the faint murmur of trickling water he looked all round and saw, only a few steps away, a small spring. He followed the watercourse to where it fell over a rock in dribbling showers of sparkling water before they fell into a wide pool. He slipped off his clothing and slipped beneath the icy shower as he washed away the grime from the previous day and the sleep out of his eyes. Feeling much refreshed, he ran around in the early sunshine while he dried. He dressed quickly and decided that, as he still had his bronze knife strapped below his right knee, he would try to smarten himself up, as he had not shaved for the last few days. He was in the habit of scraping his face with a sharpened knife ever since his days in the army, as the Greeks did. Although a lot of men had beards, he still preferred a smooth skin on his face and thought it suited him more. As he finished shaving, he thought, I wonder if she will tell me that my hair is a mess, like Lialah used to. He returned to the cave to find that people were beginning to stir. Crossing over to Naomi who was awake and sitting up looking around, he said, "It is a lovely morning outside, and you can have a bathe in the little stream while I keep watch to see that you are undisturbed."

"Thank you, Ruben," she said rubbing her eyes. "I will take you up on your kind offer."

They left the cave together, telling Samson that they would not be long, after which they made their way to where the pool was full from the droplets that showered over a flat rock.

"You may bathe whilst I keep the Philistines at bay," he laughed.

Without worrying whether or not he was watching, she slipped out of her dress and disappeared under the water droplet curtain. She soon joined him again rubbing her long golden hair with the blanket that he had given her.

"Thank you, I feel a lot fresher for that. I noticed that you have shaved, I like that, it is a shame you have no comb for your hair."

"I had a feeling that you would say that," said Ruben smiling. They left the pool and went back to the cave's entrance from where Samson had emerged. "It is a lovely day and there are no Philistines in sight, do we have far to go, Samson?" he enquired.

"We will be there in half a morning's march," said Samson. "Go inside again, Naomi, as it is too much of a squeeze for me to keep going in and out, and get everyone to hurry up as I want to get started."

As Naomi went dutifully inside the cave, Samson put his large hand on Ruben's shoulder saying, "There should be no danger of the Philistines from here on, so I would appreciate it if you walked beside me as there are a few matters I wish to discuss with you."

"Certainly," replied Ruben, realising this was his chance to find out more about the Israelites and some of their customs, but realising that he would no longer be able to chat with Naomi. Additionally he felt sure that Samson had already begun to make plans for using his services, which greatly pleased him.

They started out on their journey, Ruben soon realising that Samson must have mentioned to those who followed immediately that discretion was required and to keep twenty paces behind. It was Samson who started the conversation by asking, "Have you ever trained soldiers before?"

"Strange that you should ask," replied Ruben. "I have recently been doing some training for a Greek lord in Canaan, so the answer is, yes and I think I am a reasonably good instructor. Why do you ask, do you have some troops to train?"

"We do not have any at present," replied Samson. "But we need to build up our army. You see, people have been relying on me for too long. Admittedly a lot of that has been my own fault, as I have for a long time now shunned the assistance as it was my job to free our people from the Philistine yoke."

"Who appointed you to this task?" asked Ruben, mystified.

"Why, the Lord of course," remonstrated Samson at what seemed to him a stupid question.

"Of course," responded Ruben, feeling that this would not be the time for such questions, but nonetheless feeling that he must have missed something.

Fortunately Samson simply concentrated. "There may well come a time when I am not around, even though I cannot imagine the Lord allowing it. Fortunately some of our young people are keen to fight as well, but they need proper training. Even my fighting is not educated, that is why I did not kill you." Ruben was about to protest, and point out that if it were not for Naomi's intervention, he would have killed Samson. However, he felt it would be wise not to suggest this possibility, but nodded in agreement, hoping that Samson would continue. He was correct, as the huge man said, "Now, young Saul, who likes to consider himself as one of my captains, says that we should build a strong army to defeat the Philistines. Admittedly this is logical, but if the Lord wanted me to build an army, he would tell me."

"Oh yes, undoubtedly," responded Ruben, at a loss at what to say and hoping to ask Naomi for an explanation.

Samson continued, oblivious to Ruben's confusion. "You can see Sabasti now, it is at the top of the next ridge," he pointed. "We now will let the others catch up, as I must speak to one of the elders, but I will introduce you to Saul when we get to Sabasti. He is a nice lad, but strange as well, he even wants to marry Naomi and is saving up the bride price. She is a good girl, but that golden hair, anything like that is unnatural."

Ruben had heard this before from the odious Assyrian king, the tyrant Tiglath-Pileser. He also knew that he was now committed to these people, for better or for worse, so he desperately needed clarification, which he knew he would get from Naomi. Accordingly, he slipped away while Samson was talking to the others and went in search of her. He found her near the end of the party and drew her aside, pleading, "You must help me, there is so much your uncle has not explained." He then repeated to her the gist of his conversation and to his relief she smiled, understanding his dilemma.

"I told you he was insensitive, he obviously thinks you know everything about him." She went on to explain about his immaculate conception, saying, "He believes that he comes from God, who plans everything, and when things go badly for us, it must be because we have sinned."

"Wow," gasped Ruben. "And what do you think?"

She hesitated, and then said, "I am not sure, but everybody accepts it and it seems undeniable. It is sensible for me to go along with it, and I think the same should go for you, unless you want to start another argument, and another fight."

"I see," he said, scratching his head. "And who is this Saul who wants to marry you?"

"One of the town's main young men. I suppose he is reasonable, but I don't really like him. But if he gives my father the bride price, I will have to marry him," she said looking at him imploringly.

"Tell your father that I wish to speak to him," he advised her, as he hurried back to Samson.

"You will probably meet him before I do, his name is Ezekiel," she had to shout after him.

"Ah! There you are, Ruben," Samson said, dismissing Ruben's apology for keeping him waiting. "Here comes the young man I was talking about earlier."

Five young men ran out of the walled town to meet them. Their obvious leader was a tall, dark haired man of sturdy build, but not as tall or as well muscled as Ruben. He had black curly hair, with a short trimmed beard. He was pleased to see Samson, or so it appeared from his smile, but his dark eyes told another story as he carefully looked over all the party.

"I see you have brought my potential wife safely back," said Saul. "We had heard reports that they had been captured, but, as usual, you probably rescued them, and you have brought a stranger with you, did you rescue him as well?" Although this assumption was annoying to Ruben, he tried to dismiss it, as Saul was holding out his hand in welcome greeting.

"Not exactly, my friend, but Samson will tell you about that in due course. My name is Ruben, and Samson tells me that you are his best captain and that you need some help training your soldiers."

"I am pleased to meet you, Ruben," said Saul, with a firm handshake. "Are you an expert trainer?" he queried.

"Not expert," replied Ruben. "But I do have some experience."

Saul's searching eyes gave him a slightly sinister appearance, and although he seemed friendly enough, Ruben could understand why Naomi did not like him.

"What has been happening in my absence, Saul?" demanded Samson.

"And why have you brought a delegation to meet me?"

"I came to tell you that the Philistines have been active again not far from here," Saul warned him. "And I wanted to advise you of their actions before you speak to the town's elders."

"Give me your version first, you mean," laughed Samson, as they all turned and walked towards the town's main gate.

Ruben could only half overhear what Saul was saying about the Philistines marking out an area that they had chosen, on which to build a new town, in the valley of Sorek. Half his attention was taken studying the town, its buildings and the demeanour of the people. He liked all of these. The town was neat, tidy and well cared for, the people were all busy working at one job or another, yet were all nice and friendly and all had smiling faces. Many of the buildings were new, but neatly erected, obviously to some over-all plan. There seemed to be a lot of people who wanted Samson's ear, and he found himself swept along by the crowd. They converged on one main building in the town centre and as they all trooped in, Ruben noticed that no women were allowed inside.

A tall elderly man with a pleasant face, who was clean shaven and had light brown hair that was turning grey at the temples, came up to Samson saying, "Greetings, my father's oldest son, and how is our Judge today?"

"I am extremely well, as usual, Zeke my friend," smiled Samson, pounding him on the back, almost sending him flying.

Ruben guessed correctly that this was Ezekiel, Naomi's father, as he could see the family resemblance.

Some benches and stools were brought out and it was clear that a meeting was taking place, but there appeared to be no particular order of speakers, although most people who spoke to the crowd first addressed Samson, who seemed to be the leader. Ruben took a place at the back of the room beside one of the pillars, where he was half in the shadows, so that he could see everything without being observed. This was somewhat difficult, as he was the largest person in the room, except of course for Samson. He noticed that there was a small-screened area behind where Samson was sitting that most people occasionally bowed to and everyone treated with respect. The meeting itself seemed to last well into the afternoon and generally discussed all the town's business, as well as what was happening in the area in general and of course of the new Philistine area that Saul had spoken of earlier. It appeared that this was intended to be another garrison town, as large as Beth-Shan, and was considered by Saul's young men as a threat, as it lay between Beth-Shan and Gaza, which was the Philistine capital to the southwest. Samson finally confirmed that he had been in search of the party that had been coming from Haggan and had been overdue. He found them being taken to Beth-Shan by a Philistine patrol, which he had smashed, and he finally introduced Ruben as a fine warrior who had helped him in this task. Naomi's father was one of the elders of the town, but this introduction was right at the end of the meeting, which concluded with no particular action having been decided upon. Ruben thought it was all very strange and chaotic, but as people were beginning to depart, there was a moment when Ezekiel was on his own. Feeling the thumping of his heart, Ruben approached Ezekiel, asking, "May I speak to you in private for a moment, sir?"

"Why, of course you may," Ezekiel smiled in reply. "We can go over by the Holy of Holies," pointing to the screened area.

Ruben suddenly heard himself saying to Ezekiel, "Can I buy your daughter as my wife, sir."

"Goodness me, yes, young man, but it will cost you one hundred gold pieces."

"No problem," said Ruben, producing a pouch of coins from his large bag, saying, "There are over one hundred gold pieces in there, but please keep the rest as she is worth every one of them."

Ezekiel stared in wonder at the pouch, then quickly checked its contents, noticing, as he did so, two similar pouches still in Ruben's large bag.

"You have yourself a deal, young man, will you join us for a meal this evening to talk of your plans for when the marriage is to take place?"

"I would be delighted to join you, sir," said Ruben gratefully. "But I would be happy to let Naomi finalise the arrangements."

"Will we see you later, Samson?" called Ezekiel. "I presume you will be joining us for dinner as usual? We have something to celebrate," he said, smiling at Ruben, as he led him out of the building.

On their way to Ezekiel's house, Ruben was asked, "Did I hear Samson correctly, that you are related to Abraham, our great patriarch?"

"Yes," replied Ruben. "I believe that I am a direct descendant, at least that is what I was told by my uncle, who brought me up. That was in Babylon, a long way to the east. I decided a long time ago to trace my heritage from where Abraham is believed to have set out, which is a small town called Ur."

"Well, well," exclaimed Ezekiel. "That is exactly what our Torah tells us, although there is no mention of any descendants that were left behind. But I do recall an old legend that not everyone followed him. Were there signs of the roads made by the ancient sun worshippers?"

"Yes, I have always wondered about the old caravan route," replied Ruben. "You see, Ur is in the marshlands, near where I grew up on the river Euphrates. The old caravan route goes through the marshlands and is now washed away in many places."

"That is fascinating. Obviously you do not know that I am a teacher, and I like to study much of our history," explained Ezekiel. "The sun worshippers laid the old caravan routes, upon which they travelled all the way to Egypt, where I believe the sun is still worshipped. They were apparently very fine builders and stone workers."

They had by this time reached Ezekiel's house, which was one of the largest in the town, as being a teacher he rated highly amongst the elders. As he came in, a servant came to the entrance with a bowl of water, with which Ezekiel's feet were washed. He told Ruben that this was customary, and that Ruben should now submit to this ritual. Ruben realised that he would be able to learn an enormous amount from this kind man, who was going to be his father-in-law. Ezekiel led Ruben into the main room in the house and asked him to sit down, while he went to inform his wife that they had company for the main meal of the day. Ruben could hear him speaking to his wife, telling her that he had received the bride price for their eldest daughter.

"You had better tell her to come in and meet her betrothed." He then returned, bringing with him a pitcher of wine, from which he proceeded to fill two goblets. Handing one to Ruben he said, "This is a grand occasion and deserves celebration."

A middle-aged woman, who was very well dressed, with sandy-coloured hair and vivid green eyes, came over to meet her future son-in-law. She looked puzzled as she spied Ruben, stopped and turned to her husband saying, "I told Naomi that Saul had raised the money."

"That is not what I told you," Ezekiel admonished her. "You are getting as bad as Samson, putting two and two together and making five. This young man beat him to it, he has already given me more money than I requested."

Naomi followed her mother into the room, initially with downcast eyes, but when she heard her parents' brief discussion she looked up and saw Ruben.

She threw herself at Ruben, laughing and crying at the same time, "So you did have money all the time," she said, clinging to his shoulders and standing on tiptoe, turning her face up to be kissed, which he did whilst lifting her off her feet and giving her an affectionate cuddle.

"Mind your manners, child," scolded her mother.

But her father just smiled at Ruben and said, "At least we have no fears about the union being unhappy." He then told his wife and daughter to go and start preparing the meal, which should be quite a feast, and that they would be joined later by Samson.

Whilst the food was being prepared and they were waiting for Samson to join them, Ezekiel told Ruben a great deal about the Jewish customs and the laws.

"These are kept on scrolls in the synagogue, where the meeting was held. Behind the screen that I called the Holy of Holies." Explaining that the scrolls were copies of the laws that Moses had received from God, that were on stone tablets in the Ark of the Covenant that was itself kept hidden and one day would be placed in a Temple. Whilst Ezekiel was telling Ruben all about their laws, he explained that a lot of these were still being sorted out and slightly modified in interpretation, slipping in to the conversation an important question, "Have you been circumcised?" He had been delighted and surprised, when Ruben told him that he had been circumcised, as it was practiced in quite a few places, but Ruben had no idea that it was part of their laws.

"Although," said Ezekiel with a shrug, "even Samson flouted this law when he took his first wife from the uncircumcised Philistines."

He was later talking about his studies of the old sun worshippers, telling Ruben that he believed they were a whole race, who had been massacred by the Shepherd Kings, who called themselves Hyskos. This war-like race had appeared when their people had fled south into Egypt due to famine. It was there that they had been enslaved by the Hyskos, who had finally been vanquished, in their turn, by the Southern Kingdom of Egypt that had temporarily fled south. The Egyptians then had returned, maintaining the slavery of their people until Moses freed them people, and led the Israelites home," he said. "You see, this land was given to Abraham by the Lord who is the only true God, and presumably is now the God that you acknowledge?"

"If he is The Creator who made all the animals and plants, then yes, he certainly is," replied Ruben.

Samson joined them at that point and told Ruben that Saul and his men had started building somewhere to train soldiers, where he had arranged for Ruben to stay.

"Is this new place within the town walls?" Ruben enquired.

"The main housing is, it is beside the eastern gateway in the wall," replied Samson. "But there is no room for any training to be practiced there, that will have to be organised outside the town walls."

"I understand, Samson," said Ruben. "But in all honesty this hardly seems to be an ideal situation. Certainly it will be quite sufficient to start with, but the best solution would be to extend the town walls to incorporate the barracks and a training ground."

"Possibly," growled Samson. "That is what young Saul said, but that could only be done with everyone's agreement, and I for one am not entirely sure about the whole prospect." Ruben realised that it would be futile to argue the point, so he simply smiled at Samson and thanked him for arranging somewhere for him to stay.

The meal was finally brought in, and it was extremely fine. Ruben only then realised how hungry he was, as he had not eaten since before leaving Sam two days previously. He ate with his normal gusto, finishing plate after plate, at which Ezekiel laughed and said to his daughter, "It is a good job that you like cooking, because I think you will be spending a lot of your time in the kitchen."

"That is where all women should be," echoed Samson. "Either there or in bed, ha, ha!"

Nobody challenged him on this, but Ruben felt that the sentiment was not shared by everyone in the room, certainly not by Naomi and the eldest of her two younger sisters, who was only a year younger than she was, the other being only four, there being two brothers in between. Ruben had noticed that Samson ate an entirely different meal and did not drink wine. In answer to his surprised glance, Ezekiel broke the silence by explaining that Samson maintained a strict diet because he was a Nazarine.

"The Lord even forbade his mother to eat or drink certain foods," Naomi explained, turning to her mother for confirmation, which was given with a smile of agreement.

"That is correct, Ruben," her mother informed him, adding, "he must only eat naturally occurring foods, and no meat."

"I knew a doctor in the marshlands in Babylon who lived like that," Ruben told them, giving a minute shake of the head to Naomi as he could guess that she was about to question whether it had been his father. "I stayed with him for some time and it is, I believe, quite healthy."

"Only if the Lord grants," cut in Samson.

"Yes, of course," said Ruben, placating the large man, then adding, as an afterthought, "but surely, wine is naturally occurring."

"Rubbish," roared Samson. "It is fermented and other ingredients are added."

"Certainly, the wine we are drinking is, but when I was in the mountains, I picked some berries that were over ripe, and the baby eagle that I was looking after became drunk when he ate them."

"Ha, ha, ha, ha! A fine story," roared Samson. "You will make a fine addition to this family, your silly ideas are as daft as this crazy old man," he said pointing at Ezekiel. "Ho, ho, ho!" he roared again. "Come along Ruben, it is getting late, I will take you to your new home." This clearly indicated that the evening was at an end and Naomi's mother and the children quickly cleared up.

"May I go with Ruben to help him sort out his new home?" Naomi asked her mother.

"Certainly not, you say goodnight here, you may go and see the place tomorrow," she said sternly. "Only if you have time after doing other duties."

"You will have a whole life together, starting as soon as you can arrange the wedding," smiled Ezekiel, preventing an argument.

"Surely you mean as soon as Ruben organises the wedding," interjected his wife.

"He has already given her that responsibility," said Ezekiel, terminating the conversation.

"Goodnight, everybody," said Ruben, going round to Naomi's mother, whom he kissed and thanked for the meal, before kissing Naomi and giving her an affectionate squeeze, and finally giving her two younger sisters a kiss on the cheek. The youngest he picked up and tossed in the air, to squeals of delight, before catching her and gently setting her back on her feet, which he knew most children enjoyed. He then ruffled the hair of Naomi's two young brothers, who had initially been in awe of him, before he left the room and left the house, shaking Ezekiel's hand and thanking him for the introduction to their customs.

"You are very welcome, my boy," said Ezekiel, warmly shaking his hand and saying, "Tonight has been a great pleasure and I hope we can spend many further evenings in discussion."

"Come along, you cackling young cockerel," demanded Samson.

******

As he lay on his hastily made bed in the half finished building, next to the town's eastern gateway, Ruben looked up at the stars through the half finished roof, reflecting on the events of the day. It had been a day of many hasty decisions, possibly bringing an end to his travels, knowing full well that tomorrow he would face a difficult job with Saul as well as establishing the training camp, which would require Samson's backing. He finally fell asleep, content with his choice of a partner to share his life, knowing that he had picked the best of a good family and thanking his new God for the crazy old man, who was now his friend.

# 23
# TRAINING AND PREPARATION

As usual, Ruben woke early, and after his ablutions and eating the cold breakfast that Naomi's mother had provided, he was wondering where to start, when Naomi came along.

"You must have made an early start to be able to be with me so early?" He gratefully acknowledged her presence, giving her a comforting cuddle that he hoped would soon be the standard start to every day.

"I just had to pop along to ensure that yesterday wasn't all a dream," she whispered breathlessly in his ear, disentangling herself, stepping back and holding him at arm's length. "I will have to go back home shortly, but I will be back to tidy up and make the place more comfortable, but I have just seen Saul coming along the road."

"You run along then, leave Saul to me and I will see you later," he told her, smiling as he watched her dash away.

"Morning, lover boy," said Saul, with a perfectly straight face that showed no emotion. "I understand that you are shortly to be married," holding out his hand in congratulation.

"Thank you, Saul," replied Ruben, accepting and welcoming his handshake. "I now learn that you had your eyes on Naomi too."

"Never mind, I don't think she was keen on me anyway and there are plenty of other girls from whom I can take my pick," he shrugged his shoulders, dismissing the subject. "I apologise for the place being only half finished, but the weather should hold so there is no rush to finish the roof, but the training area will have to be outside and I don't really know how to start."

"Let's go and have a look," suggested Ruben. "By the way, I agree with you about having the whole area inside the town walls. That was my first observation to Samson, but I think he will require a lot of convincing."

They went outside the town wall in the early morning light, and strolled around on the large flat area to the southeast, as the northeast sloped away sharply. Finally, Ruben squatted down beside Saul and drew a plan of the town and the area with his dagger in the sand. About three hundred paces directly east from the town was a small valley that ran in a semicircle to the southern edge of the town wall, and this was the area that was very flat. As the northwest fell away sharply to the north from where the town walls turned to run northerly from the eastern gate. Ruben marked this flat area.

"What we need to do is fence off along the top of the valley from the south wall, leaving this area," which he pointed out on his plan. "This is the area we will use, creating a low building beside the town wall and others along by the top of the valley that eventually can form a new city wall. This will leave a V-shape that will run in to the eastern gateway. These buildings will be the barracks by the top of the valley and the armoury by the town wall. That will make it easy to extend the town wall to cover our training ground and make the area up to the eastern gate easy to defend."

"I see what you have in mind, it looks good," acknowledged Saul, smiling his agreement at Ruben's plan.

"What do we have in the way of people to train?" Ruben asked.

"Possibly between fifty and seventy men," was Saul's reply, "But if we are successful I am sure more will join."

"What weapons, if any, do we have?" was Ruben's next question.

"Nothing as yet," said Saul shaking his head sadly. "Except what the men have, which are mainly swords, but a few have spears and war clubs in addition to bows and arrows."

"Well, we must make good use of what is available and plan a small raid capturing as many Philistines as possible," explained Ruben. "That way we will show Samson the potential of building an army."

"If you can train as well as you can plan," laughed Saul, "we will soon be meeting the Philistines in open battle. If I can leave the training to you, I will supply the men and start working on plans for a sortie."

Their friendship started here, and they strolled back together, as Ruben said, "Send the men to me, firstly with building tools, so that we can make a start on the training ground and buildings."

Young men began to arrive in small numbers and Ruben started allotting tasks, according to people's ability, size and strength. By mid-morning, he had the area marked out and gangs of men working on cutting surrounding posts and digging the foundations for the new buildings. By the middle of the day he was standing on a stool hammering sharpened stakes into the surrounding area that he had previously marked off. By the end of the day, the area had all been staked out and flexible narrow branches had been interwoven between the stakes to form a temporary wall. The buildings had been started and his enthusiasm was spreading amongst all the willing pairs of hands, who worked long into the night. When he finally dismissed everyone to go home, asking them to return early in the morning, he went back to his own half finished building. Here he found Naomi, who had not simply tidied up, but had organised the room, bringing in more furniture and starting an evening meal for him.

"This is marvellous," he congratulated her as they sat down together to eat the tasty meal that she had produced. "Your father was not joking when he said that you liked cooking, this is an excellent meal."

"You are just easy to please," she laughed. "As I think you would eat anything."

"It is true that I am not a fussy eater," he replied, as he replenished his plate. "Now tell me what you have been up to today?" She told him of the plans that she had already made and that they would be married in twenty days, if he was in agreement to such haste. "That will suit me fine, but by then I hope to have started the training of our small force, so I do not think that we will be able to spend the normal period of festivities."

"That does not matter, I believe that the way people use wedding feasts as an excuse for having a good time is hardly good sense, particularly if there is lots of work to be done. You have already made a great start," she said in admiration of all they had accomplished in just the one day.

"Will you be very busy organising everything?" he enquired.

"Not particularly," she responded. "Why, what did you have in mind?"

"What I would really like, is someone to organise a group of women to start making uniforms. Would it be too much to ask you to organise that?" he requested.

"I would be happy to help," she replied. "I think a lot of the girls in the town would be happy to encourage the men in this venture, it would also help raise enthusiasm. Can you give me an idea of what you have in mind?"

He went over to his large bag and took out another pouch of gold coins. "Here, take these, I think all we need to start with is a simple shift and kilt. I think that white, as it is a natural colour, is best. Use half of the money to start a fund that I will tell the men to try to add to. And use the other half for provisions that we will need ourselves in this new house."

Her eyes widened in surprise at the sight of so many gold coins. "Gosh, you are generous." Then thinking for a moment, she said, "White is not really natural, but it is easy to bleach the cloth and maintain it."

During the next few days, the town became extremely active, with the young women meeting to design and make the new uniforms and the young men busy with building the new training ground. Ruben soon took an evening off building work and the next day he told all the men to start bringing their basic belongings into their training ground, where they would be staying until their training was finished. The next day, when they arrived, he placed them in the huts, in groups that he thought would work together, as he had already chosen people who he thought would be the best leaders. He told them to put their weapons in the already completed armoury, for which he had the only key. He then told them that in the afternoon they would start their training, but when he was asked if they should collect their weapons, he surprised them all by saying, "You are not yet fit enough to even play at being soldiers."

One of the young men, whose father was a worker in bonds and had a furnace, in which he had been an apprentice and considered himself very strong, considered this was an insult and said, "I am as fit as you are."

To prove his point, Ruben produced four heavy boxes, each with rope handles, which he placed on the ground. He then asked one of the men to fill two of the boxes with sand, so that they were much heavier than the other two, then led the men around the course that he had been constructing the previous evening, after which he picked up the two heavier boxes and asked the young man who had complained to pick up the two lighter boxes, telling the other man that if he could complete the course faster than he could, then the young man was ready to start his weapon training. His challenge was accepted and Saul was asked to judge. The challenger set off at a trot but soon became tired, as although he was strong he was unused to running. He was overtaken by Ruben, who was walking at a fast pace and then broke into a run on the final hundred paces of the course. After that, there were no further disputes and the fitness training commenced, leaving them shattered by evening.

Naomi had organised, in addition to the dress making, a cooking and eating area, where the wives and friends of some of the men prepared the evening meal, which was eaten with much appreciation. The training had started with Saul in charge of one of the barrack huts, himself taking part in all the exercises, with the bronze worker's son, Mischa, happily taking charge of the other barrack hut.

After a few days of rigorous training, Saul came to Ruben one evening and said, "I have plans for what we can do to prove our worth to Samson. But it will also involve using him as bait. Do you think that he would be willing to give the idea a try?"

"I think," replied Ruben, "that you had better tell me what you have in mind."

"It will mean going to the valley of Sorek, where Samson often goes to visit a woman," Saul explained, adding as an afterthought, "We had better take one of the captives that you rescued to confirm that this woman used to live in Haggan, as maybe she is the informant to the Philistines."

"I think," responded Ruben, "that we had better take Naomi, as nearly all the others are old. Leave it with me and I will talk to her father, to allow her out one evening."

The next day, he spoke to Ezekiel and told him what he had in mind, to which Ezekiel agreed, after making Ruben promise not to take advantage of the situation. "As if I would," grinned Ruben.

"I too was young once," replied Ezekiel. "Now off you go, before I change my mind."

The next day, Ruben told Saul that they would go ahead with their plan and it was all arranged for the next evening, when they could be sure that Samson would go to Sorek, as he had been away in Hebron, east of Gaza, for the last two days. Naomi came with them, after the evening meal had been served and the young men had retired, exhausted, to their barrack huts. Ruben had allowed Saul to rest in the afternoon, making an excuse that he had to organise the fighting fund with a treasurer that Ezekiel had appointed, which allowed Saul time enough to rest so that he was not too tired by evening.

The three of them were covered in grey hooded cloaks and flitted along behind Samson, ensuring that he was unaware of being followed. He left by the western gate and made his way directly toward the valley of Sorek, where this woman lived. They reached the valley, which was some distance away, and it was after nightfall when they stopped in a clump of trees at the top of the ridge outside of the valley. They watched from behind the trees as Samson went down the valley, to where he was met at the far side by a woman, who was standing by a small wooden bridge that crossed a small wadi. The woman was cloaked, but held a light to show the way for Samson. When he arrived, the woman threw back her cloak and embraced the huge man, almost disappearing beneath his great shaggy head.

"Do you recognise that woman?" Ruben asked Naomi.

"Yes," she replied. "That is Delilah, a woman who used to live in Haggan. She is just the type that Samson likes, small and pretty, with dark curly hair."

"Right," said Saul. "Now we can get back."

"Hang on just a moment," instructed Ruben. "There are some markings on the ground down there that I would like to check on." He left them both and was soon on the valley floor, flitting around the rocks, hardly noticeable in his grey cloak. They did not have long to wait and he was back with them. "It is rather puzzling and I will have to think about it, but let us go back now."

On the long walk back to Sabasti, Ruben was unusually quiet for a long period, so Naomi squeezed his hand and asked, "Are you all right, my love?"

After a pause he said, "I am sorry, what did you ask?"

She repeated her question and answered it herself. "You are not allright, something is troubling you. Please tell me what is wrong?"

"I am sorry, there is nothing really wrong," he lied, "I was just trying to work out something about the training, concerning how to tackle people in chariots." This, he admitted to himself, was only half the problem, but hoped to waylay her anxiety. Fortunately this he managed and they eventually arrived back, and he sent Saul back to the barracks and took Naomi directly home. Ezekiel opened to the light knock on the door, as he was awaiting their return.

"One daughter returned unmolested, sir." He kissed Naomi goodnight and returned to his own bed, still wrestling with his thoughts. There had been some unusual markings on the ground that were nothing to do with new building foundations, also there were stones that were placed in a pattern that the casual eye would not notice. Ruben neither trusted Delilah, nor did he believe that there was no Philistine involvement. However, he could not work out what the Philistines were planning.

The following day, he had driven his trainee soldiers hard all morning on the recently completed obstacle course. During the midday break, he went over to where Saul was chatting to his companions, who were all bathed in sweat. He drew Saul aside for a brief chat.

"Do you think you can find a couple of reliable people? Not from the trainees, as I require old men or children for this task?"

"What is it that they need to do?" asked Saul in perplexity.

"I need a constant watch kept on the valley of Sorek," admitted Ruben. "But I require everything, no matter how trivial, reported to me, can you arrange that?"

"There are a couple of lame beggars who I could ask to do the job, they have eyes like hawks and will be reliable, but not cheap," he told Ruben, giving him a mysterious look, as he was himself quite mystified. But Ruben asked him to go ahead and to have them report to him.

The lookouts had been in place for a couple of days and were being visited in the evening by Ruben, who ran all the way, both there and back, simply to keep in trim. Ruben listened carefully to reports of the excavation works on the valley floor that were obviously unconnected to any construction work. He considered that he knew what the Philistines were planning and decided that he required a chariot to foil their plan. He chose a couple of the trainee soldiers to come with him. These two were twins and both about fifteen years old and were fine bowmen who knew the area. Leaving Saul and Mischa in charge of the training that was progressing satisfactorily, which he did not want to disrupt, he led the way, now fully armed and having issued weapons to the two trainees, whom he had sworn to secrecy. They followed the route that would lead them to the valley of Sorek, but branched south just before the final ridge.

This, Ruben knew, would intercept the road between Beth-Shan and Gaza, which he felt sure would be used by chariots driven by the Philistines. When they reached the road he asked the twins if there was a hill that overlooked the road in both directions. The lads nodded agreement and led him to the left, where a short distance away the road made a turn around a small hill, which had ample coverage of thorn bushes and boulders on its summit. They went up the hill and after a while spotted a Philistine patrol coming from the northeast, headed towards Gaza, so that it would pass beneath them. This patrol was comprised of ten foot soldiers with two accompanying chariots, one in front of the patrol, the other bringing up the rear. Realising that this was about the smallest patrol that they would be likely to encounter, Ruben told the lads that although they would be vastly outnumbered, they had the element of surprise and that the plan was simply to steal a chariot. The twins readily agreed to this daring escapade, feeling privileged that they had been chosen. Ruben told them to wait at the top of the hill until the first chariot and the soldiers had rounded the bend. Then as he intercepted the following chariot, they were to rain arrows down on the Philistines, making the soldiers run for cover and causing the horses drawing the leading chariot to bolt. The rest he knew was up to him. He issued his final instructions to both young men, that after loosing most of their arrows, they should retreat down the hill, to join him on the road before the Philistines could retaliate. His plan was made easier by one of the horses pulling the second chariot having to have a stone removed from its hoof, which left a fifty pace gap between the foot patrol and the second chariot.

    He could hear the commotion as the arrows rained down on the leading chariot and foot soldiers. He leapt out in front of the second chariot just as it had restarted. The astonished charioteer reined in his horses, causing his companion to momentarily lose his footing. The charioteer's startled cry was cut short as a javelin, hurled with great force at only ten paces distance, slammed into his chest, penetrating right to the backbone, and threw him from the foot-plate. The second man had only just recovered his footing and drawn his sword as Ruben's large sword crashed through his neck and shoulder; he died before he hit the ground in a pool of his own blood. Jerking his large sword free, Ruben ran round and cut the traces freeing the panicking horses, which fled westwards prompted by a slap on the rump. Ruben was joined by the two bowmen, as the Philistines had not yet emerged from their hiding places beside the road, on which the leading chariot was only just being brought under control. Ruben and the two lads ran the captured chariot off the road to the west as if it was still being drawn by the fleeing the horses. When on the grass beside the dusty road they turned the chariot back and recrossed the road twenty paces behind where the attack had taken place and where the two bodies lay. Leaving the two lads pulling the chariot off the road, Ruben ran back to recover his javelin and swept the chariot marks from the road with a branch of brushwood that he had cut for that purpose. The three of them hauled the chariot another two hundred paces into cover where they lay still waiting for the commotion to die down. By this time the leading chariot with the commanding officer had been brought back to join the men, who had realised that the attack had been brief and were now scaling the hill from where the arrows had come. A few moments later the two dead bodies were found and some soldiers were sent in pursuit of the fleeing horses, which they believed were still attached to the chariot. A short while later the commander realised that the attackers had all disappeared and his men had not yet returned with the horses, so he still believed that the chariot was behind them.

"Blasted Israelites," swore the commander. "Not even that wretched hairy giant did this, not one of his games, this is something completely new, but the attack has come from Sabasti, that's for sure. Get those men to bring the other chariot back to the road further south, while we get back on the road to Gaza to report this outrage," were his words of command. This was overheard by Ruben and his two companions, who had crawled forward to overhear and grinned at one another.

After watching the Philistines resume their journey, and waiting a few moments to ensure that they had all gone, Ruben said, "We must now get the chariot up the hill to where I have a watch being maintained on the valley of Sorek." With Ruben hauling on the main shaft, where the horse traces were attached, and the two lads either pushing the back of the chariot or helping the wheels over the rough ground, they finally heaved the chariot to the top of the ridge. Ruben gave his familiar whistle to alert the watchers of his arrival, and they brought the chariot into the covering trees.

"I have another job for you two fellows," he advised them. "I require you to ensure that this chariot remains hidden from the Philistines, but we will make that easier by covering it with branches, will you do that for me in addition to keeping your lookout?"

"No problem guv'nor!" chirped one of the beggars, as they were being well paid for this job, as well as being provided with ample food, brought by Ruben when he came each evening to check on any work carried out in the valley. He and the twins soon had the chariot shielded by branches, which they cut from the other trees, and it could only be recognised as a chariot if someone walked into it. After a final chat with the beggars, Ruben and the twins hurried away towards Sabasti. "That is another aspect of my plan that I need to be kept secret," he told the lads. He knew that there was no great danger in any of the trainees knowing of his plans, but the less people who knew made it more certain that Samson knew nothing of the Philistine plan, otherwise he would not fulfil his role. Ruben returned the lads to the training ground, as the day's training finished and the evening meal was being served. Ruben was relocking the weapons that he had issued to the lads, as Saul and Mischa came up to him to report on how the day's training had progressed.

"Where have you been while we have been slaving away?" asked Saul.

"I took the Manuel brothers out to turn a nosy Philistine into a hedgehog," laughed Ruben. "It was good target practise and great fun. Our watchers have informed me that someone from in the valley had been nosing about around where they were." He lied to Saul, considering it the safest way to keep secret about the chariot.

"Anyway," interjected Mischa, "the training went really well today, we both feel that the trainees are ready to start weapon training."

"That is brilliant," said Ruben. "I was hoping for your agreement to start weapon training tomorrow, so you can tell everyone whilst they eat."

That evening, he told Naomi what he had been doing, and asked her if she knew of someone in the town who could make a form of ladder type gang plank, whilst keeping the whole issue secret.

"I will also require hooks added to the sides at every arm's length?" he requested, drawing her a plan with chalk on a slate.

"Leave the plan with me," she replied. "And consider the job done." He marvelled that she did not ask him any questions and thought for the hundredth time that he had chosen the ideal wife and smiled broadly at her, as she told him, "Our wedding is in eight days time, I hope that will be convenient?"

"I think it will all work out splendidly," he assured her, giving her a hug and telling her that she was not safe to be in his company any longer.

Weapon training started the very next morning, but this was an entirely new situation to Ruben as there were no standard weapons to start with. Therefore, he said to the assembled trainees, "The normal training, if we had sufficient equipment, would be sword and shield practise with blunt weapons. This is purely because we obviously try to minimise anyone being seriously hurt. However, I have obtained some makeshift wooden swords for everyone." He saw that many of the young men were rather crestfallen and some of the older trainees actually sneered.

"Now, I know most of you have swords of your own that are currently kept in the armoury, but are of different sizes. So I would appreciate your using these wooden swords to give you an idea of how to fight, the areas to aim for and how to defend yourself without a shield. The shield is primarily a defensive weapon, used mainly to provide defence whilst attacking." Ignoring many of the mumbled comments he went over to the armoury, which he unlocked and came out with a large pile of crudely made wooden swords.

"Here, catch!" he said as he threw three of the wooden swords to the main complainants. "You are obviously so good that you think that I am treating you like children. Well, perhaps I am, but it is because you behave like children." This was deliberately said to annoy the three who now had wooden swords in their hands, and allowing time for their anger to flare, he took one of the wooden swords himself. "All three of you attack me and if any one of you lays a part of your wooden blade on me, I will give that man a gold coin," he challenged. The three men all looked at one another. They had heard accounts of Ruben's fight with Samson and knew of his awesome power and speed, but this challenge sounded nonetheless too easy. All three attacked at the same time, expecting him to parry the blows aimed at him. As they charged, he also ran straight at the men at the centre, whacking the man's sword arm that sent his wooden blade flying. As he raced between the other two he hit one of them on both ankles in a low sweep of his sword and the men fell face down clasping his bruised ankles. He turned immediately and before the other man could defend himself he thrust the point of his sword deep into the man's stomach, sending him sprawling on his back.

"One has lost his right hand, the second has lost both his feet and the third will die within a short while in great agony, or would do had we been using real weapons. The first lesson is never to underestimate your opponent and remember that attack is often the best form of defence," here he paused, and then asked, "how else could I have avoided taking at least one blow?"

After a long silence, Mischa said, "You could have run away, we have all seen you run and you could have easily left them behind."

"Perfectly correct," returned Ruben. "It is always sensible to know when to run." Allowing this to sink in he reminded them, "We are just beginning, so we will always be fighting a larger force than our own. And also remember we need their weapons, armour and money. Even Philistine gold and silver is useful."

There was no further dissent, only respect, as he handed out the wooden swords, paired them off and then demonstrated the basic attacking blows, the places to aim for and the main defensive moves, ending his brief introduction by telling them, "You can certainly kill or mortally wound without the edge of the sword, but the majority of people who are killed quickly, are killed with the point of the sword. It is far better to kill your opponent quickly, than to leave them partly dead, screaming for their mothers or wives and alerting their comrades."

The basic sword practise continued for another two days without interruption, except for Ruben demonstrating moves to individuals, particularly in moving their feet. All the men went to bed with aching sword arms and bruised limbs where they had been too slow to avoid or parry their opponents' blows. They were quickly improving, in ability, strength and stamina.

Ruben's special ladder gangplank had been finished, and late in the evening he carried this construction himself, even though it was heavy and cumbersome, out to his watchers on the ridge overlooking the valley of Sorek. That night he was told by the watchers that the excavation work in the valley seemed to have been completed, but had been left uncovered when it was normally disguised. Ruben was sure that this was because the Philistines knew, obviously from Delilah, that Samson was away for a few days visiting settlements in Hebron. He took advantage of this opportunity to go down into the valley by night and observe the excavation works. They were of a U-shaped ditch, four paces wide and waist deep with sheer sides. They were excavated into the valley from the wadi either side of the bridge that led to Delilah's home. This meant that the wadi crossed the top of the U-shape, which confirmed Ruben's original guess. The following evening, he was told that the ditch had been mainly filled with brush wood around stone jars full of oil that was the covered by loose slates, rubble and sand. This made it indistinguishable from the rest of the valley floor, particularly to the unexpected visitor at night. Ruben now knew that the Philistine trap was almost ready and could be sprung within half a day's, or more likely a night's notice. He therefore knew that he had to keep Samson at Sabasti on his return from Hebron, to stop his visits to Delilah to satisfy his carnal lust.

He was trotting back to Sabasti, pondering this problem and how to overcome it, when some small fires away to the right caught his attention. He crept up to find a Philistine encampment and crawled nearer to overhear a discussion by the guards. He learnt that there was a force of about fifty men, with four chariots. They had come in reprisal to the attack on the patrol where two men had been killed and a chariot had vanished, although they could not understand this mystery, the reprisal attack on Sabasti was also to reconnoitre the town. Having learnt this, he withdrew and made his way back to Sabasti, where he went to wake Saul and Mischa.

He woke them and brought them, complaining at having been woken, to his half completed home. "There is a force of approximately fifty Philistines with four chariots camped in the next valley. I believe they are going to pay us a visit tomorrow, they have probably been told of the enlargement to Sabasti by our training camp."

"Do you think we have a traitor in Sabasti?" demanded Saul. "I thought everyone here was loyal."

"If we have a traitor, I will tear them limb from limb," interposed Mischa.

"No, I don't think that is the case," Ruben informed them. "The extension to the town is obvious to the outside observer, they are probably on reconnaissance."

"A large party just for that," mused Saul.

"Possibly," replied Ruben. "Your guess is as good as mine, in fact it is probably better, as you know them. It is too early to try out our men, but we must keep the training camp secret for a while. Do you think you could go and persuade Samson to come back, we may then be able to capture some more weapons."

"Yes, I will leave at once," said Saul. "But you must tell me exactly where the encampment is."

"You cannot miss it, Saul," exclaimed Ruben, trying to keep the irritation out of his voice. "They have watch fires all over their encampment, which is in the next valley, to the southwest."

"I will be back with the big man tomorrow," announced Saul, his tiredness forgotten and replaced by eagerness at the prospect of action. "Samson will enjoy taking them from behind." He quickly disappeared with his weapons, which Ruben had already retrieved from the armoury.

"Now, Mischa," continued Ruben. "I would like you to rouse the men early. I want to disguise the woven wood wall with blankets, to make it look like stone when viewed from a long way off, that will ensure that they come closer to investigate. We must then take the men, fully armed, but not to attack them. I want that point made perfectly clear; we leave Samson to do the attacking. Our job is to ensure that none of them escape, particularly in a chariot, we have to place our bowmen in the best positions." He and Mischa stayed making plans until just before dawn, when Mischa went to wake the men and Ruben went to call on Naomi, to ask her to organise an early breakfast for the men.

They left the encampment having eaten a light early breakfast, and having draped blankets over the woven wood wall. Leaving Sabasti by the eastern gate and splitting their numbers into two groups, each to encircle the Philistine advance, but under strict instruction to prevent escaping from the Philistines, yet not to even show their whereabouts. Around mid-morning, a watcher, strategically placed on the city walls, saw the Philistines to the southwest. The watchers and other young lads, just too young for army training, but who were undoubtedly very keen and possessed the sharp eyesight of the young, managed to convey, by using a group of signallers, that the Philistines were in argument over what they saw. Subsequently they advanced, as Ruben had predicted, into the trap. They were then to the southwest of the town, in the valley below the city walls and the new extension and could only escape to the east or the north, both ways that were now covered by the new Israelite force. The attack on the unsuspecting Philistines came as Saul had promised in the form of Samson, bellowing like an enraged bull, whilst throwing Philistines asunder, slicing them like a harvester reaping corn. He overturned two chariots and killed their occupants, as the remainder of the Philistine force all tried to escape his wrath. The two remaining chariots tried to flee, one to the north and one to the east, but were foiled in their bid by the forces under Ruben's command, who ensured that there were no escapees, and all were put to the sword.

Saul managed to stop Samson decapitating the horses on the chariots that he had overturned. These and the other two chariot horse teams that were also brought safely into Sabasti when the horses were calmed, were treated kindly, with their minor abrasions being treated with a salve and being well fed. The Philistine dead were stripped of all armour, weapons and money and their bodies were stacked in large funeral pyres that Ruben insisted were built and then burned, which lasted for three days. The tally of stolen equipment, apart from the chariots, included thirty-five sound swords, ten javelins, from the chariots and a selection of daggers, axes, knives and other weapons, as well as shields and body armour.

Ruben went amongst the trainees while they were eating the evening meal, laughing and joining in their camaraderie as they were all buoyed up with the success of the encounter, in which he had very little part to play, although he was ever present, with his javelin in hand to stop one of the chariots if necessary, or to prevent any Philistines escaping their net. But the young men completed an excellent job and felt they earned the praise he lavished upon them.

After the trainees had gone to bed, he and Saul went by arrangement to see Samson, who was dining at Ezekiel's house.

"Bloody Samson was not impressed by our work," complained Saul as they were walking to Ezekiel's house together. "As usual he feels he should get all the credit, and pays little heed to what we did."

"I feared that would be the case," commented Ruben. "He will hopefully see things differently when we allow him to walk into the Philistine trap, rescuing him at the last minute. But, we now have to arrange that he does not visit Delilah until we are ready."

"And when pray will that be?" demanded Saul. "I think we are ready now."

"Two more days polishing up the lads, then it is my wedding, to which everyone will be invited," he explained as they reached Ezekiel's house and knocked.

The door was promptly opened by Naomi who had been expecting them. "Hello, my darling," she whispered into his ear. She came and gave him a kiss and cuddle before her mother could say anything.

"I suppose you have come to claim some of the credit, like that cockerel?" sneered Samson, pointing at Saul.

"On the contrary," smiled Ruben. "I wished to thank you for such a devastating attack. All we had to do was to kill a few stragglers, but we now have a good collection of weapons that will help the training, which is not yet complete."

This had taken Samson by surprise and the big man laughed, spreading his hands wide. "Ho, ho, ho, ho. It has always been like that and probably will be, as I told you it is the way of the Lord." Whilst Samson had been talking, Ruben squeezed Naomi's hand, indicating that he needed her help and then relied on the telepathy that had developed between them.

"You have not forgotten that you will now be barred from this house until after the wedding," interposed Naomi's mother, giving them both a stern stare.

"By your command, my dear mother-in-law to be," said Ruben, thumping his chest in salute. "One of the other things I came to request is that you," he pointed at Samson, "go and bring Naomi's old aunt and uncle from Jericho, as you know they are elderly and will need help coming here."

"You should send some of your own men on an errand like that," growled Samson in reply.

"Oh please, Uncle," pleaded Naomi, running to Samson and throwing her arms around the huge man's neck. "They would really love to see you."

"We still have lots of training to do, particularly with the new chariots," interposed Saul, pressing the opportunity that Ruben had made.

"All right," muttered Samson. "Now get off me, girl," he said pushing Naomi away and straightening his beard.

"That is great," joined in Ezekiel, responding to Ruben's wink. "You can sleep here and leave first thing in the morning, you can use the spare room tonight. Now I am afraid, my young friends," he said turning to Ruben and Saul, "I must bid you a good night as I have important business to discuss."

"Great," breathed Ruben, with a sigh of relief. "Thanks a lot for your timely intervention, Saul," he added as they walked back to the training ground and bed. This was greatly welcomed by Saul, as he had only had a brief sleep during the last two days. However, for Ruben there was work to be done before he could retire. He set off for the valley of Sorek to arrange a warning system for when Samson paid his next visit, and also to ensure that he did not leave Ezekiel's house that night. Giving his pre-emptory warning whistle, he ran up the hill to check with his watchers.

"The Philistines have planted a load of brushwood in the small wadi and have done something to the bridge, although we are not sure what," one of them told Ruben.

"Possibly some form of collapsing device," he said. "That is as I expected. Now, I will be back tomorrow evening with three lads, who will take it in turns to stay with you and bring you provisions. What you must do is send whoever is with you at the time back to Sabasti, the moment Samson walks into Delilah's house." After checking everything else under the trees was ready, he said goodbye, and promised them a good meal at his own home in compensation for not being able to come to his wedding, which the rest of the town seemed to be attending.

He hurried back to town, grateful that he did not meet Samson on the way, which meant that Ezekiel had kept him in Sabasti, and he knew that Naomi would ensure he left for Jericho the next morning. So he was now sure that Samson would not visit Delilah until after his wedding. Gratefully he went to bed and slept soundly until the next morning, when he awoke and rose early to recommence training. He kept the young men working hard all day, alternating them between sword practice and dashing up and down the training ground in teams pulling and pushing the chariot.

"What is all the activity with the chariots for?" enquired a confused Saul. "When we use the chariots, surely we will use horses to pull them."

"Oh yes, certainly," returned Ruben. "It is primarily to keep them fit, as they will all have time off for the wedding, but could then be called on at short notice."

That evening he returned to the valley of Sorek, as he had promised, with three of the lads who had acted as signallers on the Philistine reconnaissance. He informed them of the task that they were to perform, stressing how urgent it was for him to be notified as soon as Samson was in Delilah's house. He additionally promised them the same invitation that he had extended to the watchers, as at least one of them would miss out on the festivities. On the next day the training continued, but there was an air of revelry in the whole town, which was preparing for a major celebration, as Ezekiel was one of the senior members of the town's elders.

The wedding was a triumph. The whole town seemed to be present, overflowing from the synagogue, which for once was opened to females.

Ruben looked resplendent in a brand new white shift and kilt, but insisted on wearing his crocodile skin jerkin, which it had been especially cleaned and polished for the occasion. Naomi, however, stole the show. She wore a simple white dress with a silver chain around her waist and a garland of white lilies in her golden hair, which shimmered and shone in the sunlight. Everyone claimed that she was the most beautiful girl the town had ever known.

****

    Dathram knew that he was not that far from Ruben when he left Antioch, which was confirmed by Amos, who sold him fish when on the coast below Mount Carmel. This feeling was with him all the time that he walked down the coastal road, but he knew the dangers of travelling inland from all the warring tribes, it was far safer to stay by the coast. He was now in Gaza, where he had other merchant contacts and was considering whether it was worth setting up a trade post with the Philistine governor of Gaza, when he dined with him that evening. The invitation to eat with the Governor was quite unexpected and had been channelled through his merchant contacts, but he thought that before he made any decisions like that, he must be sure of the foundation. So he decided to try to find out more of their status within the land even though the Philistines seemed a reasonable people. His journey with Joself, who led him safely from Ashkilon to the Lord Coronus in Canaan, via Thrax, had been safe even though it had been arduous, and for that he had to thank Ruben.

    He left the inn where he was staying, after first checking on his cargo and his mules, as he was planning an early start the next morning on the final leg of his journey to Egypt. Having satisfied himself that everything was in order, he made his way to the governor's house. It was a splendid building, right next to the new amphitheatre where they held contests, games and even administered public floggings and executions when necessary. He was told that the subjects were often held as prisoners in cells beneath the main public gallery. I would not like to be held there, he thought to himself as he entered the governor's residence.

    "I understand you have come all the way from Babylon," said the governor, as he welcomed Dathram.

    "Yes, that is correct," replied Dathram. "It is now quite a difficult journey as the Assyrians are at war with the Babylonians. I had to find a new route into Canaan, as the old route went north of the River Euphrates and you could even go through Nineveh, the Assyrian capital on the river Tigris. But I found a new way and I am now setting up a trade route between Babylon and Egypt."

"Fascinating," yawned the governor, only half listening. "I would like to be able to offer you safe passage to Canaan on your return, but even that is not possible at the moment."

"Oh dear, why is that?" enquired Dathram, interested.

"Well, it's these blasted Israelites," said the governor. "They are giving us such a headache at the moment, not even our own patrols are safe."

"Dear me, that is sad," muttered Dathram, slowly shaking his head. "Has this trouble been going on for long?"

"Well, yes and no, it is all rather strange and dates back since before my appointment. But at that time all the trouble came from just one man. A huge giant of a man they call Samson. But do not let our troubles worry you."

Dathram found that he was soon passed on to other people and realised that he was here purely to make up the numbers. So he decided that rather than mention that he was trying to set up a new trade route, acting as Babylon's ambassador to Egypt and that he carried the authority of the Babylonian king, he would keep quiet and learn as much as possible. He was sitting next to a senior soldier at the meal and thought that this might be a good chance to learn more.

"I understand, that your roads are no longer safe, sir?" he ventured.

"Whatever gives you that idea?" replied the soldier, clearly affronted by such a suggestion.

"I did not mean to be rude," apologised Dathram. "But your governor was telling me you have some problems with the Israelites, particularly a man called Samson."

"Oh yes, that bloody nuisance," replied the soldier. "But we will catch him soon, we have a clever plan to trap him."

"Oh, so it will all be safe then?" asked Dathram.

"I certainly hope so," said the soldier. "Because he has been brewing some devilry. Or at least it probably stems from him."

"Tell me more?" persisted Dathram. "You see, I am a merchant who travels a lot, often with expensive goods, so I like to know if I can expect any trouble."

"Well, there have been some strange happenings of late," the soldier continued. "Only last month when I was travelling on the road back here from our northern garrison at Beth-Shan, the bloody Israelites stole one of our chariots, but not the horses. At least we think it was them. We sent out a small force to the town that we suspected, but now even that seems to have disappeared.

To a large extent that was most of the information that Dathram could gather. So he said nothing about what he was trying to do, as he considered the wisest option was to wait until his return journey from Egypt, perhaps things would have sorted themselves out by then. Or could this be Ruben's doing? he mused to himself, after learning what he had done in Ashkilon, and of his escapades with Joself, the lad seemed capable of most things. He decided that he would definitely wait and set out on the final lap of his journey the next morning.

****

The wedding had been a splendid occasion and was enjoyed by everybody. The festivities were still in full swing when Ruben finally managed to get Naomi on her own.

"Let the party continue without us," suggested Ruben. "We can slip out the back way and go to my house."

"My husband, what are you suggesting?" enquired Naomi with an impish smile.

"You will see," replied Ruben, as he half dragged, half carried Naomi out the back way from her parents' home.

Before long they were in Ruben's still unfinished house, making ardent love under the half finished roof, and it was there that Ezekiel roused them only a short while later. As Ruben came to the door with just a towel hastily wrapped around his waist, ready to give the interpreter a clout, his annoyance turned to surprise when he opened the persistently rapped-on door to be confronted by Ezekiel, accompanied by a young lad.

"I am terribly sorry to trouble you, my boy, but this lad would not leave me alone until I had woken you," apologised Ezekiel.

# 24

## SAMSON'S FATE

Samson had at last decided that he could wait no longer and had slipped away from the festivities at virtually the same time as Ruben and Naomi. He had been in such a rush to return to his lover that he would not have even noticed the carefully hidden trench, which contained the brushwood and oil. It could have been left open and he would still have crossed without noticing. He also paid no attention to the watchers and the young lad whom he almost tripped over before going down into the valley to meet Delilah and his possible fate. As soon as Samson was inside the door, the watchers had sent the lad dashing back to Sabasti, running as fast as his legs and breathing would allow, as if Lucifer himself were behind him with a pronged trident, trying to stab his backside. He ran, as he had been directed, to Ezekiel's house and demanded that Ezekiel take him to see Ruben.

Ruben stood staring uncomprehending at Ezekiel and the boy. He shook his head, as if trying to rationalise them in his surroundings. All of a sudden, things fell into place and his immediate reaction to Samson was, 'Let the bastard fry.' Rationality then regained control and he said to Ezekiel, "Go and find Saul and Mischa, tell them to rouse all the trainees. They are to meet me by the armoury as soon as possible. It is urgent." He turned and ran back into the bedroom, as Naomi sat up in bed, naked and glistening with sweat.

"What is it, my beloved?" she asked Ruben, who was swiftly getting dressed. "What is happening?" she persisted.

"Your Uncle Samson is doing what we were," he replied, slipping on his jerkin and weapons. "I am sorry, my dearest, but starting our family will have to wait." He leaned over and kissed her tenderly and was then gone, snatching the key to the armoury as he went. When he reached the armoury, he saw Saul and Mischa running to meet him.

"Chose a great time, the randy old sod," complained Saul.

"No worse than the rest of us!" said Mischa. "You were trying to get your leg over that little tart, Rebecca."

"Not as bad as you with Trieste," laughed Saul, making an explicit gesture with his fingers.

"All right lads, calm down and let's get moving," snapped Ruben. "Mischa, go and get those thirty old wine skins that I put under the table in the eating area and get them filled with water and issued to the lads." He then turned to Saul and ordered him, "Start issuing the weapons. All the men are then to meet as soon as possible where the watchers are in the trees overlooking the valley of Sorek. I will meet you all there, come fast but not noisily." With that he ran off towards the western gate.

The watchers were amazed to see him so quickly, as he came running up the hill, trying to blow his customary warning signal with gasping lungs.

"Lord above!" said one of the watchers. "You must have flown!"

"Not really," explained Ruben, still panting. "But I do know every stone on the road between here and Sabasti by now. What is happening in the valley?"

"There seem to be two or three Philistines pouring oil onto the sand covering the trenches," said the other watcher.

"Right, just keep watch and let me know as soon as anything else happens," instructed Ruben, as he went and removed the cover off the ladder planking, which he brought over and then returned dragging the chariot, which he had uncovered. He was then joined by the rest of the men, who came up the hill as fast as they could, every second man bringing a full goatskin of water. Many of them still wondering with amazement what he was doing with the chariot and the ladder gangplank, which he laid on top of the chariot. The Manuel twins, who had aided him in capturing the chariot, assisted him in his work.

"Where the bloody heck did that come from?" demanded Saul.

"Well, it's on loan actually," answered Ruben. "But the Philistines were somewhat reluctant to let us have it," he grinned at the two brothers who had helped him. They soon assembled everything to his satisfaction, and hung twenty of the old wineskins, some of which were already leaking, on the ladder racks. He carefully positioned the chariot, telling the twins to take the horses' positions and himself taking the rear. He ordered Mischa and Saul to fan out on both sides when the Philistines sprang their trap, which he explained.

"You've got it all worked out haven't you?" exclaimed Saul in admiration.

"Yes, well I hope so," returned Ruben. "With luck it will work, otherwise Samson will turn into a large charred steak." He detailed six of the men to carry additional goatskins and had the four remaining goatskins emptied over the chariot and ladder gangplanks, so all was dripping wet. Just as the sun rose in the valley below them, shortly after the Philistines had disappeared behind other cover, Delilah's door opened and Samson came out yawning, with Delilah at his side, carrying a lamp.

"I had better be back in Sabasti before I am missed," said Samson as he yawned again.

"I will come with you as far as the bridge to light your way," she offered.

"There is no need for that, my little one, as it is now sunrise and I am not yet blind, ho, ho! But come with me if you wish so that I can give you a final squeeze," which he did, and half carried her with him. He let her go at the edge of the bridge over the wadi and without looking down stepped on to the bridge saying, "I will be back to see you in a couple of days. Goodbye, my little nymph."

It seemed to Ruben and the others in the shadow of the trees, that Delilah reached down to her feet and pulled a rope, at the same time flinging the lamp onto the brushwood. However, it was early morning when everything is grey and eyesight can easily be fooled, therefore no one could be definite. She was also half shielded by Samson's great bulk as he bounded over the bridge. Everything happened at that moment, the bridge collapsed and from the wadi a sheet of flame sprang up from the oiled brushwood immediately behind Samson. He wheeled around but was blown back by the blast of hot air and as he staggered back the flames spread along the wadi in both directions. Then, as the loosely buried brushwood under oiled sand sprang into fire, the sides of the U-shaped trench, containing those combustible materials, leapt into flame. Realising his plight, but not knowing the reason for it, Samson ran towards the end of the U. Much to his horror, the flaming ground spread faster than he could run and the two sides of the U met, encircling him in flame. He could see no way of escape and as he watched the mysteriously burning ground, the sunken pots of oil began to explode, turning the fire into an inferno. The heat was so intense that his hair began to singe but, as happens on such occasions, unrealised by the Philistines who had emerged from their hiding places to watch him burn, he collapsed through lack of oxygen. Fortunately, where he collapsed a few of the surrounding stones, which littered the valley floor, protected his flesh from being charred. The watching Philistines, who numbered about forty, were astonished to see a contraption, balanced on a chariot, come hurtling down from the trees, drawn by two men who suddenly peeled off to either side at the command of a large man pushing the chariot from behind. Ruben gave the contraption a final heave and watched it continue in gathering speed until it finally crashed through the flaming sand covering the brushwood. The old wineskins full of water began exploding as the flames heated the water. The water doused the flames, but then became steam due to the intense heat. Ruben continued his charge and leapt through the steam into the furnace beyond. There was no air to breathe, but with a final effort he locked his arms under Samson's huge shoulders and dragged him backwards to the leather gangplanks. He was suddenly refreshed as the six extra wineskins were thrown into the steam cloud and burst sending a fine spray of cool water and fresh air over him.

"Give me a hand," he shouted through the spray, and the two Manuel brothers ran to his assistance, each lifting one of the huge legs of Samson's inert body, which they carried over the gangplanks for a few more paces into safety, before collapsing. The astonished Philistines, deprived of their fun, were then attacked on both sides by Saul and Mischa's men, who forced them back towards the flaming trenches.

More Philistines came over the wadi on a hastily erected makeshift bridge, which spanned the wadi to the right of the affray. Mischa's men had cut down the Philistines on the left and rushed to the aid of Saul's party that was being attacked from behind. With a Samson-like bellow, a revived Ruben joined the melee, swinging his large sword, which decapitated his first Philistine adversary. He was there, taking on opponents who streamed over the makeshift bridge amid the welter of blood and death that surrounded them. The stream of Philistines crossing the makeshift bridge soon checked and drew back, as they saw the fate of their comrades who were being cut to ribbons by a large blood-covered warlord who wielded in his right hand a large shining sword which cut through shield and body armour alike. This formidable warrior also had a short sword in his left hand, which created almost as much damage. They hastily abandoned the bridge and were soon running back to their chariots. Those Philistines who had crossed were soon despatched by the fierce and terrible wrath of Ruben's men. The Israelites stripped the Philistines and flung their bodies into the still burning ditch. The steaming chariot was miraculously still working, although badly charred and twisted. It was hauled up the valley carrying the still inert but breathing Samson, who lay amid the captured weapons of the Philistines. Ruben, who was drenched in blood, was the last to leave the Vale of Carnage, which was the name then given to the valley of Sorek. The Israelites had five dead, who they carried on litters back to Sabasti, where they were to be buried with great honour.

They arrived back in Sabasti around mid-morning, to find the town rather hungover from the previous day's festivities. Those who greeted the weary warriors were mainly youngsters, who gave them a great cheer, as it had been a resounding victory for the new army. They went directly to their training ground, where the captured haul of weapons was locked into the armoury, and their own dead were reverentially laid in state on tables brought out from the dining area. Naomi was appalled by Ruben's appearance, but he assured her that as he had both arms and both legs all with the correct number of digits, the blood had merely come from his adversaries. Her appeal to him to immediately wash was rejected, in favour of his ensuring that Samson was well looked after.

"Take him to father's house," she suggested. "My mother and sisters will care for him." The chariot was wheeled back to Ezekiel's house, where Naomi's mother met them with great consternation, demanding to know what had happened to Samson.

"He has suffered greatly, but as you can see is still alive," Ruben told them. He then went on to try to explain the horrors of the trap that the Philistines had prepared. "I would never have let him walk into such a trap had I realised how terrible it was in there."

"It was his own fault for going to see that treacherous bitch," cut in Saul.

"But I should have warned Samson," apologised Ruben. "It was like being in an oven, there was no air to breathe. I only pray that he is not deranged when he recovers."

"We don't need him now," said Saul. "We have a great army, or at least the beginnings of a great army. We killed many of them and sustained so few casualties." His face was alight with triumph.

"Did you see the corpses that were stripped?" objected Ruben. "Many of them were senior ranking officials, their armour and weapons were mainly for decoration, that was why they were beaten so easily. The soldiers who attacked your party from behind were more experienced troops and could fight."

"Yes, but we soon saw them off," crowed Saul. He went away with some of the other soldiers, accepting the cheering from the crowd.

Ruben said nothing, although he had been the prime cause of the Philistine withdrawal. He turned back to Ezekiel and asked, "Please keep me informed of how he recovers." He then allowed Naomi to lead him back to their own home, where she told him to undress and carefully washed him down from head to foot. The hair on his forearms had been burnt off completely and his shoulders were slightly burnt. Some of the hair on his head was singed and had to be cut off and although, as he had said, the blood was mainly from his adversaries, there were quite a few smaller wounds on his arms and legs, which had been inflicted by his enemies. When she came to wash his private parts, he requested that she did not linger as he was very tired, and she led him to the bed where he collapsed, falling asleep before she could put a pillow beneath his head. He slept for the rest of that day and half the next. When he awoke, he found her sitting beside his bed, carefully changing the dressings that she had put on his wounds.

"Good morning, my dear, or should I say good afternoon," she smiled down at him. "Promise me now that you will not give me such a fright again."

"I will certainly try not to," he answered, "More than that, I cannot promise. Now, tell me how Samson is faring?"

"Mother says he is mending, but he has not regained consciousness yet, so we do not really know how grievously he has been affected. You mustn't blame yourself, from what many of the men are saying, even the Philistines were shocked by the furnace that they created. Will you take some refreshment and we can then go and see him if you like?"

"Yes, I am ravenous."

"So what else is new?" she laughed. "If you wait here, I will go and bring something to eat." He did not have long to wait, as she soon returned with a tray of freshly baked bread, which she lavishly coated with honey.

After he had eaten all that she had cooked, which she told him should last for a week, they went to her father's house and were greeted by Ezekiel himself, who said, before they could ask, "There is no change, I am afraid." Regardless of that, Ruben insisted on going to the room that Samson occupied. Ruben was pleased to see that he was well cared for, with clean bandages on his burns, and he was snoring regularly.

"Did I see some herb leaves, of dark green, growing by the pond to the rear of your house?" he asked his mother-in-law.

"Yes," she replied. "But I don't know what they are or how they came to be there."

"They are a fairly common marshland plant, probably brought by a bird," he explained, then asked Naomi to go and pick some of the leaves and bring them to him with some hot water. When she returned with the leaves, he crushed them between his thumb and fingers, onto which he poured hot water. The room was full of a sweet aromatic scent and, after a while, Samson began to stir.

In answer to her mother's quizzical look, Naomi said, "It is all right, mother, Ruben knows what he is doing, you see, his father was a doctor in the marshlands."

"Oohh!" groaned Samson. "Where am I, is my hair and beard burnt?"

"Only a little, Judge," Ezekiel said.

"Do not worry," said Naomi. "I can soon cut away the burnt bits."

"No, you must not do that," shouted Samson, sitting up. "It is against the will of the Lord."

"Well, he does not seem so bad after all," laughed Ruben, as he left the room, leaving Naomi's mother to tell Samson how he came to be there.

During their walk back home, Naomi told Ruben, "You really must have some time off to fully recover."

"That is what I would like to do," agreed Ruben. "The basic training has been completed, as well as needing time to recover, I must finish our house. I can leave Saul and Mischa to practice with the chariots because I have never used one myself. The main situation is really one that the town's elders must decide."

"What exactly do you mean?" asked Naomi.

"The situation is this," Ruben explained. "What we have built is a training ground, not an army barracks. The object was to convince the elders that we need an army, not whether that army, if they decide we need it, should be based here. Do you follow my argument?"

"Oh yes, I can follow your reasoning," she replied. "And possibly you wish to keep this as a training ground?"

"Right again," he replied. "Training I like, but although everybody tells me that I am good with weapons, I do not really like killing people," he shrugged. "But nobody seems concerned about my wishes."

"I am," she stressed most strongly. "I do not want you being repeatedly injured or possibly killed." This they both agreed upon and Naomi suggested they ask her father to put this suggestion before the elders, saying, "Sabasti should be retained as a training camp, with you in charge."

"Yes," agreed Ruben. "Let Saul have his army, they can live elsewhere and probably will have to do so, as they will have to keep on the move, certainly until they are very much larger."

They had, by this time reached their home and she was full of ideas of what they would do in each room, including plenty of space for children. "Speaking of which, let us go to bed and continue our attempts to start a family," suggested Ruben.

"But it is only late afternoon and I am not tired," she protested.

"All the more reason why we should," he exclaimed, leading her, unresisting, into the bedroom.

Over the next few days they asked Ezekiel to put the plan before the town's elders, with the addition that the training base be made part of the town by turning the wooden fence into a solid wall. Ruben also requested that he should be in charge of the training ground, rather than lead the army, as many people had suggested. This Ezekiel told him was a sound idea and it would have his undoubted backing. Any army that was formed would probably have to be constantly on the move, until it was far larger and the land established as their own, which the Lord had promised. Further, he promised Ruben that he would receive an answer after the next meeting of the elders, which would be in two day's time.

Ruben had almost completed the roof of their house and promised Naomi that if the agreed proposal was given, they could extend the house to the other side of the old town wall into the new area, which would give Ruben direct access to the training ground. He then mentioned, "Before I forget, I promised a special meal to the beggars who acted as watchers over the valley of Sorek, to which I also invited the three lads who had to convey the knowledge of Samson's arrival."

"That was most considerate of you, perhaps you might have asked me first?" she said, jokingly admonishing him.

"Do as you are told woman!" he replied, imitating Samson's growl. "Or I will put you across my knee." At which she fled into the kitchen, returning after a little while to request that Samson should also be invited, "That is a good idea, it would be nice to invite him as he was the unwitting key member of the whole escapade."

"Let us make invitations for the day after the meeting of the town's elders," Naomi suggested. "I hope we will have the agreement to celebrate as well."

The day arrived, with Ezekiel telling them first thing in the morning that the plan had been unanimously agreed upon, and in addition Ruben had been invited onto the elder's council, which was totally unexpected. His protestations of 'being too young to be an elder', were brushed aside by Ezekiel, who told him that it was about time they had some young blood on the town's governing council. This gave the dinner party an air of festivity into which Samson joined, arriving carrying the two watchers, who were lame brothers who had decided to stop begging for a living and offer their services as town lookouts. The evening was a great success and the watchers, as well as the boys who had been the runners, were all amazed that Ruben helped Naomi to serve the meal. The evening was almost over when there was a loud hammering on Ruben's door. It was opened to admit an intoxicated Saul.

"I suppose you want all the weapons, as well as kicking us out," shouted Saul, as he lurched into the room.

Ruben was about to explain when Samson stood up, walked round in front of Saul, bodily picked him up and literally threw him out of the house, bellowing, "You mind your manners when you speak to a member of the Elder's Council," adding afterwards. "A fine leader of our army you will be."

From that time on, there was no love lost between Saul and Samson. Saul was given all the weapons, as well as the chariots by Ruben, who also gave him plenty of time to vacate the training ground and set up a temporary camp a little way beyond the town's western gate. However, this ended Saul's friendship with Ruben, which Ruben had to admit was always strained at the best of times.

The work on the new walls had begun and there was going to be a short delay until Ruben's new intake of trainees could start. Sensing this fine opportunity, Naomi suggested that she and Ruben go away for a few days to see her elderly relations in Jericho, which she told Ruben was in the Jordan valley just north of the salt sea, which he really must visit. Their short absence from the town was accordingly planned.

As they left their house, heading towards the east, Naomi told Ruben, "The journey is all downhill, as the Jordan valley is very low and far beneath the level of the sea to the west." Jericho was always hot, and was often called the city of palms. It was lovely at this time of year when there were plenty of dates, as well as grapes that flourished in the valley. She went on to explain to Ruben that the salt sea was a strange place, in which he could swim, but not in the normal way and should simply lie in the water that would not let him sink.

"I never sink at the worst of times," he laughed. "It sounds fascinating, are there any fish in the salt sea?"

"I do not think so, there is nothing, absolutely nothing," she emphasised. "That, I believe, is why it is also called the Dead Sea."

"How far is it from Jericho?" he asked.

"You can easily walk it in less than half a day, or in your case you may be able to run there, but do keep close to the river, which you can drink as it is fresh water, like Lake Kinneret from where the river begins. But it is very hot in the valley, and do not drink the water when you get near the sea as it is terribly salty. Also, you must not get the water in your eyes as it will sting."

"It is not surprising that there are no fish, it does not sound such good fun after all, even though it sounds well worth the visit."

They were soon on the edge of the valley, which dropped down below them alarmingly steeply; it was a sight that Ruben was totally unprepared for. The valley was wide, although you could see the opposite valley walls, which were both of a reddish brown and contrasted sharply with the varying shades of green vegetation that bordered the sides of the River Jordan that wound, like a snake, in great loops, doubling back on itself.

"That really is incredible!" announced Ruben who was quite awestruck. He pointed away to his right, to where there seemed a darker green in the hazy valley. "Is that Jericho down there?" he asked.

"Yes, that is where we are headed," she replied. "But we must keep to the high ground, until we come to just above Jericho, where there is an easier way down into the valley. Apart from which, there is often more of a breeze up here."

"Let's get going then, it all sounds and looks so fantastic, I must have a closer look."

"Can we wait for just a short break, I am not feeling too well this morning," she said, sitting in the shade of a tree.

He stared down at her for a long time saying nothing, until she finally looked up at him, her green eyes, with yellow flecks, meeting his bright piercing blue eyes. "Am I going to be a father?" he asked.

"I am not sure yet, but I think so," she said quietly, smiling up at him.

"But this time we are going down, so I am sure that everything will be fine. Oh, you are wonderful," he laughed, kissed her and said, "This is possibly the most wonderful day I have ever experienced!"

She had absolutely no idea what he was talking about, but his joy was so infectious that she too was soon laughing and in a short while she felt a lot better, so they moved on above the valley heading south.

They finally arrived in the early evening. Although it was not far, there were two reasons for their delay. First, they were in no hurry and Ruben kept stopping to look down into the valley at the mysterious and fascinating sights below. The blue-greenish river and its tortuous progress, as well as the distant hazy salt sea shimmering in the heat haze, set in its harsh volcanic surroundings. Secondly, when they started descending into the valley, it seemed to get warmer and warmer with every step they descended. When they reached Jericho, they were both bathed in sweat. Ruben also asked why a well-trampled pathway circled the town and there was still a lot of rubble around what appeared to be fairly new walls, at least they were not as old as many of the buildings.

Naomi laughed and said, "You will have to ask my Uncle Jonah. He loves to tell people about what happened. He is now very old as you know and was only a young boy when they arrived and captured the town."

When they arrived, they were greeted by a shriek of delight from Naomi's old aunt who was incredibly pleased to see Naomi so soon after the wedding. Over the meal that evening, Ruben was fascinated by Uncle Jonah's story, which he said was exactly what happened. That night it took them a long time to get used to the humidity, which was far greater than Ruben had ever experienced. There was no damp mist like in the marshlands.

The next day Ruben realised one of the reasons why the rubble had not been cleared away, as it was so hot in Jericho, the pace of life was conducted at a far slower rate. It was two days before Ruben could get away to visit the salt sea, as Naomi's aunt kept telling them that there was no rush and that they could stay for as long as they wished. But she kept finding lots of little jobs that needed doing, which of course Ruben was pleased to do, as they seemed so happy to have their company. However, when he did get away he left Naomi chatting to her aunt and he went on his own wandering along the river, at intervals swimming some of the way, wading in the shallows. Finally he arrived and discovered that everything Naomi had told him was correct. He lay on his back in the water, even putting heavy stones on his stomach to try to make him float less high, or even sink into the water. He managed it once but found the effect of keeping his eyes closed very unnerving. He did once get some in his eyes and had to wash his eyes out with fresh water to stop them smarting. It was nightfall before he returned and found that he was extremely hungry, but he slept well that night.

He insisted on returning a few days later with Naomi for a whole day, leaving as soon as the sky began to pale towards the east before the sun had risen. They walked hand in hand along the edge of the sea, which Ruben realised was no wider than Lake Kinneret although it was a lot longer. They walked along completely naked as although it was hot, it was not the blistering heat of Lagash in high summer and of the marshlands. It was very pleasant when they became used to it, when they came to a freshwater spring that came out of the cliffs to the west of the sea and tumbled down through a series of rock pools. He delighted in deepening the pools by building rock dams from flat stones from the pools. Naomi laughed at him and said he was like a little boy playing in the water, but enjoyed bathing in the fresh water when they had been floating in the sea, allowing them to wash away all the salt from their bodies, which dried hard on the skin if left and also became itchy and sticky in the hair. It was late before they returned and they realised when they approached the town that they had not seen anybody else all day.

They finally insisted on leaving, having stayed for longer than they originally intended, but had to promise the old people that they would return, probably at the end of next summer. They arrived back in Sabasti much refreshed, to discover that the new town wall had been completed and the training ground finished, but were shocked and could not believe their ears when they were told that Samson had been captured when he had visited the valley of Sorek.

Ruben demanded to know how it had happened and was told that only a small patrol had captured him. He had been led away in chains as meekly as a lamb from Delilah's house, as she watched him depart, laughing at his cropped hair and beard. Ezekiel and all the elders were most concerned and asked Ruben to raise the army into action, as they did not seem worried.

Ruben barged over to the army encampment and demanded to see Saul, who steadfastly refused to raise a force of men, even though Ruben grabbed him by the hair and lifted him off the ground and stared into his dark eyes, threatening to beat him to a pulp.

After he dropped the shrieking man, Saul said, "Raise your own force, you ask the men and see how many will come with you. He would not believe that the bitch betrayed him, despite everyone saying what they saw."

Ruben did just that, but found that when he asked, the only people who offered to come with him were the Manuel twins. When nobody else came forward, he put his hands on their shoulders and said, "Thank you for offering, but it would be impossible for the three of us." He returned to Ezekiel to tell him the sad news, but said, "I will go myself to see if there is any possibility of rescuing him."

Naomi said, "Do be careful Ruben, please remember your responsibilities."

Ezekiel echoed this sentiment saying, "His arrogance has probably upset many of the young men and from what Naomi told me, you yourself had to be restrained from using your sword when he was at your mercy."

"Yes, that is true," replied Ruben. "But I would not be where I am today without him, apart from which, your people owe him their freedom."

"There is not much you can do tonight," Naomi insisted. "Let us go home and if you must leave you can go first thing in the morning."

"Where did they take Samson?" asked Ruben, addressing Ezekiel. "Presumably to Beth-Shan."

"No Ruben, I am afraid not," said Ezekiel despairingly. "They have taken him to Gaza, where they will probably make an exhibition of his execution."

That night Ruben was restless. What should have been a happy homecoming, full of happy memories of their time in Jericho and at the salt sea were forgotten. Naomi awoke before dawn to find the bed next to her was empty, in a moment of panic she thought that Ruben had left, but then noticed him standing by the window. She rose from bed and came to him, put her arms around his neck and laid her head on his chest saying, "Please do not do anything stupid, I could not bear to lose you."

"That I promise," he replied. "Yet I have to make an effort, not so much for my sake, but I think the Lord expects it."

"It will be light soon, let me go and prepare some food for you to take on the journey," she offered and disappeared out of the room and could then be heard in the kitchen. Ruben got dressed, strapping on all his weapons and by the time he was ready to leave, Naomi returned with a small knapsack with ample food for at least two days.

Ruben trotted out of the western gate, bypassing the army camp, following the road that the Philistine force had used when they came to investigate. He pressed on until he finally reached the main road that ran between Gaza and Beth-Shan. By now, the sun had risen and he made his way to the small hillside that overlooked the road, from where they had previously ambushed the Philistine patrol and captured the chariot that they used to rescue Samson. He sat on the hilltop, watching the road, while he started on the provisions that Naomi had hastily prepared. He was considering how ironic it was that his life had finally found some order, he was beginning to really enjoy life and was getting back in harmony with nature and everything that The Creator had provided. He was hoping to once again experience the sight of the aura that surrounds a person, the trick that Simeon had taught him all those years previously in the marshlands. He knew, however, that he had witnessed and caused too much bloodshed to attempt it now, still, perhaps next year, when he and Naomi had returned from Jericho, this time taking their new baby with them. And he realised that he must keep that thought in the back of his mind to make it come true.

He noticed, away to the northeast, a large party of Philistines on the way to where they had originally been ambushed. He quietly moved down behind the rocks to where he hoped that he would be able to overhear some of their conversation. The party of Philistines made sure that they were all together when they entered the narrow gorge and here the leading chariot stopped. The commanding officer climbed down from the chariot and went to the party behind him. This party, surrounded by soldiers, contained a few other presumably important people, who were riding on donkeys. Ruben noticed that one of them was Delilah, he had to compose himself to stop him impaling her with his javelin. A quick clean death is too good for that bitch, he thought as he listened to what the commanding officer was saying.

"This is the spot where they ambushed the chariot that they used to rescue Samson from the fire trap. But how they got it back over the road I have no idea, we could easily see the chariot marks leading after the horses."

A new voice then spoke, "Samson told me that they had been led by a new warrior."

"That must be the big man who killed so many of our men in the valley of Sorek, after you had so nicely completed your task, Delilah," said the commander. "He is obviously a fine, skilful soldier, with plenty of brains, but he is only a normal man, unlike Samson, who you tell us came from their God, our men simply froze in terror at the mention of his name." The commander climbed back into his chariot and the party moved off towards Gaza.

Ruben had heard Ezekiel say, "The Lord works in mysterious ways, his wonders to perform," and considered that he may be being used by the Lord.

Ruben shadowed the party all the way to Gaza, which took the best part of the day, but was unable to get close enough to overhear any further conversation. The party had entered the gates of the city, which were well guarded and ran round the city from the harbour wall that jutted out into the sea, very much like that of Lagash, which formed a harbour. Realising that there was probably a southern gate, as well as an eastern gate, Ruben made his way around the city, seeking an entrance. The eastern gateway, that looked towards Hebron was also well guarded and everything coming in or out was carefully investigated. He made his way south to the southern gate and was dismayed to find the guards were there as well, although they were not as vigilant. He was sitting behind some boulders, surrounded by blackberry bushes, when he spotted a large merchant coming along the road leading four mules, all of whom were heavily burdened. He realised he knew the merchant and, as the merchant drew near, he called out to him. "Dathram, stop for a moment and come to join me."

Dathram recognised the voice instantly and he hobbled the leading mule and went to the last mule, making a display of inspecting the mule's hoof. "Is it really you, Ruben?" he called back.

"Yes, it most certainly is. I presume that you received my scroll, from Joself, advising you of how to make your way to Egypt."

"That is correct," replied Dathram. "It was good of you to send that message."

"Can you help smuggle me into the city?" Ruben requested.

"I will, if I can," replied Dathram. "It is the least I can do, but I am not sure how, as you see the gates are guarded and everything is inspected. You are far too big to be done up like a parcel and put on my mules," he laughed.

"I have an idea. Can you pass over a jar and wait a few moments?" Dathram did as Ruben requested and spent the next few moments inspecting his mules. A large black man emerged from behind the boulders, covered in only a loincloth, with a turban wrapped around his head, which on close inspection had been his shift. Ruben had covered his body in blackberry juice and said, "If you go behind the boulders with some wrapping and bundle up my weapons and Jerkin, you can pretend I am a Nubian slave you are taking to Timon."

"Just keep your head down, as the guards will know you are an impostor if they see your eyes," Dathram laughed, thinking it was preposterous enough to succeed.

Dathram led his mules and the large Nubian slave, who did not look up from the road, when the guards by the gate inspected Dathram's baggage. After questioning him about where he had been and what he was doing, they finally allowed him, his mules and his Nubian slave into Gaza.

The sun sank into the sea like a huge orange globe, reflecting rays of golden light that shone from Ruben's black skin, enhancing his muscular body. Dathram could not be seen chatting to a Nubian slave, so he led the mules followed by the slave to the inn that he had stayed in on his way to Egypt earlier in the year. He arranged with the innkeeper to stable his mules where the Nubian slave would also sleep. He went behind the inn and went inside the stable, where nobody was watching, and finally asked Ruben, "Can you tell me what this is all about?"

Ruben said, "It is a long story, but basically the Philistines have captured a friend of mine and I wish to see if I can help him to escape."

"You would be surprised at how much I know. Is this the giant that has caused a great many problems for the Philistines?" Dathram replied.

Surprised that Dathram knew so much, Ruben asked him, "Have you any idea where he will be held prisoner?"

"He is probably being held in the cells below the great amphitheatre. That is where they hold prisoners that are waiting to be publicly executed. I can show you exactly where it is later tonight when you can move along the street in the shadows. Now then, Ruben, I have a proper turban that is of black silk, which will look better as a covering to your light hair. Hang on a moment and I will bring it out to you and safely fasten it, then you can help me unload the mules and tell me just what is going on in this land. I know a lot of your story from Latich, who now works for me, and also from Commander Mithrandir at Ashkilon and also from your friend Joself." He lifted his finger to cut short Ruben's surprised interruption before continuing. "You see I have also learned a lot from the Lord Coronus and your good friend Druselus. Even right up to when you turned inland from Mount Carmel when I spoke to Amos, that is when I had to leave your trail to continue down the coast."

After removing Ruben's shift, Dathram tied the silk turban onto his head. Standing back in admiration of his work he said, "I can now pass you off as a Nubian Prince," at which he laughed merrily. Whilst they unloaded the mules, Dathram also said, "I was sorry to learn of the death of Lialah, she was such a nice girl."

"Thank you, Dathram," acknowledged Ruben. "But I have now a new wife who is possibly more beautiful and is wonderful."

It was Dathram's turn to be shocked and he replied, "My word you do not hang around."

"No, I suppose not," said Ruben. "But what is this about Latich working for you?"

"Ah, that is another long story," replied Dathram. "To cut it short, you are now looking at Babylon's Ambassador to Egypt, and Latich works for me. He is also married to that girl Miriam, to whom you gave a message to deliver."

"So I did," remembered Ruben recalling his words. "I thought she would be good for him, but now you tell me that he has left the army and works for you." They continued talking, bringing each other to up to date on what had been happening as they finished unloading the mules. After this, Ruben said, "You had better go and eat at the inn, and see what you can find out. But then come back later this evening on the pretext of checking your animals and then going out for a stroll before going to bed, during which time you can take me to where they are probably holding my friend Samson."

"Do you want me to bring you any food?" inquired Dathram.

"No, do not bother," replied Ruben. "My wife made me bring some food with me."

Dathram went to the inn, promising to return later. Ruben unpacked his weapons, continued dressing and rearmed before setting down and eating a little more food, but not a great deal as he always remembered Lieutenant Abzher's comments about hunger sharpening the wits.

True to his word, Dathram returned late in the evening, with interesting news. "There is going to be a great show tomorrow, when the Philistines are going to execute your friend, Samson. They told me it will be quite a spectacle and they hope to torment him before they kill him slowly. It sounds gruesome and they invited me, which I declined, saying that I did not have the stomach for that sort of thing."

"If you could get me into the place, I will try to alter the arrangements." They left the stables and skirted round the back of the inn and Dathram led them to the amphitheatre, the cells being heavily guarded. "There does not seem to be a way I can slip in there," Ruben whispered. "Let us try the main entrance to the public gallery." They went round to the main entrance, and here there was only one guard on duty. "Try to get him to show you around, so that I can slip in unobserved."

Dathram went over to the guard and said, "Good evening, my fine fellow. I wonder if you can show me what they intend doing tomorrow? I am fascinated but unfortunately I am leaving by boat early tomorrow morning and will miss the fun."

The guard was getting lonely and welcomed the opportunity to show someone round. He led Dathram in through a small side gate, which Dathram left slightly opened. The guard took pleasure in giving Dathram a guided tour of the place, oblivious to the large dark figure that slipped in the gate quietly behind them. The guard was overheard by Ruben as he showed Dathram the main pillars under the public gallery, where all the important watchers had reserved seats. The guard explained that they would lead Samson out beneath the pillars into the main auditorium and then went on to explain the horrors that they had planned. Dathram followed the guard as he explained, with the occasional, "Fascinating," and then, "Serves him right," and similar observations. Finally he went back with the guard out of the gate, thanking the man for his courtesy. This left Ruben, who now looked round the vast stadium with the knowledge of where the cells were. Before making his way to the cells, he had a good look at the public gallery. With his knowledge of building he could see that the whole structure was based upon two large pillars that formed the entrance from the cells.

He went down the corridor that led from the auditorium and followed it round as it turned to the right. There were brackets on the walls every twenty paces, which held an illuminating torch of flickering flame. Here the tunnel reached a T-junction with an illuminated passage going right, that led up a flight of stairs. There was another passage leading down another flight to the left, this was not illuminated. It seemed obvious that the dungeons were to the left, with the other passage leading to the guards' quarters. Standing quietly in the shadows, Ruben could faintly hear the tumble of dice and muffled laughter from the passage to the right, which confirmed his assumption. He turned left and went down the flight of stairs, where there was an overpowering rank odour of human excretion and vermin infestation. There was now no light so he took his javelin and used the blunt end as a blind man uses his walking stick. His faint tapping noises were soon lost amid the growls and occasional rattle of chains coming from those incarcerated in this evil place, overlaid by the scurrying and squeaking of rats plus the soft murmur of insects in the straw bedding. He could also hear, high above, the sound of patrolling footsteps and the faint muttered conversation of the guards outside the cells. He felt sure that Samson would be kept in a special chamber in the deepest and most secure part of the prison, so he continued past the other cells and came to another turn to the right and another flight of steps, which led deeper below the amphitheatre. There was another flaming torch in a wall-bracket, which showed the bars of yet another cell and a wide illuminated area that contained a table and a chair, on which the large form of a jailer sat. This grotesque creature was barely human and took occasional swigs from a stone jar, whilst occasionally throwing pebbles at a huge form that whimpered and yelled as it was repeatedly struck. The jailer guffawed with delight every time one of his missiles struck and produced more pain from his target. The huge creature that was the target was obviously Samson, although Ruben could not make out the shape clearly in the flickering half light, neither could he understand why Samson was undergoing this, but something had to be done immediately. He did not want to give the jailer a chance to alert the other guards and neither did he want blood everywhere. Remembering Lialah's death, he took careful aim at the jailer's ear and threw the javelin with adequate but not excessive force. As the jailer was in good light and only ten paces away, Ruben's throw was unerringly accurate and he fell dead on the ground with the javelin quivering upright from the skull where it penetrated through the ear. Ruben went and took the torch from its bracket on the wall; from here he went nearer to Samson's cage, throwing light directly into the huge man's face. He recoiled from shock, as if struck in the face. Samson had turned in his direction at the sound of his footsteps, no sight could be seen by those hideous gouged eye sockets. Samson had been blinded, his eyes brutally gouged out leaving a ghastly mask of a face half caked in dried blood. Ruben's fears of not being recognised were groundless and even if he could get Samson out of the cage, trying to take him back to Sabasti would be a formidable task. But then, remembering what the guard who gave Dathram the guided tour had said, and remembering the pillars supporting the gallery, an idea materialised in his mind. Trying to avert his eyes from Samson's hideous face, he called out, "Samson, it is I, your friend, Ruben."

At least Samson's hearing had not been harmed and he replied immediately, "Oh, Ruben, they have blinded me as well as taking away my strength. It was that bitch, Delilah. Why did I not listen to you?" he sobbed. Or what would have been a sob, had he had any eyes to cry from.

"Samson, the Lord will give you back your strength," Ruben told him emphatically.

"No, he will not," replied Samson sadly, shaking his head. "For I have sinned and disobeyed him, because Delilah cut my hair and beard."

"But I know he will," pleaded Ruben. "He has led me directly to you and showed me what he wants you to do. Only you could perform this task, which requires incredible strength."

"Do not mock me, Ruben, I cannot even break this flimsy chain holding my hands," he held up the narrow bronze chain holding his wrists.

"They have fooled you, Samson, because you cannot see there are other chains holding your arms. Wait a moment while I come over." He went over, first drawing back the large bolts that secured the door and entered into Samson's cell, he closely inspected the chains that held his wrists about two hands' span apart. It was a well-made chain of bronze. He could not break it himself but he knew that his sword could cut through it. He brought over the stool and placed it between Samson's hands and said, "Wait a moment whilst I unfasten the other chains," knowing that Samson could not see what he was doing. He withdrew his large sword and with one sweep it cut through the bronze chain as well as the stool top. There was a sharp snap as the chain parted.

Samson said, "What is that?"

"Just me being rather clumsy. I am sorry, it will only take a little while." He picked up some material from the floor and quickly tied the two ends of the chain together. "There you are," he said making another clutter as he kicked away the stool, "Now, try again."

The chain parted easily with a slight tug by Samson who said, "You are right, my friend, my strength is returning."

Ruben told him the rest of the plan, and that he must pray to the Lord for additional strength as what he had to do required the strength of hundreds of men.

"Now I must retie your arms, sit with your back to the door and wait until they come for you in the morning. Remember the way, it is one flight of steps, turn right, then you turn right again and walk on until the last flight of steps, turn left and up the slope until you feel the fresh air on your face. The pillars will be in front of you. Now pray to the Lord for the additional strength you will need. Goodbye, my dear friend, and die in the glory that you rightly deserve."

He locked the door on the back of Samson who had bent his head in ardent prayer, in which pose Ruben felt sure he would remain until collected by the guards in the morning. Ruben went over to the dead jailer to remove his javelin from the man's skull. He had been correct in believing that this form of mortal injury did not result in a large loss of blood. He extracted the javelin and returned it onto its holder on his back, then dragged his body into the corner, soaking it with strong liquor from the stone jar, as if the man was totally inebriated. He received another shock as he rolled the body on its back, the gruesome face that stared up was that of Gershnarl, but it must have been another almost identical, as he had witnessed Gershnarl's death himself. He said to the corpse, "Well, you started it, let the killing end with you," and he heaved the body into the corner, hoping that his ploy would succeed. It was then a simple matter of retracing his footsteps and leaving the prison and auditorium, but during his quiet passage down the corridors, he found he was weeping for his friend, knowing that he would neither see him nor hear his arrogant laughter again.

He was soon back at the stables behind the inn with Dathram's mules, he undressed back to the loincloth and repackaged his clothes and weapons, ready for the morning, before finishing the food that Naomi had prepared. Dathram was delighted to see him when he entered the stables first thing in the morning.

"Would you like me to bring something to eat so that we can make an early start?" he asked.

"Yes, please," replied Ruben, while he was reloading all Dathram's baggage. Dathram returned with some maize porridge, fresh oranges, and some wheat cakes that the innkeeper had just made, explaining to Ruben that everyone else was going to watch the public execution.

"Could you not release your friend?" enquired Dathram.

"I may have been able to," replied Ruben. "But he had been blinded and I am not sure that we could have engineered his escape from the amphitheatre."

"It is actually a temple to their god, Dagon, it says so above the entrance," he corrected Ruben. "But you were not to know, as you have not seen it in daylight."

They left the inn, passing all the crowds who were going in to watch the spectacle. By the time they came to the city gates, almost everyone else was in the temple and they could hear, "Bring out Samson," being chanted by the crowd. The guard on the gate checked Dathram's identity and gave a cursory glance over his baggage and the slave, who kept his eyes on the road. Dathram whispered to Ruben, "Presumably you gave him something to take his own life, rather than having to endure the horrors that they had in preparation?"

"I did no such thing," replied Ruben. "But I did free him from his bondage and told him what the Lord wanted."

The guard had just waved them through the city gate, when a huge bellow came from the temple, there was a mighty crash as the temple collapsed before their eyes in a cloud of dust, which rose from the rubble. The guards ran back to help unearth any survivors, as the two friends walked away from Gaza followed by the mules.

"Was that your work, my young friend?" enquired a perplexed Dathram.

"No again, your guesses are not very good this morning," laughed Ruben. "But I did have a part to play simply in restoring his faith in his own ability."

"You seem good at that," said Dathram. "Just like young Latich, he had gone to pieces after he believed that you had been killed in the battle at Sousa."

Dathram had accepted Ruben's offer to come back to Sabasti and stay for a few days, before Ruben promised to return him to the coast road and resume his long journey home to Babylon. The road had been quiet until they had just turned off past the gorge where the ambush had taken place, Ruben filling in the missing parts to the story that Dathram already knew. A single chariot then came racing up the road from Gaza, not even stopping where they had turned off; it obviously carried an urgent message to Beth-Shan. Ruben had made a halfhearted attempt to clean himself, saying, "I will let my wife wash me, I enjoy it and I think she does as well."

"I am looking forward to meeting your wife," said Dathram. "I have a present for you, which I will give to her, as it is ornamental and not a weapon, so it will be better off with her as you cannot use it." They continued the journey back to Sabasti and it was just getting dark when they arrived at the town, where Naomi ran out from the gates to greet Ruben, as his return had been noticed by the watchers on the town walls.

"Yes, you can certainly pick the pretty girls," Dathram told Ruben, as they walked home to a large meal.

"She is a very good cook as well," boasted Ruben. "Which you will soon find out." He turned to Naomi and said, "Dathram has a bigger appetite than I have."

"That I cannot believe until I have seen it," laughed Naomi as she led them back to a feast. While they were eating, Dathram produced the present, which Naomi opened, from one of Dathram's mysterious parcels. It was an ivory carving of an eagle, which had a slightly bent wing.

"How on earth did you manage to get a model of Skree?" exclaimed Ruben.

"Joself described him to me," laughed Dathram. "So I had the likeness carved in ivory when I was in Egypt."

"But you did not know that you would even meet me," accused Ruben of his friend.

"Let us say that I had a premonition, or a little bird told me," laughed Dathram.

"Thank you, Dathram," said Naomi. "It is beautiful," and she gave him a big kiss. "I will let you come again, but please send warning so that I can restock my larder." Dathram had done it again, he had eaten five platefuls of food to Ruben's three. They then talked long into the night about Dathram obtaining iron weapons for them, which he promised he would try to arrange with the Babylonian king.

# EPILOGUE

Almost thirteen years had passed and the war between the Philistines and Israelites still raged, although they were now on equal terms, each having an army of almost three thousand strong. The Israelites had gradually caught up due to obtaining iron weapons in advance of the Philistines, by trading directly with the Babylonians, but iron weapons had soon become common amongst the then civilised world, the secret of its production had not been retained for long, iron deposits being discovered in many lands.

The Lord's prophet Samuel had anointed Saul as King of Israel, as the people felt that they needed a king. Samuel had not been keen, but there was no other choice as Saul was already the leader of the army. He had married shortly after Ruben and now had four sons, the eldest being a pleasant lad called Jonathan. Ruben retained control of training for the army, although he openly criticised Saul's campaigns as he felt that too many lives had been thrown away by bad judgement. But he steadfastly refused any position in the army, although he was undoubtedly the unrivalled champion, despite no contest ever being held. Saul had on many occasions sent messages requesting Ruben to come to his aid, but only as a warrior to fight individual battles, which the Philistines had adopted as a tactic – before a battle between the armies. These requests had always been refused by Ruben and the army had managed to find its own champion to fill this role. However, a final request had just been received. But this request was sent to the Elder's Council of Sabasti, pleading Ruben to come and face a giant of a man that the Philistines had suddenly produced. This man, called Goliath, was shouting a challenge every day and, as no one would fight him, the whole army was becoming demoralised; he was reputedly larger than Samson.

Ruben had not been at the Elders' Meeting, so Ezekiel had been requested by the elders to make a personal plea to Ruben, which he had just arrived to deliver. He arrived as Naomi and Ruben were preparing for the arrival of some of Ruben's old friends, complete with another mule caravan of weapons. They did not know who would be coming, except that it was unlikely to be Dathram, who was now declining in strength and said on his last visit that he was now getting too old for the long journey. Although he promised to send a suitable replacement, someone who knew Ruben from the old days, not naming anyone in particular, although the hint was that this would be Latich.

A series of signal fires burnt from Antioch to Sabasti via Mount Carmel and Mount Tabor, which was the unusually high hill that rose almost vertically like a finger from the plane of Isdralon. This was just visible from the hilltop near the ambush site on the road from Beth-Shan to Gaza. The signal fire that had been lit on this hill was visible to Sabasti, and its lighting meant that the cargo of weapons carried by the mule caravan had just left the hill, so it would shortly be arriving.

Obviously this was not the most convenient time for Ezekiel to arrive and the baby of the family was deposited in Ezekiel's arms as he entered the house.

"Look after the baby for me, Father, as I seem to be fighting a losing battle," requested Naomi. "And try to keep the other children out of the way whilst I tidy up." Ezekiel found himself confronted by all five children, all vying for their grandfather's attention, which he would normally be willing to give.

"Unfortunately," protested Ezekiel, surrounded by children, "I have come to see Ruben on urgent business."

"You will find him sorting out the guests' bedroom. Take the children with you and that will give me a chance to get back to the kitchen."

Resigned to his fate as a child-minder, Ezekiel went in search of Ruben. He was where Naomi had said, rearranging the furniture.

"Hello Ezekiel," exclaimed Ruben hardly looking up from his labours, but alerted to his presence by the children.

"I have come on urgent business from the Elders' Council, who have asked me to petition on behalf of a request that we have received from Saul," he said, raising his voice above the clamour created by the children and handing Ruben the scroll that had come from Saul. "Here, read this for yourself, the elders all feel that you should go to Saul's aid."

His brow darkened as he read the message. "You know I never go to that clown's requests?" was Ruben's irritated response.

"But this does sound alarming and if this Goliath is larger than Samson it is not surprising that everyone is afraid of him," pleaded Ezekiel.

"You always tell me in these important matters that the Lord will come to our aid," responded Ruben.

"Gosh Dad," interjected Ruben's eldest son, a boy of eight. "You can go and beat him up."

"That's enough from you, young Nathan," scolded Ruben, then turning back to Ezekiel, said, "If it really is that urgent, why has the Lord not sent me a sign?"

The question went unanswered as there was the sound of horses outside and both men turned and made their way to the door.

"Ruben!" shouted Latich as he jumped down from the back of a pony. "It is good to see you again, old friend."

"And you, my good Latich, you look very well," replied Ruben in greeting as he embraced his friend. "Dathram hinted that he would send you, and who is that with you?" he requested, trying to look round his old friend at the tall man climbing off the large bay horse. Latich finally stepped back as Ruben stared in wonder.

The purple plumes on the helmet and the height of the man gave him away. "Hello Ruben," said the large man, moving forward with an outstretched hand.

"Bel!" said the astonished Ruben, as he warmly shook the proffered hand. "What a wonderful surprise, I see they have made you a general at last."

"Yes, but I was able to get away on this errand, to act as a guard and also to check on Assyrian movements. We have a further surprise, but that is accompanying the mule caravan. Latich and I could not wait to see you," ventured Bel. Ruben finally remembered his manners and called for Naomi, who he introduced, as well as Ezekiel and his five children, starting with the girls of twelve and ten and three sons, Nathan of eight years being the eldest. Naomi was just as attractive as she had always been and had not put on any weight as her children kept her active. Naomi invited Ezekiel to dinner with the others, telling him that if possible he could bring up the discussion with Ruben that had been interrupted.

Ruben's final surprise was not long in coming. The mule caravan arrived with an escort of five Greek soldiers led by Druselus. Ruben had been advised of Lord Coronus and Druselus by Dathram, on his occasional visits. Therefore there were three extra for the evening meal in addition to Ezekiel, Druselus having insisted to Naomi that his band would cater for themselves. During the gathering, just before they sat down to eat, Naomi insisted that Bel and Ruben stood back to back, as she was not sure who was taller. It was finally decided that Ruben was a little taller and unquestionably larger around the chest. Bel thought this was amusing and he told Ruben, "I am not surprised, because it was predicted by Habib, the leatherworker who made your jerkin."

"I still have that jerkin, I would be lost without it," declared Ruben.

"He even wore it when we were married," laughed Naomi. "Now you all sit down whilst I and my daughters serve you."

It was a happy occasion, the topics of conversation being wide and including everybody. The only sad comments came from Druselus, who told them, "Regrettably I have to inform you that Lord Coronus died last winter, but his final words to me were, 'Give my regards to my other son'".

"Well, nobody lives forever," said Ezekiel profoundly. Ezekiel then went on to tell the entire gathering of the request that had not been fully answered that morning. Latich and Bel thought that the idea of single combat before a battle was quite ridiculous. However, Druselus said that the idea was occasionally adopted by the Greeks in the Trojan wars, telling of the duel between Achilles and Hector as told to him by Lord Coronus, who himself heard it from King Odysseus. After a long discussion it was finally agreed that Ruben, accompanied by Bel, Druselus and Latich, would go first thing in the morning to where the two armies faced one another, in Hebron, almost a half day's march from Gaza.

"If this Goliath does look formidable, Ruben and I will simply use him as a javelin target, as we have never managed to hold a deciding contest," Bel said to Naomi, who was slightly displeased at this decision.

The next morning, all four companions rose early and after a hasty breakfast, departed directly to where the two armies faced one another. Bel and Latich went on horseback, while Ruben took the old chariot that had rescued Samson, which he had restored and now occasionally used. Druselus came with him, as he had not ridden in a chariot for a long time. However, they had returned before nightfall, as their intervention had not been required. When questioned about this later, Ruben told Naomi an unusual story: –

"When we left here the sun had just risen, and we travelled quickly by the new road, arriving just in time to hear this Goliath shout his challenge. He was certainly a giant of a man, possibly taller than Samson, if not as broad. But then there was a cheer from our men as a lad of possibly about fourteen strode forward. This lad apparently refused to wear any armour, even though he had been offered Saul's own, and carried nothing more than a slingshot. I was told that he was a shepherd boy who had offered to meet the challenge."

"But surely you intervened?" asked Naomi in alarm.

"No," replied Ruben. "As I say, we had just arrived and were on the hilltop above our army and some distance from Saul's tent. Apart from which, I was looking through half closed eyes, you know, the way I do to see the colour that surrounds a person, depending on their thoughts. The trick that I only rediscovered when we were in Jericho shortly after Ruth was born."

She was about to interrupt again, when Ruben silenced her with a kiss and said, "Let me finish." He then continued with his story.

"Goliath hurled four spears, they were not javelins but clumsy heavy spears that anyone nimble enough could dodge. Then the lad called out in a clear voice, 'Look up at the sky Goliath and see the birds wheeling above, they are waiting to pick the flesh from your bones'. He obviously had no fear of this clumsy giant. Goliath threw back his head and laughed, not realising that this was what the lad wanted. His slingshot was whirling above his head and when Goliath looked upwards, exposing his temple, the lad let fly the stone from his slingshot. It hit the Goliath on the temple, at which he collapsed concussed. Then I intervened."

"But surely the fight was over then?" queried Naomi. "Our boy had won!"

"Well, not really, my dear," responded Ruben. "You see, with these contests, they have to end in someone's death before the winner can be announced."

"How horrible, but tell me what happened next?" Naomi requested.

"As I say, I went down to assist young David, that was the lad's name that I learnt later, as he was having great difficulty in lifting Goliath's huge sword. I drew my own large sword and offered it to David, saying, 'Use this blade, it is more fitting for a champion'."

"That was nice," said Naomi. "And did he accept?"

"Yes, most graciously. He handled the sword well and in one stroke severed Goliath's head. This he held, displaying it to our army and the Philistines. Our army let out a tremendous shout of triumph and charged the Philistines, who fled in terror. I then paid homage to the boy and said he was our new champion. He was extremely polite, handed me back my sword and said ,Only after you teach me how to fight properly, my lord'."

"How incredible, but what was his aura?" inquired Naomi.

"That was the strangest thing of all," responded Ruben. "I could see Goliath's, it was purple shot with dark red, but of the lad, there was none, except everything around him seemed brighter, as if he had his own inner light. One day, that boy will rule this land."

# GLOSSARY

**Character profile**

| | |
|---|---|
| Abraham | The main character's distant relative |
| Abzher | The expert swordsman |
| Akaad | The prophets of Nippur |
| Amos | Leading fisherman of the tribe |
| Amalekites | Tribe of fishermen |
| Andreas | Fisherman in Thrax |
| Arthermais | Timon's leading merchant |
| Ashkilon | Border town with Assyria |
| Assyrians | The people who are now called Syrians |
| Babylon | Capital city (now Baghdad) |
| Baal | Idol god worshipped in Canaan |
| Ben Uriah | Ruben's surname |
| Belthezder | Corporal in the Guards, eventually general |
| Bel | His nickname |
| Beth-Shan | Large northern town of the Philistines |
| Britzeldah | Army captain at Ashkilon |
| Canaan | Land west of Assyria and east of the sea |
| Cornelius | Cyrus platoon comedian |
| Coronus | Old general now living in Canaan |
| Cyprus | Greek island, home of Coronus |
| Dagon | The Philistine god |
| Danites | Tribe of the Israelites |
| Dathram | A well travelled merchant |
| Delilah | Samson's lover |
| Druselus | Warden to Coronus |
| Ezekiel | Naomi's father (Samson's younger brother) |
| Gershnarl | Captain of the Guards, later killed |
| Habib | The leatherworker |
| Haggan | Small town southwest of Beth-Shan |
| Harad | Man from tracks |
| Harath | Father of the two boys from Thrax |
| Hittite | An ancient empire |
| Inferior Sea | Now called the Persian Gulf |
| Ishmala | Huge servant of Mutek |
| Israelites | Tribe from the desert |
| Jericho | City north of the salt sea |

| | |
|---|---|
| Jezraal | Lieutenant in the Babylonian Guards |
| Joself | Harath's young brother |
| Judah | Land occupied by Israelites |
| Larkslip | Herbal plant |
| Latich | Trainee soldier who befriends Ruben |
| Lagash | The main town on the Euphrates |
| Lialah | Simeon's niece (Rubens first wife) |
| Laasa | A town in the marshes |
| Kinneret | Lake Galilee |
| Kish | Western end of the marshes |
| Markret | Canaanite town |
| Messuda | Canaanite witch with magical healing |
| Mithrandir | Commander of Ashkilon |
| Miriam | Ruben's cousin (sister) |
| Mischa | Bronze worker's son, Saul's lieutenant |
| Mulch | Euphrates's town below Ashkilon |
| Mutek | The merchant from Lagash |
| Mustala | Sergeant at Ashkilon |
| Nafrath | Assyrian town |
| Naomi | Relative of Samson, becomes Ruben's 2nd wife and mother of all his children |
| Neath | Assyrian town on the Euphrates |
| Nemphis | Main trading city in Egypt |
| Nippur | Ruben's home town |
| Nineveh | Capital of Assyria |
| Nozgrarot | Tiglath-Pileser's cousin, general |
| Rahki | Alcoholic drink found in Canaan |
| Rameses II | Pharaoh of Egypt |
| Ratarz | Assyrian sly man, sergeant |
| Ripotle | An elderly teacher |
| Ruben | The main character |
| Sabasti | Large Israelite town (later Samaria) |
| Samson | Israelite judge, strong man |
| Sal-e Pol-e | Northern mining town |
| Saul | One of Samson's captains (later king) |
| Schudah | Commander at Lagash |
| Shaleem | Notorious brigand chief |
| Simeon | Old man of the marshes |
| Skree | Ruben's eagle |
| S'meon | Local name for Simeon |
| Sorek | Valley near Sabasti |
| Stephen | Fisherman, Andreas' brother |

| | |
|---|---|
| Sumer | The province of Lagash |
| Sousa | Border town near Persia |
| Tasmin | Joself's wife, Lialah's look\like |
| Tiglath-Pileser | King of Assyria |
| Timon | First town in Canaan |
| Thrax | Assyrian border town |
| Tryone | Sergeant in the training camp |
| Uglis | Captain of the training camp |
| Uruk | A town in the marshes |
| Uriah | Ruben's father (Renamed Simeon) |
| Ur | Where Abraham started Chaldees |
| Zak | Old ferryman who sells his boat |
| Zohab | Town upriver from Babylon |